Cross My Heart

Cross My Heart

Cross My Heart
BY CAROL COX

Valiant Heart
BY SALLY LAITY

The Other Brother
BY LENA NELSON DOOLEY

Mail-Order Husband
BY DiAnn Mills

HeavenSent
FROM
Crossings

All Scripture quotations are taken from the King James Version of the Bible.

This edition was especially created in 2004 for Crossings by arrangement with Barbour Publishing, Inc.

Published by Crossings Book Club, 401 Franklin Avenue, Garden City, New York 11530.

ISBN: 0-7394-3960-X

Printed in the United States of America

Cross My Heart

CROSS MY HEART

BY CAROL COX

To Dave, Kevin, and Kaitlyn,
the most supportive family in the world.
Your love, patience, and great ideas made this happen.

PROLOGUE

Prescott, northern Arizona Territory
March 1885

*A*re you sure you'll be all right?"

Violet Canfield laughed and patted her older sister's arm. "Rachel, you've already asked me a thousand times. And for the thousand-and-first time I'm telling you: I'll be fine."

Her sister watched her luggage being loaded into the boot of the stagecoach and frowned. "But you've never been on your own before. What if something happens?" She appealed to her husband. "Daniel, do you think we're doing the right thing?"

Daniel Moore wrapped his arm around his wife's shoulders and gave her a reassuring squeeze. "She'll be all right. We'll only be gone for three weeks, and Tucson isn't exactly the ends of the earth. If it turns out she needs us, we can come back on the next stage."

"I guess you're right," Rachel said doubtfully.

"Of course I am," Daniel said with an assurance that earned him a laugh from both women. "I need to check out those mining properties. The work is all caught up on the farm until it's time to start planting. This is the ideal time to leave."

"All right." Rachel gave in with good grace. She gave Violet a long hug and let Daniel help her up into the coach. "You take care of yourself," she called out the window. "Don't spend the whole time with your nose stuck in a book. And don't bring home any more strays!" She wagged an admonishing finger.

Violet only laughed. She turned to give Daniel his good-bye hug. "You're not worried about me, are you?" she asked him.

"Only that you're so caught up in all those tales of knights and heroes that you never give any of the flesh-and-blood men around here a second look." He grinned and gave her a playful tap on the nose. "One of these days you're going to have to settle for one of us mere mortals, you know."

Violet laughed and arched her brows. "I'm not lowering my standards for anyone, Daniel Moore. Now you two go and have a wonderful time."

Daniel took his place beside Rachel. Violet waved until the stagecoach rolled out of sight. She walked back to their wagon with a light heart and climbed to the seat, a wistful smile crossing her lips. If she hurried home, she'd have plenty of time to finish *The Knights of the Round Table* before evening chores.

$$\textbf{1}$$

New Mexico Territory
March 1885

*C*reak. The wood of the windmill tower groaned under the weight of the two men perched thirty feet above the ground.

"Have you got it?"

"Almost." Willie Bradley gave another tug on the pump rod and pulled it sideways a fraction of an inch. "Can you shift that coupling a little more?"

The ranch hand strained at the metal shaft. "That's about all I can give you. Will it catch now?"

Willie tried again to mesh the pipe threads into place and shook his head. He spared a quick glance at the three men gripping the shaft at ground level. "Hank!" he yelled. "I need you to push it higher."

Hank and his helpers strained to lift the heavy piece of metal, and Willie felt the first thread lock in place. "Now twist it," he shouted. Within a few moments, he leaned back and flexed his shoulder muscles. "I'll go on down and prime the pump," he said. "Give it a few spins and let's see if we can get some water out of this thing."

The pump rod rose and fell with the rotation of the windmill's blades. A small trickle of water began to pour from the pump spout, signifying the success of their efforts.

Willie stared up at the turning vanes with satisfaction. Setting up the new windmill had given him some challenging moments, but he'd managed to get it done. One more small step along the road to gaining the cooperation of his father's ranch hands and winning their respect . . . and his father's. He enjoyed the small victory. Few of them had come his way of late.

He shouldered a pipe wrench and called, "That's it for today. Let's get the tools put away and head in."

"We're way ahead of you, Boss," Hank said. Willie glanced toward the men and saw them loading the last of the tools into the wagon. A hot wave of embarrassment washed over his face, and he turned away to hide his chagrin.

A hand gripped his shoulder, and he glanced up to see his brother-in-law, Adam McKenzie. "How long have you been there?"

"Long enough to know you aren't enjoying this moment as much as you have a right to."

Willie made a wry face. "It's that obvious?"

Adam shrugged. "Only because I've gone through it myself. When that itch to be your own boss takes hold of you, it's hard when things don't go the way you want them to."

Willie nodded. He appreciated Adam's understanding but hoped others wouldn't find his frustration as transparent as Adam had. Bad enough to be acknowledged as being in charge but not really accepted as the leader. It would be far worse if people knew just how much it bothered him. He watched the men ride off, then swung into his saddle, painfully aware that if his father stood in his place today, every one of them would have waited until Charles had given permission for them to leave.

"Mind if I ride along with you? I'm headed in to talk to your dad." Adam turned his mount alongside Willie's and fixed his gaze in the distance. "I guess being the boss's son isn't always the easy ride everyone thinks it is." His casual tone invited comment but didn't demand it.

"I'll say." Willie rode in silence for half a mile, then burst forth. "I'm twenty-one, Adam. By the time my father was my age, he'd been married for a year and Lizzie had been born. He'd already started a ranch back in Texas, with ten men working for him. But look at me. I've spent my life learning about cattle, but will anyone give me credit for knowing a thing?"

He snorted. "I'm nothing more than the boss's wet-behind-the-ears kid, and there isn't much chance of me ever being more than that. Not around here, anyway." He braced himself for a rebuke.

"I know." Adam's quiet comment earned him a surprised glance from Willie. "Lizzie and I have talked about it lately. We both know it must be hard to want to spread your wings and not have the opportunity to do it."

"It's not like anyone's trying to hold me down," Willie said. "I know Pa doesn't set out to undermine me; neither does Uncle Jeff. They don't have to. All the hands who've worked for us for years just look to them for direction as a matter of course. When I try to see it from their point of view, I know that to them, I'm still the little kid who put a whole bottle of pepper sauce in the bunkhouse beans. Why should they take orders from me?"

Adam took his time before replying. "What would you think about coming in with me as a partner?" He grinned at Willie's look of astonishment.

"Think about it. You're good with livestock. Like you said, you've been learning about them all your life. It would give you a chance to have something of your own and more say in what goes on. What do you think?"

Willie swallowed hard and scanned the distant horizon. Maybe Adam would assume his silence indicated deep thought instead of a struggle with emotions that threatened to choke him. The knowledge that his sister's husband thought enough of him to open up an opportunity like this meant more to him than Adam could dream.

"I appreciate it," he said in a voice rough with suppressed feeling. "But it still wouldn't be like being out on my own. I need a chance to find out what I can do. You're good with horses, Adam. You have a gift for taking a broomtail and turning it into a good cow horse. You went with the gift you've been given and proved yourself. But I'm a cattleman; always have been, always will be. I'd love to have my own say on my own spread." He set his jaw. "But I don't guess that's likely to happen."

He shot a sideways glance at his brother-in-law. "I hope you know I appreciate the offer."

Adam nodded. "I understand. That's how I felt a few years ago, when I worked for your dad and uncle. I couldn't have asked for better men to work for, but I wanted my own place so bad it just about twisted me apart inside."

"That's how it is with me," Willie agreed, grateful for the opportunity to share the dream that had gnawed at him for so long. "I don't want to sound ungrateful; I just want to find out what I can do on my own."

They topped a rise, and the ranch buildings came into view. Willie pulled his mount to a stop and squinted into the sun. "Is that a buggy parked in front of the house?" he asked, more to himself than to Adam. "Mother didn't say anything about having company. Wonder who it is?" The two men touched their horses' flanks with their heels and rode toward the house at a trot.

A cozy scene greeted them when they stepped onto the front porch after tending to their horses. Willie's parents, Charles and Abby, sat in matching rocking chairs facing a man Willie didn't recognize. Three towheaded children sat quietly nearby.

Abby sprang to her feet with a glad cry when Willie approached. "You'll never guess who's here!" She laid one hand on Willie's arm and held the other out to indicate their dignified-looking visitor. "Do you remember my cousin, Lewis Monroe? You were just a little boy the last time you saw him."

The older gentleman stood and clasped Willie's outstretched hand in a damp grip that made Willie want to wipe his palm on his pants leg. He had only foggy memories of his visit to his mother's childhood home in Virginia and none at all of Lewis Monroe.

"And this is my son-in-law, Adam McKenzie," Abby continued. "He and Lizzie have been married four and a half years now, and their horse ranch adjoins our property on the northwest."

"Finest horses anywhere in this territory," Charles put in, giving Adam an approving nod. "He's done a good job of building his place from scratch."

Willie tried to stifle the spasm of envy at Charles's evident pride in Adam's accomplishments. What wouldn't he give to have his father speak of him in the same admiring tone!

Lewis Monroe shook hands with Adam and remained standing, smoothing his salt-and-pepper hair into place. "I was just explaining the purpose of my visit to Charles and Cousin Abby," he said. "I am an attorney, and I have fallen heir to a most unpleasant duty on behalf of a longtime client, now deceased."

He waved the three youngsters to their feet with an imperious gesture. "The mother of these children departed this mortal coil several years ago. Sadly, their father also passed on quite recently. In his last will and testament, he named a lifelong friend as their guardian, a man whose whereabouts I found it extremely difficult to trace." A peevish expression flickered across his face, then was gone.

"After making diligent inquiries, I ascertained that the gentleman in question currently resides in Arizona Territory. Accordingly, I am accompanying these little orphans to their new home." He paused and bowed his head, as if awaiting some sort of accolade.

"Do they have names?" Willie's outburst surprised even him. He knew better than to do anything that would violate his mother's code of hospitality. At the same time, the way Monroe pointedly ignored the youngsters rankled. Willie knew all too well how it felt to be overlooked.

Monroe looked up with an expression that told Willie he didn't appreciate the lack of regard for his tale of self-sacrifice. Nevertheless, he turned to the silent children and pointed them out one by one.

"The Wingates," he announced. "Frederick, age ten; Jessica, age seven; and Tobias, age five."

"Toby," the small boy corrected, then lapsed into silence.

The other children didn't speak but focused hostile gazes on Monroe. Willie couldn't blame them. The lawyer obviously resented the intrusion of their father's death into his neatly-ordered existence. In the same circumstances, he wouldn't be Willie's favorite person, either.

"As I was saying before you rode up," Monroe continued with a sniff, "it has been so many years since I'd seen dear Cousin Abby, I decided to break our journey and take a brief respite from the train."

"And I've asked him to stay with us for a couple of days to rest up before they continue their trip," Abby put in with a fond glance toward her cousin and his young charges. "It will be such a delight to hear children's voices in this house again.

"Speaking of children . . ." She turned her gaze to Adam. "How is Lizzie?"

"Tired a lot of the time, but Doc says that's to be expected," Adam answered with a grin. "She's about ready for the waiting to be over."

"Aren't we all!" Abby laughed. "We hadn't gotten to that bit of news yet, Lewis. I'm going to become a grandmother in just a couple of months."

"What delightful news! Children are a blessing." He cast a swift glance at the three young Wingates and cleared his throat. "My heartiest congratulations," he added in a more subdued tone.

"Yep. In a couple more months, I'll be married to an old grandma," Charles quipped, earning an outraged sputter from his wife. He turned his attention to Willie. "How's the windmill coming, Son?"

"We pumped water today. It's ready to be plumbed to the tank. I'll get the men on it first thing in the morning."

Charles waved his hand. "Hank can see to that. You're going to be busy riding herd on these three." He nodded at the children huddled near Monroe.

Willie turned to his mother in disbelief. She smiled and nodded gently. "Yes, Dear. Your father has to meet with some of the territorial legislators tomorrow, and I'll be catching up on family news with Cousin Lewis. I'm sure these little ones would much rather have you show them the ranch than sit around listening to us reminisce. You won't mind, will you?"

A fist to the stomach couldn't have knocked the wind out of Willie more effectively. Hard as he tried, he couldn't get anyone around here to take him seriously. He'd overseen the windmill, felt immense pride at its imminent completion. Now the ranch hands would finish it without any need of his help, since he'd been elected as the first choice for a nursemaid. He clenched his teeth so tightly his jaw ached.

Watching kids, of all things! Just the thing to prove his worth. A quick glance at the three little orphans showed him they studied him with about as much enthusiasm as he felt toward them. The realization caught him up short. At least he still had a father and mother and the hope of future opportunities to win their approval. These youngsters had nothing left but memories. What would a couple of days brightening their lives matter?

He slanted a look at Monroe and made his decision. Time spent in the stuffy lawyer's company would be enough to try the patience of anyone, much less a child who'd lost both parents and wound up being foisted off on a total stranger. Giving them a chance to see the West through the eyes of someone who knew and loved it would be the best preparation they could have for a smooth start to their new life. Besides, it might even be fun.

"Not at all." He returned his mother's smile. "I'll be happy to show them around."

2

"Willliiee!" Jessica's plaintive voice set every nerve in his body jangling.

Willie winced and turned around, hoping the smile plastered on his face looked friendly. How could one little girl produce such a shrill tone? And one with so much volume? He noted the sun's position, almost straight overhead. Had he only had charge of these youngsters for one short morning?

"What is it?" he asked, trying to keep his voice even. At least he could count on his family's company during lunch. Adult conversation had never looked more appealing.

"My bonnet blew off. It's caught in the top of that tree!" China blue eyes puddled with tears.

Willie craned his neck to view the uppermost branches of the stately cottonwood. The bonnet dangled by one string, flapping in the spring breeze like a billowing flag. *Not quite at the top,* he consoled himself. *Maybe only forty feet or so up there.*

He looked down at Jessica again. Both brothers now flanked her on either side, and they each rested a hand on one of her shoulders. Three solemn pairs of eyes stared at him without blinking.

He sighed, accepting the inevitable. "All right, I'll go up and get it." He gripped either side of the broad trunk with his boots and tried to shinny up to the lowest branch. The slick leather soles gave him no purchase, and he slid down faster than he could climb. Muttering, he pulled the boots off and set them at the base of the tree.

His socks would never be fit to wear again after this climb. Willie felt the cottonwood's rough bark snag the knitted fabric and poke at his tender insteps. He gritted his teeth and inched his way upward, determined to retrieve the bonnet. No one would be able to say Willie Bradley couldn't even nursemaid a bunch of babies.

Having reached the first branch, his climb became easier. He moved from limb to limb, testing the ever-smaller branches before trusting them with his weight. At last he reached the level of the bonnet. Wrapping one arm securely around the trunk, he stretched the other out to its fullest extent. The bonnet dangled out of reach.

Willie glanced toward the ground, where Jessica looked up at him with trusting eyes. "Don't you have another bonnet?" he called. She shook her head violently. Even from his present height he could see her chin tremble.

Calling himself every kind of idiot, he released his hold on the trunk and eased himself along the branch, trying not to envision the path he'd take through those projecting limbs if he lost his grip and plunged to earth. The branch dipped precariously, and Willie froze until it stopped swaying. Not even daring to breathe, he extended his arm with infinite care and snagged the elusive bonnet with the tips of his fingers.

Going down didn't take nearly as much time as the climb up. Willie maneuvered his way to increasingly larger branches, reaching the lowermost limb at last and then sliding the rest of the way down the trunk. His abused feet protested when he hit the ground, and he had to force himself not to flinch. He handed the bonnet to Jessica with a flourish.

"Thank you." She flashed a dimpled smile and tied the strings into a prim bow under her chin.

That smile made him feel like he had when water streamed from the windmill. He patted her on the head and picked his way over to his boots, closing his eyes with relief when his foot slid into the protection of the sturdy leather sole. He stepped into the other boot.

"Yeoww!" A sharp pain shot through the sole of his foot. Willie flung the boot on the ground and grabbed the injured member with both hands, hopping around on his good foot, all the while wondering how long it took for a scorpion sting to render its victim incapable of walking.

When the pain subsided somewhat, he picked up his boot and

carefully upended it. A jagged chunk of obsidian rolled out and landed at his feet. Willie picked it up and studied it. Unless it had developed the ability to jump, he didn't see how it could have landed in his upright boot on its own.

He jammed his foot back into the boot. Ignoring the throbbing pain, he stood over the children. He balled his hands into fists. "How did that rock get in there?" he demanded.

Three innocent faces turned upward to meet his outraged glare. "We don't know," Frederick said. "Do we?" He looked at his brother and sister for confirmation. Three blond heads wagged back and forth in solemn denial.

"Cross my heart," Toby affirmed.

Willie gritted his teeth and turned back toward the ranch buildings. It wouldn't take more than ten minutes to get back there at a slow limp. No point in pressing this issue. They'd only be around another day and a half.

A giggle stopped him in midstride. He whirled, ready to pounce on the offender and wring out a confession. Three guileless pairs of eyes met his angry gaze. "All right," he began, "which one of you—"

The clanging of the dinner bell broke into his tirade, and the children scampered off with squeals of delight. Willie limped along behind them, deep in thought.

꙳

That night he lay in bed with his lamp turned low and studied the dancing shadows on the ceiling. Scattered thoughts flitted through his mind, changing as quickly as the dark shapes on the plaster overhead.

He'd always considered himself a fairly patient man, but not anymore. Not after today. Only twelve hours spent in the company of the Wingate children had completely altered his perception of himself. He turned down the lamp wick until the tiny flame went out and rolled over on his side.

It didn't make sense. He'd spent plenty of time around his uncle Jeff's kids, and they'd never produced this reaction. And goodness knew, Jeff and Judith's four offspring had enough feistiness to make every ranch hand on the place go into hiding whenever they came around.

Lizzie's baby was due to come along in just a few more weeks. The idea of being an uncle had thrilled him . . . up to now. Maybe he just couldn't take a joke.

No, he couldn't accept that idea. He and Lizzie had pulled more than their share of ornery pranks in their day. He understood the need for kids to let off some steam. He accepted that as part of growing up. But these kids. . . .

What was it about them that got under his skin so? He couldn't put his finger on it. In fact, he hadn't caught them doing anything outright. He had his suspicions, though, and plenty of them. That rock in his boot, for instance. Looking back, the whole episode of the bonnet in the tree didn't ring true—no matter how many times they crossed their hearts and proclaimed their innocence. The breeze hadn't been all that strong, after all.

If only he could catch them in the act. Those cherubic faces didn't line up with the tricks Willie felt sure they'd pulled. To look at them, a body would think they were the embodiment of innocence. In their case, though, Willie had the uneasy feeling that innocence might only run skin deep.

The strain of the day took its toll and his eyelids drifted shut. One more day. Just one more morning and afternoon with them. In the evening, they'd be busy packing; and by the following morning, they'd be safely on their way to Arizona Territory and their new guardian. *And may the Lord have mercy on his soul.*

❧

How many ways could three little kids find to aggravate a person beyond endurance? If many more existed than what the Wingates had already dished out that day, Willie didn't want to know about them.

And the worst of it wasn't even the things they came up with to antagonize him, but the fact that no one but him seemed to be aware of it. Unless . . . Lewis Monroe's odd behavior puzzled Willie. The way he skittered away with a furtive look in his eye every time they came near made Willie wonder just how much the man had endured on the trip west. Maybe he had good reason for keeping them at arm's length.

When he'd voiced that thought to his father, though, Charles only laughed.

"Seems to me I remember you playing a prank or two yourself," he reminded Willie, clapping him on the shoulder.

Twice that morning, Willie appealed to his mother, only to be admonished about the need to show kindness to three little waifs whose lives had been turned upside down. "Really, Son, you must have a little patience. Think how upset and frightened those poor little orphans must be. This is your opportunity to set a good example and plant some seeds of kindness."

Willie stared at her, goggle-eyed. What had happened to the woman who'd been able to spot every one of his misdeeds while he was growing up? Granted, she'd been in a dreamy state about children ever since Lizzie and Adam announced their forthcoming new arrival. *Even so, you'd think she'd be able to see past that angelic front of theirs.*

"Patience," he muttered. "I'll show them 'patience' if they try to set me up again." So far that day, he'd survived a loose cinch when he saddled up the horses to give the kids a ride and a pile of hay "accidentally" knocked down from the loft when he walked underneath—he had tolerated those with fairly good grace. He hadn't even given them the satisfaction of losing his temper over the salt in his coffee at lunch. But when he encountered—painfully—the gravel on the outhouse seat, his long-suffering reached its limit.

Afterward, he couldn't remember everything he'd said to the kids. He only knew that whatever it was, it seemed to put the fear in them. All afternoon, they behaved more like normal children than ever before. Willie's good nature reasserted itself. As long as they chose to cooperate, he would meet them halfway. He could be friendly and still maintain a degree of caution.

His resolve lasted throughout the remainder of the afternoon and into the evening. *Just another hour,* he congratulated himself, *and they'll be getting ready for bed. In the morning they'll be gone.* He walked down the hall, whistling a cheerful tune.

Frederick approached him with a serious expression. "Could you help me with something?"

Willie fixed the youngster with a suspicious gaze. "What do you need?"

The boy's forehead creased in a frown. "I heard somebody say it couldn't be done. I think they're wrong, and I'd like you to help me prove it. Would you?"

"Depends." Willie shifted from one foot to the other, his uneasiness growing. "What exactly do you want to prove?"

Frederick's face blossomed into a smile, seeming to take Willie's response for acquiescence. "It's about physical coordination. You're able to do so many things that it ought to be easy. Come on."

He led the way a short distance down the hallway to the door of Willie's bedroom and swung it open. "Now you stand behind the door and stick two fingers through the crack, like this. Good, there's just enough room for you to get your fingers through. I'll go stand on the other side." He suited action to his words, then produced an egg from his jacket pocket and balanced it on Willie's outstretched fingers.

"Hey!" Willie protested.

"I'll take the egg from you," Frederick continued, slipping his fingers through Willie's, "and slide it a couple of inches higher. Then you bring your fingers up to mine, and we'll take turns moving it up. See?"

"Like this?" Willie maneuvered his fingers through the crack and successfully retrieved the egg. "And what's this supposed to prove?"

"I heard Mr. Monroe say he'd read an article that said most people didn't have the coordination to do this. But I think he's wrong." The boy slid the egg a notch higher, his face a study in concentration.

"Seems simple enough to me," Willie agreed, getting into the spirit of the endeavor. "Looks like it just takes a good eye and a steady hand." He eased his fingers between Frederick's and moved the egg up an inch.

"That's what I thought." Frederick nodded solemnly. "I knew you'd be good at this." His fingertips touched Willie's, then moved back just out of reach. "What's that?"

"What's what?" Focused on maintaining the egg's delicate balance, Willie gave him scant attention.

Frederick craned his neck and cupped a hand to his ear in a dramatic gesture. "Someone's calling. I think it's your mother. I'll go see." He sprinted off down the hallway and rounded the corner toward the parlor.

"Wait a minute! What about the egg?" Only the sound of Frederick's retreating footsteps met his ears. "Frederick!" he bellowed.

Silence.

The truth dawned. "I've been had by a ten year old! Wait'll I get my hands on that little guttersnipe." He peered through the crack and studied the egg, which had begun to wobble. "Easy now. Easy," he told himself. There had to be a way to lower it to the ground without breaking it. Holding his breath, Willie tilted his fingers every so slightly back toward the door and bent his knees, inching toward the floor.

True to his expectations, bracing the egg against the door gave it the added stability it needed to follow his fingers smoothly along the groove between the door and the frame. Willie grinned. "Thought he could put one over on me, did he?" he gloated. Little did young Frederick know he'd pitted his wits against those of an expert jokester. With a triumphant grin, Willie slid lower until one knee rested on the floor . . . and his fingers met the top of the lower hinge.

He stared a moment, then slipped the fingers of his other hand below the hinge. No good. He'd never be able to drop the egg, then catch it again. Maybe . . . he stretched his arm out, then groaned when he realized he couldn't reach completely around the door.

"Frederick?" he called again. "Jessica? Toby? *Anyone?*" With a sigh, Willie accepted the inevitable and withdrew his cramped fingers. The egg splatted on the floor.

He poured water from the pitcher on his dresser into the basin and grabbed an old shirt to clean up the slimy mess, his ire mounting higher with every swipe.

"Little sneak. Rotten little coyote." Willie stormed down the hallway and burst into the parlor. The gathering there looked the picture of domestic tranquility. Charles leaned back contentedly in his armchair, while Abby stitched a nightdress for the coming grandchild. Frederick, Jessica, and Toby sprawled on the rug, looking at a picture book, while Lewis Monroe eyed them with a wariness Willie recognized all too well.

"You." His pointing finger quivered in the direction of Frederick's nose. "Did you really think you could get away with that?"

"Sir?" Frederick looked up, his face registering puzzled innocence.

"Willie, what are you going on about?" Abby set her sewing aside and leaned forward in her chair.

"The little wretch set me up. Gave me an egg to hold from behind the door, then went chasing off and left me standing there. I just now finished cleaning up the mess."

Abby's brow knitted in confusion. "Why would you stand behind a door with an egg, Dear? And why blame Frederick if you dropped it?"

Willie opened his mouth to speak, but the words caught in his throat. He'd been set up . . . again. No one would take his word against that of a "poor little orphan," with the possible exception of Lewis Monroe, who gazed at him with an air of commiseration. He turned on his heel and strode from the room. They'd be gone early tomorrow. If he could just hold out a few hours more, his troubles would be over and life could get back to normal.

3

*L*ook at them. Have you ever seen such little cherubs?"

Willie stared at his mother in disbelief. After living through all the havoc he and Lizzie had created during their growing-up years, how could she be fooled by a pair of blue eyes? Three pairs, he amended, turning to examine the Wingate children, who stood next to the waiting wagon. He had to admit they put on a good act, and he should know—he'd mustered up that same guileless mien a good many times in his day. But on his best day, he'd never achieved that degree of polished perfection.

His mother had a point. *Cherubic* seemed the only way to describe the faces staring back at him. To look at them now, scrubbed and fresh in the early morning sunlight, one would never think those sweet-looking angels could devise such devilish schemes. He had to acknowledge mastery when he saw it.

"Good-bye, my dears." Abby gathered first Jessica, then the two boys in a warm hug. "May you have a safe trip and find a warm, happy home waiting for you at journey's end." She turned to Willie. "What's keeping your father and Cousin Lewis?"

"I'll go see," he volunteered, relieved at the opportunity to get away. He hurried into the house and collided with Charles just inside the doorway.

"Get Hank," his father ordered. "I need to send him for the doctor." He drew a deep breath. "Lewis seems to have broken his leg." A pitiful moan came from farther down the hallway.

"How'd it happen?" Willie asked, trying to fight down his rising suspicion. The kids had been standing outside for a good twenty minutes. Surely they couldn't have had anything to do with it.

"He must have tripped over his valise. But that isn't important right now. Just get Hank on his way!" Charles turned back to the stricken lawyer, calling for Abby as he went.

The next few hours remained a blur in Willie's memory. He helped his father lift the groaning man and carry him to bed, fetched items his mother called for, and grudgingly watched over the Wingate children until the doctor arrived and Abby felt free to leave her cousin's side.

"Poor Lewis," she sighed. "He's in such pain, and it's making him terribly agitated. He seems convinced that someone tied a string across the bottom of his doorway. I tried to tell him that was impossible. He must have fallen over his valise. I went out into the hallway a few moments ago and checked just to reassure him. Of course there was no string there, but he keeps insisting on it."

Her voice took on a tender note. "He takes his responsibility to those children so seriously. Even in his pain, he keeps calling their names." She shook her head. "I'd better go tell the poor little things their trip will have to be delayed."

Willie flinched. Having the Wingates underfoot any longer than necessary was the last thing he wanted. He hurried to the sickroom himself to see about the probability of a speedy departure. The doctor appeared ready to take his leave, smoothing his coat and giving his patient an encouraging pat on the shoulder. "Take heart that it's only a simple fracture," he said in a comforting tone. "You'll be up and around again in just a few weeks."

"Weeks?" The word slipped out before Willie could stop himself. He saw his own horror reflected in the lawyer's eyes.

"Are you telling me I'll be confined to this bed, helpless, for all that time?" Monroe demanded in a shaky voice.

"Probably not," the doctor replied with a jovial air that struck Willie as all too unconcerned. "If you mend well, you'll likely be up in a chair in ten days or so. You may even be able to walk with the aid of a crutch in a couple of weeks." He snapped the clasp shut on his medical bag and wagged a playful finger at Monroe. "Just remember where you set your things from now on so you don't fall over that valise again."

After the doctor had gone, Willie leaned against the doorjamb and eyed Monroe thoughtfully. "My mother says you've been mentioning the children. Would you like them to come pay their regards?"

Monroe's pale face took on an even more ashen hue. "No!" he yelped. "That is . . . not right away. I have been their protector for so long on this trip, it might cause them undue distress to see me in this weakened condition." He gave Willie a wan smile. "Perhaps in another day. Or maybe two."

Willie nodded and took refuge in the barn to work out his thoughts. He had no way to prove it, but if he didn't miss his guess, those kids had been involved in Monroe's so-called accident . . . right up to their angelic little necks.

He kicked at a dried corncob, sending it spinning across the barn floor in a crazy arc. There had to be some way to get that bunch back on the road again, and soon. Maybe they could ride on the train by themselves.

Willie brightened at the thought. Surely after one glimpse of those sweet little faces, some motherly soul could be prevailed upon to make sure they got as far as the stop where they'd take the stagecoach into Prescott. After that, it would be a matter of making sure they'd been safely stowed on the stage and were met by their guardian. A well-worded telegram or two should do the trick. It would be simple. He walked back to the house, growing more pleased with his plan by the minute.

He entered the door and stepped into a flurry of activity. "There you are. Thank goodness! I've been looking everywhere." His mother grabbed his shirtsleeve and pulled him along the corridor in her wake.

"What's wrong now? Did they—That is, Cousin Lewis hasn't taken a turn for the worse, has he?"

Without answering, his mother towed him to the invalid's room with the air of a conjurer producing a rabbit from a hat. "Here he is," she announced.

"Good," Charles said in a crisp tone. "There's just time enough to make it."

"Make what?" Willie looked from one parent to the other, trying to make some sense of the conversation.

"Lewis feels it's important for the children to continue their journey immediately," his father told him.

"He's right," Willie said with conviction.

His mother beamed. "That's wonderful, Dear. I'm so glad you agree." She lowered her voice to a conspiratorial whisper. "Actually, the idea of them staying here any longer distresses him so much, your father and I are afraid it will affect his recovery. Poor Cousin Lewis! He takes his responsibilities so seriously."

Willie forbore to mention his suspicions of Cousin Lewis's real motive for wanting the children on their way. The reason didn't matter so long as those little troublemakers got on the train and left.

"Good, then it's settled." His father rose with the air of one satisfied with his accomplishment. "I knew we could count on you. The wagon's loaded and they're waiting on you."

"I'm on my way," Willie exulted. "Believe me, I wouldn't want to miss the chance to say good-bye."

His parents exchanged startled glances. "Didn't you tell him?" Charles demanded.

"There wasn't time," Abby explained. "I brought him straight here as soon as I found him." She laid her hand on Willie's arm. "You're not saying good-bye to them just yet. You're going to take them there. I've already packed a bag for you."

"To the train? I thought Hank—" He stopped himself in midsentence. It didn't matter; he could put up with them a bit longer. Nothing mattered, so long as they got out of his hair today.

"Not *to* the train, Dear. *On* the train."

A sick feeling of dread began in Willie's stomach and spread its tentacles through his chest and into every limb. "On?" His voice came out in a hoarse croak.

"That's right." His father clapped him on the shoulder. "We needed someone to get those little tykes to Arizona, and you're just the man for the job. Now, hurry, or you'll miss your train."

Propelled between his parents, Willie exited the room. He turned for one last look at his traitorous cousin and met Monroe's gaze. In it, he felt sure he saw an expression of relief . . . mingled with a look of pity.

25

❧

"Jessica, sit down. Toby, you too." Willie picked up the little boy and plopped him into the seat next to his sister, wincing when Toby's flailing boot connected with his shin.

"We've been on this train forever!" Jessica wailed.

"It hasn't been forever," Willie grumbled. It only seemed like it. Before this trip, he'd never have believed that three little kids could make a mere two days feel like an eternity. His eyelids drooped and his head began to nod. He caught himself up with a jolt. Every time he'd allowed himself to drowse, the kids had come up with yet another scheme to torment some unsuspecting passenger and make Willie look like the villain.

After a long night of horrified looks and scathing reprimands from the ladies on the train, Willie decided his only hope lay in staying awake until they'd reached the relative safety of the stagecoach. Surely even these three couldn't do too much within its confines. For now, though, he had to remain alert to prevent whatever devilment they might think of next.

He rolled his head from side to side and stifled a yawn. It would only take them another four hours to reach the junction at Ash Fork. He could hold out that long.

He angled himself so he could keep a watchful eye on the lot of them and fixed them with a stern glare. They stared back, all three chins jutted out in identical mutinous expressions. At least they'd dropped any pretense at being angelic so far as Willie was concerned. To the rest of the world, though, they kept up their cherubic facade while continuing to carry out their schemes and lay the blame at Willie's feet. He shuddered. He didn't think he'd ever forget the expression on that elderly woman's face just before she went after him with her umbrella.

He only hoped their guardian had an iron constitution and nerves of steel. He'd need them.

❧

"Next stop, Flagstaff." The conductor's voiced boomed through the car. "We'll only be here twenty minutes, folks. If you leave the train, don't go far."

Willie stretched and rubbed eyes that felt like they'd been filled with sand. His stomach rumbled. What could they find to eat in twenty minutes? He had to have something to keep up his strength. A hot meal might even make the kids mellow a bit. He got to his feet, ready to leave as soon as the car stopped.

The train lurched to a halt, and Willie shepherded his charges into a line in front of him. "Remember, I want you on your best behavior. Don't do anything that'll get us in trouble. Understand?"

Jessica sniffed and folded her arms. The boys merely scuffed their feet. Willie leaned forward and took the boys by the shoulders to make sure they'd paid attention to him, then felt his head jerked backward, his ear caught in a pincerlike grip. He turned to meet the baleful gaze of the heavyset woman who'd ridden across the aisle from them since Holbrook.

"Lay one hand on those precious babes, and I'll have the law after you," she threatened. "I've been watching you. You've badgered and hounded them ever since I got on this train. You're nothing but a bully."

Willie rubbed his ear and bit back a retort. Maybe he should have let Toby drop that bug into her open mouth while she was sleeping, after all. No, she'd only have found some reason to blame him for it. They all had.

He grabbed the younger children by the hand and led them across the dirt road to a clapboard building with the word *Café* lettered on its front. Three small tables filled the tiny space in front of the counter. Willie cast a quick glance at the chalkboard on the wall where the day's offerings were listed. "Could we get four bowls of venison stew as quickly as possible?"

The dour woman in charge nodded and set the bowls in front of them a few moments later. Willie relished each bite of the savory mixture, then set his spoon down with a sharp click. Wonderful! He felt better already. "Ready to go?" he asked the kids.

To his amazement, they'd barely touched their meals. "It's too hot," Toby complained.

"Well, hurry. We don't have too much time." He prodded at them, alternately pleading and threatening, until their bowls were empty. A warning whistle blast pierced the air. Good, they'd finished just in time.

"All right, back to the train," he commanded. To his relief, the Wingate trio filed out the door without protest. Outside, a spectacular sunset splayed streaks of crimson, pink, and gold across the sky. All four of them halted to take in the sight.

Willie closed his eyes in thanks for this reminder of the Lord's presence. If he focused on that truth instead of worrying what mischief the children might be plotting, he'd be able to manage the rest of the trip without losing his sanity. He stretched and breathed in a lungful of clear mountain air. With that dinner inside them, the kids just might fall asleep and give him the opportunity for a nap.

A bell began to ring, preparatory to the train leaving. "We'd better get going." He opened his eyes and froze. "Where's Toby?"

Frederick blinked up at him. "He said he needed to use the out-house. Didn't you hear?"

"There's no time for that now! Where did he go?"

"Back there somewhere." Jessica pointed behind the café. "Do you want us to go ahead and get on the train?"

Willie darted a frantic glance from the children to the train, then to the shadows behind the building. He could hear the engine building up steam. "No, stay with me." He plunged into the alleyway, calling Toby's name.

"Over there!" Frederick cried.

Willie sprinted to the small wooden structure and pounded on the door. "Toby? Are you in there?"

"Yep."

"Get out here! We're going to miss the train." Another whistle punctuated his command.

"Can't."

Willie rattled the door against the latch. "What do you mean, you can't? The train's ready to leave." If he grabbed Toby under one arm and towed Jessica by the hand, maybe they could run fast enough to make it.

"Booaarrd!" The conductor's cry echoed along the alleyway.

"Toby, open this door!"

"Wait'll I get this button fastened."

"*Now!*" The locomotive's drive wheels squealed as they slipped, then caught on the steel rail.

"Almost got it. There!" Toby swung the outhouse door open, a triumphant smile on his face.

Willie scooped him up and grabbed Jessica's hand. "Hurry!" he shouted to Frederick. They raced onto the platform in time to see the last of the cars sweep past.

"Look!" Toby cried gleefully. "The man on the caboose is waving to me."

Jessica tugged at Willie's pant leg. "I'm tired," she whimpered.

"Me too," Frederick told him. "You'd probably better find us a room, since you didn't get us back here in time to catch the train."

Willie clenched his hands, bringing a yelp from Toby and a curious look from a passing lumberjack. With a supreme effort, he set the boy down and walked toward a board-and-batten building whose weathered front held a sign labeled Hotel.

❧

"Are we almost there yet?"

Willie stared at Frederick through bleary eyes and nodded. A day late, but almost there, ready to board the stagecoach for the last leg of this interminable journey.

He scrubbed his face with his hands, feeling the bristle of a day's worth of whiskers. It would be good to catch up with his luggage and his razor again. He probably looked down-right scary, what with his haggard face and rumpled clothing. Sitting in a chair in front of their hotel room door last night hadn't given him the slightest bit of rest, but it had been the only way he felt sure he could keep the kids from doing another disappearing act.

"Next stop, Ash Fork." The train slowed and rumbled to a stop.

Willie pushed himself to his feet. "Come on," he said. "We have to pick up our luggage, then find the stage station."

"Will the stage leave right away, or will we stay in another hotel?" Toby asked. "I liked the hotel."

Willie stifled a growl and led his young charges to the station agent. "Where do we catch the stage?"

"Stage left this morning," the barrel-chested man told him, peering at Willie over his half-moon spectacles. "Won't be another one for three day days. You the ones that missed the train yesterday? Your luggage is right over there."

Willie stared at the man, sure he'd heard wrong. "You mean there's no way to get to Prescott for three days?"

"Didn't say that," his informant replied. He paused to send a neat arc of tobacco juice into a nearby spittoon. "There's more than one way to get on down the road. You can ride, or you can rent a wagon over at the livery. You can even walk if you don't mind sand in your boots. Your choice." He walked away to inspect the freight that had just been delivered.

"Where's the stable?" Willie called to his retreating form.

"Right there." The man pointed with a stubby pencil, indicating a point halfway down the dusty street. " 'Cept the owner had to go out and check on his ranch. Won't be back 'til morning."

Willie bowed to the inevitable. "Grab those bags, Frederick," he said, picking up the largest two himself. "Looks like we'll be spending the night here."

Toby beamed. "Goody, another hotel!"

❧

Willie directed a sullen stare at the slowly unfolding landscape and shifted on the wagon seat. Bundled in warm blankets purchased from the dry goods store, the three children dozed in the cool morning air, undisturbed by the wagon's constant jolting. Fine for them, getting to sleep all night and nap again during the day. He hadn't had a decent night's rest since they left the Double B.

Even the chair in the Flagstaff hotel room sounded good right about now, especially since their Ash Fork lodgings hadn't even boasted a chair and he'd wound up spending the night stretched out on the floor in front of the doorway. And that had been two nights ago. Last night's bed had been a blanket on the dirt at the side of the trail.

His head sagged, and he fought to hold it up again. If he figured right, they should get into Prescott by the following evening . . . if the wagon didn't lose a wheel, if they didn't encounter another canyon like the one they'd gone through yesterday, or if the rented horse didn't up and die on him.

Another day and a half. Then he'd hand the kids over to their guardian and head for the nearest hotel room. One he didn't have to share. One he could actually sleep in. A wistful smile curved his lips. He might not wake up for days.

"Williiee!" Jessica's shrill wail brought him out of his reverie. "I need to stop."

Muttering, he pulled the horse to a halt. When he'd figured the time the trip should take by wagon, he hadn't counted on all the stops a young child would need to make. Times three. Maybe they'd make it by summer.

꩜

The next evening, Willie stopped the wagon at the top of a low rise and watched the gathering colors of his fifth Arizona sunset. By his calculations, Prescott should only be about five miles down the road. If he kept on, they could make it into town in another couple of hours or so. Not too late to locate Thurman Hadlock, their guardian, and effect the transfer of the Wingates and their belongings. Not too late to find the bed that beckoned so tantalizingly in his imagination.

On the other hand . . . He glanced over his shoulder at the grubby children slumped in the wagon bed. The long, bumpy drive had taken the starch out of both them and their clothing. At the moment, they looked more like street urchins than heirs of a fair-sized inheritance. This job hadn't been his idea, but he wouldn't want to give Hadlock the impression he'd slacked off on his responsibilities. And he might as well give the poor man hope, at least in the beginning.

An hour later, the kids had been scrubbed until their faces glowed a rosy hue. The boys had their hair combed, and Jessica's hung in a neat braid. Their good clothes lay spread across the wagon bed, ready to don first thing in the morning. With sweet smiles, the three siblings snuggled down into their blankets on the far side of the fire.

Willie stared at their slumbering forms in wonder. They really did look angelic when they were asleep. Too bad he couldn't deliver them to their guardian before they woke up.

He took a few weary steps toward the water bucket, then looked at his bedroll and hesitated. With all three children safely asleep, he couldn't pass up this opportunity to catch up on some much needed rest. He could just as well clean up and shave in the morning.

He pulled off his boots and stretched out on his blanket with a blissful sigh. He wouldn't do more than doze. Just the chance to close his eyes without worrying what the kids might be getting into would be heavenly. He settled his head on his rolled-up coat and pulled the blanket around his shoulders to ward off the chill evening air. Just a few minutes' sleep; that's all he needed.

$$\textbf{4}$$

*F*ingers of light probed at Willie's eyelids. He cracked one eye open, blinked, then came fully awake when he realized the sun had already topped the mountains. He leaped to his feet. He couldn't remember the last time he'd slept this late. That's what came of trying to stay awake for days on end. At least now he'd be rested and ready to face the day and the kids.

They must have slept late, too. He hadn't heard a peep out of them. Maybe he'd wait to wake them until he spruced up. Then they'd head into town, find Thurman Hadlock, and say their farewells. Grinning at the thought of imminent freedom, he got up to draw some water from the barrel and froze.

The wagon was gone.

So were the kids.

On closer inspection, so were his boots.

Willie raked his fingers through his hair and stared wildly, unable to take in the meaning of the empty campsite. He circled their camp area in his stocking feet, looking for something that would tell him what had happened. This didn't make a bit of sense. Maybe he was still asleep.

"Ouch!" A pinecone jabbed his foot, assuring him he was awake. Choosing his steps with care, he went to the spot where he'd parked the wagon the night before. The tracks told the story. Three small sets of footprints led to the rear of the wagon and dug more deeply into the dirt where they'd pushed it thirty yards away from camp. At the bottom of the gentle incline, the largest set of prints left the wagon, then returned, accompanied by the hoofprints of the missing horse.

It didn't take much of a tracker to figure out the rest of the tale.

33

The little miscreants had harnessed the horse and started it out at a slow walk until safely out of earshot. Then they'd picked up the pace and gone on their merry way, following the road to town. Willie shaded his eyes against the sun and scanned the terrain ahead but couldn't spot them even as a speck in the distance.

"Of all the lowdown, rotten tricks!" Willie kicked at the ground in disgust and yelped when he stubbed his toe on a rock. Wait until he got his hands on those little thieves. He pulled on his coat, threw his blanket over his shoulder, and hobbled off down the road muttering dire threats between clenched teeth.

A mile down the road, he peeled off his socks. With the soles worn away to mere shreds, they did no more than irritate his feet. A mile farther, he spotted something dangling from an oak branch and whooped when he recognized his boots. After checking inside them first, he pulled them on and immediately wished he'd kept his socks. The leather rubbed the raw spots on his tender feet. He could envision the crop of blisters he'd get from this.

Dust rose up in little clouds with every step he took. The chill of the spring morning had long since worn off. He tossed the blanket under a scrubby bush, then pulled off his coat and slung it over his shoulder. When he topped a low hill, he paused, frowning.

The road forked here. The well-traveled road to town ran straight ahead, winding down the other side of the hill to disappear in the distance, while the smaller fork curved off. The wagon tracks followed the curve.

What could those kids be up to? The thought of them wandering off course so close to their destination made him quicken his painful strides. It wouldn't do to let them get lost, tempting though it might be.

Up ahead the tracks turned to the left, and Willie pulled up short when he spotted the empty wagon sitting in front of a neatly kept farmhouse. All the frustration and humiliation of the past week rose up to blur his thinking. With visions of mayhem dancing in his head, he crossed the open farmyard, stomped up the porch steps, and pounded on the front door.

A moment later, the door swung open to reveal a slender young woman with glossy dark hair and startling blue eyes that focused on him with ill-concealed dislike.

"Yes?" she said in a glacial tone.

Willie was in no mood for polite conversation. "The three kids who came in that wagon—are they here?"

The woman regarded him coolly. "They are." She made no move to call them but gripped the door with one hand and planted the other firmly on the doorjamb.

"Well, send them out!" Willie barked.

"Absolutely not." She lifted her chin and stared at him defiantly.

Willie gaped. "Why not? I'm supposed to have them." When she only glared at him in silence, he tried again. "They are my responsibility," he told her, enunciating each word with care. She didn't seem simpleminded, but appearances could be deceiving. "You don't need to be bothered with them anymore."

"Bothered?" Angry sparks flashed in those amazing blue eyes. "Is that all those children are to you, a bother? No wonder they don't want to be anywhere near you."

"Don't want to—"

"They came here early this morning and asked for sanctuary." A crystal droplet formed in one corner of her eye at the recollection. "I didn't understand it at first, but after meeting you, I can fully comprehend why." She drew herself up to her full height, which put the top of her head in the vicinity of Willie's shoulder.

"I don't want to keep them," he spluttered. "Not permanently, anyway. I'm bringing them out here to deliver them to their guardian. As soon as I turn them over to him, they'll never have to look at me again."

He made a quick mental calculation. If they left in the next few minutes, they could probably reach Prescott in a little over an hour. Allow another hour or so to locate Hadlock and effect the transfer of responsibility. By early afternoon, he ought to be soaking in the hottest bathwater he could persuade the local hotel keeper to provide. If this misguided female would quit interfering with his plans.

Her look thawed a few degrees. "Their guardian? Then the poor little dears are orphans? Oh, how sad."

Willie bit his tongue and refrained from telling her to save her sympathy for Hadlock, the citizens of Prescott, and quite possibly the whole of Arizona Territory.

She appeared to waver. "I suppose that does put it in a different light, Mister . . ."

"Bradley. Willie Bradley," he said heartily. "Sure it does. So if you'll just call them now, we'll be on our way. You wouldn't be able to tell me where to find Mr. Hadlock, I suppose?"

"Hadlock? Thurman Hadlock?"

"That's right. Do you know him?"

Her softening expression congealed into one of horrified distaste. "Thurman Hadlock isn't fit to raise a dog, much less these precious little ones. You might as well be on your way, Mr. Bradley. I will not be a party to sending innocent children into the care of the likes of that man. They were right; they do need protection." She slammed the door, missing Willie's nose by a mere inch.

"Hey!" He raised his hand to knock again but heard the *thunk* of the bar dropping firmly into place. He stared at the solid panel, non-plussed, then moved to one side to see if he could glimpse anything through a crack in the curtains covering the front window.

An alarming sight met his eyes: a wild-eyed, unshaven creature with tufts of hair standing on end like a porcupine's quills. Willie grimaced at the sight of his image reflected in the glass. No wonder she hadn't trusted him. He wouldn't trust anyone who looked like that, either.

Now what? He stepped down off the porch and kicked at a rock. He had to get those kids back, but how could he convince—why hadn't he asked her name?—how could he convince that human watchdog to talk to him again? The sooner he shed those kids, the sooner he could get back to the Double B. He aimed another kick at the hapless stone. An idea took shape in his mind. He found the rented horse in the barn, hitched it to the wagon, and set off toward Prescott.

❧

"Is he gone?"

Violet Canfield knelt before the wide-eyed youngsters clustered in the hallway and touched the little girl's flaxen hair in a comforting manner. "He's gone, Jessie. You don't need to worry anymore."

"Thank you, Miss Violet," the older boy said solemnly. "You saved us."

Violet blinked back tears at their gratitude and obvious relief. She couldn't blame them a bit for being glad to see that odious man leave. How frightened the poor dears must have been! Why, his unkempt appearance had been enough to unnerve the stoutest heart, much less these tender children.

"Can we stay with you?" the littlest one asked, speaking around the finger stuck in his mouth.

"Of course you can," she reassured him.

"Cross your heart?"

"Absolutely. Let's find places for all of you to sleep." She led the way to the cupboard, where she pulled out fresh linens, then set about assigning the children to their places.

"Frederick, you and Toby will stay in here." She pushed aside the brief flicker of uneasiness at the thought of Rachel and Daniel's probable reaction to learning their bedroom had been taken over by a pair of young boys. They wouldn't be back for weeks yet. By then, the question of the children's permanent residence would have been settled. She stripped the sheets off the bed, replaced them with the clean bedding, and pulled the comforter neatly into place.

Leaving the boys to settle their belongings in their temporary home, she led Jessica along the short hallway. "And how would you like to stay in this room? It belonged to my father." She swept open the curtains to let light flood the room and turned to see the little girl's reaction.

Jessie gazed at the cozy bed and offered her a shy smile. "I like it," she said. "It's much nicer than sleeping on the ground."

"I don't doubt it." Violet pressed her lips together in a prim line while she set about making the bed. *The man must be a monster,* she concluded, shaking the pillow into a clean, crisp case. *Forcing these tiny things to sleep out in the open. The very idea!* She thumped the pillow into place.

Rachel often accused her of being flighty and dreamy, but there had been nothing dreamy about the way she'd sent Mr. Willie Bradley packing, she remembered with satisfaction. Recalling the look on his face when she swung the door closed, she almost wished Rachel had been there to see her in action.

Almost.

"Don't bring home any strays." Her sister's teasing admonition echoed in her ears. But surely Rachel had been referring to stray animals, not these adorable, homeless waifs.

And, she reminded herself virtuously, she hadn't brought them home; they had come to her of their own volition. The Lord must have directed them straight to her door for protection. Even Rachel wouldn't ask her to fly in the face of divine guidance. In a way, all the wounded creatures she'd cared for over the years—the countless injured birds, rabbits, and squirrels she'd taken in and tended—might have been practice for just this purpose.

The story of Queen Esther flashed into her mind. What was it Esther's uncle told her when she shrank from putting herself in danger in order to save her people? "Who knoweth whether thou art come to the kingdom for such a time as this?"

"That's it," Violet murmured. "God prepared me for such a time as this." She gave Jessica a quick squeeze and headed for the kitchen to decide what she'd fix for dinner. For herself, a slice of bread with honey would have sufficed, but her new houseguests needed a more nourishing meal. No telling what that contemptible man had forced them to eat while on the trail, if he'd fed them at all.

Violet lifted her book from the dining table and closed it with a tender smile. She'd been looking forward to continuing her perusal of knightly adventures and daring rescues while she ate her lunch, but it could wait. Now she was in the midst of her own adventure. A shiver of delight ran up her arms.

She hummed while she prepared a hearty soup. She hated to admit it, but even her storybook heroes with their tales of derring-do hadn't kept her from being a trifle lonely these past few days. Not that she'd grown tired of them. Who could grow weary of reading the exploits of Robin Hood and Sir Galahad again and again? But it did make a wonderful change to be needed by living, breathing people.

She stirred the bubbling soup, savoring its rich aroma. Rachel and Daniel both teased her mercilessly about her penchant for tales of high adventure and romance, urging her to get her head out of the clouds and look at the young men available in the area instead of waiting for a white knight to appear and sweep her off her feet.

Violet had always ignored them, determined to hold out for the man of her dreams. She knew as surely as she breathed that one day he would come into her life and nothing would ever be the same again.

"And just where do you think this hero of yours will come from?" Rachel would scoff. "Do you expect him to appear out of nowhere?"

It would happen. It couldn't be as impossible as her sister made it sound. After all, she reasoned, that disreputable Bradley person had dropped into her life right out of the blue only that morning. But he hardly fit the picture of a hero.

The sound of children's voices drifted in through the window. Violet smiled. Good, they'd found something to play with outside. How nice that they felt so much at home already! She pulled out a bowl and began to mix up a batch of biscuits. A flash of gray caught her attention and she glanced outside. One of the farm cats ran streaking off toward the barn, emitting a plaintive yowl.

Odd, she thought. The cats didn't usually run from people. But then, they weren't used to children.

⑤

*T*ime spent with soap and water made a man feel almost as good as a good night's sleep, Willie decided. Having the water barrel, his luggage, and a bit of privacy again, he'd taken the opportunity to clean up and shave. He squared his shoulders, feeling more like himself than he had in days.

He hoped his efforts improved his appearance as much as his morale; he didn't want anyone else looking at him the way that stubborn young woman had. His high spirits dropped a notch, remembering her disdainful expression. He might not have the authority his father did, but he had grown used to people treating him with a certain amount of respect as the son of the Double B's owner. Being viewed as though he were some loathsome insect was a new experience for him, and an unwelcome one.

After making arrangements for the horse and wagon to be returned to Ash Fork and renting a light gray gelding for use during his brief stay, he asked for directions and soon found himself seated in a straight-backed chair explaining his predicament to Sheriff John Dolan.

The lanky, slow-talking lawman leaned back in his chair and pursed his lips. "Sounds like you have yourself a problem, all right. Now, who did you say you left the kids with?"

Willie gulped. "We didn't exactly get as far as introductions," he admitted.

The flicker of a smile lifted one corner of Dolan's mouth. "All right. Can you describe the place and the woman?" He listened to Willie's account and nodded. "That'd be Violet Canfield, from the sound of it."

He squinted his eyes into thoughtful slits and gave Willie a measuring look. "She does tend to be a mite dreamy, but all in all she's got a good head on her shoulders. I can't see why she'd hesitate to do the right thing." He leaned forward and drummed his fingers on the desktop. "You didn't do anything to make her suspicious, did you? Or uncomfortable?" He eyed Willie with a narrow gaze that sent chills of apprehension racing up and down his spine.

"No!" Willie's conscience prodded him. "Well, maybe I did look a little wild, not having washed up and shaved and all. That might not have set well with her."

"Uh-huh."

"And I might have raised my voice a bit a time or two," he mumbled.

"Mm."

Willie felt a flush rise up his neck and heat his face. "You don't know what those kids are like," he protested. "They'd try the patience of a saint. All right, I admit she probably thought I was some kind of thug. The bottom line is, those kids are my responsibility until I can turn them over to Thurman Hadlock. And speaking of Hadlock, I don't suppose you could tell me where to find him? We could get this whole thing straightened out in a matter of minutes."

Dolan, who'd seemed to accept his report readily enough up to this point, gauged him again with a gaze that made Willie want to squirm in his chair. "Hadlock, eh? You know the man?"

"I've never met him. All I know is what I was told by my mother's cousin, the lawyer I told you about. Hadlock was a close friend of the kids' father and was designated as their legal guardian in the event of his death." He produced a letter of introduction and handed it over to Dolan, who perused it briefly.

"Looks sound enough." Dolan slid the letter across the desk and tipped his chair back on two legs.

Willie breathed freely again. This would not be a man he'd choose to cross if he could help it.

Dolan rocked forward, appearing to have reached a decision. He planted his hands on his desk and pushed himself upright. "I can tell you where Hadlock lives and where he usually spends his time. Don't know that it'll do you a lot of good, though. I can't recall seeing him recently. In the meantime," he said, settling his hat on his head, "let's head out to the farm and see if we can't get your situation with Miss Canfield squared away."

Willie's misgivings returned during their ride out. "I hope the place is still standing," he told Dolan, and detailed his experiences with the young Wingates. "I've never seen anything like them."

Dolan shook his head dismissively. "Sounds to me like all they need is a firm hand and someone who won't put up with nonsense."

Willie started to argue, then broke off. "You may be right," he said, eyeing the sheriff appraisingly. "I don't suppose you'd be interested in taking care of them until I can turn them over to Hadlock? You sound like just the man for the job."

"Nope." Dolan dashed Willie's rising hopes with the single word. "My job's to maintain law and order, not nursemaid a passel of young'uns." He turned his horse into the path to Violet's home. With a sigh of resignation, Willie followed.

❧

Violet sloshed her hands through the soapy water, checking for any errant dishes that might have escaped her notice. Lunch had gone well, she thought smugly. The children's table manners showed they'd received proper training. Now Toby lay stretched out on Rachel and Daniel's bed, and Jessie and Frederick played a quiet game of checkers in the living room. Violet grinned. What was so hard about taking care of children?

She wiped the last plate and set it in the cupboard, then glanced out the kitchen window. Two riders approached the hitching rail out front. *If this isn't the day for unexpected arrivals!* Violet dried her hands and hung her apron on its hook. Smoothing her skirt, she hurried to the front door and peeped out the adjacent window.

She smiled when she recognized John Dolan's tall bay. His easygoing personality and dry humor always made him a welcome guest. But who could the other man be? The slim rider dismounted in one fluid movement. The gray horse he rode gleamed in the afternoon sunlight. *Is it my white knight at last?* Violet chuckled at her flight of fancy.

Waiting until the men's boots rang on the wooden porch, she swung the door open wide with a smile of welcome. "Sheriff! It's good to see you."

She peered past him to see if she could identify his companion. The tall man's chestnut hair fell across his forehead above lively blue eyes. Eyes that reminded her of . . . who? With a start, Violet recognized her unwelcome visitor of that morning. Her eyes narrowed to slits.

"Afternoon, Violet," Dolan said. "I see you remember Mr. Bradley here."

Violet crossed her arms and blocked the doorway. "Unfortunately." She felt gratified when Dolan's companion looked away.

The sheriff leaned back on the porch rail. "What's this I hear about you sending him away with a flea in his ear and not letting him have those kids that came out with him?"

She lifted her chin. "It's true, Sheriff. You see, when I went out to sweep the porch this morning, I saw three children turning their wagon into the drive. They were obviously frightened and told me all about Mr. Bradley and his treatment of them."

Distracted only momentarily by Bradley's sputter of protest, she refocused her attention on the lawman and went on. "They asked for shelter; I gave it to them. It's as simple as that. When he turned up several hours later, his behavior only confirmed everything they had told me. I refused to allow him near them," she said, "and what's more, I still do."

Dolan lifted his hand in a placating gesture. "Now, Violet—"

"Mr. Bradley has obviously managed to worm his way into your good graces. You wouldn't have been so quick to approve of him if you'd seen him in his previous state."

Bradley fixed her with a hostile stare and opened his mouth for the first time since his arrival. "I wouldn't have looked like that if those kids hadn't made off with the wagon and the water and my clean clothes." His voice rose louder with every word.

Violet looked at the sheriff triumphantly. "See what I mean?"

"Hmm." Dolan stroked his chin. "He has some papers with him, though, drawn up all legal and proper. He's supposed to be taking these young'uns to their guardian."

"Thurman Hadlock!" Violet summed up her opinion of the man in one contemptuous sniff.

Dolan drew himself up into a more official-looking stance. "Be that as it may, the law's the law, and I have to see that it's carried out. This man not only has a legal right but a moral responsibility to turn those children over to the person their father chose to raise them, whether any of us would approve of that choice or not."

He turned to the man beside him, who stood grinning at Violet's discomfiture. "On the other hand," he drawled, "there's no telling where all you'll have to look to find Hadlock, and you probably won't want the kids underfoot the whole time."

Violet suppressed a laugh when the grin faded and a puzzled frown appeared below the lock of hair that insisted on falling over his forehead.

"I'm suggesting a compromise," Dolan continued. "Why not let the kids stay here under Violet's care while you do your searching? That way you'll both be happier, and those youngsters won't have to be dragged around from pillar to post. Sounds to me like they've been through enough already." He rocked back on his heels and looked from one to the other. "What do you think?"

Violet gave him her brightest smile. "It suits me fine, Sheriff."

Obvious relief broke across Bradley's face. "Sounds good to me, too. That's probably the best thing for everyone all around, especially if it takes a day or so to find this fellow."

"Then it's settled." Dolan nodded to Violet with a pleased smile. "You'll know they're being well cared for, and you'll have your sister to help in case things get out of hand."

Violet cleared her throat. "Well . . ."

The sheriff gave her a questioning look.

She drew herself erect. "Actually, Rachel and Daniel are in Tucson right now." She bristled at Dolan's skeptical frown. Why did everyone always assume she couldn't handle the smallest job without help? "But I'm sure I'll do fine without them."

"You mean you're here all by yourself?" Bradley's tone went from agreeable to worried. "Just you and the kids? Alone?"

Violet stiffened. "I assure you, I am more than capable of caring for three small children."

"Lady, you have no idea what you're taking on. Just be grateful those three haven't burned your house down . . . yet."

Dolan inserted himself between them and laid his hand on the other man's shoulder. "Son, you'd best never question a woman's ability. I'm sure Miss Violet will do a fine job." He glanced at Violet, concern shadowing his face. "Won't you?"

"Of course I will," she snapped. "How much trouble can three youngsters be?"

❧

It took all Willie's self-control to keep from chortling aloud at that last remark. It showed just how little Miss Violet Canfield knew about children. He smirked, remembering that defiant tilt to her chin when she'd declared herself equal to the task of taking care of the Wingates. The Wingates! He nearly hooted out loud. She had no idea what she'd gotten herself into, no idea at all . . . but she'd find out soon enough. He'd be willing to bank on it.

In all honesty, Willie had to admit she probably could handle any normal child who crossed her path. When her eyes weren't shooting out angry blue sparks or gazing at him with cold suspicion, they held a gentle, friendly light. More than likely, she got along with most kids just fine. Children in general weren't all that bad. Even his four young cousins, rowdy as they could be at times, could be brought under control with just a bit of effort.

But Miss Canfield wasn't dealing with normal children. She'd elected to take on a handful of Wingates. And regardless of her good intentions, until the legalities had been observed, the final responsibility for them and their conduct lay at Willie's feet.

He supposed he ought to show some concern for their wellbeing. "Are they really all right? Well fed and all that?"

Violet fixed him with an austere gaze. "I can assure you they've settled in and are quite comfortable."

As if to corroborate her statement, a sleepy-eyed Toby appeared in the doorway. When he saw Willie, he clung to Violet's skirt. She smoothed his hair with a gentle hand and smiled down at him. The little boy looked up at her with what Willie could only describe as a nauseating simper. Violet turned a triumphant glance upon Willie. Immediately, the little boy stuck out his tongue. Willie took a half step toward him, and at once Toby began to whimper.

"There, there," Violet soothed him. "You're going to stay right here with me, Sweetheart." The little boy looked up at her with a questioning gaze. Violet gave the tip of his nose a playful tap with her finger. "Cross my heart," she whispered.

Sweetheart? The endearment made Willie want to gag, but he forced himself to step back and assume what he hoped looked like a nonthreatening expression. He shot a glance toward Dolan, wondering if the sharp-eyed sheriff had caught the little byplay. He'd be willing to bet the man didn't miss much. Dolan, however, maintained an impassive mien. Willie sighed. It would boost his spirits to know that someone besides himself recognized the Wingates' subterfuge.

Instead, the sheriff straightened and settled his Stetson on his head. "Seeing as how you folks are all set, it looks like it's time for me to be moving on."

"Then I'll say good-bye to you both," Violet said. "Where may I contact you if I need you, Mr. Bradley?"

Willie's jaw sagged. Up until that moment, he hadn't considered what his lodging arrangements might be. He'd noticed a hotel in town, but since he hadn't completed his mission by handing over the kids, he hadn't gotten around to inquiring about a room. Surely they wouldn't be booked up, though. He opened his mouth to say he could be found there, but his conscience stopped him.

Much as he'd love being away from the Wingates, they were still his responsibility. He couldn't foist them off on a total stranger. Besides, the idea of stranding her alone with that threesome, no matter how angelic she believed them to be, made his blood run cold. No telling what they might get up to if they didn't have a restraining influence close at hand.

"I'm still accountable for them." He chose his words with care. "It wouldn't do for me to just take off and leave them."

Violet pressed one hand to her throat and her brow crinkled. "I hadn't thought about that. I'll admit you have a right to want to be close by, but . . ." Her voice trailed away, then her face brightened.

"I think I have a solution," she said with a radiant smile that made Willie blink. "There's a small cabin on the far side of the barn that might suit your purpose nicely. My brother-in-law, Daniel, put it up some time ago. You're welcome to use it if you like. It might take a bit of fixing up and cleaning," she added sweetly, "but I'm sure you won't mind . . . and I certainly won't have time to do it with three children to cook and care for."

She flashed another dazzling smile at the men. "Good-bye, Sheriff. Thank you for taking care of this little difficulty so easily. Come, Toby. We need to see what your brother and sister are doing." With that, she shepherded the little boy back inside the house and closed the door. Softly, this time.

Willie beamed at the sheriff. "Looks like things are going to work out just fine. I'll spend a few minutes straightening up my new digs and start looking for Hadlock this evening."

"Mm." Dolan rubbed his hand across his chin. "That place out back of the barn, huh? Last time I saw it . . . well, you may not want to plan on going much of anywhere today." With that cryptic remark, he untied his horse from the hitching rail and swung into his saddle. "If I remember right," he called over his shoulder, "Daniel keeps his tools just inside the barn door."

Willie stared after Dolan's departing figure, then scratched his head and circled around the barn. Maybe the sheriff assumed he wouldn't be used to roughing it a bit. But why? He didn't look like some slicked-up city dude, did he? The cabin might not be anything special, but he could surely put up with a little privation for a night or two.

He rounded the barn and stopped dead in his tracks. A cabin, did she say? More like a pile of rubble. He walked around the tumbledown shack, moving carefully so as not to knock it over. As far as he could tell, it had only been a ramshackle, thrown-together affair to begin with. With the passage of time, the walls leaned inward in an attempt to meet one another, and the roof had begun to droop below wall level.

A little fixing up, huh? Willie snorted. He had a notion to go back and tell Violet just what he thought of her little cabin, but he had a feeling she'd enjoy it too much. He headed toward the barn to search for a hammer and nails.

When the sun hovered at the edge of the horizon, Willie stood back and appraised his progress. The four walls stood more or less erect, and the roof no longer threatened imminent collapse. Underneath the rubble he had found what could pass for a cot, once he beat the dust out of the thin mattress. Not much, but then, he didn't need much more than a roof over his head for the next night or two.

At least the place had a door. After a moment's reflection, he scrounged through the pile of scrap lumber and fashioned a sturdy latch. He didn't intend to stay awake all through his limited stay, and he had no desire for the Wingates to catch him napping. Memories of Lewis Monroe's "accident" remained all too fresh in his mind.

After a final scrutiny, he walked up to the house and rapped on the kitchen door. Violet answered his knock and clapped one hand to her mouth. Her eyes flared wide. "Oh, dear," she said in a choked voice.

Willie rolled his eyes. He hoped she didn't plan to do a repeat performance of their first meeting every time he came to the house alone. "I'd like to borrow a broom," he said. "And a scrub brush and pail, if you don't mind."

Muffled giggles met his ears when she moved to fetch the cleaning supplies, and he saw the three children seated at the table, staring at him with undisguised glee. What was the matter with everyone around here?

Violet returned and handed him the requested items. "Here you are, Mr. Bradley. While you're scrubbing out the cabin, I'll try to find a spare pitcher and basin for you." She tilted her head and gave him an appraising glance. "You have a much less frightening appearance when you're clean, you know."

Willie looked down at his clothes. If the rest of him looked anything like his filthy shirt and pants, no wonder his arrival had created a sensation.

"We haven't used the place much since my sister and brother-in-law got married," Violet went on. Her lips twitched. "I guess we really haven't done much to keep it up, have we?" She reached out and brushed at his ear, then held out her hand. "Here. You might be able to find a better place for this." She draped a large cobweb across his outstretched palm. More giggles erupted from behind her.

Without a word, Willie picked up the things he had asked for and stomped back down the path to scrub his sorry cabin, knock the dust out of his sorry mattress, and settle down on his sorry cot for his first night in his temporary home.

6

*T*he late afternoon sun's rays found their way under Willie's hat brim and hit him square in the eyes. He tipped the brim forward and lowered his chin. Settling back in the saddle, he let his horse have its head. After ten days of traveling back and forth between the Canfield farm and Prescott, he had no problem finding the way.

Another day of dead ends. Willie's stomach knotted. How hard should it be to locate one man in a close-knit frontier community? The territorial capital boasted two thousand souls, and not one of them claimed to know the whereabouts of Thurman Hadlock.

Most seemed to know about him, though. Willie winced, recalling the names he'd heard Hadlock called just that day: lush, gambler, and reprobate being the most repeatable terms. His shoulder still ached where a gray-haired woman swatted it repeatedly with her broom at the mere mention of Hadlock's name.

The most charitable opinion he'd heard came from a storekeeper who told him, "When Hadlock came here four years ago, he seemed respectable enough. Probably was. But being out on the frontier like this either makes or breaks a man. Hadlock's one who broke."

To top it all off, Willie's conscience started sending out annoying messages, asking whether it would really be right to place three children with a man who had popular opinion so firmly set against him. He still held the notion that the Wingate progeny were little fiends with angels' faces, but even so, he didn't know if he could leave them with someone like that with any sense of indifference.

He straightened in the saddle, as though by doing so he could shake off his doubts. Their father knew the man well enough to trust

50

him with the upbringing of his children, he reminded himself. And his mother's cousin Lewis, a bona fide lawyer, seemed comfortable enough in bringing them out here to him.

True, a niggling inner voice carped at him, *but Monroe hadn't gotten this far and seen what you have.*

On the other hand, Monroe was currently laid up in bed suffering from a mysteriously broken leg. He'd do well to remember that when his sympathies threatened to get the best of him.

The horse took the turn off the main road without any prodding, and Willie reviewed that day's progress. He had finally located Hadlock's place. The pitiful collection of rawhide and baling wire hadn't eased Willie's misgivings one whit. It might be several steps above the shack Willie resided in at the moment, but nowhere near the kind of home a fellow ought to have to raise a family.

He'd looked around but couldn't find any trace of the man. Worse, he hadn't been able to see any indication he'd been home at all in recent days. A check of the usual haunts Dolan mentioned turned up nothing but a sense of distaste both for the places Hadlock frequented and the company he kept. The horse flinched when a cottontail scampered across the trail, and Willie gave him a soothing pat on the neck.

When he left New Mexico, he never dreamed the job would take so long. There had to be some way to resolve his dilemma, but he didn't know what. He'd even gone to the extreme of sending Monroe a telegram, asking if he should take the kids back to the Double B until the lawyer had recovered sufficiently to return with them himself. It cost his ego plenty to hint he might not be able to handle this job, but he didn't know what else to do.

There had been one bright moment in his otherwise unprofitable day. He brightened at the memory. Coming out of Grady's Market, he'd walked straight into a passing young lady. The collision sent her parcels flying out of her arms and knocked her flat.

Mortified by his clumsiness, he rushed to help her up, then scrambled to retrieve the packages scattered across the boardwalk. Much to his relief, she accepted his fumbling apology with grace.

"Goodness me, I should have been watching where I was going," she said, peeping up at him past the flowered brim of her bonnet.

Eyes the color of spring grass shone with good humor, and she favored him with a brilliant smile that caused a tiny dimple to appear on her ivory cheek.

Willie's jaw dropped so far he wouldn't have been surprised to hear it echo off the boardwalk. He made an effort to raise it back into place. He'd already acted like a blundering idiot in bowling her over; no point in making a complete fool of himself besides. "I'm . . . I'm so sorry."

She tilted her head back and gave a merry laugh. Under the bon- net's wide brim, strands of golden hair shimmered in the sunlight. "You're forgiven. Would you mind escorting me home? I got a bit carried away with my shopping, and I'm afraid these parcels are going to be too much for me."

Willie didn't wait for another chance to redeem himself. With a gallant sweep of his hat, he took her packages with one arm and offered her the other.

"I'm Mary Rose Downey, by the way," she said, her enchanting face turned up to his. "And you're . . . ?"

Willie felt a flush creep up his neck. Couldn't he remember the simplest manners his mother had instilled over the years? "I'm Willie Bradley. And I'm pleased to meet you."

Mary Rose strolled down the street at an easy pace. "How long have you been in Prescott? You're either new here or you've been keeping to yourself. Otherwise I certainly would have noticed you."

The flush rose to his cheeks and forehead. Did she mean what he hoped she did? "I've been here just over a week. I'm staying out at the Canfield place."

Mary Rose raised a delicate eyebrow. "Are you a relative, or . . . ?" Her voice trailed away into silence.

"No, nothing like that," he hastened to explain. "I brought three orphaned kids out here to meet their guardian. A man named Thur- man Hadlock." He waited for her reaction and felt relieved when she only nodded. "Miss Canfield's watching the kids for me while I look for him."

"Miss Canfield? Violet, you mean?" The unblemished brow puck- ered in a tiny frown. "But I thought I heard she'd gone to Tucson."

Willie chuckled. "No, her sister and her husband are the ones who are gone. Violet's still here."

Both eyebrows raised at that revelation.

Willie thought he'd burn up with embarrassment. What was it about this woman that made him unable to express the simplest thought clearly? "It's not what you're thinking," he sputtered. "Not at all. The children are staying in the house with her. I'm in a cabin out back." He watched her face intently and relaxed when her radiant smile returned.

"I see." She squeezed his arm in an intimate gesture that sent his pulse from a trot to a gallop. "I have a suggestion," she said, slowing her steps to stop in front of a handsome two-story house. "I know just about everybody in town. Why don't I help you look for Mr. Hadlock?"

"Why, sure. If you really want to." Had he really found someone willing to help instead of running him off at the mention of Hadlock's name?

"Wonderful." The dimple appeared once more. "Why don't you pick me up right here tomorrow morning? My father has a lot of business connections. He might be able to use his influence to help too."

"That would be great. I'm sure glad I bumped into you. I mean . . . I would appreciate that very much." He left with her musical laugh ringing in his ears.

Mary Rose's help might not locate Hadlock any sooner, he reflected while he turned his horse into Violet's drive, but it would sure make looking for him a lot more pleasant.

❧

"More potatoes?" Violet passed the earthenware bowl in response to Willie's nod and tried to maintain the bright smile she'd plastered on her face in preparation for the evening meal. Every weary bone in her body cried out for rest, but she had no intention of letting him know how exhausted she felt. Everyone seemed to think she had her head in the clouds too much to be able to do anything useful on her own. That assumption tired her as much as taking care of the children did.

She slid Toby's plate closer, the better to cut his chicken into smaller bites. How could three little children add so many extra duties to her day? When Daniel and Rachel first left for Tucson, time stretched before her like an unending ribbon of days, hers to fill in any way she chose. Today the happy hours she'd whiled away with her favorite books seemed a distant dream.

Instead, her days were filled with chores from sunup to sunset with no time to even think of having a few spare minutes to spend reading. Taking care of injured animals had involved little more than binding up their wounds, fashioning some sort of bed, and feeding them at intervals. Plenty of time remained for whatever chores awaited her, with hours left over to follow her own pursuits.

Now her waking hours revolved around cooking, cleaning, and doing laundry, plus gathering eggs and taking care of the livestock. Doing these household chores for herself hadn't presented a problem; the additional load of three people—four, counting Willie, since he ate with them and had taken her up on her offer to do his laundry— threatened to overwhelm her.

Not that she intended to admit that to a living soul! She took a bite of mashed potatoes and gravy, and her gaze fell on her most recent letter from Rachel, in its place on the sideboard. All was well, she wrote. She and Daniel were enjoying the warmer weather in the southern part of the territory. Daniel still had several mining properties to look over, which might take a couple of weeks longer than they'd thought. If Violet had no objection, they might delay their return for awhile.

Violet's guilty glance rested momentarily on the reply she'd penned that afternoon, waiting for Willie to take it to town with him tomorrow on his latest foray in search of Thurman Hadlock.

Had she done wrong by letting Rachel think nothing had changed since her departure? She'd filled her letter with cheery talk about the weather and signs of the approaching spring, news about the farm, and the latest news from town, all written in a bright, breezy tone.

She hadn't lied—exactly—by failing to let her sister know their home had four new residents, but the omission gnawed at her.

It would only worry Rachel, she rationalized. *Time enough to let her know when she gets back. She's had little enough time alone with Daniel since they married; no point in making her feel she needs to rush home to be sure I'm not botching everything.*

Rachel and Daniel hadn't taken the time for a honeymoon when they married a little more than three years before, busying themselves with the work involved on the farm the girls' father had left Rachel. They welcomed having Violet as a part of their lives, but she always felt a little guilty about them never having time to themselves. How could she think of spoiling the first opportunity they'd had to be off on their own?

She couldn't. Pushing her qualms firmly to the back of her mind, she patted her mouth with her napkin and sent a determined smile around the table. By the time Rachel returned, the Wingate children would be settled with their new guardian and the whole episode would make an amusing tale to share. Especially if she got some rest between now and then.

Frederick folded his napkin and tucked it under the edge of his plate. "May we be excused, Miss Violet?"

"Of course." She watched the three children scamper off. "It's still light outside," she called after them. "Why don't you play outdoors a bit before bedtime?" Shrill cheers and the slam of the front door told her they approved her suggestion.

She leaned back in her chair, glad for the moment's respite. "More coffee?" At Willie's nod, she poured fresh cups for them both. She sipped her coffee and considered the man across the table from her. He hadn't made one derogatory comment during the meal. Amazing. He didn't seem so bad when he left off badmouthing the children.

Tonight he seemed preoccupied by something. Apparently he hadn't had any more success in finding Hadlock. She took another sip, taking advantage of his distraction to study him more closely. The rigors of ranch life had given him a lean, sinewy build, she noted, along with a tanned complexion from hours spent outdoors. His work-hardened hands carried the calluses of manual labor, but his easy familiarity with table manners indicated a proper upbringing.

At the moment, he had his gaze fixed on the tablecloth; but she knew if he glanced up, she'd look into eyes that matched the color of a summer sky. And that stubborn lock of hair still insisted on falling down over his forehead. She noted the wayward strands with a smile. He could almost be the knight of her imagination, if he just didn't seem to hate children so much.

Willie chose that moment to look up, and his gaze locked onto hers. A funny tingle started in the region of her stomach, then spread up into her throat. Strange, she'd felt just fine up until then. Her fingers were trembling too. She clasped her hands together, hoping Willie wouldn't notice.

Her lips parted and she pressed them together. They opened again of their own accord. Really, she ought to say something, if only to keep from looking like a gaping fish. "How did your search go today?"

Willie shook his head and the light in his eyes dimmed. "Still no sign of him. I've checked every place and every person Sheriff Dolan told me about. It's almost like the man's vanished off the face of the earth."

For the first time, Violet felt a tender concern for him. How frustrating it must be, to have left home and family on what amounted to a mission of mercy, only to find oneself stymied at every turn. She opened her mouth—intentionally, this time—to offer some consolation, when Willie continued his story.

"One good thing happened, though." A flicker of hope rekindled the spark in his eyes. "It looks like I'm going to have some help from now on."

"Really?" Violet felt a sudden surge of joy at this sign of encouragement.

"I met someone in town who knows just about everybody. Once she found out how much trouble I've had finding Hadlock, she offered to help me look for him." He brushed his forehead, pushing the errant strands of hair back into place. "Having someone local help me ask questions should make people open up more."

Cross My Heart

"Oh." Violet tried to recapture her earlier happiness for him. He had a point; getting assistance from someone who knew the lay of the land ought to prove most helpful. Sheriff Dolan didn't have time to poke around looking for Hadlock, and goodness knew her own schedule didn't allow for that. She ought to be happy for both him and the children, not feel like the proverbial dog in the manger.

"Who is it?" She tried to inject a bright note into her voice. She could sound pleased, even if she didn't feel that way.

"It's a Miss Downey." He tilted his head back to swallow the last drop of coffee. "Mary Rose Downey." He rose as if to leave, then stopped and stared at Violet. "Is anything wrong?"

"Mary Rose Downey and Thurman Hadlock." Violet forced the words out past the constriction in her throat. If he had reached across the table and slapped her, she couldn't have felt more stunned. "You do choose interesting companions, don't you?"

"Now, wait a minute!" Willie planted his hands on the table and leaned toward her. "Leaving those kids to Hadlock wasn't my idea. And I didn't ask Mary Rose to help out; she just offered. As a friendly gesture. Some people reach out to help instead of biting other people's heads off."

"And you have to accept every offer that's given, is that it?"

"If you remember," Willie shouted, "it wasn't even my idea to come out here in the first place. If my cousin had kept his guard up just a little while longer, he'd be the one out here being unappreciated, not me."

"What a shame it didn't happen that way." Violet rose to her feet and flounced across the room. "If you'll excuse me," she said, sweeping past Willie with the regal air of royalty side-stepping a minion, "I need to send the children to gather the eggs. I got so busy earlier I didn't get around to it, and there's just enough light left, if they hurry."

Willie put his hand out to stop her. "Eggs? You're letting those kids get the eggs?"

Violet raised her chin and fixed him with a lofty stare. "And why not? Don't you believe in teaching children responsibility?"

"Oh, absolutely." His mouth worked. "Yes, Ma'am, I surely do.

You just go right ahead and send those little darlings after the eggs. Just stay away from doorways." He picked up his hat and exited, chuckling.

Violet stared after him. What had gotten into him? What had gotten into her, for that matter? She couldn't remember a time she'd gone from fluttery trembling to outright rudeness like that. What on earth had set her off like that? She pressed her fists against her temples, trying to recall the course of their conversation.

Oh, yes. Mary Rose Downey and her offer to help. And which bothered her most, the memory of Mary Rose or the knowledge she'd be spending time with Willie? *Be honest, Violet. Would you feel like this if a man had offered to help him?*

But he had no idea of Mary Rose's character . . . or lack of it. He'd be like a fly caught in her skillfully woven web before he knew it. And what did it matter to her? Willie Bradley was a grown man and didn't need her advice on how to run his life. He'd dropped into her neatly ordered existence out of the blue and would go out of it just as quickly. He probably wouldn't welcome her advice, anyway.

With a wistful sigh, she hooked the egg basket over her arm and went outside to call the children.

7

*W*illie made his way back to his cabin, enjoying the warmer evening air. Tonight the light breeze felt almost balmy. Leaning against the side of the barn, he looked up at the darkening sky and waited for his favorite constellations to appear: Orion the Hunter with his belt of three stars and the Big and Little Dippers in their constant rotation around the North Star. In another hour, when the sky had become truly dark, the faint cluster of the Seven Sisters would be visible in the East.

As children, he and Lizzie spent hours staring at the stars each evening. His sister might even be looking at them right now, he thought. With the supper dishes cleaned up and put away, maybe she and Adam sat on their broad front porch at that very moment, watching the timeless display.

He entered his cabin and lit the lamp, his meager furnishings becoming visible when the match flared up. For some reason he couldn't begin to name, he felt more content than he'd been in a long time. His circumstances had changed dramatically over the past few weeks, but he saw the same stars tonight he would have seen at home in New Mexico. The God who created them—and him—was as present with him here as back at the ranch. He sat on the edge of his cot and pulled off one of his boots.

For the first time since leaving home, he measured his problems against the backdrop of the heavens' grandeur and saw them as small indeed. Surely he could trust the Creator of the universe to solve his minor troubles. Even a trio of Wingates didn't pose too big a problem for the Almighty.

The reminder of the children caused him to stop in the act of tugging off his other boot. Violet had sent them to get eggs, and he hadn't given her much in the way of a word of caution. He should have warned her about Frederick's egg trick.

Nah, let her find out on her own just how adorable those three can be. He chuckled and undid the buttons on his work shirt, wondering just how long it would be before they showed their true colors.

Why would anyone in their right mind volunteer to take on those hoodlums in training? He pulled his shirt over his head and hung it on a peg, turning the question over in his mind. He knew firsthand how disarming the trio could be at first sight; he'd been bamboozled himself, until he spent time alone with them. Understandable, then, that a tender heart like Violet's would feel sympathy for them in the beginning.

But after spending days on end in their company? It didn't make sense.

Willie ran his fingers through his hair and prepared to stretch out on the thin mattress. He'd posed that puzzle to Mary Rose earlier in the day, while they walked down the boardwalk, her dainty hand tucked trustingly in the crook of his arm.

He closed his eyes and inhaled, as if he could bring back the scent of lilac water that surrounded her in a fragrant cloud. Unlike Violet, she hadn't despised him on sight. In fact, she'd seemed pretty impressed by his description of his home and family. And she'd patted his arm in consolation when he related his misadventures in trying to connect the Wingate children with their new home. Overall, her frank admiration and sympathy bolstered his badly wounded pride and made Willie feel like a hero.

"And you say Violet Canfield is caring for them?" Mary Rose fluttered eyelashes like fans in his direction. "Is she an old friend of your family? Or the children's, perhaps?"

Willie shook his head. "Not at all. I'd never seen her in my life before I tracked the kids to her door."

"And she agreed, just like that, when you asked her to care for children she didn't know?"

"I didn't ask; she told me that's how it was going to be." Willie flushed at the memory. "At the time, it didn't set real well with me;

but I have to admit, it's all worked out for the best. I've been able to spend my time looking for Hadlock without the three of them underfoot." No need to add that he wouldn't have been able to squire a certain young lady along the streets of Prescott if the kids had been his to watch.

"But I still can't figure out why she keeps on doing it. I know what those kids are like. Either they've done a grand job of keeping her fooled, or she has more grit than I gave her credit for."

"Or maybe she thinks it's worth her while to put up with them in spite of all their mischief." Mary Rose looked up at him with speculative green eyes. "Money, perhaps?"

Willie knew the start he gave answered her question before he ever opened his mouth. "They do stand to inherit a fair amount," he said slowly, remembering the sum Monroe had mentioned. "But she'd have no way of knowing that."

Mary Rose laughed again and gave his arm a playful swat. "Men can be so innocent," she teased. "She had plenty of time to cozy up to them and learn every little detail long before you showed up. Maybe there really is more to Violet than that delicate exterior she shows to the world."

Mary Rose's words swirled through Willie's head while he lay on his cot, arms pillowing his head. Could it be true? Did Violet know about the Wingate money and have plans to latch onto it if Hadlock couldn't be found? Even given their unending friction, he wouldn't have thought it of her; but women knew other women, or so he'd always heard.

Did Mary Rose know something about Violet he didn't? She hadn't said she disliked Violet in so many words, but her tone carried that implication clearly enough. And Violet's reaction to his mention of Mary Rose at the supper table made her feelings about the other woman abundantly clear. It didn't take a genius to see the two women shared a mutual lack of regard. But did either of them have a valid reason? As far as he could see, neither had a solid basis for their attitude.

He frowned into the darkness, trying to assess the situation. It seemed clear that Mary Rose's offer of help came purely from the goodness of her heart; there could be no other motive. And only that morning, he would have sworn Violet's affection for the children was genuine, if misguided. He hadn't seen a thing to make him believe otherwise.

Until Mary Rose put the thought into his mind. Willie sat up and combed his fingers through his tousled hair, then yanked his shirt on over his head and stepped into his boots. He wouldn't sleep a wink until he knew for sure whether Violet had heard about the kids' inheritance.

Lights still burned inside the house. Good. If everyone had already gone to bed, he'd have had to turn back and stay awake all night, chewing on the question. He rapped on the front door and drew back, startled, when Jessica answered his knock.

"Miss Violet's putting Toby to bed," she told him. "My turn's next."

Willie responded with an unwilling grin. Jessica's blond hair streamed down her back in silky waves. Bare toes peeked out from under the hem of her white nightdress. If he didn't have all too much insight into her true nature, she'd look awfully cute. Could it be that Violet's loving care had given the kids sufficient motivation to mend their ways? Maybe they'd decided to settle down and behave. If they did, it would sure make his job easier.

No point in carrying a grudge; if they were willing to turn around, he could meet them halfway. He knelt down in front of the little girl to put himself at her eye level. "Do you think she'd have time to talk to me when she's finished?"

Jessica smiled and nodded. "Probably."

Willie's heart warmed. When she wasn't plotting or carrying out some nefarious scheme, she could be one little charmer. He started to speak, ready to draw out their conversation, when approaching footsteps caught his attention.

"Did I hear someone at the door?" Violet walked into the room and stopped short at the sight of Willie. He rose to his feet, suddenly self-conscious about the question he'd come to ask.

"It's just me," he said, adding with a grin at his small companion, "Jessica and I were having a little chat."

Jessica drew herself up ramrod straight and took two steps backward. "And I don't care what you say," she huffed, "I don't believe Miss Violet would ever do a thing like that." She flounced off toward the rear of the house without a backward glance.

Violet stared at him wide-eyed. "And may I ask just what you've been telling her about me?" She advanced on him, fists on her hips and fire smoldering in the gaze she turned on him.

He opened and closed his mouth, but no sound came forth. He swallowed hard. "I have no idea," he managed to say.

Violet raised a disbelieving eyebrow. "Surely you can do better than that."

"So help me, all I'd done was ask whether you could spare the time to talk to me."

"And I'm supposed to believe she came up with a remark like that on her own?" The look she gave him could have withered a small oak at twenty yards. "I'd been foolish enough to think you were finished casting aspersions on the children."

"Well, no—I mean—" Willie clamped his lips together. He sounded like a moron, even to himself.

Violet fixed him with a haughty gaze. "Did you have something specific you wanted to discuss, or did you just come by to talk about me behind my back?"

"I was going to ask you—" He broke off, knowing full well how his question would sound in light of their current conversation.

He gulped and tried again. Hadn't he already made enough mess of things for one night? Nothing could make him look much worse in her eyes than he did already . . . unless it was the question he was about to ask. Still, he had to know.

"Do you know anything about the money the kids are going to come into?" There, it was out. He waited for the roof to cave in. To his amazement, Violet threw back her head and laughed.

"You mean their inheritance?" At Willie's dumbfounded nod, she chortled again. "Yes, the little scamps told me all about the money their father left them. I suppose they thought it might make them look more important, poor little things. As if they needed to do something to impress me. But you needn't worry that I took them seriously."

"But—"

"How on earth did they manage to come up with such a fanciful story?" Violet tilted her head to one side and cast a quizzical glance at Willie. "To think a wild tale like that could come from the imaginations of such young children. What put it in their heads, do you suppose?"

Willie's mind reeled. "You don't believe it then?"

Violet shook her head and gave him a pitying smile. "How could I? It's hardly logical. If their father had that kind of means, would he have chosen someone like Thurman Hadlock as their guardian?" She erupted once more into peals of laughter.

"I guess that would be hard to figure, wouldn't it?" Willie attempted a grin and edged toward the porch steps. "Well, that was all I wanted to ask you. Good night."

The soft smile left Violet's lips and her stern expression returned. "Please don't try to malign the children again. You're much more likable, you know, when you don't tell stories about them."

Willie's foot slipped, and he saved himself from a fall only by twisting his body into wild contortions between the top step and the ground. Behind him he heard a soft giggle before Violet closed the door. Within minutes he had regained the solitude of his cabin and once more stretched out on the cot.

"What do You think about that, Lord?" he whispered. "She'll believe any crazy story those kids make up about me, but she doesn't recognize the truth when it up and stares her in the face. I know You created women, so You must understand them. But it sure is a tough proposition for the rest of us."

He laced his fingers behind his head and considered the other women he'd known. That pretty much narrowed the field down to his mother, his sister, and his aunt, all basically normal females. True, his mother seemed to have gone a bit softheaded with the advent of her first grandchild; but in her usual state, she had plenty of common sense. If she hadn't been so addled by Lizzie's coming confinement and the arrival of Cousin Lewis, he knew she'd never have been taken in by the Wingate tribe, sweet faces or no.

What about Lizzie? She had been Willie's closest friend and playmate all through their growing-up years. He knew her almost as well as he knew himself. *It's a pity she couldn't get over to visit before I left,* he mused. *She would have seen right through those three.*

On the other hand, every woman they'd run across in their travels to Prescott seemed to feel an immediate need to take on a protective role toward the children. Even when it meant protecting them from him. It just proved his point: There was no figuring women.

So where did that put Violet? If he'd met her under different circumstances, unencumbered and Wingate-free, they might have started off on better footing. Her delicate figure and graceful walk were enough to catch a man's notice right off. With the addition of glossy sable hair framing her heart-shaped face, it made for a stunning combination.

And those eyes! Willie pursed his lips in a silent whistle. He'd seen plenty of blue eyes in his family. He had blue eyes himself. So did his father, Uncle Jeff, Aunt Judith, and his cousins. But *these* . . . He'd never encountered the likes of them before. Blue as a delphinium, blue as the hottest part of a flame. With their intensity, they could scorch a man or melt his heart. He'd met a beauty, no doubt about it.

But what went on beneath that lovely exterior? He reflected on this dilemma, fighting off the drowsiness that made his eyelids drift closed despite his attempts to keep them open. She didn't seem like an empty-headed dreamer, but to all appearances she'd been taken in hook, line, and sinker by every story the kids had told her, save the one about the money their father had left them. *Funny,* he mused, *that she missed the truth about that one.*

Or had she? The thought jolted him wide awake. What if that slim body housed a devious brain, one that did indeed recognize the inheritance story as the truth and had decided to benefit from it?

Could lovely Violet be capable of such duplicity? The thought gnawed at him, and sleep fled.

8

"iss Violet, I don't feel so good."

Violet scooped the last of the scrambled eggs from the frying pan onto a serving dish and set it on the table next to the platter of bacon. "What's wrong, Honey?" She turned back to the counter and sliced a freshly baked loaf of bread with smooth, practiced strokes.

"My throat hurts."

"Probably from talking too much." Willie's comment, though mumbled, carried clearly.

Violet swung around and pointed the bread knife at him. "I thought we had an agreement."

He raised his hands in surrender. "You're right. I apologize." His sullen demeanor didn't match his words, but she decided to let it go. Might as well take any concession he was willing to give.

She handed the bread plate to Frederick and circled the table to lay her hand on Jessica's forehead. A flutter of concern knotted her stomach.

"Willie." Even to her own ears, her voice sounded strange. He paused in the act of loading his breakfast plate and looked up. A frown creased his forehead when he met her gaze. "What's wrong?"

"I need you to go into town and fetch the doctor." She could hear her voice rising, tight with fear. She cleared her throat before she continued, hoping to inject a more casual note into her tone. "Since you're going in for supplies, anyway, it won't take but a few moments extra. His office is right over the mercantile." There, that sounded much calmer.

"Fine." His face cleared and he picked up his fork. "I'll head out as soon as I've finished eating."

Maybe she'd sounded too calm. She spooned a mound of eggs from his plate onto a slice of bread, laid two strips of bacon across the eggs, and piled another slice of bread on top, ignoring his startled yip. "Here. You can eat this on the way." When he opened his mouth to protest, she shook her head and laid her finger across her lips, nodding toward the door. She breathed a sigh of relief when he followed her out onto the kitchen stoop without further argument.

"She's running a fever," she told him. "A high one. You need to leave as soon as you can get the horse hitched up." She shoved the improvised sandwich into his hands.

"Hurry," she pleaded. "I'm truly worried about her."

Willie responded with a gratifying air of concern and hurried toward the barn. Violet returned to the kitchen, where the two boys mopped up the remains of the bacon and eggs with their bread and Jessica stared listlessly at her untouched plate.

Violet put an arm around the little girl and helped her out of her chair. "Come on, Jessie. Let's get you back to bed."

"She just got up," Toby argued around a mouthful of eggs.

"Things are a little different this morning. You boys help yourselves to seconds, if you'd like." She scooped Jessie into her arms and hastened down the hall.

In the bedroom, she helped Jessie out of her pinafore and into her nightdress and tied her hair back with a ribbon. After tucking the little girl in bed, she hurried to the kitchen and returned with a cloth and a basin of water.

"This should make you feel better." She sponged Jessie's forehead with the cool water, remembering how Rachel had once cared for her the same way during a bout with influenza. "Does that help any?"

Jessie closed her eyes and tossed her head in fretful denial. Moist wisps of her wheat-colored hair clung to her forehead. Violet smoothed them back with her fingertips and winced at the heat emanating from the little girl's body. If only the doctor would arrive! She stared at the small form on the bed and felt her throat tighten. No matter how her heart had gone out to her animal patients in the past, this was far different than taking care of a bird or a squirrel, and the stakes were much higher. For the first time during one of her rescue efforts, Violet felt burdened by a sense of inadequacy.

She dipped the cloth in the basin again, this time wiping Jessie's arms and hands. Jessie whimpered and pulled away. Violet studied the little girl. Heat from the fever had added color to her fair complexion, almost as if . . . Padding across the floor so as not to disturb the sick child, she pulled the curtain back to admit the morning sun. Light filled the room and washed across the bed. She peered at Jessie's face.

"Honey, were you outside without your bonnet yesterday? It looks like the sun has burned your poor little face."

Jessica murmured an unintelligible reply. Violet resumed her seat at the bedside and continued bathing her face and arms. She'd had sunburns herself, enough to turn her nose pink and even make it peel at times, but she'd never gotten sick from it. She'd never been burned as badly as Jessie seemed to be, though.

Remorse smote her. She ought to have noticed whether or not the child had worn her bonnet. Jessie's fair skin was no match for the intense northern Arizona sun. Why had she let yesterday's turmoil keep her from fulfilling her responsibility? If she hadn't been so caught up in talk of Mary Rose Downey and its aftermath, she *would* have noticed. She felt sure of that.

Don't let anything bad happen to Jessie because I wasn't paying attention, Lord. Help me know what to do.

An overwhelming weariness swept through her. How did mothers manage to take care of the myriad details of housekeeping plus tend to their children's needs and watch out for their safety? It seemed so simple on the surface, but carrying it out proved to be another matter altogether. Her shoulders settled against the back of the chair. Her eyelids drifted shut, and she dropped her hands into her lap. It felt so good to relax for just a moment.

A light breeze drifted in through the window, and Violet roused with a start when she heard the voices of her two other charges. How could she have forgotten about them? She shook her head to clear it and glanced at Jessie. The little girl appeared to be asleep. Violet noted her steady breathing and felt reassured. Satisfied her absence wouldn't be noticed for a time, she rose, grimacing at the damp coolness on her lap. She'd dropped the cloth without noticing when she became drowsy, and now a large circle marred the front of her skirt.

No matter. She had more important concerns at the moment than the state of her clothes. She hurried outdoors to see what the boys were doing. On second thought, she retrieved their hats from the hooks in their room and carried them with her. No point in risking any more sunburns.

❧

Stupid! Willie berated himself all during the wagon ride into town. Just how much of an idiot could one man be? As if he needed to add to the black marks on his slate from the night before, he had to go and make that snide comment about Jessica's sore throat being caused by too much talking.

The memory of it made him want to bite his tongue. For all their perfidy, the Wingates were only little kids; but he was a grown man, supposedly able to control his tongue and keep his temper in check. *What's wrong with me, Lord? Haven't I heard those verses about a gentle answer turning away wrath often enough?*

Violet's concern for Jessica's health had been evident in the way her voice tightened and her hands trembled. And what had he done? Only added to her worries by his thoughtless quip. Hopefully, his quick departure once she made the situation clear had reassured her that he could be more of a gentleman than he'd shown her up to now.

He clucked to the horse to pick up the pace. The sorrel gelding could rest while he ran his errands in town. Right now, the important thing was to find that doctor and get him started on his way. Where did Violet say his office was located? He spied the gilt lettering— Phineas Hathaway, M.D.—on the door above the mercantile and set the wagon brake.

With the doctor alerted, Willie felt free to go about his business. Jessica did have a fever, he reasoned, but surely it would turn out to be nothing more than a bad cold or some other innocuous complaint.

An hour later, Willie looked at the wagonload of supplies with satisfaction. He decided to take just a few more minutes in town and turned his steps toward the telegraph office. A sweet voice called his name just as he reached the door. He looked back over his shoulder and saw a smiling Mary Rose heading his way.

He felt a broad grin spread over his face. Maybe the day wouldn't turn out to be a total loss after all. Mary Rose's company could take a load of care off a man in a hurry.

The scent of lilacs wafted toward him when she approached. "I didn't know whether I'd ever see you again," she pouted, tucking her hand into the crook of his arm in a proprietary gesture that made his heart race. "I thought you might have finished your business here and gone off to that ranch of yours without another thought for poor little me."

Willie's mouth went dry as a drought-parched pasture. Did it really matter to a lovely woman like Mary Rose whether she saw him again or not? They had only met a bare twenty-four hours before, after all. He peered at her more closely and saw her lower lip quiver. The sight stirred a feeling of protectiveness, and he pressed a reassuring hand over her fingertips.

The smile she turned on him could have lit up the whole town on a moonless night. Willie nodded toward the office doors. "I was just going to see if I'd had a reply to a telegram I sent home. Would you care to join me?"

"Only if you'll join me for a cup of tea when you've finished your business here." Her inviting gaze made his heart lurch.

Monroe's response to Willie's query about bringing the children home until he could return with them himself was succinct and to the point. The word *NO* sat alone in the center of the yellow paper, leaving no room for doubt.

Willie thanked the clerk, folded the missive, and tucked it into his coat pocket, surprised at how little the abrupt refusal disturbed him. Somehow with Mary Rose clinging to his arm, staying around

Prescott a while longer didn't seem like such a bad idea. Not to mention the prospect of another train trip with the three Wingates no longer hung over his head.

He passed a pleasant half hour drinking tea with Mary Rose, then walked her to her home once again and went on his way. Recounting her every word, look, and gesture filled the drive back to the farm in a most pleasant manner.

He started into the curve leading to the farm and turned his horse to the side to avoid the buckboard that rattled along the road toward him. The grizzled driver pulled on the reins and studied him. His face broke into a broad smile, revealing several missing teeth.

"You must be the young feller with all the kids who's staying here with Violet."

Willie stared at the scruffy newcomer. "I guess that would be me," he agreed slowly.

The other man beamed. "Thought so." He held out a calloused hand. "Put 'er there. My name's Jeb McCurdy. I live just down the road." He pointed a gnarled finger over his shoulder.

"Willie Bradley." He returned the older man's grip, surprised at its strength. McCurdy seemed in no hurry to leave. He might as well question him while he had the opportunity. "I'm looking for a man named Thurman Hadlock. Do you know him?"

The benevolent glow faded from McCurdy's eyes. "I should say I do. What do you want with him? You don't look like the sort he usually hangs out with."

After learning something of Hadlock's reputation, Willie felt glad to hear that. "He's been named guardian of the children. I've come to take them to him."

McCurdy shook his head somberly. "I don't know where he is, and if I did, I'm not sure I'd tell you. That man doesn't have a decent bone in his body." Then he brightened. "Tell you what. You stop by my place one of these days and we'll figure out someone else who can take those kids. How about it?"

Willie chuckled at the earnest offer. "We'll see, Jeb. At any rate, it's been nice talking to you."

"Likewise," his neighbor said. He picked up the reins and shook them. "Come see me if you get in a bind."

Willie nudged his horse forward and continued around the curve. He frowned in surprise when he saw the doctor's buggy still standing in front of the house and the doctor himself busy nailing a brightly colored placard to the gate post.

"What's going on?" he called, as soon as he was within earshot.

Doc Hathaway pounded in the final nail before taking any notice of Willie's presence. "I'm putting the place under quarantine," he told him brusquely. "I'm afraid young Jessica has scarlet fever."

"Scarlet . . . But she seemed fine yesterday. All she said this morning was that her throat hurt."

The doctor nodded. "That's how it often begins. By the time I arrived, the rash had already started on her face and spread to her neck. Right now she's one sick little girl."

"How about the boys? They don't have it, do they?"

"Not yet, but with as much close contact as family members have, there's a good chance they'll catch it from her." He dusted his hands together and shook his head. "Violet's going to have her hands full."

"Surely some of the neighbors or people from town . . ." Willie's voice trailed off when the doctor tapped the quarantine notice.

"I don't want this spreading if I can help it. No one but me goes in or out past this sign until further notice."

Indecision tore at Willie. The idea of staying cooped up with Violet and the kids for an indeterminate period held all the appeal of building a mile of fence singlehandly, especially when it would put an end to his search for Hadlock for all that time. He eyed the provisions in the wagon bed. Surely he could unload them on the porch, unhitch the wagon, and hightail it back to town without the doctor objecting. They'd have plenty of food, and he could continue looking for the elusive guardian without interruption.

An image of Violet flashed into his mind, and he remembered the dark circles under her eyes that morning, her drooping shoulders, and the worry etched on her face. Tempting as it might be to be shed of the kids for awhile, he couldn't subject her to caring for the three of them without help. And what would happen if she came down with the disease herself, leaving her at the mercy of those renegades? The recollection of Monroe's fractured leg made up his mind for him.

He clicked his tongue and urged the horse past the gate. "I'm staying," he told the bushy-browed doctor. "I picked up supplies this morning, so we'll be set for however long it takes. We'll be fine." He hoped he could live up to that brave assurance.

Doc Hathaway stiffened and fixed him with a stern gaze, then relaxed, apparently reassured by what he saw. He dipped his head in reluctant acquiescence. "I'll say this to your face: I'd be more inclined to horsewhip you than let you stay if I hadn't already heard about you from the sheriff. Dolan's a good man. If he vouches for you, I guess you're all right."

The halfhearted compliment sent a jolt of unexpected encouragement through Willie. Dolan had stopped by a time or two to see how his search was progressing. They'd spent time talking and seemed to get along all right, but he had no idea the sheriff had formed such a positive opinion of him. Coming from a man like Dolan, the accolade meant a lot.

Doc stepped up into his buggy and picked up the reins. "I'll look in later," he promised. "If you need anything from town, nail a list to the gate post and McCurdy can pick them up for you." He flicked the buggy whip and drove away.

Willie stopped the horse at the foot of the porch steps and started unloading bags and boxes. He looked at the pile of supplies, gauging how long they would last. Realization struck him with a sense of finality: As long as the quarantine lasted, they wouldn't be able to count on anyone else's presence or help. If the boys contracted the disease one after the other, it might be a month before he could leave the farm again.

9

*I*t tastes good, Miss Violet." Jessie smiled, the first sign of animation Violet had seen in her since she'd taken sick.

"I'm glad, Honey. You need to keep eating so you can get better." Violet spooned the last of the chicken broth into the little girl's mouth, then set the bowl on the bedside table. She dipped the cloth into the basin and sponged Jessica's forehead.

"That feels so nice," the little girl murmured, her voice slurred with drowsiness. Her eyelids batted once, then twice, then drifted shut and stayed that way.

Violet continued bathing her head and arms, hoping her ministrations would help bring that high temperature down soon. When her arms tired, she sat watching Jessie's chest rise and fall with her breathing, giving a quick little catch from time to time. Damp ringlets of wheat-colored hair clung to the little girl's forehead, and Violet brushed them back tenderly, trying not to waken the sleeping child.

Surely this wouldn't last much longer. When the rash she'd mistaken for sunburn started to spread from Jessie's face to her chest and back, then her arms and legs, Violet had been able to do nothing but watch the disease's progress with horror . . . and prayer. Thank the Lord, it had begun to fade, although red streaks remained in the creases under her arms and inside the crook of her elbows. Those would go away soon, according to what Doc Hathaway said on his visit earlier that afternoon.

"You've done a fine job," he said in his gravelly voice. "If all my patients had the diligent care you've given this little sprite, my job would be a lot easier." He pulled his stethoscope from around his neck and placed it back in his medical bag. "With the rash fading like it is, you can expect her fever to go away in another day or so. Once that happens, she should begin to recover quickly."

Violet felt a surge of hope for the first time in the days since his first visit to Jessie. "Does that mean you'll remove the quarantine sign soon?"

The doctor picked up his bag and pursed his lips in thought, skewing his bristly white mustache to one side. He shook his head. "It stays in place. Nobody goes in or out of here but me. This little scamp is doing well—" He tweaked Jessie's toes through the comforter, eliciting a weak giggle from the sick girl. "—but I don't want to risk having an outbreak on my hands. I look for the boys to come down with it anytime within the next few days. We'll see what happens then.

"In the meantime . . ." He turned to Violet and wagged a finger under her nose. "You take better care of yourself, young lady. That means plenty of food and plenty of rest. I won't have you jeopardizing your own health. Do you understand?"

Violet essayed a bright smile of agreement and kept it fixed on her face until the sound of the front door closing told her the doctor had gone and she could safely slump against the bedstead in despair.

Fine for him to tell her to eat and sleep, she reflected, wearily dipping the cloth in the basin and beginning the sponging procedure once more. He didn't have to worry about two lively boys in addition to their sick sister. He didn't have to plan meals, clean the house, and do the laundry.

He didn't have to find time to prepare meals for three hearty male appetites on top of fixing the nourishing soups and pots of strong tea he'd recommended for Jessie. And that didn't include the time spent cajoling the reluctant child to allow Violet to spoon tea and soup down her throat.

He didn't have to find time to take care of personal needs in the midst of the multitude of chores that faced her.

Speaking of chores . . . She heaved herself out of the chair. She gathered up the bowl and cup and tiptoed out of the room.

❧

Unwashed dishes, unscrubbed counter, unswept floor. Violet surveyed the disaster in the kitchen through fatigue-dulled eyes. Willie and the boys had taken over the outdoor chores, and she would ever be grateful for that, but the housework still fell to her, and she didn't know how she'd begin to catch up.

With a weary sigh, she placed Jessie's empty bowl atop the pile of dirty dishes and ladled out some soup for herself. She swallowed two spoonfuls, then set the bowl aside. With all the responsibility she carried these days, who had the time or energy to eat? She leaned against the counter and propped up her forehead with one hand. Even before Jessie's illness, she'd had the uneasy feeling she might have bitten off more than she could chew. Today she felt as though her myriad duties were choking her.

Violet forced her exhausted body upright and began to stack the dishes in the sink. If she didn't make a dent in this mess soon, there wouldn't be a clean dish left in the house. Her eyes brimmed with unbidden tears. She felt tired, more tired than she could ever remember being in her life, even during that awful period just after Pa's death when she and Rachel had been forced to run the farm on their own. Not only did she have the physical chores to do; the sheer responsibility of keeping tabs on the children and ensuring their safety weighed on her like an anvil.

Despite the relief their departure would bring, she dreaded the day Willie located Thurman Hadlock. The specter of his guardianship never left her mind for long.

How would the three children she had grown to love fare under his dubious care? Try as she might, she could only envision a grim future for them. Nearly as grim as the prospect of Rachel's imminent return. Violet could only imagine what her sister would say when she found her home had been taken over by strangers. Such thoughts were best left alone. Reality would come soon enough. Any hope that the Wingate family would have relocated to their new home by the time

Rachel and Daniel returned had flown out the window with the onset of Jessie's illness.

She placed the last of the cups on top of the towering pile. Just having the crockery arranged in a more orderly heap made a definite improvement to the appearance of the room, and Violet's spirits rose accordingly. As soon as she drew water and heated it, she could start on the actual cleanup. She lifted the bucket from its place and made it halfway to the door before her knees threatened to buckle. She swayed and wiped her forehead with the back of her hand.

What had come over her? Going out to draw a bucket of water seemed a small enough task. Goodness knew, she'd done the same chore countless times before. But today, she simply couldn't face the simple act. Feeling like a lazy quitter, she replaced the bucket and stumbled back to the sickroom. She would have to wash the dishes later. Right now, she just didn't have the strength.

She sagged into the chair at Jessie's bedside, willing herself to keep her spine erect and not lean back against the cushions. If she relaxed even that much, she knew she'd never be able to remain awake.

Her thoughts drifted back to Rachel and her probable reaction when she came home. Maybe she should have mentioned something about her current situation in a letter, just to prepare her sister for the children's presence. Not to mention Willie's.

What would her sister think when she discovered a strange man had been living on their property? Violet shuddered at the prospect. Rachel would not be pleased, not at all. She afforded herself the tiny luxury of letting her shoulder blades make contact with the back of the chair. She could allow that much comfort and still be able to remain alert.

She would have to convince Rachel of Willie's upright character. That wouldn't be the insurmountable task it would have seemed when they first met, she reflected. Willie had lost a lot of his aggravating ways. And thank goodness he had chosen to stay, or she never would have been able to cope. She would not soon forget the relief that swept over her when she found out he'd chosen to share the quarantine of his own free will. She didn't want to contemplate what would have happened had she been left to handle all three children completely on her own.

Not for the first time, Violet wondered whether she'd done a terribly foolish thing in taking on such a huge responsibility. Tending to her former animal patients had used up only an hour or two of her day. It hadn't taken long for her to realize that caring for a human child involved a whole different level of commitment, one she didn't know if she could handle much longer. Could she live up to the trust the children and Doc Hathaway placed in her?

It would be different once Rachel got back and she had a little help. She let her head rest against the tufted cushion, then shook it impatiently. How could she think of asking her sister to assume a workload like this when she hadn't had a thing to do with inviting a crew of strange children and their irascible escort to stay? This wasn't Rachel's responsibility. It was hers, Violet's, and she would handle it on her own.

If she could just get some rest, she'd be able to manage. Her chin sagged, and she nodded, then jerked her head up with a start. She didn't dare nap now. Too many chores awaited her. But surely a few moments relaxation wouldn't hurt. She let her head slip back against the chair once more and let out a blissful sigh. She didn't have to go to sleep; she could simply sit still and enjoy a brief respite. Then she'd be able to pull herself up and go on. Just a few blessed minutes . . .

Her eyelids fluttered, then closed.

*W*ant me to throw the hay down?"

Willie looked at Frederick, already halfway up the ladder to the hayloft, and shook his head. "I'll do it." He waited for the disgruntled youngster to descend, then climbed up and tossed forkfuls of hay to the two boys below. *Give one of them the advantage of height? And equip him with a pitchfork? No, thank you.*

He watched the brothers gather up the hay and carry it to the manger. He had to admit they'd done pretty well at keeping up with him while he split wood, fed the livestock, and milked the cow. Not many complaints, either, and not a single attempt at a practical joke. But he couldn't quite bring himself to let down his guard completely, not after what they'd put him through. He descended the ladder rungs and helped the boys throw the last of the hay to the milk cow.

"That's it for tonight, Fellas. You put in a good day's work." Might as well give them credit when he could. Maybe it would inspire them to live up to a higher standard. He took a last look around the barn, then carried the lantern to the doorway and waited for the boys to exit so he could swing the heavy doors shut for the night. Instead, they stood unmoving, their faces solemn in the lantern's dim glow.

They looked at each other as though passing some kind of silent communication between them, then turned to Willie. "Can we ask you something?" Frederick's voice sounded a faint echo in the barn's shadowy interior.

Willie's stomach clenched. Had they managed to set up some kind of trap without his seeing them? "Sure." He strode back to join them, keeping a careful watch for hidden snares. He stopped just short of the boys, holding the lantern high so as to get a clear look at them. "What is it?"

Again the boys exchanged glances, then Toby looked up to meet Willie's gaze. "What happens when you die?" The question hung suspended on the night air.

Willie bent down to scrutinize the small boy's face, seeing the worried puckers in the lamplight. "Any special reason you're asking?" he queried, hoping he'd just come up against a normal childish query and that the inquiry hadn't been prompted by any plans the two might have made for his immediate future.

Toby's chin quivered, and he clapped a grimy hand over his mouth. Frederick took up the line of questioning. "We were wondering about Jessie. Is she going to die?" Two pairs of somber eyes stared into Willie's face with an intensity that put to rest any doubts about the sincerity of their question.

Willie hung the lantern from a nail and dropped to one knee to put himself on their level. "Listen to me," he commanded, placing a hand on each boy's shoulder. "Your sister is sick, I'll grant you that. But the doctor's been in to see her every day, and he's satisfied with the way she's coming along. She's not going to die."

"But they only put up quarantine signs for really bad things." Frederick's voice came out in a quaver, despite his attempts to sound manly.

"You're right. Scarlet fever is nothing to fool around with, and the doctor doesn't want any more people catching it than he can help. That's why the sign is out there, to protect the rest of the people around here. Miss Violet's watching over Jessie every minute; you know that. She's taking good care of your sister so she can be up and around again and playing with both of you in no time."

He searched the two young faces for signs that they believed him, but their expressions still registered fear. A sudden thought came to Willie. "Did they hang out a quarantine sign when your pa took sick?"

Frederick nodded. "They hung it up when he got sick, just like with Jessie, and Papa died." He swallowed hard and his Adam's apple bobbed in his throat.

Willie's grip on their shoulders tightened. "I still have my ma and pa, but I know what it's like to worry when one of them is sick. You've all been through a lot, but I promise you, you can quit worrying now. Jessie is going to be just fine."

"Cross your heart?" Toby asked, his voice muffled by his fingers.

Willie flinched at hearing the phrase but made a show of drawing an X on his chest with his finger. His heart swelled with relief at the flicker of acceptance he saw in their eyes, and he got to his feet, ready to walk them to the house. The boys didn't follow.

Toby pulled his hand away from his mouth. "But we still want to know," he told Willie. "What happens when you die?"

Willie knelt again, then settled back on his heel. It looked like this discussion might take some time. He cleared his throat, trying to decide what to say to the two youngsters. Just how much would they be able to understand? Plenty, he reminded himself. He'd only been about Frederick's age when he decided he wanted to belong to God's family, and Lizzie had been even younger. They could understand all they needed to. Maybe he ought to find out first just how much they did know, so he'd know where to start.

"What do you think happens?"

Toby sat cross-legged in front of him, and Frederick followed suit. "My teacher says you become an angel," Frederick confided with a hopeful gleam in his eye. "She said our ma's an angel now. I guess that means Papa is too. Is that right?"

Willie passed his hand across his face. This was going to be even harder than he thought. How did you tell two little boys something that might shake their hope for their parents' destiny? You told them the truth. "Not exactly," he began. "If you go to heaven, there are angels there, but the angels weren't people first. Understand?" Two blank faces told him he'd missed the mark. He took a deep breath and prepared to try again.

"Look," he said, trying to remember how his parents had explained it to him when he was younger, "it's like this. Everyone does bad things sometimes, right?" Both blond heads nodded in sober agreement. "Well, God calls those bad things sin. And since God can't be around sin, He can't be around us when we've sinned. Are you with me so far?"

Toby's face puckered in bemused concentration, but he didn't say a word. Frederick eyed him intently. "So if God's in heaven and if we want to go to heaven, we can't if we do wrong things?"

"That's the idea."

Frederick studied the toes of his shoes. "But if everyone does bad things," he said, shredding a piece of straw into slivers, "how does anyone get to heaven?"

Willie grinned and relaxed. The hardest part was over; from here on out, he felt on familiar ground. "That's where Jesus comes in." He paused. "You have heard of Jesus, haven't you?"

Toby swiped his sleeve across his nose. "The baby in the manger at Christmastime?"

"Well, yes. But that was when He first came to earth. Jesus is God's Son, and God sent Him here to tell people how to get right with Him. You see, He knows how people are and how we just can't always do the right things no matter how hard we try."

Frederick leaned forward, lips parted. "So how do we get to heaven if we can't do right on our own?"

Willie's heart pounded. Could it be possible that one or both boys were ready to make the decision to turn their lives over to the Lord right here and now? "We trust in Jesus. Like I said, He came to earth from heaven and never did anything wrong in His whole life."

"Not even once?" Toby's face twisted in amazement at the idea of such a feat.

"Not once." Willie's face softened into a smile. "He loved us so much, He took our punishment for us when He died on the cross. If we trust in what He did, God looks at us as though we're just as perfect as Jesus."

Frederick leaned back, his face a mask of skepticism. "That's all we have to do, say we trust Him?"

"Well, it's more than just giving Him lip service. You show you really trust Him by giving Him control of your life." He paused and wet his lips. "So what do you think, boys? Do you want to pray and ask Him to save you right now?" *Lord, please don't let me ruin this.*

A lengthy pause ensued. Willie continued to send up prayers of intercession. Toby looked at Frederick; Frederick stared at the floor, frowning fiercely. Finally, he raised his head and met Willie's gaze. "Not right now. It's too much to figure out all in one night." His face pinched in worry. "Is that all right?"

"It's okay," Willie told him, fighting down his sense of disappointment. "It wouldn't do you a bit of good to say the words if you didn't really mean them. But I want you to keep thinking about what I've said, will you promise me that?"

Frederick considered this for a moment, then nodded. "I will," he said. "Something like that is too important not to think about a lot. Right?"

"Right." Willie reached out and tousled the boy's hair, realizing it was the first friendly gesture he'd made toward any of the Wingates since their first meeting. The knowledge smote him with shame. These kids had been through the loss of both parents, plus being uprooted and hauled out West to be raised by a total stranger. That would be enough to make anyone cut up a bit.

This time the boys followed him readily when he left the barn and swung the wide door shut. He shepherded them back to the house, where he oversaw their washing up and their preparations for bed. Before blowing out the lamp in their bedroom, he stopped to lay his hand on each boy's head and say a gentle good night. Maybe all they needed was to be shown a little godly love.

What if no one had cared enough to show a loving concern for him and tell him about God's great gift in his younger years? For the first time, he began to grasp just how blessed his upbringing had been. Not only his parents, but his aunt and uncle, too, had lived out a faithful model of God's sacrificial love in their every action toward him.

Even with their good example, his path hadn't been without its pitfalls. He remembered uneasily how, only a few years before, he had rebelled against his upbringing and chosen for his hero the notorious gunman Billy the Kid. It had taken the combined forces of constant prayer and a stiff dose of reality to bring him to his senses and set him back on the right path. What if no one had been praying for him or taken the time to try to set him straight?

The thought sobered him. The Wingates needed God in their lives, and in order to comprehend His love for them, they needed to see it exemplified in the lives of those who knew Him. Violet was doing a fine job of that already, Willie thought with a pang of guilt. His behavior, on the other hand, would have to undergo some major changes in order to reflect any semblance of Christlikeness.

At least they'd made some progress tonight. What a question to be asked right out of the blue! Apparently, Jessie's illness had a more sobering effect on them than he'd thought. It would have been nice if they'd followed through tonight, but he could take heart in knowing he'd presented the gospel clearly enough that they could understand. At least that seed had been planted.

He ought to tell Violet. She'd be thrilled to hear of their interest, and she could pray with him that all three of the young Wingates would come to trust Jesus as their Savior in the near future. The thought buoyed him and he headed to the kitchen.

∽

He found a mountain of unwashed dishes, but no Violet. Come to think of it, he hadn't heard her once since bringing the boys into the house. Thoroughly concerned, he hurried down the hallway to Jessie's room, his boots ringing on the wooden floor with each long stride.

He halted three feet short of the door to Jessie's bedroom. Their agreement during the quarantine had been to keep himself and the boys completely away from the sick child. He and Violet hadn't even been in the same room since the morning Jessie got sick. Now he hesitated, not wanting to take a chance on spreading the disease to Jessie's brothers, but feeling deep inside himself that something must be wrong.

Even though he and Violet kept their distance, he could always discern her presence. He couldn't remember being in the house the past few days without hearing the low murmur of her voice comforting Jessie or her light footsteps while she hurried from one household chore to another. This sudden silence unnerved him.

He crept closer to the doorway. Light from the kerosene lamp spilled out into the hallway, painting a bright rectangle at his feet.

Willie steeled himself for whatever he might find and peered into the room.

Jessie lay deep in slumber on the bed, her hair spreading around her pale face in a golden pool. The gentle rise and fall of her chest assured Willie she slept peacefully. His gaze moved to the chair next to the bed. Violet slumped back against the cushion, eyes closed and head sagging. The cloth she used to wipe Jessie's brow dangled from one limp hand.

Willie's throat constricted. Had Violet succumbed to the disease as well? He started to enter the room, then stopped and observed her more closely from where he stood. Her color seemed good, he noted with relief, except for those dark smudges under her eyes. Probably the result of all those sleepless nights sitting up with Jessie. He watched her breathing. Good, smooth and even. From all appearances, she merely slept the sleep of utter exhaustion, and who could blame her?

He hesitated in the doorway, wondering if he should wake Violet. She would be mortified to think she had dozed off while tending to her charge. No, he decided, let her sleep. She needed all the rest she could get, from the looks of her.

Willie studied her face, fascinated by the way her dark lashes fanned out over her cheeks. With those loose strands of hair floating about her face, she almost looked like a little girl herself. Better not tell her that, he thought with a chuckle.

A wave of tenderness engulfed him. How could such a frail-looking creature accomplish so much? He felt an overpowering desire to shelter Violet, to protect her from life's storms. She'd had no reason to pour out her love to three children she didn't know, except for the kindness of her heart; but she took on the responsibility without a moment's hesitation. She bore no legal obligation for them, yet here she sat, selflessly attending a little girl she met only recently, risking her own health to do so.

Hardly the actions of a woman after easy money. The thought sent a pang of contrition straight through him. Why had he taken Mary Rose and her suggestion seriously for even a moment? He had to admit the woman had charm and looks, along with ways that made a man feel special. But with all her frills and fripperies, he knew beyond a doubt that Mary Rose Downey didn't possess one-tenth of Violet's character.

The desire to ask Violet to join her prayers for Toby and Frederick to his had entered his mind the moment he'd finished his talk with the boys. Had she been awake when he found her, he knew without question she would have welcomed the opportunity. Violet didn't flaunt her faith; she lived it out in every aspect of her life. He'd been aware of it without noticing it since the beginning. Now that he took the time to think things through, he wondered at not picking up on such an obvious character trait more quickly.

He sent one last lingering glance her way, then withdrew back down the hallway and let himself out the front door, treading lightly so as not to waken the sleeping occupants. His footsteps made little sound on the hard-packed path between the house and his cabin. A hundred thoughts clamored for attention, most having to do with the change he'd experienced that evening. What had happened in that brief span of time to make him look at the Wingate children and Violet in an entirely new way?

Only You, Lord. Only You. He lay on his back and pondered, marveling at the ways God had shown Himself to be at work in his life. The boys' subdued attitudes evidenced a depth of concern for their sister he hadn't suspected before now. And then those questions they'd peppered him with!

Willie chuckled softly. He sure hadn't seen them coming. Had he given the boys the information they needed to fully understand Christ's sacrifice? Explaining the most important decision life held wasn't something he did on a regular basis, but his parents and pastor had always made it clear that being equipped to do so was the responsibility of every believer, not just the clergy.

He thought back over the answers he'd given, then nodded. Both Frederick and Toby seemed to understand the concept of sin and their need to be saved from its penalty.

Willie snuggled his blanket closer under his chin and fell asleep whispering a prayer for the salvation of both the boys and their sister.

11

*H*ello there!"

Willie looked up from the woodpile to see a man and woman standing next to the gatepost where the quarantine sign glinted in the noontime sun. Must be neighbors he hadn't met yet. He waved to acknowledge the greeting and sauntered over to exchange a few words, pleased at the prospect of seeing new faces. Aside from Doc's visits and the occasional howdy Jeb McCurdy hollered from the road, he hadn't talked to anyone but Violet and the kids since the quarantine began.

He stopped at the prescribed distance from the newcomers and dipped his head in greeting. The couple stared back at him without speaking, then the man turned and jabbed a finger at the quarantine notice.

"What's the meaning of this?" he barked.

Willie felt the hackles rise on the back of his neck. He hadn't been in the area long, but he'd met enough locals to know he could expect friendly treatment from most of them. Apparently this fellow didn't belong to the majority.

"Just what it says," he responded, not bothering to temper the frosty tone in his voice. "There's scarlet fever here. We're under quarantine."

The woman's clear brown eyes widened. She gasped and clapped a hand to her throat. "Violet?" she faltered.

Willie relaxed a fraction. At least she seemed to care somewhat about the farm's occupants. "No, Ma'am," he replied. "It's Jessie, the little girl who's staying here." Instead of the relief he expected to see, the woman's expression grew more confused.

Her companion glowered. "What little girl?" he demanded. "And who on earth are you?"

Willie bristled at the peremptory tone. "Name's Willie Bradley." He drew himself erect and took on a combative stance. "Of the Double B Ranch in northern New Mexico Territory. And you are . . . ?"

The man's face darkened like a thundercloud. He planted both fists on his hips and scowled. "I'm Daniel Moore, and this is my wife, Rachel. We live here."

～

Once, Willie had watched a cowboy stun a wild-eyed steer by delivering a well-aimed blow between its eyes with a two-by-four. Now he knew just how that steer must have felt. He drew his lower jaw up from its sagging position and tried to gather his whirling thoughts into some semblance of order.

Rachel and Daniel. Of course. He'd heard Violet mention them often enough. He'd even seen a photograph of the two of them on the mantel. Why hadn't he made the connection himself?

What brought them back from their trip so soon? Mentally, he calculated the date and groaned inwardly. Their return wasn't early at all. With all the upheaval surrounding Jessie's illness, he'd lost track of time. *Violet must have too, or she would have mentioned something about expecting them any day.*

He had to quit standing there like a dunce. Willie struggled to find something suitable to say. "Welcome home. How was your trip?"

Judging from Rachel and Daniel's startled expressions, his overture hadn't had the desired effect. Daniel's sandy brows drew together in a straight line, and he took a step forward. Rachel grasped his arm. "Let's hear what he has to say," she counseled.

Daniel halted in midstride and crossed his arms. "All right." He threw Willie a challenging glance. "Let's hear it. I want to know who you are and why you're here and why I shouldn't horsewhip you off this property."

Much as he wanted to turn tail and run, Willie forced himself to stand his ground. Up to now, given the isolation of the farm, he hadn't paid much thought to how their situation might look to outside eyes. And he'd never considered how this scene might appear to Violet's relatives. He knew his behavior had been above reproach; so did Violet. But how would her sister and brother-in-law take his being there with Violet, alone except for three children who were strangers to them? A hard knot of worry formed in his stomach.

"It's kind of a long story," he began, feeling his way along like a man crossing a raging stream. "I brought three orphaned kids out here to meet their guardian, but I've had trouble locating him. Your sister met them and wanted to take them in until he'd been found. The sheriff thought that was a good idea too, so the kids have been staying in the house with Violet and I've been sleeping in the cabin out back."

He took note of Daniel's grim expression. He hadn't relaxed, but he hadn't come through the gate either. That might be a promising sign. "The little girl—Jessie—came down with scarlet fever, and Doc Hathaway put up the quarantine sign. We've tried to keep the boys away from her, and so far they haven't caught it. If all goes well, the quarantine should be lifted before too long."

Daniel glared at him through slitted eyes. "You're telling me you've been staying out here, unchaperoned, for all that time? And you expect me not to shoot you?"

Willie tried to moisten his lips, but his mouth had gone bone dry. He had an idea how his father might have felt had Lizzie been in a similar situation. Squaring his shoulders, he returned Daniel's unblinking stare as steadily as he could. "That's what I'm saying, all right. It's not a normal situation, I'll grant you that. But I can tell you, and I'm sure Violet will too, that nothing untoward has happened . . . and nothing will."

He maintained his position, willing himself not to look away, even when he heard the creak of approaching buggy wheels. A raspy voice broke the tense silence.

"Well, look who's back. You catching the folks up on what all's happened lately, Willie?"

Willie darted a glance sideways and caught a glimpse of Jeb McCurdy's face, aglow with neighborly benevolence. "Something like that." He shifted his gaze back to Daniel's stony countenance.

"It's a good thing Willie was around when all this happened," Jeb went on, not seeming to catch the underlying tension of the moment. "If Miss Violet hadn't had his help, she'd have been plumb snowed under, trying to take care of all those young'uns on her own."

The knot in Willie's stomach loosened a fraction. Thank goodness for Jeb's timing. He couldn't have asked for a more fortuitous circumstance than to have his behavior vouched for by a trusted neighbor.

"You seem to be forgetting one thing, Jeb," Daniel replied in a dry tone. "If he and his crew hadn't been around, none of this would have happened, would it?"

Jeb scratched his grizzled chin and shot an unerring stream of tobacco juice toward a manzanita bush. "I s'pose you may have a point there," he muttered. Then he brightened. "Be that as it may, I can't recall ever seeing Miss Violet so full of life as she's been since those younguns showed up. Tended to 'em like a mother hen, she has, and happy as can be to do it. A body could see that right off.

"As for this young feller here," he continued, "he's been every inch the gentleman, doing everything he could to help ease the burden. Why, he even hustled into town to fetch Doc Hathaway when the little girl took sick. Got him out here in record time, he did. And he wasn't even on the premises when Doc posted the quarantine notice; but as soon as he got back, he took it on himself to cross over and look after the boys and the chores to give Violet a free hand at taking care of that little one. I got that from Doc hisself," he added with an emphatic nod. "He was plumb impressed by that, and I guess you should be too."

He nodded to punctuate his lengthy speech, gathered up the reins, and clucked to his horse. Willie watched his progress down the road for a moment, struck by the fortuitous arrival of his unexpected champion. A spark of hope flickered. Surely Daniel and Rachel couldn't help but be moved by McCurdy's impassioned defense. He cast a hopeful look in their direction.

Daniel eyed him thoughtfully, then looked at his wife. "Old Jeb seems quite taken with him."

Rachel, whose demeanor had gone from amazed to suspicious during McCurdy's recitation, exchanged glances with her husband, then lifted her chin in a way that reminded Willie of Violet and looked directly at him. "Just for your information, Mr. Bradley, a recommendation from Jeb McCurdy doesn't go a long way toward setting my mind at ease. Don't think we're going to accept this situation just on his say-so. I'd like to speak to my sister."

Willie swallowed again. The knot seemed to move from his stomach to his throat. He tried to force the words past the obstruction. "She's resting right now, and I hate to disturb her," he said, hoping his words carried a ring of sincerity. "She's worked so hard at taking care of Jessie that she's just about worn herself out."

Rachel turned a troubled face toward Daniel. "Do you think we ought to go on in, as Mr. Bradley did?"

Her husband gave her a long, appraising look, then drew a deep breath and let it out slowly. "I don't want to leave Violet in this situation any more than you do. But I'm not willing to risk your health either. Let's look at the facts. This situation has apparently been going on practically since we left. There's nothing we can do to change that. Why don't we go into town and check things out with Doc and see what he says? I'd feel a lot better if he gives this whole thing his approval."

"Why don't you talk to Sheriff Dolan too?" put in Willie. "We've gotten to know each other fairly well, and I'm sure he'd be willing to vouch for me." The measuring look Daniel gave him told Willie his shot had hit home. Dolan held the respect of people in these parts; a good word from him would do a lot to allay their doubts.

Daniel paused as if considering, then gave a decisive nod. "That's what we'll do." He helped Rachel back into the buggy and climbed into the seat. "If they both put in a good word for you, we'll find a room in town and check in with you every day until the quarantine's over. If they don't . . . well, you'd better pray we don't hear anything to contradict that glowing recommendation you got from McCurdy." He flicked the whip and set the horse off down the road.

Willie watched the buggy recede until it disappeared in the distance. He rubbed the taut muscles in the back of his neck with one hand. He knew he had won a reprieve. How temporary that reprieve might be remained to be seen.

❧

"Well, Doc?" Violet watched the gray-haired physician put his stethoscope away and purse his lips.

He regarded Jessica with a long, surveying look, then his face broke into a pleased smile. "She's past it," he announced. "Have her take it easy for the next week or so, but for all intents and purposes, you can consider her recovered."

The air left Violet's lungs in a whoosh of gratitude. "Thank goodness! What about the boys?"

Doc bent to fasten the latch on his medical bag. "I checked them before I looked young Jessica over. They're fine. No sign of scarlet fever . . . or anything else, barring a streak of boyish orneriness." Faded blue eyes twinkled over half-moon glasses, and Doc squeezed her shoulder in a fatherly gesture. "I'm ready to lift the quarantine, Violet. You've done a fine job, just fine. You should feel proud of yourself."

All Violet felt was a profound sense of relief. She had done it. She had weathered the most difficult challenge of her life and prevailed. She tilted her head back and a laugh gurgled from her throat. No more worries about keeping the children apart. No more strain of wondering whether one of the boys would contract the disease, prolonging their separation from the rest of the world. She could sleep for a whole night in her own bed without having to keep watch on Jessie. She could . . .

"Rachel!" Violet exclaimed. "Doc, does this mean Rachel and Daniel can come home?"

"Just as soon as I take the sign down, if your sister doesn't rip it loose before I can get my hands on it." Doc chuckled. "She's been after me every time I came back into town. When I told her there was a good chance your ordeal was nearly over, she followed me out in her buggy. Want to come out with me?"

"Yes! Well . . . maybe not just yet." Violet's gaze swept around the room, taking in the unsightly disarray. More clutter awaited her in the kitchen, and goodness only knew what chaos lurked in other parts of the house. She fixed Doc with a pleading gaze. "Do you think you could take your time getting out there? Give me just a few more minutes?"

His eyes widened. "After all this time, you want to stretch it out even longer?" He watched her scurry around the room to snatch up dishes and soiled clothes with frantic haste and smiled. "I'll see what I can do, but I won't promise much. Your sister's just as eager to get inside as you are to stall her." He strode down the hallway at an easy pace, his rumbling laughter audible until the closing of the front door cut it off.

Violet hefted her armload and headed for the kitchen. A quick glance as she passed the living room door confirmed her worst fears. Seeing to Jessie's needs during her illness and making sure no one else came down with scarlet fever had been preeminent. Now that Doc had declared the crisis over, routine chores reared their heads again, needing her attention.

What to do with the dirty clothes? She darted a glance around the kitchen and stuffed them into a cupboard, then turned to grab the broom. If she could just—

"Violet!" The glad cry from the doorway stopped her in her tracks. She pivoted and ran to embrace her sister.

"Oh, Rachel, it's so good to have you home! I've missed you." She would have continued to hold her sister close, savoring the comfort of her presence, but Rachel pulled away and stepped back to study her at arm's length.

Worry lines appeared in Rachel's forehead. "Violet Canfield, what on earth has been going on here? You look like you've been dragged behind a team of runaway horses."

Violet raked her fingers through her hair, encountering a mass of snarls and tangles. Maybe her first move should have been to spend time in front of her mirror preparing for their reunion. "We've had quite a time, I'll admit that. But things are going to get back to normal again right away, you'll see. It's been a little hectic with Jessie sick and all. I'm just happy the boys didn't catch it too."

"Ah, yes. Let's talk about this little family you've acquired while we've been gone. What happened? We leave you alone one time and come back to find four strangers have taken up residence and there's a quarantine notice on our gate." Rachel raised an eyebrow and planted both hands on her hips in a gesture Violet recognized from innumerable encounters in the past.

She lifted her chin in a gesture she hoped would hide its trembling from Rachel's keen gaze. "It's no great mystery. The children needed help; I helped them. It's as simple as that."

Rachel rolled her eyes and huffed. "Simple? Violet, there has to be more to it than that. What kind of help did they need, and why did they need it from you? Why couldn't Mr. Bradley help them?"

"Oh." She turned and traced her finger across the windowsill. "Well, it seems rather silly now, but at the beginning they were looking for protection *from* Wil—Mr. Bradley." She squeezed her eyes shut and waited for the explosion.

She didn't wait long.

"And so you just told them to come in and live with you—then invited this man they were afraid of to stay here too, is that it? Honestly, Violet, don't you ever think? He could have been some kind of criminal, or worse! And here you are by yourself, opening the place up to total strangers and not mentioning a word of it in your letters."

"Sheriff Dolan came out here with him," Violet muttered, keeping her face averted. "He thought it was okay for them all to stay."

Rachel gripped Violet by the shoulders and turned her around. Anxiety darkened her eyes and her taut facial features showed the depth of her concern. "Honey, you have to understand that this is not the same as bringing home a baby squirrel or a bird with a broken wing. There's more responsibility involved in taking care of children. A lot more."

Violet swept away Rachel's hands and put the width of the kitchen between them. "Don't you think I know that by now? I've done nothing but tend to their needs since they got here. I've cooked and cleaned and mended and washed. I've read stories and played games and settled squabbles and tucked them into bed at night. Since Jessie's been sick, I've spent nearly every moment keeping her fever down and racking my brain to try to find something to tempt her appetite. Don't try to tell me how much responsibility's involved," she cried, her voice breaking. "I know good and well just how hard it is to take care of a child!"

The pent-up emotions of the recent ordeal broke through the dam she'd erected, and the tears poured forth. Violet wrapped her arms around herself and bent double, racked with sobs. Through the turbulent storm, she was vaguely aware of Rachel's arms supporting her, then settling her in a chair. She savored the luxury of leaning into her sister's embrace and listening to her comforting voice.

"I'm sorry, Violet," Rachel crooned. "I didn't mean to hurt you. I've been so worried ever since we got back, and I guess it just all spilled out." She stroked Violet's hair back from her forehead. "Go ahead and cry it out, Honey. You've been through a lot."

Violet tried to speak, but sobs still shook her body. Over the sound of her own weeping she heard Daniel's voice: "She's not getting sick, is she?"

"I don't think so," Rachel replied. "She's just tired and overworked, and I lit into her without thinking."

Violet could tell by the creaking of the floor that Daniel had moved to a position near the living room doorway. "I've been talking to the Bradley fellow," he said. "Seems like a decent enough sort. From what he tells me, Violet's done an amazing job looking after the kids. To tell you the truth," he said, lowering his voice, "I never thought she had it in her. We ought to be real proud."

"I am." Rachel dropped her voice to a whisper and held Violet close while the tempest subsided. "Look at her, Daniel. This isn't the dreamy-eyed little sister we left behind just a few weeks ago."

"It isn't the same house we left behind either." Daniel's chuckle removed any sting from his words.

"I know. But with some extra hands helping, it won't take long to get it back in shape."

The warmth of her sister's caring offer lifted the burden of guilt from Violet's shoulders. She drew a shaky breath and mopped at her face with her sleeve. Daniel pressed a handkerchief into her hand, and she gave him a wobbly smile.

"Welcome home," she told him in a voice that trembled only a little.

"It's good to be back." He smiled down at her, his deep green eyes gleaming with humor. "Even if it isn't quite the welcome we'd expected. It sounds like you've had a time of it."

"It's been a challenge," she conceded, giving her cheeks a final swipe and getting to her feet. "But we managed."

"So I hear." Daniel folded his arms and regarded her thoughtfully. "You certainly have a champion in Willie Bradley. He couldn't say enough good things about the way you took on the kids and kept things running."

"Did he?" Violet felt the blood rush to her cheeks and used the handkerchief to fan herself. Goodness, she wasn't coming down with a fever after all, was she?

Rachel's brows drew together in a quick frown. "But I thought the two of you weren't on good terms, with you feeling you had to protect the children and all."

The heat rose in Violet's face. She didn't exactly feel sick, but maybe she'd better get a cool drink and lie down for a while, just to make sure. "That was just at the beginning," she reassured her sister. "The children felt he didn't like them, and I'll admit I thought the same thing at first. But he's been wonderful to them lately . . . to all of us," she added softly.

Rachel raised her brows and looked at Daniel. "And where is this remarkable man? I'd like to get a chance to speak with him under better circumstances."

"He headed into town as soon as we finished talking," Daniel replied. "Said he needed to make up for lost time and get back to looking for Thurman Hadlock, although a less likely prospect for raising children is hard to imagine. At any rate, now that he's free to check around again, it surely won't be too much longer before he can turn the kids over to him and get on back to his ranch."

Violet blinked. "I guess he'll be happy to be leaving," she said. The Wingates and Willie had become such a regular part of her life of late, she hadn't thought much about the fact that they wouldn't be staying on permanently. She changed her mind about having a fever. The warm glow departed in a rush, to be replaced by a cold, leaden feeling she couldn't explain.

⑫

adlock? Sure, I know him." The whiskered miner leaned against the wall of the mercantile and scratched his chest through holes in a shirt that looked like it hadn't been washed in months.

Willie moved upwind. *Somehow, that doesn't surprise me. He looks just like the type of person I'd picture Hadlock with.* Odd how Hadlock had taken on such a clear image in his mind after listening to Violet's perceptions of the man. She had influenced him more than he'd realized. "Can you tell me where to find him?"

His grubby companion shrugged and cocked his head. "How far you willin' to travel?" He cackled at Willie's bewildered expression. "He took off for San Francisco over a month ago. Just one more of his harebrained schemes for gettin' rich, I reckon, but he was plumb fired up about it."

Willie tried not to show how much this news rocked him. "Any idea when he'll be back?"

"Hard to tell. I would have expected him back before this, but if he got sidetracked by some blond gold digger, who's to say? It oughtn't be more than another week or two, though. If he did make any money, he'll run through it all by then. If I see him, you want me to tell him anything for you?"

Willie considered the man's probable trustworthiness at conveying a message. "No, thanks. I'll wait and talk to him myself." He strode back along Montezuma Street, trying to keep an impassive expression while he assessed this new information.

A week or two to wait! And here he'd already spent three weeks chasing his tail trying to find the man, when all along he hadn't even been in the territory. Willie slammed his fist into the rough wood of the market and received a reproving glance from a passing matron. He continued on his way, fighting to keep his frustration under control.

He thought back. When had Monroe come to the Double B? And how long before that had he sent word to Hadlock to expect his arrival with the Wingates? Willie made a quick mental calculation and groaned aloud, earning him another uneasy look from a passerby. In all likelihood, Hadlock hadn't even received Monroe's message before heading for parts west. In that case, he had no idea he would be welcoming the children of his late friend into his home upon his return.

Could things possibly get any worse? It hadn't even been his idea to make this trip in the first place, he reminded himself on the way back to the farm. He never volunteered to ride herd on a group of kids who made a pack of wolves look tame in comparison. He shuddered, remembering how they'd run him ragged on the way out, caused him to miss their train, then left him stranded out in the middle of nowhere.

If that hadn't been enough, they'd made him out to be some kind of wild-eyed monster. And people had believed it of him. Gloomy memories of their trip came back to haunt him, memories that even the boys' improved behavior of late couldn't displace.

What on earth was he going to do now? Another week of trying to cope with those three would be enough to send him around the bend. And where would he go? Did he dare ask if he and the kids could stay on at the farm? There had to be a way. He simply couldn't handle them all on his own.

Slow down. Take it easy. God's in control. It took every bit of his willpower to remind himself of this fact on the trip back to the farm. Gradually, the truth of God's sovereignty seeped into his mind and calmed his soul. A week wasn't forever. Even two weeks didn't compare with eternity. He could hold out that long.

By then, surely Hadlock would have returned. And if not, Monroe should be able to travel soon. He could come out and take the kids off Willie's hands, reclaiming the responsibility that had been his to begin with. Cheered by this thought, Willie turned his mind to how he might persuade Daniel to let his little band stay on.

❧

"Let me get this straight." Daniel climbed down from the loft and slapped the hay dust off his clothes. "You want to stay around and work for me to earn your keep and the kids'?"

"That's about the size of it." Willie coiled and uncoiled his lariat to give his jittery hands something to do. He tried in vain to read Daniel's expression and gauge the other man's probable reaction to the proposal he'd just made.

Daniel gave Willie a long, measuring look, then grinned and stuck out his hand. "Sounds good to me. I could use some help with the planting, and it'll be a way to keep the kids around here a while longer. I have a feeling we'd have a hard time prying them loose from Violet," he said with a chuckle. "She's grown mighty attached to them. So have Rachel and I, for that matter. It'll be hard to see them go when the time comes."

Willie returned his firm handclasp with a silent prayer of gratitude and tried not to show his astonishment at this news. How anyone as levelheaded as Daniel Moore could cotton to those kids was beyond him, but he didn't have any intention of jeopardizing his position by enlightening the man as to their true natures. He could only pray they'd maintain their current level of behavior until after they left the farm.

"I appreciate it," he told Daniel. "And I'll be sure to make good on my part of the deal."

Daniel nodded agreement with a readiness that took Willie by surprise. "I know you will. Out here, you learn to size up a man pretty quickly. Truth to tell, I have a feeling I'll come out ahead in this bargain. Why don't you start out by fixing that fence at the south end of the pasture?" He pointed out the tools Willie would need and a pile of posts and left.

Willie watched him walk away, then began loading the fencing material into the back of the wagon with a thrill of gratification. For the first time in his life, he'd been judged on his own merit and found worthy of approval; it was enough to make a man walk mighty tall.

❧

A gentle breeze teased the young spring grass coming up in the pasture. Toby romped across the yard, kicking up his heels like a young colt. On the porch, Frederick pondered his next move on the checkerboard set up on a low table between his chair and Jessica's, while Violet fussed over the little girl, making sure she was safely bundled up against the evening air.

Daniel watched from his seat in one of the matching rocking chairs and shook his head. "It's plenty warm out here, Violet," he said with a tolerant smile. "She's not going to take a chill."

Violet finished tucking a light shawl around Jessie, then gave a self-deprecating laugh. "You're right; I'm hovering over her like a mother hen. I just want to make sure. That was quite a scare we had with her." She tenderly stroked Jessie's head and took a seat on the other side of Rachel, who rummaged through her mending basket. She picked up a piece of embroidery and began stitching.

Willie watched the homey scene from his seat on the porch steps, savoring the memory of the roast chicken dinner he'd enjoyed a short time before. He laced his fingers around one knee and stretched the other leg out with a sigh of satisfaction. Kids playing while the adults sat around the porch sharing an easy camaraderie—the scene could have been taken straight from his own family.

He closed his eyes and drew a long, slow breath, enjoying the smell of fresh-turned earth. How long had it been since he'd felt so content? Well before the advent of the Wingate clan in his life, he thought with a wry chuckle. Life hadn't seemed this idyllic for a long time.

With every day that passed, Willie felt increasingly comfortable around Daniel. The man had his unqualified respect. The more time he spent with Daniel, the more he found him to be hard-working, expecting much from himself and those around him; but he balanced that expectation with an innate sense of fairness. Much of what he saw in Daniel reminded him of the traits he admired in his father and uncle, including his deep faith.

Daniel's relationship with Rachel reminded him of his parents' too. Their obvious love for each other was the same kind he longed for in his own marriage someday. And after the awkwardness of their first meeting, both of them had gone out of their way to make him feel like he fit right into the family circle as an accepted part of the group. No wonder it didn't take any effort to feel right at home.

"What's this, Miss Violet?" Toby ran up the porch steps. His pounding boots narrowly avoided contact with Willie's shin. "I found it over by the well." He held up a delicate yellow flower trailing long spurs for her inspection.

Violet lifted the drooping blossom with the tip of her finger. "Do you remember its name?" She gave him an encouraging smile. "We talked about it the other day."

Toby frowned and studied his specimen with the tip of his tongue protruding from one corner of his mouth. "Clummine?" He looked up at Violet for confirmation.

"That's close. It's a columbine."

"Col-um-bine." Toby pronounced each syllable with care.

"Good for you!" Violet gave him a squeeze. "Can you find some other flowers we've studied? Look around; there are lots of them just starting to bloom."

Willie moved his legs out of Toby's way, and the little boy scampered away from the house in search of more specimens. Jessie watched him with a wistful expression that tugged at Willie's heart.

"Can I look for flowers too?" she pleaded.

Violet looked askance at the request, then appeared to reconsider. "Poor Jessie. You haven't gotten to play outdoors for ages, have you? All right, but no running. You can still find plenty of flowers to pick if you just walk between here and the edge of the field."

"I promise." Jessie's smile fairly shone. "Cross my heart." She stepped past Willie and bent her head to study the ground, with Frederick at her heels. A moment later, she squealed in delight and stooped to pluck a tiny bloom hidden in the grass.

Willie watched them, a warm glow spreading through him at their childish enjoyment. Maybe all these kids had needed all along was a little love and attention. Violet provided plenty of that, all right. Hard to imagine how such a delicate frame could hold so much affection, but she had all they needed and plenty to spare.

"You just made Jessie one happy little girl," he told her, meeting her gaze straight on. Her smile shone as radiantly as Jessie's had.

"I almost didn't let her go," she admitted. "But then she gave me that look. . . ." She shook her head and laughed. "How could anyone argue with those incredible eyes?"

Willie knew exactly what she meant. Just looking into Violet's blue eyes made him feel like he was falling into a deep forest pool. If a man didn't watch his step, he could be in over his head before he knew it.

The scrape of Rachel's rocker on the wooden porch floor brought him back to the moment. Willie blinked and tried to assume a nonchalant air. He didn't know just where that errant thought had come from, and he sure didn't want anyone else to suspect the direction his mind had just taken. He had enough problems on his hands without making the Moores worry about his intentions.

He shot a quick glance at Daniel and felt his neck grow warm under the older man's scrutiny. Daniel's face held a knowing smirk that told Willie his calf-eyed stare hadn't gone unnoticed. Toby ran up on the porch again, his arrival providing a welcome distraction.

"Look at this one. Isn't it pretty?" He held aloft a pinkish flower that reminded Willie of his mother's snapdragons.

"I've got some too," Jessie called. She and Frederick climbed onto the porch behind their brother, each clutching a handful of blooms for Violet's perusal.

Rachel chuckled. "It looks like you have your work cut out for you this evening. It's a good thing you're the flower expert in the family."

"Mama was a good teacher," Violet replied and turned her attention to the samples before her. "Oh, my. Look at these beautiful things." She took her time examining each specimen. Toby danced from one foot to the other, awaiting her verdict. "This," she announced, twirling the slender stalk of Jessie's offering between her fingers, "is blue flax." She placed it back in Jessie's hands, and the little girl stared at it in wonder.

"Look at mine next." Frederick pointed at the clump of small white flowers in Violet's hand. "Mine have lots more petals than the others do."

"They do, don't they?" Violet held up the tiny blossoms so all the children could see them. "That's one way of identifying it. This one is a baby aster."

"There's a whole bunch of them over near the corral," Frederick volunteered. "Want me to pick more for you?"

"Why don't we let them grow right where they are?" Violet's eyes sparkled with amusement at the boy's enthusiasm. "That way, we'll be able to keep on enjoying them."

"What about mine?" Toby demanded. "What's its name?"

Violet grinned. "It's called penstemon," she told him, enunciating the word with care.

Frederick snickered at the odd name, and Toby glared at him. "It's still a pretty flower," he muttered, then descended the steps again. "I'm gonna go find another one that has a pretty name to go with it." He trotted over near the barn and gave a cry of triumph. "Look at this great big white one!" He reached for it with both hands.

"Don't touch it!" Willie hollered. "That's—" His words were cut off by a yowl from Toby. "Prickly poppy," he finished. He loped across the yard with Violet right behind him and scooped the little boy into his arms. "Are you okay? Let me see those fingers." He studied them, noting that the skin hadn't been broken. "You'll be fine, just a little sore for awhile," he told him. He set the youngster back on the ground and watched him run back to recount his injury for the others, then turned to Violet. "No real damage, but he won't be grabbing for those flowers again anytime soon."

She nodded in sympathy. "It seems like it takes a painful lesson to get through to us sometimes." She tilted her head up to look at him. "I didn't know you were acquainted with flower names."

Willie laughed. "I'm not. I just happened to recognize that one from an encounter I had with the stuff when I was about Toby's age.

It was one of those painful lessons, all right." He grinned at Violet and their gazes locked. There was that sensation of diving into dangerous water again. He could feel himself plunging down farther into its depths with every passing moment. He didn't know if he'd ever reach the surface again and wasn't sure he wanted to.

Violet, too, seemed to recognize their special connection. He could see the pulse flutter at the base of her throat, and she probed him with a questioning gaze. She laid her hand on his arm.

Her fingers sent shafts of fire right through the fabric of his shirt. Willie flinched as though stung and regretted the involuntary reaction when Violet snatched her hand away and clasped it against her stomach. Neither of them spoke, but a message seemed to pass between them just the same.

13

*W*illie hung up the heavy harness and went into his cabin full of satisfaction at the amount of plowing he'd done. He poured water into the basin on the tiny table beside his bed and sluiced it over his face and hands. Sputtering, he reached for the towel hanging on a nail in front of him and shivered. The weather might be getting warmer by the day, but that water felt downright cold.

He combed his hair and checked his appearance in the cracked mirror he'd fastened to the wall. He smoothed a stray lock of wavy hair back off his forehead and decided his appearance would pass muster. After a day spent hauling sacks of seed, Daniel wouldn't look much more energetic than he did. He just hoped his inner feelings wouldn't show on his face.

Not even to himself did he want to admit how his pulse quickened around Violet these days. He sure didn't want Rachel or Daniel to have any inkling of the turmoil he felt when Violet was anywhere near him, not after they had extended their hospitality by letting him and the Wingate kids stay with them. And they wouldn't, if he could help it.

He tried not to think about Violet's response, or her lack of it. She hadn't said a word since their conversation near the barn, and he wasn't about to bring it up.

Willie tucked his shirttail in and took a deep breath, then headed up the familiar path to the house, determined to act as though he felt no different tonight than any other. He gave a perfunctory tap on the kitchen door and walked inside, ready to dole out a light compliment about the savory aroma coming from the oven. His words of praise died on his lips when he saw the white-faced group seated at the table.

A quick glance told him only the three other adults were in the room and a sick feeling of dread wrenched at his stomach. "What's wrong? Is it one of the kids?"

Rachel gazed at him wordlessly and shook her head. Violet merely stared down at her hands, clasped together in a white-knuckled grip on the tablecloth. Finally, Daniel broke the uneasy silence.

"You'd better hear what's going around town. I don't know any other way to tell you than just to say it straight out." He pressed his lips together and cleared his throat, then went on. "There's talk circulating, Willie, and it's bad. Real bad."

Willie looked from face to face, but still couldn't find a clue. "What kind of talk?"

"About you . . . and Violet. Seems there's quite a bit of speculation as to your real reason for staying out here during the quarantine." Daniel regarded him steadily.

If not for the steady ticking of the mantel clock, Willie would have believed that time had frozen. Even his heart seemed to have quit beating. He stared at the people who had given him their trust and taken him in. Did he detect a difference in Daniel's and Rachel's attitude toward him? "I swear to you—" he began.

Daniel held up his hand. "I believe you. We both do. We know Violet and we've come to know you. No one can convince me anything happened out here that shouldn't have, but the story is flying around, just the same. I left half my load of seed on Samson's loading dock and came home as soon as I heard."

"Who started it?" Anger surged through Willie with an intensity that shocked him. He'd been in plenty of scraps in his younger years, but never before had he wanted so badly to strangle someone. He clenched his fists and wished he could use them on whoever said such a thing. "Give me a name and I'll put an end to it before another day is over."

Daniel held up a restraining hand. "I asked the same question. It's like trying to track down a wisp of smoke. No telling how it got started . . . or how it'll end. We'll just have to ride it out, I guess."

Willie's stomach churned with suppressed rage. He grasped the door handle.

Rachel reached out a hand. "Aren't you going to eat?"

"I'm not hungry." With that blunt statement, Willie stepped out into the fresh spring evening. He stood on the porch a moment, listening. Crickets chirped; blades of new grass whispered together in the soft breeze. To all outward appearances, life went on just as it always had. But Willie felt the difference deep within him, a burning fury that demanded satisfaction. With angry strides, he started toward his cabin.

"Willie."

He registered the quiet voice even through the pounding of blood in his temples. He stopped, turned, and walked slowly back to the porch where Violet stood in the glow of light from the kitchen window. He took a step nearer. Even in the dimness, he could discern her pallor.

His heart melted and guilt threatened to gnaw a hole straight through him. Violet had only reached out to minister to some needy orphans and their testy keeper. She didn't deserve this kind of ugly talk or the pain it caused. Why on earth hadn't he had the sense to foresee something like this happening? He knew the answer, and it galled him. He'd been so focused on his own troubles that he never considered what staying there might cost her. At the moment, he didn't know who he wanted to vent his anger on more—the purveyor of the rumor or himself.

"Willie," she said again. The pale golden light shimmered on her hair. He wished he could see those amazing blue eyes of hers, but they remained in shadow.

"I won't let whoever's responsible get away with this."

"It's going to be all right."

"All right?" The words tore out of him. How could anything be all right again?

She nodded, sorrow and resignation evident in her movement. "Let it go. There's nothing you can do."

Wasn't there? As soon as he figured out who'd set such vicious slander in motion, he'd be only too happy to throttle him.

"There's no point in trying to track this down," she continued, as if she'd read his mind. "A rumor is like a pillow that bursts and sends feathers floating everywhere. You can mend the rip, but all those feathers will keep on floating around, especially if you keep stirring them up even more. It's best just to let them all settle down of their own accord. They will eventually, you know."

"But in the meantime—"

"There's no truth to the story, is there?"

Willie jerked his head back. "You know there isn't!"

"Of course I do. We both know the truth, and that's what we have to hang on to. People will either believe the story or they won't; there's nothing you or I can do to change that. All we can do is hold our heads high and walk tall through this. God is our witness, and He knows we have nothing to be ashamed of."

True enough, but it didn't help assuage his sense of justice. "I'm sorry I got you into this."

Violet turned her head slightly, and her lips parted in a tiny smile. "It seems to me this started out as my idea. As I recall, you had rather strong feelings against it in the beginning."

Willie grinned in spite of himself at the memory of their earliest encounter. "All the same, I'd still like to find the fellow who started all this."

"I understand, Willie, believe me. I've felt the same way ever since Daniel came home with the news. But adding wrong to wrong won't make it any better. We'll just have to weather this and remember that God is in control."

Her gentle voice held a confidence that echoed in Willie's mind through the long hours of that sleepless night. He'd known that Violet Canfield had an abiding faith, but he never suspected its depth before now. It put his own reaction to shame.

Back home he'd chafed at the feeling that no one took him seriously, but that didn't begin to compare to the gravity of his present position. Being considered a well-meaning, if incompetent, kid bore no resemblance to being labeled a philanderer.

And he'd dragged Violet down with him. The knowledge only added to the bitterness of his despair.

One thing he knew: He had to shed the kids as quickly as possible.

He needed to get out of there so he wouldn't do anything else to bring more pain to Violet.

～❦～

Just after first light, Willie took the wagon and headed into town to pick up the rest of Daniel's seed. He pulled the horses to a halt in front of Samson's Market and took his time setting the brake and climbing down from the seat.

He scanned the people passing by, trying to discern any telltale glances that might be cast his way. Did anyone look at him differently this morning than they had a week ago? Several men nodded when they walked past him, and he couldn't decide whether their smiles were genuine or held a note of sly amusement.

Hard to tell. With his feelings so much on edge, it would be all too easy to see scorn where none existed. Not only that, but he had no idea how long this story had been circulating. The attitudes he had accepted as normal might have been covering disdain for weeks. The thought left a sour taste in his mouth.

He finished his business in short order, then walked to the telegraph office on the off chance Monroe had sent a wire to tell him when to expect his arrival. To his surprise, the clerk reached for a yellow slip of paper even before he gave his name. He hurried outside and found a spot away from any curious eyes.

Let it be soon. He opened the paper.

> *Regret to inform Lewis ill with pleurisy STOP*
> *Will advise when able to travel to Arizona STOP*
> *Pa*

Willie read the message three times, hoping he'd somehow misunderstood its import. Each time, he came to the same conclusion: Once again, his cousin had managed to leave him stranded. His fist crumpled the telegram into a wrinkled yellow wad. It seemed the longer he stayed in Prescott, the deeper he got into a situation he never wanted to be a part of in the first place.

—&—

"Cow pats, Miss Violet? Are you sure?"

Violet looked at the astonishment on the three upturned faces before her and put a hand over her mouth to cover her smile. "Quite sure," she said when she had regained her composure. "The pioneers used them for fuel on their travels west. And more often than not, it was the children's job to collect them."

Jessica's lips curled in horror. "Did they have to wait behind the cows while they . . . they . . ."

This time Violet couldn't control the laugh that burst forth. "No, Honey. There had been plenty of cows on the trail long before them. Remember we talked about how people often used oxen to pull their wagons? The pats those children picked up had been out there for some time. They were quite dry, I promise you."

Frederick raised a skeptical eyebrow. "Well, if they were dry, I suppose it wouldn't be too bad."

"No worse than the ones out there." She rose from her seat on the front porch and waved a hand to indicate the open area where their milk cow grazed in the summertime. "I've seen you kicking them when you cut across the pasture. So you see, it really wasn't so bad. They'd just go out and fill up a sheet with them and bring them in during the day so they'd have a way to start their fires at night."

Toby's face scrunched up in thought. "I guess it's nice to know it's good for something." He joined his brother and sister on their way to the pasture to take a fresh look at the previously unappreciated material.

The sound of boots thudded on the porch steps, and she turned to see Willie smiling down at her. An answering smile spread across her face without any conscious effort on her part. He'd seemed somewhat distant since that moment near the barn, even more so since learning about the rumors. Today the liveliness had returned to his eyes, and for the second time she felt that fiery tingle dart back and forth between them.

"What got you onto that topic?" he asked with a low laugh that sent a pleasant warmth all through her.

She stared up at his sun-browned face, taking in the even features and the wavy chestnut hair that glinted flashes of red in the sunlight. His composure didn't appear to have been disturbed the slightest bit. Apparently he hadn't experienced the same reaction to their proximity. "I ran out of flower names to teach them, so I decided they could learn about how this part of the country was settled. They've been playing pioneers all morning and loving every minute of it. Up to the part about the cow pats, anyway."

Willie grinned, crinkling the creases at the corners of his eyes and doing strange things to the rhythm of Violet's heartbeat. "You've worked wonders with them. They don't seem like the same kids I brought out here."

"I've said all along they were wonderful. I don't understand how you happened to get off on the wrong foot." She noted the furrow between his eyebrows and hastened to add, "But I'm glad you've worked things out with them." She felt a warm glow of pleasure when the furrow disappeared, and his smile returned before he tipped her a nod and went back to mending fence.

The smile suited him better, she decided. Much better. How glad she was that their relationship had improved so much since his arrival! It would have been a shame to have him leave with her still thinking him a cold, uncaring man.

The thought of him leaving left a cold feeling of its own deep inside her, and she tried to keep her dismay from showing on her face. She'd gotten used to having him around. *Too* used to it, she suspected. It would be harder to see him go than she'd ever have dreamed when she first met him. Back then, she would have rejoiced in his departure and done everything she could to speed him on his way. Now . . .

Saying good-bye had never been easy for her, especially not to someone she cared about. And Willie Bradley had somehow slipped into the category of a person she cared about without her even realizing it. She shook her head and blinked back the sting of tears. She would just have to be strong and make the best of it. He'd soon be going back to a life she had no part in, and she might as well get used to that fact.

❧

Willie tamped in the last of the dirt around the fence post and shook it to test his work. Good, it didn't budge. From across the field, childish voices echoed in the twilight. With the lengthening days, the kids were determined to take advantage of every bit of daylight they could. He leaned against his shovel and watched them drag what looked like an old sheet around the pasture, tossing in cow pats as they went. From the way the sheet drooped, it looked like they'd collected quite a load.

Willie grinned at their enjoyment and gathered up his tools. Quite an idea of Violet's, getting them to play pioneer. It gave them a way to run off their energy without getting into trouble, something he heartily approved. He didn't know if he'd go quite as far as Violet and call them wonderful, but he had to admit they no longer acted like the little hoodlums he'd known at first.

He yawned and stretched. He'd done his share of slapping on brands and riding countless hours in all sorts of weather. It had hardened him physically, no doubt about it, but this farmwork used a whole different set of muscles. He hoped he could stay awake long enough to pull the blankets up over him once he stretched out on his cot.

$$\left(14\right)$$

A full night of dreamless sleep. Just what a man needed to set him back up for another day. Willie raised his head and blinked, puzzled by the weak light that filtered into the cabin. Usually sunlight aplenty made its way through the ample cracks around the door, even in the moments just after daybreak. Could it be earlier than he supposed?

From outside came the sound of Daniel rattling the latch that opened the barn door, ready to start his after-breakfast chores. Willie sprang from his cot and pulled his shirt over his head. Dim light or not, he'd managed to oversleep.

He frowned again at the door, puzzled by the lack of illumination. Maybe a heavy bank of clouds had moved in, although he wouldn't have thought it from the looks of last night's sky. Shoving his shirttail into his waistband, he yanked open the door and jumped back when an avalanche of cascading objects showered over him.

Willie coughed and waved his hand to drive away the swirling cloud of dust and tried to get his foggy mind to figure out what was going on. Something still partially blocked the light from the doorway. He pulled down the offending object and recognized it as a sheet. It looked like the same one the kids had used to carry their collection in the night before.

No. Even those kids wouldn't . . . He glanced down at the ankle-deep pile. The bright sunshine of a perfect spring morning streamed inside, clearly illuminating an ample heap of pioneer fire fuel. Most of which was dry.

Even when his mind had to accept the evidence at his feet, Willie could do nothing but stand and stare. How had they managed it? He moved to examine the outside of the door and saw where the sheet had been tacked into place along both sides and the bottom, leaving an opening in the top wide enough for loading it with their ammunition. That explained the lack of light. He must have slept even more soundly than he thought, for them to be able to make their preparations without waking him.

He prodded one of the dry pats with the toe of his boot and looked down at his shirt and pants. No point in changing until he'd swept out the cabin. He reached for the broom.

It didn't take more than ten minutes to sweep the mess back onto the sheet and redeposit it in the pasture, but that provided more than enough time for Willie's emotional temperature to soar. By the time he'd cleaned up and changed clothes, he'd reached his boiling point. He mounted the porch steps in a single stride and entered the kitchen in a state of high dudgeon.

Three expectant faces looked up from their breakfast. "Good morning, Willie," they chorused.

"Did you sleep well?" Frederick asked.

Willie fought the urge to up-end Frederick and give some serious attention to his backside. Their intent had been to make him lose his temper and look like a wild-eyed maniac in front of Violet and her family. He would not give them that satisfaction. He drew up a chair and reached for a slice of toast.

"I slept fine. How about you?"

"Well, we were up kind of late," Jessica said. She swallowed the last of her milk as though nothing significant had occurred.

"Yeah," Toby added. "We were playing pioneer." Three muffled giggles followed his announcement.

The laughter did what outright provocation couldn't. Willie stood, sending his chair over with a clatter. "Of all the underhanded—" He broke off when Violet entered the room.

She favored him with a bright smile. "Leaving already? But you haven't even had breakfast yet."

"I thought I'd just grab this and go." He scooped the toast into his hand and slathered jam on top of it. "I got a bit of a late start this morning." He picked up his chair and set it back in place, then turned to leave.

Violet waved away his explanation. "Don't feel bad. We all over-sleep sooner or later."

Willie choked but refrained from answering. He stepped past the snickering Wingates and reached for the door handle. "Don't you go giving Miss Violet any trouble today," he admonished them.

"We won't," Toby said. "Cross our hearts." He turned a loving glance on Violet, who rewarded him with a quick pat on the head.

"We'll probably play pioneer some more," Jessica put in.

Violet beamed. "Isn't it wonderful how they've taken to that game? And they seem to be learning so much from it."

Willie clenched his hands, squeezing his toast into a sticky, doughy mass.

❧

All during the rest of the day, Willie plotted ways to teach his tormentors a lesson. They had gone too far this time. He might never be able to convince Violet of their two-faced treachery, but those kids deserved a comeuppance, and it looked like he would have to be the one to do it. Thoughts of some of his own childhood pranks drifted through his mind, evoking a reminiscent smile. The three of them had no idea who they were tangling with. They had chosen to take on a master of practical jokes who had a considerable arsenal of his own at his disposal.

He pondered ways and means, discarding one idea after another. Then the memory of his tenth summer and how he'd dealt with one particularly obnoxious visitor to the ranch came to mind. He considered the possibilities. It seemed to have all the qualities he needed. Quick. Easy to set up. Simple, yet effective. Yes, that would do nicely. He propped the shovel up against a nearby tree and set off in search of a bucket.

❧

Just a little wider . . . no, too far. There. Willie stood back and surveyed his handiwork. The chicken coop door stood slightly ajar, as though it sagged a bit on its hinges. No one would be likely to think any more of it than that, certainly not three young kids in search of eggs. He lifted his gaze and stared proudly at the bucket he had procured from the barn, now half filled with water and impeccably balanced between the door and the building.

It would only take a slight tug on the door to bring the water splashing down on the three kids. Nothing that would hurt them, just enough to let them know they'd met their match and had better watch their step in the future. Willie chuckled, savoring his moment of triumph in advance. He checked the angle of the sun and went back for his shovel to dig the last posthole. He could finish that and still get back in time to see the action.

The hole dug, he slipped up behind the woodshed and hid in the shelter of its walls. They should be along any minute. He strained to pick up the first indication of footsteps. He didn't plan to make a move until he heard the splash. It wouldn't do to give his position away and alert his target.

There they came, right on time. Willie grinned and prepared to enjoy his victory. The steps quickened, then paused. A slight creak from the door and then . . . *Clang!* A muffled shriek followed.

Willie leaped out from his hiding place, ready to whoop with laughter at the sight of three dripping children. Instead, he beheld a lone figure standing stock still in the henhouse doorway, an inverted bucket covering its head, and realized with a feeling of doom that he'd managed to catch Violet in his trap.

Before his horrified gaze, she staggered around in a tiny circle, arms flailing. His jaw sagged, and a jumble of bewildered thoughts whirled through his brain. Thank goodness he'd picked out the lightest bucket he could find. But where were the kids? He looked around for some sign of the Wingates, but they were nowhere to be seen.

He needed to get a towel, something to dry Violet off. He started toward the house, then stopped, struck by a peculiarity that had escaped his notice until that moment. Violet hadn't gotten a bit wet.

How could that be? Maybe the water had spilled before the bucket came tumbling down upon her? A quick glance showed no puddle, no splash, no sign of water anywhere.

Mystified, Willie moved to help, but Violet tugged the bucket off before he could reach her. He skidded to a halt, stricken by the sight that met his eyes. Instead of water, a gummy substance coated Violet's head. With agonizingly slow movement, globs of the amber stuff rolled from her forehead to her nose to her chin. More oozed its way down the length of her hair. Her eyes gaped wide. Her mouth opened and closed, but she made no sound.

Willie stared, completely baffled. No water in the world looked or acted like this stuff. What on earth had happened? He sniffed, trying to place the heavy smell that emanated from Violet.

No, it couldn't be. He reached out and touched her shoulder with a tentative finger, picked up a drop of the treacly goo, and touched it to his tongue.

Molasses? Another taste convinced him.

Violet turned a stunned face toward him. "What . . . ? How . . . ?"

"I don't know," Willie said. "It was supposed to be water."

Violet's features froze. She narrowed her eyes into angry blue slits. "What do you mean, 'it was supposed to be water?' "

"That's what I put in the bucket," he began, then stopped, aghast, when he realized his error.

"You set this up? *You?*" Violet's chest heaved with the force of her emotion.

"Not exactly," he sputtered. "Well, sort of. But it wasn't meant for you."

Violet tried to wipe the molasses from her eyebrows, but only succeeded in stringing more of the syrup from forehead to fingers. "Then who?" She glared at Willie, targeting him with a gaze capable of freezing a waterfall. Without giving him time to answer, she went on. "The children were supposed to gather eggs. You knew that. You intended this for them, didn't you?"

She turned on her heel and stomped across the yard toward the house, radiating outraged fury. "You would have gotten them with your nasty trick, too, if Toby hadn't hurt his knee. Jessie and Frederick are helping him into bed, so I told them I'd come down here in their place."

"Wait a minute." Willie's suspicions flared to a high level. He had never yet seen a Wingate do anything without some purpose. "When did Toby get hurt? Is he bleeding?"

"It happened just a few minutes ago, and no, his knee is not bleeding. Does that disappoint you?" The sarcasm dripped more freely than the molasses.

"I just meant . . . well, if he only *said* he'd been hurt, it would be a way to keep them all in the house and make sure you came down here instead." His voice trailed off at the look of contempt she shot at him.

"Are you implying . . . ?" She shook her head, flinging molasses onto the ground. "Save your breath, Willie Bradley. It's bad enough you set up something like this without trying to cast the blame on three innocent children."

"Innocent! Compared to those three, a rattlesnake looks like a housepet."

"How can you even think of saying such a thing when you've already admitted you're the one responsible for this? Why, if I hadn't come down here, that bucket would have fallen on one of them. Which is exactly what you intended," she added with a dark look.

Willie raised his arms in protest, then dropped them, admitting defeat. "It was only water," he mumbled.

"Oh, really?" Violet fumed. "And which well did this particular water come from?" She pivoted and swept up the porch steps, leaving only a trail of molasses droplets to mark her passing.

❧

Violet lathered her hair for the third time, probing with her fingers to make sure she'd finally gotten rid of the last traces of molasses. When she encountered no more of the sticky syrup, she reached for the pitcher of rinse water.

"Violet, are you all right?" Rachel's concerned voice came from behind her.

Unable to talk without getting a mouthful of water, Violet contented herself with an affirmative grunt.

"But why are you washing your hair this time of day? And why is your dress all balled up in the corner like that?"

Violet squeezed the water from her hair, caught it up in a towel, and stood to face her sister. "I got something on my dress," she said, hoping Rachel wouldn't press for details. "And my hair." *And my face, and my ears, and my hands.*

Rachel knelt before the wadded dress. "I'll say you got something on it. Let's just hope it isn't a total loss. What on earth is it anyway?" She poked at the garment with an inquiring finger. "Why, it almost looks like . . . Violet Canfield, how did you manage to get molasses all over your head?"

"I don't want to talk about it." Violet toweled her hair vigorously, then pulled on a clean dress. "Leave it," she said, when Rachel would have picked up the soiled one. "I'll take care of it myself." She thinned her lips into a hard, straight line.

Rachel opened her mouth as if to argue, then appeared to reconsider. "All right, Honey. Have it your own way." She paused at the bedroom doorway for one last look at the puzzling sight and then left.

Violet wadded the towel into a ball and flung it next to the molasses-coated dress. She could hear Rachel's footsteps moving around in the kitchen. Apparently her sister had decided to take care of the supper preparations. Good. It would give her time to think about what had happened.

The moment the bucket had toppled onto her head, she'd shrieked in alarm. That first instant of shock, though, didn't begin to compare with her feelings when something thick and heavy began to spread its way over her head and face. If she hadn't managed to pull the bucket free and regain contact with her surroundings, she knew she would have dissolved into hysterics. The memory still left her shaken.

And then to find Willie right on the scene telling her she'd been covered in molasses. Molasses, of all things! His look of assumed innocence had been so well contrived she almost would have believed him blameless, if he hadn't admitted his guilt in setting up the trap. Why he insisted he'd only filled the bucket with water was something she couldn't understand. A forthright confession and apology would have gone a long way toward mollifying her feelings. Maybe when he realized the enormity of what he'd done, he'd been afraid of what she might do.

And well he should be! Violet couldn't ever remember being so utterly furious in her entire life. In any case, Willie Bradley had shown his true colors at last. Sir Willie? Ha! More like the Black Knight. She paced the width of the room, the staccato beat of her footsteps punctuating her angry thoughts.

Hadn't she given him every opportunity to prove her first impression of him wrong? He'd done a good job of pulling the wool over her eyes too. Her cheeks flamed when she remembered her tender response to the way he'd ridden off to fetch Doc Hathaway, the joy she felt when their eyes met and his smile lit up his suntanned face. She'd even begun to wonder if . . .

No. She must thrust away such foolish thoughts. It turned out her first assessment had been the right one all along, and she had to face the fact. No matter what she'd thought—what she'd hoped—might be true, today's episode only proved the children's stories correct. The man simply couldn't be trusted.

It shouldn't be difficult to come to terms with that. Why, then, did the thought leave her feeling so bereft? She'd lived a peaceful, happy existence before he barreled into her life. She could go back to that placid, dreamy state when he left. After all, he'd made it all too clear he wanted nothing more than to go his way as soon as possible ever since he arrived.

All right, then. He would be out of her life before much longer. His character, however deplorable it might be, shouldn't bother her in the least. She touched her hand to her cheek and stared at the traces of wetness on her fingertips. And thoughts of his departure surely shouldn't make her cry.

15

T'm taking this load of corn over to Zeke Thomas's " Daniel stepped up into the wagon seat and picked up the reins. "I may not be back until suppertime."

"Want me to take it for you?" Willie hoped his eagerness to get off the place didn't show.

Daniel sent him an appraising glance that told him his hope had been in vain. "It's been pretty rough on you the past few days, hasn't it?" A grin crinkled the corners of his eyes. "I've heard your version and I've heard Violet's, and I'm still not sure what to make of what happened. Whatever it was, I wish I'd been there." He leaned back and slapped his thigh. "I don't think I've ever seen Violet as stirred up over anything. It must have been a sight to see."

"Oh, it was. Believe me."

Daniel chuckled at Willie's dry tone and jumped down from the seat. "Go ahead. The time away should do you good." He clapped Willie on the back and walked toward the barn, still laughing.

Wish I could see it in the same light Daniel does. Willie guided the horses onto the road to Thomas's place and tried to get his mind to think of happier things than Violet's attitude of late. Every time he came within twenty feet of her, she sniffed and left in a pointed manner that made it clear he was the reason for her departure.

He'd tried more than once to explain to her, but she refused to stay around long enough to listen. He thought about confronting the kids and forcing them to confess their part in the fiasco, but Violet kept them firmly out of his sight. He sighed. What could a fellow do? *Go away and leave her in peace, I reckon.*

And so he would . . . just as soon as he found Thurman Hadlock.

The gloomy thought did nothing to brighten his spirits. He unloaded the corn for Zeke with barely a word of greeting and left the puzzled man scratching his head.

He glanced at the sun. It hadn't taken nearly as long as he thought it would. At this rate, he'd be home well before suppertime. He hauled back on the reins, bringing the surprised horses to a halt in the middle of the road.

He needed time away, and Daniel wouldn't expect him for several more hours. He clucked to the horses and wheeled them around in the opposite direction. For the first time since he arrived, he had the opportunity to see more of the area than the farm and the road into town. He would do a little exploring.

He paused a moment to get his bearings. To reach Zeke Thomas's place, he'd crossed a ridge about two miles east of the farm, which put him on the northeast side of Granite Mountain. Willie nodded. The craggy peak that loomed above him made an easy reference point. He snapped the reins and started the horses again.

The road meandered through broad open areas and under stands of pine trees. He filled his lungs with their pungent scent, glad he had chosen this course. For one who'd spent most of his life crossing the range on horseback, the past weeks had been unbearably confining. He'd needed this change of scene.

He stopped the wagon at the edge of a smooth, rolling meadow and set the brake. The sun sent warm beams down from an azure sky as clear as any he'd ever seen at home. Leaving the horses where they could reach the new spring growth, Willie walked across the springy meadow grass. He tried to name the trees he saw scattered throughout the expanse: cottonwoods, walnuts, and some good-sized oaks.

Once he left the meadow and entered the trees on the other side, a thick layer of leaves and pine needles cushioned his steps. He stopped at the foot of a towering pine and settled himself against its trunk. What a view! A tree-studded foothill behind him, the rolling grassland before him—what more could a man ask for?

He perused the area with an experienced eye. The winter must have brought plenty of moisture; he could tell from the new growth that lush graze would soon spring up. Would it be like that every year? If so, wouldn't this be the perfect setting for a ranch?

He grinned at his foolish notion. Making himself more comfortable on the pine needles, he rested his arms on his knees and let the quiet of the place seep into his soul. After listening to the kids' chatter for weeks on end and spending every moment he could in search of Hadlock, this quiet spot seemed like a piece of heaven. Apart from the sound of the wind soughing through the trees, nothing reached his ears but the horses' steady munching.

"You like this place as much as I do, don't you, fellas?"

A flicker of movement caught his attention and he spotted a gray, bushy tail just before it disappeared behind the trunk of a nearby pine. The squirrel peeked out from the other side and chittered at him. "But you found it first and you wish we'd get on our way, is that it?" He laughed and folded his arms behind his head. What made this place so special? Peace, he decided.

What a man could do here! He scanned the setting before him. Up on that ridge would be a perfect setting for a house. Right near those massive pines, sentinels of the forest. Then, noticing the bright stripe that spiraled down the trunk of one of them, he revised his opinion. Maybe not. It wouldn't do to build anywhere near the likelihood of another lightning strike.

He shifted his position and kept looking. All right, what about down in that sheltered hollow? It still commanded quite a view. Yes, that would work. He turned his attention to the broad expanse opposite it. In his mind's eye, he could see tawny cattle hides dotting the landscape, moving through clumps of manzanita and cliff rose.

Scooting into a reclining position, he tilted his hat low over half-closed eyes and went deeper into his pleasant daydream. The corrals would go . . . over there, he decided. The barn would be placed nearby. Both would be only a reasonable walking distance from the house. It wouldn't be a fine house like his parents' or his uncle's— not at first anyway. But he could start out small and build on as necessity demanded. In his mind, he mounted the steps to the porch. The door opened.

Willie's lips curved upward, wondering who would appear. He tried to insert Mary Rose Downey into his mental picture, but her image faded as quickly as it appeared. Mary Rose would never be suited for a life away from boardwalks and town amenities. Ranch life needed to be lived by someone like . . . Violet.

Violet? The notion made him start bolt upright, then sink back to his more relaxed position. He had to admit it: Violet fit the setting as though it had been created just for her. Mary Rose's mincing city steps would never manage to cross that broad meadow without stumbling. But Violet's easy stride would move over the land with grace.

He shook his head and the picture faded. No point in entertaining any such thoughts about Violet Canfield. The woman despised him, pure and simple. He couldn't rid himself of the image of the ranch so easily. Something about the place touched a chord deep within him, one he'd known existed but had told himself he might as well ignore. Now he wondered—could the Lord have shown him the place he could claim as his own?

In a daze, he turned the horses in the direction of the farm and gave them their heads. While they plodded homeward, Willie tried to sort out the startling thoughts that clamored for attention in his mind.

～◈～

"Jessica?" Violet pulled her shawl tighter about her shoulders and strained her ears to hear any reply the little girl might make. Jessie usually answered quicker than her brothers. Today, though, her repeated calls brought no response.

She cast another glance at the leaden sky, and a prickle of fear ran up her arms. Surely the children wouldn't have ventured too far afield on a day like this. "Toby? Frederick?" Her voice carried clearly across the pasture. They would have heard her if they were anywhere nearby.

Worry knotted her stomach. The temperature had dropped that morning, bringing a return of crispness to the air. She hadn't been overly concerned, though, not with the children bundled up against the change in the weather. But the light clouds that dotted the morning sky had become a heavy gray mass by early afternoon; and if Violet didn't miss her guess, a storm was brewing.

If only she hadn't gotten so caught up in her spring-cleaning chores. Focused on scrubbing out cupboards and cleaning behind furniture they seldom moved, she'd lost all track of time . . . and the changing weather conditions.

She needed to locate the children, and soon. But how? She'd been calling for the last twenty minutes. She'd even rung the dinner bell, hoping that would bring the three of them scampering out of the woods that bordered the farther field. Nothing.

Rachel and Daniel would pick this day to spend the afternoon with Sheriff Dolan and his wife. If she had Daniel here, she knew he'd think of a solution. But she had only herself to rely on. Everyone else was gone. . . .

Except Willie. Violet clenched her teeth and gripped the ends of her shawl in her fists. No way did she want to make that man feel he'd somehow gotten back in her good graces. Not after what he'd done. She'd avoided him ever since the molasses incident and didn't see any reason to change that now.

Except that she didn't see any other way to find the children.

Muttering, she set off for the barn. He ought to be inside, sharpening tools.

❧

Willie looked up at the sound of footsteps, and his jaw dropped when he saw Violet standing in the doorway. He sat unmoving, not knowing what she'd come for. He didn't want to do anything to set her off again. He watched while she drew herself up and hugged herself tightly.

"I can't find the children." Her voice trembled.

He didn't know what he expected, but it hadn't been that. After keeping up her steadfast silent treatment so long, he knew she wouldn't break that silence for any trifling reason. But for the life of him, he couldn't understand what inspired such anxiety in her now.

The kids had probably decided to have a little fun with her and refused to come when she called. Irritating, but not a cause for fear.

"Have you looked in the corn crib?" he asked. "What about the chicken coop or that spot over by the tree line where the boys have been playing soldier?"

"I've looked everywhere." She batted her eyelashes furiously against the brimming tears, but Willie saw how close she was to breaking down. "Have you seen what's happening outside? We're likely to be in for a storm in another hour or so, a bad one. I'm telling you, Willie, I've looked in every place I can think of, and those children are *gone*."

Willie strode to the door, galvanized by the urgency of her tone. Sure enough, heavy gray clouds massed across the sky. The wind had picked up too. Violet was right: They needed to find those kids, and they had no time to lose.

"Show me the last place you saw them," he told her.

❧

An hour later, Violet trotted her horse beside Willie's, nearly frantic with fear. They had checked all the children's usual haunts once more at Willie's insistence, but to no avail. Only when they made one last trek across the pasture did he notice three fresh sets of footprints leading away from the farm and into the trees.

"They've taken off," he told her, a grim set to his mouth. "I'll saddle up and go looking for them."

"I'm going with you."

"In this weather? I don't think so."

"When you find them, you'll need an extra hand to get them all home. I'm going, and that's all there is to it." She pivoted on her heel and walked to the house to get her warmest coat and extra blankets for the children when they found them. For once, he didn't argue with her.

Rather than hitch up the wagon, Willie saddled horses for them both. They'd never be able to maneuver the wagon far off the road, he explained, and no telling what kind of terrain they'd have to cross following the tracks. At first the trail seemed clear enough, at least to Willie. He followed without hesitation for nearly a mile, then shook his head.

"It seems to peter out right here in these rocks," he said. He twisted in his saddle, scanning the area on all sides, then turned to Violet. Worry puckered his forehead. "I don't understand it. How did they get this far from home in the first place, and where could they be heading?"

Violet only shook her head, unable to speak past the tears that clogged her throat. How could she have been so preoccupied as to not notice the children's disappearance? She shrugged her coat farther up around her neck. The storm would hit within the hour; she had no doubt. And when it did, what would happen to the children? Would Jessie suffer a relapse, or worse, because of her negligence?

"There are some caves up along the ridge," she managed to say. "Daniel mentioned them the other evening after supper. Maybe they decided to go explore them."

Willie touched his heels to his horse's flanks, and without hesitation her mount followed.

~&

If Willie hadn't been concerned when Violet first told him the kids had gone missing, he was now. Those gray skies spelled trouble, and three youngsters—even three as ornery as the Wingate brood—just might meet their match when pitted against the weather's fury. And now he had Violet's safety to think about as well. He couldn't believe it when she informed him she would be coming along; but after one look at her set face, he hadn't taken time to argue. He knew stubbornness when he saw it.

Where in the world could those three be? He'd hoped to find the three wanderers within a few minutes of beginning the search. By now, they must have traveled two or three miles from the farm. If the storm hit, he and Violet would have to take shelter themselves.

"Are those the caves?" He pointed to a series of pockmarked openings along a ledge of the limestone cliff. Violet nodded. They both dismounted and hurried up the slope, checking each cave in turn. No sign that the Wingates had ever been there.

"We're heading home," he said. "We can start looking again as soon as the storm has passed."

"But the children!" Violet's horrified gasp tore at his heart.

"They're either safe or they aren't. There isn't a thing we can do for them now, except pray." And he'd been doing plenty of that, ever since they started. He took long strides down the slope, sliding the last few feet to the bottom on the layer of loose rocks near the base. Behind him, he heard the rattle of rocks and a sharp cry. He turned to see Violet waving her arms wildly, trying to regain her lost footing.

He reached for her, but her feet shot out from under her before he could manage it. She slid to within six feet of him and lay there in a crumpled heap.

"Violet! Are you all right?" He cupped her face in his hands, willing her to open her eyes. In a few moments, she blinked slowly, then stared up at him.

"Are you hurt? Answer me."

Her eyes cleared and she pushed herself to a sitting position. "I'm fine. Just clumsy, I guess. I feel so foolish."

"I should have given you a hand." He berated himself for the oversight. Thank heaven she hadn't been injured. He slid his arm around her shoulders to help her to her feet. She stood, then sank back to the ground with a moan. "What is it? What's wrong?"

"It's my ankle. I must have twisted it when I fell."

Willie helped her ease off her boot. If they hadn't had trouble aplenty before, they did now. Violet's ankle had started to swell. It seemed to be increasing in size even while he watched. He sucked in his breath. Would she be up to making the ride back to the farm?

He probed the swollen flesh with gentle fingers. "How much does that hurt?"

Her low moan and ashen face gave him all the answer he needed. He didn't know whether the ankle was broken or not. He did know Violet was in no shape to be riding.

The first light splats of rain pattered down on him and he glanced up at the sky. The storm had come even more quickly than they thought. They needed to find shelter and find it fast. He wrapped his arms around Violet and lifted her up.

"I don't know how I'm going to make it home," she said in a weak voice.

"We aren't going home." He took a cautious step onto the loose rocks, looking for a foothold. "We're going up to the caves." Violet's head lolled against his shoulder with a weary acquiescence that worried him.

16

The unyielding hardness of the rock beneath her brought Violet back to awareness. She pressed her hands against the floor of the cave and pushed herself upright. A hot shaft of pain stabbed her ankle, and she cried out.

Pulling the hem of her skirt out of the way, she tried to examine her injury. To her surprise, her ankle was encased in a neatly bound splint. When had Willie done that? She didn't remember a thing since the moment he had scooped her into his arms and carried her back up the hill.

More to the point, where was Willie now? She swiveled her head back and forth, peering into the recesses of the cave's dim interior. She couldn't see him anywhere. Outside, the sky had unleashed a deluge of rain. What trees she could see through the darkness of the storm bent like buggy whips in the wind.

Where is he? Surely he wouldn't have gone off and left her! Panic at the thought of being alone and injured welled up inside her and threatened to overflow in a torrent of fear.

Footsteps rattled against the stones just outside the mouth of the cave. Violet bit her lip to keep back the tears of relief that sprang to her eyes. In a moment Willie appeared, swathed in a dripping slicker and staggering under the weight of their saddles, blankets, and saddlebags. "There, that ought to do it." He dropped the blankets and saddles near a pile of dry pine branches and slung the saddlebags over near the rock wall.

"Where have you been?" She hadn't meant for the question to come out in a high-pitched squeak.

Willie looked at her, compassion and amusement mingled in his gaze. "I had to get things squared away before I could come back and hole up here. This isn't any too big," he said, waving his hand at their small shelter, "but anything much larger would be too hard to heat."

He shucked off his slicker and began laying a fire at the mouth of the cave. "I put the horses in the next one over," he went on. "They should be fine. I have some jerky in my saddlebags and water in my canteen. We're in pretty good shape." He lit the kindling and blew the small flame to life.

"You call this good?" Violet wrapped her arms around herself and tried to keep from shivering.

"It could be a lot worse. We have shelter, food, and fire. We'll be fine." He added more wood to the growing blaze, then came to sit next to her. "How's your ankle?"

"It hurts," she admitted. Then, remembering the splint, she added, "Thank you for binding it up for me. Do you think it's broken?"

"I couldn't tell for sure. We'll take another look at it in the morning. You look like you're feeling a little better now. I'm glad." He gave her a gaze that rivaled the fire for its warmth.

Violet felt her cheeks flush. "I feel fine, except for my ankle." And the way she went lightheaded when he looked at her like that. "Willie . . . do you think the children are all right?"

The crease that furrowed his brow told her he'd wondered that himself. "I think so. I hope so. They're young, but they're all smart kids. They might not have known about the storm ahead of time, but once it got close, I bet they figured out a place to take shelter, just like we did."

She wanted to believe him, *needed* to hold on to his comforting words.

❧

The rain continued unabated. Willie stoked the fire yet again, then leaned back against the cave wall. In their small quarters, the modest blaze threw off enough heat to keep them from freezing without requiring too much of the wood he'd gathered earlier. Light from the fire flickered around the cave, throwing shadows into weird, dancing patterns on the walls.

He looked at Violet and saw her shiver despite the blanket he had wrapped around her hours before. He scooted closer to her and pulled the sleeping woman into his arms.

"What? Hmm?"

"Shhh. Just be quiet." He stroked her hair, smoothing loose tendrils back from her forehead. She murmured once more, then relaxed back into slumber. Willie shifted his position slightly and settled back against the wall again. Their shared body heat should help keep them both warm until morning. It wouldn't do to let Violet get sick on top of everything else.

That look on her face when she came plummeting down the slope had scared him more than he wanted to admit. That, and the way she had sagged against him, uncomplaining, when he carried her uphill. Coming back into the cave to find her sitting up and back to her old self made him want to shout with gratitude, but he contained his joy and made himself continue with his preparations for the night without comment.

Violet's injured foot had come out from beneath her blanket when he moved her, and he leaned over to cover it again. He squinted at her ankle in the firelight. Had the swelling gone down slightly? Hard to tell with the splint strapped to it. He tossed the corner of the blanket over it and gathered Violet closer to him.

Her warmth penetrated both his body and his heart, and he allowed himself to savor her nearness. *It feels right to hold her in my arms, Lord. How am I supposed to keep my distance after this?* But keep it he would. He couldn't inflict his presence on her any longer than necessary, knowing all he'd brought her had been misery, hard work, and pain.

And a passel of kids for her to love. The thought came unbidden to his mind, and he wondered for the thousandth time whether the trio had made it to some place of protection. Despite his calming words to Violet, he didn't know whether they'd have sense enough to realize the coming danger or not. And he knew they didn't have the wherewithal to light a fire. Would three small bodies huddling together be able to keep each other warm on a night like this?

Only time would tell. Tomorrow he would manage somehow to get Violet back to the farm. Then he'd round up every able-bodied man he could and comb the forest until those kids were found.

He turned his attention back to the woman in his arms and smiled when she murmured in her sleep. The constant downpour outside lulled him into drowsiness, and he let his eyelids drift closed. Immediately, he opened them again. He might never again have the opportunity to hold Violet Canfield close to him. He wanted to stay awake and enjoy the moment while it lasted.

He sat staring into the fire, holding his welcome burden and listening to the sound of the rain. It slackened by degrees, then slowed to a mere drizzle. Willie heaved a sigh. By all appearances, it would let up by morning. They would be able to get back home. The weariness he had tried to hold at bay overcame him. Despite his best intentions, he slept.

～

Violet floated in a beautiful dream in which she and Willie shared a meal before a cozy fireplace. The corners of his eyes crinkled with laughter, and he smiled at her as though there had never been any rift between them. In his blue gaze she saw an intensity that matched her own feelings, a look that hinted at something far deeper than friendship. He leaned toward her and . . .

Something shifted behind her. Strong arms moved her gently to one side. "Something's bothering the horses," Willie whispered. "I've got to go check on them." He took two quick strides to the mouth of the cave and disappeared along the ledge.

She fought to bring herself completely awake. Willie had gone to see to the horses. That made sense. But had his arms been wrapped around her, or had she confused that with her dream? And had she imagined it, or had he really dropped a gentle kiss on her temple just before he left?

She pulled the blanket back around herself and stared out into the gray dawn. The rain had finally ended. Good. There would be nothing to stop them from going home at first light and organizing a search for the children. With some misgivings, she tried rolling her foot from side to side and felt a thrill of hope when it didn't respond with the shooting pain of the day before. Maybe it wasn't broken after all.

Willie's boots scraped along the ledge, and he poked his head inside the opening. "They're all stirred up about something," he told her, "but I can't figure out what it is. I'll circle around up above the caves and be right back."

She nodded, her mind already busy planning what they should do first on their return. She scooted her way across the floor and poked another stick into the fire, not wanting to lose any of its warmth until they were ready to leave.

High-pitched whinnies sounded from the next cave, followed by the stamping of nervous hooves. Violet frowned. Normally, the horses didn't act like that unless they felt in danger. What could be bothering them so? She squinted out into the morning, hoping Willie hadn't come to any harm, and saw a tawny paw at the edge of the opening.

Her breath caught in her throat, and she watched in horror as another paw appeared beside the first and the mountain lion's face moved into view just outside the cave. The creature seemed to take notice of her at the same instant. For an endless moment, their gazes locked. Then the big cat's lips drew back in a snarl and its muscles tensed.

Violet grasped the cool end of the stick she had just added to the fire and waved its blazing end at the cougar. The movement knocked her off balance and she fell to one side. With her ankle in its splint, she couldn't hope to rise to her feet. All she could do was wriggle along on her side, continuing to brandish her improvised torch in the face of the snarling animal.

The mountain lion made a tentative swat toward her with one paw. Violet's heart pounded. If the beast chose to attack her, she could do nothing more to defend herself. The cat, seeming to understand it faced a helpless prey, crouched back on its haunches and waited for the opportunity to spring.

Yaaaahh! A shout echoed through the morning air, and Willie appeared to drop straight from the sky, landing on the ledge not ten feet from the menacing animal.

The cat twisted its body to face this new foe in one lithe movement, muscles rippling along its glossy hide. No sooner had Willie landed than a shot rang out. The cat leaped into the air, then disappeared in a tawny blur.

For a moment, neither of them moved. Violet was the first to find her voice. "Did you get it?" she asked through trembling lips.

Willie shook his head. "I shot too fast. I saw it streaking off through those trees up there." He dropped to one knee beside Violet. "Are you all right?"

"I am now." She regained a sitting position. "I never heard anything more wonderful in my life than that yell you gave a moment ago."

Willie's laugh sounded a bit shaky. "I'd spotted some sign higher up the hill. I was just coming back to tell you when I saw the lion outside our cave and you flailing at it with that burning branch." He cupped her cheek with one hand. "You are one plucky woman, Violet Canfield."

Violet closed her eyes and leaned into his touch. If he hadn't gotten there when he did . . . She opened her eyes and looked up at him. The force of his gaze rocked her. Neither of them moved; neither of them spoke.

Willie was the first to break the silence. "We'd better go," he said, pulling his hand away. "No telling how far that cat went or how long he'll stay gone."

❧

The horses picked their way, trying to find the firmest footing on the slick, muddy ground. Willie kept his attention fixed on the path before him, wanting to spot any potential trouble spots before they could cause a problem. They'd had disasters enough in the past day without adding any more.

Three lost kids, an injured woman, a night stranded in a cave, and an encounter with a cougar. He shook his head and shot a quick glance toward Violet to see how she was faring. She seemed to be holding up well, despite having to keep weight off her ankle. If she could manage to sit her horse for another mile, they'd be home.

And then they could explain to Daniel and Rachel why no one had been home when they came back from town yesterday. His stomach tightened at the thought. Couldn't he last a week without bringing some fresh calamity upon this family? They'd be as glad to see the last of him as he would be to finish his responsibilities to the Wingates and get out of there.

His mood darkened like the previous day's sky. If he had come out to Arizona with any notion of proving himself, he had been sadly mistaken. Not only couldn't he find the kids' guardian; at the moment he had no idea where the kids themselves might be or what condition they were in. He recalled his father's trust in him when he placed them in his care, and his outlook soured even further. It seemed he couldn't do anything right. *So much for being a hero.*

❧

Violet gave her horse its head, trusting the surefooted animal to follow Willie's lead. Clinging to the saddle horn with both hands, she concentrated on keeping her weight shifted away from her injured ankle. Pictures of their ordeal on the mountain flashed through her mind nonstop: her fall down the slope, Willie's quick response to their predicament, the miserable night in the cave, the heart-stopping moment when she'd locked eyes with that mountain lion, and Willie's amazing appearance out of thin air to drive the beast away.

It had taken a day of such extremes to open her eyes to the truth about Willie. When faced with an impossible task, he'd forged ahead without complaint. The moment she'd asked him for help, he'd come to her aid without hesitation, despite her previous cold treatment of him. He never upbraided her for her carelessness in losing her footing and stranding them in the downpour. And never once had he treated her with anything but the utmost courtesy and concern.

How had she failed to recognize a real-life champion from the first? The irony of the situation struck her with a bitter pang. She'd met the hero of her dreams at last and nothing could possibly come of it. How could she bring herself to tell him of her feelings, knowing how much he wanted to leave?

17

To he front door flew open by the time they'd reached the gate, and both Daniel and Rachel hurried across the yard to meet them.

"Are you all right?"

"We've been so worried."

"What on earth possessed you to take off in weather like that?"

Questions and demands for explanation tumbled over one another. Willie waited until they had run down, then held up his hand. "First off, let's get Violet onto the porch. She needs to prop up her ankle."

Rachel gave a muffled cry of dismay and stepped back to let him carry her sister up the stairs and settle her in one of the rocking chairs. She fetched a stool and helped Violet ease her foot onto it. "Is it broken?" she asked when she saw the splint.

"I don't think so," Violet replied. "It feels much better than it did yesterday. Willie took very good care of it." The smile she sent his way did a lot toward bolstering him for the ordeal of telling the others about losing the kids and the need to organize a search party.

He braced himself against the porch railing and faced Daniel. "We have to make some plans. I don't know how to tell you this——"

"We already know." Daniel gave him a solemn nod. "Although I must say, I wish you'd waited long enough to tell us yourself. We were only in town for the day, after all."

Willie exchanged a puzzled look with Violet. Obviously they knew the children weren't there, but how could they have learned the reason? And why would they have expected Willie and Violet to wait any longer to start their search with that storm headed their way? He

138

looked at Daniel for some clue as to the man's reasoning but couldn't read his expression. "We didn't have time," he said, feeling the other's disapproval even as he spoke.

Rachel stepped toward her sister with an exasperated sigh. "Honestly, Violet, this is really too much. I know Daniel and I had our wedding only a week after he proposed, but at least we let people know and took the time to do it right."

Violet's bewildered expression matched the way Willie felt. He held up both hands and took a deep breath. "Would someone please explain what's going on?" He hadn't meant for the statement to come out as loudly as that, but it had the desired effect. Everyone on the porch focused their attention on him. "We're trying to tell you why we've been gone all night," he began.

"But we already know why," Rachel responded. "The children told us."

Willie gaped. "The kids? You mean they're here?"

Daniel nodded slowly, looking at Willie as though he thought he'd lost his mind. "They got home just before we did. The little scamps had taken off on a hike and gotten as far as Jeb McCurdy's place. He bundled them up in his wagon and brought them home just before the storm hit. Good thing he did, too. It wouldn't have been any fun to be caught out in weather like that."

Willie knew that only too well. He calculated for a moment. That meant everyone had been converging on the farm just about the time Violet had hurt her ankle. That meant . . .

"They've been here all the time?" he asked in a hollow voice.

"Except for when they went off to play after you left," Rachel told him. "And I must say I'm surprised at you both for doing that. I know you expected us home fairly soon, but to leave those little things on their own just so you could run off—"

"Run off?" Willie and Violet asked in unison.

"—to get married. Really, don't you think you could have waited just a bit, even if you felt you had to elope?"

A gray mist swirled in front of Willie's eyes. He waited to speak until he could blink it away. "Let me get this straight. The kids have been here—safe—all this time? And they told you we had eloped?"

Daniel hooked his thumbs in his pockets and nodded. "That's about the size of it."

"But that's not true!" Violet's anguished cry rang out. "They ran off and we thought they were lost in the storm. We went out looking for them, and when I hurt my ankle, we were stranded overnight." Willie noted the look of horror filling Violet's eyes as she sought out Rachel. "They really said that?" Violet asked in a stunned whisper.

"They really did." Daniel answered for his wife, his lips set in a grim line. He turned to Willie. "I think we owe you an apology. Looks like we should have listened more carefully when you tried to tell us about some of the things they've pulled."

A week ago, Willie would have found immense consolation in this statement. Today any satisfaction he might feel at this vindication paled beside Violet's obvious misery. He watched her features crumple before she buried her face in her hands. When Rachel tried to comfort her, she shook her head. "Would everybody please leave me alone?" The words came out muffled, but their meaning was clear. Once again, Violet wanted no part of him.

◆

Footsteps scraped on the wooden porch, first shuffling uncertainly, then receding. Violet listened to the soft click when the front door closed behind Rachel and Daniel and heard Willie's steps stride away across the packed dirt toward the barn. She pressed her hands still tighter against her eyes, wishing she could somehow disappear into the comforting darkness and never have to face any of them again.

What must Daniel and Rachel have gone through, thinking she had run off to marry Willie? Her spirit writhed in mortification. How could they have believed such a story? *The same way you believed every awful thing the children told you about Willie.* Those sweet faces seemed incapable of housing such devious minds. He had tried to tell her over and over, but she'd refused to listen to anything that might contradict her perception of them. A fresh spasm of agony pierced her when she thought how much Willie must have suffered.

How could she have misjudged them all? Willie had shown

himself to be the kind of man she always dreamed of, while the children . . . Violet thought back to their times together: stories they'd read, games they'd played, the awful period of nursing Jessie back to health. In all that time, she hadn't once seen anything to give her the slightest qualm. Would she be able to go on caring for them after this?

After a moment's thought, she knew she would. Her love for them had grown so deep, she couldn't cut it off like the flow of water from a pump. *Is this how God feels when we hurt Him and He goes on loving us just the same?* She reflected on the number of times she'd carelessly taken His love for granted. Never again would she do so, now that she had some idea of the cost.

She pulled her hands away from her face and wiped the dampness on her skirt. She stared across the pasture, where Willie had started to work setting a new fencepost. Had she learned anything from this awful episode? Undoubtedly. She, Violet Canfield, was a terrible judge of character. She noted the strength in Willie's arms when he lifted the post into place. Those same arms had held her, given her comfort and warmth all through the night. They belonged to a good man, one to whom she feared she had already given her heart.

With a low cry, she covered her face again, trying to erase the memory of the joy she had felt in Willie's arms, and the kiss—real or imagined—he had pressed against her forehead in the night.

❧

"They did *what?*" Sheriff John Dolan pushed his hat back on his head and stared at Willie with round eyes.

Willie continued filling him in on his and Violet's supposed elopement. When he finished, Dolan puffed out his cheeks and let out a long sigh. "They're really something, aren't they? Somebody better get them straightened out before it's too late."

"I couldn't agree more," Willie said with fervor. "The sooner I find Hadlock, the better I'll like it."

"Mm." The sheriff rose from his seat on the edge of his desk and put his hand on Willie's shoulder. "I've got something to tell you. Hadlock won't be raising those kids."

"What?"

"I got into a conversation with Evan Mills yesterday. He'd just come back from San Francisco, so I asked him if he'd seen Hadlock there. Thought I'd help you out a bit if I could."

Willie nodded and waited for the blow to fall.

"Hadlock's dead. To quote Evan, 'He'd been out debauching all night and fell down a flight of stairs when he tried to go up to his room. Broke his fool, drunken neck, and good riddance.' " The sheriff gave Willie's shoulder a sympathetic squeeze and dropped his hand to his side. Eyeing Willie steadily, he asked, "What are you going to do now?"

"I have no idea." Willie tried to assimilate the news, but all he could think of was that his weeks of hard work had gone for naught. "Guess I'll wire home and see what my cousin has to say." He picked up his hat with a shaking hand and walked out the door.

"I'll be praying, Son." Dolan's words followed after him.

It took him a good while to frame a coherent message at the telegraph office. Once the wire had been sent, he felt at loose ends and decided to pick up supplies while he was in town. Daniel's new order of seeds should be in, and maybe the time spent doing something productive would help to clear his mind. He had gone a block toward the general store when he felt a hand on his arm.

"Willie Bradley, have you gone deaf? I've been calling and calling, but you just kept walking." Mary Rose Downey looked up at him with those grass-green eyes of hers. She pushed out her lower lip in a tiny pout. "It's been ages since I've seen you," she said, circling his arm with both hands. "Come have a cup of tea with me so we can catch up."

"Not today, Mary Rose. It isn't a good time." He extricated his arm and started to walk away, hoping she'd let it go at that.

Instead, she quickened her steps and planted herself in his path. "Just what is going on? Do you think you can pay attention to me one minute and ignore me the next? I won't be treated in such a way!" A dangerous emerald gleam glowed deep within her eyes, and her lips curved up in a feline smile. "It's Violet, isn't it? You prefer that insipid little farm girl to me. Well, fine, Mr. Bradley. If you want her, you can have her." With a toss of her head, she was gone.

Willie stared after her. How had he ever considered her attractive? Memories of his mother's comments about beauty being only skin deep returned in snatches. She sure had that figured out. Mary Rose's allure didn't extend one bit beneath the surface of her pretty features. What would his mother think about Violet? He smiled, remembering her glossy sable hair and startling blue eyes and going beyond that to her ready smile, her loving heart, and the faith rooted deep within her soul. No doubt about it. Violet was beautiful, inside and out.

Two hours later, his errands completed, he stepped up into the wagon. He had just taken up the reins when he heard a voice calling his name. He turned to see the clerk from the telegraph office running along the boardwalk.

"Mr. Bradley! Glad I recognized your wagon." The man clutched the off wheel and gasped for breath. "These just came for you," he said, handing over two telegrams. "I thought you might need to know about them at once, seeing as they arrived so quickly after you sent your last message."

Willie tried to hide his astonishment long enough to thank the man and drove a little way out of town before he stopped to open the wires. Could he really have received a response in such a short time? Apparently so, but why two of them? His heart filled with misgivings, he opened the first.

William Adam McKenzie born May eighth STOP
Mother and baby fine STOP
Father insufferable STOP
Pa

He took advantage of his isolation to let out a joyous whoop. So Lizzie'd had her baby, had she? He scanned the message again, letting the first sentence sink in and register. William Adam McKenzie? Why, they'd named the baby after him! Another whoop rent the air, and the horse twitched a curious ear at the uproar.

Willie laughed out loud. He felt reconnected with his family again, sure of his place in their affection. He gave the wire one more perusal and chuckled at the last line. From the sounds of it, Adam had taken to fatherhood with a substantial amount of pride. What he'd give to be with them right now. He set the paper aside and turned to the second telegram.

Bring children home STOP
Lewis

How had Monroe managed such a quick answer? He must have gone with Charles to send the wire about the baby and been on the spot when Willie's telegram arrived. Nothing else would explain it. Willie stared at the paper again.

He held in his hands the words he'd hoped to see ever since his arrival. After all the long, tormenting weeks, he'd finally gotten word to go home. He folded both wires and tucked them in his shirt pocket, waiting for the realization of his deliverance to set in. Instead, a dismal feeling settled over him like a pall. He pulled off his hat and raked his fingers through his hair, trying to understand this strange reaction. Here he'd just been given leave to go back to the ranch and get rid of the kids. He could accomplish both within the week. The whole sorry episode would finally be over. He was about to go home.

And he didn't want to.

Willie looked at the sky and gauged the sun's position. He clicked his tongue at the horse and turned it back in the direction of town. He had time enough to send one more wire.

(18)

illie shouldered his fencing tools and carried them back to the barn. Daniel waited for him in the shadowy interior, one arm propped on the sideboard of the wagon and a speculative glint in his gaze.

"Care to explain this?" He pulled a yellow slip of paper from his pocket and waved it gently up and down. "Rachel found it in the pocket of your shirt when she started the laundry this morning. It made us both a little curious."

Even from several feet away, Willie recognized his summons home from Monroe. "I—uh, well, the truth of the matter is that I didn't want to go." He took his time putting the tools away and waited for Daniel's response.

"Uh-huh. Any particular reason?"

Willie fumbled for an answer. "Just that . . . I found some property over on the other side of the ridge. I think it would make a fine ranch."

Daniel pursed his lips. "And you're thinking about buying it? You plan to stay around here?"

"If I can." Speaking the words aloud made the whole idea seem more plausible. Willie stood straighter. "I'd like your opinion on it, if you have the time."

"Saddle up," Daniel said. "Now's as good a time as any."

The trip by horseback took much less time than his first meandering visit in the wagon. Daniel listened while Willie pointed out the features that appealed to him: the mixture of forested and open ground, the promise of abundant graze, the building sites that stirred his imagination during his first visit. He talked about the feasibility of

145

driving in a herd of starter stock from the Double B. When he finished, he held his breath and waited for Daniel's assessment.

"I'd say you've picked a spot about as perfect as it gets." Daniel cast an approving glance at the setting. "It has everything you need and plenty of water. And I like the site you've set on for the house. You can start off small and add on for yourself . . . and whoever you may want to share it with in the future." His shrewd look made Willie's mouth go dry.

"What about money?" The directness of the question as well as the abrupt change of subject caught Willie off guard. "How do you plan to finance this venture?"

"I haven't quite figured that out yet," he admitted. Would Daniel think him a fool for even considering a move like this without sufficient funds at his disposal?

"Then let me put forth a possibility." Daniel leaned forward and went straight to the point. "The mining I did before Rachel and I got married paid off well—very well. I've been looking for someplace to invest the money. My first thought was to put it into another mining venture. That's why we went to Tucson, to check out some properties I'd heard about. But listening to your plans makes me think I'd rather keep the money closer to home.

"What would you say to my backing you in this? It wouldn't be a gift, strictly a business arrangement. Any kind of investment is a risk, but I'd rather take a chance on you than on the hope of someone else striking it rich. I'll provide the money, but you'll run the show. I won't get in your way. What do you think?"

Willie's mind reeled. The one obstacle to fulfilling his dream had just been waved aside as though it never existed. He looked at Daniel for any sign of uncertainty, but saw only a calm confidence in the other man's gaze.

He stretched out his hand. "It's a deal."

A week alone on his newly acquired property proved balm to Willie's soul. Taking advantage of Rachel's generous offer to watch the children while he got acquainted with his new place, he spent days marking off the exact sites for his barn and corrals and digging the foundation for his house.

His house. The thought filled him with such joy, he felt he could hardly bear it. This would be his place, his own to do with as he pleased. He knew he'd make mistakes, but he'd learn from them and grow, just as his father and uncle had done.

After a week, though, he'd learned something else. Whether Daniel intended to or not, his comment about having someone to share the place with had stirred another desire. Much as it meant to have the opportunity to strike out on his own, without someone to share his days with, acquiring the property would be a hollow victory. And that someone had to be Violet.

She was as present in his thoughts now as she'd been the first time he imagined her coming out of the house that would soon become a reality. She filled his days with dreams and his nights with longing. He saw her everywhere he looked, imagined her delight in the flowers that dotted the meadow and the tiny animals that scampered through the trees.

The day came when he knew he had to face the situation head-on. Life without Violet wouldn't be worth living. He put down his tools, scrubbed, and dressed in his best. Then he mounted his horse and rode back to the farm to propose.

He worked on his speech all the way through the foothills and over the ridge, wanting to get the words just right, to let her know beyond a doubt how much he loved and needed her. He rode into the farmyard, his heart pounding in his throat at the realization that he'd soon have her answer. *Let her say yes, Lord. Please let her say yes.*

Three blond heads looked up from their game on the porch when they heard him coming. Three children scuttled inside the house and closed the door behind them. *Just as well,* he thought grimly. He didn't need the kids around to twist his words and mess things up. He mounted the porch steps, slicked his hair back with both hands, and knocked on the door.

Rachel opened it, slid outside, and closed the door again. She stood facing him with a half smile. "The children said you'd come."

Willie passed his hat from one hand to the other. "I'd like to see Violet, please."

Daniel walked around the corner of the house to join them. "I saw you ride up. I need to talk to you."

"Later." Willie flushed and softened his tone. "I want to speak to Violet first."

"That's what we need to discuss." Daniel put an arm about his shoulders and led him to the edge of the porch. "Dolan rode out this morning. There's been more talk. Now the story says you have a wife back home. He thought you'd want to know."

Willie groaned. "All the more reason I need to talk to Violet. I want to tell her—"

"That's the point I'm trying to make. Violet doesn't want to see you." He listened to Willie sputter and gave him a compassionate smile. "I know you're solid. In her heart, I think Violet knows it, too, but she took this real hard. Give her some time; she'll probably come around."

Willie retraced the path he'd taken so hopefully only a short time before, trying to decide on his next move. A wife, of all things! How would he ever straighten that out with Violet, especially when she wouldn't talk to him? He brooded over her reaction. It would be natural for her to be angry at his supposed deception, but to be so upset she didn't want to see him? That didn't make sense, unless . . .

Willie wheeled his horse around and rode past the farm, into the forest beyond. He could wait there until nightfall. If Violet's behavior meant what he hoped it did, he needed to talk to her without delay. And she liked watching the stars of an evening as much as he did.

❧

A light breeze played with a loose strand of Violet's hair. She tucked it back behind her ear and stepped outside the circle of light coming through the kitchen window. After being shut up inside all day, she knew she had to get some fresh air. And with Rachel, Daniel, and the children all in bed, it made a good opportunity to have a quiet moment to herself.

She moved farther away from the light, the better to watch the stars come into view. There was something peaceful about the way they kept to their courses regardless of the events being played out below them, and peace was something she needed right now. Her customary tranquility had been tested beyond endurance over the past few days. She rested her hand against the porch rail and breathed deeply of the night air.

Light footsteps mounted the steps behind her and she whirled, drawing her hands to her throat when she saw the dark form before her.

"Violet? We need to talk."

Exasperation mingled with relief when she recognized Willie's voice. "I thought Daniel told you I didn't want to see you." She moved purposefully toward the kitchen door.

Willie beat her to it in two long strides and planted his shoulder against the door, barring her way. "He did. That doesn't change a thing. You need to hear what I have to say."

Violet wrapped her arms around herself and took a slow step backward. What did he think he was doing? Should she call for help?

"You know that story about us was a pack of lies," he went on. "This one is no different. I don't have a wife back home or anywhere. Not yet, anyway." He took a step toward her, and she moved away again, coming to rest against the porch rail. He closed the gap between them and caught her shoulders in a light grasp.

"I love you, Violet Canfield. I love your spirit and your courage and that love of God that shines out from you like a beacon. I've spent the past week working on the place I've dreamed about all my life, but without you it will be empty." He tightened his hold on her shoulders and drew a long, shuddering breath. "My whole life will be empty without you. What I'm trying to say—to ask you—is, will you marry me?"

Violet closed her eyes and let the lovely words wash over her like a cleansing rain. He loved her, wanted to marry her! She longed to do nothing more than melt into his embrace and give him the answer he sought. But her self-doubt held her back. Her instincts told her Willie meant exactly what he said, but her instincts had been wrong before—

so very, very wrong. She couldn't risk the heartache of saying yes now, only to find out she'd been wrong again.

Fighting the desire to fling herself into his arms, she shook her head and whispered, "I can't." She felt glad for the darkness that enveloped them. She couldn't bear to see his face reflect the hurt she had inflicted.

"Are you saying you don't love me?"

"No! It's . . . it's that story."

"But you know it's a lie."

She pressed her hands together and braced herself to deal another blow. "I asked the children. They said your mother isn't the only Mrs. Bradley at the Double B." She lifted her chin, wishing she could read the truth in his eyes. "Is there another Mrs. Bradley, Willie?"

"Well, of course there is!" he sputtered. "My aunt Judith."

His *aunt?* She hadn't considered that possibility. How could she possibly know for sure?

"Do you mean to tell me you're still listening to those kids after everything they've done? You'd trust them more than you trust me?"

She didn't have to see him to know the depth of the pain she'd caused; she could hear it in his voice. But how could she bear to give her heart, then find out she'd made the most foolish mistake of her life? Her eyes brimmed with scalding tears. "It isn't you I don't trust, Willie. It's me."

He wrapped his arms around her and held her close. "I don't know how I'm going to convince you of this, Violet, but I'll find a way. I promise you, I'll find a way."

19

he next morning, Willie woke with the dawn and stretched, surprised at how comfortable his thin cot felt after a week of sleeping on the hard ground. When he left Violet last evening, he'd chosen to stay at the farm instead of returning to his property. He saw no point in trying to fix up the place while the issue with Violet remained unresolved.

After he finished the early chores, he joined the family for breakfast. Violet must have told Rachel and Daniel about his visit, for they showed no surprise when he entered the kitchen. The kids didn't say a word but kept their attention focused on their plates, something that increased his enjoyment of the meal. Violet didn't speak, either, but cast wistful looks his way that only increased his desire to prove his sincerity to her.

Rachel excused the children to go outside and helped Violet clear the table. Willie and Daniel rose to start work in the field just when Frederick bolted in the front door. "Two riders coming," he cried.

"This early in the day?" Rachel gave Daniel a worried look. All four adults joined the children on the porch and watched the riders approach.

"It's Dolan and some slicked-up fellow," Daniel said.

Willie swallowed hard. He recognized the portly form. "My cousin, Lewis Monroe."

The two men stopped at the hitching rail, Dolan dismounting in one easy motion and Monroe laboring to regain the ground without mishap. If Willie's stomach hadn't tied itself into knots, he might have enjoyed the spectacle.

"Morning," Dolan called. "I have someone here I expect you'll be happy to see. Mr. Monroe rolled in on last night's stage. I told him I'd bring him out first thing this morning."

Daniel broke the collective silence. "We're pleased to meet you, Mr. Monroe." He introduced himself, Rachel, and Violet.

The lawyer acknowledged the introductions, then turned a bleak eye on Willie. "I must say I found your last telegram mystifying. After all those pleas to cut your time here short, I hardly expected to tell you to return to the ranch only to get a reply reading, 'Come get them.' "

Willie cleared his throat. "Actually, your wire said to bring the kids home. But I already am. Home, that is. I plan to stay right here."

Monroe's eyes widened, and he looked around the group for confirmation. "Then I suppose I can't count on your help on my return journey?" Willie's decisive shake of his head seemed to dishearten him. He stared at the ground for a moment, then regained some of his composure.

"I can't tell you how distressed I was to learn of the demise of Thurman Hadlock. This means I'll have to take them back East with me and start a new search, perhaps for a distant relative who'll be willing to take them in."

"Nooo!" All three Wingates joined in the chorus.

"We don't want to leave!" Frederick cried.

"We like it here," Jessica wailed.

"Yeah," Toby added. "We don't want to leave Miss Violet, or Miss Rachel, or Daniel . . . or even Willie."

Willie saw the faces of the other adults mirroring his own disbelief, especially at that last statement. He looked at Monroe, wondering how the pompous lawyer would handle this situation.

Monroe patted his forehead with his handkerchief. "Be that as it may, this is a legal matter, and I must follow legal guidelines. I have no choice but to take you with me, so you may as well go pack your things now. I've made arrangements for transportation back to the railroad, and we need to leave as soon as possible. This fruitless journey has cost me quite enough time already."

The children looked from one adult to the other for support. "You mean he's right?" Frederick asked on a quavering note. "We have to go?"

"I'm afraid so, Dear." Violet bent to wrap her arms around them all. "Go ahead inside and get started. I'll come help you in a few minutes."

Tears glistened in all three pairs of eyes when they traipsed slowly into the house.

Seemingly unaware of the emotional havoc he had wrought, Monroe patted his waistcoat and gazed about him. "I must confess this has been an interesting trip. Your part of the country is quite fascinating. A bit primitive for my taste, but still worth a brief visit."

Behind him, Dolan rolled his eyes and approached the group on the porch. "I thought you'd like to know, I finally found out who's behind those stories."

Willie jerked upright as though a lightning bolt had shot through him. "Who?" he cried hoarsely. He could feel Violet tremble beside him.

"None other than Miss Mary Rose Downey," the sheriff replied. "It seems the young lady got her nose out of joint when a certain gentleman didn't pay as much attention to her as she thought he ought to."

"Mary Rose?" Willie supposed he ought to feel shocked, but somehow the revelation didn't surprise him. It only confirmed what he'd seen in her at their last meeting. If only she had taken her venom out on him and left Violet out of it! He turned a worried glance toward Violet and blinked in surprise at the radiant look on her face.

"She started the stories? Both of them?" Her voice bubbled with laughter.

Dolan nodded. "Appears that way. I didn't expect it to make you quite that happy, though," he told her with a bemused smile.

Willie caught on to the reason for her excitement. "And if you need any further confirmation, you can get it right here," he told her. He waved a hand toward Monroe. "From an officer of the court, no less."

Violet's eyes sparkled, and she turned a glowing smile on the lawyer. "Mr. Monroe, there was a silly rumor going around about Willie having a wife back in New Mexico. That isn't true, is it?"

"Willie? Married?" Monroe burst into a hearty laugh. "Oh, my dear young lady, what a singularly preposterous idea! No, I can assure you most definitely that my young cousin here has no wife." He continued in his mirth.

Willie captured Violet's hand. "Would you join me at the other end of the porch? There's something I want to ask you."

"Miss Violet!" Toby's voice rang from inside the house.

Rachel gave her sister a little push. "I'll go help them. It sounds like you have some serious talking to do."

Violet returned the pressure of his fingers and followed him to the end of the porch. Willie took both her hands in his and caressed the backs of her fingers with his thumbs. "You heard what my cousin said. Are you sure now that I don't have a wife tucked away somewhere?"

Those amazing blue eyes looked into his with an expression of pure joy. "Yes," she said.

"You know beyond a doubt that it all came from Mary Rose's imagination?"

"Yes."

Willie drew a deep breath. "Then I want to ask you again. Violet, will you—"

"Yes!" she cried, flinging her arms around his neck.

He pulled her close and buried his face in her hair, savoring its sweet fragrance of spring air and sunshine. With one arm around her waist, he cupped her chin in his other hand and tilted her face to meet his.

The sweetness of their first kiss sent skyrockets shooting off inside his brain. Violet's arms twined even closer around his neck. *Lord, a lifetime of this won't be nearly enough.* When their lips parted at last, Violet leaned against his chest and stared into his eyes. She traced his jawline with her finger and said, "I love you, Willie Bradley, do you know that?"

He stroked her hair and nodded. "But I'll never get tired of hearing it."

Footsteps clattered on the porch, announcing the return of Rachel and the children. She looked at her sister nestled in Willie's embrace, then at Daniel. "Did I miss something?"

"Say hello to your future brother-in-law," he told her, coming to congratulate Willie with a slap on the back. "This is turning out to be quite a morning."

"My heartiest congratulations." Monroe joined them on the porch. "I'm glad to be able to offer you my very best wishes before I take my leave."

At the reminder of his cousin's mission, Willie swung his glance to the three Wingates. All three of them stood beside their valises, heads drooping, the very picture of despair. Their dismal faces tugged at his heart in spite of all they'd put him through. He wished their stay here could have ended differently.

Monroe turned to the children. "Come along," he said. "I'm sure if we put our minds to it, we can have a most enjoyable ride home." His eyes filled with doubt and he turned back to Willie. "You're sure you won't consider coming along?"

"Not a chance," Willie said and smiled down at Violet. "I have plans to make and a home to build."

Dolan cleared his throat. "Just for the record, does it have to be a relative who takes the kids?"

"Not at all," Monroe replied. "Merely someone who is willing to take on the responsibility and can provide them with a good home."

"In that case, I have an idea." Dolan stepped forward and hooked his thumbs in his belt. "My wife and I have always wanted kids, but none ever came along. After all this time wishing for a family, it would be right nice to start out with one ready made, so to speak. What do you think?"

Monroe stared at the sheriff, then darted quick glances between him and the children. "Sheriff," he intoned, "I can have the papers drawn up this afternoon." He stepped off the porch and wrung the man's hand. "God bless you, Sir."

Willie grinned at the way Dolan swiped his hand on his back pocket after their handshake.

The sheriff glanced up at Daniel. "All right if I borrow your wagon to take them home?"

"Be my guest."

"The three of you come to the barn with me, then," he told his new brood. "I'll expect you to help."

Frederick eyed him warily. "What if we don't—"

"Move!"

"Yes, Sir." The three Wingates lined up and followed Dolan to the barn like baby ducks trailing their mother.

Violet patted Willie's arm. "What just happened?" she asked, her voice full of wonder.

Willie chuckled. "I'd say the right man just took over the job. He'll be the best thing that ever happened to those kids."

"Like you're the best thing that ever happened to me?" Violet smiled and snuggled closer to him, and a light blush mantled her cheek. "Just think. Some day we'll be raising our own children."

Willie nodded in happy agreement. Then a thought struck him, and his mouth went dry. He looked at Violet. "You don't think . . . Our kids won't be anything like that, will they?"

Violet lifted her chin proudly. "Of course not," she said. "They'll be Bradleys . . . just like their father."

20

October 1885

*V*iolet added one last pinecone to the arrangement on the mantel and stepped back. "What do you think?" she asked.

"I think you'd better start getting ready. Guests will be arriving anytime now. I'll be along to help you in a minute."

Violet hurried to her room. After all their preparations, she could hardly believe the moment she'd looked forward to had finally arrived. She touched the yellowed satin of the wedding dress, which hung in the corner. First her mother's, then Rachel's, and now hers.

Rachel entered. "Haven't you started yet? Honestly, Violet!"

A light tap sounded at the door. "Do you need any help?" Rachel swung the door open to admit a slender blond woman.

Before she could close it again, another voice spoke. "Is there room for us, too?" Two more women, one holding a baby, slipped inside the room and took a seat on the bed.

Violet looked at the loving faces turned her way and wondered how her cup of joy could be any more full. When Willie's family—all of them—announced their plans to attend the wedding, she'd been jittery about meeting them. Five minutes after they disembarked from their rented wagons, all her uncertainty disappeared in the flurry of loving words and warm embraces. Willie's family had become hers in a matter of moments, and they made it plain they meant to include Rachel and Daniel in the bargain as well.

"For goodness' sake, Violet, quit standing there and get dressed!" Rachel plucked at the buttons on her dress, aided by Abby's nimble hands. In short order they helped her step out of the garment and held the satin gown at the ready. Judith, Willie's aunt, moved forward to lift the flowing folds of the skirt over her head. It settled over her in a shimmering wave.

"It's beautiful," Lizzie said from the bed, where she sat holding her five-month-old son. "I'm so glad we got to come. I couldn't stand the thought of missing out on this day." She chucked a finger under the baby's chin. "And this little guy needed to meet his uncle and his new aunt."

Violet tried to stand still and let the other women work with the tiny buttons in the back. "I don't think I've ever seen Willie smile as much as when he saw his nephew for the first time. He's one proud uncle. And I'm going to enjoy being an aunt." She cast a sly glance at Rachel. "I'm going to get lots of practice at it before long."

Rachel left the last of the buttons to Abby and Judith and sank onto the bed beside Lizzie. "After being married all this time, I can't believe it's finally going to happen." She pressed her hand against her abdomen. "I just wish I didn't feel so queasy all the time."

Lizzie laughed and patted her arm. "That happened to me at first. It'll pass, but it's no fun while it lasts. How far along are you?"

"Just a couple of months. The baby should be born about the time little William here turns a year old." She ran a gentle finger over the baby's coppery curls.

"Done." Abby stepped around in front of Violet and surveyed the effect with a satisfied nod. "You look absolutely beautiful, Dear. I'm so happy for you both."

Judith tucked a wayward wisp of Violet's hair back into place. "There. Looks to me like you're ready." She placed a spray of yellow asters in Violet's arms at the same moment a knock rattled the door. Abby went to open it.

"Is it safe to come in?" Daniel asked. At her nod, he squeezed inside the crowded room.

Charles peered around the doorway. "Why don't you womenfolk come on outside and give that lovely young lady a chance to breathe?" he quipped. Abby swatted him on the arm, but followed him out along with Judith and Lizzie.

Rachel stood and pulled Violet into her arms. "You've grown into a fine young woman, Honey. Ma and Pa would both be proud." She brushed a swift kiss against her sister's cheek and hurried out to take her place among the guests.

"I guess that's our cue," Daniel said with a grin. He crooked his arm and offered it to Violet. "Are you ready?"

Violet nodded, unable to speak. How could any one person deserve the blessings being poured out on her today? No one could, she decided. No one ever did. It was God's grace, pure and simple. In a few moments she would be joined to a new family, beginning a life with the man of her dreams, and all because of God's abundant love.

She walked beside Daniel to the living room, where a crowd of guests and Bradleys filled the space to overflowing. Charles's and Abby's proud faces beamed at her. Behind them stood Lizzie and her husband, Adam, then Judith and Jeff and their four children. On the other side of the room, Frederick, Jessie, and Toby Dolan stood meekly beside their new parents.

And straight ahead, Willie waited for her. The presence of everyone else in the room faded into insignificance while she walked to meet him, her gaze never leaving his face. Daniel tucked her hand into Willie's, then sat beside Rachel while the minister took up his Bible and cleared his throat.

Willie clasped her hand in his, tracing tiny circles on her fingers with his thumb while he repeated his wedding vows. In a moment it was her turn. She followed the minister's leading, speaking the words of commitment to love, honor, and obey, while her heart spoke a promise of its own.

I have learned what kind of man you are, Willie Bradley, and you're a blessing sent straight from God. With His help, I'll be the kind of wife you need, and I will never doubt you again.

The minister finished speaking. Willie looked at her expectantly. She raised her face to his and slid into his arms. When their lips met, tears of joy stung her eyes. This wasn't the storybook finish she had dreamed of; this would be better. This time the story wouldn't end.

When the kiss ended, Willie pulled her into a close embrace. She pressed her lips near his ear. "I love you," she whispered, "so very, very much."

"I love you, too, Violet Bradley," he whispered back. He turned his head and gave her a look that made her pulse race. "Cross my heart."

$\mathcal{V}$ALIANT $\mathcal{H}$EART

BY SALLY LAITY

————◆————

Dedication
To Barb,
my forever friend.

Acknowledgment
My profound gratitude to Gloria Brandt,
Dianna Crawford, and Edwina Harlander . . .
this couldn't have been done without you.
May the Lord bless you all.

Valiant Heart

By Sally Laity

The first time I laid eyes on you
    I thought you were like all the others . . .
Helpless, weepy, and a lot less bright than you should be.
    How wrong I was.
For what I perceived to be
    A stubborn streak turned out to be the opposite . . .
Fortitude. Backbone.
    A spirit of adventure.
Yet despite those admirable traits,
    What struck me most about you
Were things entirely different . . .
    Qualities I could not even name, at first.
Trust. Hope. Striving onward for what is right
    I see now that faith is something
Which stretches beyond Sunday
    to all the days of one's life.
And character comes from deep within . . .
    As intangible and enduring as a valiant heart.

Missouri
May 1848

manda Shelby stared out the window of her second-story room in the Bradford Hotel. Scattered showers had dotted the dirt streets of Independence with puddles—glossy brown mirrors that reflected the puffy clouds and blue expanse of the ever-changing spring sky above.

And everywhere were people. Young and old, whole families of them, eager and waiting to start out on the trail to the rich, fertile valleys and hills of Oregon. They had all but emptied the mercantile and hardware stores of goods until new shipments arrived, and then those, too, would be snatched up before they had time to gather dust on the shelves. The process would repeat itself over and over throughout the spring as numerous companies of travelers gathered to begin the westward trek over mountains and plains to establish new homes before the onset of winter.

As she gazed wistfully at the bustling scene below, the iron-rimmed wheels of a pair of Conestogas splashed through the puddles, rumbling toward the growing encampment near the spring on the outskirts of town. Two small boys leaned precariously out of the bowed canvas top of the second wagon, their eyes round with excitement. At the sight of a garishly dressed woman in red satin and a feather boa, in front of the Bluebird Saloon, they elbowed each other, then darted back inside the confines of their arched haven.

Amanda released a sigh and steeled her heart against a twinge of sadness. Only a few short weeks ago, Pa had driven her and Sarah Jane in their own prairie schooner over the quay and up the steep grade to Independence Square, their hearts full of hopes and plans for the trip overland to the Far West. But that seemed so long ago, almost like a dream. Nothing could alter the grim reality that Pa now occupied a fresh grave on a lonely hillside a mere stone's throw away. The cruel twist of fate had brought a swift end to the visions of their wondrous new life. Now the world felt bleak and empty, and Amanda had no idea what she and Sarah would do.

Almost as if the last thought had been an audible summons, her seventeen-year-old younger sister breezed into the room, wheat-gold curls slightly tangled by the breeze. The triumphant smile that lit her guileless face looked a little out of place against the shadows beneath her eyes. Amanda had been more than aware of Sarah's tossing and turning each night during the past few weeks—and her soft crying. But during her waking hours the younger girl flitted about in a near frenzy of activity, as if trying to keep too busy to dwell on their losses.

Sarah draped her woolen shawl over the back of a chair and held out her tote. "There were only three bottles of sarsaparilla left in the whole town! I nearly had to fend off a mob to get one of them!" Then she sobered, concern drawing her fine brows together above shimmering eyes of clearest blue. "Something wrong, Mandy?"

"Just thinking a little too much." Amanda silently regarded her sibling, who was the very picture of what she herself had always wished to be—willowy and graceful as Mama, with delicate features and a face that never failed to turn heads. But alas, that particular dream had been in vain. Amanda had conceded long ago that it was only fair that one of them resembled the plainer, sturdier Shelby side of the family, and she was the only other one there was. Twisting an errant strand of light auburn hair absently between her thumb and forefinger, she backed away from the muslin-curtained window and sank to a chair, smoothing the skirt of her somber brown cotton dress.

Sarah set down her booty on the small round table next to the door, then crossed the room and gave Amanda a hug. "As Mama always said, death is as much a part of life as birth is." She made a wry grimace, and when she spoke again, her tone sounded tart. "Maybe we should be used to it by now, after losing everyone dearest to us this past year."

Yes, everyone. Shaking off the tormenting reminder that her own losses went beyond mere beloved family members—to the death of her most cherished dream as well—Amanda quickly snuffed the thoughts that could so easily consume her in bitterness. "I'll never ever be used to it."

The younger girl smiled gently and gave Amanda's shoulder a comforting squeeze. "No, I don't suppose I will either, to be truthful. But at least we can think on what Pa said just before he passed on, about not wanting us to wear black and drown in mournful tears. He felt his time had come, and he had peace about where he was going. And he's with Mama now. Her and the baby. As for us, well, I think we owe it to him to heed his words and keep alive his dream of starting over."

"Whatever you say." Pressing her lips tightly together before she voiced a thought about the senselessness of life, Amanda heard a growing noise outside. She stood and returned to the window to see a handful of rowdy boys wrestling in the soggy dirt on the street below. Not far from them, two shaggily dressed buffalo hunters with clenched fists were in a heated debate of their own, their gruff voices spewing bursts of profanity to which no one paid the slightest heed.

From the corner of her eye, Amanda could see her sister filling two tall glasses.

Sarah offered one to her as she stepped to her side. "What's all the commotion?"

"Another fight. I'm looking forward to some peace and quiet when that train finally pulls out."

"So am I. Surely the spring grasses along the route are green and tall enough for the animals to graze on by now."

Several minutes of silence lapsed as they sipped their drinks and surveyed the harried activity that seemed never to cease. Independence, far from being a sleepy little hamlet, was second only to St. Louis as a river port. The hotel proprietor had assured them that the height of each spring season was the same—the whole town overrun with river men, steamship captains, hunters and trappers, traders, teamsters, and hordes of emigrants, the latter all fighting over the scant grazing for their thousands of horses, mules, and oxen. Even on the Lord's Day, constant movement and voices of the transients filled the air.

"What do you think will become of us?"

Amanda caught her breath. She had been wondering the very same thing herself. Staying at the hotel indefinitely was not even a remote possibility. The expense of lodging and meals was putting a serious drain on their funds and would soon make it necessary for them both to seek employment. The home and possessions that had been sold before leaving the verdant green woods of northeastern Pennsylvania now seemed not only part of some other world, but another life as well.

Unbidden memories of sailing the Great Lakes to Chicago, then boarding a steamboat to St. Louis and securing their outfit for going west, were as real in her mind as if they had occurred yesterday. Who would have imagined all of that would come to naught, all Pa's plans to relocate in Oregon Territory and use his woodcrafting talents to provide for the three of them. Now it was left to Amanda and her sister to make their own life somewhere. Somehow.

Sarah Jane stepped away from the window and moved to the dark pine four-poster abutting one wall of the room. She picked up her guitar from where it leaned against the headboard. After absently twisting the tuning pegs and adjusting the pitch, she sat down on the quilted counterpane and strummed a soft chord, then another, and a dreamy smile curved her lips.

Amanda groaned inwardly. Strumming always led to singing, and for all Sarah's innocent sincerity and melodious speaking voice, she was blissfully unaware of the fact she could not carry a tune. "I, um, think I'll go for a walk and get the cobwebs out of my head," Amanda blurted. She grabbed her gloves and warm shawl from the armoire and made a swift exit on the first few hummed notes.

Outside, the soles of Amanda's hightop shoes made hollow sounds on the board sidewalk, the rhythmic echoes blending with the voices and footfalls of others as she threaded her way through the throng, dodging loose chickens and the occasional small farm animal in her path. False fronts on the assorted wooden buildings lining both sides of the street gave the illusion they were more impressive than they actually were. After passing the bank and the barber, the wheelwright and gunsmith, she finally stopped at the last smithy's shop on the street.

The owner, a stocky, muscular man in his mid-forties, glanced up from the red-hot horseshoe he was plucking from the fire with a pair of long tongs. "Afternoon, miss." He nudged the beak of his black working cap higher, exposing a band of light skin on his soot-streaked forehead.

"Good afternoon, Mr. Plummer. No one has purchased the wagon as yet?"

" 'Fraid not. Folks what need 'em, already has 'em by the time they get to town, unless they arranged ahead of time for one of the wagonwrights to build 'em one." He set the glowing shoe down on the anvil and raised a muscled arm to administer a few whacks with his hammer.

Amanda's ears rang with each blow, and she sighed as she gazed at the big wagon Pa had bought, now parked alongside the enterprise. Such a waste, brand spanking new, and complete with foodstuffs and tools sufficient for the journey west, plus three braces of mules being housed in the livery. Surely someone should have been interested in it by this time. It galled her to think she might end up having to sell the entire outfit to that shrewd Mr. Cavanaugh, the owner of the mercantile, after all. The offer he had made for it was shockingly low— despite the ridiculous prices he charged for things in his store. The knowledge that her and her sister's loss would be very profitable to that scoundrel was a bitter pill to swallow. Amanda could just picture his smug expression of triumph if she were forced by circumstance to acquiesce. "Well, I'll check back with you tomorrow," she said, turning to leave. "Perhaps someone will still come along and want it."

"Could be. I did have a couple of people askin' after the goods." He cocked a bushy eyebrow in question.

Amanda shook her head. "No. We wouldn't want to sell things off that way except as a last resort. Certainly a full wagon would be of much more value to a latecomer, don't you think? We've been careful to leave everything intact so the entire outfit would be available for a quick sale."

" 'S'pose there's always that possibility, but time's runnin' out, miss, till the next train starts gatherin'."

"I'm aware of that. But still . . ."

He sniffed and wiped his bulbous nose with a large kerchief, then returned the cloth to his back pocket. "Well, don't worry, I won't do nothin' without your say-so. I'm keepin' an eye on it for ya."

"Thank you, Mr. Plummer. My sister and I truly appreciate all your trouble. Good day."

With a heavy heart and at a much slower pace, she strolled toward the hotel. Slanting rays of the sun at Amanda's back elongated her shadow as it flowed gracefully over the walk ahead, making her appear several inches taller than her five-foot height—and nearly as slender as Sarah. She lifted her chin.

Several hours later, kneeling at her bedside, Amanda did her best to ignore the outside racket while she formulated her heavenly petitions. When the cool breath of night rustled the curtain on the partially open bedroom window and raised gooseflesh, she rose and climbed into the warm bed.

"Your prayers took longer than usual," Sarah said.

"I have a lot on my mind," Amanda confessed.

All at once her sister's seemingly blithe acceptance of their fate irked her. Blinking back stinging tears, she raised up on one elbow to face the younger girl, unable to bite back the angry words that insisted upon tumbling out of her mouth. "Aren't you the least concerned that we're completely alone in the world now—and have only a pittance to get us by for heaven knows how long? It took everything Pa could scrape together after paying off those debts that—that—" Amanda fought to keep from choking on the name, "*Morris Jamison* dumped on him, you know, to finance this venture. And when our money is gone, I haven't the slightest idea what we're going to do."

"I never said I wasn't concerned," Sarah said quietly.

Chagrined at the sight of the moisture glistening in her sister's eyes, Amanda berated herself for her hasty words and reached over to hug Sarah. "I know. I'm sorry, Sissy. I shouldn't have said that."

"The Reverend O'Neill told us we have to trust God for the strength we need to go on. And the more I think about it, the more I agree. We can't spend the rest of our lives moping around, however tempting that might be. Pa did that after Mama died, and look what it did to him. Working day and night, not sleeping, barely eating . . ."

"Yes, you're right."

"It's no wonder his malaria came back again—only this time he wasn't strong enough to fight it off. Even if we still have days when we're so sad we can't think straight, we have to keep living. And whatever pit of trouble we're in now, we have to climb out of it ourselves, no matter what." She folded her arms over her bosom. "So I'm going to apply myself to finding a husband—one handsome and rich—so I can get as much as I can out of life."

Amanda blinked, aghast. "And how do you plan to do that, exactly . . . if you don't mind my asking. No one has bought that stupid wagon yet, and we really need the money."

Sarah's quiet, even breaths made the only sound in the room for several seconds. "Things work out for the best, don't they? I figure the wagon didn't sell because we need it."

"I beg your pardon?" Amanda sat up in bed, the covers clutched in her hands as she stared through the dim light in her sister's direction.

"We need it. You and I. We're going to go west ourselves, the two of us."

2

*A*manda's mouth fell open at her sister's statement. "That has got to be the most—" she fluttered a hand in speechless futility. "I'm surprised that even you could say such a dumb thing!"

Sarah Jane flinched and lowered her gaze.

Amanda knew her younger sister considered her pessimistic and staid, a stick-in-the-mud person, one who rarely gave the girl credit for having a sensible thought in her little blond head. But with both Pa and Mama gone and no one else left to them in this world, the crushing weight of responsibility Amanda felt made it almost impossible to temper her words. It was high time Sarah started acting more like the young woman she was than the little girl she still wished to be.

"It isn't dumb," Sarah said evenly. "Surely you can see this town is not a fit place for two unchaperoned girls. We left Pennsylvania to begin a new life out west, didn't we? Well, now that we've started in that direction, I think we should keep going."

Amanda could scarcely breathe. She stared toward the parted curtain panels, where the glow from outside cast silver outlines on the roofs across the street and glazed the edges of the furniture in the hotel room. She released a despondent huff and flopped back down on her pillow. "I just don't know. I truly don't."

Sarah, the contours of her slight body shrouded in blue-violet shadows and blankets, remained silent for a long moment as her tapered finger tapped the counterpane. "I picked some spring flowers today and took them out to Pa's grave. And something inside of me made me start singing—you know how he always loved my singing."

An inner smile struggled for release, but Amanda managed to contain it as her sister went on.

"Anyway, when my song was done, I asked him what we should do, where we should go. He always did give the best advice. And it came to me—as if Pa had said it himself—the wagon is bought and paid for. It has everything we need to go west just like we would have if he hadn't passed on. The least we can do is to try to see that dream of his through. He would want us to. We owe it to him."

Amanda didn't respond for several moments as her sister's preposterous notion warred in her mind. She gave a shaky sigh. "Know what really scares me?"

"Hm?"

"You could be right. I don't see any other choice for us at the moment. No matter where we go, we're going to be alone. We've got no one to go back to, and I sure don't want to settle in a place like this, full of ruffians and drifters." She paused again in deep thought. "If we did go west the way Pa wanted—and I'm not altogether sure we should, mind you—maybe it would feel like a part of him would be with us." She paused. "We might just find a good new life for ourselves. Those new woodworking tools of his could provide the resources we need for a while. Maybe even enable us to open a shop of our own in Oregon."

"What kind of shop?"

Unexpectedly, with the decision to go not actually settled yet, a feasible possibility came to mind. "If there's one worthwhile thing Maddie managed to teach us it was how to use a needle. Think about it. More flocks of people are heading west all the time. And they'll all be in need of clothes. They'll have their hands so full trying to clear land and build homes before the onset of winter there won't be much time for less needful things, like sewing."

"Yes!" A growing excitement colored Sarah's breathless voice. "That's a grand idea. Truly grand! And we wouldn't have to wait to settle somewhere before we got started. We could buy some bolts of dry goods right here in Independence, then one of us could ride in back and sew bonnets and aprons and baby things while the other drove."

"Maybe. It's just a thought." Amanda, feeling the first flickers of doubt after her initial enthusiasm, needed time to ponder the idea before making a definite commitment that would alter their lives forever. Then she tossed caution to the wind. "I'll get in touch with the wagon master and make the arrangements to go with the train as planned."

Sarah Jane's teeth glistened like pearls in her wide grin, and Amanda couldn't help wondering what sort of unpredictable hopes and dreams were taking shape in her sister's imaginings. It would be one huge chore keeping the flighty girl in check during a long westward journey.

Nevertheless, in that brief instant, Amanda felt a tiny bit of Sarah's optimism course through her being, accompanied by an uncharacteristic surge of adventure. Maybe for once in her life Sarah was actually right. Heading west would be far better than letting sadness and grief defeat them . . . and besides, if they really put their minds to it, perhaps they truly could make a good life out there. A small smile tugged at her lips as she relaxed and closed her eyes, sloughing off the guilt from not having sought God's guidance in the matter.

❧

Early the next morning, the crowing of the rooster out back awakened Amanda. The curtain of night had barely begun to lift, spreading a band of thin light outward from the eastern sky. She checked over her shoulder to see Sarah still in deep slumber. It was an opportune time to talk things over with the Lord.

Reaching for her flannel wrap, Amanda slipped her arms into it and tied the belt snugly, then knelt beside the bed. *Dear heavenly Father,* she prayed silently, desperately, *I don't really know what to pray. Nothing has happened the way we expected it to since we three came to Independence. And now with Pa gone, Sarah and I have nowhere to turn. We can't go back to the home we used to know, and it's a fact this town is not a fit place for us to settle. We've decided to see to Pa's wish and go west.*

She paused to gather her thoughts. *In truth, I don't know how we'll manage this long journey alone, since neither of us is used to doing for ourselves. Back home we had Maddie to cook and keep things nice while we girls wiled away our time in what I admit now were frivolous pursuits. But we're strong and healthy, and we can learn. I know that for certain. Please go with us on our way. Grant us wisdom and courage, and stay close to us in the weeks ahead.*

When there were no words left inside, she rose and crawled back into the warm bed again for a few more minutes of sleep, thankful for the blankets that chased away the chill of the early hour. She would have liked to have more inner peace over her decision, but perhaps that would come in time. Pa always said a person's steps were ordered by the Lord, and circumstances had all but forced this plan upon them. Surely it had to be God's will. Determined, she pressed her lips together and closed her heavy eyelids as peace settled over her like a quilt of down.

A short time later, Amanda awoke again to full morning brightness. She dressed in her best navy worsted dress, confident that the tailored fit and fashionable sleeves made her look older than her twenty years. After twisting her long hair into a neat figure-eight coil at the nape of her neck, she added her Sunday bonnet, tying a stylish bow just beneath her chin.

"You look divine," Sarah Jane gushed. "Ever so grown-up and important."

"I'm trying very hard to convince myself I feel important," she confessed. "Let's go have breakfast, and then I'll try to locate the man Pa made the arrangements with."

❧

At Martha's Eatery, a bustling restaurant popular with trail guides and mountain men alike, Seth Holloway shoved the empty plate away and leaned back in the chair, unfolding his cramped legs. He glanced across the table at rusty-haired Red Hanfield, his partner and longtime friend. "I had word that the O'Bradys pulled into town this morning.

That's the last family we've been waiting for. I'll see they have all their supplies so we can head out day after tomorrow. You ride point with the first wagons this time, and I'll follow along with the cow column."

"Yep, just make sure you don't ride last in line," his wiry pal quipped. "Wastes a lot of time high-steppin' them cow pies." His coppery mustache twitched in barely suppressed humor.

"I get the picture," Seth grated. Picking up his coffee mug, he drained the last bit in one gulp, then set it back down.

"Ready for a refill?" At his elbow, good-natured Martha Griffith, owner and chief cook, poured a fresh cup.

"I do thank you, ma'am," Seth said, grinning up at her with admiration. No matter the time of day, the perky woman always sported a crisp, spotless apron over her calico dress, and the ruffle on her cap was always neatly starched over her salt-and-pepper bun. The two serving girls who worked for her were similarly attired. "You never let a man run dry."

"No sense in it a'tall, when the pot's always on! I like to make sure my regulars always come back."

"As if anybody else in town cooks as good as you," Red piped up.

Martha's pink cheeks dimpled with a smile as she filled his cup also. "Mighty kind words for a busy woman. I knew there was a reason I always like to see you two comin' in off the prairie." With a cheery dip of her head, she continued making the rounds with the coffeepot.

Seth observed her efficient movements absently as he slowly drank the hot liquid, his mind recounting endless last-minute details that needed his attention before the wagon train departed Independence two days hence.

On the edge of his vision he noticed a dark-clad figure approaching the table he and his pal occupied. He looked up when the rather small, smartly dressed young woman stopped beside them. Her classic features were composed in a businesslike expression, but it was her eyes that drew his like a magnet. Large and luminous, an unmistakable sadness lurked within their clear green depths.

"I beg your pardon?" she said softly.

"Miss?"

"I'm looking for Mr. Holloway."

They both rose at once. "That's me," Seth said, mentally noting some nicely rounded curves, neat, nearly auburn hair beneath a prim bonnet, a tempting but unsmiling mouth. "Seth Holloway. This is my partner, Red Hanfield. What might I do for you?" Noticing that her hands, gloved in white kid, trembled slightly despite her confident demeanor, he returned his gaze to her eyes, caught again by the cheerlessness accented by the fringe of long lashes.

She moistened her lips. "My name is Amanda Shelby. My father—"

Seth recognized the name at once. "Oh, of course. I heard of your unfortunate loss, Miss Shelby. You have my deepest sympathy. We'll refund the fee he paid right away, if you'll just let me know where to bring it."

"That won't be necessary."

Seth frowned in confusion. "We can't keep—"

She regarded him steadily. "Well, you see, that's why I've come. My sister and I will be leaving with the rest of the group, just as planned. So the registration money our father paid you is rightfully yours."

Red Hanfield choked on the gulp of coffee he had just taken. One side of his mustache hiked upward in a comical expression of uncertainty as he sat back down.

Seth had trouble finding his own voice. Aware that patrons at the nearby tables were gawking at them, he finally managed to link a few words together. "Surely you're joking, Miss Shelby."

"No, I am quite serious. We will be ready to leave with the other wagons."

Searching for just the right reply, Seth kneaded his jaw, then met her relentless gaze. "Look, miss. I don't mean to be rude, but whatever your intentions were before you came here, you're gonna have to forget them. There's no way we can let you and your sister make the journey. In fact," he reached for the inside pocket of his leather jacket and withdrew a thick packet, from which he pulled out several bank notes. He pressed them into her hand. "Here. This is the cash your father paid for the trip. Take my advice and go back to wherever it is you came from."

He could tell just by looking at her—rooted in that spot without a change in her countenance, other than the obvious set of her teeth—that his words had not dissuaded her one bit.

"I cannot take this," she said flatly. Placing the funds intact on the table beside him, she held her ground. "My sister and I are quite set on this. We will be going west. Good day, Mr. Holloway. Mr. Hanfield." Turning on her heel, she headed for the door.

Seth cast an incredulous look at Red, who made no effort to hide his amusement. Then he snatched up the bank notes and used them to punctuate his words in his friend's face. "Thanks for backing me up, buddy!" With a huff of disgust, he started after Amanda Shelby.

He caught up with her three doors down, in front of the Bluebird Saloon, where raucous piano music from inside the swinging doors tinkled around them, creating an absurd carnival atmosphere for any intended serious conversation. Frowning, he tapped her shoulder.

She stopped and turned, and her eyes flared wider. Instantly, a soft vulnerability in her features disappeared behind a facade of purposeful determination. "Oh, it's you."

"Who'd you expect?" he spat, instantly regretting his harsh tone. "Look, take the—" Conscious of the intense interest of a growing number of passersby, Seth knew better than to wag a handful of cash out in the open, and instead slid the bank notes back within the confines of his jacket pocket. Then he grabbed Amanda Shelby's elbow, ignoring the mortification that glared at him from her narrowed eyes, and steered her to an unoccupied spot a short distance away. There he turned her to face himself. "Please, Miss Shelby. I've been called blunt at times and have probably hurt a few feelings in my day, so if I'm hurting yours I'm sorry. But you don't seem to understand. The journey west is grueling, even for tough, experienced folks, and some of the hardiest souls won't survive it, let alone a couple gals like you and your sister."

"I don't believe that."

"Do you know how to shoot?"

"No, but—"

"Can you change a wheel? The trail rattles the best wagon to shambles."

"No."

"How about repairing harness?"

The last thing he was prepared for was the sheen of tears that glazed her eyes before she lowered them in defeat. It nearly melted his resolve altogether. But she blinked quickly and brushed the imprint of his grip from her dark blue sleeve before raising her gaze to his.

"But . . . we have to go," came her small voice.

There ought to be a law against a gal crying, for what it did to a man inside, Seth thought fleetingly. He hardened himself against the sight of her whisking a stray tear from her cheek as he mustered up all his reason. "Look, if there was some way we could let you come, any way at all, we would. I mean that. But it's out of the question. Even if by some stretch of the imagination you could make the trip— and you can't, take my word for it—at best, you'd slow us down. You're too much of a risk. Now I'm taking you back to your hotel, and when we get there I'm giving you back your father's registration fee. That's my final word on the subject."

Her shoulders sagged in hopelessness, and her despair cinched itself around the middle of Seth's stomach. But he had to hold firm. It was the only thing to do, and all for the best. In time she'd see it, too. He watched her turn and walk mutely toward the Bradford.

Seth accompanied her without speaking. When they reached the hotel, he escorted her inside, then once more pressed the money her father had paid him woolen ago into her palms.

She didn't even look at him.

He cleared his throat. "Again, my deepest sympathy to you and your sister in your loss. I wish you well. Good day, Miss Shelby."

Seth felt like a heel as he strode away from her and called himself every choice name he could think of. But the entire scheme was insane. Any fool could see that. There was no way on earth two very young— not to mention unattached—females could endure the hardships that faced the emigrants on the Oregon Trail. All the overlanders started out with grandiose visions and optimism . . . but the entire route was littered with discarded furniture and household possessions, carcasses of dead horses and oxen, and worse yet, graves of every imaginable size. As if the trek weren't rough enough over rugged mountains and endless blazing prairie and desert, there were plenty enough other threats—wild animals, bizarre weather, Indians, disease—to instill fear in the stoutest heart. It took everything a person had, not to mention an unquenchable, unbeatable spirit to make that journey.

It took a much more valiant heart than Amanda Shelby possessed . . . but that didn't make Seth feel any less like a cowardly snake for being the one to shatter her dreams.

(3)

*A*manda trudged wretchedly up the enclosed staircase to the second floor. Earlier this morning she had managed to acquire at least a portion of peace after kneeling before the Lord in prayer. Now a scant few hours later the grand plans were in ashes. Hopeless. And simply because of that insufferable, overbearing Mr. Holloway with his long, rugged face and squinty eyes and morbid words. How was she going to break the news to Sarah after all their high hopes?

Reaching their room, Amanda drew a deep breath to fortify herself. Why, oh, why had life taken such a sad turn? Why did Pa have to die and leave them stranded way out here so far from everything they knew? Wasn't it heartbreaking enough that death had claimed Mama and the tiny baby her frail body had not been strong enough to bring into the world, without heaven's laying claim to Pa as well? And that, on top of—

No! her mind railed. *You cannot think about him. Not now. Not ever.*

Well, whatever the reasons the little family had been dealt such dreadful blows, Mama would have been the first to remind her girls that God's ways are often beyond understanding, and one should accept troubles just the same as good fortune. But that, Amanda reflected with a sigh, was truly hard to do. She straightened her shoulders and reached for the latch.

Sarah Jane looked up from writing in her journal and sprang to her feet, her face a portrait of bright expectation as Amanda entered the room. "Well? How did your meeting with the wagon master go? Tell me everything!"

"Not as well as we hoped," Amanda fudged. Then seeing her sister's crestfallen expression, she decided to come right out with the truth. "Mr. Holloway refuses to allow us to accompany the rest of the wagon train."

"You can't mean that!"

She nodded. "He returned the money Pa paid him and practically ordered me—and you—to go *'back where we came from,'* as he put it. I'm really sorry." Untying her bonnet, Amanda slid it off, not caring as it slipped from her fingers to the floor. The urge to give it a swift kick under the bed was hard to resist . . . but it wouldn't solve anything, and someone would only have to retrieve the thing. Instead, she flopped onto the quilted coverlet and lay staring up at the dismal ceiling.

"I don't believe it!"

"Believe it, Sissy. There was no reasoning with that obnoxious, opinionated, bullheaded man. He didn't give me a chance to explain our plight."

"How . . . perfectly horrid!" Sarah declared. "Forbidding people their destiny." With a toss of her golden curls, she flounced over to where she'd been putting her innermost thoughts down on paper and tore the half-written page out of the journal, crumpling it in her hand. An oppressive silence hovered in the room as Sarah plopped grimly back onto the chair, arms crossed in front of her, staring at the opposite wall. Her exhaled breaths came out in a succession of audible exclamation points.

Amanda finally broke the stillness. "Well, this isn't getting us anywhere. I'm going downstairs for the noon meal, and while I eat I'll think about groveling at Mr. Cavanaugh's feet to persuade him to take that wagon off our hands. Much as I hate the prospect, it's the only sensible solution left to us. At least it'll give us money to live on until we make other plans."

Sarah shrugged. "Whatever you say. I'm not hungry. In fact, I may never be hungry again. Think I'll wander on over to the mercantile and browse through the fabrics and jewelry. It doesn't cost anything just to look. And afterward I may go visit Nancy Thatcher at the bakery until she closes up."

Seated in the dining room moments later, Amanda heard scarcely a word of the cheerful chatter bantered about the rectangular pine table by other hotel guests during the meal. Her thoughts were occupied back at Martha's Eatery, upon the most infuriating man she had ever had the occasion to meet.

Seth Holloway certainly seemed taken up with his own importance, she concluded, swallowing a spoonful of beef stew. Not even allowing her an opportunity to explain the reasoning behind the decision she and Sarah had made. Who did he think he was—ruler of the world? Humph. Some king he would make, in buckskins, with a face that looked in need of a good shave, unruly dark brown hair and hooded, deep-set brown eyes that had a sneaky quality to them. Even that low voice of his rasped in her memory as the conversation mentally took place again. *Go back where you came from.* It would serve the beast right if the sky clouded over and rained for days and days, making the trail impassible for a month. Or better yet, forever. Then he'd have to give everyone's money back, leaving him flat broke.

As she bit into some warm cornbread, a glance out the window revealed the object of her scathing thoughts passing by with his partner and several other men, obviously from the wagon encampment. He wasn't exactly smiling—in fact, Amanda had serious doubts the man ever broke into a smile at all. But he did appear pleasantly cheerful and walked with long, confident strides.

What she wouldn't do to take him down a peg. He had no right to refuse her and Sarah's inclusion with the rest of the overlanders, no right at all. If only she'd become acquainted with some of the migrating families there might have been someone to stand up for them and demand they be permitted to join the company. But when Pa had come down with chills and fever it made folks leery of coming too close, so Amanda had moved the wagon to a spot some distance from the encampment. And after he expired, she and Sarah had mostly kept to themselves in the hotel. It was too late to try to make a friend now. Much too late.

"Mr. Randolph," Seth said, resting a hand on the lantern-faced man's shoulder as he, Red, and two other emigrant leaders walked toward the hardware store, "I'm calling a meeting around the campfire this evening after supper. I want all the men to be present. Think you can handle that?"

The older man stroked his close-cropped beard and gave a nod of agreement. "No problem at all, Mr. Holloway. We're all pretty anxious to leave, after sittin' around for nigh on three weeks."

The heavyset man on the end snorted. "That's an understatement—it's been four weeks for us. It's getting harder and harder to keep a handle on all the loose young'uns. Even the womenfolk are antsy."

"We understand, Mr. Thornton," Red chimed in. "But your waitin's about over, an' now we need to go over the rules we expect folks to abide by for a smooth crossin'."

He nodded. "We'll be there. Count on it."

"Soon as we get back to the wagons we'll spread the word," Randolph said, glancing to the others.

"Good." Seth touched the brim of his hat as they reached the store. "See you then, gentlemen." He turned to Red as the other men entered the establishment. "Guess I'd better start getting my own gear together."

"Me, too. Say, did you manage to smooth that little gal's feathers—about heading west?"

"Fortunately, yes. Took some convincing, though." He shook his head with a droll smirk. "Can't imagine a girl being fool enough to think she—and a sister who I know is even younger than she is—could make a journey like that all by themselves. But at least they're off our hands. I gave their pa's money back. That's the end of it, far as I'm concerned."

❧

Amanda hesitated outside the mercantile for as long as she could, dreading the inevitable. Then, knowing the task would never get any easier, she slipped inside as two chattering women exited. She didn't see Sarah Jane in the store, but spied Mr. Cavanaugh across the cluttered room, chewing on a fat cigar while he spoke with another customer beside the pickle barrel. Amanda stopped near the display of fabrics and fingered a bolt of violet watered silk as she eyed the proprietor with disdain, taking in the waistcoat that strained across his protruding belly, the shiny bald circle atop his head.

His gaze flicked her way and a snide quirk twisted his thick mouth. He excused himself and approached Amanda in self-assured calm. "Well, well. Had a feeling I'd be seeing you sooner or later, Miss Shelby."

She dipped her head slightly. "Mr. Cavanaugh."

"Come to accept my offer, did you?"

"Well, I—"

"Course, I haveta tell you, the stuff's not worth as much to me now, with the train about to leave. I'll have to lower the price some. You understand, I'm sure. I'm still doin' you a favor. Least I can do, under the circumstances."

Amanda stiffened. The man was actually gloating! All so certain that she'd hand over what amounted to the entirety of her and Sarah's worldly possessions for next to nothing! And she had no doubts whatsoever that the moment he got hold of all those supplies he'd take advantage of some other poor souls—turning her misfortune into an indecent profit for himself. She felt her spirit grow ice solid. The sudden reply that popped out of her mouth surprised even her. "I didn't come about the wagon. I'd like to arrange a trade. My father's tools for some dry goods."

"Hm." He rubbed his chin in dubious thought. "I s'pose that could be done—"

"Fine. I'll bring them to you shortly, then, and choose some yardage."

"What about the rest? The outfit. The supplies?"

She offered a cool smile. "We're only discussing Pa's tools, Mr. Cavanaugh. I'm afraid our wagon isn't for sale after all. We do thank you, however, for your . . . *generous* offer. Good day." Gathering a fold of her skirt in one gloved hand, Amanda whirled and fled before she changed her mind.

She fairly flew back to the hotel and up the contained staircase to her rented room. A depressing heaviness settled over her. Her own pride had just caused her to act prematurely—and make a decision that could end up being far more foolish than anything Sarah had ever conceived. What was that verse Pa had quoted so often? "Pride goeth before a fall"? Well, if she and Sarah were in for a big fall now, it would be all her fault.

Letting herself in, Amanda released a shaky breath of relief to discover her sister had not yet returned. At least there'd be time to reason things out, to pray. Instead of coming from the mercantile with cash in hand for the two of them to live on until they decided what to do, she had just thrown their one chance away. She sank to her knees in yet another frantic prayer.

Dear Lord, I've really done it this time. Slammed a door You left standing wide open for us . . . and all because of my silly pride. But Mr. Cavanaugh wasn't being fair to Sarah and me. He just wasn't. You must want us to go west. You must. She paused, rolling her eyes heavenward as if expecting to see the answer inscribed bright and clear on the ceiling. Finding none, she closed her eyes once more. *So we need You to help us now. I know You will see us through.*

Trusting that to be sufficient, Amanda picked up Pa's Bible and took a seat in the overstuffed chair near the window. When her sister's light step sounded outside the door a short time later, she looked up from the Psalms and met the younger girl's curious eyes with a smile.

"I take it you were successful," Sarah Jane said airily. "We have funds to tide us over for a while, until we can find some kind of employment."

"No, I'm afraid not."

"No?" The younger girl removed her shawl and draped it on the nearest chair. "You did go to see Mr. Cavanaugh."

"Yes—" Amanda felt her face growing warm, and looked away. "But I could not let that brute *steal* our things. He wanted to give me less than before. *Less!* Can you imagine? I couldn't bring myself to let him cheat us like that. I just couldn't."

Sarah crossed the room and knelt at her feet, eyes troubled and imploring. "But . . . what will we do now, Mandy, when our money runs out?"

Giving her sister's hand a pat where it rested on her own atop the Bible in her lap, Amanda shrugged nonchalantly. "You said it last night. We're going west, just as we decided."

"But the wagon master said—"

"I know what he said. But I've been thinking about it, and we're going anyway . . . just not with him."

"I don't understand."

"We'll wait until the others have all gone. Then, later on that day or the next, we'll follow behind them. No one will be the wiser."

"Do you think we can do such a thing? Truly?"

"Of course. We belong to the Lord, you and I. God will take care of us. He has to—after all, He promised, didn't He?"

"I . . . suppose."

Amanda forced herself to relax and appear calm and assured. It wouldn't do for Sarah to know how doubtful her older, wiser sister actually felt in the hidden reaches of her heart. Journey across half a continent. Alone.

4

*A*manda got barely a wink of sleep all night. One minute she was convinced she'd made the only decision that had any merit, but the next, the absurdity of considering such a monumental undertaking assaulted her. She couldn't even pray. Despite numerous attempts, the words refused to come out right. It seemed folly to expect the Lord to bless their venture, when the wagon master himself pointed out how lacking she and Sarah were in many of the basic and necessary travel skills.

Heaven only knew exactly what they might encounter ahead. Swollen rivers, swift and deep from spring rains, trouble with the wagon, possible injuries to herself or Sarah. And what about wild animals that freely roamed the open country? Or Indians? Amanda's stomach knotted just imagining the two of them alone in the wilderness, no one knowing or caring where they were. But on the other hand, she reminded herself, the Bible did say that God was all-knowing, so nothing would take Him by surprise. The Almighty, in His omnipotent wisdom, had surely known that Pa would pass on to his eternal reward and leave them to fend for themselves. The Lord must have a place for them out west. He would be with them. He would take away all their fears. Grasping that conviction, she closed her heavy eyelids and finally dozed off.

A pair of distant gunshots echoed a few hours later, awakening Amanda with a start. Sarah, next to her in bed, was still breathing in the slow, regular pattern of deep slumber. Amanda, her head aching from the lack of sleep, raised the coverlet and slid out of bed, then padded to the window.

The first pale streaks of dawn were beginning to stain the dark sky in the east. Turning her head in the opposite direction, Amanda spotted the golden lantern glow rising from the conglomeration of wagons amassed in the rocky-outcropped meadow near the spring on the edge of town. Everyone had anxiously awaited those signal shots over several unbearably long weeks. She could imagine the people milling about, hitching teams, readying their wagons. What suppressed excitement there must be, what cheerful chatter, bright hope, and sheer happiness. Last-minute preparations before setting out for a new life.

She heaved a sigh. What she would give to be part of that exhilarated throng about to depart for Oregon.

Brisk morning air ruffled over Amanda's bare arms, and she shivered. Hugging herself, she retreated to the warm sanctuary of the bed while her plan reaffirmed itself. No telling how long it would take that whole wagon train along with the vast herd of cattle and livestock to depart Independence. But once a sufficient span of time passed to allow the emigrants to put some distance between themselves and the town, she and Sarah would leave, too.

That settled, Amanda again relaxed, and her eyes fluttered closed.

"Mandy?"

Sarah's voice seemed fuzzy and far away, but the gentle hand shaking Amanda's shoulder felt very real. She raised her lashes. How could it be this bright already? Only a minute ago it was still dark.

"We'll miss breakfast if we don't hurry."

She bolted upright, noting that her sister was fully dressed. "Oh! I must have overslept! Sorry."

"I left water in the basin for you."

"Thanks." Amanda rose and dashed across the room to wash up. The cool liquid she splashed on her face felt refreshing, and she was surprisingly rested after that last unexpected snatch of sleep. After blotting her hands and face on a towel, she shimmied out of her night shift and into her chemise, then reached for the sturdy burgundy calico dress laid out the evening before.

Sarah moved up behind her and helped with the buttons. "Are we, you know . . . still going?"

Amanda peered over her shoulder. Her sister's brow bore uncharacteristic lines of worry. "Of course. Why wouldn't we?"

"I just wanted to make sure."

"But we'd best not let anyone know. If we so much as let a single word slip, good-intentioned people are sure to stop us. We'll bide our time, wait until we can leave unnoticed."

"Right." Finished with the buttons, Sarah nibbled her bottom lip with unconcealed excitement. "I've packed our things."

"Splendid!" Amanda smiled and sat down to pull on her stockings, then jammed her feet into her hightop shoes and used the buttonhook to fasten them. After some quick strokes with the brush she tied her long hair at the nape of her neck with a black velvet ribbon and stood up. "Do I look presentable?"

Sarah nodded.

"Well, what are we waiting for?" Sputtering into a giggle, she hugged her younger sibling. Arm in arm, they headed downstairs to the dining room, reaching it even as a handful of other patrons were taking their leave.

Mrs. Clark, the middle-aged widow who provided hearty meals at the Bradford Hotel, greeted them as they entered the now-empty room. Her apple-dumpling cheeks rounded with her smile. "We wondered where you two were this morning," she said pleasantly, a hand on her wide hip.

"Everything smells luscious," Amanda said, averting her attention from the gray-haired cook to the long table. She resisted the impulse to offer an explanation for their tardiness.

"You missed all the goin's on," the older woman announced. "The train pulled out first thing this morning."

"Oh, really?" Feigning nonchalance, Amanda exchanged a cursory glance with Sarah. "It certainly seems like a perfect day to begin a journey."

"Yep, that it does. Pity you two couldn't be among them. Well, set yourselves down in one of them clean spots, and I'll bring you some flapjacks and eggs right quick."

The remainder of the morning seemed interminable to Amanda and Sarah as they peered constantly out the window, checking the immense, distant trace of dust stirred up by wagons and cattle. Finally they gathered their belongings and stole down to the livery to tuck their bags unobtrusively into the wagon.

The two of them heaved down the heavy chest containing their father's woodworking equipment and lugged it to Cavanaugh's Mercantile. Amanda had to bite her tongue at the pathetic sum the storekeeper offered for the finely crafted tools, but there was no recourse but to accept. She and Sarah ignored his questions as they casually perused the bolts of material he had on hand and chose several different kinds they thought would prove most useful for their new enterprise.

In mid-afternoon, on the pretense of wanting to get current with all their affairs, Amanda settled their hotel bill, and the girls checked their room one last time to be sure they hadn't forgotten anything. No doubt they'd miss the comfort of that big four-poster soon enough, Amanda surmised. But she eagerly anticipated some solitude after the constant racket of this rowdy frontier town.

"There's no sign of dust above the trail now," Sarah Jane mused, closing the window. "Do you think it's time?"

Amanda subdued the butterflies fluttering about in her stomach and gave a solemn nod. "It's now or never. But first we must say good-bye to Pa. It's only right."

With the emigrant train gone from Independence, the diminished noise level outside seemed all the more apparent in the stillness of the grassy knoll just beyond the simple white church on the far edge of the settlement. Amanda and Sarah treaded softly over the spongy ground.

A soft, fresh breeze whispered among the scattered wooden crosses bearing the names and life years of the dear departed. It gently billowed the girls' skirts as they stood gazing down at the forlorn rectangle of mounded earth beneath which Pa lay awaiting the heavenly trumpet call.

Amanda felt a lump forming in her throat, but swallowed hard and sank to her knees to place a bouquet of wildflowers on the grave. It took every ounce of strength she could muster to force a smile. "Pa, Sarah and I've come to say good-bye now," she said, her voice wavering slightly. She drew a deep breath. "We're setting off for Oregon, just like you planned, so this will be the last time we can visit you. Tell Mama . . . we send our love. Farewell."

Beside her, Sarah Jane sniffed and brushed tears from her cheeks. "We'll keep you and Ma in our hearts . . . until we're all together again. We—we love you. Good-bye . . . for now." After a few moments of silence they met each other's eyes and stood. "We'll have an early supper, then head over to the livery and watch for Mr. Plummer to go have his," Amanda announced.

The blacksmith was busy shoeing one of a pair of work horses when they peeked around the edge of the doorway after their meal. But finally he exited his shop and walked over to Martha's Eatery. The door of the restaurant closed behind him.

"This is it." Amanda led the way around back of the livery, where they sneaked inside. Ever grateful that Pa had made her practice hitching up the mules and driving them, she located the required equipment belonging to them and followed her father's instructions to the letter. Then she went to Mr. Plummer's makeshift desk and left a packet containing sufficient funds to cover the expenses incurred from boarding and feeding the animals, along with a short note of thanks for his kindness.

Everything finally in readiness, they climbed aboard. Amanda released the brake, clucked her tongue, and slapped the traces against the backs of the mules. The heavy wagon lurched into motion, its huge wheels crunching over the gravelly dirt.

Without Pa, the cumbersome vehicle felt huge. Immense. And the mules seemed less than enthusiastic about having to work after weeks of being penned up and lazy. But Amanda gritted her teeth and held on, steering them around the sheltering grove of trees behind the livery and then guiding them in an arc that would soon intersect the trail to Oregon Territory.

Sarah leaned to peer around the arched canvas top at the busy river port they were leaving behind. "I don't think anyone even noticed us drive off. Oh, this is so exciting, Mandy! We're actually doing it . . . heading west, just like Pa dreamed. I can't wait to start writing about it in my journal. I'm going to put down every single thing that happens along the way!" Gripping the edge of the hard wooden seat, she filled her lungs and smiled, staring into the distance.

A person would have to be blind to miss the sparkle in the younger girl's wondrous blue eyes, Amanda conceded. If it weren't for the sobering knowledge that she herself was now in control of both their destinies, she might have shared some of her sibling's lilting optimism. But right now her hands were full. Returning her attention to the long trail stretching beyond the horizon, she put her full concentration on the hard job ahead.

The road west, impossible to miss, already bore deep ruts from vast hoards of wagons that had made the journey in previous years. Amanda filled her gaze with the absolutely breathtaking landscape all around them. Groves of budding trees dotted the gently rolling ground, itself a wondrous carpet of long, silky grasses. Myriad spring flowers speckled the spring green in a rainbow of glorious hues. Surely in such a delightful season of new life, nothing could spoil their adventure. To make certain, Amanda lofted yet another fervent prayer heavenward, beseeching the Lord to bless and protect them on the journey.

"I wonder when we'll reach Oregon," Sarah mused.

"Papa expected it to take months. But according to that guidebook he purchased back home, it's a fairly pleasant drive, even if it is rather long."

"Why would Mr. Holloway try to scare us off, then?"

At the mention of the wagon master's name, Amanda tightened her lips, forcing aside an exaggerated mental picture of his obnoxious smirk and insinuating eyes. "He's just a pompous beast, is all. But he isn't going to stop us now, Sissy. And neither is anybody else. We are on our way west!"

And Seth Holloway will never even know it.

5

*G*uiding the team over the gently rolling northwesterly trail that ambled along the Kansas River, Amanda drank in the breathtaking wooded ridges lining either side of the serene valley. Springs and patches of timber interspersed a serene landscape much more vast and open than the familiar dense forests and winding, irregular hills of northeastern Pennsylvania. Already she found the spaciousness refreshing, the immense sky overhead magnificent. "Space to breathe," Pa had called it, and now Amanda knew why. She loved being able to see so far in every direction, and swallowed a pang of sadness that he wasn't there to enjoy it, too.

"I'm getting thirsty," Sarah said, drawing her out of her musings.

"We'll stop at that little grove ahead. It looks like a good place to make camp."

The sun had already sunk beneath the horizon, its slanting rays painting the western sky vibrant rose and violet. Amanda halted the mules, then hopped down and began unhitching them.

"I'll gather wood before it gets too dark," Sarah offered, and bustled off out of sight.

❧

Sarah Jane found an abundance of deadfall among the trees and quickly gathered a generous armful. On her way back to the wagon she saw that Amanda had hobbled the mules and was now freshening up at the riverside. Sarah grabbed a towel. "How far do you suppose we've come?" she asked, joining her sister.

Amanda shook excess water from her hands before drying them

and her face. "Our late start only gave us a couple hours of travel time. We'd better get up early tomorrow if we ever hope to see Oregon."

After a quick light meal of bread and cheese, they returned to the wagon to dress in their night shifts.

Sarah watched her older sister brushing out her long, auburn hair with the usual regulated strokes, then gave her own curls a few dutiful brushes. "Think I'll write for a little while before I blow out the lantern."

"Just don't be long. We need to be on the road at first light." With a yawn, Amanda slid into her side of the mattress and almost instantly fell asleep.

Sarah retrieved her journal and moved closer to the glow of the lantern.

Dear Diary,

Today is the most glorious day of my entire life! Amanda and I set off on our adventure to find our destiny. I thought it would seem a little lonesome, traveling by ourselves, but instead it feels more like we have sprouted wings and are completely free. We can make our own rules, which surely must be one of the most wonderful benefits of all.

You cannot imagine how beautiful this wondrous countryside has been so far. It's as if some grand and heroic knight of old rode through the vast stretches of the land and carved out the most lovely of routes westward, full of sparkling rivers and fragrant spring flowers. Somehow it would not surprise me to discover he is still here, mounted upon his swift steed just beyond our sight as he looks after travelers on this road to Oregon, keeping them always from harm.

Smiling to herself, Sarah closed the book and hugged it. Imagine if it were true, and some handsome champion were just around the next bend in the trail, ever watchful of the weary pilgrims on their way to a new life. How wonderful to know there was nothing to fear. As glorious as it was to be free now and on their own, a tiny part of her had felt a little afraid of what lay ahead. But since heading west without Pa had been largely her idea in the first place, she'd squelched those feelings and concentrated on the mild weather and the lovely scenery instead. She leaned over and blew out the lamp, then crawled into bed.

The faraway howl of a wolf pierced the night stillness. Sarah's eyes flew open as a second howl answered from much nearer. Nervously she pulled the blankets over her head and snuggled closer to her sister's slumbering form. But not until the vision of a stalwart man astride a glorious golden horse drifted into her thoughts was she able to relax as she imagined him patrolling the grounds around them. A peacefulness settled upon her, and her eyelids fluttered closed.

Morning arrived all too quickly. When Sarah felt behind her, Amanda's side of the bed was empty. She gathered the topmost blanket around her shoulders and went to peer out of the wagon into the semidarkness.

Amanda was fully clothed and kneeling before a feeble fire she was coaxing to life.

"You're up early," Sarah called. "It's not even light yet."

"Thought we'd better not waste any of this morning if we expect to ever get anywhere."

"Of course. I'll wash up and get dressed."

Her older sister nodded and set a pot of water over the flames to boil. By the time Sarah got back, Amanda was stirring a thick mixture of mush.

"I wonder if it's supposed to be this hard to stir," she commented as Sarah handed her two tin bowls. Then with a shrug she ladled out a sticky gob for each of them, and they took seats on a fallen log. Amanda bowed her head. "We thank you, Heavenly Father, for this new day and for the food you've provided. We ask your blessing and continued presence on our journey. In Jesus' name, amen."

"Amen," Sarah whispered, then smiled. "It smells good." She spooned some of the gooey substance to her mouth, struck by the unusual taste—or lack of same—as she slowly chewed.

Amanda, beside her, spit hers out. "Blah. This is horrid."

"What did you put into it?"

She shrugged. "Just cornmeal, flour, and water."

"Not even salt?"

Amanda shook her head. "I didn't know it needed any. Maddie's mush always tasted just fine."

"I think she used a bit of sugar, too. And maybe it didn't need flour."

"Well, how was I to know?" Amanda huffed.

"Sorry." Sarah bit her lip at her sister's uncharacteristic outburst. "I'm sure if we just sprinkle some salt in it now, it'll help," she said hopefully, and went to get some at the wagon. "Anyway, I'm more thirsty than hungry. That coffee should be about finished, shouldn't it?"

Amanda's glum face brightened. "I'll pour us some." But when Sarah returned with the salt box, an irregular black stain in the dirt steamed next to the fire.

"Thank your lucky stars you didn't even taste it," Amanda said miserably. "We'll just have some water instead." She offered one of the two cups she held.

"I'm not that fond of coffee anyway," Sarah assured her, taking it. "As a rule, I'd much prefer tea." She bent over and sprinkled a pinch of salt into the pot of mush, then reached for the wooden spoon. But the mixture had hardened, and now the spoon stuck fast, right in the middle. It would not even budge. Sarah fought hard to restrain a giggle as Amanda groaned.

"We are going to starve to death, do you realize that?" her sister groused. "This breakfast wasn't even fit for pigs. And look at this pot. The mush is hard as a rock." With a grimace she tossed the container, spoon and all, into the weeds.

"Well, no matter," Sarah said brightly. "We can have more of that two-day-old bread Nancy from the bakery was going to tear up for the birds. And there's lots of cheese in the cornmeal barrel."

While her older sister put the collars on the mules and hitched them to the wagon after the meager breakfast, Sarah traipsed happily from the grove with another armload of dried wood, which she put in back. Then the two of them climbed aboard. Glancing backward shortly after they drove off, Sarah saw a small coyote prance tentatively up to the castaway pot of mush. He put his snout into it, then scampered away. She almost laughed out loud as she settled back onto the seat. It would make a funny entry in her diary, one she'd have to keep secret.

❧

Amanda hoped they would cover a decent stretch of ground before nightfall. So far there had been no trace of the wagon train ahead. She couldn't help wondering how many miles' advantage the emigrants had. But before any thought of Mr. Holloway could intrude, she glanced at Sarah, who was removing some light blue thread and a crochet hook from her sewing bag.

"Thought I'd work on a baby cap," her sister said, nimbly forming the first few loops of a chain stitch.

"Good idea. During our nooning today I'll cut out some aprons. We should be able to work by firelight in the evenings. By the time we reach Oregon we could have a fair number of things made for our store."

Sarah smiled and went on crocheting as they left their first camp behind. Before them lay even grander spring displays amid the trees and swells of the greening landscape, and the cheery songs of bobolinks echoed across the meadows.

The first narrow stretch of the Blue River to be crossed presented no difficulty, and after fording it they stopped for dinner and a rest. Amanda figured it was probably too much to hope the entire trip would pass as smoothly and effortlessly as these first days, but in any case, it was better to dwell in the moment. No sense borrowing trouble.

Another long day of lumbering onward began a set routine as the girls divided chores related to making camp each evening and breaking it the next morning. Good as her word, Sarah took over the cooking, so Amanda no longer dreaded noonings and suppertimes. The throat-closing splendor of green swells star-dusted with tiny frail blossoms and great spillings of mountain pink, larkspur, and other more vivid wildflowers continued to fill them with awe.

"The train must have spent a night here," Amanda stated, hopping down from the wagon one evening. They had stopped near a solitary elm with a trunk three feet thick. The tree towered over the headwaters of a little creek. "There've been lots of cook fires here recently."

Sarah placed a hand on her hip. "Yes, and they didn't leave much wood, you'll notice." Tightening her lips, she walked some distance away to find enough to make supper.

The middle of the following day they passed the fork where the Santa Fe Trail split off in a more southwesterly route, a landmark Amanda regarded in silence, brushing off the solemn reminder she and Sarah were in the middle of nowhere.

~&~

"What's that up ahead?" Sarah asked one afternoon, looking up from a flannel baby blanket she was hemming.

"Must be the ferry over the Kansas River." Amanda had been assessing the questionable-looking scows at the edge of the wide, swiftly running water ever since she'd first glimpsed them. And the nearer they came, the less optimistic she felt—especially considering the two somewhat dishevelled, black-haired characters in buckskin breeches and rumpled calico shirts who were manning the contraptions. She would have rather faced another cozy little stream like others they had driven through.

"They're Indians!" Sarah murmured. "Unsavory ones like we saw loitering around Independence. Is this the only spot we can cross?"

Amanda shrugged. "It's part of the trail. The rest of the train must have crossed here."

"Well, I don't like the way those two are snickering and leering at us."

Amanda took note of the more-than-interested glances the swarthy pair aimed at them while muttering comments behind their bony hands. The fine hairs on her arms prickled, and her heartbeat increased. Glancing nervously upstream and down, she saw no fordable sites and wished as never before that they were in the company of other travelers. She swallowed and sent a quick prayer heavenward, pretending a confidence that was far from her true feelings as she drew up to the edge of the steep bank and stopped the team.

"Good day."

One of the unkempt men approached. A lecherous smile curved one end of his mouth. "No more wagons?" Beady dark eyes peered around the schooner, searching the distance before exchanging a wordless look with his chum.

The second one's lips slid into a knowing grin. He stepped nearer, hungrily eyeing Sarah up and down.

Amanda's skin crawled. She barely subdued a blush as Sarah's hand latched onto hers.

The motley louts whispered something. Then, black eyes glinting with devilment, the taller one took hold of the wagon to hoist himself up.

"It's all right, Pa," Amanda said over her shoulder. "We've reached the ferry."

The man paused.

Amanda quelled her sister's questioning expression with a stern look, then returned her attention to the Indians. "He's feeling poorly. Came down with a fever early this morning." The calmness in her voice amazed even her.

"Fever?" Dark fingers instantly released their grip on the wagon. He leapt backward.

The other, with some hesitance, thrust out his palm. "Five dollar for wagon. Two more for mules. One for passengers."

Amanda was fairly sure the price was outrageous, but wasn't about to make an issue of it. She smiled politely and turned to Sarah. "Go inside, Sissy, and get the money from Pa, will you?" As the younger girl complied, Amanda prayed all the more fervently for the Lord's help and protection.

When Sarah returned, Amanda forced herself to remain casual as she placed the fee in the dark hand.

He motioned the two of them inside the rig, and the girls watched out the back while a rope that had been looped around a tree was attached to the wagon. The taller Indian led the team forward toward the boat, while the other used the rope to help slow the schooner's descent down the bank. When everything was finally positioned on the ferry, the men used poles and paddles to propel the scow across the fast current. On the other side, the larger of the dark-skinned pair drove the team through deep sands leading up the northern bank and a short ways beyond. Halting the mules, he nodded to Amanda and jumped off, then loped back to join his cohort on the return across the river.

With the greatest relief, Amanda drew what seemed like her first real breath since the entire process had begun. She emerged from the confines of the wagon bed and moved to the seat.

Sarah, inches behind, grabbed her in a hug. "I'm so glad they believed you. I was never so frightened in my whole life."

"Me neither." Returning the embrace, Amanda gathered her shattered emotions together and allowed herself a moment to stop shaking. Then she clucked her tongue to start the mules and put as many miles between them and the Kansas River as they could before stopping for the night.

After a supper of bacon and fried mush, Sarah refilled their coffee mugs. "I'm too tired to sew tonight," she said on a yawn.

"It's been a long day." Amanda looked dejectedly down at her hands, growing tender from the constant rubbing of the traces against her soft flesh.

"I think there are some of Pa's work gloves in the back," Sarah offered. "They might make the driving easier."

Amanda only stared.

"Or shall I take a turn tomorrow?"

"Actually, that's more what I had in mind, if you must know," Amanda admitted.

"Well, that's fair. You shouldn't have to do it all."

After the nooning stop, Amanda took the reins again, more relaxed after Sarah's turn driving than she would have thought possible. The rhythmic, soothing clopping of the hooves and the jangle of the harness now brought a misty half-consciousness, and she lost herself in memories of their old life, of family times.

Very few people enjoyed such a privileged existence as she and Sarah had once known. But that was before their father's partner—bile rose in Amanda's throat—her own betrothed, had swindled Pa and absconded with all the cash from the land investments, leaving him alone to face creditors and wronged clients. Amanda felt partly responsible for her pa's death, though she had never voiced the dire thought. Morris had fooled them all. Only through her father's grit and hard work, plus the sale of the grand house and most of their worldly possessions, had all the monies been repaid. The three of them were able to set out for Oregon with their heads high.

Even if we would have preferred to stay home, Amanda mused caustically, immediately cutting off thought of the dastardly blackguard whom she had foolishly trusted enough to promise her heart. Well, at least he was out of her life. She was twenty now—old enough to know better than to trust any man's sweet words, ever again. She would remain forever a spinster, one whose sole responsibility in life was to look out for her beautiful younger sister—and she would do that to the very best of her ability. Firm in that resolve, her gaze rose idly into the hazy distance.

A jolt of alarm seized her.

A sullen, angry mass of clouds churned across the faraway horizon.

"Uh-oh. Looks like we might be in for some rain."

Her sister looked up. "Well, a shower shouldn't bother us. The wagon, after all, does have a double-canvas top."

Amanda could only hope the younger girl was right. But eyeing the irregular black cloud bank crawling toward them from the west, she had a niggling fear it was no mere spring shower heading their way.

She urged the team faster as the pleasant breeze began to turn strong and cold.

All too soon the first jagged bolts of lightning forked the slate-gray sky in the distance. Amanda strained to hear the low growl of thunder, then nudged Sarah. "We'd better stop for today. We'll have an early supper."

At the nearest likely spot, they made camp in the fading light, then draped India-rubber tarps over the bedding and the barrels of supplies. Amanda tied the drawstring closure tight on their haven, and the girls wrapped in shawls and sat down in the eerie darkness, hoping the mules would fare all right.

Soon enough, a strong gust of wind rattled the wagon. The arched top shuddered. A mule brayed.

Amanda drew her lips inward as tentative raindrops spattered the canvas. Maybe Sarah was right, it was just a shower after all. But relief vanished almost as quickly as it had come.

The gentle patter turned sinister. With each second, the pounding overhead grew more deafening. The torrent roared over the heavy bowed top, pouring down the sides of the wagon and splashing onto the ground.

A bright flash of lightning glowed through the sodden fabric like daylight for a split second. An earth-shattering boom of thunder rent the night.

Sarah's scream was drowned out by another blast. Amanda huddled close to her, cringing with every flash and crash. Rain began to drip through the cover overhead, trickling down onto the tarpaulins.

"I'm c-cold," Sarah said, shivering as she inched nearer.

Thunder boomed again.

"This has to end sometime," Amanda assured her as an icy drop spattered her nose and rolled off her chin. She hugged herself and tucked her chin deeper into her shawl, pressing close to her sister.

The elements crashed around them for what seemed like forever. Then, ever so gradually, almost imperceptibly, the thunder began to lessen in degree. The spaces between lightning bolts grew longer. Amanda eased out from under the heavy tarp and went to peer through the closure to see how the trail was faring. She gawked in dismay when a bright flash revealed they were surrounded by a sea of water and mud. The wagon ruts were not even visible.

A small part of her harbored the wish they had the comforting company of the other emigrants, but she was not ready to concede that the know-it-all Mr. Holloway had been right. Surely this wasn't the first bad storm that faced an overlander on the westward trek. If others had made it through, so would she and Sarah Jane.

"If I weren't so cold, I could at least play my guitar," Sarah groused. "It would pass the time."

Amanda silently thanked the Lord for the cold. It was bad enough being soggy and chilled without adding the headache of Sarah's tone-less singing. Soon would come the blessedness of sleep, when they would be less aware of how miserable they were. Heaven only knew how long the rain would last. It had to stop sometime. It had to.

6

"Steaming! We're steaming!"

"What?" Amanda opened her eyes, momentarily blinded by bright sunshine. How had they slept so late?

"Look at everything, Mandy," Sarah insisted.

With a yawn and a stretch, Amanda lifted the drenched tarp and sat up. Fragile wisps of mist floated upward in the confining interior of the wagon bed from the scattered tarpaulins and blankets. Rising, she untied the drawstring and leaned out.

The sodden earth sparkled in newly washed glory. Beside them, the rushing stream and a thousand puddles reflected the last puffs of cloud and the blue sky. And Sarah was right. The whole wagon was steaming in the warmth of the brilliant sun. So were the hobbled mules, unharmed and grazing contentedly nearby.

"See if any of that last wood you gathered is still dry," Amanda said. "We'll have hot tea to go with our breakfast. While the water heats, we'll open the sides and set things out to dry."

Sarah stripped down to her drawers and chemise, then rooted through the piles of damp supplies to find the wood she'd wrapped in blankets. "It's not wet at all, Sissy."

Within an hour, the bushes in the surrounding area sported a colorful array of blankets, linens, and articles of clothing, and the soft spring breeze wafted over them while the girls sipped mugs of tea. The temperature warmed considerably, inching higher and higher, the opposite extreme from the previous day.

Alas, the soggy rutted road ahead looked less than hopeful. The ground remained spongy to the foot, much too soft for travel. Amanda knew they'd be stuck here for at least a couple days, but if nothing else, they'd have ample time to sew.

In the middle of the third lazy afternoon, Sarah laid aside the sunbonnet she'd finished and stretched a kink out of her spine with a sigh. "Know what I'd love right now?"

"What?" Amanda recognized that particular spark in her sister's eyes.

"I would absolutely adore a bath."

"You're kidding, right?"

"Not at all. I'm dying to wash my hair."

"But the stream is still swift and muddy from the rain."

"I know, but we can stay near the edge, can't we? And we can rinse off with rainwater from the barrel. Wouldn't you just love to be clean again—all of you, instead of just washing up?"

"That water was freezing cold when we did our clothes. And besides, we're out in the open."

"So? We haven't seen a living soul since we crossed the river on the ferry. And anyway, we can leave our drawers on."

Amanda searched all around and beyond, as far as she could see. There truly wasn't anyone in sight. For all intent and purpose, they were the only two people in this part of the world. And she had to admit, she did feel grubby. What harm would there be in taking a quick dip, so long as they stayed in shallow water? "Well, I suppose we could try it."

"Oh, good!" Sarah all but tore out of her shirtwaist and skirt and undid her hair ribbon. Grabbing a cake of rose-scented soap and a towel, she dashed, shrieking, into the rushing water.

Amanda, not far behind, gasped when she stepped into the frigid flow. This was going to be the quickest bath in history. But once she was completely wet, the water didn't seem quite so cold, and the sunshine blazing down on them felt incredibly warm. A sudden splash drenched her.

Sarah giggled.

Turning, Amanda met her sister's playful grin. "So that's how it's going to be, eh?" Leaning down, she skimmed the surface of the water with her palm, directing an arc of water at the younger girl. It cascaded down her face, and over her shoulders.

"Enough, enough! I'm sorry!" Hand upraised in a gesture of defeat, Sarah acquiesced and began wetting her hair.

Amanda followed suit. But seeing her sister bent over at the waist with her behind in the air as she rinsed her long hair was too much to resist.

A little shove, and in Sarah went, headfirst. She came up sputtering, ready to reciprocate.

Instead, she froze, eyes wide.

Amanda whirled.

In the distance, a small band of Indian braves on ponies rode straight for them.

Her mouth went dry. "Back to the wagon! Hurry!" Though what security the two of them would find there, she could only question.

After they clambered up into the back, they seized blankets and wrapped themselves up, then perched fearfully on the seat.

Any remaining doubts Amanda may have had regarding the lunacy of this westward venture now vanished. Everyone knew the sad fate that had met Narcissa Whitman and her doctor husband Marcus last November. Missionaries to the Cayuse Indians of the Far Northwest, they had been brutally massacred in their mission home by the very tribe with whom they had labored faithfully for several years.

Now Amanda's dreadful realization that she and her younger sister would soon join Ma and Pa in the hereafter dropped with a thud. She prayed the end would be swift, if not merciful. *Please, Lord, help us to be brave.*

Sarah Jane's expression was no less fearful, but she hiked her chin. "Well, if I'm about to die, I at least want to go happy." She darted into the wagon bed and returned with her guitar.

Mouth agape, Amanda could not respond.

The Indians were almost upon them now. Their skulls were shaved but for a thick strip of dark hair running from front to back that was roached into an upstanding comb. Naked, except for aprons worn about their loins, they also sported vermillion face paint applied in lurid rings about their eyes.

As if completely oblivious to the approaching uninvited audience, Sarah Jane strummed a few chords of introduction, then sang at the top of her lungs:

"Oh, don't you remember sweet Betsy from Pike,
Who crossed the wide prairies with her lover Ike,
With two yoke of cattle and one spotted hog,
A tall shanghai rooster, and an old yaller dog?"

"Sing too-ral-i, oo-ral-i, oo-ral-i-ay,
Sing too-ral-i, oo-ral-i, oo-ral-i-ay."

"They swam the wide rivers and crossed the tall peaks,
And camped on the prairie for weeks upon weeks . . ."

The young braves reined in their pinto ponies and sat motionless atop them, staring dumbfounded as Sarah completely destroyed the tune of the comical song.

Amanda didn't know whether to laugh or cry as her sister continued belting out verse upon endless verse:

"They soon reached the desert, where Betsy gave out,
And down in the sand she lay rolling about;
While he in great terror looked on in surprise,
Saying, Betsy, get up, you'll get sand in your eyes."

"Sing too-ral-i, oo-ral-i, oo-ral-i-ay,
Sing too-ral-i, oo-ral-i, oo-ral-i-ay."

Still moving nothing but their dark eyes, the Indians passed curiously astonished looks among themselves. They maintained a safe distance as Sarah launched into another four stanzas.

". . . Long Ike and sweet Betsy got married of course,
But Ike, getting jealous, obtained a divorce;

And Betsy, well satisfied, said with a shout,
Good-bye, you big lummox, I'm glad you backed out."

"Sing too-ral-i, oo-ral-i, oo-ral-i-ay . . ."

Amanda, not entirely recognizing some of the ridiculous lyrics, wondered inanely if her younger sibling had penned some of them herself. She was almost relieved when the final phrase ended. Moments of heavy silence ensued. Even the Indian ponies stood as if frozen, except for the occasional flick of a tail.

Amanda had to force herself to replenish her lungs.

"I suppose I should sing a hymn, too, as my last song." Sarah Jane drew a fortifying breath:

"I'm just a poor wayfaring stranger,
While trav'ling through this world of woe,
Yet there's no sickness, toil or danger
In that bright world to which I go."

"I'm going home to see my father,
I'm going there no more to roam,
I'm only going over Jordan,
I'm only going over home."

"I know dark clouds will gather 'round me,
I know my way is rough and steep.
Yet beauteous fields lie just before me,
Where God's redeemed their vigils keep . . ."

As the last note of the fifth stanza died away, Sarah moistened her lips and stood the guitar in the wagon bed, then bravely raised her chin.

Amanda herself had yet to move. She could feel her heart throbbing, her pulse pounding in her ears. Now, awaiting her own most certain demise, she could only wonder what form of torture the two of them faced. How sad that someone so young and pretty as Sarah would meet such a tragic fate, would never find the dashing husband she dreamed of most of her life. If only Amanda could wake up and find this whole foolish idea had been only a dream. Independence could probably have used some good seamstresses . . . there were far worse places for the two of them to live.

After an eternal moment, the brave in the center gave an almost imperceptible signal, and en masse, the band turned their mounts and galloped away. Without even looking back, they crested the top of a near rise and vanished from sight. "D-do you think they'll come back, Mandy?" Sarah asked in a small voice.

Amanda, as befuddled as her sister, merely shrugged.

A ridiculous phrase of off-key singing burst from behind the hill. Then a howl of laughter.

Sarah loosened her soggy blanket and stood. "Humph. They don't even know good music when they hear it!"

At this, Amanda, too, exploded into a giggle, then laughed hysterically until tears coursed down her cheeks. Though her sister joined halfheartedly, it was easy to see she didn't quite see the humor of the moment. Amanda suddenly realized the Indians had thought her sibling was possessed by some strange spirit . . . one they were hesitant to anger. It made her laugh all the harder.

Finally regaining control of her shattered nerves, she turned to Sarah. "Well, Sissy, we can thank the Good Lord for His protection this day. We could easily have made our entrance through the pearly gates."

Sarah paused in the process of stripping off her wet underthings. "I suppose you're right. God definitely is looking after us." But she leaned out, peering in the direction the Indians had taken, just to be sure.

7

*H*ow's it look up ahead?" Seth asked, riding alongside Red's chestnut gelding in the late afternoon.

"Well, coulda been worse." His friend's copper mustache spread with his grin. "I'd say we've wasted time aplenty. Cy an' T. J. scouted far as the river, an' say the Big Blue's still pretty high from the rain. Trail's hardening up, though. Reckon the worst of the storm passed behind us."

Seth nodded. "Yep, but we have other things to consider, pal. While I was collecting some strays, a bit ago, I spotted a handful of Kanza braves in the distance. Before they get ideas about helping themselves to the livestock, we need to double the guards till we move out of here tomorrow. Pass the word."

"Right, boss."

With a dry smile at his partner's lighthearted formality, Seth waved and headed back toward the rear of the wagon train. The heavy rainfall had necessitated a few precious days' wait for the ground to firm up again, but as Red declared, things could have been worse. Nevertheless, it was the Big Blue they had to worry about most. Always a crotchety river even at the best of times, when it was flowing high, the current was incredibly strong and swift.

Skirting a cluster of cows grazing directly in his path, Seth navigated around them and rode to the crest of the knoll. He took out his spyglass and peered toward the rise where he'd glimpsed the Indians. There was no sign of them at the moment, but no telling where they'd gotten to. He moved the glass and searched what he could see of the undulating landscape.

Just as he was about to inhale a breath of relief, the telescope picked up some movement. He blinked and looked again. No. It couldn't be. He'd counted all the wagons on his way to talk to Red. How could there be a straggler? And several miles behind them, yet! He reined in for a better view.

His heart sank at the sight of two very feminine forms in skirts and bonnets fussing about the winding, silvery ribbon that made up a narrow section of the stream. He had a very strong inclination exactly who'd be fool enough to travel alone in this sometimes-hostile country. "Of all the harebrained—"

Seth took off his hat and rubbed his forehead on his sleeve before replacing it. Another look confirmed his worst fears, and angrily he slumped back into the saddle. It would serve that empty-headed female right if he simply let her and her sister keep on the way they were until they came face to face with that cantankerous river—see what they'd do about crossing those treacherous waters without a ferry. They'd discover soon enough how idiotic they were to set out by themselves. If they had a lick of sense they'd turn around now and return to Independence. Maybe the next train out would take them under supervision, but he wanted nothing to do with them.

Red would never believe this. In fact, Seth had half a mind not to even mention the Shelby sisters to his partner. The last thing the company needed was to be slowed down by two girls who didn't have the sense the Almighty gave a fencepost.

But even as he enumerated in his mind the reasons why he should continue on as if he hadn't seen them, the possibility that those wandering Indian braves might find them easy pickings cut across his resolve. A full train wasn't likely to be attacked, but a single wagon out in the open with two vulnerable young women aboard might be another story entirely. No telling what gruesome fate would befall the Shelby girls then.

Seth realized that the next train that happened along would blame him for whatever misfortune befell the pair and spread the word that he couldn't look out for folks under his care. He'd never lost a family to Indians yet. Cholera and dysentery, yes, accidents and drownings. But even when the odd wagon rumbled apart on the rough trail, he'd always managed to find folks willing to lend a hand to the unfortunates. Emulating his idol, the famous trail guide Thomas Fitzpatrick, Seth was trying to earn a reputation for taking people all the way to their destination—and he wasn't about to let all his hard work be ruined by the likes of Amanda Shelby.

That decided, he ground his teeth and nudged his dapple-gray mount, Sagebrush, into a canter. He'd try one more lecture first, and in the unlikely event Miss Shelby still wouldn't take his advice, he'd figure out what to do then.

❧

Amanda washed up the dishes from their early supper of the usual beans and biscuits while Sarah retired to the wagon to record the events of the day in her journal. Tomorrow they would leave this restful campsite. Ahead, miles of rolling prairie in all its green glory stretched to the sky.

This had been their most pleasant stay so far, and restful, thanks to the torrential rain that had brought the journey to a halt. Of course, there had been the encounter with those half-naked Indian braves. Amanda would thank the Lord till her dying day that He'd kept them from harm. She still had qualms regarding further unknown dangers. But as long as the land remained so open, with its gently rolling hills and long prairie grasses, she and Sarah would fare well enough Amanda couldn't help wondering, though, what lay beyond the horizon.

Standing to shake the excess water off the plates, she lifted her gaze far away to the west, then frowned. It had to be her imagination, the lone rider like a speck of black against the ocean of undulating green. And coming this way! A tingle of alarm skittered up her spine. Is this what they'd be facing every livelong day of this journey? Strange men everywhere they turned? Tomorrow when they stopped for their noon meal, she would get out Pa's rifle and figure out how to use it. Amanda had seen him load and fire it often enough. Surely it couldn't be so hard to master. After all, with Sarah being as fetching and winsome as she was, there might be dozens of occasions when some overly interested man might need to be convinced he should be on his way.

That decided, she sloshed the heavy frying pan in the stream and then wiped it dry while she prayed again for protection. *What time I am afraid, I will trust in Thee.* The precious promise her parents had often quoted drifted to mind, bringing with it the assurance that God was still in control. An unexplainable calm began to soothe her jangled nerves. The cookery and utensils had been stowed away and the camp-fire doused by the time the rider was near enough for the horse's hoofbeats to be heard. The man looked vaguely familiar, which struck Amanda as curious, since they had gotten to know only a few people during their stay at the hotel. But when he pushed back the brim of his dark hat, revealing his long-faced scowl, her heart sank. The wagon master! For an instant she entertained thoughts of trying to hide, but it was too late. She inhaled a deep breath and assumed an air of indifference as he rode up.

"What do you think you are doing?" he demanded.

Amanda, sitting on a crate, placed the apron she'd been stitching on her lap and looked up. "And good day to you, Mr. Holloway," she returned sarcastically.

"You heard me." The wagon master's brown eyes sizzled with fury as he glared at her from atop his mount, his granite expression hard and rigid as his posture.

"Why, I believe it's quite evident to anyone who can see."

"Yes, well, this has gone far enough. Turn this rig around tomorrow. Won't take you any longer to get back to town than it did to get this far."

Amanda smiled thinly. "Thank you. That's quite the brilliant deduction." She rose casually and started toward the wagon to put her sewing away.

Leather creaked as he shifted position in the saddle. "So you do have some sense after all."

"I beg your pardon?" She paused and turned, arching her brows.

"You're finally giving up on this brainless notion of yours to head west."

Brainless! Amanda felt growing rage at the crass remark. Only her good breeding enabled her to restrain her tongue as she stared without blinking at the domineering, cantankerous man. "Not at all. My sister and I are getting along just fine . . . not that it's any concern of yours, I might add."

"Is everything all right, Sissy?" Sarah Jane called, leaning to peer from the confines of the wagon.

"Perfectly. Mr. Holloway came to wish us well. And now he's leaving."

"In a dog's age I am," he bellowed. "Now, see here—"

"Really, sir, whatever your purpose in forsaking your own duties to come here, you've said your piece. However, it does not change anything. So I would like you to . . . how did you put it? *'Go back where you came from,'* wasn't it?"

A muscle worked in his jaw. He dismounted and reached to grab Amanda's arm, but she shied away. He rolled his eyes. "Look, Miss Shelby," he began, his patronizing tone an obvious ploy to get her to listen. "I know I sounded a mite blunt when I first rode in. I apologize. It was no way to speak to a lady. But I can't seem to get through to you what you need to hear."

"Oh? And what might that be?" She crossed her arms in supreme disinterest.

He filled his lungs and let the breath out all at once. When he spoke, his voice was much kinder, almost pleasant. "I must admit, I was surprised when I looked back and saw you coming. I wouldn't have thought you'd make it this far."

Amanda, with an inward smile of satisfaction, had to remind herself not to gloat.

"But I have to tell you," he went on, his voice taking on a more ominous quality. "This is the easy part. When folks start out for Oregon they think the whole trail's gonna be like this. But it's not. Far from it. There's hardship coming up. Real hardship. First off, there's a mighty river just ahead. It's running high and fast now from that rain, and there's no ferry to make the crossing easy. We'll have to float every wagon over it and hope none of them gets swept away in the current. After that will come the mountains. There'll be places so steep we'll have to haul the wagons up one at a time with ropes and chains, then let them down on the other side. Course, a whole passel of them'll rattle apart long before they ever make it that far. And don't forget the watering holes we'll come to that aren't fit to drink. Folks and animals weak with thirst will drink anyway. And every one of them will get sick and die."

Amanda tapped her foot impatiently. Anything to keep from revealing that his dire predictions were beginning to get through to her.

"And that doesn't even take Indians into consideration," he continued. "Or the rattlesnakes, the cholera, and even the weather. You may think you've seen wind and lightning since that little storm we just had. But that was a spring shower compared to what we'll face once we hit the high country. We could get pounded with hail. It could even snow on us before we're through the passes, and the lot of us could freeze to death. Think about it. You've got a younger sister to be responsible for. Is that how you want her to end up?"

Amanda swallowed hard. What he was telling her was the complete opposite of what Pa had read in the guidebook he'd bought. Yet something in the wagon master's face seemed honest. Trustworthy. He'd been over this route before, and he should know more than the books reported. But still—"Well, the Lord has been with Sarah and me up till now, and the Bible says He'll take care of His own always," she reasoned.

Mr. Holloway's demeanor hardened. "I'd say that's a mite presumptuous, myself. Expecting Almighty God to come to your rescue when you don't use the sense He gave you."

Amanda broke eye contact and lowered her gaze to the gritty ground. She took a few steps away, thinking over his words. If she hadn't been enduring the railings of her own conscience along that same line, she'd have been livid. She could not deny that the Lord had already spared them from impending doom twice—and they'd barely begun the journey. Perhaps this was the last chance He was giving them to turn around.

But to what? an inner voice harped.

She stopped and turned. "I want to thank you for coming, Mr. Holloway. I know you mean well. But I'm afraid Sarah and I have to keep going west. We don't have anyplace else to go. If we die along the way, then it's God's will. But we're still going to try."

He slowly shook his head.

"We don't expect you to understand or to feel concern over us. You gave Pa's money back, and we don't have the right to count on you to look after us. We'll just keep on by ourselves. We'll be all right. Now, I'm sure your duties are calling you back to the train. I wish you good day."

He didn't respond for several moments, just stared. Then his expression flattened, along with his tone. "Well, now, that's where we differ. About the last thing I can do is leave the two of you here alone." He hesitated again, a look of resignation settling over his sun-bronzed features. "The train will camp by Alcove Spring tonight so we can start getting everyone across the Big Blue tomorrow. Pack up in the morning and come join up. Travel with the company."

"But—"

"Do it." Without further comment, he swung up into his saddle and galloped away.

Amanda wanted more than anything to ignore Seth Holloway. But for some unexplainable reason, she could not will herself to do so. Nor could she restrain her eyes from gazing after him.

8

*H*e's quite handsome, don't you think?" Sarah asked, emerging from the wagon to lounge on the seat, her journal in hand. "In an outdoors sort of way, I mean."

"Hm?" Dragging her gaze from the departing horseman, Amanda turned.

"The wagon master. He's handsome, I said. Not at all the way I pictured him from things you told me."

Amanda barely suppressed a smirk.

"Well, not that he appeals to me, of course," Sarah amended. "I fully intend to find someone much more refined, myself. But in general, Mr. Holloway seems to have a certain . . . charm."

Charm! Amanda thought incredulously. *That's the last attribute I'd assign to Seth Holloway.* "I didn't pay him that much mind," she finally said.

Sarah gave a dreamy sigh. "The man I'm looking for must be head and shoulders taller than anyone I've ever met, and stronger, with gorgeous thick hair, expressive eyes and lips, and a voice that sings across the strings of my heart. And he'll be rich, of course. I refuse to settle for less."

The raspy voice alone would eliminate Mr. Holloway, Amanda decided, but didn't bother answering. After all, his eyes were too dark to be very expressive anyway, and his lips had yet to reflect anything but his anger and irritation. She wondered absently if he ever bothered to smile.

"Are we going to do what he asked?"

"You mean *ordered,* don't you?"

"Well, are we?"

220

Amanda met her sister's questioning face as Mr. Holloway's blunt accusation about presuming upon God came to mind. Loath as she was to admit it, his remark did have merit. "Well, at—at first I didn't plan to," she hedged, "but already in the few days we've been on the trail, God has had to rescue us twice. We really shouldn't expect Him to come to our aid every time we encounter any sort of peril."

Sarah did not respond.

"The fact is," Amanda went on, "the wagon master is right. Sooner or later we're going to face some serious difficulties we won't be able to handle on our own. With the other emigrants there'd be someone who could help us. Folks look out for each other. I'm afraid if we don't join the train it could be to our folly."

"I see what you mean." Sarah glanced westward momentarily, in the direction their visitor had taken. Then she sat, opened her diary and began writing once more, a fanciful smile curving her lips.

Amanda saw that Seth Holloway was no longer within sight. Reaching into the wagon, she retrieved her sewing and returned to the crate she'd occupied earlier. If the man had not appeared at their campsite out of the blue, she'd never have guessed the other wagons were within such close proximity. They, too, must have had to wait out the horrific rain. Oh, well, she concluded, knotting the last stitches in the apron she'd been making, if she and Sarah were actually hoping to meet up with them in the near future, it would be wise to turn in soon so they could get an early start. She bit off the remaining thread. After making swift work of attending to all the evening chores, Amanda hurried to the wagon, where she discovered Sarah already asleep in bed. She shed her cotton dress and tugged on her night shift, then took her place beside the younger girl on the hard mattress. But her mind remained far too active to relinquish consciousness easily. In the stillness broken only by the uneven cadence of the night creatures, she analyzed Mr. Holloway's unexpected visit.

Something about the man disturbed her in a way she had never experienced before. It wasn't so much his domineering manner, or even his patronizing attitude toward her and her sister—those she could understand. But when he'd realized they were determined to make the trip with or without the benefit of company, he'd mellowed.

For a few seconds he'd even seemed . . . kind. And she preferred him the other way. Sarah was right. Seth Holloway did possess a certain rugged, outdoors look that some might consider handsome. But aware that the man had proclaimed her brainless and foolhardy, Amanda saw no reason to concern herself with such inane fantasies as trying to convince him otherwise. With a sigh, she fluffed her pillow and settled down on its plumpness.

⁓

Seth, on the last watch of the night, poured the dregs of the coffee into his mug, then drank it slowly as he walked the outside perimeter of the circled wagons. Spying Red keeping a lookout on the westward side, he joined him. "All's quiet, eh?"

His friend nodded. "Ain't seen hide nor hair of them Injuns or any other creatures lurkin' about."

"Me neither." Seth tossed the dregs from the mug into the bushes. He would have preferred not to have had an encounter with the Shelbys, much less have to talk about it, but it needed to be aired. His partner would also be affected by their joining up with the train. He cleared his throat. "There's something I might as well tell you."

Red looked up, his brow furrowed. "You happened on some other trouble?"

Seth shrugged. "Not exactly. Well, maybe. I, uh, spotted the Shelby sisters trailing us some ways back."

"What?" His partner's jaw went slack, his expression tinged with a combination of humor and disbelief.

"You got it. Fool females took it upon themselves to set out after us. I tried to persuade them to turn around while they still could, but it was no good. Trying to get through to that older one's like butting up against a stone wall." He grimaced and shook his head. "Stubbornest gal I ever did come across."

"Hm. Worse than that sister-in-law of yours is, eh? The one who soured you on marriage, I mean."

Seth didn't dignify the comment with anything but a glower. The mere thought of his younger brother being linked up with that conniving, sharp-tongued Eliza always made him angry. Red snickered, then rubbed his jaw in thought. "Well, if they made it this far on their own, I s'pose they have as much a shot at goin' west as anybody else."

"Maybe. At least on the easy end of things," Seth grated. "Figure if we're gonna end up playing nursemaid, we might as well have them within reach. I told them to join up with us this evening. Who knows, they might get their fill when they stare the Big Blue in the face."

Neither spoke for several seconds.

"Guess I'll head on back to my end," Seth said with resignation. "Folks'll soon be up and cooking breakfast before those cockamamie Sunday services they insist on having."

"Strange comment, if you don't mind me sayin' so—'specially comin' from the grandson of a circuit-ridin' preacher."

Seth branded him with a glare. "See you later."

"Sure. Could be an interestin' day."

Ignoring his partner's chuckle, Seth strode away.

❧

When Amanda came within sight of the train of emigrants, the next evening, the first thing she noticed was the warm glow of lantern light that crowned the circle of wagons like a halo. It bolstered her spirits, as did the happy music drifting from the encampment from fiddles and harmonicas. Drawing nearer, Amanda heard soft laughter and the sound of children and barking dogs.

"I think I'm going to like being with the others," Sarah said happily.

Before Amanda could answer, her eyes locked on to Seth Holloway's where he leaned against the nearest rig with his hands in his pockets as if waiting for the two of them to arrive.

His expression unreadable, he shoved his hands into his pockets and walked toward them. "Pull up over there," he instructed with a slight jerk of his head.

Amanda nodded, guiding the team to an empty space in the formation. As she did so, a threesome of men approached. "Evenin', ladies," a solid-chested older man said, thumbing his hat. "Name's

Randolph. Nelson Randolph. This here's Ben Martin and Zeke Sparks," he said, tipping his head to the left and right to indicate a rawboned man in his early thirties and a narrow-faced one with a long nose and prominent ears. "We'll help get you into place."

"Why, thank you." Amanda accepted his proffered hand as she climbed down. "I'm Amanda Shelby."

"And I'm Sarah, her sister."

"Glad to make your acquaintance," Mr. Randolph said, reaching to help Sarah also. "We'll be neighbors of yours along the way, so you'll soon get to know us an' some of the others in this mob."

"An' which ones ya should keep an eye out for," Ben Martin said with a good-natured wink. He nudged his lanky pal in the ribs.

In a matter of moments the mules had been unhitched and the wagon rolled into the open slot, its tongue beneath the back of the wagon ahead of it.

"When you gals get settled in," Mr. Randolph said, "make yourselves to home. Mosey in by the big fire and introduce yourselves, if you want to. Folks generally do most of their visitin' in camp. Or just sit an' listen to the music, if you druther. With it bein' Sunday, folks seem to like hymns best."

Amanda smiled. "We'll do that. Thanks for your help."

As the men left, she glanced around self-consciously at the several curious but friendly faces turned their way and returned a few smiles. No one was familiar, but then Amanda hadn't actually met more than one or two emigrants back in Independence before Pa had taken sick. The only person to whom she'd spoken was Mr. Holloway, and he was nowhere to be seen. "Well," she said turning to Sarah, "we're here."

"Yes." The younger girl's gaze swept across the open circle, where a few couples were blending their voices in song. Clusters of children frolicked everywhere.

Amanda recognized her sister's peculiar smile and its accompanying blush immediately. Habitually checking to see which young man in particular had caught Sarah's eye, she noticed a gangly youth who extracted himself from a group of others and sauntered toward them.

"Evening, ladies," he said, grinning broadly on his approach. He doffed his hat in an elaborate gesture, revealing curly brown hair, then plunked it back on, blue eyes sparkling as his attention settled on Sarah. "I'm Alvin Rivers. Delighted to welcome you to camp."

Amanda noted the young man's clothing seemed of finer cut and quality than that of the men they'd met earlier.

"Why, thank you, Mr. Rivers," Sarah gushed. "My name is Sarah Shelby, and this is my older sister, Amanda."

Amanda cringed.

Alvin gave her a respectful nod, then switched back to Sarah again. "Anything I might do to help you get settled in for the night? Check your wheels? Grease the hubs?"

"Grease the hubs?" the younger girl echoed in puzzlement.

"Right. We do it most every night, miss. With the bucket of grease hanging back by the axle."

Both girls followed his gesture.

Amanda hadn't missed his surprise at Sarah's question. She had a vague recollection of Pa mentioning something about that chore, but she'd neglected to do anything about it up until now. How fortunate that Mr. Holloway wasn't around to witness her stupidity. "Thank you, Mr. Rivers," she said. "Sarah and I would be most grateful to have you tend to greasing the hubs this evening." *While I watch to see how it's done!*

"Glad to, miss." He tipped his hat and started toward the back of the wagon, with them in his wake. "Where do you two hail from?" he asked casually over his shoulder.

"Pennsylvania," Sarah answered. "Tunkhannock. And you?"

"Baltimore, Maryland. My aunt and uncle are looking to buy some prime land in the Oregon Territory where there's room to spread out. Too many people were bottled up in the little valley we lived in back east." He took down the grease bucket and set to work.

"Excuse me, miss," Amanda heard someone say. She turned to see a pleasant-faced grandmotherly woman smiling at her, accenting deep laugh creases on either side of her smile. "Since it's late, and all, I thought you and your sister might like some stew. We've finished up,

225

but there's plenty left in the pot. Name's Minnie Randolph. Husband and me are three wagons down." She pointed in that direction.

"Why, thank you, Mrs. Randolph. You're most kind. I'm Amanda, and she's Sarah. Shelby."

"Glad to know you. When we heard you two were coming, I figured you'd be tired by the time you got here. And don't worry about a thing, you hear? A lot of folks're gonna be keeping an eye out for you gals on this trip. We didn't get to know your pa, but he seemed a decent sort the little time we saw him readyin' for the journey. Downright shame he had to pass on so suddenlike." Obviously noting the distress the reminder had caused, she quickly cleared her throat. "You just come right on down as soon as you're ready."

Amanda nodded her thanks. She turned back to Sarah, catching the end of something Alvin Rivers was saying as he finished the last wheel.

". . . so you wouldn't mind if I come by of an evening and show you around?" His voice cracked on the last word.

"That would be very nice," Sarah answered.

And once all the other eligible young men in the group catch a glimpse of my fair and lissome sister, you'll have to stand in line, Amanda couldn't help thinking.

"Sarah," she called. "We've been offered some supper. Let's go wash up."

Her sister gave a nod of assent, then turned to Alvin. "Thanks for helping out with the wagon. Perhaps I'll see you tomorrow."

"Yes, miss," he said, hanging the bucket back on its hook. He took a large kerchief from a back pocket and wiped his hands. "Tomorrow." The grin he flashed at her broadened to include Amanda. "Miss Shelby."

Amanda nodded. She bit back a giggle as he moved backward, almost stumbling over a rock in his path before he turned and strode away. Then, aware of someone else's scrutiny, she glanced curiously around. Part of her expected to find Seth Holloway's critical gaze fixed on her, ready to find fault, but it wasn't the wagon master after all.

Two wagons ahead, a tall, somber man stared unabashedly. He held a fussing little girl in his arms. Another small child, a boy a year or so older, clung to his knees. He patted the towhead and said something Amanda couldn't hear, then bent and scooped him up. He placed the two tots inside his wagon and climbed in after them.

"I'm ready," Sarah Jane said, coming to her side.

"Hm? Oh. I'll be just a minute." Accepting the dampened cloth her sister held out, Amanda scrubbed her own face and hands, then brushed her hair and retied the ribbon. "Best we not keep Mrs. Randolph waiting." Shaking some trail dirt from the hem of her skirt, she fluffed it out again, and the two went to join the kind older woman.

After enduring even those few days of their own inadequate cooking, their neighbor's hearty stew tasted like a feast fit for royalty. Amanda relished every drop, mopping the last speck from her bowl with the light biscuits, even as steady, sad crying carried from the next wagon. It caught at her heart.

"Would you like more?" the gray-haired woman asked, interrupting Amanda's musings.

"Oh, no, we've had plenty, thank you." Amanda placed a hand on the older woman's forearm. "It was truly delicious."

"I'm afraid we don't share your gift for cooking," Sarah confessed. "All I've managed so far is some pretty ordinary beans with biscuits or cornbread."

"Well, cookin's more skill than gift, I'd say. There'll be plenty of time on this trip for both of you to pick up some of the basics of makin' meals on the trail. I'd be more'n happy to pass on what I know at some of the noonings and suppertimes."

"Why, that's very kind of you." Amanda fought sudden and unexpected tears at the woman's generosity. Up until this past sad year, she hadn't been one given to displaying her emotions, and she sincerely hoped this was not becoming a habit. She must merely be overly tired. She smiled and got up. "We'll just wash up our dishes and bring them back." She nodded at Sarah, and the two hurried to the spring with the soiled things.

The beauty of Alcove Spring was not lost on either one. They gazed in rapt delight at the pure, cold water that gushed from a ledge of rocks and cascaded ten feet down into a basin. Quickly finished with their chore, they left the idyllic spot.

Mrs. Randolph graciously inclined her bonneted head on their return. "I know this has been a long day, so I won't keep you. Tomorrow I'll introduce you to some of the folks around. Meanwhile, don't waste time worryin' about anything. We'll all take real good care of you two."

A wave of reassurance washed over Amanda, and she couldn't help wondering if everyone in the train would be so kind and thoughtful. She lifted a hand in parting and took her leave. "Thanks again. Good evening."

Passing the next wagon, Amanda once more met the brooding eyes of the lanky man sitting inside as he cuddled his two forlorn children. She gave a polite nod and continued on. Tomorrow she'd ask Mrs. Randolph about those little ones.

9

At the wakeup signal the next morning, the girls expectantly threw on their clothes. From all around the camp, a curious assortment of whistles, snorts, shouts, and cracks of bull-whackers' whips filled the air as the company came to life. Women put coffee on to boil and started the bacon to sizzle over crackling fires, while the men went to gather their oxen or mules and hitch them up. Sleepy-eyed children yawned and stretched, then hustled to wash, dress, and tend to chores before the order came for the wagons to roll.

"Sure is a busy place," Sarah commented, measuring tea leaves into the tin coffeepot.

Amanda only nodded. "I'd best round up the mules while you see to that. We'll have to do like everyone else now." She stepped over the wagon tongue and hurried toward the animals.

Hardly had the company finished breakfast when the first outfit set off for the river. The girls stashed their things and boarded their schooner, waiting to take their place in line.

A movement on the edge of Amanda's vision brought a brief glimpse of Seth Holloway riding herd on the cattle. She did not allow her gaze to linger. Concentration was needed to maintain a proper distance between her mules and the wagon ahead.

"This is all so exciting," Sarah Jane gushed. "I never realized before how dead our camps were. All this organized bustle and activity . . ." Her words trailed off as she swiveled on the seat to look around the edge of the wagon.

"I liked the quiet," Amanda mused. Cutting a glance toward Sarah,

229

she found her too occupied in observing the surroundings to have heard. Amanda tightened her hold on the reins.

Soon enough, she glimpsed the belt of sycamores, oaks, and elms lining the banks of the awe-inspiring Big Blue, the sight and sound of which became more and more unnerving the nearer they got. She reined to a stop.

The long, slow process of crossing had already begun. A number of wagons dotted the opposite shore, and several more now inched across the swiftly flowing water at an upstream angle. Amanda noticed that some outfits drove right into the Blue, while others, at the river's edge, had men grunting and straining to remove the wheels so the beds could be elevated on wooden blocks. Still others were being hitched to double teams. Sarah jumped down without a word and walked ahead, where a handful of women stood watching the men at work.

Amanda's gaze returned to the brave souls traversing the roiling water, and her heartbeat increased. She tried to study the way the drivers retained control against the force of the current, knowing soon enough she would face that same challenge.

Sounds came from farther downstream, from bawling and balking cattle whose bobbing heads kept time with their sporadic movements. Several swung in wide-eyed frenzy to return to the riverbank, and a few of them lost their footing, only to be swept away by the rushing water. Amanda held her breath as outriders ignored those and quickly set to persuading the rest to continue on. She easily picked out Seth Holloway. With the determined set of his jaw and distinctive rigid posture, he stood out from the others. Watching him, she couldn't help but admire his mettle and strength.

"You'll be next, miss."

The low voice startled Amanda. She swallowed and obeyed the signal to pull up to the edge of the water. Sarah Jane climbed to the seat and clutched the edges, her knuckles white, as their schooner, somewhat lighter in weight than the more cumbersome Conestoga wagons, was checked over for the crossing.

Mr. Randolph stepped near, astutely reading the apprehension Amanda knew must be evident in her expression. "Don't worry, little gal. Just keep a firm hold on your animals. They're strong swimmers, an' I'll be right behind you, keepin' an eye out." With a grin of encouragement, he turned and strode to his own rig, parked off to one side so she could precede him.

Amanda tried to smile, but failed miserably as the men coaxed the skittish mules down the slippery bank and into the dark current that whooshed by unimpeded as it swirled over the animals' shoulders. They hee-hawed in protest, but began their unhappy swim.

The wagon bed rocked fore and aft, jouncing uncertainly on the choppy waves, and cold wetness splashed over the wooden sides to slosh about Amanda's feet. She couldn't have spoken if her life depended on it, but sent a frantic prayer aloft and held on for dear life.

The churning water surrounding them now seemed wide as an ocean. Hoping her own inexperience would not hinder the mules from following the rig ahead at a similar angle, Amanda clutched the reins, watching anxiously as the animals labored toward the opposite shore. Sarah, huddled beside her, kept her eyes closed the whole time. Amanda only hoped her sister was adding fervent prayers to her own.

An eternity later, forelegs and hind legs gained footing on the other bank, where men armed with strong ropes and other teams lent a hand and ushered the mules up to dry ground. It took all Amanda's stamina not to collapse in relief.

Moments later, the Randolph wagon followed and pulled alongside. A grin of satisfaction spread across the lined face of the older man, but his wife's was devoid of color. "Land sakes," she murmured. "Thank the good Lord we made that one!"

❧

As soon as Amanda had parked the wagon out of the way of the last remaining rigs and got down to unhitch the team, Sarah Jane climbed into the back and settled down with her journal:

Dear Diary,
*   I cannot even describe how good it feels to have come to the end of this busiest and most frightening day! Poor Mandy shook*

like a leaf when we had finally made it across the Big Blue—a curious name for a river flowing with such brown water! But when word reached us to make camp, both of us could have jumped for joy. Everyone else seemed grateful, too, since so many hours of daylight had been given to the effort of getting the entire assemblage to the westward side.

Now it is oddly peaceful. The animals graze contentedly on the shining grass, while the setting sun haloes the slim trees with a border of hazy gold. Most of the songbirds whose sweet trills lighten our journey have returned to their nests, and the twilight air is filled with the pungent smell of wood smoke. I wonder what tomorrow will bring.

"That was some mighty fine driving you did earlier."

At the sound of Alvin Rivers' voice outside, Sarah quickly closed her book, set it down, and exited the wagon.

The young man's freckled face bore a grin from ear to ear at her sister, but his gaze immediately sought Sarah's. "If I hadn't had my own hands full helping out my aunt and uncle, I'd have gladly taken the reins for you."

Sarah saw Amanda smile her thanks.

"Mandy's almost as strong as Pa," she blurted.

Rolling her eyes, Amanda shook her head and began getting into the wagon. "I'll see if there's enough dry wood and kindling to make a cook fire."

"Anyway," Alvin went on, "I'll see that the hubs get a good greasing after all that water."

"Why, how very sweet." Sarah tied her apron ties more snugly about her waist, then got out the cook pot while Alvin tended to the wheels. She returned to the fire Amanda was laying.

They both looked up at the sound of footsteps.

"No use botherin' with viddles tonight," Mrs. Randolph said. "One of our neighbors shot a fine pair of rabbits while the rest of us were comin' over the water. I'm just about to fry one of them right now, and you gals are more than welcome to join us. There's wild honey for the biscuits, too, thanks to him."

Coming after the trying day, the invitation was more than welcome. "We'd be delighted," Sarah said.

"If we can contribute something," Amanda quickly added. "Potatoes and carrots, at least? And may we watch?"

The older woman's bonnet dipped with her nod. "Don't mind if you do. Come anytime."

"Thanks ever so much. We'll be there soon as we put these things back inside." Amanda flashed a grin of relief at Sarah.

❧

At the close of the delicious meal, the girls made fast work of washing the dishes. When Alvin and some of his friends came by to claim Sarah for a walk, Amanda chose to linger over a second cup of coffee with their kind neighbor.

Twilight was deepening, and the cacophony of music made by the night creatures began to fill the air . . . pleasant sounds against the intermittent crying coming from the next wagon. Mrs. Randolph heaved a sigh. "Poor little thing starts up every night about this time."

Amanda dragged her gaze back to her hostess. "Where's her mama?" she couldn't help asking.

"That's a sorry tale." The older woman paused in raising her cup to her lips and slowly wagged her head. "While we were camped at Independence, the child's mother—scarcely more than a kid herself—was cavorting with her brood out in one of the fields, gathering wildflowers, racing to see who could pick the most. Running toward a real purty bunch of flowers, she turned to look over her shoulder at the little ones, and tripped over a root. Hit her head on a jagged rock, she did. Prit' near bled to death on the spot."

"How awful."

"Somebody went and fetched the doc right quick, but by the time he came, it was too late. Little gal was so weak she never even come to. She was in the family way, too, which didn't help matters." Mrs. Randolph gazed toward the motherless children.

A raft of sad memories flooded Amanda's mind, and her eyes swam with tears. She quickly blinked them away.

"Had ourselves our first funeral before we even left town," the older woman continued. "And now those precious babes are without a mother's love." Then, as if suddenly recalling that hadn't been the only death among the families gathering to migrate west this spring, she blanched. Her hand flew to her throat. "Mercy me. I'm as sorry as sorry can be, child. You losin' your own pa, too. I should be more careful to think before I talk."

Amanda reached to pat her gnarled hand. "It's all right. Truly. I've accepted Pa's passing on. We both have. And at least we're grown. What must those poor darlings be going through?" Her curiosity once again drew her stare toward the sobbing child—and met the somber gaze of the widowed father.

Amanda quickly averted her eyes, focusing on the half-empty cup in her hands. She gulped some of the lukewarm coffee. "What are the children's names, Mrs. Randolph? Perhaps there's something Sarah or I could do to help."

She nodded thoughtfully. "You know, there just might be, now that you mention it. The little girl's Bethany, as I recall. The boy, now . . . Hm." Frowning, she folded her arms over her generous bosom and tapped an index finger against her mouth. "Thomas, maybe. No, Timothy. Goes by the nickname Tad."

"And the father?" Amanda prompted, aware of a rising flush at her boldness.

The older woman seemed not to notice. "Name's Jared Hill. Seems a decent sort, leastwise from what we've gotten to know of him since we been on the trail. He's a mite standoffish."

Jared Hill. It suited him, Amanda decided—or did from a distance. She had yet to see him close up. The important thing was that the poor man had his hands full, and anyone with a sense of Christian duty should be more than willing to help in whatever small way she could.

By the time Amanda finished her coffee and made her way back to her own wagon, Bethany's sobs had ceased. She surmised that the children had been tucked in for the night. Mr. Hill, however, remained outside, kneeling in the circle of firelight, checking a section of harness. He looked up as Amanda neared.

She felt it only polite to smile. "Good evening."

"Evening, miss." Putting the traces aside, he rose, straightening his long limbs to tower a head above her. The eyes beneath his sandy hair appeared dark in the dim glow, their color indistinct, but a pronounced downward turn at the outer corners gave evidence of his grief.

Amanda stopped. "I—I couldn't help hearing your little girl cry."

He shrugged in resignation.

"So sorry to hear of your loss." Taking a step forward, she reached out her hand. "I'm Amanda Shelby, your new neighbor."

"Hill," he replied, shaking her hand. "Jared Hill. I'll do my best to see Bethy doesn't disturb you anymore."

"No!" Amanda gasped. "Please don't think—" Flustered that he'd mistaken her remark as criticism, she started over. "I—I only wanted to offer help. My sister Sarah's especially good with children. If there's anything we can do, please don't hesitate to ask."

His fingers raked through the tousled strands of his hair. "Well, thanks. Don't see as I need help, though. Or pity. We'll get by." One side of his mouth turned upward in the barest hint of a smile, softening his narrow face.

Amanda nodded. "Oh. But—Well, I just wanted to offer, that's all. Good night." At his nod of dismissal, she walked briskly away trying not to feel utterly humiliated.

10

ou'd be surprised what an interesting life Alvin has led," Sarah Jane declared as the wagon rumbled onward the following morning, the harness jangling in time with the clopping of the mules. "His great passion is art. Last year his aunt and uncle took him to Europe to art museums in Spain, Italy, France, and England, just to view the work of the great masters. He even showed me some of his own drawings. He's got wonderful talent."

"Oh, really?"

"Um-hmm. He's working on a book of sketches of the various terrain and landmarks along the trail. He's planning to try to interest a publisher in putting together a project of that sort for other folks thinking of heading west. Someday Alvin hopes to become a real artist. Maybe paint portraits, or—"

Her sister's sigh indicated she was only half listening.

Sarah paused and turned her head, a ringlet falling forward on her shoulder with the movement. She flicked it back. "You're awfully quiet this morning. Something wrong?"

Staring at her for a few seconds, Amanda finally spoke. "It's that man and the two young children, in the wagon behind the Randolphs."

"What about them?"

"The mother died accidentally back in Independence. The kids—especially the daughter—have taken it real hard."

At the sad news, Sarah's mouth gaped in dismay. "How very tragic. That would account for the crying I've heard from time to time. How old are those little ones?" She peered ahead, in the direction of their wagon.

"The boy, Tad, looks to be about four. Bethany must be three, or nearly so."

"Maybe we could help out somehow."

Amanda gave a soft huff. "That's what I thought, too. Only their father as much as told me to mind my own business."

Recalling her own first experience in the valley of the shadow of death, Sarah could easily identify with other people's sorrow. "Well, I'm sure he must not have meant to put you off so rudely. He might just be hurting, too. Remember how we felt when Mama died?"

Her elder sibling momentarily appeared lost in the sad memory of their own wrenching loss. "We knew our lives would never be the same. Nor had we expected to stand before another open grave so soon," she added with a pang of near bitterness.

"Maybe I'll make a doll for the little girl and take it by. She needs to be around women."

"I think that's a splendid idea." Amanda visibly relaxed.

Sarah lifted her gaze to the countryside, making mental notes she would enter into her diary later. There were considerably fewer trees since they'd crossed the river, no forests filled with glorious red-budded maples, no thickly wooded groves like those in the East, which seemed like nap on earth's carpet. Now she saw only the occasional solitary tree standing alone to face the elements.

The grasses, too, were taller, growing to a height of six or eight feet in the moist areas. The land itself was more open, allowing the wagons to spread out, some of them even traveling side by side as they meandered westward along the Little Blue River, a calm glistening ribbon of satin accented by the floral beauty of spring. Most of the womenfolk and youngsters had taken to walking now, in deference to the hard, springless wagon seats. Sarah often walked with them herself, taking part in the cheerful chatting as they gathered wood or colorful bouquets of wildflowers to pass the miles.

"Does Alvin Rivers have any other family?" Amanda asked, reverting to the previous topic.

"Not since he was quite young. His relatives have been raising him. He's pretty happy, though. Apparently they have a lot of money."

Her sister quirked a brow at her.

"Well, Alvin can't help that," Sarah said, her prickles up. "It isn't as if he lords it over anyone. He's just had advantages a lot of other young people have never enjoyed. Anyway," she added, lifting her chin, "we were quite comfortable ourselves not too long ago, if you recall."

"True."

"So maybe you shouldn't judge someone you don't even know."

Amanda flushed. "Yes, Mother," she said wryly.

"Well, if I'm going to make little Bethany a new doll, I'd best get to work." Sarah Jane swung her legs over the seat and retreated into the back, where she began rooting through the sewing supplies.

❧

After a quiet supper of beans and fried mush, Amanda took the dirty dishes over to the river and knelt to wash them. The drowsy sultriness of the spring evening was crowned by the tranquil richness of a glorious sunset, which spread deepening violet shadows everywhere. She filled her lungs with the perfumes emitted by blue lupine and other flowers.

Splashing sounds from nearby ceased. Not twenty feet away, a man rose to his feet behind a curve in the riverbank that had concealed him from view. Stripped to the waist, he stood motionless for several seconds, his skin glistening like purest gold. When he pulled on his shirt, it clung to his muscular contours in a few enticingly damp places. Amanda caught herself staring.

So did he.

Her cheeks flamed.

Seth Holloway held her gaze, his expression altering not a whit as he fastened the last shirt button. He bent and retrieved his wide-brimmed hat, then nodded ever so slightly before plunking it on his wet head.

Amanda tried to quell the flush of heat in her face. Why hadn't she looked away, for pity's sake? She busied herself scrubbing the heavy iron frying pan in the flowing water with added vigor.

"Miss Shelby."

The sloshing water had covered the sound of his approaching footsteps. Amanda nearly lost her balance as she jerked her head to peer up at him. "Mr. Holloway . . ." She wondered what else to say, but needn't have been concerned. He was already striding away without a backward glance.

Thank heaven.

After returning to her rig, Amanda did her best to dismiss the mental picture of the wagon master from her mind. Had she been Sarah, she conjectured with a smile, she'd have flown right to her journal to pen flowery phrases of the magnificent vision Seth Holloway had made against the vibrant sky. But she wasn't Sarah . . . and anyway, a spinster shouldn't dwell on such nonsense.

With new resolve, she gathered her sewing and sat on a crate outside to enjoy the pleasant music and banter of camp as she hemmed the ties of another apron. It was quite gratifying to see the stock for the future store accumulating. Besides the half-dozen other aprons she had completed herself, Sarah had finished quite a pile of calico bonnets and flannel baby blankets. But with the younger girl's evenings so often taken up by Alvin Rivers and other young people, Amanda knew her own items would soon outnumber her sister's. Sarah had never lacked for friends. Amanda released a resigned breath.

A tall shadow fell across her work, blocking the glow from the big center fire. "Excuse me, miss?"

Startled, Amanda looked up to see that the low voice belonged to Jared Hill. "Yes?"

He removed the hat from his sandy hair and cleared his throat, then shifted his weight from one foot to the other, as if working up courage to speak. "I came to apologize. Had no call to be short with you when you asked after my kids. I know you meant well."

"Oh. Well, thank you. I took no offense, Mr. Hill." The statement wasn't quite true, but after Sarah's comments had put the whole thing into perspective, Amanda felt better about it and had been able to make allowances for the widower.

He nodded. "Well, I said my piece. I won't keep you from your chore." Offering a faint smile, he turned and walked away.

Amanda's spirit was lighter as she watched him go back to his own wagon. She had no intentions of forcing herself on the man's children, but it was nice to know that if she did have occasion to befriend them their father wouldn't shoo her away.

❧

Seth laid his hat on a rock, then spread out his bedroll and climbed in between the blankets, resting his head on his saddle. Face up, he clasped his hands behind his neck and stared idly at the myriad stars speckling the midnight sky. It reminded him of something. He searched his memory and grimaced . . . the Shelby girl had been wearing navy calico. That had to be it. He rolled over onto his side.

Truth was—and he'd be the last to admit it even to Red—it completely astounded him that those two young women had actually made it across the Big Blue on their own. Or rather, Amanda Shelby had done it on her own. Who would have expected a female of her tender age to have such pluck! A low chuckle rumbled from deep inside him.

On the other hand, he reasoned, that river was but one of numerous obstacles the train would face. There'd be plenty more opportunities for her to give up and turn back for Missouri. Yep, for all her faith that God would see her through, Seth knew they had to be merely brave words. Most people he'd met only put on that religious act to go along with their Sunday go-to-meeting duds. Come Monday morning, they all reverted back to their normal selves. She wouldn't be any different.

Course, when he'd been a tadpole, Seth had possessed quite the religious bent himself, much to his chagrin. His grandfather had seen to that. But after Gramps passed on, and Seth had grown up enough to see a few too many prime examples of church folk, he had wised up.

Too bad his brother Andrew hadn't been so perceptive, letting the wool be pulled over his eyes that way by that beautiful but scheming Eliza. Once a female had a man where she wanted him, she went in for the kill. Seth winced. That would be the day he would fall for any woman's goody ways or holy-sounding words. He was bright enough to see right through people, thanks to her.

Far in the distance, the lonely howl of a wolf carried on the wind. Seth raised his head to see the men on the night watch add wood and buffalo chips to the fires. He lay back down.

Enough time wasted thinking about women. There wasn't one of them worth the time of day.

But his mind refused to keep in line with his intentions. Seth found himself grinning. He had pretty near scared the prim Miss Shelby out of her skin, earlier. She'd all but toppled right into the Little Blue—and he could just imagine the sight she'd have made, all sputtering and flustered, water streaming off that long hair, her dress clinging to those fetching curves of hers . . .

Quickly reining in his wayward thoughts, Seth deliberately forced aside the vision of troubled green eyes that had a way of lingering in his mind as if he had no say in the matter. It was beginning to aggravate him how that at times he found himself comparing the variegated greens of the prairie grasses to the shade of those eyes. He'd best start keeping some distance between that gal and himself and concentrate on doing what he was hired to do—get these folks out west. Once he dumped them all off on that side of the world, he'd have no more cause to cross paths with that Shelby girl. End of problem. He squeezed his eyelids closed . . . but sleep was a long time coming.

11

*W*ood, water, and grass were plentiful along the friendly Little Blue, and so were flies and mosquitoes. Several evenings in a row, the wagons stopped to park alongside one another on its shady banks instead of drawing into the customary circle. A big common fire continued to draw forth fiddles, harmonicas, flutes, and lithe feet of emigrants eager to lose the weary monotony of travel in dancing and music. The menfolk, after tending to needed wagon repairs, would loll about and smoke their pipes, and the women would ignore the pesky insects long enough to visit and swap life stories.

During noon stops, Minnie Randolph had introduced Amanda to many of the other travelers. Added to the younger set she'd been meeting through Sarah and Alvin, Amanda now felt more a part of the company.

"I'll tell ye," Ma Phelps, a tall, rawboned woman, was saying as Amanda carried her sewing over by the great fire. "I've yet to find a better way to make johnnycakes."

A wave of murmured assents made the rounds, followed by a "Hello, Amanda-girl."

Amanda smiled and took a seat on the blanket that frail little Rosalie Bertram patted with her multiveined hand. The woman kept right on subject. "Hazel Withers just gave me a recipe for the most mouth-waterin' dried-apple pies t'other day. Y'all need to try it." Her nod loosened one of the skimpy braids in her graying coronet, and her nimble fingers quickly repositioned the hairpins.

Thin, weak-eyed Jennie Thornton squinted through her gold-rimmed spectacles at a nearby wagon as another muffled birthing scream contrasted sharply with the happy music. She exchanged knowing nods with the other women, then picked up the conversation again. "I'm still hankerin' for some of that buffalo steak the outriders rave about. Ain't even seen one o' them critters yet."

"We'll come across them soon enough, from what I hear," Mrs. Randolph said confidently. "Then there'll be meat to spare and enough to make jerky, to boot."

During a lull in the music, a soft slap sounded from the wagon confines, followed by a tiny cry. "Ohhh, that be our first young'un born on the trip," Ma Phelps breathed. "Shore hope the little angel makes it."

Several seconds of silent contemplation followed. Then the fiddles broke into another tune, and laughing couples linked elbows for the next jig

Amanda felt a cool gust of wind. Pulling her shawl more closely about her shoulders, she noticed gathering clouds.

"Another shower's likely," Mrs. Randolph said. "Guess I'll go make sure everything's closed up nice and tight."

"Me, too." Amanda folded her project and went to shake out tarps and cover supplies in the wagon.

Sarah Jane came soon afterward. "Whew!" she breathed airily. "Sure is breezy out there. I hope it's just another nice rain like we had last night. I might be able to finish that doll for the little Hill girl. There's only the dress left to do." Reaching for the blue calico and the shears, she moved nearer to the lantern.

Amanda nodded. "It's turning out really cute. Where'd you get the hair?"

With a slightly embarrassed grin, Sarah flinched. "That old shawl of mine . . . the brown one. It was getting rather worn, so I pulled a thread and unraveled the bottom row."

"Bethany is sure to love her."

"You're not mad at me for being wasteful?"

"Heavens, no. It was very unselfish—and industrious of you." Amanda picked up the small muslin figure and examined it more closely, from the tiny embroidered face to the ingenious woolen braids. It was sure to make one sad little girl perk up.

"I couldn't think of anything to give the boy," Sarah said.

"Well, I can!" Amanda jumped up. "Didn't Pa bring along that slingshot Johnny Parker gave him for luck?"

"Now that you mention it, yes, I think so. It's probably in with the wagon tools."

Amanda untied the canvas opening and went to dig through the tools in the jockey box. "It's here!" she exclaimed upon returning. "It brought us luck after all!"

Sarah Jane giggled. "Now, should I make the dress with full sleeves, or fitted? And it needs an apron, don't you think—which, by odd coincidence, just happens to be your specialty."

❧

A few nights later, Mrs. Randolph again extended an invitation to supper. Sarah tucked the newly completed dolly deep into her pocket and handed the slingshot to Amanda to do the same, in case the opportunity arose to present the gifts. "What if they don't like them?" she asked, voicing her worst fear.

Amanda looked askance at her. "How could they not?"

"I don't know. I'm just wondering if we did right, is all. It really isn't interfering—is it?" Nervously she nibbled her lip, trying to recall when she'd last spent time with children.

"Don't be a goose. You're trying to befriend a lonely little girl, that's all."

"And her brother. And I'm not used to little boys. What if he doesn't like me?"

"Really, Sarah," Amanda sighed. "He doesn't have to like you, just the slingshot. He probably doesn't own one yet."

"You're right. I'm being silly. If they don't like me, I just won't bother them." *Ever again,* she added silently.

Coming up on the Randolph wagon, the tantalizing smells of crispy fresh fish and amazingly light biscuits greeted them. Sarah swallowed the lump in her throat and drew a calming breath.

"Oh, you're here," Mrs. Randolph said warmly, accepting with a nod of thanks the cheese and the tin of peaches they'd brought along. "Sit right down. Everything's ready. Nelson? You say grace, will ya?"

He gave a gruff nod, settling his husky frame on one of the crates by their cook fire. "Almighty God, we thank you for the traveling mercies and for the food you provide us every day. Bless it now, we pray, and make us fit by it. Amen."

Raising her head, Mrs. Randolph whisked away an annoying fly. "I swear, such pests," she remarked, forking a portion of fish onto a plate and handing it to her husband. She passed the next serving to Amanda. "Hear tell somebody up front has come down with the fever."

The older man nodded gravely. "And once we come to the bad water spots, there'll be lots more of it."

A shudder went through Sarah. "What'll they do? The sick folks, I mean."

"Pull off by themselves, I 'spect," he answered. "Wait it out. See how they fare. Won't stop the rest of the train."

"It won't?" Amanda asked, obviously shocked. "That's hardly Christian."

"Mebbe. But it's what we all voted, back in Independence—and the only way to keep other folks from catchin' it. If they live, the next train along'll pick 'em up."

But what if they don't live? Sarah looked from one troubled face to the next. Things had gone so smoothly up until this point, she'd actually believed the whole trip would continue on in the same pleasant fashion. Now she felt a deep foreboding that this was just the beginning of woes to come. Who knew how many of this company would be called home to their eternal reward before ever reaching the western shores? Accepting the food Mrs. Randolph held out, she settled back in thought.

"We'll wash everything up, Mrs. Randolph," she heard Amanda say sometime later. Looking down at the plate in her own lap, Sarah noticed it was empty—yet she couldn't remember eating. Brushing crumbs from her skirt, she stood and helped her sister gather the soiled dishes, then walked woodenly beside her to the stream. "Mandy? Do you think we'll really make it out west? Truly?"

"All we can do is try," came her sister's honest answer. "We do our best, same as everybody else . . . and trust God, same as everybody else. In the end it's up to Him."

Sarah pondered the words in silence. "I—I haven't been keeping up with my prayers," she admitted at long last, regretting her laxness. "The days seem so busy. There's so little chance to find quiet times for prayer. I haven't touched Pa's Bible—haven't opened it once since Independence."

She felt an encouraging pat on her forearm. "Fortunately, the Lord's faithfulness isn't dependent on ours, Sissy, or we'd really be up a crick. It's never too late to get back to reading the Scriptures or talking to the Lord. He's always there."

"Good. I'm going to start praying and reading the Bible again tonight."

"And I'm going to be more faithful myself," Amanda replied. "Lots of nights I've been tired and skipped my prayers. That has got to stop. Right now."

New hope dawned in Sarah Jane as they finished the dishes and returned to the Randolphs'. No one could be sure about the future, that was true. But at least she would keep her hand in that of the One who, as the Bible said, knew the end from the beginning.

The train had stopped early for the night because of the onset of sickness. In the remaining daylight, Sarah peered expectantly at the next wagon. It was empty. But she caught Jared Hill on the edge of her vision, strolling along the river, a child's hand in each of his. "Mandy?" She nodded in the direction of the threesome. "Shall we go see them now?"

"Now or never, I suppose."

They took their leave and headed toward the water. Sarah Jane, slightly less at ease in the presence of a man easily ten years older than herself, had to muster all her courage when the tall widower glanced their way and stopped. "Good evening," she said politely. "I'm Sarah Jane Shelby."

"Miss Shelby," he answered with a nod, a look of surprise on his narrow face. "Jared Hill." Releasing Bethany's hand, he took the brim of his hat between his thumb and forefinger and dipped it slightly as he met Amanda's eye. "Miss."

"And who have we here?" Sarah added cheerily, more than glad to switch her attention to the little ones. She bent down to smile at the somber little girl.

Huge blue eyes grew even wider in the delicate face beneath fine blond hair. The child pressed closer to her father's leg.

"She's Bethy," her brother announced with four-year-old importance. "Her real name's Bethany. I'm Tad."

Sarah Jane beamed at the towhead, liking him at once—especially the sprinkling of freckles across his nose. "And you must be the big brother."

"Yep."

"Well, I'm very glad to meet you. I have a sister, too. Right here. This is my big sister. Amanda." She gestured behind herself as she spoke.

"Aw, I saw her lots of times. She comes to the Randolphs'."

"That's 'cause they're our friends," Sarah replied. "Do you have friends in the train?"

He shrugged. "Mama used to let me play with Sammy and Pete sometimes. They're over thataway." He pointed down the line. Then his bright expression faded. "We . . . we don't have a ma anymore."

Sarah noted the catch in his voice. "Oh, how sad," she murmured. "I know just how you feel. Our ma and pa live up in Heaven with Jesus, too. And you know what?" she added brightly. "I'll bet our mas are friends already."

"Think so?"

She nodded. "And they'd probably like us to be friends, too. What do you say?"

"I dunno." Tad sought his father's approval. "I guess."

"Good." Expelling a breath of relief, Sarah stood and motioned to Amanda. "We found something in our wagon you might like—that is—" She looked anxiously to Mr. Hill, feeling her color heightening. "—if your pa says you can have it."

Tentatively, Amanda held out the slingshot.

The lad's mouth dropped open. "Oh, boy! Can I keep it, Pa? Can I? Can I?"

No one could have resisted the pleading in that impish face, least of all his father. Nor could Sarah miss the depth of love that softened Jared Hill's demeanor as he gazed down at his young son. It warmed her heart. "Sure. I'll teach you how to use it, so you can do it right."

"Thank you! Thank you!" Tad said, awed by his new treasure.

Sarah touched his shoulder. "You're most welcome. Friends, remember?"

"Friends," he parroted.

Noting the way Bethany seemed drawn to the conversation, Sarah next knelt by her. "Would you be our friend, too, honey?"

The little girl pressed her heart-shaped lips together in mute silence, clutching her father's hand all the harder.

"It's all right," Sarah assured her. "Sometimes it takes a while to make a real friend. But my sister and I made something for you." Retrieving the dolly from her pocket, she offered it to Bethany.

The child stared longingly. Then, after glancing up and receiving her father's nod of approval, she slowly reached out and took it, hugging it for all it was worth.

Sarah Jane smiled. "She'll be a real true friend, you'll see. Pretty soon we'll come by and see you again, to make sure she's been minding her manners. Would you like that? My sister might even tell you a story. She knows lots of them."

A tiny smile curved her lips upward at the corners.

"Thank you, miss," Mr. Hill said with sincere gratitude. "Thank you both."

Completely charmed by the man's offspring, Sarah lifted her gaze to his and would have responded, but Amanda beat her to it.

"People like to help each other, Mr. Hill," her sister said kindly. "It's what neighbors are for. Do have a pleasant evening." With a smile at the children, she took Sarah's hand and started for their prairie schooner.

Sarah's backward glance revealed the tender sight of a father sweeping his two little ones up into his arms.

No crying issued from the Hill wagon that night.

*T*hree more families fell prey to sickness the next day. Then two more. The number of wagons in the train began to dwindle as those afflicted dropped out of the column while the rest continued on—a concept the girls found utterly appalling. Even though other brave Good Samaritans willingly stayed behind to look after the sick—or worse, dig needed graves, the fate of the unfortunates weighed heavily on Amanda's mind. *O Lord,* she prayed fervently, *be with them. Please, take care of them. Bring them back to us.*

Weeks passed in tedious sameness as the wagon train rumbled through Nebraska in an upward slope of terrain so gradual the travelers were unaware they were going uphill until the bullwhackers' whips cracked more frequently and oxen and mules strained against the harness.

Amanda often watched her sister silently observing the world around them and knew she was memorizing scenes, sounds, and sensations to record the minute they stopped for the noon meal or evening camp. From the various passages the younger girl had already related to her, Amanda knew entries in Sarah's journal chronicled how the grass along the route now grew shorter, the trail sandier, and the weather more changeable, and the way a day could dawn in mild and colorful splendor—only to cloud over and turn cold, pelting the travelers with rain or even hail. But with spring's fragile beauty lingering into early summer, the younger girl's spirits—along with everyone else's—remained high. Especially considering the plentiful elk and antelope to provide respite from the daily fare of smoked or salted meats.

On one of the meal stops along the arid plain between the Platte

River and the low hillsides lining the valley, Amanda watched Sarah scribbling furiously in her diary. "Does it help much?" she teased.

Sarah stopped writing and crimped her lips together. Then she smiled. "Well, not that I'm likely to ever forget the way the wagon wheels screech in protest with every turn lately—or the huge clouds of dust they throw up into our faces. But I thought I'd jot it down for posterity anyway. At least we can breathe through our handkerchiefs or apron hems. I'll be glad to see the end of this section."

Amanda had to giggle.

One afternoon, lulled into a state of half-awareness by the clopping of the animals, Amanda was brought rudely back to the present by an ear-shattering crack. Horrified, she watched as the wagon ahead tipped crazily, then crashed to the ground over its splintered rear wheel. She struggled to maintain control of her own startled mules, then steered cautiously around the disabled outfit so she wouldn't be in the way of the men who would immediately assist in replacing the wheel.

"That's the second one today," Sarah Jane whispered.

Amanda nodded. "The dryness of the air is making the wood shrink. I wonder when our turn will come."

"Alvin says that when he finishes helping his uncle tonight, he and his friend Jason will soak our wheels in the river."

Despite the comforting news, Amanda's unrest persisted. So many, many miles lay ahead. Could she have been wrong to presume the Lord wanted her and Sarah to go west after all? Pa had often teased her about her stubborn streak. What if she had placed her own will above God's? The two of them might make the entire trip—only to meet with unhappiness and misfortune in the Oregon Territory! She couldn't help recalling the incident in the Bible where the Israelites demanded meat in the wilderness rather than the manna God so graciously provided. He granted their request, but sent leanness to their souls.

"Let's teach the kids some songs tonight."

"Hm?" Amanda swallowed, forcing aside her disquiet.

"I said," Sarah Jane repeated, "Bethany and Tad might like to learn some songs."

With her mind occupied by more serious concerns, Amanda merely shrugged. "Sure."

"Good. Tonight when we go to see them, I'll take my guitar." Reaching around for the instrument, Sarah unwrapped the sheet shrouding it, plucked a few strings, then adjusted the tuning pegs. "What with all my sewing and visiting, it's been ages since I practiced. I wonder which tunes they might particularly like." Her face scrunched in thought as she strummed a chord.

The slightly flat tones brought a smile to Amanda. So did the realization of how the children had grown to welcome their visits. It seemed a fair exchange when Mr. Hill offered to look after repairs on both wagons while she or Sarah—sometimes both—took the little ones for walks along the rocky outcroppings on the hills or near the shallow river.

But when this evening finally came, Amanda's pensive mood knew the further aggravation of a dull headache, precluding even the enjoyment of the usual camp music. She left the visiting and singing to her sister and strolled somewhat apart from the train.

The night breeze rustled the dry grasses beneath the huge dome of starry sky as she walked, and nightly cricket sounds blended with the familiar lowing of the cattle. Amanda sank to her knees and clasped her hands. *Dear Father,* began her silent plea. To her frustration, no further words would come. She loosened her shawl and lay back, losing herself in the display of the twinkling host so high above her . . . almost wishing she had never left Independence.

❧

"Isn't that the Shelby gal?" Red asked, with a jut of his chin toward the open prairie beyond the camp perimeter.

Seth followed his friend's gesture as if it was news to him . . . as if he hadn't seen Amanda's slender form depart, hadn't observed nearly her every step. "Probably. Just like her to go off by herself as if there isn't a wolf or rattler for miles."

"Want me to go bring her back?"

"Naw." Rubbing a hand across the bridge of his nose, Seth let out a slow breath. "I'll just keep an eye on her from here."

"Don't appear as if you're the only one. I've noticed a certain widower's a lot less sorrowful lately, since her an' her sister have been ridin' herd on those little ones of his. I s'pose it would solve more'n a few problems if he hitched up with one of 'em."

Seth huffed. "No never mind to me." But the confirmation of a niggling suspicion sank slowly to the pit of his stomach.

❧

"This a private party?"

Amanda bolted upright with a start. "Not at all, Mr. Hill. I was just looking for some quiet."

He sank down a few feet away, propping an elbow on one bent knee and followed her gaze to the starry heavens. "Does get pretty noisy some nights."

Neither spoke for several seconds.

"Don't you think it's time you quit being so formal?" he finally asked. "We're not strangers anymore."

Amanda regarded him in the twinkling light. "No, we aren't strangers."

"Friends, then?"

"I guess so."

"Then it's Jared. And Amanda—unless you say otherwise."

She shook her head, then looked away. Everyone needed friends. There was no reason to keep always to herself. But she wasn't silly enough to expect—or even desire—anything more than friendship again. Once was enough. And anyway, she assured herself resolutely, Jared Hill couldn't possibly be putting more into this relationship than there was. It was far too soon for him to even be thinking about replacing his dear late wife. Amanda relaxed and began idly plucking at the stiff grass. Another span of silent seconds passed.

Jared raked his fingers through his hair. "Helped two young fellows take your wheels down to soak in the river a while ago. Should keep you going a ways now."

She smiled. "I don't know how we'd make it but for the kindness of folks on the train. Thanks."

"Least I can do after what you and Sarah have done for my boy and girl." He filled his lungs, quietly releasing the breath through his nostrils.

"They really miss their mama."

Jared didn't respond immediately, but Amanda felt his gaze switch to her. "Well, guess I'll head back." Standing up, he offered a hand.

She grinned and placed hers inside his more calloused one, and he raised her effortlessly to her feet. They walked in companionable silence back to camp.

The crossing of the shallow but fierce, mile-wide south fork of the Platte went without mishap. Advised about the threat of quicksand, no one ignored the order to water all animals beforehand to prevent them from stopping in the middle of the chocolate-colored river.

But Amanda would never forget the terror that seized her some miles later, poised on the brink of Windlass Hill. She and Sarah Jane gaped down the steep grade, watching the harried descent of other wagons. Even with the back wheels chained to prevent them from turning, and with dozens of men tugging on ropes to slow the downward progress, gravity sucked mercilessly at the rigs skidding and sliding to the bottom. To the girls' horror, midway down the slope, one outfit broke free of restraint. Amid screams of onlookers, it teetered and toppled over the side, careening end over end till it came to rest, a shattered heap of rubble. For a moment of stunned silence, no one so much as breathed.

"That does it," Jared Hill announced, climbing up to the seat and taking the reins from Amanda. "No way I'm gonna let the two of you try this one." A jerk of his head ordered the girls out to walk with the other women. "See that my kids keep out of the way, will you?" He wrapped the traces firmly around his hands and eased the mules forward, already applying pressure to the brake. Neither girl could bear to watch their schooner's descent to the reaches below.

When the nerve-wracking day came to a merciful end with the arrival of the last wagon in Ash Hollow, the cool, bountiful meadow at the base of Windlass Hill seemed a glorious oasis. The very air was fragrant with the mingled perfume of the wild rose and scents of other flowers and shrubs in the underwood of majestic ash and dwarf cedar trees.

"Why, there's actual shade!" Sarah Jane cried, as she and her small group reached the bottom of the hill. Taking Bethany and Tad by the hand, she bolted ahead of Amanda and Mrs. Randolph, with the children in her wake. Under the green canopy of a huge ash, she swooped the little girl up and swung her around. Tad ran circles around them both.

Mrs. Randolph joined in with their gleeful laughter. "I declare! It's the Garden of Eden, that's what it is." Joining Sarah, she kicked off her worn boots and wiggled her plump toes in the silky grass, her expression almost dreamlike.

Amanda's gaze drifted to the center of the meadow, where prattling little streams merged together in a translucent pond, sparkling now in the late afternoon sun. She hadn't realized how thirsty she had been. The last truly decent water had been long since passed. Glancing around, she spotted her wagon parked beside Jared Hill's and hurried over to get a pitcher.

Her neighbor was tightening the straps on his rig's canvas top when she approached. "Some place, huh?" he said pleasantly. "Almost feels like we deserve it after a day like today."

Amanda laughed lightly and clambered aboard her schooner.

Jared's low voice carried easily through the bowed fabric. "Wagon master says we're stopping here for a day or two. Plenty of folks have a whole bunch of new repairs to see to. And most everyone will pitch in to help the Morrises salvage what they can from their wreck."

"That was truly a horror," Amanda said, emerging with the coveted pitcher in hand. "On the way down the hill, at least half a dozen ladies speculated on which of them could best make room for the family, bless their hearts. And I couldn't be more grateful for a day of rest. Tomorrow's Sunday anyway, isn't it?"

"Come to think of it, you're right."

"Pa! Pa!" two young voices called out above their scampering footsteps. They made a beeline for him and flung their arms around his long legs.

Gratified at the sweet display of affection, Amanda averted her gaze and hopped to the ground.

Sarah Jane stepped beside her at the spring. "Alvin's aunt has invited me to supper. Do you mind, Mandy?"

"Of course not. Just don't stay out late."

"Yes, Mother." With a wry grimace, her sister joined her curly-haired escort.

Oh well, Amanda decided, watching the pair walk away, I've been wishing for solitude lately. This should provide a nice quiet night of sewing.

Or praying, her mind added. What she needed above all was to know inner peace again. There had to be some way to find it.

$$\textbf{(13)}$$

The summer sun warmed the faithful flock gathered in the meadow for Sunday service on a curious collection of wooden chairs, crates, blankets, and the odd fallen log. The breeze rustling the leaves in the glen was gloriously free of the mosquitoes that had plagued the encampment late last evening. Now the voices blended in harmony with the fiddle and harmonica.

Amanda had known "Abide With Me" most of her life but had never paid close attention to the words. But as Sarah had pointed out a week ago, it must have been a lot of folks' favorite, the way it got requested almost every Sunday. Going into the second verse, Amanda listened even as she sang:

> "Swift to its close ebbs out life's little day;
> Earth's joys grow dim, its glories pass away;
> Change and decay in all around I see;
> O Thou who changest not, abide with me."

Certainly this trip had brought about drastic changes. Amanda surmised that other folks' dreams of a new life had probably been every bit as grand as hers. Yet despite the fact that many of them had already lost friends and loved ones to sickness or accident, they found strength to continue on. Lonely, saddened, they somehow remained hopeful. It had to be of tremendous comfort to know that the Lord stayed ever constant. She observed the peaceful countenances of some of the folks within her range of sight and went on to the third stanza:

"I fear no foe, with Thee at hand to bless;
Ills have no weight, and tears no bitterness.
Where is death's sting? Where, grave, thy victory?
I triumph still, if Thou abide with me."

When Amanda saw a woman blot tears on her apron as she sang, her own eyes stung, rendering her unable to voice the lyrics herself. She finally managed to regain her composure for the final lines:

"Heaven's morning breaks, and earth's vain shadows flee;
In life, in death, O Lord, abide with me."

Never again would that hymn carry so little meaning. Amanda realized for the first time that it had not been her own strength that had held her together after the loss of her parents. It had been the Lord all along. His strength, His faithfulness—and those, without a doubt, loving answers to her mama and papa's faithful prayers. Humbly she bowed her head and breathed a prayer of gratitude.

She opened her eyes to see the jug-eared man most folks had started calling "Deacon Franklin" rise from his seat and move to the vacant spot the fiddler left behind at the close of the song.

"Folks," he began. "As you've figured out by now, I'm not much of a preacher. But like I said before, I love the Lord, and I love His Word. Thought I'd read a favorite verse that has been a real blessing to me for a lot of years. It's in Romans, the eighth chapter, verse twenty-eight." He opened his worn Bible to the page his finger had held at the ready. " 'And we know that all things work together for good to them that love God, to them who are the called according to his purpose.' "

Looking up from his text, he scanned the rapt faces before him and smiled gently. "There's hardly a one of us who hasn't at some time or other questioned the Lord's doings. Especially these last hard weeks, as we've all of us watched helplessly at the hardships that came to folks who were once part of this travelin' family of ours."

Bonneted heads nodded, and murmurs circulated in the ranks.

"But in spite of all that comes by," the leader continued, "whether sickness, or death, or accident, I know we can still trust God. There's no lack of people in this world who don't give Him any part of their lives a'tall. Can't help wonderin' what gets them through the hard times, or where they turn for help. There'd be none to find if we just threw up our hands and turned our backs on the One who made us, the One who is workin' out His purposes through all the circumstances of our lives. Yes, I said *all*," he injected without a pause. "There's not one among us who's here by chance."

Amanda's ears perked up.

"It doesn't make a lick of difference what made us choose to make this trip," the speaker said with a firm nod. "What does count is that the God who brought us here will never let us down. Think about that today and tomorrow—and all the tomorrows yet to come. Trust your well-being to the Lord and keep a good hold on His strong hand. And whatever effort you've been givin' to complainin' about hills or rivers or dust or mud, spend instead in thankin' God for takin' you through it. If you see somebody beside you startin' to sag, bolster him up with a kind word—or better yet, lend a hand. This journey is gonna take all of us pullin' together, helpin' one another along."

Deacon Franklin rocked back onto his heels and tucked his Bible under one arm, and a twinkle in his eye accompanied his smile. "Well, that's all I have to say this morning. Be sure and enjoy this nice purty restin' spot the Good Lord put here just for us, right enough! Now, let's close in prayer."

A new calmness began to flow through Amanda's being as she closed her eyes. The words hadn't come from behind a proper pulpit. The speaker was not in reality a man called to be a preacher to the masses, and the speech hadn't even been what one might term a sermon. Yet her spirit felt strangely comforted and encouraged. She almost felt like dancing.

⮟

Behind the furrowed gray trunk of a swamp ash, Seth flicked a crumbled leaf through his fingers and headed for the cook wagon. No sense having Red catch him listening in on a sermon, that's for sure! It wasn't worth the endless mocking that was certain to follow.

It beat all, though, how this bunch seemed to handle the misfortunes and tragedies that struck so relentlessly now. Unlike some of the travelers he'd taken west in previous years, these folks even seemed sincere in believing what that farmer told them. Took it right to heart. Of course, Grandpa had been that way, too, he remembered. Never once doubting the Good Book or the Lord above. Seth could still picture the shock of white hair above the aged face, could still see the piercing eyes that seemed to see clear into a person's soul. The old man's voice contained a gravelly quality, as if preaching had used it up somewhere along the way. But those long arms of his, which could spread so wide to make a point, had felt mighty warm and strong wrapped around a young boy's shoulders.

An unbidden memory came to the fore of times he and Drew had ridden double on old Lulabelle while Gramps took them along on a preaching trip. He'd sit the two of them right in the front row, where one look could still their squirming through the longest sermon. Seth smiled, knowing if he thought back far enough, he'd have to admit there was a time he thought of becoming a circuit-riding preacher himself! Wouldn't Red get a kick out of that!

Seth emitted a ragged breath. A lot of years had passed since then. He'd ended up on a far different path . . . but a very small part of him was starting to hunger for the kind of sincere faith he'd known as a young lad.

🖎

"Sarah?" Alvin extended a hand as they left the service. "Will you come for a walk with the rest of us? Aunt Harriet wants me to pick her some currants and chokecherries."

She smiled, but shook her head, mildly disappointed. "Can't. I promised Bethany I'd help her make a flower crown."

"You could do that later."

Sarah felt compelled to refuse. "I wouldn't want to disappoint her, Alvin. She's only a little girl, and I—"

"—sure spend a lot of time with kids that aren't even related to you," he finished. "You used to be more fun."

Ignoring the critical note in her friend's usually jovial tone, Sarah just nodded. "I still like to have fun, Alvin. But sometimes there are other things that need doing. Anyway, it's hard to resist a pair of big blue eyes."

"Exactly." A rakish gleam lit the hazel depths of Alvin's. "Won't I ever get to finish that sketch I started of you?"

"Sure you will. We'll have plenty of time together, you'll see. Now, I really must go. Thanks for the invitation, though."

"Right." The edge of his lip took on a strange curl before he turned and strode away.

Almost wishing she'd accepted, Sarah stared after him. She felt Amanda step to her side.

"It's really sweet of you to turn down an afternoon's frolic just to keep a little girl happy."

"I promised," Sarah Jane said simply.

"I know. I'm very proud of you."

"Really?"

A blush tinted her sister's cheeks. "Well, it's just—You know. When we first spoke of coming west, I was afraid you'd get in one pickle after another. But you're changing by the day."

Sarah cocked her head back and forth. "I imagine it's called growing up."

"I suppose. Just wanted you to know, I like the change."

"Thanks, Sissy. And while we're at it, I'd like to say I'm sorry for not being more help sewing, cooking, driving . . . I've let you down. That's going to change, too."

❧

When the company again took up the journey, a new, lighter mood prevailed . . . until the nine-year-old Thornton boy, riding the tongue of his family's wagon on a dare, plunged under the wheels shortly after departing Ash Hollow. An unexpected funeral took place that noon. The little body was laid to rest in a grave dug right beneath the rutted trail. The wagons to follow would pack the earth hard again, too hard for wolves to ravage.

And another new baby came into the world that night.

" 'The Lord giveth, and the Lord taketh away,' " Mrs. Randolph muttered as Amanda poured a cup of coffee for them both outside the schooner. "My old heart goes out to Jennie. He was their only boy, you know. The others are girls. He'd have been a big help when they got settled in Oregon."

Sipping her own coffee, Amanda could barely swallow.

"Say, these are right fine apple fritters your Sarah made."

"She's been—well, we've been practicing."

"And it shows."

"Thanks to you."

The older woman sloughed off the compliment. "Pshaw. You'd have picked up all the cookin' you needed in time anyway."

"Even if that's true," Amanda said, patting her friend's arm, "you surely made it much easier for us. We both appreciate it." She paused with a smile. "I don't know if I'm going to want to part with you when we get to the California Trail and you and Mr. Randolph head off to go be with your sons. What did you say their names were?"

"Nelson Junior an' Charlie," the older woman said proudly. "Don't mind admittin', though, if I had my druthers I'd still be back home in our Allegheny Mountains. At my age, thought of sittin' in my rockin' chair in front of a cracklin' fire was soundin' mighty pleasurable. But when Nelson, the oldest, got the notion to go see what lay beyond the hills, he up and took our other'n and they lit out. Ended up in northern California—far as they could get—then convinced their pa an' me to come, too. One of 'em might even come to meet us partway."

Amanda smiled. "Well, it'll truly be a whole new life for you then—without having to start from scratch, like most of us. You might even arrive to discover they've built you a nice little cabin, fireplace and all, complete with a rocker."

"If not, I brung my own along," she admitted with chagrin. "Didn't want to take a chance. It was my own ma's. Our two boys got rocked on it, so did our girl. Course, little Rosie wasn't with us too long . . ." Blinking away a sudden sheen in her faded blue eyes, she looked

Amanda up and down, then tapped a crooked finger against her bottom lip in thought. "You'd make our Charlie a pretty fair wife, if you don't mind my sayin' so."

Amanda, having raised her mug for another sip, swallowed too quickly and choked instead.

"There, there," her neighbor crooned, thumping her on the back. "Just take a deep breath, now. You'll be right as rain." Barely stopping, she resumed the conversation where she'd left off. "Nelson Junior took himself a wife out west. Found her in Sacramento. Name's Cora. But our Charlie's still loose."

Amanda had to giggle.

Barely stopping for breath, Mrs. Randolph rambled on. "Course, I know you an' Sarah Jane have high hopes of openin' a store an' all— which sounds fine. Real fine. I think folks will need new clothes, just like you said." Handing Amanda her empty mug, she ambled to her feet. "Well, I'd best be gettin' back. But store or no store, give some thought to my Charlie, would you? Don't mind tellin' you, a body could do worse havin' you for a daughter-in-law."

At this, Amanda couldn't resist hugging her. "Or you for a mother-in-law. Thanks for coming by."

14

or three more weeks, the train continued along the sandy banks of the North Platte. A mile or two off to the left and right, two lines of sand hills, often broken into wild forms, flanked the valley beneath the enormous sky. But before and behind, the plain was level and monotonous as far as the eye could see.

"Nights are growing colder now," Sarah read to Amanda from her open journal. Tired of walking, she had hopped aboard for a short rest. "Even though it's still the dead of summer, the temperature continues to drop as we go higher. Soon we'll glimpse the peaks of the Laramie Mountains, I'm told, their frosted caps sparkling diamond-white against crystal blue sky." Amanda smiled to herself. Her sibling had always possessed a gift for writing, and the abundant wonders of the trail brought that talent to the fore. More and more often she would look up after finishing a paragraph, obviously eager to share her latest entry—whether it chronicled the pesky sand flies that replaced the mosquitoes everyone found such a torment during the nights at Ash Hollow, the thunderous sound of a buffalo herd on the move, the delicate appeal of grazing antelope, or how the landscape was becoming more brown than green and was empty now of timber, sage, and even dry grass.

And Amanda couldn't help noting a vast improvement in the younger girl's vocabulary as the miles passed. Sarah's association with artist Alvin Rivers revealed itself in new, eloquent words and phrases she now used in her diary. She did not share all of her innermost thoughts concerning Alvin, but had no qualms about revealing passages about special times she spent with the Hill children.

But best of all, in Amanda's estimation, had been her sister's written accounts of the various landmarks whose unique formations had come into view while still a whole day's travel away. Sarah painted word pictures . . . visions of glorious rainbow hues cast over the towering shapes by the ever-changing play of sunlight between dawn and dusk. She likened the mounds of stone to castles and ships and slumbering animals. Amanda felt those images would remain forever in her mind.

She truly appreciated the diversions in the tiresome journey. More than once she had caught herself straining for a glimpse of the wagon master and that gray horse of his, then would quickly chide herself for such foolishness. Having Sarah's daily narratives to concentrate on kept her wandering thoughts in line.

Not long after the snow-patched Laramie Mountains appeared on the far horizon, cheers and whistles came from the front of the company. Sarah, walking beside the wagon, jumped onto the slow-moving vehicle, then craned her neck to see around the outfits ahead. "Mandy! It's Fort Laramie! And I'm just covered with trail dust. I do wish we had time to freshen up." She grabbed the hairbrush from a basket beneath the seat and tugged it through her curls, then removed her apron and fluffed out her skirt. "Do I look all right? I hear we'll be able to replace the flour and other supplies."

"If there's any to be had after everyone else restocks, of course," Amanda reminded her. "No doubt it'll cost us dearly."

"Well, whatever the price, we'll have to bear it. We've still a long, long way to go." She paused. "Oh! Look at the sparkly river—and all the Indian shelters everywhere!"

Amanda nodded, her gaze lost in the sharp contrast between the Black Hills, thick with cedar, and the area's red sandstone. Speckled with sage, the sparse grass was turning yellow. She flicked the reins to keep pace with the others, urging the mules up the steep bank leading to the entrance of the fort, where huge double doors had been raised to permit the train to enter.

"Not as impressive as I expected," Sarah murmured, nearing the cracked, decrepit adobe walls. But exhaling a deep breath, she waved to the sentry perched in the blockhouse erected above the gateway as they pulled inside, where Indians in buffalo robes stared down at the new arrivals from perches on the rampart. After stopping the team, Amanda glanced around the interior. Long, low buildings stretched out in a large circle, forming the walls around a great open area crowded with Indians and traders. Among the horde strolled lean, rough-looking frontiersmen, their long rifles at the ready for any sign of trouble. The noise and bustle of the bargaining reminded Amanda of Independence. Within moments, Alvin Rivers came to offer a hand to Sarah, then to Amanda. "Word has it we're to rest here for two whole days. Mind if your sister and I explore a bit?"

Amanda smiled as she stepped to the ground and arranged her skirt. "Not at all. I'll likely do some of that myself, once I've tended the animals." That evening, the replenished emigrants joined forces and shared their bounty with some of the fort folk. The men quickly assembled makeshift banquet tables from wagon boards propped up on barrels, and the women filled them end to end with heaping platters of roast hen, antelope, buffalo steak, fried fish, and all manner of vegetables and breads, followed by a delectable assortment of berry pies, tarts, and jelly cakes.

Much laughter and banter passed to and fro as everyone caught up with the latest news from back east. Word regarding conditions of the trail ahead brought raised brows and shakes of the head, then expressions of resignation and determination.

When at last every appetite was sated, an even grander celebration began. Double the usual number of instruments broke forth in song, aided by clapping hands and stomping feet, which drew the more energetic souls to frolic.

"You should go have some fun with the other young folks, Amanda," Mrs. Randolph said, gesturing after them. "Leave the cleanin' up to us old fogies."

"I'd rather not. Really," Amanda assured her friend. "I prefer to be useful." But a small part of her wished she still felt as young as Sarah and her friends. In an effort to tamp down the wistful longing, she began humming along with the happy tune while she worked.

"Land sakes," Mrs. Randolph exclaimed, putting leftover bread and biscuits into a sack. "I'm full near to burstin'!"

"Me, too," Ma Phelps chimed in. "I might never take another bite of food as long as I live. Or at least till tomorrow." She guffawed at her own levity.

Amanda had to grin as she gathered some half-empty tins and scooped the remaining portions of the pies into them. She licked berry juice from her sticky index finger and glanced around for another chore.

Disassembling tables with some of the other men a few yards away, Jared Hill looked up and caught her gaze with a smile. "Care to go for another stroll with me and the kids?" he asked.

Spending time with the little family had become a commonplace activity by now. She shrugged a shoulder and nodded.

A sudden movement in the shadows between two of the warehouses revealed Seth Holloway as he spun on the heel of his boot and stalked away.

❧

"Oh, Alvin," Sarah breathed, flipping through his sketchbook as they sat on crates outside his uncle's wagon, somewhat apart from the noise. "These are truly wonderful." She studied a sketch of a vast buffalo herd, then one of a valley filled with the animals' whitened bones and skulls, before turning to the more pleasing views of Chimney Rock and the majestic Courthouse Rock. "I was certain nothing could be more beautiful than your drawing of Devil's Gate, but this . . ." She leaned closer to examine his most recent landscape— Fort Laramie and the Laramie River, with the Black Hills as a backdrop. She ran her fingers lightly over one of the bastions.

"What about these?" he asked tentatively, taking down a second drawing pad and holding it out.

Sarah observed the peculiar gleam in the young man's blue eyes as she took the proffered book from him and opened it. The warmth of a blush rose in her face. Page after page presented renditions of her. All were very good . . . and almost too flattering. She swallowed. "But I never posed for these."

"You didn't have to. Everywhere I look, I see you. Don't you know that by now?" Taking the sketches from her unresisting fingers, he stood and drew her to her feet, encircling her with his long arms.

He had been a perfect gentleman over the hundreds of miles the train had traveled, almost always sharing her company with other young people. Now, Sarah's heart raced erratically as she felt Alvin's breath feather her neck. "Please, don't—" she whispered.

But his head moved closer, until his lips brushed hers. "You're so beautiful, sweet Sarah. I could spend my whole life drawing you, painting you. You could become famous right along with me."

Though the last was said in a jesting tone, his previous remarks had been anything but so. Uncomfortable, she drew away. Mixed emotions—confusing emotions—rushed through her being. "But we're friends . . . Neither of us knows for sure where our paths will lead at the end of this trip."

Alvin's expression did not alter a whit. "It's afterward I'm thinking about, Sarah. You, me, the two of us. Forever. I won't be a pauper when we reach Oregon, you know, unlike most folks. I'll have a lot to offer . . . and I want you to think about that." He took one of her hands in his and pressed it to his lips.

Sarah searched his eyes, afraid to utter the question closest to her innermost longings. How could she ask something so deeply intimate as whether or not he ever wanted children? She didn't know him well enough yet—and she wasn't sure she truly wanted more than friendship from him . . . now or ever.

Gently she pulled her fingers from his grasp. "I—I—" But words failed her. She turned and ran blindly for the wagon.

～❧～

"Sure is a pleasant evening," Jared said.

Amanda, walking by his side, could only agree as she drank in the star-dusted night sky, the warm lantern glow from the many rooms and buildings of the fort. She smiled after Bethany and Tad, who were skipping ahead of them. "Everyone's so happy to have their barrels refilled. And to rest, I might add."

He nodded, and his gaze returned to his children. "They're a lot happier, too. Thanks to you . . . and your sister."

Something in Jared's tone sounded an alarm in Amanda. She moistened her lips. "Well, the whole train was eager to lend a hand—" she began.

"But no one did, except you."

Amanda felt an inward shiver and drew her shawl tighter around her shoulders.

"They're almost their old selves, now," he went on. "The way they used to be."

Determined to keep the conversation casual, Amanda responded only generally. "It's nice to see them smiling."

"I sure don't have to tell you they think a lot of you, Amanda. And so d—"

"I think we should head back now, Jared, don't you?" she blurted. "Bethy! Tad! Time to go." Grabbing them one by one in a hug as they ran to her, Amanda turned them around and pointed them toward the clustered wagons. "March."

"Like soldiers?" Tad asked. "Yes, sir!" Immediately he straightened to his full height and puffed out his chest. "Hup, two, three, four . . . hup, two, three, four."

A giggling Bethany did her best to mimic her older brother's longer strides. The effect was enchantingly comical.

Grateful for the lightened mood, Amanda picked up the pace to discourage further conversation. This night she would be spending more time than usual at her prayers.

❧

"Ah! Some real, actual rest. At long last." Red yawned and straightened his legs as he leaned against the wheel of the supply wagon and crossed his arms. "Let somebody else do the lookin' out, for a change." He tugged his hat over his eyes.

In no mood to make small talk, Seth only grimaced. The rowdy music was giving him a headache. Above the camp smells he could detect rain coming. And he detested wasting travel time when early snow could close the mountain passes.

His pal plucked the hat away and leaned his head to peer at him. "Boy, you sure do have a burr under your saddle."

"Why do you say that?"

"Oh, nothin'. 'Cept, you ain't said a word for the last three hundred miles or so, that's all."

"Nothing to say."

Red nodded, a lopsided smirk pulling his mustache off kilter.

"Look. Do me a favor, will you?" Seth rasped. "If you want to talk about trail hazards or the trip in general or the storm that's coming, go ahead. We'll plan accordingly. Otherwise, clamp those jaws of yours shut and give me some peace."

"Right, boss. Will do." With a mock salute, Red replaced his hat over his eyes and nose and resumed his relaxed pose.

A pair of pregnant minutes ticked by.

The hat fell to Red's lap. "Er, get the letter that was waitin' for you?"

Seth slanted him a glare.

"I just asked. None of my business, I know. Even if it was wrote by a woman. Same last name as yours, I noticed."

Releasing a lungful of air all at once, Seth lurched to his feet, whacking dust off the seat of his britches.

Red jumped up, too, and grabbed Seth's sleeve. "Hey, buddy, I ain't pryin'."

"Oh, really?"

"Sure. Your brother's got the same last name, too. Figure it must be from her. That wife of his."

"So?"

"So nothin'. Figure you know what you're doin'." He rubbed his mouth. "Just hope you're not foolin' around with—"

Seth's fist sent his partner sprawling backward in the dust. Immediately he regretted the hasty act and leaned over to help Red up. "Sorry. I didn't mean that. And I'm not."

Kneading his jaw and working it back and forth, Red shrugged and gave a nod. "Didn't really think you were." He smirked again. "You really hated that woman Andrew married, didn't you?"

"Hated her?" Seth looked him straight in the eye. "On the contrary, pal. I was in love with her, but she refused me." Turning, he left Red gaping after him as he walked away.

15

en exhausting days after leaving Fort Laramie, the wagon train labored up and down the slopes of the Black Hills, where sweet-scented herbs and pungent sage permeated the air. Mountain cherry, currants, and tangles of wild roses lay against brushstrokes of blue flax, larkspur, and tulips. Game was prevalent, and solitary buffalo bulls roamed the ravines of terrain so rough it tested even the most recent wagon repairs, to say nothing of the most rested soul. Trudging a little off to one side while Sarah Jane took a turn driving, Amanda observed for the first time how rickety most of the rigs appeared. Even their own prairie schooner, once so new and sleek against the more clumsy Conestogas, showed the same deterioration. Hardly a wheel in the company was without a wedge or two hammered between it and the rim to fill gaps in the shrinking wood. Canvas tops above the rattling, creaking wagons were stained with grease and dust and bore patches or gaping holes from hail and wind. Animals that had begun the journey hale and hearty now appeared jaded and bony . . . and ahead lay even rougher country. So many, many miles yet to cover.

"Mandy?" Sarah barely paused. "What do you think of Alvin?"

"He's quite nice looking," Amanda fudged, then ventured further. "He has very gentlemanly manners, shows definite artistic talent, and will be quite rich someday, from what you've told me."

"Yes. That's true. All of it."

"Why do you ask?" With sadness Amanda skirted a child's rocking horse that had been discarded by someone up ahead.

"I was just wondering."

"Has he . . . I mean, has he done something . . . ungentlemanly?"

271

Sarah shook her head. "No. But he's beginning to care. For me." Her voice vibrated with the jouncing of the seat.

The news did not come as much of a surprise, considering all the time the two had spent in each other's company. Glancing at her sister, Amanda expected to see a hint of excitement—even happiness—in her expression, yet Sarah seemed glum. Amanda could only pray that her sibling's trust in men would not be shattered as her own had been. "What about you, Sissy?"

Sarah's gaze drifted away, and she smiled. "He does meet a lot of the qualifications I set out when we first started this journey, doesn't he? He is rich. He is quite handsome."

"But?"

The smile wilted.

"I couldn't help but notice you seemed to be avoiding him, at Fort Laramie, while you spent more time with Bethany and Tad."

"I . . . needed time. To think."

Amanda could see her sister's unrest. "Tonight at camp we'll pray about things. Together, like we used to. Would you like that?"

Sarah only nodded.

❧

After Amanda fell asleep, Sarah Jane eased off the pallet. The sudden absence of its comforting warmth became even more apparent as the chill of night crept around her. Shivering, she shook out an extra blanket and wrapped it about herself, lit a small candle, and opened her journal.

Dear Diary,

It's been days and days since last I visited with you. The rest at Fort Laramie did wonders for both people and animals. A hard rain made the river too swift to cross, so our departure was delayed an extra day. The upper crossing of the North Platte, however, was without mishap, thanks to the Mormon ferry . . . eight dugout canoes with logs laid across the tops—an effective, if flimsy, method of transport.

Now, heading into the mountains, the land is bleak and barren. Things that appear green in the distance turn out to be only dry sand and rock, sprinkled with stunted clumps of sage and greasewood.

It makes me sad whenever we pass castoff treasures along the trail, but folks are trying to ease the burden on the animals lumbering so earnestly in this upward climb. We've been examining our own meager stores, wondering what we might be able to do without, should our mules begin to falter.

I pray we all make it through this rough section of country, so full of ravines and treacherous slopes. Progress sometimes slows to a point that tempers flare at the least provocation, and the men remain on their guard for rattlesnakes and other wild animals.

Tapping her pencil against her chin in thought, Sarah frowned. Then after a short pause she continued writing.

Alvin has expressed a desire for some kind of commitment from me, but I've managed to put him off, suggesting we remain friends for a while longer. I always thought wealth was important, along with one's outward appearance . . . But now such things seem trivial. Especially in the face of true loss and real struggle, like poor Bethy and Tad endure every day. I feel a little guilty about hiding behind those little ones, though, while I try to decipher my true feelings regarding Alvin. Mr. Hill seems greatly appreciative of any thoughtfulness shown to his children. He's quite a sensitive man—and ever so much more mature than Alvin. I—

She stopped writing and nibbled at her lip, trying to put her feelings on paper. Then she erased the last word.

❧

Two of the hard days following the ferrying of the river were made all the more loathsome by scummy water, alkali springs, choking dust, and the putrid stench of animal carcasses lying in gruesome little pools of poisonous water. Then came a hideous stretch of deformed rock strata that tore relentlessly at hooves, boots, and wheels.

Finally, to everyone's relief, the valley of the Sweetwater River came in sight, with its easier grades, fine water, and grass to be enjoyed for more than a week's travel. Cheers again rang out when the huge bulk of Independence Rock loomed on the distant horizon.

"We'll be there to celebrate July fourth, Mandy," Sarah Jane exclaimed. "Right on time."

Amanda nodded. No one appreciated rest days more than she. Of all the recent tortures—steaming marshes, odorous sulphur springs, and the like—most horrendous had been the huge crawling crickets that crunched sickeningly beneath wheels and boots for a seemingly endless stretch of miles. Each day took increased effort to remain optimistic for Sarah's sake, while inwardly her feelings were anything but pleasant. Surmising that other women appeared to have things so much easier than she, with men to drive the wagons and look after repairs and animals, Amanda gritted her teeth, fighting feelings of jealousy and self-pity.

". . . so I said to him—" Sarah stepped closer to the wagon. "You're not even listening to me, are you?"

"Hm?"

"Oh, never mind. Do you feel all right, Mandy? You look flushed."

"I'm fine. Fine!" At her own uncharacteristic outburst, Amanda watched the scenery blur behind a curtain of tears.

"No, you're not. You're not fine at all."

Even Sarah's voice sounded faint, sort of fuzzy as she scrambled aboard. "You need to go lie down in back. I'll take over."

You can't. I'm the oldest. The one in charge. But the words wouldn't come out. In a wave of dizziness, Amanda relinquished the reins without a fuss and nearly toppled off the seat. She crawled back to the pallet. The rumble and rattle of the wheels made her head pound and pound . . .

Voices. Everywhere. Loud and laughing. Noise. Too much noise. And it was hot, so hot . . . or cold. How could one shiver so much when it was hot? Why couldn't the world just stop and be still. There had to be quiet somewhere. Where was Oregon? All a body really needed was peace and quiet, a place to rest. To sleep.

&

"Do you think she'll be all right?" Sarah looked anxiously to Mrs. Randolph, hating the waver in her own voice as she peered down again at Amanda's flushed face. At least her sister had stopped thrashing about and now appeared to be sleeping peacefully.

"Right as rain, soon enough," came the soothing reply. "Poor child's plumb exhausted, that's what. She's been workin' herself near to death, always doin', doin', never takin' time to be young."

"It's my fault," Sarah moaned miserably. "I've let her carry the whole load this entire journey. Now I'm being punished. What if—"

"Don't even think such nonsense," the older woman chided. She removed the wet cloth from Amanda's brow and rinsed it out in cool water before replacing it again. "Your sister's a person who takes responsibility serious, is all. She likes makin' it easy for you, seein' you having fun with the others. It makes her happy."

The truth of the statement only made Sarah feel worse. "And I was only too glad to run off and leave everything to her—even after declaring I'd help out more. I hate myself."

"Now, now." Mrs. Randolph patted Sarah's arm. "These days of rest here at Independence Rock will do her a world of good, you'll see. And when we're on the road again, she'll perk right up, wantin' to take over. See if she don't."

"I hope you're right. Mandy's all I've got left in this world. I'm sure not about to give her up!"

"Well, I'll be bringin' some broth by in a little while. See if you can get her to take some." With a nod, their kindly neighbor took her leave.

Sarah took Amanda's limp hand in hers and softly massaged it, praying she would open her eyes, be herself again . . . her dear strong Mandy, who was everything she wished to be herself. Confident, independent, capable . . . A rush of tears threatened to spill over, until a shuffling at the rear of the wagon brought her emotions back in check.

A voice cleared, and a familiar face peered through the back opening. "How's the patient?"

"Doing better, Mr. Holloway," Sarah answered. "Resting comfortably now."

He nodded and his expression appeared to relax. "Well, if you need anything, let me know."

"Thank you. That's very kind. I will."

More visitors came by throughout the day, one by one. Jared Hill, Alvin, Ma Pruett, all of them speaking in quiet voices.

Even Bethany tapped gently on the side of the wagon, her smudged face scrunched with concern. "I brought Miss Amanda some flowers," she whispered, clutching a raggedy bouquet in her hands. The stems were too short to put in water.

Sarah accepted the offering with a gracious smile. "Thank you, sweetheart. She'll just love them when she wakes up."

"Papa said I can't stay, so I'd best go now."

Sending her off with a hug, Sarah felt comforted and hopeful. Maybe she and Mandy had a family after all, one given to them by God. She bowed her head in a prayer of thanks.

❧

"So I missed the whole celebration," Amanda said in amazement as the train meandered past the spectacular slash in the granite mountains known as Devil's Gate, heading toward Split Rock and the much anticipated Ice Slough folks were eager to see, still a few days hence.

At the reins, her sister nodded. "Fireworks, gunshots, the raising of the flag, everything! I'd have thought the racket would have disturbed you."

"I never heard it. Any of it! Sorry I was such a bother."

"You weren't. You earned that rest—I'm just sorry you had to get sick to get it!"

"Well, I'm better now. Did you get to climb the rock, at least?"

Sarah's smile held a hint of guilt. "Actually, when I saw you were doing all right, I did go up with some of the others while Mrs. Randolph stayed with you. Alvin took a pot of axle grease along and wrote his name and mine together for all the world to see. Do you believe that?" She giggled. "When he went with Jason to catch the view from the far side, I added a few other names to the list. By the time we left to come back down, the list read, 'Jason and Alvin and Sarah Jane and Amanda and Mary Katharine, Bethany, and Tad.' Alvin never noticed."

Amanda couldn't help laughing. She adjusted her shawl over her warm coat as they rode in mountain air crisp with pine and the sweet perfume of wildflowers. Tomorrow she would either walk or drive, to spare the mules, but today it did feel good to ride—even on the hard, springless seat. She just wished she hadn't missed the festivities at Independence Rock.

"You sure had a lot of visitors while you were sick."

"Oh?"

Sarah guided the team around a fallen log. "Mrs. Randolph, of course, was a godsend. She was the one who knew it wasn't cholera, just exhaustion, and was a great encouragement to me. She made you that good broth."

"Sounds just like her. She's a dear."

"And then Jared Hill came, and Alvin, and Ma Pruett. Bethy picked the sweetest flowers and brought them to you. Even the wagon master checked on you."

Amanda's heart tripped over itself. "Mr. Holloway?"

"Mm-hmm. Told me to let him know if we needed anything. I know you think he's domineering and stodgy, but I found him to be rather . . . nice."

"Well, I suppose everyone has his good points," Amanda hedged. The man probably kept tabs on everyone in his train. Yes, that had to be it. Of course, chances were he'd come to see if the problem was cholera, even yet hoping to force her and Sarah to stay behind!

But, on the other hand, there was no harm in allowing a tiny part of her to dream he truly cared . . . as long as she didn't voice the thought aloud. No one needed to know such a seemingly inconsequential gesture would be locked inside the treasurehouse of her heart forever. After all, someone destined for spinsterhood could probably use a few secret dreams to look back on in later lonely years. Pretending to adjust her bonnet during an elaborate stretch, Amanda turned to see if the wagon master was anywhere within sight.

Seth nudged his mount over a knoll, keeping an eye on the straggling cattle that plodded in the wake of the wagon train. Not many head had been lost up to this point. Not many travelers, either, considering how quickly and effectively an outbreak of cholera could wipe out an entire company. They'd been pretty lucky so far.

He'd noticed Amanda Shelby was up and about, too, after wearing herself out. Not that he cared, particularly, but someone with her spirit deserved a quick recovery, and he was glad the Almighty saw fit to give her one.

Strange, how he'd started attributing occasional circumstances to God's hand of late. Gramps would like that. Could he be smiling down from the pearly gates now? Next thing, Seth would find himself going back to praying on a regular basis, dusting off the little black Bible he'd kept out of Gramps' possessions. Wouldn't that be something. He smirked, hardly bothered by the fact that the concept no longer seemed so unthinkable. He must be getting old.

Shifting in his saddle, Seth felt the letter he'd gotten at the fort crinkle in the pocket of his trousers. He compressed his lips. So Liza wanted him back. The gall of that woman! After worming her way into his younger brother's life for no other reason than to spite Seth, she'd seen the error of her ways and wanted to call it quits. As if he'd go behind Drew's back like that! He grimaced and shook his head.

Time to get rid of that fool thing before Red came across it. Removing the papers from his pocket, Seth tore them to shreds and let the wind scatter the pieces far and wide.

Women. There sure was a shortage of truly honest and decent ones. Ones with real spirit who could bring out the best in a man, make him want to settle down.

When a certain feminine face and form drifted across his consciousness, Seth wasn't quite so quick to squelch the green-eyed vision . . . even though he figured he had a lot of good years left to boss trails while he saved up for that thoroughbred horse ranch he'd always dreamed of.

Urging Sagebrush after a cow that was too far off the trail, Seth spotted a familiar-looking cloth item on the ground and swung down to pick it up.

16

*J*ust before going over the sloping shoulder of the mountains, the girls paused for a last glance backward in the sage-scented morning, memorizing a scene they were unlikely ever to see again. The shining Sweetwater River, after its tempestuous roar through Devil's Gap, meandered lazily beneath a lucid aquamarine sky. Independence Rock looked like a slumbering turtle in the vast expanse of dry sage, and on the eastern horizon, misty hills discreetly hid their cache of new graves.

The trail ascending into the Rockies was lined with crusted snowbanks soiled with mud, twigs, and animal tracks. The route grew increasingly rough and rugged, some portions necessitating the use of chains and double teams to drag wagons one at a time up the steep grades. The temperature, too, reached new extremes. In the pleasant sunshine, rivulets of melted ice would trickle downhill to water sporadic patches of green starred with brilliant yellow flowers and clumped with iris. But at night, folks shivered around the insufficient sagebrush fires, longing for some of the spare blankets only recently discarded.

Hard days later they crested the summit, where massive clouds churned threateningly across the curved sky. Early snow dusted the range to the north. Sarah hunkered down into the turned-up collar of her coat and frowned at her sister as Amanda drove onward. "Isn't this where we're supposed to cross the Great Divide?" she hollered above the howling wind. "Somehow, I expected to see a dramatic gorge, or something spectacular—but it's only a grassy meadow!" She perused the wide, bumpy plain between two solid walls of impassible mountains.

"My thoughts exactly." Amanda grinned as a gust flailed her scarf. Then she sobered. "They say Doctor Marcus Whitman knelt with a flag and a Bible and prayed over the West on his first trip through this pass, before he ever set up the mission where he and his wife ministered to the Cayuse Indians."

Sarah pondered the tragic end of the courageous missionaries a moment before turning to a cheerier thought. "Well, at least the place isn't as rough and rugged as the route we had to take to get here. But I still would have expected some unforgettable landmark to indicate the crossing of the *Great Divide!*"

Amanda nodded in agreement.

The train rolled steadily through South Pass, then began the downward grade to the west. They paused at a spring for an icy ceremonial toast from the westward flowing water, then continued down to camp beneath the willows at Little Sandy Creek.

After supper, Sarah Jane left Amanda working on sewing projects and headed toward the Hill wagon.

Bethany and Tad came running the minute they saw her.

"Look at the pretty flowers I picked, Miss Sarah," Bethany said, proudly displaying the colorful wildflowers in her hand.

"And I found a real nice stone." Tad held out his open palm. "Pa says I can keep it, too."

Sarah smiled. "That's nice. I'm happy for both of you." Their father laid aside the worn harness he was examining and stood. "Mind keeping an eye on my pair while I go talk to your sister?" he asked.

Meeting his gaze, Sarah felt the color heighten in her cheeks. "Not at all. I'll take the children for a walk."

"Thanks. Much obliged." With that, he strode away.

Sarah wondered what he and Amanda would be discussing, then filled her lungs and exhaled. A person could have all kinds of things to talk about on an extended journey like this one. Maybe he was weary of having to look after their wagon in addition to his. Maybe he needed some mending done.

"Will you tell us a story, Miss Sarah?" Bethy's huge blue eyes rounded as she gazed raptly up at her.

"A scary one," Tad chimed in. "With dragons and sailing ships and—"

His sister pouted. "No. One with princesses and castles."

Sarah Jane wrapped an arm around each of them and gave a light squeeze. "Tell you what. I'll tell you my very favorite Bible story, about Naaman the leper and his little slave girl."

"Oh, goody!" Bethany clapped. "I like that one, too!"

❧

Sewing the hem in a flannel baby gown, Amanda looked up as Jared came toward her. "Good evening," she said politely.

He removed his hat and inclined his head, then without waiting for an invitation, lowered himself to a corner of the blanket. His posture remained rigid. "Where is everybody?" she asked lightly, gazing hopefully past him for his brood.

"The kids, you mean? Sarah took them for a walk."

Amanda gave an understanding nod. Something was in the air, she could feel it. Taking up her sewing again, her fingers trembled unaccountably, and she pricked her finger.

He appeared nervous too, fiddling with the brim of his hat, not quite meeting her gaze. "Amanda, I . . . have something to ask you," he began.

Now she was more than a little uneasy. "Something wrong with one of the children?" she asked, trying to steer the conversation in a safe direction.

"No, no. Nothing like that. Nothing like that at all."

"Oh, well, have we been making pests of ourselves, then? Sarah and I? Taking up too much of their time?"

He let out a slow breath. "This has nothing to do with Tad or Beth. Well, actually it does, sort of."

"I don't understand." Alarm bells were clanging in earnest inside Amanda's head. *Please, please, don't let it be what I think it is,* she prayed silently even as her heart began to throb with dread. Laying aside her project, she expended the enormous amount of effort required to look directly at him.

"This'll probably come as a shock, but I want you to hear me out. Don't say a word till I'm done."

"But—"

Jared's straight brows dipped slightly, silencing her. He cleared his throat and looked around. Then his eyes met hers. "I don't have to tell you how hard it's been on my kids—and me—losing their mother."

"I understand, but—"

This time a pleading look cut her off. "I came pretty near changing my mind about heading west, when she died. But there was nothing to go back to."

Feeling a shiver course through her, Amanda held her hands out to the warmth of the fire a few feet away.

"Gave more thought to dropping out when it seemed the trip was gonna be too hard on the young'uns. But then you and your sister stepped in." He shrugged. "Now they're normal kids again. Happy, enthusiastic about living out west. And you know what? So am I."

"Jared—"

"Not till I'm done, remember? I might never have enough gumption to bring this up again."

Amanda clamped her lips together.

"What I'm trying to say is, the kids and I would be mighty pleased if you were to go with us to wherever we settle. It's not right for them to grow up without a ma. I'd marry you, of course, make no mistake about that. And I'd be good to you, Amanda. Real good. I think the world of you, and so do my little ones."

Her mouth parted, whether in shock or dismay, she really wasn't sure. But her heart truly went out to Jared Hill. No one had to tell her he was a kind man, a sensitive and caring father. And she felt instinctively that he'd make a wonderful husband, too . . . if a woman were so inclined.

He tipped his head self-consciously. "Oh, I know I'm not much to look at. You could do lots better than me, that's for sure."

Amanda reached over with her hand and covered one of his, stilling its assault on the poor hat. "You, Jared Hill, are one of the nicest,

283

most decent men I have ever met in my entire life. And you've done twice as much for us as we've ever done for you."

He smiled wryly. "Pretty sure I hear a but coming."

"Not for the reason you think," she admitted, then rattled off the first thing that came to her head. "It isn't you. It's me. I already have my future all planned out . . . and it doesn't include marriage—to any-one. There are things I want to do, on my own. And there's Sarah to consider. I'm the only family she has."

"But your sister's welcome to come with us, too," he insisted. "We'd both look after her until she found someone she wanted to spend her life with. You wouldn't have to worry about her at all."

Amanda hesitated.

Jared filled the silence. "Well, it'd be enough if you'd just think on it. Would you do that? Who knows, maybe by the time we go the rest of the way to Oregon you might change your mind."

"I wouldn't count on it," she answered in what she sincerely hoped was a kind tone. "It's not fair for you to get your hopes up too high."

"Then, I won't. But just know the offer stands. I'll not beat you over the head with it. It's up to you."

"Thank you, Jared. I really mean that. It's the kindest, nicest offer I've had in my life."

He grinned, a touch of embarrassment tugging it off center. "I might have figured you'd had others."

"Only one. One too many," she confessed bitterly.

His expression softened into one of understanding. "Must have been a dimwit to let a fine woman like you slip away." His face grew solemn and he cleared his throat once more, then ambled to his feet. "Well, I'd be obliged if you just gave the matter some thought. It's all I ask."

Amanda got up also. "I will. Truly. But—"

"I know." With a cockeyed smile, Jared turned and went back in the direction of his wagon.

A host of conflicting emotions made her watch after him until he was out of sight.

That night, when the majority of folks gathered around the camp-fire for a hymn sing, Amanda remained behind. Taking down the empty wooden pail outside her wagon, she glanced toward the gathering. Hardships of the journey showed on everyone, clothing ragged and worn hung loosely on the thinner forms, but the faces aglow with the golden light of the big fire looked peaceful. It was no surprise to hear "Abide With Me" issue forth soon after the singing began. Smiling, she drew away and strolled the short distance to the stream.

The quiet, gurgling brook had been pretty in the fading light of day, but now in the growing darkness it surpassed its former beauty as the ripples spilled over rocks in the stream bed, catching remnants of firelight in shining ribbons of silver and gold. Amanda set down the bucket. Stooping near the edge, she trailed her fingers in the cold current, then licked her fingertips, enjoying the sweetness of pure water after so many bitter and cloudy springs.

"Nice crisp evening," a low voice said quietly.

Amanda sprang to her feet.

Several yards away, the wagon master stood after filling and capping his canteen. He thumbed the brim of his hat in a polite gesture.

"Mr. Holloway." She returned her attention to the creek as, to her dismay, the rate of her pulse increased.

"You don't cotton to singing?"

Her hands slid into her coat pockets in an effort to remain casual. "Normally I would. Just not tonight."

From the corner of her eye, she saw him nod slightly. "I was glad to see you back on your feet so soon after being sick."

Slowly raising her lashes, she peered toward him. Warmth coursed through her, almost making the cool, fall evening feel more like a midsummer night. She swallowed. "I heard you'd come by. Thank you for the concern."

His dark eyes were completely lost in the shadow of his hat brim, but Amanda could feel the intensity of his fixed gaze. "I like to make sure my company stays healthy."

Amanda didn't respond.

"You've been kind of a surprise—or rather, amazement—to me," the man went on. "Never thought you'd stick out the hardships of the trip."

"I hope you didn't lose any bets over it," she blurted, immediately hating herself.

But he chuckled.

Amanda felt compelled to smooth over the hasty remark. "We're thankful God has brought us this far."

With a soft huff, he started toward her. "You're really serious about giving the Almighty all the credit, even though you're the one doing all the work?"

Sensing that he was baiting her, Amanda frowned. It seemed immensely important for the wagon master to understand her simple logic, her simple faith. "He gives us strength to do it."

"I suppose." Closer now, he picked up the pail and dipped it into the stream, filling it to the brim, then set it next to her on the grass.

Her surprise over the act of kindness almost clouded over the realization that he hadn't made light of her convictions this time.

Mr. Holloway continued to stare. "Oh." He reached into an inside pocket of his buckskin jacket and drew out a calico bonnet. "I believe this belongs to you."

"Y-yes," she gasped. "It does. I lost it a few days ago." Taking the article from him, her fingers brushed his calloused hand, and a maddening blush flamed her face. It intensified with the awareness that the cloth retained the heat of his body. She knew better than to trust her voice. "Thank you," she could only whisper.

He nearly smiled. "Wouldn't want you coming down with something else, now, would we?" he teased.

Amanda's lips parted in disbelief at this glimpse of yet another aspect of his personality. He was far more complex than she'd given him credit for . . . and perhaps, far more *fascinating*. Realizing the dangerous turn her imaginings were taking, Amanda became aware that she was gawking at the man and clamped her mouth closed.

"Well, I wouldn't stay out here too long, Miss Shelby. Night brings out all kinds of thirsty animals." He bent to pick up the water bucket, then motioned with his head for her to walk beside him.

"Do you—?" Both of them spoke at once.

Having paused at the same time as well, they smiled. He gestured for her to go first.

Amanda only shook her head. "Never mind." In an attempt to prolong the conversation she was on the verge of making some inane query regarding the trail. She was more curious as to what he had to say.

"I . . . don't suppose you like horses."

Completely taken by surprise, she turned her gaze fully on him. "I—they're beautiful creatures. I've never had one of my own, of course, but who wouldn't think they're wonderful animals?"

He showed no visible reaction. They had reached her wagon. Setting the pail up on the schooner within her easy reach, he then assisted her up as well.

Conscious of the touch of his hands on her waist, Amanda had to remember to breathe as he lightly set her down. "Thank you, Mr. Holloway," she managed as, with a half smile, he walked away.

Inside the warmer confines of the bowed top, Amanda fought a peculiar assortment of giddy, fluttery sensations she had never before experienced. Left over from her bout with sickness, she rationalized. That was it. Surely her imaginings were getting the best of her. It was time to calm down.

When at last she had regained her composure, she thought again of the unexpected marriage proposal—more than likely the cause of all this confusion—and knelt in the honey-colored lantern light.

Dear Heavenly Father, I thank you for the opportunity to come to you in prayer. You've been so merciful to Sarah and me over the many miles we've traveled. You've looked after us, kept us from harm, and given us so many blessings, so many friends.

Surely You know of this new predicament I face. A proposal—after all the time I've spent convincing myself never to trust a man again, much less expect one to look upon me with favor. I don't think I've given Mr. Hill the slightest indication of my desiring to replace his dear dead wife. Nor have his actions toward me, to be truthful. More than likely he's thinking of his children, trying to do what's best for them.

She paused and sighed. *But I couldn't imagine committing myself to another man unless I truly, truly loved him. And the affection I feel for Jared is not of that nature. In fact, I—*

Refusing even to finish the stunning thought trying to come to life within her heart, Amanda steeled herself against it and returned to her petition with renewed urgency. *Please give me wisdom to make the right choice. Help me to do your will, to do what's best. In Jesus' name, Amen.*

Not exactly at peace, Amanda draped her coat over one of the barrels and slid into the warm quilts and blankets on the pallet.

But it was not Jared Hill's face that remained in her thoughts.

17

While they camped at Little Sandy, a vote was taken to bypass Fort Bridger and navigate the shorter route to Bear Valley known as Sublett's Cutoff. The idea of saving eighty-five miles—even at the price of heading straight out into a grassless desert tableland—seemed of more import than the difficulties they knew would have to be faced. Every available water container was filled to the brim in the clear cool river before leaving, and the men cut a supply of long grass for the animals.

The thought of seven days' less travel appealed to Amanda, whatever the hardships. Considering all she and Sarah Jane had endured up to this point, she had no qualms about trusting the Lord to take them through a dry march as well.

The memory of Seth Holloway's unexpected kindness last evening had kept her awake long into the night, try as she might to slough it off as mere good-neighbor courtesy. The man was an enigma. Though usually displaying a hard, domineering side of his character, he also possessed a caring, thoughtful side. The latter caused Amanda the most unrest and was hardest to ignore.

And there was Jared Hill's proposal to consider. The more she thought about it, the more convinced she became that the needs of the motherless children were uppermost in the widower's mind. After all, a remote homestead in sparsely settled territory demanded the combined efforts of a man and a woman to provide a nurturing environment for little ones. And she truly loved Bethany and Tad as if they were her own younger brother and sister . . . yet—

"Mandy?" Sarah asked, keeping pace with the plodding mules. "Would you like me to drive? You look tired."

Amanda shook her head. "I'm fine, really. It was just kind of a short night." She paused, debating whether or not to seek her younger sister's advice. But who else was there to ask? "Sissy . . . what do you think of Mr. Hill?"

Sarah turned her head so abruptly she stumbled on the uneven terrain. "Why?"

"He . . . he's asked me to marry him." Amanda watched the color drain from her sister's face.

"D-do you love him?" she asked, her words barely audible over the hoof falls and the rattle and creak of the wagon.

Amanda averted her gaze to the countryside, still amazingly pleasant for all the dire predictions of what lay ahead. "I like and respect him very much. It would be hard to find a more decent man." Hearing no reply, she glanced at her sibling again.

Sarah moistened her lips. "Does he . . . love you?"

A ragged breath emptied Amanda's lungs. She tipped her head in thought. "We both love the children. I think that's what's most important to him at the moment."

"They are dear, aren't they? Truly dear." A wistful smile played over Sarah's lips.

Amanda thought she detected a mistiness in her sister's eyes before Sarah quickly cut a glance to the earth. But the tear her sibling brushed away while trying to hide the action was not imagined. "Are you all right, Sissy?"

Sarah merely nodded. But she did not speak another word for hours.

❧

Crossing the crucible of sand speckled with prickly creosote and mesquite shrubs, the temperature climbed with the merciless sun. The bone-weary emigrants decided to rest during the day under the meager shade of canvas or wagon and journey at night, to spare the animals. But at least half a dozen beasts perished anyway, dropping right where they stood in the extreme scorching temperatures. People began abandoning wagons and doubling what remained of their teams.

Days later, the sight of the Green River on the far western side couldn't have been more welcome. The animals practically stampeded toward the swift, deep water. When everyone's thirst had been sated, the necessary preparations began for transporting the company across the formidable river. Some people by now routinely unpacked their heavy wagons and floated their stores over the water on rafts, then had to repack everything once the empty wagons reached the other side.

Amanda, having successfully forded numerous rivers, decided to chance this one as well. She tied down everything and inched the team into the Green after one of the other rigs.

The mules balked at the force of the flow, but started toward the opposite bank, making slow but steady progress.

Part way across, a front wheel struck something and buckled. The wagon pitched sharply to the left.

With Sarah's scream still ringing in her ears, Amanda plunged headlong into the frigid mountain flow. The roiling water whisked her away, hiding any view of her sister or the wagon.

Helpless against the force of the current, she made a futile attempt to swim, but the weight of her sodden skirts pulled her under, tangling about her legs—and her shoes felt as heavy as anvils. With the icy river roaring over her head and shoulders, Amanda fought desperately to keep her face above the surface, but each time she gasped for air she swallowed more water. She had to try to make it to shallower water—but no amount of thrashing with her arms could overcome the force of the relentless current. And the cold mercilessly sapped her strength. *I'm going to drown!* The sick realization clenched her heart. What would become of poor Sarah! *Dear God,* she prayed desperately, *take care of her. Don't let anything happen to her.*

Suddenly something snagged her around the shoulders. Cut off her air.

Amanda writhed frantically to get free.

"Don't fight me!"

As the command penetrated her numbed mind, Amanda became aware of a strong arm encircling her. Exhausted, she gave in, aware only of a man's labored breathing as he attempted to get them both to shore.

Coughing water from her lungs, Amanda clung to her rescuer. She blinked to clear her vision, then raised her lashes—and discovered that the masculine body pressed to hers was the wagon master's! The two of them were being pulled toward the bank by a rope.

When Amanda's feet grazed the sandy bottom, she was scooped up and carried to dry land. Still coughing as Seth Holloway set her down and loosed her death grip from his neck, she shivered uncontrollably in the wind.

His partner quickly wrapped the blanket from behind his saddle around her, while Mr. Holloway, enshrouded in his own, mounted his horse. Then she was lifted again into the wagon master's arms, and he started back toward the crossing site.

Deep shudders racked Amanda as the horse plodded along. She relived the ordeal as if it were a dream that hadn't ended yet—and she wondered if she would ever again in her life feel warm enough. Gathering the pitiful remnants of her remaining energy, she tried to speak over her violent shivers as they jounced along. Nothing would come out. "S-Sarah," she finally managed between chatters of her teeth.

"The others are probably looking after her."

"Y-you s-saved my life. Th-thank you."

An angry whoosh deflated his chest. "You almost got us both killed!" he ranted. "You had no business driving that wagon across by yourself. But you're bound and determined to prove me wrong." With another furious huff he shook his head. "I swear, you've been nothing but trouble from the first time I saw you!"

Utterly crushed by the attack, Amanda felt welling tears, but she had no time to respond. They had arrived at camp.

"Mandy!" Sarah ran up and yanked her to the ground in a bone-crushing hug. "Thank heaven you're all right!"

"Poor thing's near froze to death," she heard Mrs. Randolph say as another blanket was thrown about her. "Bring her over by the fire. Give a hustle, now. We have some good strong coffee on to help warm her up."

Amanda allowed them to lead her to the blazing campfire. Glancing over her shoulder, she saw Seth Holloway headed in the opposite direction. But she was far too spent to give further thought to her reluctant rescuer or his insulting tongue-lashing.

Shielded from view by a wall of blankets and concerned women, Sarah Jane stripped Amanda's sodden clothing from her stiff, shivering frame. Then layers of dry covers and quilts wrapped her from head to toe, providing the first measure of real warmth she'd felt since being drawn from the frigid river.

Much sooner than she would have expected, the ministrations of her sister and the kind older woman who'd become such a friend to them began thawing her out. With her stiff fingers wrapped around a hot mug, Amanda drained the last drop of coffee, then asked the question foremost in her mind. "When can I go lie down in the wagon?"

Sarah paled. "That's the bad news. But the men were able to salvage most of our things, and Mr. Hill is trying to fashion a cart for us from what's left of the schooner. When it tipped, he and another man came to help me. They saved the mules, too. Poor things were scared silly, braying their heads off."

"But don't you worry none, darlin'," Mrs. Randolph said gently. "You and Sarah Jane can sleep under our rig every night. We'll look after you."

Still stunned by the dire fate of the prairie schooner, Amanda drew little comfort from her neighbor's offer. Her expression must have been transparent, for Sarah Jane swiftly took command of the conversation, saying more all at once than she'd said for days. "Your heroic rescue was the talk of the camp, Mandy," she announced much too brightly.

Amanda just stared at her.

Her sister nodded. "Everyone gasped when that wheel snapped and you were flung into the river. Mr. Holloway had already crossed with the herd and was riding along the bank when you fell in. You should have seen him!" Sarah's eyes grew large. "He yelled something to that Mr. Hanfield and charged after you. Honestly, if ever a real

true knight existed, that man fits the bill. It was almost . . . romantic."
A smile gave emphasis to her airy sigh.

But Amanda felt tears gathering inside her soul. All she wanted
was to be alone so she could cry her heart out. And she knew it had
nothing to do with her harrowing experience.

Having merged from the cutoff onto the rugged hills of the main trail
once more, Amanda truly appreciated the way the much smaller cart
handled. It wasn't exactly as stylish as something back east, but considering the poor shape of the materials used to make it, it rolled over
the high ridges and through the pine forests as well—if not better—
than many of the heavy wagons. Best of all, hitched to only four mules
rather than six, it gave the animals an easier lot, too. Amanda could
rotate them. And Jared Hill had thoughtfully made a canvas cover,
which provided at least some shelter, in a pinch.

She had not seen Mr. Holloway since the incident at the Green
River. Nor did she intend to see or speak to him for the remainder of
the journey. Sarah, too, she noticed, had reverted to that oddly quiet
way she'd acquired of late. She rarely spent time with Alvin or his
friends, and even her moments with Bethany and Tad seemed
weighted by her countenance.

Jared Hill had insisted the girls drive in front of him so he could
keep an eye on their tentative conveyance, so the children normally
walked beside either her or Sarah Jane, whichever one of them was
afoot. Their endless chatter kept Amanda's mind occupied—another
of life's blessings—while yet another ten, twenty, fifty miles ticked by.
Would this tedious journey never end? Points of interest they passed
along the way no longer held the slightest appeal, not even the amazing
springs where the water tasted like soda.

Lost in moody depression, one afternoon, Amanda thought she
imagined a cry in the distance. She peered ahead at a tiny cloud of
dust that appeared to be coming toward them.

The shout came again.

"Gold!"

And again. *"Gold!"*

Much clearer now. Folks up front hollered it back to the rest and halted their teams.

Upon reaching the company, the galloping rider skidded his mount to a stop. "There's gold in California!" he yelled for all to hear, panting between breaths. "At Sutter's Mill, on the American River. Enough for all! I'm ridin' east to fetch my brothers." With that, he spurred his lathered horse and sped on.

A moment of silent shock swiftly evolved into an excited murmur, then erupted to hoots and howls.

"Well, I, for one, am headin' to Californy," one man bellowed. "Soon as we pass the fort!" Waving his hat, he kicked up his heels and jumped aboard his outfit, clucking his team to motion.

"Me, too," another hollered.

A virtual shouting match broke out down the line, between folks bound and determined to grab this chance to get rich, and others who declared they were continuing to Oregon despite what could turn out to be a rumor started by some practical joker.

Just listening to the melee, Amanda and Sarah exchanged questioning frowns.

Then Mr. Holloway cantered by, one hand raised, on his way to the front of the line. "Let's not get all het up, folks," he said a number of times. "Stay calm. Whether there's gold or not, there's plenty of time for you and your animals to rest up at the fort while you think the matter through. Then if you decide to turn off on the California Trail when we come to it, at least you'll have a better chance of getting there in one piece."

But there was no slowing down some of the determined travelers. Breaking off from the rest of the train, those wagons pulled ahead, anxious to set out on fortune's path.

A much smaller group made camp that night.

Amanda felt exposed as she and Sarah were forced to sleep out in the open. Listening to plaintiff yips and howls of coyotes and wolves, the rustlings in the sagebrush that could be any number of wild things, she rolled up in her blanket like a mummy and lay awake waiting for utter exhaustion to claim her.

All she wanted was to get somewhere. *Anywhere.* Never to go another mile again. Someplace where she never had to set eyes on Seth Holloway as long as she lived. As they had for the past several nights, burning tears slid out from behind her closed eyes and into her hair.

18

rom a distance of five miles the whitewashed fur-trading
post of Fort Hall was visible, occupying half an acre of sagebrush plain alongside the shining Snake River. The breeze
played over the red flag on the pole, ruffling the initials of the Hud-
son's Bay Company. But this time upon approaching a fort, the mood
of the company was a peculiar mixture of excitement and subdued
resignation.

Amanda gave no more than a cursory glance to the five-foot wall
surrounding the two-story bastion or the hewn log buildings inside.
Word had it there was no meat, flour, or rice to be had. Only a small
supply of coffee and sugar—and that at fifty cents a pint. Nevertheless,
two days of rest would be appreciated. "Look, Pa!" she heard Tad
shout. "A cannon! A real cannon!"

But before the lad could skip off to the piece of artillery parked
in the courtyard, his father reined him in. "Slow down, son. That's
nothing to fool with."

The boy groaned in disappointment.

Jared tousled the towhead's hair on his approach to Amanda and
Sarah. "If you two would look after the young'uns, I'd like to go hunting with the other men. See if I can replenish our stores."

Amanda nodded. "Go on. I'll see to your oxen."

With a grateful smile at her and Sarah, he retrieved his rifle and
walked toward the loose horses among the animals that had trailed
the company. Amanda thought she caught a wistful longing in her
sister's expression as he left.

"I'm hungry, Miss Sarah," Bethany implored.

Her brother perked up. "Me, too."

"Well, let's see what we can scrape together," Amanda heard her say, "while Sissy takes care of the animals."

❧

That night, the camp was anything but quiet. News of the gold strike had the whole place abuzz, precluding the customary music and dancing while folks made plans for the remainder of the journey. Amanda and Sarah sipped coffee by their evening fire until Jared tucked his little ones into bed.

Moments after he came to join them, the Randolphs paid a visit as well. Beaming from ear to ear, the older couple had a stranger in tow. It took Amanda only one look to guess the young man was their son. He bore an uncanny resemblance to his father, already possessing similar body structure and bearing, and the same pear-shaped face. But one striking difference stood out—he had the brightest red hair Amanda had ever seen.

"We'd like you all to meet our Charlie," Minnie Randolph said proudly, her small blue eyes aglow as they rested on him. "He's just come over from California to meet his pa an' me. Charlie, this is Amanda—the sweetest little gal a body could know—and her sister Sarah Jane, and Jared Hill, our neighbor." She indicated each in turn.

Amanda blushed at the emphasis of her name.

"Howdy," he managed, fair sunburnt skin turning an even deeper hue up to his hairline as he nodded to her, then Sarah. He shook hands with Jared, who had risen to his feet.

"How'd you find the desert trail?" Jared asked.

"Not much good a person can say about that," the young man admitted candidly. "But I figured my folks would do all right with me to help out."

"Would any of you care for some coffee?" Amanda asked, regaining her composure as Sarah spread out an extra blanket.

"Don't mind if we do," the elder Mr. Randolph said, kneading his bearded jaw. He assisted his wife, then settled his solid bulk between her and their son as they accepted the proffered refreshment.

"Mm. Tastes mighty good," the old man commented. "Near as good as Minnie's, if I do say so."

His spouse beamed in agreement. "Reason we come by," she said, centering her attention on Amanda, "is to invite you an' your sister to come to California with us when we take the cutoff."

Aware of the woman's son on the fringe of her vision, Amanda blanched. "We—"

She held up a gnarled hand. "I know, the store an' all. But seems like the Good Lord's layin' a real good chance at your feet. You won't know a soul when you get to Oregon, and more'n likely, folks who've suffered the hot sands and dry waste of the desert will be needin' clothes as much as anybody else. Might be, you could even happen across a few nuggets of gold to help get you started. We'll be passin' nigh Sutter's Fort on the way to our new place, a handful of miles farther."

"I've been considering heading off on that fork myself," Jared announced out of the blue before Amanda had opportunity to reply. "I was gonna make you and Sarah Jane the same offer."

Sarah, raising her mug to her lips, halted midway and lowered it to her lap instead.

Amanda had never once considered branching off the main trail and settling in California. Her sights had been fixed on Oregon since before leaving Independence. She looked to Sarah for a response and found her sister's expression unreadable as the younger girl stared at Alvin Rivers' wagon.

"My other offer still stands, too," Jared told Amanda quietly when the others began talking among themselves.

It was all too much to take in at once. Amanda felt torn in two. Either route had definite merit as well as dreaded pitfalls. But she wasn't exactly up to committing her entire future in marriage just yet, either. Looking to her sibling once more, her gaze drifted above Sarah's shoulder and happened upon Seth Holloway, exiting the fort's general store with his partner. That same instant, his attention flicked her way. He tipped his head slightly in Amanda's direction and said something to Mr. Hanfield. They both laughed.

Amanda set her jaw. One good thing about the Lord, she reasoned, He always provides a way of escape, just as He promised in First Corinthians. With a glance encompassing the Randolphs, Jared Hill, and her sister, she hiked her chin. "We'll do it. We'll go to California!"

◆

"You're not serious!" Alvin snapped his sketchpad closed in the only true display of his temper Sarah had ever witnessed. His charcoal pencil and blending stick fell unheeded to the sandy ground outside the fort, where he'd been working on a new landscape.

"I'm afraid I am," she replied, shielding her eyes from the bright sun. "When the wagon train leaves this fort tomorrow morning, Mandy and I have decided to take the California Trail with the Randolphs, Mr. Hill, and whoever else will be splitting off from the company."

"But why would you do a fool thing like that?" Not to be put off, he sidled up to her, his fingertips lightly grazing up and down her forearm. "For—gold? I'm already in line for a considerable fortune, you know. I'm not about to waste weeks and months grubbing through a bunch of rocks and mud for a few paltry nuggets."

"I never suggested you should."

His movements halted. "I see." The light that dawned in his head was almost visible in his eyes and lent them a steely glitter. "So this is good-bye, then. Fare thee well and all that."

Sarah nodded, brushing aside a loose tendril the fall breeze whisked over her face. "I thought I'd tell you now, while there's still time to talk. But please don't think ill of me, Alvin. I'll always remember you. I'll think back with pleasure on the happy times we shared on this journey. And I truly hope one day you'll find someone who'll fulfill all your dreams. She'll be a very fortunate person."

"Indeed." A smirk lifted a corner of his mouth. "I thought I already had."

"No." Slowly shaking her head, Sarah smiled thinly. "There was only room in your heart for me. My dream is to be part of a family . . . the bigger the better. To bear children and watch them grow and have

300

children of their own. Even if I were poor and had to scratch for my existence I could never settle for less than that."

He raked long fingers through his wiry curls and shook his head. Then, reaching for both her hands, he pulled her into a warm hug, his heart beating against hers for several seconds until finally he eased her to arm's length. "Tell you one thing, Sarah Jane Shelby. If it were a few years down the line and I'd already been to all the places I plan to see, I just might be tempted to *settle for* a piece of that dream of yours. But not right now."

She smiled sadly.

Alvin paused and searched her face as though committing it to memory. Then he raised her chin with the edge of an index finger and lightly brushed her lips with his. "Well, do be happy . . . little *friend*. Any young lady who happens across my path in the future is sure going to have a lot to measure up to. Who knows, perhaps one day we'll meet again, and you'll be able to show me your brood of little ones."

Fighting tears, Sarah could only attempt to smile as she took his hand and squeezed it in mute silence. Then she turned away and walked slowly back to the gate.

❧

Amanda braced her heart against even a twinge of regret the next day as the cutoff to California loomed ever nearer. Ignoring an inner sense of guilt over not having prayed about her rash decision, she purposefully closed her mind to scenery and everyday matters and focused on the future, on the blessed time when she would no longer be forced to suffer the unbearable presence of wagon master Holloway. She determined not to even announce her change in plan to the man. Likely he would be relieved anyway that she and Sarah would no longer be his responsibility. And Amanda had no desire to provide another opportunity for him to gloat. Nor would she permit her gaze to seek him out during nooning stops or evening camps. Whatever strange fascination she might have felt toward the man, it was time it died a quick, natural death. So decided, she ceased the solitary evening walks she had previously enjoyed and expended the supreme effort required to center her attention within the three- or four-yard circumference around her person. After all, she had mules to tend, meals to cook and clean up. It would do well to get used to being with the lesser number of travelers who would be turning off at the split tomorrow.

That night at the campfire, Deacon Franklin prayed for those who on the morrow would part company with the remainder of the Oregon Trail travelers. Reflecting on his thoughtful words, afterward, Amanda finally willed herself to sleep. Morning dawned in grayness, and Amanda drew perverse pleasure that it matched her mood. After what seemed an interminable length of time to dispose of breakfast and early chores, the signal finally sounded to roll.

"This is it," Sarah breathed, her excitement barely concealed. With Bethany on one side of her and Tad on the other, she waved to their father and began walking at a brisk pace.

Amanda mustered all her resolve. Tonight, camped on a new trail, her heart would sing a victory song. She was sure of it. Refusing to acknowledge the silly tear that teetered over her lower lashes and plopped onto her hand, she clucked the team forward.

❧

Riding at the rear end of the column, Seth watched the company dwindle as, one by one, wagons turned off onto the California Trail, taking along several head of cattle that they had cut out of the herd earlier this morning. Granted, some folks retained sense enough to continue on to Oregon Territory, but out of the nearly thirty families who had begun this journey at Independence three months ago, it appeared only a handful would stay with the original plan.

Oh well, he mused, it would make the job easier on him, Red, and the scouts. There were some pretty rugged mountains yet to be crossed. He shook his head. The hardships on this route were nothing compared to what lay ahead of those gold-crazy fools. His friend, Thomas Fitzpatrick, had related some amazing tales of overlanders he had bossed across that frying pan.

Only three wagons had yet to come to the branch. Seth watched the Randolphs turn off. He'd known from the onset their destination was to be northern California. He'd found Nelson Randolph a decent man, one who had acquired respect from a lot of the folks during this journey. Having a son come to meet them with the foresight to trail a string of extra mules and water, Seth figured the old couple would make out okay—provided the heat didn't do them in.

Nearby, a bony heifer meandered away from the fringe. Seth nudged his mount in that direction and brought the wanderer back in line.

He glanced ahead once more, and his heart lurched. The Shelby cart had veered onto the southerly trail toward the Raft River—with that widower, Hill, right behind!

A battle raged as Seth fought the irrational desire to chase after Amanda and spare her from the horrific dangers of that route. After all, he had somewhat enjoyed playing rescuer once. But on the other hand, he reminded himself, she was no longer his responsibility now—wasn't that what he'd wanted all along?

He shifted grimly in the saddle and watched the rickety cart growing smaller in the distance. Once Amanda crossed the river, she would be on her way to an entirely different world.

Leaving his own profoundly empty.

19

*S*arah Jane studied her sister as Amanda walked with the children along the blistered sagebrush trail. For days, ever since they had foregone their original plan and taken the California branch, Amanda had been moody and quiet. She seemed to be doing her best to be cheerful around Bethy and Tad and polite to Jared and the Randolphs . . . but she had changed drastically after her near drowning.

Before the incident Amanda had been her normal, jovial self most of the time. Even inwardly happy, as if she had come to terms with the shameful way Pa's dastardly partner had humiliated them all, before thoughts of heading west ever came up. For some time, now, there'd been nary a shred of the bitterness only Sarah could discern in her sibling's eyes. That close brush with death had disturbed Amanda far more deeply than she let on. With a deep sigh, Sarah sent a prayer aloft that God would bring her sister through this hard time.

That night she waited until Amanda's even breathing indicated sleep, then lit a candle and opened her journal to the next page.

Dear Diary,

In my worst imaginings, I never would have dreamed a more sterile, desolate region than is all around us on this California Trail. After crossing the river, we descended upon a landscape consisting entirely of burnt rocks and cinders. High, blackened cliffs towered above our camp the first night.

We found surprisingly good grass and water when we reached the Humboldt River, whose benefits we enjoyed for nearly two weeks—but one day it disappeared into a most distressing alkali swamp, and we left it behind to make our way across a vast sea of hot sand.

The sun beats down upon us mercilessly, sucking the very moisture from our bodies, while the wagon wheels churn up an unbearable cloud of dust. It coats man and beast alike from head to foot, filling our nostrils and burning our eyes. How I yearn to see another glorious waterfall like those we passed after departing Fort Hall.

A snore drifted her way from the confines of the Randolph wagon. Sarah peeked around to see if the sound had roused any of the others, then resumed her writing.

We should reach the mountains tomorrow. We've been looking at them for the past two days as they sat on the horizon like a mirage. Hopefully there will be water there—and grass for our poor, weary animals.

Mandy and I both long to see the end of this journey.

A cool gust of night wind caused Sarah to shiver. Marveling at the vacillating desert temperatures, she tucked the journal away and snuggled deep into her covers.

❧

It was a delightful treat to camp beside a stream again, to have actual shade and lush grasses. For one whole day, the company rested, bathed, and washed clothing in readiness for the trek up the rugged mountain trail.

Amanda had never enjoyed a bath so much—even such a cold one. After the tortures of the desert, she was beginning to feel her spirit come to life again. It seemed the passing of miles helped ease the ache in her heart as well, but she knew it would take some time before it dissipated completely . . . if ever. Surely the worst of the journey must be over. Traipsing back toward the cart with some wet laundry draped over her arm, she saw Jared staring her way as he leaned against the trunk of a tree. "Jared," she said pleasantly.

"Amanda." He tossed a handful of pebbles aside that he'd been rolling around in his hand. "Mind if we talk a spell? Your sister's got the kids."

"Not at all." But a trickle of uneasiness crept along her spine. She carefully laid the clothes on the grass.

Jared sank to the ground and brushed a spot smooth for her, then offered a hand. "Give any more thought to the offer I made a while back?" he asked, his long face became serious as he came right to the point.

She chewed the inside corner of her lip and nodded.

"And?" he prompted.

Turning to him, Amanda let out a nervous breath. Loath as she was to hurt the man, leading him on would be ten times worse. "I cannot accept it," she said softly. "I'm truly sorry."

Jared stared at her for a timeless moment, then expelled a resigned breath as he looked off into the distance. "Figured as much."

"Somehow, I knew you might," she replied, "but I also knew you probably wouldn't understand my reasons."

He plucked a handful of grass and let the breeze take a few blades. "Mind if I ask what they are?"

"One of them, you might be surprised to hear, is love." At his perplexed expression, she went on. "I've grown to love you a lot, on this journey, Jared . . . but it isn't the right sort of love to build a life on."

"Sure about that?"

She nodded. "I told you once that I had no plans ever to marry, and that's truer now than the day I said it. You're an incredible, wonderful man. You deserve a wife who will love you with all her heart . . . and it wouldn't be fair for me to stand in her way."

Jared slowly filled his lungs, obviously mulling her words over in his mind. Averting his gaze once more, he cocked his head back and forth. "Well, I only asked you to consider it. I'll do my best to accept your decision. Even if I don't agree."

"One day you will," Amanda said with a smile. "You'll see."

~&~

"It'd be a shame not to share some of these apple fritters," Amanda remarked, "after hoarding the last of our dried apples so long." She gathered several and wrapped them in a cloth.

Sarah tried to ignore a peculiar awkwardness within as her sister left her and Jared and crossed the small wagon circle toward the Randolphs, seated around their own evening fire. "You've gotten to be a mighty fine cook, Sarah Jane," the widower said, popping the final bite of his own fritter into his mouth. "You and Amanda both." He refilled his mug from the coffeepot and relaxed against the wheel of his Conestoga.

More than a little aware of Jared's presence and close proximity, the scant width of a blanket from her, Sarah Jane tried not to blush as her eyes met his. She wished she had courage enough to lose herself in their sad blue depths, but quickly looked away instead. "I think Sissy and I are more surprised than anyone! You would not believe the awful fare we had to choke down when we first started out on the trail. Of course," she rambled on in her nervousness, "we had a pretty good teacher in Mrs. Randolph. She's taught us a lot."

"Fine woman."

"Yes. A great friend. Mandy thinks the absolute world of her and her husband after all they've done for us. That's probably the main reason she wanted to share our dessert with them tonight."

He nodded, idly taking another gulp of the strong brew.

"Mr. Hill—"

"Jared," he corrected. "Fits better."

Sarah swallowed. "I know," she said breathlessly. "It's just that— Well—You're so much older than the boys I've been around all my life."

He gave her a pained look.

She wanted to crawl into a hole. "I—I don't mean you're old. Not at all."

A chuckle rumbled from deep inside his chest.

Drawing a huge breath to calm herself, Sarah tried again. "What I mean is, you're different. Not like any man I've ever met before. That's what I was trying to say."

"Thanks. I think." A strange grin curved one side of his mouth. "A pity your sister doesn't share those sentiments."

"What do you mean? She admires you a lot."

"Right." His sarcasm was evident.

"Truly."

"Just not enough to marry me, is all."

Certain she was dreaming, Sarah's heart skipped a beat. "Mandy told you that?" She cast a disbelieving look toward the Randolph wagon and held her breath, waiting for his reply.

"Yep. Well, no use bothering a young gal like you with my troubles, is there?" Dumping out the remains of his coffee, Jared got up and brushed off his backside, then stepped over the tongue of his wagon, exiting the circle.

Nibbling her lip, Sarah flicked a cautious glance around to make sure no one was paying them any mind. Then she gathered every ounce of gumption she possessed and rose to follow him, not even sure what she'd say. "I'm not exactly a child, you know," she blurted, flushing scarlet at being so brazen. What on earth would he think of her?

Jared, about to take a stride, stopped mid-motion and turned.

Sarah's pulse began to throb. She could barely hear over the rush in her ears. "Just because Mandy's the oldest, that doesn't mean she's the smartest. I—"

A small incredulous smile crept across the widower's mouth. He didn't move, didn't interrupt. His countenance softened considerably as he gazed down at her.

Sarah felt her insides quiver. She couldn't hold back a shuddering breath. Amanda would certainly call her to task for such boldness— but there were so few occasions to be alone with Jared Hill. And now to take a chance she never would have considered had Amanda accepted his proposal. But with her sister's rejection, he could easily turn off the trail at the next branch—and neither of them would ever see him again. Sarah pressed onward, hoping her voice and her shaking legs wouldn't fail her. "I . . . wouldn't have refused you." There. She'd said it, even if the utterance had been barely audible. Now she waited—almost prayed—for the world to open up and swallow her. She would positively die if he made light of her declaration.

He stared for a heartbeat. That merest hint of a smile reappeared as his even brows rose a notch. "Sarah . . . if you're—" He stopped, kneaded his temples, then began again. "A beautiful young girl like you—"

"Woman," she corrected bravely. *Desperately.*

"But I'm old enough—"

"To need someone who loves you," she whispered, unable to stop now without baring her soul. "And loves Bethy and Tad, too. And can't bear even the thought of having to say good-bye when we get to the end of—wherever it is we're going."

"You mean that?" he asked, appearing utterly astonished. "You'd actually settle for me? With that face of yours you could have your choice of a thousand young bucks!" He wagged his head in wonder even as undeniable hope rose in his eyes.

"My heart has already made its choice."

Jared searched her face for a moment, as if still uncertain whether to believe this was really happening. Then ever so gently, he reached toward her.

Sarah melted into his arms, barely able to hold back tears of profoundest relief as she felt his strong heart keeping pace with hers.

"I never thought for a moment I could have you," he said softly, cradling the back of her head in his palm as he rocked her in his embrace. "I figured, I mean, with you being young, you deserve somebody just starting out in life, same as you. Your sister didn't seem as taken up with fellows her age."

"Does that mean you might grow to love me, too, someday?"

His embrace tightened as he hugged her closer. "It means I won't have to go on fighting the feelings I've had for you since the first time I saw you with my young'uns. When I was sure I'd never have this chance."

Sarah turned her face up to his with a slightly teary smile. "Life's filled with chances, isn't it?"

"It is at that, Sarah Jane. It is at that." And Jared's lips at last claimed hers.

Seth stared up at the midnight sky. It seemed as if every star that had ever been created was out tonight, each of them representing one of the countless ways he'd been a fool. If he lived to be a hundred he would never forget the sight of Amanda's cart turning off the trail.

Or the anguish in her eyes on that day at the river.

He turned in his bedroll, seeking comfort in the stillness while Red was on watch. What had possessed him that he'd railed at her after she'd nearly drowned? Thinking back on the event, he realized those had been the last words he'd spoken—no, bellowed—to her. After that, she'd given him a wide berth. And he sure didn't blame her.

But Amanda should have known he'd reacted out of anger. Anger at the Green for wrecking her wagon, nearly wiping out everything she owned in this world. And maybe foremost, anger at the fact widower Hill was paying her so much attention.

But there was one thing she couldn't have known. He had only now come to where he could admit it himself. He loved her.

Loved her.

He'd set ridiculous standards after Liza dumped him. They had him scrutinizing a woman against some insane checklist. Truthful? Check. Reliable? Check. Sensitive? He deflated his lungs in exasperation. What were all those traits anyway, compared to spunk, an unquenchable spirit, or a valiant heart?

Come to think of it, Seth realized, there was nothing he didn't like about Amanda Shelby. Including her faith. In its utter simplicity, it took him back to his own roots, when his deepest desire was to do justly, love mercy, and walk humbly with his God, as the Old Testament said. Since he'd turned his back on the Lord, his life had been nothing but a sham. Amanda, not Liza, was the example of true Christianity . . . and much too good for the likes of him. Maybe it was for the best that she ended up with someone else. After all, he'd practically pushed her into Jared Hill's arms himself!

Seth waited for the pain of that thought to subside.

It would take some time before the emptiness would go away, though. And inside, he knew where he had to go for the strength to live the rest of his life without her. Easing out of his blankets, he knelt beneath the stars and sought forgiveness from the God of his youth.

April 1849

"Do I look all right, Sissy? Oh, I'm still so thin."

Standing in the Randolphs' spare bedroom, which she and her sister had shared through the winter months, Amanda had to fight tears as she fluffed out Sarah's veil. Throughout the long trek over the Oregon Trail she had envisioned life with the two of them together, running a store . . . for several years, at least, if not forever. But God's plans had proven to be vastly different from hers. She would content herself with the few months that dream had been reality.

"He'll be rendered speechless," Amanda finally murmured, mustering a smile. Her fingertips lightly touched a cluster of seed pearls and alabaster sequins adorning the fitted lace bodice. "You've done a beautiful job on your gown. Maddie would be pleased to see how those years of stitching and samplers paid off."

Sarah covered Amanda's hand with hers. "I only wish I weren't moving away. Won't you please reconsider closing the shop and coming with us to Mount Shasta?" she pleaded. "Jared always said you were more than welcome. And you know how Bethy and Tad became enamored of you while they stayed here and Jared went off to find a place of our own."

With a stoic smile, Amanda met the younger girl's shimmering eyes in the oval cheval glass. "Not just yet. It's so convenient here on the farm, with Sacramento only a few miles away. You know how busy we've been, what with that tide of newcomers pouring west. Mr. Randolph doesn't seem to mind my using the wagon to drive to town and back every day—and besides, you need some time to be alone with that new little family of yours. You're a bride, remember?"

"I . . . sometimes feel a little guilty about that," Sarah confessed quietly. "After all, he did ask you first." Taking a fold of the lacy skirt in hand, she stepped away from the mirror and sat on the multihued counterpane draping the four-poster.

Amanda eased gently onto the rocker, so as not to crush the cerulean taffeta gown she wore. "Well, it's time to put those feelings to rest. You and I both know I never loved him in that way. And *I* could hardly miss seeing that *you* did."

A light pink tinted her sister's delicate cheekbones.

Increasingly conscious that soon enough the buckboard would bring Jared and his children, Amanda was determined to keep the mood light . . . the last sweet moments before Sarah's wedding ceremony would bring the younger girl's old life to an end and embark her upon the new. "It'll be ever so exciting," she gushed. "I wonder what your house looks like. I'm surprised Jared was able to finish it so quickly."

"Probably not quite as grand as this one, I'd venture. He wouldn't even give me a hint in his letters—and no doubt the little ones have been sworn to secrecy, too. I only hope the curtains I've sewn will fit the windows. It'll be nice having those braided rugs Mrs. Randolph taught me how to make, though, and the pretty needlepoint pillows you've done. But no matter what, I'm determined to like it—and to be the best wife and stepmother in the world. Perhaps one day the Lord will see fit to bless me with a child of my own."

Amanda felt tears welling deep inside. Tomorrow the shop in town would seem unbearably quiet and empty without Sarah's bubbliness. Happy as she was for her sister, it was difficult to dismiss the waves of sad reality that insisted upon washing over her.

The sound of approaching wagon wheels drifted from the lane leading into the rolling section of land.

Sarah sprang to her feet. "He's here!" she whispered breathlessly, and moved to peer out the window.

"Don't let him see you," Amanda teased. "I'll go downstairs and find out if everything's ready."

There was a soft rap on the door. Mrs. Randolph opened it and peeked around the jamb. "It'll be just a few minutes, my dears." Her glance fell upon the bride, and her eyes misted over. She stepped inside the room. "Oh, now, just look at my sweet Sarah. Almost too purty to look at, I swear. I couldn't be prouder of you if I was your own ma."

Sarah Jane flew into the older woman's arms. "Don't you dare make me cry. I'll spoil your pretty new dress."

"Pshaw!" Mrs. Randolph clucked her tongue. "Don't pay me no mind, even if some of my mountain of happiness spills out of these old eyes." She switched her attention to Amanda, slowly assessing her from head to toe. "And my other sweet gal. Never were spring flowers as purty as the two of you."

Barely containing her own emotions, Amanda joined the huge hug.

Mrs. Randolph's bosom rose and fell as she tightened the embrace, then stepped back. "I'd imagine everybody's in the right spot by now. I'll go tell Cora to start the organ. Nelson Junior never told us his wife could play."

As the first reedy notes drifted to their ears, Amanda moved to the top landing. Her eyes grew wide at the breathtaking transformation of the staircase and parlor. While she and Sarah had been fussing with curls and gowns, masses of brilliant orange poppies and blue lupine had been gathered to fill garlands, vases, and centerpieces to near overflowing. Here and there, tall tapers lent a golden aura of candlelight to the lovely scene. Taking one of the nosegays of spring beauties that Mrs. Randolph had thoughtfully left on the hall table, Amanda slowly started down, aware that all eyes in the house were upon her.

Hair slicked back and in his Sunday best, Charlie Randolph met her at the bottom landing and offered an arm, then escorted her toward the fireplace, where Jared Hill, in a crisp new shirt and black suit, waited with the minister. Bethany and Tad, seated off to one side with Mrs. Randolph, waved and smothered giggles.

Amanda took her place, then watched Jared flick his attention toward the top of the stairs to his bride. His expression of awe almost shattered her fragile composure. It was all she could do to hold herself together as Mr. Randolph escorted Sarah Jane to the side of her husband-to-be.

Lost in remembrances of all that had transpired to bring this moment about, Amanda witnessed the simple ceremony as if it were a dream . . . a blur of loving looks, tender smiles and murmured vows, the breathless kiss. Soft laughter at the end brought her back to reality. She blinked away threatening tears and fortified herself to extend her best wishes to the newlyweds. "Much happiness," she managed to whisper as she hugged Sarah.

Returning the embrace, her sister kissed Amanda's cheek. "Oh, Mandy . . . I never knew there could be so much happiness as I feel right at this moment."

Amanda moved into Jared's open arms next. "I always wanted a brother," she told him. "I'm so glad Sarah chose you. May God bless you both."

He gave a light squeeze. "I'll take care of her for you. I promise."

"I'm sure you will. Be happy. God bless you both."

He nodded. "When you come to visit, the kids will sing you a whole raft of new songs, I'll wager. They begged me to make sure she brings her guitar home with us."

Amanda's lips parted. "You really like her music?"

"Well, sure! Can't carry a tune in a bucket, myself, but Sarah's pretty voice pleasures me."

Amanda had to laugh. After a lavish celebration of Mrs. Randolph's grandest fare, everyone went outside to see the newlyweds off.

Daylight was fading into a watercolor glory of muted rose and mauve as the setting sun gilded the edges of slender clouds low on the western horizon. A perfect end to a perfect day, Amanda decided. She bent to kiss Bethany and Tad, then their father swept them up into the wagon bed.

Sarah Jane threw her arms around Amanda once more, and they hugged hard for a long silent moment. Amanda knew instinctively that her sister was no more able to utter a word than she. Finally they eased apart with a teary smile. "Be happy," Amanda whispered again as Jared came to whisk his bride away.

Waving after them, watching until the wagon was but a speck in the distance, Amanda's heart was filled to bursting. She had never known such happiness.

Or such sadness.

❧

Amanda plucked her shawl from a hook by the door and tossed it about her shoulders, then grabbed the parcel containing the men's shirts she'd finished the night before. "Goodbye, Mrs. Randolph," she called out. "I'm going now."

"Take care on the road," came the older woman's answer from the backyard, where she was beating rugs on a clothesline.

Amanda drove the wagon at a leisurely pace toward the teeming settlement of Sacramento, whose level of noise and activity seemed to increase constantly. Every day brought more and more newcomers to replace those who had pulled up stakes and moved on to the next gold field. New businesses sprang up overnight in the very structures abandoned only days before. And an amazing number of lonesome, homesick men appeared at Amanda's shop on the pretext of needing a button sewed on or a tear mended. She never imagined she'd receive so many proposals! But after having her heart shattered two times already, marriage was the last thing on her mind. Inhaling the heady scent of the spring flowers adorning the greening countryside, Amanda wondered if there were as many farther north, where Sarah had gone two weeks past. Perhaps one day soon, after the newlyweds had settled in, it might be fun to take the stage and visit. After all, the store was hers, and she could close it up whenever she took a fancy. Smiling at the thought, Amanda felt considerably more cheerful.

Dear Lord, her heart prayed. *Please watch after my dear Sarah Jane. I'm lost without my sister, my best friend, my confidant. I miss her so, yet I would never begrudge her this happiness. It still humbles me to think back on the indescribable journey You kept us through. Deserts, swamps, horrific storms, torturous mountains—to say nothing of how easily I might have drowned that day . . .*

As happened so often despite all her best efforts to the contrary, the memory of Seth Holloway intruded. Amanda had never so much as spoken his name aloud since the incident at the Green River . . . but a small, secret part of her couldn't help wondering what had become of the man. "Oh, what does it matter?" she hissed. The farm horse twitched an ear her way. Chagrined, Amanda returned her attention to the road.

Guiding the gelding along the bustling dirt streets of town, she took pride coming into view of the painted sign above her own enterprise. *Apparel and Alterations,* grand forest green letters proclaimed, then in much finer print, *A. J. Shelby, Proprietor.* She turned alongside and drove around to park in back of the small square building Mr. Randolph and Charlie had fitted with shelves and counters months ago.

Using the rear entrance, Amanda hung her floral-trimmed bonnet on a peg, then went through the swinging half-doors to the sales room. There she slid the shirred curtains apart on the front window and turned the Open sign out . . . duties she would perform every day, save Sundays, for the rest of her life. It was her lot, and what she had planned—or, nearly so, anyway. She would get used to the solitude. To help matters, she would look for a room to rent this afternoon as well, so it would no longer be necessary to burden the kind Randolphs or tie up their wagon. Thus decided, she began tidying the simple shop in readiness for the day's business.

After eating a bite at noon, Amanda walked several doors down the street to Mrs. Patterson's boarding house and put a deposit on a room that only that day had been vacated by a former tenant. Then, returning to her own shop, she tackled the ledgers.

The bell above the entrance interrupted the chore. Amanda set her quill aside and peered toward the dark figure silhouetted against the bright daylight. "How may I—?"

He removed his hat.

"W-why, Mr. Holloway!" Amanda gasped, rising to her feet.

Seth watched the blood drain from her face. He had been similarly shocked himself when, moments ago, he'd exited the Crown Hotel a few doors beyond the boarding house and glimpsed Amanda as she strolled to a clothing store up the street. He'd have recognized her anywhere, even with that long hair of hers tucked ever so primly into her bonnet.

He gave a perfunctory nod and settled for a simple greeting. "Good day," emerged on his second try.

"W-what are you doing here? I mean, you're the last person I ever—" Amanda's expression was one of utter confusion as she stood still, her mouth agape.

Another nod. Seth suddenly realized his hand was crushing his good hat and eased his grip. Lost in those glorious green eyes, he couldn't recall a word of the great speech he'd worked out so carefully in his head through the Oregon winter. He cleared his throat. "You're well?" *Great beginning, idiot!*

"Yes . . . fine . . . and you?"

"Not bad. Your sister, she's well?" It was all he could do not to roll his eyes at this inane conversation.

She nodded, then blinked quite suddenly and shook her head as if to clear it. "What are you doing in Sacramento?"

No point beating around the bush, when the truth was so much easier to get out. He shored up his insides. "Looking for you, actually."

"I-I don't understand," she said, her fine eyebrows arching higher. "Why would you—?"

Seth raked his fingers through his hair. "Sorry, I never asked if you were busy, Miss Sh—I mean—are you? I won't take much of your time."

She frowned, still perplexed. "I'm not busy just now."

"Good." A tiny flicker of hope coursed through him. He breathed a quick prayer that the Lord would loosen his tongue. "I must have asked at a hundred gold camps if anyone had seen you or knew of you. I was just about to give up, when you appeared out of the blue, just down the street."

Her expression remained fixed.

"I've been wanting very much to apologize," he went on, "for the callous things I said that day at the river. They were rude and completely uncalled for."

Amanda moved nearer the swinging doors and sank slowly to one of the chairs occupying either side of them. "Really, Mr. Holloway, the incident has long since been forgotten, I assure you."

"Not by me, it hasn't." He paused. "Do you mind if I sit down?"

"Oh. Not at all." She indicated the other chair.

Noticing the absence of a wedding band during her gesture, Seth thought it odd, but figured her preferences were none of his business. Obviously Hill must be an addle brain, unconcerned about letting the world know she's taken. "As I was saying, I came to tell you how sorry I am. My partner seemed to take singular pleasure in pointing out what a cad I was—which is true. It's gnawed at me ever since."

"Well, pray, suffer no more, then. I accept your apology." A tiny smile softened her face, revealing a touch of her old feisty spirit. He didn't realize how much he'd missed it. Missed her.

"Splendid." Swallowing, Seth stood to his feet. "Then I won't keep you from your work any longer. Thank you for hearing me out. I wish you well."

"And you," she whispered.

Watching him cross to the door, Amanda rose, still in shock over his sudden appearance. "Mr. Holloway?" He paused, his hand on the latch, and turned.

"Since you've come so far, and all . . . might I offer you some tea?" At her rash invitation, Amanda felt her knees wobble as she rose. The whole thing seemed unreal, dreamlike.

"That would be . . . kind. Yes, thank you."

She waved toward the chair again. "I'll be only a moment. I had some brewing in the back room." Hastening there, she filled two cups and returned. By sheer determination she willed her hand not to tremble as she gave one of the cups to him. There was certainly no reason to be nervous.

"Thank you."

"I don't see any familiar faces in town," she said, noting the presence of circles under his dark eyes, a day or two's growth of beard. And his boots were dusty. He really must have been traveling. For some unaccountable reason, she thought that was sweet. Touching. She felt her face growing warm. He couldn't be the ogre she had painted him after all. His gaze, wandering about the premises, re-turned to her. "This your place?"

She nodded, gathering herself. "Didn't you see the sign?"

"I wasn't paying much attention."

"Oh. Well, it was Sarah's and mine, until she left."

"Left?" He raised the tea to his mouth.

"Moved, actually. To Mount Shasta, after she and Jared married."

He swallowed too quickly and choked, and some of the scalding brew spilled over on his hand. The cup crashed to the floor and shat-tered in a thousand pieces as russet spokes of tea stained the plank floor. He knelt to collect the shards. "How clumsy. Sorry."

Amanda was more concerned about him. "But you've burned yourself. Let me look at it." Before he could argue, she knelt beside him and took his work-roughened hand in hers. Gently she unraveled the clenched fingers, turning them this way and that to assess the reddened skin. "It's not—" she raised her lashes, finding his face mere inches from her own, "not too bad." The last words were barely au-dible.

She released her hold even as her face turned every bit as scarlet as his burn. Why had she been so impetuous? This man somehow managed to bring out the absolute worst in her—and had since the first time their paths had crossed a summer ago. She'd never been more humiliated . . . unless she counted those half dozen other times she'd been in his presence. She tried to regather her dignity while easing graciously back onto her chair seat.

He sputtered into a laugh. Then roared.

Hiking her chin, Amanda turned her back. Perhaps he wasn't the gentleman she'd thought she'd glimpsed mere moments ago. "I'll thank you not to make fun of me."

"Oh, I'd never make fun of you, Amanda," he said in all sincerity. "I promise you that."

It was the first time he had ever called her by her given name. And it sounded so—different, in that raspy voice of his. Her heart hammered erratically against her ribs as she turned and shyly met his gaze.

He wasn't laughing now . . . but a strange almost-smile caught at her, stealing her breath. "You truly came all this way just to see me?" she asked in wonder.

"Mostly. I'm trying to acquire some good horseflesh for my new venture, so I answer every advertisement I come across. But in my travels, I've been looking for you." He reached to brush a few stray hairs from her temple as his intense gaze focused on her eyes. "Everywhere."

Her mouth went dry. "That's—that's really—" Unable to think straight, she moistened her lips.

"I thought I could forget you, Amanda Shelby," he continued. "Tried my hardest to. Drove Red crazy with my mutterings. That day I saw you turn off the trail, I figured you would be marrying that widower. Even when I saw you today, I thought you'd become his wife by now." His face blanched. "Or someone else's. Are you promised to anyone?"

She shook her head, wondering where this was all leading, fearing the hope that it could go anywhere at all. And did she want it to? "Good." He appeared visibly relieved. "Then I might as well go for broke. If I were to stay on at the hotel here for a while—" He swallowed nervously. "What I mean is, would you be opposed to being courted? By me?"

Amanda felt suddenly lightheaded and took hold of a spindle of the chair to steady herself. "Aren't you forgetting the matter of my being—how did you put it—brainless and foolhardy, wasn't it?"

Seth had the grace to smile, though it was tinged with more than a little guilt. "I deserve that. I've been unbearably thoughtless to you. But I know now that I was way off course, Amanda. After you drove off the trail and out of my life, I had to face up to the way I'd mistreated you—and forsaken the Lord. I finally sought His forgiveness and then knew that to have true peace I needed to seek yours as well. I'm no longer the man you met in Independence. I've changed. Because of you. I'm asking for a chance to undo that bad impression I made on you . . . if you'll allow me to."

Looking at him, Amanda could see how vulnerable he was. There had been a considerable amount of ill feeling between them, but thinking back, she could recall sensing almost from the onset of the journey west that he was trustworthy and honest. He affected her in ways she'd never before experienced, stirred chords within her soul as no man she had ever known. And she felt profound inner peace about his offer, because for longer than she cared to admit, she had been in love with Seth Holloway.

All things considered, she had only one choice . . . to be honest in return. "I would be truly honored, Seth, to have you court me."

His vulnerability evaporated, leaving a fragile hopefulness in its place. He expelled a ragged breath and drew her close, close to the beating of his heart. "I promise you, Amanda, you will never be sorry."

Raising her lashes, Amanda tipped her head back, needing to glimpse again the intensity of the love he made no effort to disguise. Seeing it, she smiled.

Seth held her gaze for a heartbeat, then slowly lowered his head, until his lips were barely a breath from hers. Then with tenderest reverence, he kissed her.

Amanda felt her heart sing and wanted the moment to last forever. But all too soon he eased away.

"I've wanted to do that for a long time," he murmured huskily.

"And I wished for a long time that you had." The remark came in all honesty.

He wrapped his arms about her just as the bell above the door tinkled, announcing a customer.

Seth took a step back, and a comical spark of mischief glinted in his dark eyes. "Well, thank you kindly, miss," he said with a mock bow. "That's mighty friendly service, I must say. I'll be by later for that new shirt." With that, he exited, whistling.

Amanda smiled after him. *Yes, come back later, my love. I'll be here waiting.*

The Other Brother

by Lena Nelson Dooley

This book is dedicated to my two daughters, Marilyn Van Zant and Jennifer Waldron, who provided the catalyst that started me writing inspirational romance novels. Now they have given me the four most wonderful grandchildren in the world. And no book is ever written in our home without the support of my wonderful husband, James, whom I love more today than I ever imagined when I married him in 1964. He is the second most wonderful gift God ever gave me.

1

April 1891

*O*lina Sandstrom stood by the railing of the *North Star,* her face turned away from the biting wind. A wayward curl persistently crept from her upswept hairdo and fluttered against her chilled cheeks. The wind flapped the hem of her heavy traveling suit as well, threatening to sweep her into the choppy sea. Thank goodness for the ship's railing. Even though the hard metal chilled her fingers until they were almost numb, she didn't want to let go.

The dark gray waters of the Atlantic Ocean spread from horizon to horizon. The ocean seemed to be a living thing, constantly moving and changing, never still. As waves lapped against the dark hull of the ocean liner, the deck where she stood dipped and rose in rhythm. It had taken Olina over a day to get used to the feeling. The movement unsettled more than her stomach. Never before had her foundation constantly shifted.

Oh, to be on land again, to feel safe. But would she ever feel safe again? Although Olina was excited to be on the grand adventure that would culminate in her reunion with her beloved, her heart was heavy with knowing what she had given up. Knowing what she left behind, maybe forever.

The ocean fascinated Olina. Lars Nilsson's eyes were that shade of gray, and they were always alive with plans and new ideas. Even during storms, which had occurred more than once in the week since they had left Sweden, the ocean reminded Olina of Lars. When he was unhappy, his eyes took on that same brooding darkness. But when he was happy, they danced and flashed as the waves did when the sun sparkled across them. So day after day, Olina stood by the rail of the ship and longed for the time when she would look into those eyes again. It had been so long since she had seen them. This crossing seemed to be never ending.

"What are you looking at?" The soft voice of Johanna Nordstrom, Olina's traveling companion, penetrated Olina's concentration.

Olina gave a soft reply without looking away from the water that surrounded the ship. "The ocean."

"What do you find so interesting out there?" Johanna turned toward the churning water. Johanna had spent most of her time on the ship inside one of the salons. She told Olina that she preferred the warmth to the cold deck. Even in second class, the ship seemed luxurious to both of the young women.

Olina turned to face Johanna, one hand finally leaving the rail to swipe at a tendril that tickled her nose. "It reminds me of Lars. This voyage can't end soon enough for me. It has been so long since I saw him."

Looking out across the waves, Olina pictured Lars the last time they had been together. They had been alone in their favorite meadow. Soft green grass, dotted with tiny white flowers, spread around them. Jagged rocks broke through the ground cover farther up the slope, and the sound of the water in the *fjord* was a constant background melody punctuated by the calls of the birds that circled in the cerulean sky.

Lars came to tell her good-bye. When Olina started to cry, Lars pulled her into his arms. His gentle kiss brushed the hair from her temple. She didn't want to think of life without Lars. Ever since they were very young, they had known they would someday marry. Lars was an essential part of her. How could she go on without seeing him almost every day?

America was so far away. So far that she couldn't even imagine the distance. She just knew they would never see each other again. And it had taken years. Five long years.

"I'll work," Lars whispered against her coronet of braids, "and I'll save up until I can send you the money to come to America. Then we will be married. Even if it takes years, it'll be worth it." Lars placed a gentle kiss upon her willing lips before he left to meet his family at the docks.

Olina stayed in the meadow the rest of the afternoon. She relived every precious moment they had spent together. Every few minutes, she had touched the lips his tender kiss had covered for the first time, lost in the wonder of it.

"You know, Olina." Johanna's voice interrupted Olina's memories. "I haven't questioned you about your quick decision to accompany me to America. All you told me was that Lars had sent you the money for passage." Johanna patted one of Olina's icy hands. "I don't understand why none of your family came to see you off."

Olina wondered what she could tell her friend without making *Fader* sound bad. But Johanna deserved the truth. Without her help, Olina wouldn't be making this journey.

After turning away from the frothy water, Olina leaned on the railing, her hands still clutching it for support. "I wasn't trying to be mysterious. I just had a hard time talking about it." Thinking about it caused tears to pool in her eyes. She reached one hand into the pocket of her skirt and took out her pristine linen handkerchief to dab the tears away. "Fader didn't want me to go to America. He didn't understand. I love Lars so much, and there is no one else who can stir my heart as he does. I had to go to Lars."

Olina swallowed a sob. "Fader told me that I was old enough to make my own decision . . . but if I went, he would disown me. No one in my family would ever be allowed to contact me. *Tant* Olga said he didn't mean it, so I waited awhile before I made my decision, hoping he would change his mind. He didn't." Olina wept so hard that she could not continue her explanation.

"He probably didn't mean it. He thought you would do what he wanted." Johanna pulled Olina into her arms and let her cry. "He'll change his mind when you get to America, and you can tell him how happy you are. If not then, at least when you and Lars have children, he'll want to know his grandchildren."

Olina was warmed by the embrace. Her mother often hugged her when she was still living at home. She hadn't realized how much she had missed it.

When Olina stopped crying, she moved from Johanna's embrace

and dried her face with her handkerchief. "*Tack så.* A good friend you are, for sure."

The ship dipped, and Johanna grabbed the railing. "I'm sorry I didn't realize something was wrong. I was excited about going to America to be with Olaf. Even though I'm married, my mother didn't want me to travel alone."

Olina tried to smile at her friend. "You and Olaf hadn't been married long when he went to America, *ja?*"

"Only a few months."

"It must have been hard for you."

Johanna nodded. "It was. But your decision was a difficult one, too. I'm not sure I could have made it."

Olina studied the waves with their whitecaps. "It was the hardest thing I've ever done, choosing Lars over my family."

࿋

Gustaf Nilsson was angrier than he had been in a long time. "*Gud,* why did You let this happen?" When he was alone, Gustaf often talked to God. Was he ever alone today. Driving his wagon across the rolling plains in Minnesota toward Litchfield, all he could think about was taking the train to New York City.

Five years ago when his family had left New York, headed toward Minnesota, Gustaf had vowed never to set foot in that town again. It was too big for him. It was too dirty . . . and too noisy . . . and too crowded with people. Not at all the sort of place he wanted to be. He didn't like to be hemmed in. He needed fresh, clean air. He was a farmer. He tilled the land. And there was a Swedish settlement in Minnesota. That was why they had emigrated.

The winter before the move had been harder than usual in Sweden. With the crop failure that summer, the family finally heeded the pleas of their friends, who were already landowners in America, and sold everything they owned. God had been good to them in Minnesota. They bought a large farm, which Gustaf and Papa couldn't run alone. They had to hire several men to help them.

August, Gustaf's younger brother, had wanted to be a blacksmith.

Papa thought it was a good idea, so August had moved to town. Then there was Lars, his youngest brother. Gustaf didn't want to think about Lars and what he had done. He didn't like to be this angry, but every time he thought of Lars, anger bubbled up inside him like the spring that had fed icy water to the family on their farm back in Sweden. But the anger did not cool him. It made him grow hotter and hotter. Even though the spring winds still blew, they couldn't touch the heat that was building in Gustaf.

"Fader, what am I going to do when I get there?" Gustaf looked into the wide blue sky, but the puffy white clouds didn't tell him anything. And he didn't hear the voice of God thundering the answer. Not that he expected it to. Gustaf had never heard the audible voice of God. He knew some people claimed to, but Gustaf always heard God's voice speak deep within his soul. That was where he hoped to hear something, but God was quiet today.

Why did Gustaf always have to clean up the messes Lars made? He knew he was the oldest, but that didn't mean he should have to leave the farm, where he had so many things that needed to get done, and travel to that awful place to meet that girl. Why hadn't she stayed in Sweden where she belonged? What would he do with the sturdy farm girl?

When the Nilssons had first arrived in Minnesota, the spring had been so wet that the roads were impassable. Lars had tried to go to town anyway. By the time Gustaf pulled the bogged-down wagon out of the mud, one of the axles had broken. He had taken it to town for August to fix before Papa found out. He hadn't minded that too much. Gustaf was glad August hadn't caused trouble like Lars had. One brother giving him grief was enough.

After a year, Lars decided he needed to work in town to make money to send for Olina. At first, Gustaf had been unhappy about that. So much of the time, Lars didn't complete what he was supposed to on the farm, and Gustaf was the one who finished the job. It was easier to do the whole thing himself. Besides, his sister, Gerda, helped more than Lars ever had.

Since he hardly ever finished anything he started, Gustaf had been sure that Lars would give up on the idea before he had earned enough money. That hadn't been the case. Lars took to merchandising. Before long, Mr. Braxton gave him more responsibility. Although it had taken another four years for Lars to save enough money to pay for Olina's passage, he never deviated from that plan. Then six months ago, Lars had sent Olina the money.

Soon after the letter was mailed, Mr. Braxton's brother from Denver came to Litchfield. He had been impressed with Lars's abilities, so he offered him a position in his mercantile. Lars moved to Denver. He said he would be better able to provide for a family with the increased income. The whole Nilsson family assumed that Lars had written Olina about the change in plans.

It took a long time for mail to cross half of the United States, the ocean, and part of Europe. However, Gustaf had expected to hear before now that Olina had arrived in Denver. He didn't know why it took her so long to start the journey. Yesterday, they had received two messages. A letter from Lars and a telegram from Olina to Lars. Papa had opened the telegram because he thought it might be something important.

Olina's note told them when she would be arriving on the *North Star* in New York City. The letter from Lars was disturbing. He had fallen in love with Mr. Braxton's daughter, and they would be married by the time the letter reached Minnesota. He said he had only thought he loved Olina. Until he met Janice, he had not known what real love was. He would write to Olina and explain things, but Gustaf knew it was too late for that. Olina was already on her way when Lars wrote the letter, if he did.

Papa should have been the one to go to New York to meet Olina, but Mama didn't feel well. She had been extremely upset by the letter from Lars. Gustaf was sure that was the reason she felt so bad. She begged Papa to send Gustaf, so here he was.

Gustaf had half a mind to send Olina back where she came from. He would if she had enough money for the passage. He certainly didn't.

This would never have happened if Lars hadn't started working in that store. Why couldn't he love the farm as much as Gustaf did? Or if he had to work in a store, why had Lars not stayed in Litchfield with Mr. Braxton and his mercantile? Why did Lars wait to leave town until after he had sent Olina the money to come to Minnesota?

It was a good thing Gustaf's horses knew the way to town without much help from Gustaf. If they hadn't, he would have never made it to the train on time.

❧

The seemingly never-ending journey was finally over. The ship docked at something called the Battery in New York. Such a huge place it was. So many docks. So many ships. So many people. Olina was overwhelmed. She had never heard such a din in all her life. It was so loud it was hard to distinguish one sound from another—voices speaking in many languages, which Olina couldn't understand, clanging, banging, the hooting of ship's horns, the clatter of horses' hooves on the brick streets.

"It's a good thing we came when we did." Johanna looked out over the crowd that had gathered as the ship docked. It was a constantly moving sea of humanity.

"What do you mean?" Olina took time out from trying to find Lars in the crowd to look at her friend. "What difference would another time make?"

Johanna turned toward Olina. "I was talking to one of the other passengers. She told me that there are so many people coming to America that they are building a place on an island where they will process many of the emigrants. It's called Ellis Island, and it will be open for business in a few months. It'll take longer to be processed there before you get to come ashore. I want to be with Olaf as soon as possible." Just then she spied her husband's tall frame pushing through the crowd. She raised her hand as high as she could and waved her handkerchief.

❧

It had taken long enough to get off the ship and through Immigration—much longer than either woman wanted it to take. But now

Johanna was hanging onto Olaf's arm as Olina scanned the thinning crowd for Lars. Where could he be? She had sent a telegraph message before she boarded the ship. Surely he received it. It wasn't pleasant waiting here. Of course with fewer people around, Olina wasn't overcome with the strong smell of unwashed bodies as she had been when they first stepped on shore, but there were other unpleasant odors. Garbage and human waste were too strong for the ocean breezes to cleanse. Many of the men must have been drinking in nearby taverns before they came to the wharf. Stale alcohol mingled with all the other smells. Besides, the large ships blocked many of the breezes. There was also the odor of fish and fumes from the many boats. Olina thought about covering her nose with her handkerchief as some of the other women on the dock were doing, but she didn't.

❧

Gustaf had lost his good humor before he left home. Now it was so far away he didn't know if he would ever find it again. He was angry and frustrated. The train ride had been long and noisy. No one could sleep with all the babble from the passengers. Add to that the chugging engine and the *clackity-clack* of the rails. Gustaf had nursed a headache since he left Minnesota. The stuffy cars didn't help him feel any better. When he went out on the platform between cars to get a whiff of air, it wasn't fresh. Smoke from the engine, which enveloped the train itself, was no more pleasant than the unwashed bodies and bad breath inside the car. When he turned to go back inside, a cinder caught in the corner of his eye. After he removed it, tears formed in the injured eye for over an hour. For sure, he didn't want people to think he was crying.

When he had finally reached New York, it was a race against the other passengers to find a cabby who could take him to the docks. He had gotten the slowest cabby in New York City.

"Hey." Gustaf reached up and tapped the driver on the shoulder.

The driver didn't take his attention off the road. "Sir?"

"You aren't driving around and around trying to make my fare larger, are you?" Gustaf didn't try to disguise his anger.

"No, this is the most direct route to the Battery. That's where you said you was going, ain't it?" The man leaned away from a right turn, easily controlling the horses and buggy. "It's not far now."

"I'm glad." Gustaf scooted back in the seat, holding on tight. If not, he might be thrown from the buggy as it lurched and groaned its way through the traffic. "I'm meeting a young lady, and her ship should have docked over an hour ago."

"Why didn't you say so? We wouldn't want to leave a lady waiting in that mob." The man flicked the reins across the rumps of the horses, and they trotted at a much faster pace.

Gustaf glared blankly. He was trying to remember what Olina Sandstrom looked like. He didn't want to spend a lot of time looking for her. Blond braids loosely encircled her head the last time he saw her. She had a round face with rosy cheeks and big blue eyes. He thought Olina's eyes were the prettiest of any of the girls in their village. She helped her family with farm chores, so she was strong. Butter and cheese, from the family dairy, and rich pastries had kept her figure rounded. She should be easy to spot in New York. He hadn't seen that kind of girl anywhere he had been in the city.

"Here we are. Would you like me to wait to take you and your lady to a hotel?" The cabby looked around the area. "I don't see any other conveyance that ain't being used by someone else."

"How much is that going to cost?" Gustaf could feel his purse shrinking as they talked.

"Tell you what." The cabby winked down at him. "I wait for half an hour, and I won't charge nothing but the fare here and to where you're going. If you ain't back by then, I'll have to take any fare I can get."

"It's a deal."

Gustaf loped off, seething inside. The cheeky cabby thought he was coming for his own lady, not for his brother's castoff. If that didn't cap the day. Gustaf hurried toward the wharves, where he saw several ships docked. There was the vessel she had sailed on. Quickly, Gustaf scanned the scattered clusters of people near the *North Star*. Not one of the women looked like Olina. What if she hadn't boarded the ship? What if he had made the journey in vain? Gustaf's anger built even higher than it had been—if that were possible. Had he wasted all this time and money for nothing?

❧

Once again, Olina looked around the large wharf area. Where was Lars? She didn't know what she would do if he didn't come. She had so little money left. Johanna had insisted that they book passage in second class. She didn't want to travel in steerage, where everyone was treated like cattle, sharing rooms and bathrooms and who knew what else. Olina had enjoyed the relative luxury. She knew it was not like first class, but she had never known that kind of life, so she didn't miss it. But she would have missed the money it would have cost. Olina didn't have that kind of money to start with. Now she almost wished she had talked Johanna into steerage. At least she would have enough money to make her way to Minnesota on her own if Lars was unable to meet her in New York.

"I wonder what's keeping Lars." Olaf turned from his conversation with Johanna to talk to Olina. "You could go with us to the hotel. I'm sure there's another room available. Of course, tomorrow we'll be leaving for Cincinnati, but we'd be glad to have you with us tonight."

Olina looked at Johanna, clutching her husband's arm as if she would never let go. She knew that the young couple didn't need her tagging along on their first night together in over a year.

"Lars wouldn't know where to find me if I went with you." Once again Olina looked around the wharf. "I think I'll wait a little longer."

"We can't leave you here alone." Johanna took Olina's arm. "It wouldn't be proper, and you might not be safe. I would worry instead of enjoying my husband." She smiled a secret smile at Olaf.

That smile made Olina uncomfortable, so she quickly looked away. That's when Olina noticed a man who seemed to be looking for someone. He was built like Lars, strong and muscular, and blond hair stuck out from under his navy blue cap. He looked a lot like Lars, but he was taller than she remembered Lars being. Maybe it was Lars. He could have grown taller since he had come to America. All that work and good food in the land of plenty. Maybe he had grown. Lars, or whoever he was, started toward them. Now he was close enough for her to see all of his face.

Just as Olina realized that, she looked into icy blue eyes. Sky blue and cold as the ice in the fjords in winter. They jolted her. But it wasn't Lars. His were gray, not blue.

❧

Gustaf recognized Olina's eyes the moment he saw them. It was a good thing. He would never have known who she was otherwise. She stood as if she were holding herself upright by the strength of her will. She was slender, with curves in all the right places. Instead of the braids he remembered encircling her head, her upswept hairdo was topped with a fashionable small hat that had ribbons and feathers and a small veil that was turned up. Wispy curls brushed her cheeks and neck.

Gustaf didn't know a lot about fashion, but he knew that the traveling suit she was wearing was fashionable. Olina had changed, all for the better. But she was fragile looking, as if the journey had worn her out. As if she would wilt if given the chance. He couldn't tell her what he had come to tell her until she had rested. He would have to wait for the right time. But what *was* the right time to tell a woman who had come halfway around the world that she had been jilted?

2

*G*ustaf?" Olina was surprised she hadn't realized who he was right away.

He nodded as he glanced at the luggage. "How many of these are yours?"

"Those two trunks and this carpetbag." After Olina pointed out the pieces, she looked past Gustaf, scanning the thinning crowd. "Where—?"

"I have a cab waiting. We need to hurry." Gustaf hefted one trunk up on his back.

"Wait." Olina's hand on his arm stopped him. "I want you to meet my traveling companion and her husband." She turned toward the Nordstroms.

Olaf held out his hand. "I'm Olaf, and this is Johanna."

"I'm pleased to meet you." Gustaf let the trunk slip back to the dock before he shook Olaf's hand.

"Do we have to hurry to catch the train?" Olina had a lot of questions she wanted answered. "And is—?"

"No," Gustaf interrupted. "Our train doesn't leave until in the morning."

"But where will you spend the night?" Johanna sounded worried.

Olina smiled at her. How like Johanna to be more concerned for her friend than herself.

"I hadn't thought of that," Gustaf answered. "I guess I was planning on waiting at Grand Central Station tonight."

"Why don't you come to the hotel with us?" Olaf said. "I'm sure they have another room."

Gustaf looked angry, but he agreed. "We can share my cab if we hurry. The driver said he wouldn't wait long for us."

Each man picked up a trunk and started toward the cabstand, leaving the women to guard the other luggage. When they returned for the other two trunks, Olina and Johanna went with them, each carrying a carpetbag, as well as their reticules.

The cab was crowded. Olina had to sit very close to Gustaf. After they had gone a couple of blocks, she leaned close to his ear. "Where is—?"

"That's our hotel." Olaf pointed toward a three-story building with a red brick facade.

When the three men had unloaded the baggage, Olaf and Gustaf went to the front desk.

"I booked you a room on the same floor as your friends, but on the other side of the hotel," Gustaf told Olina when they returned. "My room is on the next floor."

As they walked across the lobby to the staircase, the carpet softened Olina's tired steps. It was a good thing Gustaf had brought her here. Olina wouldn't have been able to afford a hotel room at all in this big city. New York City. It was so confusing and noisy.

After the baggage was stored in the three hotel rooms, the four went to the restaurant on the ground floor. Another time, Olina would have enjoyed the beauty of the place, aglow with gas lights on the walls, as well as candles on each table. Delicious smells wafted through the room, making Olina aware that she had not eaten much that day. She had been too excited, knowing they were landing in New York. She was supposed to see Lars waiting for her. That had added to her excitement, but that had not happened. Now here she was in a hotel restaurant with Gustaf. Maybe he would soon tell her where Lars was and why he didn't come to meet her.

As soon as they were seated, a young woman in a long black dress with a white apron and cap served them. Gustaf and Olaf were able to converse with her in English. Neither Olina nor Johanna understood anything they said. But the two men sounded as if they had spoken the language all their lives. Olina hoped she would be able to learn the strange way of speaking. It felt uncomfortable being an outsider. Surely Lars could speak English as well as Gustaf. Lars would help her learn. He wouldn't want her feeling uncomfortable around others.

The meal was congenial, but Olina waited for Gustaf to bring up Lars's whereabouts. Lars hadn't even been mentioned during the meal. Gustaf seemed rather aloof. Maybe he didn't want to talk about Lars in front of the Nordstroms. Olina was beginning to worry. She hoped Lars was not sick or injured. Just wait until Gustaf walked her to her room. She would get to the bottom of this.

❦

All through the meal, Gustaf was distracted. He tried to carry on a sensible conversation with his companions, but his thoughts were otherwise engaged.

Here they were in a hotel, using up more of the hard-earned money he had brought with him. He felt each dollar as it slipped through his fingers, his precious store dwindling at an alarming rate. He had better get Olina back to the farm quickly, before he ran out of money. Why had he not brought more with him? He had enough put away that it wouldn't have hurt to bring extra so he wouldn't feel the pinch, but he had been angry. He only wanted to get the trip over with. He hadn't wanted to spend one penny more than was necessary, and he had planned to send Olina back to her parents. Besides, he would need his money when he and Anna married.

Gustaf hadn't thought about spending time at a hotel. He was going to go back to the train station and wait for the train to Minnesota, even if it took all night. When he first saw Olina standing there, he knew he couldn't treat her that way. Now look at the mess he was in. It was a good thing Fader had told him to buy both tickets before he left home. He had planned to turn Olina's ticket in and get his money back after he put her on a ship to Sweden. Now he barely had enough money for food until they got to Litchfield.

Gustaf hadn't even mentioned Lars to Olina. How could he bring up his name without exploding with anger? She didn't need to see that, not in her condition. She was so tired; she looked as if she was having a hard time staying awake. There was not one detail of her actions or appearance that escaped him.

If he could get his hands on Lars right now, he would likely hurt him. How could Lars do this to Olina? Why couldn't he be man enough to face this on his own?

Olina said she was hungry, but she didn't eat like the farm girl of his memory. She ate more like his mother did, with grace and poise. She had stopped eating before her plate was empty. She insisted the food tasted good, but she left some, as his mother often did.

What was he doing comparing her to his mother? Was he mad? How was he going to tell her about Lars? He would have to wait until the right time.

❧

When Gustaf finished the last bite on his plate, Olina stood up. "I'm tired." She looked right at him. "Will you walk me to my room?"

Olaf stood when Olina and Gustaf did. Then he sat back down with his wife.

At the top of the stairs, Olina could wait no longer. "Where is Lars?" she asked as they walked down the hall.

"I'm not sure."

Olina stopped and placed her hands on her hips. "What do you mean, you're not sure? Is something the matter with him?"

Anger blazed from Gustaf. "Yes, something's the matter with him. He's married."

Olina couldn't believe her ears. Surely he hadn't said what she thought she heard. "Married?"

She didn't realize she had voiced the question until she saw the expression on Gustaf's face. He reached toward her, but she stepped back from him.

"Olina, I'm sorry. I didn't mean to tell you this way." He took her arm, but she pulled away.

"How could he be married?" The question ended on a squeak. Here she was worried that Lars was sick or hurt, and he had done this to her. Olina clutched her arms around her waist as if something inside hurt. And it did. Everything hurt. She felt as if she couldn't stand up another minute.

Gustaf must have realized this, because he put his arms around her and pulled her against his chest. Olina began to sob. What was she going to do now?

Gustaf helped her walk to her room. "We need to talk. If we leave the door open, I can come in for a few minutes."

He eased her into a chair and hunkered on the floor beside her. Olina didn't look at his face. How could she? She didn't want to see pity there. First Fader rejected her, and now Lars had jilted her. How could God have let this happen?

"What am I going to do?" It was hard to get the words past the lump in her throat.

"What do you want to do, Olina?"

"I don't have the money to go back to Sweden."

Gustaf stood and walked over to the window. "I came to take you to Litchfield with me."

"Do your *moder* and *fader* want me to come?"

Gustaf turned from the window. He looked at her, but she didn't read pity in his expression. "Yes. They're not happy about what Lars did."

Olina sat up straighter. "What exactly did Lars do?"

"Didn't he write you at all after he went to Denver?"

"Denver?" Olina quickly stood and paced across the floor. "The last letter I received from him contained the money for my passage." She stopped walking and turned toward Gustaf. "What is he doing in Denver?"

"I don't want to talk about Lars right now." Gustaf stomped to the window again. "He's always making messes and leaving them for me to clean up. You are one of those messes, and I will take care of you, as I have all the others."

Olina could hardly believe her ears. "Did you just call me a mess?" She stood a little taller, the starch returning to her backbone. "I'm not sure I want to spend any time with you."

"Well, you're going to have to . . . until we get to Minnesota, at least!"

Why was he shouting at her? Did he want everyone in the hotel to know what had happened to her?

Olina walked over to the door. "I'll thank you to leave my room."

"All right. I'll go, but I'll be here to pick you up early in the morning so we can catch our train." At least he had moderated his tone. "When we get to Litchfield, you and my parents can decide what to do."

After Olina closed the door behind him, she resumed pacing the floor, sure she would never be able to sleep tonight. Everything in her life had turned to darkness. Fader had rejected her because she wanted to come to America to marry the man she loved. She stopped by the window and stared out, unseeing.

How could Olina love a man who could do that to her? How could she turn off a love that had consumed most of her life? Here she was in a strange place where she couldn't even speak the language. Tomorrow she would board a train with the most insufferable man she had ever known.

Olina didn't remember Gustaf much from when they had been in Sweden. He was older than Lars and she, so he hadn't paid much attention to her, or she him. She never noticed him acting the way he was now.

Olina walked over and sat on the side of the bed. It had been so long since she slept in such a soft one. She had been looking forward to it, but with what had happened today, she didn't know if she would sleep a wink.

Olina didn't like to feel helpless, but that was what she felt right now. Helpless and alone. Alone and unloved. How much worse could it get? She didn't want to know. She wished she couldn't feel anything. That's what she could do. Stop feeling anything. Then maybe the hurt would go away.

Olina knew she could trust no one except herself. She would have to face this alone.

Gustaf had been quiet at breakfast, and then he rushed her to Grand Central Station. What a large place it was! So fancy with arches and columns and all kinds of mosaic tiles. Olina had never seen anything like it. The ceiling seemed to be a million miles above them. People were everywhere, all talking in their own languages or the language of this new country. Occasionally, Olina heard a Swedish word as they made their way through the throng. It was like music to her ears, even though it was buried in the multilingual cacophony. The place was so large, they had barely made it to their train on time.

Olina was fighting a headache. The *clackity-clack* of the train was much louder than she had expected. Some people carried on conversations, which only added to the confusing din. She pressed her fingers to her temples as she tried to ignore all the noise.

This America was big. They had traveled for two days, and they hadn't reached Minnesota yet. At first Olina looked out the windows to see everything . . . and to keep from looking at Gustaf. Although she tried not to feel anything, every time she saw him, it brought all those feelings back; so she ignored him as much as she could.

There was a lot to see. Before they left the state of New York, Olina saw lots of trees—tall trees, many kinds that were new to her. As they traveled across other states, hills gave way to prairies with tall grasses blowing in the wind. Soon vast fields of wheat and other crops were interspersed with farmhouses and barns.

The train passed through small settlements as well as a few cities. It often stopped to let off and take on passengers. Soon the cities all looked a lot alike. They had crossed several states—Pennsylvania, Ohio, and Indiana—before they reached Chicago, Illinois, which was the largest city since they left New York City.

Every so often, she sat back and glanced at Gustaf in the seat facing hers. Every time she looked at him, Gustaf was reading the newspaper he bought in Grand Central Station . . . or he was asleep . . . or he was reading from his Bible, which he had in the carpetbag he carried. The only time he talked to her was when he needed to tell her something about the trip or when they were getting something to eat. That was fine with her.

Although Olina tried not to, she missed Lars. She also missed *Mor* . . . and her brothers. She could not even keep from missing Fader, even though he had hurt her so much. Maybe if she closed her eyes and rested her head against the back of the seat, her headache would go away.

◆

Gustaf glanced up when he heard the soft breathy sound. Olina's head rested on the window beside her. Her eyes were closed, and her lips were slightly parted. She must be asleep, because the soft sounds that came from her small mouth were almost snores, but not quite. Gustaf wished he sat beside her. If he did, he would ease her head from the hard glass onto his softer broad shoulder. He would love to cushion her sleep there.

What was he thinking? He loved Anna, didn't he? The sweet honey smell of Olina had teased him when they were in the cab, but he had tried to ignore it.

Gustaf pulled his Bible out of his carpetbag again. His thoughts were not the thoughts of a man who planned to ask Anna to marry him the next time they were alone together. The sooner he got this mess with Olina fixed, the better for him. Gustaf leafed through the book, trying to find something that would ease his mind. But he went from one verse here to another verse there without gaining the peace he was seeking.

How had Olina gotten under his skin so much? Was it because he wanted to make up for what Lars did to hurt her? When she broke down and cried at the hotel, it touched Gustaf's heart. What he felt was pity, wasn't it? Then the next morning, Olina was somehow stronger. He had watched her, and he could see an iron will that kept her from showing the outside world how much she had been hurt. He admired that.

3

ould this train ride never end? The benches that had felt comfortable when they left New York were now almost too hard to bear. Olina squirmed, trying to find a softer spot, but to no avail. Most of her body was sore. She thought about Lars, and tears pooled in her eyes. When she thought about her family back in Sweden, the same thing happened. She would not cry. Crying didn't help anything. Olina wished she had something to read, but the newspaper Gustaf bought in New York City was in English. She couldn't read a word of it.

Olina's thoughts drifted to Tant Olga. What would she have done without her great-aunt?

About a year after Lars moved to America, Tant Olga asked if Olina would move into town to take care of her. At first Olina hadn't wanted to leave her beloved farm near the fjords. But she was glad when she did.

Tant Olga had fallen in love with a sailor when she was young. She married him against her family's wishes. *Farbror* Art had worked hard until he bought his own ship. As the wife of a merchant seaman, Tant Olga had enjoyed a life of plenty. Then her husband had been swept from the deck of his ship in a storm, leaving Tant Olga a wealthy woman. Art and Olga never had children of their own.

Tant Olga was an old woman when she asked Olina to live with her. She said she would pay Olina to take care of her. Olina had been worried that all she would do would be a drudge for Tant Olga. That had not been the case.

The two women, so far apart in age, were kindred spirits. Tant Olga helped Olina become the woman she was today. Climbing the stairs in the three-story house and eating smaller portions of foods that weren't so rich helped Olina slim down. Tant Olga taught Olina to be a lady instead of a farm girl.

They enjoyed taking outings. The two of them even read the newspapers together, because they wanted to know what was going on in the world. Olina had written about these things in her letters to Lars. They discussed current events through their letters.

When Lars sent the money to come to America, Olina hadn't known what to do. Her father had forbidden her to go. But Tant Olga hadn't. When Tant Olga learned that her nephew opposed the trip, she assured Olina that he didn't mean it. She was convinced that when Olina asserted her independence and started on the journey, he would come to his senses and change his mind. Her father had changed his mind after she married Art. Olina hoped that would be the case with her own fader.

She didn't want to think about her father. She didn't want to cry again, so she pushed thoughts of him out of her head. Instead she returned to those days before her journey started.

Tant Olga helped her buy new clothes with the money she had saved. Tant Olga hadn't let Olina pay for anything she needed while she was staying with her, and she still paid her a wage for taking care of her. Over and over again, Olina told Tant Olga that she felt as though she were taking advantage of her, but Tant Olga didn't agree.

They studied the fashion books and bought the most popular fabrics. Tant Olga taught Olina how to sew and embroider and make lace. So when Olina made many of her clothes, they were the latest fashions, with extra touches. Tant Olga also helped her find a dressmaker who made other things for Olina when she was preparing for the journey to America.

Tant Olga even asked around until she found that Johanna needed someone to go with her so she could join her husband in America. Without Tant Olga's help, Olina wouldn't be on this train somewhere in the interior of the vast country of America.

The train whistle cut through Olina's thoughts.

"This is our stop, Olina." Gustaf's words followed the sound. "Welcome to Litchfield, Minnesota."

Olina peeked out the window as the train slowed. The town of Litchfield spread on both sides of the tracks. It looked like many of the small towns they had come through on the long trip from New York City. Olina saw a mercantile and a livery stable near the tracks on one side. Other buildings surrounded them. One looked like a hotel. Even a building that appeared to be a saloon was nearby. On the other side of the tracks, the buildings looked more like homes. She saw a church steeple sticking up from a grove of trees that obscured much of that side of the town.

When the train came to a stop, Gustaf took Olina's hand to help her stand. Olina couldn't explain the funny feeling she had every time Gustaf touched her. Maybe it was because she had been traveling so long.

Olina stood poised on the platform and looked around. Beyond the depot, dirt streets were trimmed with wooden sidewalks. Hitching posts stood sentinel in front of various buildings, but they were different from the hitching posts in most of Europe. These were connected by a board. Many people were making use of both the sidewalks and the hitching posts. Single horses, horses with buggies, and horses with wagons were tied to several of the posts. Litchfield was a town full of life. Olina liked that.

As Olina continued her perusal of the town, she noticed that there were several stores down one street away from the depot. Maybe Litchfield was a larger town than she had first thought. She turned, looking for Gustaf. She spied him claiming her trunks from the baggage wagon. He pulled one up on his shoulders as if it didn't weigh much, but Olina knew better. She couldn't get the trunks down the stairs at Tant Olga's. The wagon driver helped bring them down when she was going to the ship.

Gustaf deposited the trunk beside the two carpetbags, which he had placed on a bench that ran the full length of the depot. Then he went back for the other. Olina walked over to stand beside the luggage.

"I'm going to leave you here to guard our bags." He didn't look at her while he was talking. Instead he looked around as if trying to see who was at the station. "I left my wagon at the livery. I'll go get it. You'll be safe waiting with our bags. I'll be back soon."

With long strides, he stepped off the station platform and marched to the livery. Olina sat beside the trunk. She was glad the bench was in the shade. The late morning sun was hotter than she thought it would be in April. Olina would be glad when they got to the Nilssons' farm. She could hardly wait to freshen up. And she wanted clean clothes. On the trip from New York City, she had changed her waist a couple of times with fresh waists she had packed in her carpetbag. But she had worn these clothes too long.

What she actually needed was a bath. She would love to soak in a bathtub, such as Tant Olga had in her upstairs bathroom, filled with tepid water. One like she used in the hotel in New York City. She needed to wash her hair. It felt as if it were sticking to her scalp. They couldn't get to the farm any too soon for her.

When Olina heard a wagon pull up beside the platform, she turned to see if it was Gustaf. It was, but he didn't look happy.

"I'm afraid we're not going straight to the farm. Mother sent a list to August at the livery, asking that I pick some things up at the mercantile. I hope that doesn't inconvenience you."

Why did he sound so formal? It made Olina uncomfortable. "No, that'll be just fine, for sure."

Gustaf helped her up from the bench, then took her arm and lifted her into the wagon. While she was busy arranging her skirt on the seat, Gustaf crossed in front of the team of matched black horses. He took time to whisper to the horses and caress their faces before he climbed into the wagon. The seat was wide, but Gustaf was a big man. His presence beside her seemed to crowd Olina.

"Just wait here," Gustaf said as he stopped the wagon in front of a store that was about a block from the train station. "I'll be right back." Gustaf stepped down and tied the horses to the hitching post.

At least he had parked in the shade. Olina was still hotter than she wanted to be. She glanced into the open door of the store. It looked cool inside. What could it hurt if she moved out of the heat?

With that thought, Olina clambered down from the wagon and stepped into the cool interior of the store. What a lot of merchandise they carried. Why, she could probably get anything she would ever need right here. Olina noticed a display of fabrics on a far wall. She made her way through the crowded store and started feeling the texture of various pieces.

A soft feminine voice sounded behind Olina. Olina turned and glanced at the blond girl who stood there. Then she moved as close to the fabric as she could. She had not understood what the young woman said. She guessed that she might want to get by.

"Olina Sandstrom?" Now the voice was excited.

Olina looked once again. "Were you talking to me?" she asked in Swedish.

"Ja," the girl answered and continued in Swedish. "Don't you know me? It's Merta Petersson. We used to live near you."

"Of course." Olina reached to hug the girl. Finally someone she knew and who spoke the same language she did. "But I would have never known you. How old were we when you moved? Seven or eight? You've really changed, for sure."

"You have, too." Merta nodded. "But I would recognize you anywhere. You always had the most beautiful eyes."

Olina blushed at the compliment. "Do you live here in Litchfield?"

"I do now. Until last week, I lived on a farm with my family, but I got married." Now Merta was blushing. "How did you get here?" Merta looked around the store to see who was there. "Who are you with?"

"I'm with Gustaf Nilsson." Olina couldn't help wondering if Merta knew that Lars sent her the money to come to America, but she didn't want to ask her, in case she didn't. She also wondered if Merta knew about Lars's marriage. Gustaf had indicated that the family had just found out about it. Maybe no one else in town knew yet.

"Yes. I saw his wagon outside," Merta said. "I'm so glad you are visiting here. I hope we can spend some time together before you go home."

"I'm sure we can." Olina noticed Gustaf heading toward the door. "I would like that," she added before turning and following him out the door.

4

*G*ustaf started the horses moving toward the edge of town. Olina had a lot to think about. Merta was married now. *She didn't even tell me what her married name was. Maybe Gustaf knows.*

"Did you see Merta in the store?" she asked as she turned her gaze toward him.

"Yes."

"She told me she was married, but she didn't tell me her married name."

"It's Swenson." The curt answer spurted from Gustaf's stiff lips.

What's wrong with him now? Is he always in a bad mood?

Olina hoped the farm wasn't too far from town. She was ready to talk to someone besides this sullen man. She took a deep breath to keep from sighing. How easy it would be to give in to the desolation that threatened to engulf her. At this moment, she had no one to depend on. No matter what awaited her at the farm, she would take care of herself.

Olina didn't know what the rest of the Nilsson family thought about what had happened. She wasn't even sure what Gustaf thought about it. Except he called her a mess that had to be cleaned up. He said he would take care of her, but she didn't want him taking care of her.

Olina liked this Minnesota. Although the land was flat with a few small rolling hills, it was beautiful. Tall green prairie grass blew in the gentle breeze. Dotted over the green were patches of prairie flowers. Some were white, some pink or yellow. Olina wondered what they were called. They were unlike any flowers she had seen in Sweden.

No wonder everything looked so green. She often caught glimpses of water shining through the grass. The farms they passed had many of their fields in cultivation, covered with bright green shoots of some kind.

When they first left town, Olina asked a few questions, but Gustaf answered in monosyllables. Soon she gave up.

❧

After the few attempts at conversation, Gustaf also rode quietly, thinking his own thoughts. He didn't point out the beautiful wild flowers, or the small lakes, or even the road to their neighbor's farm. He sat berating himself. Maybe if he had made Lars face his own mistakes, he would have learned to be more responsible.

He couldn't even imagine what Olina must be going through, but he was beginning to admire her. He wished he could be more help to her; but whenever he thought about the last few days, anger still boiled up inside him. He didn't know who he was the angriest at, Lars or himself.

When they reached the farm, decisions had to be made about Olina. Would he have any say in what happened? He hoped that he would. He wanted to help this young woman who shared the wagon seat with him, so close that he could feel her even though they were not touching. He wanted to help her. Occasionally on the train, he caught a glimpse of the hurt that lingered deep within her. What could he have done to help prevent it?

❧

"Our farm starts right here." Gustaf pointed toward the fence line that divided the land on their right.

The sound of his voice, after riding so far without talking, startled Olina. She jerked, then turned to look where he was pointing.

"It's still a ways before we come to the drive up to the house."

How could Gustaf sound as if everything were normal? Maybe he was right. Soon she would face the whole Nilsson family. She didn't want to fall apart the first time someone spoke to her.

"The crops look good." Olina was surprised that her voice didn't tremble. "What is growing in that field?"

"This one has winter wheat," Gustaf answered. "We'll plant corn in the next field, though."

Olina didn't think she had ever seen corn growing. She wondered if she would be here to see it.

"Just past that field, we'll turn in and head toward the house."

Olina gazed over the fields toward a grove of trees growing back from the road. "Is the house up there among the trees?"

"Yes. We bought the farm from Ben Johnson's widow. They had been on the farm for a long time. He was the one who built the house. The trees keep it cool in the summertime and protect it from some of the harsh winds in the winter."

Olina tried to see the house from where they were, but it was too far away. "Why did Mrs. Johnson sell such a wonderful farm?" Olina turned to look at Gustaf.

"They didn't have children, and she was getting older. She couldn't run the farm by herself."

"Couldn't she hire someone to help her?"

"Yes, but she felt alone when Mr. Johnson died. She wanted to move back East with her sister. It was our good luck that she was ready to sell about the time we got here. No one else tried to buy it. It's a big farm, so it cost quite a lot. After we sold everything we had in Sweden to come to Minnesota, we had enough money to buy it from her."

Gustaf turned the horses down a long drive bordered on one side by a plowed field and on the other side by another field of wheat. "She didn't want to move all of her furniture across the country. I think her sister had married a wealthy merchant in some city back east. She already had a nice house full of furniture. We were able to move in and live right away. Of course, over time, Mother has made the house into her own home."

When Gustaf chuckled at that, Olina was able to laugh along with him, at least a little. She remembered how homey Ingrid Nilsson's house always was. How happy it made Ingrid and her family.

✧

It was a little laugh, but Gustaf felt part of the heavy weight he had been carrying slip with the sound of it.

Maybe, just maybe, Olina will be able to get over what Lars has done to her. And maybe someday she will forgive me.

5

erda Nilsson must have heard the wagon coming up the long drive to the house, because she rushed out onto the porch. Olina was glad to see the friend she had grown up with. But the young woman standing on the porch was no longer the girl who had romped through the meadows with her. Gerda's hair was up in the new pompadour style that was coming into fashion. The pouf formed a soft blond halo that framed her delicate features, features that were so like the ones Olina remembered, and yet so different. But then, they both were.

As Olina climbed down from the wagon seat, her gaze was drawn to the two-story farmhouse so different from the houses she was used to seeing in Sweden. Farmhouses back home were usually only one story. Instead of rock that was used over there, this American home was built of wood and painted white. Dark green shutters framed the windows on both the lower story and the upper story. Porches at home were small, but this house had a covered porch that spread along the lower story, covering at least three-fourths of it. White columns supported the roof of the porch, and a railing connected the columns except where steps led up to the porch.

Olina thought it must be wonderful to sit in the inviting rocking chairs that were scattered the length of it. Three sat on either side of the front door. The house looked enormous to Olina, much larger than farmhouses in Sweden.

"Olina!" Gerda rushed down the steps.

"Gerda!" Olina scrambled over the side of the wagon, catching her foot in the hem of her skirt. She would have fallen if strong hands hadn't caught her. She didn't want to look at Gustaf. He might be able to see how much his touch affected her, even though she didn't want it to. Her emotions were too close to the surface.

Gerda threw her arms around Olina and held her as if she would never let go. "I'm so glad you're here. I've missed you so much." She sounded as if she were about to cry.

Maybe she would think that Olina was only emotional about seeing her. "I've missed you, too. It seems like forever since you left."

When the two girls finally pulled apart, tears were streaming down their faces. Gerda pulled a handkerchief from the pocket of her apron and gently wiped Olina's face. Then she dried her own tears.

Gerda took Olina by the arm and drew her toward the porch. Flower beds spread in front, and young plants were beginning to bud. There were even a few rose bushes. Olina had always loved the smell of roses. She doubted that she would be here when the buds opened enough to share their delightful fragrance.

"Mor has just left to take dinner to *Far* and the hired men, but she left food in case you got here before she returned. She wanted to be here when you arrived, but the men have to be fed. I was glad she let me stay at the house and wait for you." Gerda opened the door that led into the formal parlor.

Gustaf followed them in, carrying Olina's smaller bag.

Olina liked the furniture, upholstered in wine-colored velvet. It was different from what she was used to in Sweden, but it was attractive. A thick carpet spread to within a foot of each wall. Even Tant Olga's house didn't have carpet. Everything matched so well, not like the hodgepodge of furniture her family had collected over the years. Lace curtains and doilies knitted the decor together. Mor would love to see this beautiful place.

"What room do you want Olina to have?" Gustaf was heading toward the hall that was behind the parlor.

"I wanted her to share mine, so we could really catch up." Gerda glanced at Olina before she continued, "But Mor said we should give her the bedroom on the front corner. That way she can have her privacy, but we'll still spend time together when we want to."

Gustaf nodded and ducked through the doorway. In the hallway outside the parlor was the stairway. He climbed up the steep stairs as if they were level ground. Olina followed him at a slower pace.

"When you've freshened up, come down to eat." Gerda stood looking up after her friend. "I put fresh water in your room."

❧

Olina met Gustaf as he came from the bedroom that would be hers. His presence made the narrow hall feel even narrower. Olina needed to have more room between them. Why did his presence unsettle her? He was like all the other men in her life. He didn't want her, but she felt drawn to him even though she wanted to push him away. She felt as if the dark hall did not have enough air. She was having a hard time taking a breath.

"I can wait to bring up your trunks." Gustaf looked down at her. "That way you'll have plenty of time to freshen up."

"What I really need"—Olina moved toward the beckoning doorway—"is a long, soaking bath. It feels as though it's been a lifetime since we were in New York."

"Wouldn't you like to eat first?"

Olina slowly nodded.

Gustaf pointed to another door halfway down the hallway. "That's the bathroom. We have a large tub in there. A man from Norway invented an automatic storage water heater a few years ago, and we've just installed one, so we don't have to carry hot water upstairs for the bathtub."

Again Olina nodded. Then she stepped into the bedroom that would be hers for awhile. How long, she could only guess. She was going to have to make some decisions, but she didn't want to think about them right now. She pulled out her hat pin and removed her hat. Dropping her hat on the table by the bed, she walked over and looked out the window that faced the front of the house. There was another window on the side of the house, and a gentle breeze blew through the room. More lace curtains covered these windows, and matching lace draped across the bed. How inviting that bed looked.

Maybe she should lie down and forget everything. But she couldn't. It was there in her heart . . . in her mind . . . in every part of her.

After picking up the pitcher of water, she poured some into the matching bowl. Both of them were decorated with hand-painted roses. As she splashed the water on her face, its coolness soothed her. Gerda must have filled the pitcher right before they arrived.

Taking off the jacket of her traveling suit, she looked down at her wilted, dusty white waist. It didn't matter. Gerda and Gustaf had already seen it. She decided not to change until after her bath. Olina picked up the rose-scented soap and washed her hands. She dried her face and hands with the embroidered linen towel that lay on the washstand beside the pitcher and bowl. How was she ever going to get through the evening? She crossed the hardwood floor and descended the stairs, trying to rein in her emotions.

Gerda and Gustaf kept the conversation light and informative as they all ate homemade bread and ham, accompanied by applesauce that Gerda and her mother canned last autumn. Olina learned a lot about the farm, the neighbors, and the many activities that occurred in the close-knit community. Although they were a ways from town, many of the neighbors were from Norway or Sweden, and they often got together. Women visited over tea or held quilting bees as well as other bees. They had helped Merta Swenson make her linens before her marriage. It sounded like a lot of fun, but Olina wondered if she would ever have fun again. Men helped each other harvest crops, build barns, or mend broken farming equipment. But no one could help fix her broken heart.

They had even established a school close by. The school building was also used to hold church services when the weather was too bad to get into town. Olina would have loved getting married here and establishing her family in this community. Now there would not be any family. At least not for Olina and Lars.

And who else was there? Unbidden, a face swam into Olina's mind. A face so like Lars, only more mature. A face with icy blue eyes, but she had seen those eyes warm when he had looked at his sister. Why was she thinking about Gustaf? He was nothing to her. Nothing but her best friend's brother.

Olina needed to make a decision. What was she going to do? What could she do? She had very little money. Not enough to go back to Sweden. The only thing she could do was write her father and beg his forgiveness for going against his wishes. If he forgave her, maybe he would send her the money to come home. That is, if he had enough money to send.

Olina was soaking in a tub of warm water when she heard Mrs. Nilsson return. The sound of voices rumbled below her, but she couldn't make out what they were saying. She did recognize their voices as both Gerda and Gustaf talked to their mother. Was their conversation about her? Soon the talking ceased, and Olina heard Gerda and Gustaf leave the house.

Tears streamed down Olina's face and plopped in the cooling bath water. She felt chilled, inside and out. She got out of the bathtub and pulled the plug. As the water gurgled down the drain, Olina dried off and put on fresh clothes. At least she felt better being clean again. Tonight, when she was once more alone in her room, she would write her father a letter.

❧

Mrs. Nilsson was waiting in the kitchen for Olina when she came down the stairs. She opened her arms and gathered Olina close.

"My precious child." There was a catch in her voice. "I'm sorry that my son treated you so wrong." By the end of the second sentence, both Olina and Mrs. Nilsson were crying.

Olina quickly regained her composure and pulled out of the embrace. She reached for the handkerchief she had earlier stuffed into her sleeve. After wiping her face, she turned toward the woman she once thought would be her mother-in-law.

Mrs. Nilsson was also wiping tears from her cheeks. "Since we received the letter, I have asked myself if I did something wrong when I was rearing Lars. How could my son have done something so irresponsible and hurtful?"

"For sure, it's not your fault that this has happened," Olina said. "But I don't know what I'm going to do now."

Mrs. Nilsson pulled a chair out from the table for Olina. "After supper tonight, we'll have a talk with Bennel. He'll know what we should do."

❧

Evidently Gustaf had gone out to help Mr. Nilsson in the fields, because they both came in for the evening meal at the same time. Mr. Nilsson didn't say anything about Lars to Olina before they ate, but when the meal was over, he asked Olina and Mrs. Nilsson to accompany him into the parlor. Gustaf followed them. Evidently his fader didn't mind, because he didn't tell him to go away.

Mr. Nilsson indicated that Olina should sit on the sofa beside his wife. Mrs. Nilsson took Olina's hand and squeezed it. Olina knew she was trying to make Olina relax, but she couldn't. Maybe it was because of what her fader had done to her. Mr. Nilsson felt too much like her fader. The stern expression on his face caused her to be nervous.

"First, Olina, I want to apologize to you for what my son did. I can imagine that you are extremely hurt."

Olina could tell that he meant what he said. She nodded.

The expression on Mr. Nilsson's face softened. "I can never make up for what Lars did, but I want you to know that we love you as if you were our own daughter. You have a home here as long as you want one."

"Thank you." It was hard for Olina to get the words out because her throat was dry.

"We'll do anything we can to help you." Mr. Nilsson got up from the chair where he was sitting and stood beside his wife, placing his hand on her shoulder. "While you are in our home, we hope you'll think of us as your parents."

Olina bowed her head a moment before she raised it and answered. "Thank you. I'd like that."

Mrs. Nilsson patted Olina's hand, which rested on the sofa between them. "Do you have any plans for now?"

"Well, I don't have the money to go back to Sweden." Olina tried to swallow the lump that had come in her throat. "I plan to write

Fader a letter tonight, asking him to help me come home." Olina couldn't tell them what her father had said before she left Sweden. She hoped she never would have to tell anyone.

Gustaf didn't say anything while this conversation was going on, but Olina could feel his gaze on her. She glanced and caught an expression on his face that she had never seen before. It made her feel as if he cared what happened to her, not at all like the man in New York City who called her a mess.

6

*O*lina wondered how long she would have to wait for an answer to her letter. Knowing it would take a long time, she tried to hide her hurt from the members of the Nilsson family. She thought she was doing it quite well. However, after only a few of days, Gerda came to her room a little while before supper.

"Olina." Gerda sat on the side of Olina's bed and watched her friend as she fussed with her hair. "I haven't wanted to pry. I wanted to wait until you shared with me, but you haven't." Gerda got up and went to stand behind Olina, looking directly into the reflection of her face in the mirror. "It's hard for me to watch you hurting so badly. We've been friends a long time. Can't you let me help you?"

Olina turned from the mirror and walked over to the window. She pulled back the curtain that gently blew in the breeze, trying to find something to fix her gaze on. Although her focus wandered from the birds in the trees, to the open barn door, to the sparkle of water barely visible beyond the roof of the barn, none of these things interested her. She paused a minute before answering, trying to decide how much to tell Gerda. Then she turned to face her dear friend.

"Oh, Gerda." A shuddering breath shook her frame. "I haven't known what to say . . . or if I could say anything without crying." The sentence ended with a soft sob.

Gerda pulled Olina into her arms and hugged her, gently rubbing her back as she broke into sobs muffled against Gerda's soft calico dress. The soothing touch brought comfort to Olina. It had been too long since someone who loved her had held her. She missed her mother's touch. Tant Olga had hugged her occasionally, too.

When Olina stopped crying, she pulled away and swiped, with

both hands, at the tears on her face. Gerda picked up a soft white handkerchief and helped Olina mop away the moisture that had completely covered her face and soaked the shoulder of Gerda's dress.

"Oh my, I must look a fright." Olina turned toward the oval mirror on the wall. "My face is all puffy and red." She patted some hairs into place before turning back toward Gerda. "I don't think I'll have any supper tonight. I'm not really hungry." She didn't want anyone else in the family to see her like this.

Gerda gazed deep into her eyes before turning toward the door. "I know you helped feed the chickens and gather the eggs. And you insisted on hanging the clothes on the line for Mother. That's enough to work up an appetite. I'll make both of us sandwiches out of cold roast beef and cheese. We'll grab an apple apiece and go down to the creek for a picnic supper."

Olina had no answer for her, except to nod. After Gerda left, Olina glanced down at her white blouse that had become soiled when she was gathering the eggs. While Gerda went down to fix their supper, she changed into a soft green calico. Looking at the white collar and cuffs trimmed with lace that she usually wore with the dress, she decided to leave them off. She was glad that she had plaited her hair and wound it around her head that morning. It was suitable for a picnic on the banks of a stream.

After tramping down the fencerow of a large field, the two girls ambled out across a pasture toward the grove of trees that lined the banks of the stream. Each girl carried her supper in a small tin lard bucket. Gerda told her that they were the ones the Nilsson children had used when they were younger to carry their lunches to school. It made Olina feel young and almost carefree. But not completely. She could not bury her hurt that deep.

The day had been warm for late spring, and it was a long walk. Both girls began to perspire before they entered the cool shadows of the trees. Taking a well-worn path through the underbrush, they soon arrived at the bank of the flowing water. A small sandbar led from the verdant growth to the stream, and a few large stones jutted out into the water. One even formed a flat shelf above the flow.

Gerda walked out on the stone shelf that was still warm from the sun, although it was now shaded from the branches of the trees that hung over it. Olina followed her, watching bubbles and gurgles burst from the water as it swirled around the rocks. Gerda sat cross-legged on the rock and arranged her skirt to cover her legs. Then she put her lard bucket in her lap. After prying off the lid with a stick she had picked up as they walked through the woods, Gerda pulled out a sandwich wrapped in paper.

Olina did the same. Before she laid her sandwich on the full skirt that spread around her on the rock, she took a bite. It tasted heavenly. Olina hadn't realized how hungry she really was. After taking another bite, she looked back into the bucket. It contained more than just an apple. She pulled out another lump of paper and unrolled a sweet pickle. When Olina sank her teeth into it, pickle juice dripped down her chin. She reached up with her free hand, trying to catch it before it stained her dress.

"This tastes good." Olina wiped her mouth on a napkin that was also in her bucket.

"Mother and I made those last summer." Gerda unwrapped her own pickle. "It's a recipe Anna Jenson gave us. We all like it, especially Gustaf." Gerda took a bite of her sandwich. After she finished chewing it, she said, "Of course, Gustaf likes everything Anna makes."

Olina looked up. "Is she a wonderful cook?" She didn't know why she was so interested, but she was.

"Oh, she's a good cook," Gerda answered, "but I think Gustaf would like it even if it wasn't that good. He likes everything about Anna. The whole family expects them to marry sometime soon."

Olina didn't know why that should bother her, but it did. She looked up at Gerda, who was now digging other packages out of her bucket. "Why did you say that?"

Gerda looked up. "Say what?"

"That the family expects them to marry. Has he asked her to marry him?"

Gerda went back to unwrapping her supper. "I don't think so. She would have told us . . . or he would have. They're together a lot. I think he's calling on her."

Olina nodded even though Gerda wasn't looking. She took a bite of the sandwich again, and what had tasted heavenly a few minutes ago now turned to sand in her mouth, making her throat dry. She looked around for something to dip the water with.

Gerda dipped her empty bucket into the cool, moving water and handed it to Olina. "Drink this. You look as though you need it right now."

Olina turned the bucket up and gulped the soothing water, dripping some down the front of her dress. Then she emptied her own bucket of food and handed it to Gerda. "Here you can use mine."

The rest of the meal was eaten in silence by the two girls. Olina tried to force the food past the large lump in her throat. At any other time, the sandwich, pickle, chocolate cake, and apple would have tasted good. But not tonight. They were only so much sawdust to chew and wash down with lots of water. She was glad when all the packages were empty. She hadn't wanted to hurt Gerda by not finishing what she had fixed for them.

When Gerda was through with her food, she pulled off her shoes and stockings and dangled her feet into the water. "Are you ever going to talk to me? I know Lars hurt you, and I know that Gustaf didn't tell you about it as soon as he should have. But I thought we were best friends. I want to help you if I can."

Olina followed Gerda's lead and soon splashed her feet in the refreshing stream. As they sat there, Olina did reveal part of her heart to her friend. They discussed Lars and how he had hurt her and how Gustaf had treated her in New York City and on the trip to Minnesota. But Olina couldn't tell her friend about her own father rejecting her. Or that she no longer felt she could trust God.

❧

Since it was such a warm spring day, Gustaf soon worked up a sweat. He loaded the wagon full of hay and took it to the pasture where the dairy cattle were kept. There he scattered the hay into four piles in different parts of the pasture, helping supplement the meager grass. Then he plowed the only field that hadn't been done before he went to New York. All the time he was following the horses pulling the large implement, he thought about that fateful journey, his anger on the trip there, and his confusion on the journey back.

It wasn't long before his thoughts settled on Olina. He would never be able to remove some images from his memory. Olina as she stood on the dock waiting for Lars. Olina at dinner at the hotel. Olina in the hall of the hotel when he had blurted out the truth about Lars. How different Olina was the next morning. She had strength and poise.

He couldn't understand what it was about her that drew him. But something did. Olina filled his thoughts as Anna never had. He couldn't remember thinking about Anna so much while he was working. He had a hard time concentrating on making the rows straight while his thoughts were in captivity to Olina.

What was he going to do? He knew that everyone, including Anna and his family, expected him to ask Anna to marry him. He wasn't sure he could do that now. How could he hurt her that way? Anna had meant a lot to him for a long time. But did he love her enough to marry her? That was a question he would have to answer soon. When he tried to bring her image to mind, Olina's face sometimes took its place. A lot of good his thoughts of Olina were. She didn't trust him, and he didn't know if she ever would. How could he have said those things to her in New York? What had he been thinking?

Gustaf didn't know what he was going to do. He knew that what he already felt for Olina was a major impediment to his stagnant relationship with Anna.

Gustaf worked even harder trying to clear the thoughts from his mind, but they wouldn't leave. He was glad when he finished the last row of the field. After unhitching the plow, he drove the horses into the barn before removing their harness. While he rubbed them down, he decided to go to the creek to take a swim before supper.

Because his mind was on other things, he didn't notice that the prairie grass, on the way to the grove of trees, was trampled down. It never entered his mind that someone had beaten him to the quiet haven.

As Gustaf walked the path through the underbrush, he pulled down his suspenders. Then he stripped off the sweat-soaked shirt and threw it onto a bush near the end of the path. He had started unbuttoning his trousers when he emerged from the woods and first heard the soft murmur of feminine voices. Startled, he froze just as Olina turned her eyes toward the rustle he made coming through the brush.

Shock registered on her face as her gaze swept from his unbuttoned waistband across his naked chest to his face. Blood rushed to color her cheeks, and she swiftly looked away.

Gustaf's first inclination was to cover up, but his shirt was nowhere near him. So he dove into the deep swimming hole formed by a small cove on the creek. He didn't even take time to remove his work boots. He was thankful that the creek wasn't over his head there because his heavy boots pulled his feet to the bottom, and he stood chest high in the water.

"Gustaf, what are you doing here?" Gerda started gathering up the scattered papers and putting them in her bucket. "We didn't know you were coming for a swim."

"I didn't know you were here, either." Gustaf pushed his wet hair back over his head.

"Is that why you went in swimming with your boots on?" Gerda covered her mouth to hide a giggle.

Gustaf looked down into the clear water. "Well, so I have. No wonder I'm having trouble swimming." He burst out laughing. The sound reverberated from the rocks and trees that surrounded them.

Gustaf noticed that Olina was laughing, too. A high musical sound. It was wonderful to hear. Before they had left Sweden, she had been a happy, fun-loving girl. He had often heard her laugh peal across the fields as she and Lars, or she and Gerda, were playing. He hadn't realized how much he had missed the sound of it until it wafted across the water to him. Maybe his being all wet was a good thing if it could start her laughing again.

Gerda and Olina both pulled their feet from the water and picked up their shoes and stockings. After looping their buckets over their arms, they started back toward the path.

"We'll let you swim in peace." Gerda smiled at her brother before following Olina through the opening in the bushes.

As they walked away, Gustaf could hear them giggling as if they were little girls. He was sure they were discussing him, but that was all right. Olina was laughing again.

❧

The day after they washed the clothes, Mrs. Nilsson wanted to wash all the sheets and towels. Olina was glad to help her. While the water was heating, she went upstairs and started taking all the sheets off the beds. She made a pile in the hall at the top of the stairs. When she finished in the last bedroom, she spread out one of the sheets and placed the others on it. After pulling the corners together, she tied them in a soft knot and picked them up to carry downstairs. It was hard to see around the large bundle, and her mind was on her problem.

When Olina had gone down about half of the steep stairs, her foot slipped, and she was unable to regain her balance. Her elbow struck one of the stairs, and a pain shot up and down that arm. She shut her eyes and groaned as she hit another step.

Something stopped her descent, and a concerned voice sounded near her ear. "Olina, are you all right?"

Olina opened her eyes and stared up into Gustaf's face, which was very near hers. "I think so."

She lost her precarious hold on the bundle, and it fell to the bottom of the stairs. Gustaf eased himself down on the step beside Olina. He reached up and wiped a tear that had made its way down her cheek.

"You're crying. Are you sure you're not hurt?"

Olina rubbed the elbow and couldn't keep from wincing. It did hurt. "I hit my elbow on the stairs."

Gustaf carefully assisted her to stand. "Is that all that hurts?"

"I think so."

"Can you walk?"

Olina nodded.

Gustaf helped her the rest of the way down the stairs. He took her into the kitchen and pulled out a chair. "Sit here. Let me look at your elbow."

His touch was gentle as his fingers probed the area. "I think your arm is swelling."

He went to the sink and dipped a towel into cool water. When he came back, he made a pad with the wet cloth and tied another around it to keep it on her arm.

Olina watched all these ministrations with interest. This man was different from the man who met her in New York City. She would have never thought that Gustaf could be so caring, especially to her.

"Thank you." Olina started to get up.

His hand on her shoulder kept her in the chair. "You need to sit here and let the cool water ease your pain."

"But your moder is waiting for me to bring her the sheets to wash."

Gustaf glanced to the bundle that lay in a heap in the hall between the kitchen and the parlor. "I'll take them to her. She would want you to take care of yourself."

Olina watched in amazement as Gustaf hefted the bundle onto his shoulder as if it were as light as a feather and carried it out the back door. Maybe she should rethink her opinion of him.

❧

Gustaf wasn't sure why he went into the house at that moment, but when he saw Olina's foot slip, his heart jumped into his throat. He rushed to stop her from tumbling all the way to the bottom of the stairs. She would have hurt more than her elbow if that had happened. Something deep inside him reached out to her. It wasn't just her beauty that called to him.

Olina had faced her terrible dilemma with more strength than most men would have had in the same circumstances. He admired the way she fit right into the family, sharing the workload with Mor and Gerda. Of course, she was kind of quiet when the family was all together, but he was sure she had a lot to think about. It would be awhile before she had an answer from her father. Gustaf hoped that when it came, Olina's troubles would be over. But something within him didn't want her to leave Minnesota.

⤧

After supper, the family went into the parlor. Mrs. Nilsson picked up her knitting, and Mr. Nilsson read to the family from the newspaper he had picked up in town. Gerda and Olina sat on the sofa. Gustaf sat on the floor beside it.

"How is your arm, Olina?" he asked when his father stopped reading out loud.

She looked down at his upturned face. "It's much better."

"I'm glad."

Mr. Nilsson folded up the newspaper and laid it on the table beside his chair. "What happened to Olina?" He sounded compassionate.

"She was helping me," Mrs. Nilsson told him, "and she fell on the stairs."

"But Gustaf stopped me from going all the way down." She turned back to Gustaf. "I didn't thank you, did I?"

This was the first time Olina really took part in the conversation. She felt more comfortable and a part of the family.

The next day, Olina was helping Mrs. Nilsson once again. Several times during the day, Gustaf came by wherever she was and spent a few minutes talking to her. Soon this became a daily habit. The friendship continued to develop, but Olina wanted to be careful. Of course, it was just a friendship. Gustaf was spoken for, wasn't he?

7

*O*lina had been in Minnesota for three weeks. The Nilsson family planned a party to introduce her to the neighbors. Olina dreaded that celebration. She didn't know how she could face all the people when they found out that she had come to America to marry Lars. Maybe if she had a headache or stomachache or something, she wouldn't have to go. Everyone else could enjoy the gathering whether she was there or not. Then she found out that the doctor was coming. If she pretended to be sick, Mrs. Nilsson would have him look at her. He would surely know that nothing was wrong with her.

Things had gotten better since the day she and Gerda had the picnic. Maybe she could make it through the party. If things got tough, she could remember how Gustaf looked when he jumped into the water, the way the cool stream had darkened his white blond hair to a honey color. But that memory also recalled his broad muscular chest liberally sprinkled with blond hairs. With that picture came feelings that Olina didn't understand, a tightness deep within her that she had never felt before. It made her feel breathless. She had to remind herself that she didn't trust men. Besides, Gustaf was promised to Anna, wasn't he?

At least the party would bring one good thing. She would finally get to see this Anna. What would she look like? She wondered if Anna was prettier than she was. What did it matter? She didn't mean anything special to Gustaf, and he wasn't special to her. Was he?

❧

The schoolhouse looked festive when Olina and Gerda walked in. Whenever there was a party, the whole farming community helped. Chains made from colored paper draped around the rafters, and lanterns hung on hooks all around the walls. The young women were drawn toward long tables made from lumber laid across sawhorses and covered with tablecloths in various colors. Holding down the cloths were fancy dishes containing all kinds of goodies. Everyone must have brought their most cherished glass plates and bowls. Cakes and pastries took up half of one table.

Olina loved pastry, especially *munk*. The fried pieces of slightly sweet dough were especially good when they were rolled in sugar as soon as they came from the kettle. She could even see that one plate held *äppelmunk,* tasty doughnuts filled with apples and cinnamon before they were fried. She couldn't identify all of the kinds of cake, but she did see *gräddbakelse*. This cream cake was a favorite of hers. Olina knew she would have to be careful not to eat too much or she would look just as she had when she first went to live with Tant Olga.

Every one of the neighbor women had fixed several of their best recipes for the party. Olina decided that a large crowd must be coming to eat that much food.

"How many people will be here tonight?" she asked Gerda as they hung their shawls on two of the empty hooks on the wall near the door.

Turning around, Gerda looked across the group that already filled the room. "Everyone is here." Then she looked again. "But I don't see Anna. The Jensons are late as usual. I think Anna likes to make an entrance."

The two friends walked over to the table where Mrs. Nilsson was pouring apple cider into a variety of cups. "Here, Olina." Gerda handed her a cup before she took one for herself. "Mrs. Swenson, Merta's mother-in-law, makes the best cider."

Just as Olina reached for the proffered beverage, a large family came through the door accompanied by a lot of noise.

"There are the Jensons." Gerda took a slow sip of cider. "The one with the dark hair is Anna."

Olina was surprised. Anna Jenson was pretty enough, with bright eyes and a smiling face, but she stood tall and sturdy. Olina could tell by looking at her that she was a hard worker and strong. Her upswept hair braided and looped into a figure-eight bun low on the back of her head. Her laugh, though infectious, was a little too loud.

Olina looked around for Gustaf. She was surprised that he hadn't gone to greet his intended. If Olina were promised to someone, she would want him by her side at a party, especially one given to introduce a new girl to the community. Now why was she thinking about that? It didn't matter to her what kind of relationship Anna and Gustaf had, did it?

The night was a great success. Olina enjoyed meeting the neighbors, and they welcomed her with open arms. Some of the neighbors had emigrated from the same area where she had lived in Sweden. She renewed acquaintances with them. After inquiring about her family, they moved on to asking her how she liked Minnesota. No one wondered why she came, so she soon relaxed and enjoyed herself, pushing to the back of her mind and heart the fact that she was still hurting. She needed to get on with her life. Maybe soon her visit would be over, after her reply from her father arrived.

When Anna and her family came in the door, Gustaf started to go to her, but his attention was drawn to Olina, where she stood by Gerda, drinking cider. He couldn't keep from comparing the two women.

Anna was familiar and comfortable. Olina caused something inside Gustaf to tug his heart. The last week or so, their friendship had grown, and he liked that. But would a man who intended to marry one woman develop such a strong friendship with another? Of course not. He knew he couldn't pursue the feelings Olina caused until he talked to Anna. He would wait until the end of the evening and ask if he could drive her home. Gustaf didn't want her hurt at the party, and what he needed to say to her would be upsetting. He knew that if he loved her as a husband should love his wife, he wouldn't be so interested in Olina. Anna deserved more than that from the man she would marry.

❧

During the evening, Gerda or her mother made sure Olina met every-one in attendance. When the dancing started, accompanied by a fiddle and an accordion, playing some American music and some Scandi-navian music, Olina was never without a partner. All the young men, and even some of the older men, asked her to dance. All the men except Gustaf.

That Gustaf didn't dance with her shouldn't have mattered, but it did. Why did he stay so far away from her? Olina watched him covertly all through the evening. He didn't dance with Anna any more often than he did with the other young women. Maybe Gerda was wrong. Maybe there wasn't an understanding between them. And what dif-ference did that make to her? Nothing. Not any difference at all.

However, several hours later while the women were gathering up their nearly empty dishes, Olina noticed Gustaf talking earnestly with Anna. Anna stood smiling up at him. Although Anna was a tall woman, he was several inches taller. After a moment, they walked together to the hooks along the back wall. Gustaf took a long blue cape off one hook and draped it around Anna's shoulders. Then they left together.

A dull ache started in Olina's heart. Trying to hide it, she helped Mrs. Nilsson gather up all the things they had brought.

"Where is a broom?" Olina asked as she put the last tablecloth in the basket. "I'll sweep the floor. Most everyone is gone."

"Oh no, you won't." Gerda took the basket from her hands and started out the door to take it to the wagon. "You were the guest of honor. You won't be cleaning up," she called back over her shoulder.

"It's all right." Mrs. Nilsson was standing beside Olina now. "To-morrow Gerda and Merta will come and clean up the schoolhouse. No one wants to stay tonight, and they already planned to do it that way."

Olina allowed herself to be led out of the warm building into the cold of a spring midnight in Minnesota. Stars twinkled in the clear inky sky above. Shivering, she pulled her woolen shawl tighter around her and threw the loose end across her shoulder. She had done a good job of not thinking about Lars, but for a moment, she couldn't stop thinking how good it would feel to have his arms around her to help keep out the cold. She imagined glancing up into his gray eyes, but instead the eyes she saw in her mind were glittering, icy blue.

❧

Anna smiled up at Gustaf. "I missed you while you were on your trip to New York. I've been surprised that you haven't come over since you returned. You've been back three weeks, haven't you?"

Gustaf's nod was accompanied by a grunt of assent.

"I suppose you've been busy catching up with the things that didn't get done while you were gone."

"That's right." Gustaf steered her toward the door. "I'm glad you wore this cape. It'll be warm on the ride home." Gustaf was trying to change the subject, but this was not a good subject to change to.

"Well, you could keep me warm," Anna purred in a voice unlike her usual clear one.

It was a good thing Gustaf was walking behind her. She couldn't see him gritting his teeth. How was he going to do this without hurting her too much? Even though the cold air caressed them as they walked to the buggy, Gustaf was beginning to sweat. This night was going to end in disaster. It wouldn't end well for him and not for Anna, either.

After helping Anna into the buggy, Gustaf walked around in front of the horses, giving them an encouraging pat as he passed. When he climbed up on the seat, he noticed that Anna was sitting closer to the middle than the side. Gustaf didn't want to sit so close to her.

He didn't want her upset the whole way home. It would take about half an hour to get to the Jenson farm. He would wait until they were within sight of the farmhouse to talk to her.

As they drove along, Anna kept up a steady stream of chatter. Gustaf wasn't sure what she was talking about because he was trying to think how to say what he needed to say with the least amount of hurt. He hoped his occasional comments of *yes, right,* and *interesting* were appropriate and at the right time.

When they were still about a mile from the Jenson farmhouse,

Anna broke through his thoughts. "All right, Gustaf." Her voice was louder and harsher than it had been on the rest of the trip. "Are you going to tell me what's bothering you?"

Gustaf pulled the team off the road and parked under a tree. He tied the reins to the front of the buggy and sat there a minute. Then he turned to look at Anna in the dark shadows. Her luminous eyes sparkled through the darkness. "What makes you think something's the matter?" It was a stupid question. They had spent enough time together for her to read his moods.

"I've been carrying on a one-sided conversation all the way home. You haven't heard a single word I've said." Anna sat with her arms crossed defiantly across her chest.

Gustaf wanted to deny her allegation, but then thought better of it. "You're right. My thoughts have been engaged otherwise."

"And who has engaged your thoughts?"

Gustaf was amazed that her question had cut straight to the root of the problem, but he didn't want to tell her that right now.

Sensing his hesitation, Anna continued, "Are you going to tell me what's going on?"

"Anna." Gustaf tried to take her hand in his, but she pulled stiffly to the far end of the buggy seat. He was afraid if he reached for her again, she might tumble off into the dirt. He didn't want that.

"I've been thinking about our relationship." Gustaf stopped and cleared his throat, trying to dislodge the large lump that had taken up residence there.

"And?" Anna wasn't going to make this any easier.

"And . . ." Gustaf tried again. "And I think . . . maybe . . . we shouldn't spend so much time together."

"Is there someone else?" Anna's bitter question surprised Gustaf.

"What kind of man do you think I am?" he asked in anger.

"I don't know what kind of man you are." Anna shivered, but she pulled even farther away from him, if that was possible. "I thought—" Anna stopped to swallow a sob. "I thought we had something. You've been calling on me for some time now."

An owl hooted in a nearby tree, and the wind picked up, swishing the branches above their heads.

"Well . . . I have been." That lump had grown to be a boulder. "Calling on you, I mean." Why did this have to be so hard to say? "I'm not sure we're supposed to be together for life."

Even in the dark, he could see Anna glare at him. "What is that supposed to mean?" Her tone was harder and more brittle. "I thought you were going to ask me to marry you tonight." Anna ended on a sob, and Gustaf could see the tears glistening on her cheeks, making trails that she didn't wipe off.

It felt as if there were a dagger in his heart. He reached out to her, but hesitated when he saw her expression. Gustaf pulled his big white handkerchief from his back pocket and handed it to her, knowing she wouldn't want him touching her right now. As she mopped her tears away, they were replaced by others.

"I know that's what you thought, and that makes this even harder." Gustaf tried to sound gentle, but he didn't. The words sounded harsh to his own ears. "You're important to me, but I know I don't love you the way you should be loved by your future husband. You deserve better than that. Can't we remain friends?"

"And are we friends right now?" Anna's question was forced from between stiff lips. "Is friendship what we have had all this time? Nothing more?"

Gustaf bowed his head and covered his face with both hands. Could the evening get any worse? "I'm so sorry. I didn't want to hurt you." He wasn't even sure Anna heard his muffled words, so he looked up, dropping his hands into his lap.

"Would you please take me home now?"

Gustaf untied the reins and clucked to the waiting horses. Ominous silence accompanied them the last mile to the farmhouse, covering them in an oppressive blanket. When the buggy stopped, Anna didn't wait for Gustaf to help her down. Instead, she scrambled over the wheel, almost falling in her haste.

"Wait, Anna. I'll help you." He tried to follow her.

"Don't bother," she yelled back over her shoulder and ran into the house.

Gustaf hoped some day she would speak to him again.

8

After the party, Olina settled into life on the Minnesota farm. She gladly helped with her share of the chores. It was good for Gerda and Olina to be together again. It was as if they had never been separated. Gerda helped Olina become a part of the community, and Olina caught Gerda up on what had happened in the old country after the Nilssons left.

Before long, the two girls spent most of their evenings doing needlework as they talked. Gerda took an interest in all the fashionable clothes Olina had brought with her from Europe.

"Stand still, Olina." Gerda walked around her friend, looking at the darts and flounces on the dark green traveling suit Olina was modeling. "I want to see how she made this."

"I could take it off." Olina unbuttoned the suit. "That way we could look at the seams from the inside. The jacket is lined, but the waist and skirt aren't." When the coat was completely removed, it revealed a soft creamy cotton waist with a lace-edged, ruffled jabot gracefully draping around Olina's neck.

Just then, the back door burst open and Gustaf entered, followed by his brother August. Gerda and Olina watched them from the parlor.

"I tell you, Gustaf." August raised his voice. "You'll never get him to sell it."

"What need does he have for a plow horse?" Gustaf sounded disgusted. "That horse will stay in his barn and pasture and never do another day's work." He threw his cap on the table, stomped over to the sink, and started washing his hands. "I could use another plow horse."

August glanced through the door to the parlor and saw the two girls. "Gerda, how are you?" He rushed to his sister, picked her up and twirled her around, then set her on her feet. "It's been a long time since I saw you."

Gustaf followed him, drying his hands as he went. "You saw her on Sunday. It's only Thursday. That's not a long time."

He stopped short when he saw Olina. She was standing between him and the window. The sun coming through the pane gave her a gilt edge, turning the soft hairs that had escaped her chignon into a golden halo. The creamy-colored blouse and dark green skirt looked like something from one of the *Godey's Lady's Books* Gerda often received. Olina took his breath away.

It had been like this ever since he talked to Anna. He had felt a freedom from his ties to her, releasing all the pent-up feelings for Olina he had been fighting before.

Sometimes the pain he glimpsed deep in her eyes, when she didn't know anyone was looking, cut him to the quick. He knew Lars had hurt her, but Gustaf felt that there was even more hurt he didn't know about. What could it be?

Besides, Olina didn't ever participate in worship when they were in church. The Sandstrom family and the Nilsson family had been part of the same church in Sweden. Both families fully participated in everything together. During the services now, Olina looked as if she had been turned to stone. If only he could reach across the barriers and ease the pain in her. But how could he do that? He prayed for her every day. He tried to reach out to her in subtle ways.

"Are you men coming in for the evening?" Gerda turned from August to Gustaf.

"We thought we'd sit and talk awhile before August returns to town." Gustaf lowered himself onto the horsehair sofa. "Do you girls want to visit with us?"

Olina looked at Gerda. "If we want to discover how the seamstress made this suit, maybe we should go up to my room." She swept out of the parlor and up the stairs without waiting for an answer.

When the two young women reached the bedroom, Olina stepped out of the skirt. She handed the garment to Gerda before also shedding her waist and putting on her dressing gown.

"Look at all the tucks and ruffles she made on this waist." She knew she was hiding from Gustaf, but she didn't like the way he unsettled her. The feelings aroused by being near him were at war with the decision she made not to trust a man again. Turning from her musings, she looked into the questioning face of Gerda. "I wonder how long it took her to finish the waist of the suit."

This question didn't deter Gerda. "Olina, what's the matter?"

Olina looked away and picked up the garment she had been talking about.

"Oh, don't worry." Gerda stood looking into Olina's troubled eyes. "I don't think anyone else has noticed. But I've known you too long not to see that something more is wrong."

Olina crumpled onto the side of the bed. Gerda sat beside Olina and pulled her into her arms. How could she comfort her? She didn't even know exactly what was wrong.

"You can tell me what it is. I'll keep your secret." The whispered words went to Olina's heart. "Sometimes it helps to have someone to talk to. Someone who knows everything. You know that nothing you could tell me would ever change the way I feel about you. We're too good of friends for that, ja?"

Olina nodded as she raised her head from her friend's shoulder. "I have been carrying this a long time, and it has become an unbearable burden. . . . But I don't know where to begin."

"Since I know about Lars"—Gerda reached up to brush back the hair that had fallen across Olina's forehead—"why not tell me what else is bothering you?"

Olina stood and walked across the room. She stood at the window and pulled back the filmy curtains. Dusk was falling on the farm, wrapping all the buildings and trees in shadows. She stared into the shifting darkness.

"It's hard to tell you that my own father doesn't love me."

Gerda's quickly indrawn breath preceded her question. "How can you say that? Your family has always been close."

"I thought so." Olina looked toward the sky to see the first twinklings of starlight. "But you know that father was always stern. He's a very controlling man."

Gerda stood and crossed the room to stand beside her. "That doesn't mean he doesn't love you."

Olina turned and gazed into her friend's face. "He disowned me when I chose to come to America and marry Lars."

Gerda stood speechless. Olina could see that she was trying to digest what she had just heard. "Disowned you? What do you mean?"

"He told me that I was no longer a part of the family . . . that I was to have no contact with anyone in my family." She started pacing back and forth across the bedroom, before returning to stand beside the window.

"What about your mother and your brothers?" Gerda demanded.

"They could say nothing. Father was in a high temper. I think he thought I would change my mind, but I couldn't. Lars and I were so in love." Olina finished on a sob, dropping to the floor. She crossed her arms on the windowsill and placed her chin on her hands. "At least I *was* in love with him," she wailed.

Gerda dropped beside Olina and once again held her in her arms. "Your father will change his mind."

Olina looked up. "That's what Tant Olga said. She said he'd change his mind when we had his grandchildren. But now that will never happen." Olina felt completely drained. "How could God have allowed all this?"

The question hung in the air between the two young women. A question without an answer.

Gerda got up and started picking up the clothing they had dropped at various places around the room. "Olina, didn't you write your father a letter right after you arrived?"

Olina nodded. "I told him what happened, and I asked him to send me the money to come home. I told him I would work and pay back every cent as soon as I could."

"Well, see. Everything will be all right. He'll send you the money." Gerda folded the skirt and laid it across the end of the bed.

Olina stood and picked up the crumpled waist from where the

two girls had sat on it. Smoothing out the wrinkles the best she could, she put it beside the skirt. "But what if he doesn't? What will I do then?" She turned a forlorn face toward her friend.

Gerda took Olina by the shoulders. "He will. He has to." She let go and picked up the jacket. "But if he doesn't, you'll stay right here."

"I can't stay here. I would be a burden to your family."

"A burden? I don't think so." Gerda turned the jacket wrong side out. "You've been doing your part. Besides that, maybe we could move to town together and become seamstresses. We're both good at making quality clothing. The only ready-made clothing at the mercantile has to be ordered from other places, and they never fit right. We could probably make a good living as seamstresses. The only way Father will let me move to town is if I have someone to live with. It would work out well for both of us." Gerda smiled at Olina. "Besides, it won't come to that. You'll be going home before you know it. So let's do all we can to learn how she made your lovely clothes. *Jaha?*"

9

When Olina came, the Nilsson family had started speaking Swedish most of the time around Olina so she would not feel left out. Olina asked Gerda to help her learn English, and Gerda was good about helping her. After the second week, she asked the whole family to speak mostly English, so she could learn it. Even if she went back to Sweden, she would be glad she knew the language. Olina was surprised how quickly she picked it up. It wasn't easy, but when she heard it all the time, it was easier to learn. Now that she had been there nearly two months, only a few Swedish words crept into their conversations.

Gerda and Olina took each of the garments Olina had brought as part of her trousseau and studied it inside and out. They drew diagrams of how each piece was shaped and how the pieces fit together. Then they made new summer dresses from some fabric they had at the farm.

"Moder," Gerda called out as the two girls came down the stairs carrying one of the new dresses. "Come see what we have for you." Both girls were excited.

Mrs. Nilsson wiped her hands on her big white apron as she came from the kitchen into the hallway. "Now what could you possibly have for me? No one has been to town today."

"We wanted to surprise you." Olina held the dress up by the shoulders. It fell to the floor in a graceful sweep. "Here, try it on."

Mrs. Nilsson was surprised, but pleased. "All this time I thought you girls were making something pretty for yourselves."

"We did." Gerda twirled to show off her new dress. "This is mine." Balloon sleeves, gathered at the shoulder and tightly cuffed at her wrists, had five rows of tucks running the entire length. Intricate white lace set off the powder blue material with a dainty flower pattern. The dress was full at the bust, but had the new wasp waist that was accented by the full skirt. Yards of material gathered at the waist and swept to dust the floor with a lace trimmed ruffle flounce.

"See, Mrs. Nilsson, we made you one like hers." Olina held it out to her. "Only in an old rose floral print."

"I'm too old to wear such frippery." Mrs. Nilsson couldn't keep a smile from flitting across her face as she reached for the dress and held it up in front of her.

"You are not." Gerda hugged her mother. "It'll look good on you."

The girls went into the parlor to wait for Mrs. Nilsson to return. Someone had brought in the mail, and it contained a new *Godey's*. The two girls pored over the pages while they waited.

"Mrs. Johnson gave me a stack of these magazines that she had collected over the years. I had a good time looking through them. I don't think the book is as good since Sarah Hale sold it." Gerda was looking at some of the pictures. "I'm not sure how long I will continue to take it."

"It does help you keep up with fashion, doesn't it?"

"Anna has been taking another magazine. It's called *Ladies Home Journal*. I'm sure she would let us borrow one to compare them."

Just then Mrs. Nilsson came in wearing the new dress. "This is wonderful." She smoothed the fabric over her hips. "You put more lace on mine than you did yours." Lace lined the tucks on her sleeve and outlined the waspish waist. The delicate rose color of the dress brought out the natural color in her cheeks, making her look younger. "I'm sure you had a hand in this." She smiled at Olina.

"Gerda helped. And she picked out the fabric for you. It does look good." Olina had a feeling of accomplishment when she looked at the beautiful picture made by the woman standing before her.

Mrs. Nilsson continued to finger the delicate lace. "When the other women see these dresses and how well they fit, you'll probably have some asking you to make them a dress."

That sounded good to Olina. If her father refused to send her the money to come home, maybe she and Gerda could work together.

"What have we here?" Mr. Nilsson's voice boomed, preceding him from the hallway into the parlor. "Who is this vision of loveliness?" He picked his wife up from behind and twirled her around before setting her feet back on the floor.

"Bennel, behave yourself." Mrs. Nilsson blushed and patted a hair back in place.

"Where did my Ingrid get this pretty dress? I haven't seen it before, have I?" His expression told the girls how much he liked the garment.

"No. The girls made it for me as a surprise."

Mr. Nilsson looked astonished. "I thought you had to try it on several times to check the fit."

"I did, too. But they made it in secret, and it fits so well." She turned around so he could see the dress from every angle.

"You girls are good." Pride tinged his voice. "Very good."

"Mother," Gerda interrupted, "we used the last of the lightweight fabric we have here. Maybe Olina and I need to go to town and pick out some more."

"I could take you," Gustaf said from the hallway.

His voice startled Olina. When had he come in? She hadn't heard the door open. She had been too wrapped up in what was going on.

"I'm going to town tomorrow." Gustaf was drying his hands on a towel from the kitchen, so he had been in the house long enough to wash his hands. "You girls can ride along. How about it?"

"Sure," Gerda answered before Olina could decline.

Olina knew she should refuse. She had little money. She wanted to keep what little she had in case her father refused to send her the money to go home.

All eyes had turned to her, and she needed to give an answer. It might not hurt to ride along with them. She might have to tell Gerda why she was not spending her money, but she didn't want the rest of the family to know that Fader had rejected her when she left Sweden. That was one secret she was in no hurry to share.

After supper, the girls were upstairs in Olina's room looking at more of the drawings they had made. Gerda picked out four of them.

"I want to get fabric to make these four for me." She pointed out two more of them. "Mother would look good in these. What kind of fabric are you going to buy?"

Olina looked at the floor for a minute. She traced the pattern in the carpet with the toe of her black high-top shoe. "I won't be buying any."

"Why not?"

"I don't want to spend the money I have left. I might need it."

"Don't worry about that. We'll get you some fabric with our order."

"I couldn't take it." Olina looked up at her friend. "Besides, I have all these new clothes I brought with me."

❧

Soon after breakfast, Gustaf pulled the wagon to the front of the house. The day was fresh and new as the girls stepped out into the brisk morning air. The sun had come up, and the rooster was still occasionally crowing as he pranced across the yard.

When they reached the wagon, Olina was trying to figure out how she could get up without Gustaf touching her. Then he placed his hands on her waist and swung her effortlessly across the wagon wheel. In the blink of an eye, she was sitting on the bench seat beside Gerda.

Gustaf walked around the front of the wagon. He stopped by each horse and gave it a bite of something he had in his pocket. Olina watched him, all the while still feeling where the heat of his hands had touched her. Her skin burned, and her stomach was in turmoil. This was going to be a long day.

"You haven't been to town, except to go to church, have you, Olina?" Gustaf's voice broke through her thoughts.

"No, not since the day I arrived," she whispered.

"How long have you been here?" Gustaf picked up the reins and clicked his tongue to start the horses.

Was the man going to ask her questions all the way to town? "It's been about two months, hasn't it?" she said.

Gerda looked at Olina and must have noticed how uncomfortable she was, because she changed the subject. "Gustaf, we haven't seen

Anna since the night of the party. And you have not gone over to the Jensons', have you?"

Gustaf's face seemed to close up. "No," he grunted.

"I'm not trying to make you mad." Gerda looked frustrated. "I was just wondering."

Gustaf heaved a gigantic sigh. "Well, wonder no longer, Little Sister. I have not said anything about it, but Anna and I are not seeing each other any more."

Why did that unsettle Olina? It shouldn't make any difference to her, but a small weight lifted from her heart.

When they reached Litchfield, Gustaf took the young women to the mercantile. He needed to get some work done at the blacksmith's, and he was going by the bank. He promised to return for them in time for the three of them to go to the restaurant at the hotel for lunch.

Gerda pulled Olina along with her as she rushed to see if there were any new bolts of fabric on the shelves. Looking past Gerda, Olina spied several bolts of colorful silk on the shelf beside the cotton bolts.

"Oh, look, Gerda." She pointed to a color that was neither pink nor lavender. "Isn't it lovely?"

Gerda reached for the bolt just as Mrs. Braxton came to help them. "Is this new?"

"We have never had silk this color before. They call it mauve. I think the name is French. Would you like me to cut you some?" Mrs. Braxton reached for the scissors under the counter. "We have refinished this counter so it won't damage the silk."

Olina smoothed her hand across the wooden counter. "It feels nice. It shouldn't snag anything."

Gerda put her finger on her cheek and thought a minute. "I want ten yards of the silk."

"What are you going to make with it?" Olina fingered the fabric, enjoying the smoothness.

"I want to copy one of the dresses you brought with you, and I think I'll make a matching bonnet."

Mrs. Braxton looked at the new dress Gerda was wearing. "Where did you get the pattern for that dress you have on? I like the sleeves. I might want a similar dress myself."

Gerda waved toward her friend. "Olina brought a lot of new clothes with her. We've been studying them. This is the first one we duplicated. Hers was made from a soft, lightweight wool. But it made up really well in this cotton."

"Do you think you could make one to fit me?" Mrs. Braxton turned around so the girls could study her figure. "You could take measurements today."

Gerda looked at Olina with a question in her expression. Olina nodded slightly. It would give her something to do until she heard from Fader.

"I think we could manage that." Gerda turned toward the shop owner's wife. "What fabric do you want us to use?"

Mrs. Braxton reached up and removed a bolt of emerald green silk. "I want it out of this. If you make it for me, I'll give each of you enough fabric to make yourself a dress. . . . Or I could pay you instead."

"I would love to have this sea green silk." Olina held it against herself. "Would I look good in it?"

Gerda nodded. "And I want this . . . what did you call it?"

"Mauve."

"Yes, I'll take the mauve. We each want ten yards."

Mrs. Braxton began cutting the fabric as Gerda and Olina chose thread, buttons, and lace to trim the dresses. Mrs. Braxton added an extra packet of needles to the order before she wrapped it. Then she took the young women upstairs to her living quarters. They spent an hour visiting with Mrs. Braxton while they measured her for her dress and shared a cup of tea with her. They returned downstairs to buy several pieces of calico and gingham to take home. They had finished getting all the notions they needed when Gustaf came for them.

"Are you ready for lunch?"

When Olina heard his voice, she looked up. For a moment she felt drawn to him. What was she thinking? She didn't even trust him. She couldn't risk getting hurt again. All of her pain was still too new. She had tried to deal with it the best she knew how, but she would never risk being hurt like that again.

The three went across the street and entered the dining room of the Excelsior Hotel. It wasn't as luxurious as the hotel where they had stayed in New York City, but it was nice. During the meal, several people Olina met at the party came by the table to visit with them. Lunch passed rather pleasantly.

Just after they finished dessert, Gustaf reached into his pocket for his money. When he did, something crinkled. "I forgot. I picked this up at the post office when I went in to mail some letters." He handed a letter with a Swedish postmark to Olina. "It looks as though you have a letter from home. I know you'll be glad."

Olina didn't want to be impolite, but she couldn't help it. While Gustaf paid the waitress, she tore into the envelope. The thickness of the envelope felt as if the letter would be long and newsy. Instead, the letter she had written home dropped onto the table, unopened. Accompanying it was a short terse note.

> *The person whose return address is on this envelope is considered dead. The Sandstorm family does not want to receive any more mail from that person.*

Olina sat and stared at her father's signature on the bottom of the note.

❦

Gustaf had turned to say something to Gerda when he heard Olina gasp. As he whipped back around, he saw that every bit of color had drained from her face. Her eyes were glazed with unshed tears. Gustaf wanted to shield her from other people, so he got up, gathered the dropped papers from the table, and helped her from the chair. Placing himself between her and the other people in the room, he ushered Olina out the door and through the lobby to the waiting wagon. Gerda followed right behind them.

This time, Gustaf picked Olina up first and put her on the middle of the wagon seat. Gerda could sit on the outside to shield her from curious onlookers. As soon as he was in the wagon, he started the horses toward home. He didn't stop until they pulled up in front of the house.

No one had said anything on the way home. Olina sat quiet and still. When he helped her down from the wagon, she rushed into the house.

"Go to her, Little Sister. She needs someone." Gustaf drove the wagon to the barn, praying for Olina all the way.

10

e really means it. Olina paced her room, tears streaming down her face. *How can I go on like this?*

Olina wished she could still depend on God. Knowing God was with her had given her comfort when she was younger. She needed comfort now as never before. Gerda had tried to help her, but what could anyone do? Olina dropped in a heap beside her bed, leaning her head on the Flower Garden quilt that draped to the floor. Her shoulders slumped against the side of the bed.

Thinking hurt so much, so Olina tried to clear the horrid thoughts from her mind. However, memories flitted in and out of her head. As she rejected one, another attacked her from the other side. Fader's harsh words the last time she had seen him rang through her consciousness undergirded by the written words on the letter she clutched in a crumpled ball, unable to let go of it. Olina had no hope.

Child, please let me help you. Olina had heard that voice before, but today she turned a deaf ear to it. *I know the plans I have for you.* Olina put her hands on her ears as if to shut out an audible voice and moaned loud enough to drown it out.

Olina stayed in her room for two days, not letting anyone come in except Gerda when she brought food and fresh water. Gerda would return later in the day to pick up the dishes, often containing most of the food, uneaten. But Olina did eat enough to keep from starving. If Gerda hugged Olina, she let her, but when Gerda tried to talk, Olina wouldn't listen. She would busy herself rearranging her silver-handled hairbrush and mirror on the dresser or opening a drawer and moving things around, but she never touched the wad of paper she had finally dropped beside her bed.

The third day, Olina came downstairs after the family had eaten breakfast. When she arrived in the kitchen, Mrs. Nilsson looked up expectantly.

"I don't want to talk about it right now." Olina tried to keep her hostess from asking any questions. "If it's all right, I'll tell the whole family after dinner. That way, I only have to say it once."

Mrs. Nilsson nodded and turned back toward the cabinet. "We have some bacon and biscuits left from breakfast. Are you hungry? I could fix you some eggs." She picked up the cast-iron skillet and placed it on the stove.

"No, thank you." Olina went to the cupboard and got out a plate and glass. "I don't want any eggs, but the biscuits and bacon sound good." She helped herself.

"Would you like some butter and jelly on your biscuits?" Mrs. Nilsson placed a jar of jelly on the table beside the dish of butter.

"That sounds good." Olina pulled out a drawer and picked up a knife and spoon.

"Well, sit down and enjoy your breakfast." Mrs. Nilsson reached for the glass Olina had left on the cabinet. "I'll go to the springhouse and get you some milk."

Olina turned. "Oh, I can get the milk."

"Let me wait on you this one time." Mrs. Nilsson patted Olina on the shoulder. "You haven't let me do much for you since you came here." She turned and started out the back door, but she turned back. "Olina, I want you to know that we've all been praying for you. We were worried, but Gustaf convinced us to let you take your time. He told us that you would talk to us soon." Then she walked into the bright summer sunshine.

Olina sank into a chair by the table. Maybe this wouldn't be so bad. She had been able to function and even carry on a conversation without bursting into tears. If she could get through the day and then the evening, she might make it. Olina hadn't realized how hungry she was. She had eaten two biscuits and two slices of bacon by the time Mrs. Nilsson returned.

"Would you like to finish these other two biscuits and the rest of the bacon?" Mrs. Nilsson picked up the uncovered plate and placed it on the table in front of Olina. "Then I could go ahead and wash up all the dishes."

After breakfast, Olina helped Mrs. Nilsson clean the kitchen before she went out to gather the eggs. Performing regular chores brought the illusion of normalcy to Olina. Egg production had picked up. Although the chickens had a nice house with wooden nests filled with straw, a few of the hens laid their eggs in strange places. When Olina had filled the egg basket from the nests in the henhouse, she searched the weeds that grew along the fence between that building and the barn. There she found three more eggs. Olina went into the barn and looked in the scattered hay at the base of the mound that filled one end of the barn. Four more eggs were added to her basket before she returned to the kitchen.

"Those hens." Olina set the basket on the cabinet. "Why don't they use the nests you've provided for them?"

"I've wondered that myself." Gerda came into the kitchen and put the empty laundry basket on the table.

Olina turned to look at her friend. "At least the ones that lay their eggs somewhere else always lay them in the same places."

Gerda's gaze held Olina's for a minute or two before she turned away. "Ja, that's a good thing. It would take a long time to gather the eggs if we had to search everywhere for them."

Olina was glad that she had seen understanding in Gerda's expression before she turned away. Having a friend who loved her no matter what could get her through the rest of the day.

∼❧

Dinner was delicious that night. Mrs. Nilsson had baked two large hens. She served them on a platter surrounded by potatoes and carrots. That afternoon, she had also baked fresh bread and an apple pie. It was a feast worthy of a special occasion. Olina tried to eat the wonderful food, but after a few bites, she pushed it around her plate instead of putting it in her mouth. When she thought about the evening ahead, her stomach started jumping and her throat tightened, making it hard to swallow her food.

Mrs. Nilsson looked around the table. "Olina would like to talk to us in the parlor when you're all finished eating."

Gustaf looked up and stared at Olina. Surely he would look away soon. However, he didn't. And Olina couldn't look away, either. Everything in the room faded from her consciousness. It was as if there were only two people in the room, Gustaf and herself. The moment stretched into what seemed like an eternity, and Olina felt more confused than ever. If anyone else noticed, they didn't comment on it.

"We'll help you clean up, Moder." Gustaf got up from his chair and picked up some empty dishes from the table.

"You don't have to do that." Mrs. Nilsson reached for them.

"Yes, we do." Gustaf continued toward the sink with his hands full. "That way we'll all get to the parlor at the same time."

Even Mr. Nilsson helped. Gustaf and Gerda started talking about what they had done during the day. Soon the dishes were washed and put away. Mrs. Nilsson removed her big white apron and hung it on a hook beside the back door.

By the time Olina reached the parlor, the only place to sit was beside Gerda on the sofa. When she was seated, everyone turned toward Olina. The time had come for her to share. She closed her eyes and took a deep breath. Before she opened them again, Gerda reached over, took her hand, and squeezed it.

❧

Gustaf's heart ached as he watched Olina prepare to talk to them. When he had looked at her during dinner, he could see the wall she had erected around her heart. It was painted with painful strokes trying to hide what was inside, but he could see more hurt than he ever wanted to feel himself. He wondered how she could take it. She didn't look that strong, but she must be.

When Gustaf had gone into the kitchen for dinner, she had been standing beside her chair. He thought she looked fragile when he had met her on the dock, but that woman would look strong beside the woman standing by the table. She had to have inner strength to stand there, as if nothing were wrong. But something was wrong, terribly wrong, *Gud, what can I do to help her. Please tell me.*

He wished he could sit beside her, where Gerda was. He wanted to be the one to comfort her and take away her pain. This feeling was new and stronger than anything he had ever felt for a woman. Was this love? If it was, what could he do about it if she wouldn't let him come near her?

Just love her, My son. She needs so much love.

When Olina opened her eyes, Gustaf tried to communicate that love to her through his expression. He knew he would have to go slowly and let God heal Olina's hurts before he could ever say anything to her about his feelings. That thought caused his heart to beat a little faster. Gustaf felt hope for a day when Olina might be his wife.

❧

Olina glanced at Gustaf. He was looking right at her. His expression was trying to tell her something, but she felt uncomfortable, so she quickly looked away. What was he trying to communicate to her?

Olina took a deep breath again. Still holding Gerda's hand, she looked at Mr. Nilsson and then Mrs. Nilsson before fixing her gaze on the pattern in the carpet. As she began to talk, she studied the design.

"I'm sorry I have not been sociable these last two days."

Gerda didn't let her continue. "Olina, it's all right."

"Yes," Mrs. Nilsson added. "You have no need to apologize."

Olina nodded. "Thank you." She looked into Mrs. Nilsson's sweet face. "I seem to have a serious problem." For a moment she couldn't go on. A large lump formed in her throat, and she couldn't get any words around it.

Gustaf jumped up from the chair where he was sitting and went to the kitchen. He could be heard rummaging around before he returned with a glass of water. When he reached toward Olina, she gladly took the proffered liquid refreshment.

After a few sips of the cool well water, she was able to continue.

"My father didn't want me to come to America. He told me that if I did, he would disown me. I didn't think he really meant it . . . until I received the reply to my letter."

Olina's hands started shaking, so she set the glass on the table beside the sofa. "He didn't even open my letter. Instead, he wrote that the person who mailed it was considered dead by the family. He doesn't want me to write again."

A sob was working its way up Olina's throat, but by sheer will, she swallowed it. She wouldn't cry in front of everyone.

"I have no home."

"You certainly do," Mr. Nilsson thundered. "Your home is right here." He jumped out of his chair as if catapulted and stomped toward the hall. He leaned one hand on the door frame, looking as if he needed the support. With his head down, he paused before he turned around and continued. "We are your family now." He looked as if he wanted to say something more, but instead, he turned and walked through the kitchen. Before he went out the back door, Olina saw him grab his hat from the hook and slam it on his head.

Mrs. Nilsson spoke softly. "You'll have to forgive him, Olina. When he's disturbed, he tends to get too loud."

Olina nodded. "That's all right."

"He really does love you." Mrs. Nilsson got up from the rocking chair and walked over to Olina. "I know you are concerned about not having any money. You're doing your share around here, so you will be treated like the others."

Olina started to say something, but Gerda interrupted. "Besides, we've started making dresses. Perhaps we'll soon make enough money to live on."

Gustaf had been sitting listening to everyone else. When he heard what Gerda said, he stood up and made a noise that sounded like a snort. Olina looked up at him, and he said, "Neither one of you needs to make enough money to live on. We'll take care of you." Then he followed his father out the back door.

What was it about men that they felt they had to take care of women? The two men who should have taken care of Olina hadn't. She never wanted to have to depend on a man again.

11

*G*erda and Olina were hanging clothes on the line when they noticed a horse-drawn surrey turn from the country road and start up the long drive to the house. With her right hand, Gerda shaded her eyes from the bright sunlight and gazed at the approaching vehicle.

Olina removed a wooden peg-shaped clothespin from her mouth and secured a sheet to the rope line. "Is that someone you know?"

"The surrey belongs to the Braxtons." Gerda picked up another pillowcase from the laundry basket. "It looks as if Mrs. Braxton is driving, and she has another woman with her. Did Moder say anything this morning at breakfast about expecting company?"

"I didn't hear her." Olina stopped and, while Gerda hung the final piece of laundry on the line, watched the two women as they moved closer and closer to the house.

Gerda picked up the empty laundry basket. "I thought maybe I wasn't paying attention. Come on. We don't often get unexpected company."

The young women went in through the back door before the knock sounded on the front. Mrs. Nilsson looked up from the stove, where she was stirring a pot of stew.

"Now who can that be?" She patted a stray lock of hair into place and started untying her apron strings. "Did you see anyone drive up?"

"Mrs. Braxton and another woman," Olina answered while Gerda hung the laundry basket on a hook beside the back door.

Gerda turned to her mother. "I think it might be her sister-in-law. The one who is married to Mr. Braxton's brother."

Mrs. Nilsson brushed her hands down her skirt to smooth it. "The one from Denver?" When Gerda frowned and glanced at Olina, she stopped talking.

"I forgot they were coming to town for a visit." Mrs. Nilsson started toward the front door.

"Denver?" Olina looked at Gerda. "Is he the man who owns the store where Lars went to work when he moved to Denver?"

Gerda slowly nodded, not taking her gaze from her friend's face.

Olina took a deep breath. "I think I'll go to my room." She hurried through the hall and up the stairs before Mrs. Nilsson had invited her guests into the house.

❧

"Do come in." Mrs. Nilsson opened the door wide and gestured toward the parlor.

The two women preceded her into the room. After sitting on the sofa, they started removing their gloves.

Mrs. Nilsson sat in her favorite rocker. "It's always a nice surprise to have guests come to your door. Besides, I want to know how Lars is doing."

Mrs. Braxton glanced at her sister-in-law, who said, "He was fine when we left Denver."

"Actually . . ." Mrs. Braxton looked around. "We were hoping to talk to Gerda and Olina."

Gerda was starting up the stairs to check on Olina when she heard her own name spoken. She came back down the steps and entered the parlor.

"Gerda is right here." Mrs. Nilsson looked at her. "Do you know where Olina is?"

"She went upstairs." Gerda sat in the straight chair where she could see both the staircase and the other women in the parlor.

"Let me go put some tea to steep while you talk to Gerda." Mrs. Nilsson started toward the kitchen. "Then I'll go see about Olina."

❧

Olina was standing at her favorite place beside the window, watching two birds with their babies in a nest in the tree by the barn, when she heard a soft knock on her door. She had been expecting someone, but she had figured it would be Gerda, not her mother. Gerda always knocked harder. Olina glanced one more time at the industrious birds before she started toward the door. *I wish I could be like you. You don't seem to have a worry in the world.*

Olina took a deep breath before she opened the door and peeked around the edge. "Yes?"

"The ladies would like to see you and Gerda." Mrs. Nilsson's compassionate look went to Olina's heart. "But you don't have to come down . . . if you don't want to."

Olina sighed. "It's okay. I have to face people sooner or later." She fluffed her hair where the kerchief had mashed it while she was hanging up the clothes. "I'm feeling better since I told your family everything last week." She stepped through the door and closed it behind her.

Mrs. Nilsson put her arm around Olina's waist. "I'm proud of you, Olina."

They went down the stairs together. When they entered the parlor, Mrs. Braxton looked up eagerly.

"Olina, there you are." She stood and took Olina's hand in both of hers. "My sister-in-law wanted to meet you two."

Olina looked at the other woman still sitting on the sofa. The woman was smiling at her. Olina wondered how much she might know about what had happened, if she knew that Olina had come to America to marry Lars.

"Olina, this is Sophia." Mrs. Braxton took Olina by the arm and led her farther into the room. "She was wondering how long it would take you and Gerda to make her some dresses."

Olina looked at Gerda. This was what they were hoping for. "How many dresses are we talking about?"

Sophia Braxton rose from where she was sitting. "We're going to be here in Litchfield for a week before we return to Denver. We were in Chicago, but I didn't see any clothes there that could compare with the dress you made Marja." She looked at her sister-in-law. "Without a dressmaker, I can't get clothes that fit as well as her dress does. I would like to have as many dresses as you can make during the week we are here. I understand that you brought several European fashions with you when you came."

Olina wondered if she looked as surprised as Gerda did. How many dresses could they make in a week? They didn't know.

Marja looked from one girl to the other. "I have an idea."

"What?" Olina and Gerda both said at once.

Marja clapped her hands before clasping them under her chin. "You girls could stay in town this week. That way you would be close if you need to do any fitting."

Olina was amazed. She would have never thought of that.

"But where would they stay?" Mrs. Nilsson looked worried.

"They could stay at the hotel." Sophia stood up. "What a wonderful idea. Adolph could rent the room next to ours. I think it's empty."

The idea presented interesting possibilities to Olina. If all they did that week was sew, they might make quite a bit of money.

Marja chuckled. "I'm full of ideas. The price on treadle sewing machines has dropped, so we ordered one for the store. It came last week. Maybe you girls could use it. I've heard that you can sew much faster that way."

Olina looked at Gerda. Sew with a machine? She had never used one. All the dresses she had made were by hand. "I wouldn't know how to use it."

"It has a manual." Marja patted Olina's arm. "We could learn how to use it together. That would help Mr. Braxton and me sell more of the machines, if we know how well they work."

It would be a change from staying on the farm. Maybe it was not a bad idea. Olina turned toward Mrs. Nilsson.

"Do you think Mr. Nilsson would mind?"

"We could ask him."

When the men came in for dinner, Gerda and Olina had a hard time keeping their questions to themselves. They wanted to blurt out what Mrs. Braxton had said, but they knew they needed to wait. It seemed as if the men took an eternity washing up, but finally, they were all seated around the table. After the blessing, Mrs. Nilsson started passing food around the table.

"We had some visitors today." She smiled at the girls as she made the casual comment. "Marja Braxton and her sister-in-law Sophia came by."

Mr. Nilsson put a large scoop of gravy on his mashed potatoes, then passed the gravy boat along to Gustaf. "What did Mrs. Braxton have to say? Did she have any news of Lars?" After realizing what he had said, Mr. Nilsson blushed and looked at Olina.

Mrs. Nilsson took a bite of her baked chicken. She chewed and swallowed it before answering. "She said he was fine when she left Denver. She didn't come to see me. She wanted to talk to the girls."

Mr. Nilsson looked first at Gerda, then Olina. "Why would she want to talk to our lovely girls?"

Gerda giggled. "She wants us to sew for her sister-in-law."

"You remember when the girls made the dress for Marja?" Mrs. Nilsson put her hand on her husband's arm. "They did such a good job that she recommended them to Sophia."

Mr. Nilsson nodded. "Good work speaks for itself."

"They want the girls to spend the week in town, so they can sew all week for Sophia."

The girls held their breath while they waited for Mr. Nilsson to answer. However, they knew he couldn't be rushed.

Mr. Nilsson thought for a moment. "That might not be a bad idea. Where would they stay? Do the Braxtons have enough room for all the extra people?"

"Well." Mrs. Nilsson took a drink of water. "The Braxtons' living quarters are small, so Adolph and Sophia are staying at the hotel. They want to rent the room next to them for the girls."

Mr. Nilsson put his fork down and rested his forearms on the table. He looked from his wife to his daughter to Olina. "Is that right?"

"Oh, Fader, Mrs. Braxton has a treadle sewing machine in the store." Gerda pleaded with her father. "She wants us to use it so we can get several dresses done this week. Would it be all right if we go? Please?"

Mr. Nilsson looked at his wife. "Do you think it's a good idea? I wouldn't want anything to happen to the girls."

Mrs. Nilsson nodded. "I'm sure Johan and Marja and Adolph and Sophia would protect them."

"Let me think about it a bit." Mr. Nilsson picked up his fork.

"If you decide it's all right, I would be glad to take Gerda and Olina into town in the morning." Gustaf looked at his father. "I need to pick up a plow August is fixing for me. He said it would be ready by tomorrow."

Mr. Nilsson took another bite and laid his fork down while he chewed his food. He looked at Gerda, then Olina. "I think that is a good idea."

Gerda jumped up from her chair. "That's wonderful." She went to her father and hugged him.

Olina had finished packing her carpetbag when Gerda knocked on her door.

"I can hardly believe Father agreed to let us go. It'll be so much fun."

"It will be a lot of work, too." Olina smiled at her friend's enthusiasm. She walked over to the window for a last look at the birds. "I wonder if the babies will learn to fly by the time we get back from town?"

"What?" Gerda came up beside her.

Olina pointed toward a fork in a high branch. "See that nest? I have been watching the birds with their babies."

"Maybe they will." Gerda picked up Olina's bag. It felt light. "You aren't taking much for a week's stay."

"I don't need much to work all day." Olina laughed.

Gerda stopped at the door and turned around. "We'll do more than just sew all the time. There's always something going on in town."

Olina wasn't interested in what was going on in town. She wanted to see how much money she could make as a dressmaker. Maybe she could soon support herself. But would Mr. Nilsson let her live on her own?

The ride into town was a happy affair. Gustaf and Gerda teased each other and told funny stories. Olina relaxed and enjoyed the comradery. She missed being around her brothers, and this brought back pleasant memories. If only she could keep from thinking about Fader and the pain he had caused her. Because of him, she would never see her brothers again. She couldn't think about that or she would cry. So she shut out those thoughts and chuckled at Gerda and Gustaf.

❧

When Olina first laughed, Gustaf almost fell off the wagon seat. He thought he would never hear that laugh again. Ever since Olina had told them about her family, she had hardly smiled when he was around. He didn't know if she smiled at other times. He turned to look at her.

She was wearing a light green dress and bonnet. Probably one she and Gerda had been working on. He remembered their buying green fabric when they went to town. The color brought out the peachy texture of her skin. A light wind tugged some of her hair free from the confines of the hat, and the sun shining through it made it look like liquid gold floating in the air around her head. She was so beautiful. It almost hurt to look at her. He wanted to take her in his arms and hold her close, but he knew he couldn't do that yet.

"Gustaf." Gerda was looking at him. "You haven't answered my question."

He dragged his gaze from the beautiful image he was enjoying and glanced at his sister. "What did you ask?"

"See," she said to Olina. "He wasn't even listening to me."

Olina laughed. "I guess not."

"Well, what did you want to know?" Gustaf tried to sound gruff.

"How long will you stay in town today?"

Gustaf looked at Olina again. A sinking feeling settled in his stomach. He didn't want to leave her in town. Every day he looked forward to sitting across from her at the dinner table. Often he saw her during the day as she worked around the farm, gathering eggs or hanging up clothes or walking around and enjoying the outdoors. He was always finding excuses to work near her, so they could talk to each other. The longer he was around her, the more he found to admire about her.

"I may be there most of the day." He turned toward the outskirts of town that were up ahead. "If that's all right with you."

"Of course it is." Gerda hugged his arm. "You can help us get settled. That way, you can assure Father that we are all right."

"Sounds like a good idea." Gustaf smiled. *A very good idea. Maybe I'll have to find several reasons to come to town this week. So I can assure Father that they're all right.* But he didn't fool himself. He wanted to come to town to see Olina as much as possible. *Yes, this week could get interesting.*

12

When Gustaf stopped the wagon in front of the mercantile, Marja and Sophia Braxton hurried out the front door. They must have been as eager as Gerda and Olina, since they had been watching for them.

"Mrs. Braxton." Gustaf doffed his cap. "Should I take the girls to the hotel? Their bags are in the wagon."

"What a wonderful idea." Marja clapped her hands. "Sophia and I'll walk over right now."

"I'm sorry I can't offer you a ride." Gustaf gave a rueful smile. "The wagon seat is full. If you want to wait, I can come back for you."

"It's not far, and the walk will do us good." Sophia waved them off.

Gerda's eyes sparkled as she looked around. "I'm so excited. I didn't think Father would let us do this."

Gustaf chuckled. "You're a grown woman, Gerda. Father wants the best for you. He's just careful because sometimes there are rough men in town."

"I know." Gerda put her hands around his powerful arm and looked up into his face. "We'll be careful." She turned to look at her friend. "Right, Olina?"

"Of course." Olina made the mistake of looking at Gustaf. His gaze was fastened on her, and when she looked at him, she was drawn to those blue eyes. Sometimes, they could look so icy, but now they held the warmth of a sunshiny day. That warmth reached all the way to her toes. She couldn't look away, even if she had wanted to. But she didn't want to. That warmth was melting something deep inside her, as the sunshine melted ice in the fjords back home.

Home? Where was home? Was it in Sweden? Or was it right here in Minnesota with people who accepted her for who she was. People who didn't try to change her. Yes, it was starting to feel like home. With a tremulous smile, Olina finally looked away from Gustaf's mesmerizing eyes. Today was a new day. Minnesota was her new home. Olina was going to make the best of it.

Child, let Me help you.

Olina almost heeded the quiet voice. Almost, but not quite.

When Olina smiled, Gustaf could feel it touch his heart. It felt like the wings of a butterfly as it flitted across the flowers Gerda planted around the front porch. Soft, gentle, but a smile nonetheless. Olina needed to smile more. Maybe this was the start of something in her life. She looked as if she had made a discovery . . . or a resolution. Gustaf didn't know which. But whichever it was, it would have far-reaching consequences in her life. He hoped those consequences would include him. *Please, Gud.*

Adolph Braxton was waiting in the hotel lobby for them. He took them up to the third floor, the top floor. "We wanted to be away from the noise in the street."

He opened the door to a large room that was at the back corner of the hotel. Windows on adjoining walls bathed the interior with sunlight.

Olina walked over to check the view. Since the hotel was taller than the building next door, she could look across the rooftops. The hotel was at the end of Main Street, so the windows at the back overlooked an open field.

Olina turned around. "This is a wonderful room. We'll have lots of light to work by."

Just then, Marja and Sophia walked in. Marja smiled and clapped her hands. "We thought this would be just right. Sophia and Adolph moved next door so you girls could have this room."

"You didn't have to do that," Gerda exclaimed.

"Nonsense." Sophia put her arm through her husband's. "This room is the largest in the hotel. It'll give you plenty of space to work. Our room is nice, too." She smiled up at her husband. "Right, Dear?"

Adolph nodded. It looked to Olina as if his fair skin blushed a little under his bushy sideburns.

"We'll bring the sewing machine up later today," Marja said.

"Mrs. Braxton." Gustaf walked to the door. "Would you like me to bring it in my wagon? I would be glad to."

With a harrumph, Adolph said he would help Gustaf, and the two men left. Olina looked around. Heavy drapes hung at the windows. Olina walked over and discovered ties hanging high beside the window. She used them to hold the drapes open and allow the maximum of light to enter the room. Gerda went to the large canopy bed that was in one corner of the room. She sat on the side. Olina turned and surveyed the room. Even with the substantial wardrobe on the wall near the door and the table that sat against the other wall without a window, there was lots of space. There were even two straight chairs by the table. This would be a wonderful place to work.

"This room is as large as some people's houses," Gerda said as she walked to one of the two rocking chairs that flanked a small round table.

Sophia sat in one of the rockers. "That's why we wanted you to have this room. You can spread out all over while you are working."

While they were waiting for the men to return, Olina and Gerda showed their drawings of the clothing to the two Mrs. Braxtons. Sophia exclaimed over most of them.

"How am I ever going to choose which dresses for you to make for me?"

Marja Braxton sat on one of the straight chairs. She folded her hands in her lap. "That is a real problem. When Gerda and Olina made my new dress, I had only seen the one style."

Olina stood looking out one of the windows at the back of the hotel. She could see a cluster of trees in the field. As the wind gently blew the branches, birds flitted in and out among the treetops, much as the birds at the farm had. It would be pleasant to watch them when she needed a break from the tedium of sewing. But maybe it wouldn't be quite so tedious when they used the treadle machine. She hoped not.

Olina turned back toward the other three women. "I have an idea, Mrs. Braxton."

"What?" Both women spoke in unison.

Marja laughed, then added, "You should call us Marja and Sophia. It would be a lot easier."

Sophia nodded. "I agree. Now Olina, dear, what was your idea?"

Olina spread the drawings out on the table. "You should pick your favorite drawing. Bring us the fabric you want to use. We'll start on that dress. Then you can choose the next favorite. That'll give you a little time to decide what fabric to make it from while we are working on the first. We'll make as many as we have time to this week, doing them one at a time like that."

Marja clapped her hands. "What a wonderful idea. Olina, you are a smart girl. I'm so glad you came to Minnesota." She pulled Olina into her arms and hugged her hard.

That hug reminded Olina of her mother. Maybe the people here did accept her for who she was. She could make a home for herself. Perhaps in time, she would find peace in her heart again.

When the men returned with the sewing machine, Olina was amazed. She had never seen anything like it. The black iron machine was attached to a small wooden table with iron legs. Under the table, a mesh contraption near the floor was attached to the machine above it. She had no idea how it could work, but she was eager to find out.

"Where is the manual?" Marja looked at the two men.

"Right here." Gustaf pulled a booklet from his back pocket and handed it to her. "Sorry I had to fold it, but I couldn't carry it and the machine at the same time."

Marja gave it to Olina. "Tonight you girls can read this and try to see how it works. Sophia and I will come in the morning for you to take her measurements. We'll bring the first fabric and notions." She clapped her hands. "Oh, I'm getting so excited."

"So am I," Sophia agreed as she took Marja's arm. "We need to go look at the fabric in the store. I have my eye on a couple of those drawings." Adolph quietly joined the two women as they walked down the hall, chattering about the different dresses.

Gustaf turned to Gerda, but he watched Olina out of the corner of his eye. "Could I take you and Olina to lunch downstairs?"

Gerda stood up. "Is it noon already? Where has the morning gone?"

"One, it took awhile to get to town." Gustaf counted on his fingers. "Two, we had to move your bags into your room. Three, we brought that heavy machine up two flights of stairs. That took time."

"Oh, you." Gerda playfully hit his arm. "That's not what I meant."

"I know." Gustaf laughed with her. Then he turned to Olina. "May I escort you to lunch?" When Olina nodded, he continued, "We'll let my sister come with us, if she'll behave herself."

Olina couldn't help herself. She burst out laughing with them. It felt so good to share a fun time. Maybe her heart could heal.

In the dining room, they were served a rich beef stew with hot corn bread slathered with fresh butter. While they were eating, several people from church stopped to visit. When they found out that the girls were staying in town for a week, they issued many invitations. Gerda and Olina wouldn't have to eat at the hotel very often, and they would have time to renew acquaintances and establish new friendships.

"I guess we'll not be sewing all the time." Gerda smiled at Olina.

"We need to sew a lot." Olina kept thinking about the money they would earn.

"I know that Marja and Sophia won't expect us to sew all our waking hours as if we were slaves."

When the waitress brought apple cobbler for dessert, she asked if they had heard about the brush arbor meeting that was going on that week. Olina didn't know what she was talking about, so Gustaf explained.

"We don't have many of these since we have our own church building. Traveling evangelists hold meetings in an open-air structure with a roof made out of tree limbs. I've heard that wonderful things happen at them." He got a faraway look on his face. "I've always wanted to attend one, and I hear this preacher has a powerful message." He looked back at the young women. "I think I'll come to town for the meeting tomorrow night." Turning toward Olina, he asked, "May I escort the two of you?"

Before Olina could decline, she heard Gerda accept with eagerness. How could she not agree to accompany them? Maybe later she could think of a way out of it.

❧

Thank You, Father. On the way home late that afternoon, Gustaf was glad he had a reason to come to town tomorrow. He would have thought up some excuse, but this meeting was a good opportunity. He couldn't imagine worshiping out in the open like that. The services in their church were formal. This sounded as though it would be a chance to relax and worship with abandon. Of course, he sometimes did that when he was out working in the fields. He would take a break and sit under the shade and sing praises to the Lord. He had even been known to walk around praising the Lord with a loud voice, but only when he knew no one was near.

Gustaf had heard people talk about the old-time brush arbor meetings and how they would contain a lot of praise and worship; the ministers presented the gospel in a forceful, but understandable manner. Gustaf wanted to hear that kind of sermon. And he wanted to see Olina touched in a service. Maybe this meeting would be the time God could reach her in a new way, bringing healing to her wounded heart.

13

When Marja and Sophia arrived the next morning, the four women spent an hour learning to use the sewing machine. It wasn't as hard as Olina had feared it would be. Then Olina and Gerda measured Sophia. After Sophia showed them which dress she wanted them to make out of the fabric they brought, she and Marja left the young women to their work.

Olina and Gerda cut out the bodice first. While Gerda cut out the rest of the dress, Olina started sewing the bodice, using the machine. By lunchtime, the dress was far enough along that the girls were sure they could finish it that day.

With a spring in their steps, Gerda and Olina started down the stairs to see what the restaurant was serving for lunch. Before they reached the bottom step, Merta Swenson came through the front door.

After greeting them, she asked, "Have you eaten yet?" When they shook their heads, she continued, "I want you to come to my house for lunch."

Merta served them chicken and dumplings, followed by gingerbread. This visit was the break from sewing that Gerda and Olina needed. After they were finished eating, Merta accompanied them on the walk back to the hotel.

"Remember how you said that you would like to move to town and be dressmakers here?" Merta asked as they reached the hotel.

"Yes," Gerda answered, and Olina nodded.

Merta pointed to a house down the road a ways, but still clearly visible from town. "The Winslow house is for sale. An older widow lived there, but her son wanted her to move to California with him, so she did."

Gerda studied the cottage for a minute. "From here, it looks as though it's in good shape."

"It is," Merta agreed. "Everyone in church made sure she was taken care of. Some of the men are still taking care of things at the house until it sells."

Olina could tell that it was a nice place and not at all small. She turned to Merta. "Do you have time to walk down there with us?"

"Please do." Gerda stepped off the wooden sidewalk. "We could look around, couldn't we?"

Merta took Olina's arm and pulled her with them. "It's not far. It won't take long."

The three young women walked along talking as they approached the cottage, set back from the road and surrounded by trees. When they reached the gate, Olina opened it and walked up on the front porch. It covered over half of the front of the house, with the front door at the end by whatever room projected beyond the porch. Olina stood in one of the two arches of the porch, which were held up by columns. She liked the shrubbery growing at the end and flowers beginning to bloom in the flower bed in front.

"I like this porch." Olina turned and looked back toward town. "It would be pleasant to sit out here in the cool of the evening." She slid down to sit on the top step. "I wish I had the money to buy this house, but I don't."

"Neither do I." Gerda sat beside her. "Maybe Father and Gustaf could work out a deal with the owner. I would like to move closer to town. This is far enough out from town to be away from all the noise, but close enough to be safe and convenient." She stood up and stepped away from the house. After turning, she looked up at the second story. "Merta, have you ever been inside?"

"Oh, yes." Merta joined her and looked up, too. "The second floor has two bedrooms in the front. There are two smaller rooms behind them. She used them for storage." Merta pointed to the room that was beside the porch. "That is the parlor. On the other side, she had a library. I think she used to be a schoolteacher, so she had lots of books. Behind those two rooms are a kitchen, with a large area for a table and chairs, and a big pantry."

Olina stood up and looked back toward town. "It sounds perfect. If only . . ."

"We need to pray about this. Maybe the Lord wants us here." Gerda took hold of both Olina's hand and Merta's. Then she asked God to provide a way . . . if He wanted them to live in this house.

～

Just as Gerda and Olina sewed the last button on the dress, a knock sounded at the door.

"That must be Sophia." Olina was glad for the opportunity to get up and move around. She stretched her arms over her head for a minute before she opened the door. "You're just in ti—" She was startled and stopped with a gasp.

"Well, what a welcome." Gustaf's laughing gaze met her startled one. "I didn't know you were expecting me."

Olina could feel her cheeks redden. She wanted to hide them, but she couldn't look away from him. She liked to see the merriment in his eyes. Was that something more? Whatever could it be? She shook her head. Why did Gustaf have this effect on her? Maybe it was because she had not expected to see him filling her doorway.

"We thought you were Sophia." Gerda jumped up and came over to hug her brother. "But I'm glad you're here, even though I don't know why." She stepped back. "Come in."

Gustaf seemed to fill the room, too. Olina turned back to the dress they had dropped in a heap on the bed. She picked it up and started folding it as she listened to Gustaf and Gerda.

"Do I have to have a reason to come see my little sister?" With his finger, he flicked a curl that was drooping on her forehead.

Gerda playfully hit him on the arm. "You are a big tease. Isn't that right, Olina?"

Olina looked at Gerda. "Yes, he does tease a lot."

"So what brings you to town?" Gerda came over to help Olina finish folding the dress.

"Remember yesterday at lunch, I said I would be coming into town for the brush arbor meeting." Gustaf looked from Gerda to Olina. "I came a little early. I wanted to check on the two of you so I can assure Father that you're all right."

Gerda rolled her eyes.

"I thought maybe you two lovely ladies would join me for dinner before the meeting." Gustaf looked at Olina, waiting for her to answer.

They did have to eat. Olina picked up the dress and moved it to the table. With her back turned from Gustaf, she answered, "We could do that."

All afternoon Olina and Gerda had been smelling roast beef cooking. "I think we are having roast." Olina sniffed the air. "It smells like they are cooking yeast rolls. It should be good."

Their meal was a congenial affair. Gustaf and Gerda kept up a lively conversation. Although Olina was quieter, she enjoyed listening to them.

"Gustaf." Gerda sounded excited. "Merta, Olina, and I went to the Winslow house today."

Gustaf swallowed a mouthful. "Why did you do that?"

"It's for sale." Gerda buttered a hot roll.

Gustaf looked at Gerda, then at Olina. "Why would you be interested in a house that's for sale?"

"I know that we don't have the money to buy it." Gerda put down the roll and clasped her hands in her lap. "But Olina and I would like to move closer to town."

Gustaf raised his eyebrows. Olina looked down at her plate, but she peeked at Gustaf through her eyelashes. He turned toward Gerda. "Why is that?"

"Oh, Gustaf." Gerda placed her forearms on the table and eagerly leaned toward him. "There's no dressmaker in Litchfield. Olina and I think we could make a living here."

Gustaf looked thoughtful. "You might be able to."

"It's no use to think about it though." Gerda sighed and picked up her forgotten roll. "Father would never let us do it. But the house would be perfect for us. The woman who lived there was a teacher, and she had a library with lots of windows. That room would make a wonderful workroom for us."

Just then the waitress brought their dessert to them. In a moment, she returned with a large pitcher of water to refill their glasses and a cup of coffee for Gustaf.

When they had finished eating rice pudding with raisins and cinnamon, Gerda wiped her mouth with the napkin. "I would like to go to the meeting with you, Gustaf."

"I had hoped you would say that." He turned toward Olina. "What about you?"

"Of course she'll go. She won't want to sit alone in the hotel room." Gerda got up from her chair. "We need to go freshen up before we leave. What time does it start?"

"You have plenty of time." Gustaf helped Olina push her chair away from the table. He walked them into the lobby. As he watched the two go up the stairs, he called after them, "I'll be waiting right here for you."

When the young women came back down the stairs, August had joined Gustaf. The two men looked as if they were praying together. Surely they weren't doing that right there in the lobby of the hotel. They must be having a private conversation.

"Wonderful." Gerda pulled Olina across the lobby. "August is here, too."

The two men glanced up when they heard Gerda's exclamation. August grabbed her in a bear hug and swung her feet off the floor. When he put her down, he turned toward Olina. "You look nice tonight. I'm glad Gustaf talked me into going with the three of you."

Olina looked at Gustaf. Once again, she felt a blush rise to color her cheeks. She had known other women who didn't turn red every time a man looked at them. Why couldn't she be like them?

The evening was cool but pleasant when they arrived at the structure covered with fresh branches. Olina hoped that the four of them would sit on the back bench, but Gustaf led them down the center aisle. He stopped about halfway between the back and the front. He motioned for August, Gerda, and Olina to precede him on the bench, leaving him sitting on the aisle. He probably needed to sit there so he would have somewhere to put his long legs. The benches weren't far apart.

Olina wondered if many people would come to the meeting. Soon most of the benches were full, and men stood outside the arbor, looking in. Olina was glad. At least they wouldn't be conspicuous. When everyone was crowded into the structure, it warmed up a bit.

A large man with snow-white hair stood from the front bench and stepped onto the short platform. When he turned around, he unbuttoned his black frock coat and raised his hands. All talking ceased. His booming voice led in an opening prayer. Olina had never heard a prayer like the one he prayed. He sounded as if God was his friend, not just someone who lived in heaven and kept His distance. In the Swedish church they attended here, as well as the church back in Sweden, God had seemed far from Olina.

She used to love Him. She had liked learning about Him, but she hadn't thought of Him as a friend. When this man said "Father," his voice held love and warmth, not just awe. Olina didn't know what to think about that.

After the man finished praying, he started singing a song Olina had never heard before. However, the words and the music touched something in her that she had been hiding. The first line, "Love divine, all loves excelling, Joy of heaven to earth come down," awakened a longing. Olina felt uncomfortable. If she had been sitting on the back bench, she would have slipped out and returned to the hotel room. The longer the singing continued, the more uncomfortable she became. Her mother had always told her not to squirm in church, but the wooden bench was hard even through the layers of her clothing.

When the first song ended, the leader started another, without announcing what it would be. That didn't bother the other people. By the second word, most of them were singing with him.

Olina didn't sing along. She had never heard this song, either. She didn't want to "survey the wondrous cross." Olina didn't want to think about Jesus dying for her. She didn't want to think that He loved her. By now she was fidgeting a lot. Maybe she could tell Gerda that she needed to use the necessary.

When the singer started the third song and everyone joined in, Olina couldn't shut the words out of her mind. "Amazing Grace, how sweet the sound." How she would like to believe in that amazing grace, but she knew that God had not protected her from grievous hurt.

Gustaf was attuned to Olina's every move. He could tell that she was uncomfortable. Maybe it would have been better not to bring her. He and August had prayed for Olina while they waited for the two young women to come down to the lobby. Perhaps it wasn't the time for God to speak to her yet.

Gustaf had been humming along after he caught on to the melody of the songs. The words had gone right to his heart, making it joyful, but that didn't seem to be the case with Olina. Maybe he should offer to walk her back to the hotel. But something stopped him from asking her.

The last song started. *Holy Spirit, Truth divine, dawn upon this soul of mine; Word of God and inward light, wake my spirit, clear my sight.*

Those words calmed Olina. Could the Spirit of God clear her sight? By the time the song ended, she had stopped fidgeting. She let the music pour over her, hoping it would indeed bring her lasting peace. But how could she trust God?

When the singer finished, he returned to his seat on the front bench, and another man stepped onto the platform. He was a small, wiry man carrying a big black Bible under his arm. He turned and looked out across the group that was gathered. It seemed to Olina that his gaze stopped when he reached her. For a moment suspended in time, he continued to look at her before he continued on across the crowd. She felt as if he could see everything in her heart. Why was he interested in her?

He stood there for several moments. The crowd was quiet except for a mother in the back, shushing her fussy baby. After the long pause, the preacher cleared his throat, pulled a large white handkerchief from his pocket, and mopped beads of perspiration from his forehead. Then he opened the Bible near the middle.

"I'm going to read to you from the book of Jeremiah, the twenty-ninth chapter, verses eleven through thirteen." Once more, he cleared his throat before continuing. " 'For I know the thoughts that I think toward you, saith the Lord, thoughts of peace, and not of evil, to give you an expected end. Then shall ye call upon me, and ye shall go and pray unto me, and I will hearken unto you. And ye shall seek me, and find me, when ye shall search for me with all your heart.' "

When he once again cleared his throat, the singer moved to the platform and handed the preacher a tin cup of water. After taking a swig, he gave it back to the man with a whisper of thanks. "I'm also going to read the first part of the fourteenth verse: 'And I will be found of you, saith the Lord.' "

Olina didn't remember those words from the Bible. Maybe it was because she didn't really like the Old Testament. It was harder for her to understand than the New Testament. She hadn't paid much attention when Fader read to the family from the Old Testament. But she thought she would have remembered those words. They had lodged in her heart after the preacher read them.

"I believe God is talking about His plans for us." The preacher closed the Bible and walked back and forth across the small platform. "God has plans for us, and they are plans that are good, not bad. He knows what He wants to happen in our lives. Sometimes it doesn't seem that way, but in the end, the good He intends will come to pass."

Could this be true? Olina didn't know. She only knew that God had allowed so much to happen to her. If He wanted good to come from it, when was it going to happen? Olina didn't hear any more of the preacher's sermon, but his opening words kept ringing through her heart and mind. God had plans for her good. Did He? Could she trust Him to bring them about?

(14)

hen Sophia and Marja came to the hotel late Monday afternoon, Olina and Gerda had finished two dresses that day. These would be the last, since Sophia and Adolph were leaving on the train Tuesday morning. Because they had been so busy, the week had flown by.

On Wednesday and Thursday, Olina and Gerda had made one dress per day. Once they became used to the sewing machine, everything went more quickly. Starting on Friday, they were able to finish two dresses per day. They had taken turns with each new dress. On one, Gerda cut the dress out while Olina sewed the pieces together. On the next one, they switched places. That way they both learned to use the machine. They shared the handwork, sewing on buttons and hemming.

"I can hardly believe I have eight new dresses at one time. These will last me for years." Sophia held up the light blue dimity, and its full skirt spread around her. "I've never had such a fine wardrobe as this." Her smile warmed Olina's heart. "What are you girls doing tonight?"

Olina looked at Gerda, who was making a bundle of the fabric scraps. She would take them home so her mother could use them in a quilt. "We'll be packing, getting ready for Gustaf to come for us tomorrow morning."

Sophia glanced down at the dress again. "I want to wear this before I leave town. Adolph and I would like to have you girls as our guests for dinner tonight."

Marja clapped her hands. "What a wonderful idea. We could all eat together."

"Of course," Sophia agreed. "It can be a dinner party. I'll check with the hotel to see if we can get festive food for tonight."

Sophia and Marja gathered up their things. They had started toward the door when Sophia turned back.

"I almost forgot to give you this." She opened her reticule and pulled a sealed envelope from it, thrusting it into Olina's hands. "I've put a little bonus in this along with what I agreed to pay you. You've done such a good job."

Before the young women could demur, Marja and Sophia had bustled out the door, chattering about the plans for the evening.

Gerda looked at Olina, who was using both hands to test the weight of the envelope. Olina could tell that it held quite a bit of money.

"Well, look at it, Olina." Gerda was anxious.

Olina was careful not to tear the paper as she looked inside. Several greenbacks spilled from the envelope onto the bed. Olina dumped the rest and sat beside the pile to divide it into two stacks. She had never seen that much money at one time in her whole life. At first, she just sat and looked at it. *What a blessing!* Now why did she think that? Did she still believe in blessings?

Since the first night of the brush arbor meetings, Olina had pondered the words of the evangelist. She wanted to read the words he shared from the Bible in her mother tongue, but she had not brought her Bible with her. Because of what her father had told her, she had left it at her aunt's house. After that Wednesday night meeting, Olina had written her aunt a letter, asking her to send the Bible to America. She wanted to wait to face the words until it came, but they kept popping into her head at the oddest times.

The preacher had said things on Thursday and Friday night that piqued her interest, but none as strongly as that first night. Did God have plans for her? If so, what were they?

"This is a lot of money." Gerda's comment interrupted Olina's musings.

"Yes, it is." Olina still stared at the two piles.

Gerda sat on the bed across from Olina, the money between them. "I have an idea."

Olina looked up at Gerda. "What?"

"Do you remember how much Marja said the sewing machine cost?"

Olina nodded.

"Look at all this." Gerda picked up her share of the bounty and let it drift back to the bed. "If we put our shares together, we could buy that machine and still have plenty of money left."

Olina's eyes widened as she looked at her friend. She hadn't even thought about anything like that. Maybe Gerda's idea was a good one.

"Remember at church?" Gerda started stacking her money in a neat pile. "When the other women saw Marja's and Sophia's new dresses, we got orders from four other women."

Olina was getting interested. "We could make those dresses much faster with the machine." She walked over to the piece of equipment and rubbed her hand over the wooden table that held the machine head. "If we are going to be dressmakers, we need this."

Gerda joined her. "It would be wonderful if somehow we could move to the house we saw and sew from there." She got a dreamy look in her eyes. "We did pray and ask God to provide for us. Look what He has already provided."

Olina could only agree. Maybe, just maybe, she had been wrong, and God had not deserted her as she had thought.

❧

The party that evening was festive. The glow of candlelight glistened from polished silver and crystal goblets, and a floral centerpiece graced the table. Instead of the roast beef most people were having for dinner, they each had a tender steak, surrounded by fresh vegetables. The dainty rolls were fluffy and browned to perfection. Dessert was a light chocolate pastry with a custard filling. Olina had never tasted anything like it.

While the guests enjoyed their meals, several people came over to talk to Olina and Gerda. Some of them were visiting with Sophia and Adolph before they went back to Denver. Other couples came for the wives to look at the dresses all four women wore. Olina and Gerda had worn the pastel silk frocks they had made before they had come to town to sew for Sophia. Three more women wanted to talk to them about making them dresses.

"Marja," Gerda said as they were getting ready to go up to their rooms. "You said that Johan would pick up the sewing machine in the morning when we are getting ready to leave."

"Yes, Dear, I hope that's all right." Marja patted Gerda on the arm.

"Well, Olina and I have decided that we want to buy the machine with the money we made this week."

Marja clapped her hands. "What a wonderful idea." Then she put her arms around both young women. "You have so many more dresses to make already."

The three women started up the staircase. "We thought it would be a good investment," Olina added.

⁓

"I'm glad Johan came to help me carry that heavy machine down to the wagon." Gustaf made a clucking sound to the horses, and they started out of town. "Here I thought I had carried it on those stairs for the last time." He chuckled. "It's a good thing we needed to pick up some feed for the horses. If not, I would have brought the buggy, not the wagon."

Gerda was seated between Gustaf and Olina on the wagon seat. She poked Olina with her elbow. "He always has something to complain about, doesn't he?" The young women giggled. "I think he likes helping us."

Olina peeked around Gerda to see that Gustaf was looking right at her. "Do you agree?" he asked.

Goose bumps ran up her arms. "I think . . ." Olina swallowed and looked away.

"What do you think, Olina?" Gerda seemed oblivious to the charge in the air.

"I think that Gustaf does like to help . . . us." Olina ducked her head. "But I don't think he complains much. At least I don't hear him."

When a robust laugh burst from Gustaf, another feeling ran up

Olina's spine. She was not sure what it was, but she knew that she liked to hear Gustaf's hearty laugh. It sounded musical to her, like the symphony she and Tant Olga attended before she came to America— rich, full, and heartwarming. At least it warmed her heart today. But it wasn't just the laugh. That was only part of what warmed her heart. After all, she and Gerda really became professional dressmakers when they bought that treadle sewing machine. Her life was taking shape. It had a purpose now.

Ingrid Nilsson prepared a special feast to celebrate the return of the young women. Even August came home to have dinner with them. He said that Gustaf invited him when he came to town to pick them up. The meal was a lively, happy time, with much talking and teasing among the Nilsson family. However, Olina remained silent, listening to the others and remembering such evenings with her family back in Sweden. The times she thought of them were not as often, but since writing the letter to Tant Olga, Olina couldn't get them off her mind. A veritable smorgasbord of thoughts tumbled through her head. Dressmaking. The house on the edge of town. Her family. In the midst of all those thoughts, Gustaf's face often appeared.

"Isn't that right, Olina?" Gerda's voice penetrated her reverie.

Olina looked at her friend.

"I was telling Father about all the women who want us to make dresses for them." Gerda smiled at Olina.

"Oh, yes. It's amazing. Even with the sewing machine, we will be busy for a couple of weeks." Olina could feel a blush creeping up her neck. She should pay attention to what the others were saying.

"By the time we're finished," Gerda added, "perhaps more women will want our dresses."

"What sewing machine?" Mr. Nilsson had a puzzled expression.

Olina looked at Gerda, wondering if she shouldn't have said anything about the machine. She assumed that Mr. Nilsson knew about it by now.

"Olina and I used some of the money we made this week to buy the treadle sewing machine Mrs. Braxton let us use to make her sister-in-law's dresses." Gerda smiled at her father.

Olina noticed that the puzzlement in his face softened. "Since we have so many other dresses to make, it was a good investment."

Mr. Nilsson's face softened even more. "That is so, for sure. You girls used your heads." He took another bite of creamy mashed potatoes. "Ja, it was a good investment."

"I made a good investment this week, too." Everyone stopped eating and looked at Gustaf as he continued. "Father, remember the Winslow house right outside town?" He waited for his father to nod. "Brian Winslow moved to California."

"I remember hearing that," Mr. Nilsson said.

Mrs. Nilsson passed the fried chicken to August, who didn't have any more on his plate. "I heard that he took his mother with him."

"He did." Gerda picked up another hot roll and buttered it.

Olina wondered where this discussion was headed. She didn't have to wait long to find out.

Gustaf put his fork on his plate and tented his fingers over it. "The Winslow house was for sale. I talked to their lawyer last week. This morning I signed the papers making the house mine."

Olina and Gerda looked at each other with stunned expressions. Gustaf had bought their house. The house they had prayed for God to find a way for them to rent. A plan was forming in Olina's mind, and she could tell that Gerda's thoughts were running along the same lines. Maybe. But it could never be. Mr. Nilsson wouldn't agree to let two young women live alone, even though it was near town.

"Gustaf." Mr. Nilsson laid his fork down and looked at his son. "Why did you buy the house?"

Gustaf looked at his father, man to man. "The price was reasonable, and I had more than enough money saved. Some day, I may want to live there with my wife."

"Son, you know that you'll always have a home here on the farm."

Gustaf smiled. "I know that. But when I marry, we might want to live closer to town. It wouldn't mean that I couldn't work the farm. It's not that far from here."

August couldn't let that comment pass. "Just when are you planning on getting married?" He jabbed Gustaf in the ribs, laughing.

Gustaf ignored the teasing. "I don't know when God will have me marry, but I know He doesn't want me to be a solitary man all my life."

He looked at Olina when he made that solemn declaration. Her heart began to beat double time at the sound of his voice and the words he said.

"What will you do with the house right now?" Mr. Nilsson took the conversation back to the heart of the matter. "It isn't good for a house to sit empty for long."

"I know that." With a smile, Gustaf glanced at Gerda and then Olina. "Since the girls have several clients in town, they could live in the house."

Olina expected a negative exclamation from Mr. Nilsson about that statement. Her father would have vehemently denied the request. But the room was silent except for August's fork scraping on his plate. Everyone else in the room had stopped eating. The silence lengthened, while Olina held her breath.

Finally Mr. Nilsson answered Gustaf. "I'm not sure I like that idea. The girls are under my protection, and I don't want anything happening to them."

"Father, I know that." Gustaf once more leaned his forearms on the table with his fingers tented over his plate. "Look at Gerda and Olina. They aren't girls. They are women."

Mr. Nilsson looked at Olina first, then turned his attention toward his daughter. Olina could tell that he was seeing them differently than he ever had before.

"You're right, my son, but they still need protection."

Gustaf nodded. "That can be arranged. Several men in the church have been looking after the property since the Winslows left. I'm sure they would help look after the young women."

It sounded to Olina as if Gustaf emphasized the words *young women.*

August put his fork down. "I could check on them every day, too, Father. It would be nice to have part of the family living closer to me."

"I know we don't have locks on this house," Gustaf continued, "but I had locks installed on that one. It would make Gerda and Olina feel safer at night."

August looked at Gerda with a smile. "I could make a big dinner bell for the girls to hang outside. Then if they need help, they can ring it. I could hear it from where I work and where I live."

Mr. Nilsson looked around the table at each of his children. "You have all given convincing arguments." Then he looked at Olina. "Is this what you would like to do, Olina?"

A large lump had grown in her throat, and she couldn't get any words around it, so she nodded. Mr. Nilsson studied her face as if he were trying to read her thoughts. Then he picked up his fork. "Let's finish this wonderful meal, so we can have a piece of that apple pie I smelled as I came into the house. I'll think on this discussion and give you my decision in the morning."

15

*G*ustaf knew that his father was a fair man with a strong sense of responsibility for his family. He would pray about the decision he had to make before morning.

Gustaf had prayed before he bought the house. God hadn't given him that check in his spirit that helped keep him from making wrong decisions. He felt complete peace about buying the property and couldn't help thinking about the possibility that he would one day live there with Olina as his wife. The house was perfect for a newlywed couple. Olina could continue to be a dressmaker, if she wanted to. When God blessed their marriage with children, he would build onto the house to accommodate however many children God blessed them with. There was plenty of room for expansion.

He imagined little girls with blond curls blowing in the wind as they played in the yard or even swung from limbs of trees. When they were younger, Gerda and Olina had climbed trees right along with their brothers. His sons would accompany him to the farm to help their grandfather.

What was he thinking? In his mind, he had children when he didn't even know whether Olina would ever forgive him. If she did, she might never come to love him as he already loved her. He needed to turn his thoughts to more profitable pursuits.

Gustaf got on his knees with his Bible open on the bed beside him. He prayed for a few minutes. Then he read a passage of Scripture about God hearing and answering prayers before he returned to his supplications. After over an hour spent in the presence of his heavenly Father, peace descended over Gustaf's soul. He knew that no matter what his earthly father decided, it would be the will of the heavenly

Father. Clothed in that peace, Gustaf climbed into his bed and fell into a deep, restful sleep.

❧

Olina paced the floor of her room, thinking about the discussion at dinner. Could it be possible that Mr. Nilsson would let them move to the house?

Trust Me, Olina. The voice sounded in her mind. A voice that was getting harder to ignore since the first night at the brush arbor meeting. Did God have a plan for her? Did it include living in the house? Olina never imagined that it would be so simple to establish herself as a dressmaker. Had God been a part of that?

She wanted to pray for Mr. Nilsson as he made the decision, but it had been a long time since she trusted God enough to ask Him for anything. She knew that Gerda was probably praying right now, if she hadn't already gone to sleep. Maybe even Gustaf was talking to God about his father's decision. Olina hoped so. Gerda and Gustaf still trusted God. He would listen to them.

I will listen to you, too, Olina.

Olina wished that were true, but she had ignored God for so long, how could He want to hear what she said?

When Olina awoke, she could tell that she had overslept. The sun, streaming through her window, was too high in the sky for it to be early morning. She quickly dressed and went downstairs to the kitchen, where she was met by the smells of bacon and biscuits.

"I'm so sorry I overslept."

Mrs. Nilsson turned at the sound of Olina's voice. "That's all right, Olina. We decided to let you sleep until you awoke. Gerda heard you moving around in your room late into the night."

Olina frowned. "I didn't want to disturb anyone."

Mrs. Nilsson put her arms around Olina and pulled her into a maternal hug. "Olina, Dear, you didn't disturb anyone. I think Gerda was awake a long time, too. She was probably praying about her father's decision." She patted Olina's arm before turning back to the skillet on the wood stove. "I've kept the bacon and biscuits warm. Would you like one egg or two?"

"Only one, but let me cook it." Olina started toward the extra apron hanging on the hook beside the back door.

"No, please let me do this for you." Mrs. Nilsson broke an egg into the skillet. She started basting the egg with the warm bacon grease as she continued. "After all, I won't be cooking for you much longer."

Olina sat down hard in the chair she had pulled out from the table. "Do you mean what I think you mean?" She was afraid to believe what she had heard.

"Yes, Dear. Bennel said that you and Gerda could move into Gustaf's house."

Olina was speechless. It was too wonderful to imagine. Was this part of God's plans for her? Whether it was or not, Olina was ecstatic. She couldn't hold back a giggle that bubbled from deep within.

"I'm glad that makes you happy." Mrs. Nilsson set the plate of food in front of Olina. "Now eat up. Gustaf and Gerda are finishing the chores, so the three of you can look at the house. They want to see what needs to be done to get it ready for you to move in."

Olina was so excited that she thought she couldn't eat, but when she took the first bite of the light fluffy bread, it whetted her appetite. By the time Gerda and Gustaf came in from outdoors, she had cleaned up everything on her plate.

Gerda burst through the back door like a whirlwind. "Olina, has Mother told you?" When Olina nodded, she continued. "Isn't it wonderful?" She ran around the table and pulled Olina up into a hug. Olina felt as if Gerda were cutting her in two with her strong arms, but she hugged Gerda back just as hard.

Gustaf soon followed Gerda into the kitchen. "If you girls . . . young women . . . would get ready, we'll be off to town."

Gerda and Olina turned to look at him. His smile was as big as theirs.

"We'll be ready in ten minutes. Right, Olina?" Gerda hurried out into the hall.

Olina couldn't tear her gaze from Gustaf. He looked so strong and masculine. The freshness of the warm summer morning surrounded him, and his eyes communicated something to her soul. She didn't know, or recognize, what it was, but she liked it. It made her feel fresh and warm as the morning.

~&

While Gustaf unlocked the front door of his house, Olina stood on the porch, looking out toward the road. Everything around them was in the full bloom of summer. Trees were clothed in various shades of green above their brown or gray trunks. Birds were singing in some of the trees. Prairie grasses, blowing in the wind, were dotted with white, pink, and yellow wild flowers. When she looked down the road to her right, Litchfield looked rooted in the prairie as much as the trees were. It felt as if it were part of the landscape, a close neighbor to keep the house from being lonely. Taking a deep breath of the fresh air, Olina let out a sigh of contentment. This would soon be her home. But she had to ask Gustaf one question.

Olina turned to look toward him, only to find him smiling at her. Gerda had already entered the house.

"So, how much rent are you going to charge us?"

The look that passed over his face was one of hurt, then understanding. "I won't charge rent to anyone in the family."

"Oh, but I'm not—"

Before Olina could finish, Gustaf interrupted with a teasing comment as he walked over to stand in front of her. "But you can cook me a hot meal every once in awhile. That would be a fair rent."

Olina had to look up to meet the challenge in his face. "Why would you need a hot meal when your mother cooks so well?"

Her question, which had started on a strong note, ended with a soft breathy word. Gustaf leaned closer as if he were having a hard time hearing her. Olina didn't know whether to step back or stay where she was. He was entirely too close for comfort. But she would not allow him to cause her to move.

"Does that mean I can't enjoy another woman's cooking?"

There he was emphasizing the word *woman* again. Olina liked the fact that he knew she was a woman, but that knowledge caused unfamiliar feelings within her. She couldn't decide whether they were comfortable feelings or not.

His gaze held hers, and time stood still. The fragrance of soap and something else that Olina couldn't define enveloped her in a world inhabited by the two of them. Olina couldn't ever remember any man she had known smelling quite like that. Sweat, she had smelled, and soap, but not this masculine aroma. It was heady and scary at the same time.

Gustaf reached toward her when the sound of Gerda's voice came from inside the house. "Olina, look. The house has furniture in almost every room."

Gustaf pulled back as Olina turned toward the door.

"Yes, there was too much furniture to take to California, so they left most of it. If the person who bought the house didn't want the furnishings, they would have been sold at an auction for the Winslows. I thought we could use most of it."

Olina was still dazed by what had happened on the porch, but she looked around her, trying to get her bearings back. The Chesterfield in the parlor looked to be in good condition. She decided to try it out. It might help to sit for a minute. While she walked to the sofa, she looked at the chairs and tables arranged around the room. A large rug covered the floor. The room had a homey feel.

Olina dropped onto the comfortable sofa. She ran her finger across the table that sat beside it.

"Merta swept and dusted the house for me yesterday while I was in town." Olina raised her head at the sound of Gustaf's voice from the doorway. Now that she was across the room from him, she had her equilibrium back.

"That was nice." Olina didn't look into Gustaf's eyes. She focused on the wall beside the door.

"I told her someone might be moving in pretty soon." Gustaf looked at the wall, too. "Do you think we should put up new wallpaper?"

Gerda walked up behind him. "This wallpaper is lovely. Isn't it, Olina?"

Olina nodded, for the first time noticing the ivy pattern. "Everything is wonderful."

Gustaf stepped into the room. "Do you think the curtains need washing?"

Gerda walked over and lifted the edge of one. "Of course they do. They'll be filled with dust. Come, Olina. Let me show you the rest of the house."

After the tour, the trio decided to have a workday the next day. They would bring all the things needed to wash the curtains in the house. Their search of the cupboards revealed that there were enough dishes, pots and pans, and utensils for the young women to set up housekeeping. They could add to them as needed. One of the closets even held bed linens. They would want to wash them when they washed the curtains.

The room that Mrs. Winslow used as a library had shelves on two walls and windows on the other two. It would be ideal for the sewing room. They could utilize the shelves to showcase fabrics and notions, and the windows gave it a light, airy feeling. Since the room contained no furniture, there was plenty of space for a cutting table, the sewing machine, and whatever chairs Gerda and Olina needed in their business. It might take them a little time to completely furnish it as they would like, but the possibilities made both girls excited.

"It won't take long to get the house ready to move in," Gerda gushed. "One or two workdays, and we'll be living here."

She hugged Olina hard again. Olina felt like dancing as she had when she was an excited little girl. But today she was no longer a girl. She must act as a woman would. She never wanted Gustaf to think of her as a little girl again.

❧

The whole family decided to participate in the workday at Gustaf's house. Even August took the day off from the blacksmith's. Mrs. Nilsson decided to cook dinner at the house, and Mr. Nilsson wanted to check everything out before Gerda and Olina moved in.

After chores were finished, they piled into the wagon. Mrs. Nilsson sat on the seat between Mr. Nilsson and Gustaf. Gerda and Olina sat in the back of the wagon, surrounded by cleaning supplies and various items they were taking to the house.

When they stopped the wagon, they sat for a minute while Mr. and Mrs. Nilsson looked at the cottage and its surroundings.

Mrs. Nilsson was the first to break the silence. "Oh, Gustaf, I like it. It's so pretty from the outside."

Mr. Nilsson nodded his agreement before he stepped to the ground. While he was helping his wife out of the wagon, August called to them from down the road toward town.

They all pitched in and soon the windows were open wide, letting in the summer breeze to air out all the rooms. While the women put water on to boil, the men took down the curtains. August tested the clothesline to make sure it was stable. Then he used a wet rag to wipe the dust off the wire before the women hung clean items over it.

When the first load of water was hot, Mrs. Nilsson put another pot on the back of the stove to heat. She placed the pot of beef stew that she had brought from home on the front of the stove to heat for lunch.

About the time they were going to stop to eat, Merta pulled up in her buggy. Two other women from the church were with her. They brought hot corn bread and butter, lemonade, and a pound cake. The women insisted on taking over the work in the kitchen, making Ingrid sit down and rest while they served everyone.

Lunch was like a party to Olina. She enjoyed having Merta there, but she also got to know the other two women better.

"Are you a good cook?" August asked Olina. "I've eaten some things that Gerda made that weren't so good."

Gerda, who was sitting beside him, hit him playfully on the arm. "That was a long time ago."

"Yes, both Mother and Tant Olga insisted that I learn to cook." Olina smiled at August. "Maybe you could eat with us sometime, since we're so close now."

"That would be wonderful," Gerda exclaimed. "I would love to fix you breakfast and dinner every day. I'm not sure about lunch every day, though. We'll be busy in the daytime. We have a lot of orders to fill."

"I might take you up on that." August smiled as if he had been given a special present.

And I might take you up on it sometime, too. For the first time in his life, Gustaf envied his brother.

16

It took only one day to finish getting the cottage ready, so Gerda and Olina planned to move on Friday. Mrs. Nilsson gathered some of her kitchen items to add to the things left in the house. She also packed a few towels, more sheets, and two good goose-down pillows.

With Gerda and Olina in her bedroom, she opened the large cedar chest. Inside were a number of handmade quilts. She let each of the young women pick two for their own beds. While adding some cutwork kitchen towels and crocheted doilies to the growing stack, she furtively wiped a tear from the corner of her eye, but Olina noticed the movement.

Perhaps her own mother had shed tears about her daughter leaving home. For a moment, Olina's heart yearned to see her mother's dear face. *Please, Gud, let me see Mor again, at least once.* After she had that thought, Olina realized that it was a prayer.

When they had unloaded the first wagon full of things at the house, Gustaf and his father returned to the farm to bring another load. Olina was surprised that there was more than would fill one wagon. In addition to her hand luggage, she had brought two trunks full of things with her when she moved from Sweden. Gerda had a lifetime of possessions to move. She didn't seem to be leaving anything at her parents' home.

Mrs. Nilsson insisted on giving a large table to Gerda and Olina for them to use in the sewing room. Besides that, she gave them two rocking chairs that were in the attic of the farmhouse, along with two straight chairs. Olina couldn't imagine that they would need anything else at their new home. Her small hoard of money wouldn't have to be used for furnishings. That was a blessing.

When the men returned and unloaded the wagon the second time, Merta arrived. She said that some of the women had prepared lunch for them. They had the table set at Merta's house waiting for them to come.

"We can't possibly go looking like this." Olina pushed a stray curl back under the scarf she had tied around her head.

"Yes, you can." Gustaf touched her cheek with one finger, rubbing at a spot. "You have some dust on your face, but it won't take you long to clean up."

Olina turned away to hide the blush she could feel staining her cheeks. More than her cheek was affected by the touch of his finger.

"Of course not," Gerda agreed. After filling a white pitcher with a rose pattern on the side, she picked up the matching bowl and invited her mother to accompany her to her bedroom to freshen up.

Olina soon followed with a pure white bowl and pitcher of fresh water for her own bedroom. Setting it on the washstand, she peered into the looking glass on the wall above it. After removing the scarf, she fluffed her hair with her brush and pulled it back, tying it at the nape of her neck with the scarf. That would have to do. She didn't have time to put it up properly.

Olina was descending the stairs when Gustaf returned from washing at the pump in the kitchen. He caught his breath when he looked up at her. He hadn't seen her like that since she arrived in America. Even though her hair was tied back, curls cascaded past her waist. It reminded him of the bubbling waterfall on the farm in Sweden, as it sparkled in the sun. He had seen her many times back in Sweden. When she hadn't had her hair in braids as a young girl, she wore it tied back, but he didn't remember it like this. Gustaf wished he had the right to run his fingers through the silky-looking strands. He had to just imagine what they would feel like curled around his fingers.

"Is everyone ready?" His father's voice sounded from behind him.

Gustaf was glad that his father hadn't been watching his face. He knew Gustaf too well, and he might realize what Gustaf was thinking.

Gustaf wasn't ready to discuss his feelings for Olina with anyone, especially not his father.

While they were eating, the women from church asked if there was anything else they could do to help Gerda and Olina get settled in the Winslow house.

"I guess it's no longer the Winslow house." Gustaf couldn't keep the pride out of his voice. "From now on, it will be the Nilsson house."

Olina knew what he was saying, but she was not a Nilsson. It felt different to be living in a Nilsson house when Gustaf owned it instead of his father, but she wasn't yet ready to explore the reason.

Two of the women had talked to Gerda and Olina about sewing for them. They made arrangements to bring fabric to the cottage on Monday, so that Gerda and Olina could get started making their dresses. Olina felt so professional. She thought Gerda felt the same, because they shared a secret smile across the table.

It didn't take long for Gerda and Olina to settle into a routine. In the mornings, after doing whatever cleaning the house needed, they started sewing on dresses for customers. Working together, they had no trouble finishing a dress, sometimes more, in a day. As women began wearing their new frocks, more were ordered, both by the same women and others. By the end of the first month they lived in the house, their business was thriving.

August quickly formed the habit of eating breakfast with the young women. Sometimes when they were busy, he would invite them to join him for lunch at his boardinghouse. The food there was good, and it kept Gerda and Olina from having to take time to cook. They took turns fixing dinner.

It soon became apparent that Gustaf meant what he said about the rent being a hot meal. It wasn't at all unusual for him to arrive in town to share lunch or dinner with them four or more times a week. Not that Olina minded. It was pleasant to have him around. When he was there, he checked to see if there were any repairs that needed to be done at the house.

❧

Two months had passed when Gustaf arrived carrying a package. "Olina, I have something for you." He strode into the sewing room and stopped short. She was standing on a straight chair, trying to reach something on a high shelf. "What do you think you are doing?" His voice exploded.

The loudness and harshness must have startled Olina because she lost her balance, teetering on the chair before her feet flew out from under her. Gustaf hurled the package to the floor and lunged toward her, barely catching her. He pulled her hard against his heaving chest. What a scare she had given him. He didn't realize how hard he was clutching her to himself until he heard her soft sob. That sound cut right to his heart.

Gustaf loosened his hold, cradling her gently against his still pounding heart. "I'm so sorry. I didn't mean to hurt you."

Olina hiccoughed. "You scared me," she whispered against his chest.

Gustaf set her on her feet, but he didn't let her go. She felt so right in his arms. He tried not to sound harsh. "What you were doing was dangerous. I was afraid you would fall."

She pushed against his chest until there was room between them. "Actually, you caused me to fall. Your shout startled me." At least she didn't sound as though she were accusing him of anything bad.

"Do you often climb like that?" Gustaf stepped away from Olina, giving himself room to breathe.

"Only when I need something from a top shelf." She looked defiantly up at him.

"I can get you anything you want."

"What about when you are not here?" The question came out in a whisper.

"I will bring you a step stool the next time I come." Gustaf looked at the package lying on the floor near the wall. "I brought you something. It's from Sweden."

Olina looked from his face to the box.

"My Bible. Tant Olga has sent my Bible." Olina grabbed the box and clutched it to her heart. "Thank you for bringing it to me."

Gustaf was confused for a moment, then he nodded. He was surprised, but encouraged by Olina's actions. He had been praying for her so long, worrying about her relationship with the Lord. The fact that she had asked her aunt to send her Bible must be a good sign. He decided it would be best to let her open the package alone, so he said a quick good-bye and went to look for Gerda.

❧

Olina knew that Gerda would come back into the house at any moment. She had been out checking the small garden they planted. Olina wanted privacy when she opened the box, so she took it up to her bedroom and closed the door.

Dropping into the rocking chair by the window, she continued to hold the package close as tears streamed down her cheeks. She wasn't sure she was ready to read the words for herself, but she knew she must.

Olina took the package and laid it on the bed. She wondered why Tant Olga had used such a large box to send the Bible. When she opened it, she found out. Letters and two smaller parcels accompanied the book. One letter was in Tant Olga's handwriting, but the writing on the other cried out to her heart. It had been so long since she had seen anything her mother had written.

Grabbing that letter, Olina returned to the rocking chair. Very slowly, she read her mother's words, savoring every one of them.

Olina,

I miss you very much. Olga has let me read your letters. I am so sorry about Lars, but Olina, you are better off without him. If you had married, he might have hurt you later. I am praying for God to heal that pain in your heart.

Olina paused and gazed at the fluffy clouds floating in the azure sky. She felt disappointment from what had happened with Lars, but the deep hurt was no longer there. When had that happened?

Peter has gotten married. I don't think you know the girl.
Mary's family had moved here not long before you left for Amer-
ica. They are living with us on the farm. Of course, he is working
the farm with your father and John.

Speaking of your father, I pray daily that he will change his
mind about you, but he hasn't yet. Olga said she will pass on my
letters to you. And you may write me at Olga's. I visit her as
often as I can.

It was as if Olina could hear her mother's voice as she read.

When she finished the rest of the letter, she placed it lovingly
among her handkerchiefs. She knew that she would take it out and
read it many times. Tonight, she would write a long letter in return.
Hope about her family crept back into Olina's heart.

She went over to the bed and picked up one of the small packages.
Turning it over, she saw her mother's handwriting on it. *This belonged*
to your grandmother. I want you to have it.

Olina quickly tore the paper from the box. It contained a cameo
brooch set in gold. Olina held it in her hand, carefully studying the
dainty carved features of a young woman. Her mother's thoughtfulness
touched her heart. She would treasure this link with her past.

The other small package was from Tant Olga. The cameo earrings
it contained had to be carved by the same craftsman. Olina quickly
opened Tant Olga's letter. In it she told that the brooch and earrings
had been a set when they were first purchased.

After reading Tant Olga's letter, Olina opened her Bible. The pages
fell open to the words she was looking for. She read the verses again
and again. The evangelist was right. God did care about what was
going on in her life. Olina had never heard anyone explain those
particular verses in quite that way, but there was no doubt in her mind
what the words were saying.

Father God, forgive me for doubting You. I have been so hurt. Please
help me get past that hurt to what You have for me.

It was a simple prayer, but a peace Olina hadn't felt for a long time invaded her heart, returning it to familiar territory. Olina still didn't know what would happen about her father, but her heavenly Father was once again in her life. However, she wondered if He had ever left. Maybe, she had just shut herself off from His presence.

$\mathcal{L}$ife in the little house bustled. Besides the thriving dress-making business, Gerda and Olina often had women from town call on them. Sometimes women from the surrounding farms also stopped by on their way to or from town. When that happened, the two young women took time from their busy schedules to share conversations accompanied by refreshments. Olina liked using her grandmother's china teapot to brew the invigorating tea they all enjoyed. Gerda was the one who liked to bake, and she kept a pie, a cake, or dainty pastries on hand for those times of fellowship.

Soon after her Bible had come from Sweden, Gustaf arrived at the house just as Olina was making herself a light lunch. That day, Gerda had gone into town to help Merta make new curtains for her kitchen.

"Are you hungry?" Olina asked when she answered Gustaf's knock. After he nodded, she continued, "I can make us a picnic, and we can eat down by the stream."

Gustaf helped Olina gather together the cold chicken, applesauce, and bread. They put them in a basket, along with a tablecloth to spread on the ground.

After they had finished eating, Olina asked Gustaf, "Do you think that God has specific plans for each person?"

Gustaf took a moment to think about her question. Olina was glad. She wasn't looking for the easy, quick answer.

First, Gustaf asked her a question. "Why are you asking me this?"

Olina watched a cloud that resembled a calf drift across the sky above them. It was hard to put her thoughts into words. "A lot has happened in my life that didn't seem to be good at the time."

Gustaf nodded as if he agreed.

"When we went to the brush arbor meeting, the preacher said that God has plans for us. He read a Scripture that I had never heard before, and he said that it was about the plans God has for us. Do you remember?"

"Vaguely." Gustaf looked as if he were trying to remember.

"That is one reason I asked Tant Olga to send me my Bible. I wanted to read those verses for myself." Olina wasn't sure she should have started this conversation. It was hard to put into words. "I have memorized the words now."

"Tell them to me." Gustaf sounded eager.

" 'For I know the thoughts that I think toward you, saith the Lord, thoughts of peace, and not of evil, to give you an expected end. Then shall ye call upon me, and ye shall go and pray unto me, and I will hearken unto you. And ye shall seek me, and find me, when ye shall search for me with all your heart.' Do you think God was talking about His plans for us like the preacher said?"

Gustaf didn't answer right away. "It could mean that. I know that when I try to make a decision without asking God about it, I often make the wrong decision."

"How do you know whether your decision is right or wrong?"

"Olina, when a decision is the one God would have me make, He gives me peace deep in my heart. It is hard to explain, but that's what it is. Real peace."

When Gustaf left, Olina didn't go back to work. Instead, she took out her Bible and read the verses again. Since her Bible had come from Tant Olga, Olina read it every day. Her relationship with God had grown.

It had been so long since she had read the words of God that her thirst was almost unquenchable. She looked forward to Sunday, when the Nilsson family attended services at the Lutheran church in Litchfield. Every Sunday, Olina listened eagerly to the words spoken by the pastor. Her whole outlook on life had changed dramatically.

"Olina." Gerda came down the stairs wearing her bonnet and carrying a basket on her arm. "I'm going to the mercantile. We have no more eggs, and we'll soon be out of flour. Do you need anything?"

Olina looked up from the hem she was stitching. "We only have one more needle. It's surprising how many we break."

Gerda laughed. "Maybe we work them too hard. They can't keep up with our speed."

Olina put the dress down on the table and walked over to the sewing machine. "I've been wondering what we would do if the machine needle breaks. Maybe we should have Marja order us a couple of replacement needles, just in case something happens."

"That's a good idea." Gerda took a list from her pocket and wrote on it. "Do you want to come to the store with me?"

Olina picked up the dress again. She sat in the chair by the window and reached into the sewing basket at her feet, taking out the spool of thread. "We promised this dress today, but we don't know when she'll come for it. I think I should work on the hem. I want it finished whenever she comes to pick it up."

After Gerda left, Olina's fingers flew as they made the dainty stitches for which she and Gerda were so famous. Although her hands were busy, her mind kept wandering. It had been three days since Gustaf had come to eat with them. She wondered where he was and why he had stayed away so long. For a moment, she dropped the dress in her lap and looked out the open window. Gustaf's face filled her thoughts as if he were standing there. She could even feel the touch of his hand against her waist. He had been walking beside her on Sunday. When they walked up the steps at church, his hand had touched her back as he guided her. Olina wondered if he even noticed. Probably not. She picked up the dress and continued working on the hem. She should keep her mind on what she was doing and not daydream.

❧

Gustaf drove the wagon into town to pick up supplies for his mother. It was the first day that week he could get away from the farm. One of the hired men was sick, and Gustaf had to do this man's work as well as his own.

He was glad that the horses knew the way to Litchfield. It allowed his thoughts to ramble wherever he wanted. They naturally turned toward Olina. When he was finished in town, he planned to stop by the Nilsson house to check on things, especially Olina. Maybe he would stay for dinner.

Sunday, when they started up the steps at the church, Olina stumbled on the second step, and he touched her to steady her. While it had helped Olina, it did nothing to steady the beat of his heart. Just thinking about it, his hand tingled as it had on Sunday. Whenever there was any kind of physical contact between them, his heart beat double time. Gustaf would hurry gathering the supplies so he could see Olina sooner.

The eastbound train was leaving town when Gustaf pulled up in front of the mercantile. Trains fascinated him. He didn't think he would ever tire of riding them. At the sound of the whistle, Gustaf looked down the street toward the station. A couple standing on the platform beside a pile of luggage looked familiar. At least the man did. If he didn't know better, Gustaf would have been convinced that the man was Lars. But Lars was in Denver. They had received a letter from Lars two weeks ago, and he had not said anything about coming to Minnesota.

The tall man raised a hand and gave a broad wave to Gustaf. Instead of getting out of the wagon, he clucked to the horses, urging them toward the station. Soon he was convinced that the man was Lars. That must be his wife with him. Gustaf had never seen her. She was almost as tall as Lars.

Gustaf had not stopped the wagon before Lars leapt from the platform into the street and shouted, "I thought that was you, Big Brother." Lars stood as if waiting for him to jump from the wagon, but Gustaf just sat where he was.

"Lars, what are you doing here?"

Lars laughed. "You sound as if you aren't glad to see me."

"Of course, I'm glad to see you. I'm a little . . . surprised."

"That's what we wanted to do. Surprise everyone."

Gustaf frowned. "Surprises aren't always a good thing. There are some people who might be uncomfortable by your surprise."

"Who would that be?"

Gustaf jumped down from the wagon seat and spoke quietly to Lars. "Do you know that Olina is still here?"

"Yes." Lars looked a little uncomfortable. "I need to talk to Olina face-to-face."

"That might not be a good idea." Gustaf tried not to sound too angry, but when he thought about what Lars had done to Olina, the anger came anyway.

Lars spoke to Gustaf, man to man. "It's something I have to do. I'm not proud of what I did to Olina. I need to make amends for it."

"Lars, is everything all right?" The feminine voice called from the station platform.

Lars gestured toward the woman standing on the platform, and Gustaf looked up at her.

The woman smiled.

"Come meet my wife." Lars took Gustaf by the arm and pulled him along up the steps. "Janice, this is my oldest brother."

She placed her gloved hand into Gustaf's. "I think I would have known you anywhere, Gustaf. Lars has told me so much about you." Her voice had a lyrical quality to it.

Gustaf hadn't known what to expect in his sister-in-law. She was tall and willowy. Her friendly face was surrounded by abundant black hair, styled in the current pompadour fashion. Her eyes were her most arresting feature. They were green, sparkling with life. For a moment Gustaf questioned his brother's sanity. Janice was beautiful, but she didn't come close to Olina in any area that he could see.

Gustaf gave Lars and Janice a ride to the hotel. They had decided to stay there for the first few nights of their visit. They thought it would make everything less awkward. It was a good thing that Gustaf hadn't yet bought the supplies. There wouldn't have been room in the wagon for all of their luggage and everything he came to pick up.

When they came back out of the hotel after taking the luggage up to their room, Gerda was walking down the sidewalk near the mercantile. She saw Lars before he saw her, and she came hurrying across the street, calling out to them.

Gustaf suggested that Gerda, Lars, and Janice go into the hotel. He told them he would pick up Olina and bring her back so they could have lunch together. When Gerda looked concerned, he told her that he would prepare Olina for the confrontation.

As Gustaf drove the wagon toward his house, he started praying for Olina. He wanted to warn her about Lars, and he wanted to be with her when she learned that he was in Litchfield. If need be, Gustaf was prepared to stay at the house with Olina until she didn't need him anymore. He hoped that Lars and Janice's presence wouldn't set Olina back in her walk with the Lord. Most of all, Gustaf didn't want Olina hurt again.

❧

Olina was finishing the last stitch in the hem of the ruffled skirt when she noticed Gustaf's wagon coming from Litchfield. She hadn't seen him go by on the way to town. It was hard to miss him now. He was driving fast. That was unusual for Gustaf. He was always careful with the horses. Olina stood up and stretched. Then she took the dress to the table to fold it. She was glad that she could see outside from every spot in the room. With one eye on what she was doing, she kept part of her attention on the wagon that was approaching the house.

When Gustaf stopped the wagon in front, Olina went to the door. Maybe he was coming to eat lunch with them. It was too bad that they hadn't cooked anything today. Olina was planning to make a sandwich with some of the tomatoes out of the garden and the piece of ham left from breakfast. That would barely feed her. It wouldn't be enough for a hardworking man like Gustaf.

Olina opened the door just as Gustaf stepped onto the porch. "Hello. Have you come for—?" The look on Gustaf's face stopped the question in midsentence. She rushed through the door. "Oh, Gustaf, what's the matter?" Without thinking, she reached up and cupped her hand on his cheek.

Gustaf placed his calloused fingers on top of hers as if to hold them in place. "Olina, I must talk to you."

"You're scaring me. Whatever has happened to cause you this distress?" Olina couldn't pull her gaze from his.

He looked as if he were worried about her. Why would he be worried about her? Had he heard something in town? She glanced down at his other hand. It didn't hold any mail, so it couldn't be anything bad about her family.

Gustaf pulled her hand from his face and held it in both his hands. "Let's sit here."

Olina and Gerda loved sitting on the porch in the cool of the evening, so Gustaf and August had built a wooden swing for them. Gustaf guided her toward the swing. When they were seated, he leaned his forearms on his knees and clasped his hands.

"I've come to tell you something."

Olina was exasperated. "So tell me. Don't keep me wondering any longer."

Gustaf leaned back and placed his arm along the back of the swing. "Someone came to Litchfield on the train that just went through."

"So?" Olina knew that people often came to Litchfield on the train. She looked up into his troubled eyes and waited.

"It was Lars and his wife." The statement hung in the air between them while Gustaf seemed to be studying every expression on Olina's face. What was he looking for?

"Lars . . . and his wife?" Olina was puzzled.

"Yes." Gustaf took one of her hands in his.

"I didn't know that he was coming home."

"No one did." He rubbed the back of her hand with his thumb while he continued to study her. "It's a surprise visit."

Olina waited for the hurt to settle in her chest, but all she felt was surprised. *Oh, Father, did You take that hurt away, too? Will I be able to forgive Lars as You have forgiven me?*

"Where are they?"

Gustaf must have been holding his breath because he had to let it out to answer her. "I left them at the hotel with Gerda. Do you feel like going into town to see them?"

Olina stood up and walked to the porch railing. She leaned against it, looking toward town as if she could see into the hotel. Then she turned back to Gustaf. "It was inevitable that this would happen. We might as well get it over with, but I need to freshen up a bit."

Gustaf's smile went right to Olina's heart. "I'll be here when you are ready."

"I'll hurry."

Gerda, Lars, and his wife were sitting in the lobby visiting when Gustaf and Olina arrived. Lars stood as if he had been watching the door for them. Standing across the room from her was the man she had planned to marry. For a moment, all the pain lanced through Olina's heart. How was she going to get through the next few minutes? She just had to. She closed her eyes and took a deep breath. Did she need to stop all feeling again as she had before? Would it help?

Lars introduced Olina to Janice. *What does he see in her that he didn't see in me?* Olina recognized the wariness in Janice's expression. It wasn't her fault, was it? Lars hadn't been a real man. He hadn't taken responsibility for his actions, and two women were paying a price for that irresponsibility. When Lars met Janice, did he even tell her about Olina?

After introducing Olina to Janice, Lars asked Olina if she would take a walk with him. She looked at Janice, who nodded.

They walked around the hotel and out across a field toward a small grove of trees. When they reached the shade, Lars stopped Olina with a gentle touch on her arm. She turned toward him.

"Olina, we came to visit with our family, but you're the main reason I've come."

She looked up at him and waited. It was a minute or two before he continued. During that time, he studied her as if he were looking for something specific.

"I know that I did you a grave injustice." Lars seemed ill at ease. He shifted his weight from one foot to the other. "I was blind to my faults. And I was impulsive."

Olina nodded. She agreed wholeheartedly.

"I should have met you in New York City. I apologize for that. Can you forgive me?"

Olina gazed up at a cloud that was drifting by. It looked like a little lamb, gamboling in the pasture around his mother. The lamb reminded her of Jesus, who died to bring her forgiveness.

Looking back at Lars, she whispered, "Yes, I will work on forgiving you." She paused, then continued. "Why did you go to Denver in the first place, Lars?" She had to know.

Once again, Lars shuffled his feet in the grass. "I thought we could start our new life together in Denver. I was offered a better paying job, and I planned to get us a home, then come back here before you arrived. I planned for us to be married here and then go to our new home." He looked everywhere but at her, taking a long time before he blurted, "I thought I loved you, Olina, but I didn't know what love really was until I met Janice."

Olina waited for the pain to lance though her midsection. She felt disappointment, but not the agony she expected. "And what is love . . . really?"

"It's not just that she's beautiful. You're beautiful, too. Janice and I were made for each other. She has strengths where I have weaknesses, and I have strengths in the areas where she is weak. I know God created someone for you, just as he created Janice and me to be together."

When Lars said that, Olina looked across the field toward town, and her thoughts drifted to Gustaf. Could he be the one?

"I have great fondness for you." Lars's voice sounded stronger, more sure. "You will always have a special place in my heart."

Olina glanced back at him. "Maybe that's not good."

"Janice knows all about you . . . us . . . what we were to each other. At least now she knows. I was not man enough to tell her about you until after we were engaged." Lars rubbed the back of his neck. "We were not meant for each other, you and I. We just thought we were. I know it'll be hard for you to forgive me for all of this, but that's what I came here for. To apologize to you face-to-face. I pray that someday we can be friends."

Olina glanced at the grass, then across the field to some cows that were grazing in the adjoining pasture. "I'll not deny that you hurt me very much. I don't know when I've ever been so hurt." She looked down at her skirt that the gentle wind was swirling around her ankles. "I'm trying to forgive you. In time, maybe we'll be comfortable around each other." She gazed up at Lars. "We should go back. I don't want the others to be worried about us."

Lars took her arm and guided her back to the front of the hotel.

On the way across the field, Olina thought about all she had gone through. Had God allowed those things to happen because He had created someone for her, someone besides Lars? Was he here in Litchfield, Minnesota, right now?

What about Janice? She had been caught in the middle of the dilemma Lars had caused by his irresponsible actions.

Just as she stepped up on the wooden sidewalk, Olina said, "I'm glad you've come. I do want to get to know your wife."

❧

When Gustaf drove Olina home, Gerda stayed in town with Lars and Janice. He was glad, because he wanted to talk to Olina alone.

After stopping the horses by the front gate, Gustaf turned to Olina. "Are you all right?"

Olina looked up at Gustaf. "You mean about Lars and Janice?"

"That . . . and about Lars being here . . . and about Lars and you."

Olina blinked as if her eyes were watering. "There is no 'Lars and me.' "

Gustaf reached over and took both her hands in his. "I know that, but how are you handling everything?"

When Olina looked down at their clasped hands, so did Gustaf. Hers looked so small and smooth, engulfed in his large, calloused ones. He would gladly take all the pain out of her life, but he knew he couldn't.

Olina looked back up at him. "I want to forgive Lars, but it is so hard, for sure. How can I completely forgive him? The hurt goes deep."

Gustaf didn't know if he had an answer for her, so he got out of the wagon, then helped Olina down. They walked to the front door in silence.

"Let's look in the Bible, Olina." Gustaf opened the door and waited for her to enter.

Olina went into the parlor and picked her Bible up from the table where she had put it when she finished reading it last night. "What do you want to show me?"

Gustaf sat on the sofa, and Olina sat beside him. Gustaf searched for a verse. "In Matthew, chapter six, it says, 'And forgive us our debts, as we forgive our debtors.' "

Olina nodded. "I remember reading that. It's where Jesus teaches His disciples how to pray, isn't it?"

"Yes. But it was more than that." Gustaf cleared his throat. He didn't want to hurt Olina, but he wanted her to understand what he was talking about. "I believe it means that if we don't forgive others, then the Lord won't forgive us."

"That's a hard word, Gustaf."

"I know, but when you forgive others, it allows your forgiveness from God to flow freely. Does that make any sense?"

Olina nodded. "I see what you mean. And I think I agree, but it's not easy sometimes."

Gustaf stood and walked to the front window. "God didn't say that everything would be easy, but it would be worth it. I had a hard time forgiving Lars for what he did. God used this verse to teach me that I had to. It took me awhile, and I thought I had totally forgiven him."

Gustaf rubbed the back of his neck with one hand. "Then today when I saw him on that platform . . . and knew that his coming could cause you pain, my anger came back. While I was coming for you, God reminded me that I had forgiven Lars. If you are never able to forgive Lars, there'll be a root of bitterness growing inside your heart. Soon it will consume you." He turned back toward Olina. "You don't want that, do you?"

Olina shook her head. "No, I don't. Would you pray for me?"

"We can do that right now." Gustaf sat back down beside Olina.

"Father God, please help Olina turn loose of the bitterness and un-forgiveness she has in her heart. Give her Your strength. Let Your love for Lars flow through her heart and take its place. We pray this in Jesus' name. Amen."

18

*L*ars and Janice stayed at Litchfield for a month. Because Lars decided to help with the harvesting at the farm, after a few days, he and Janice moved into the house with his parents. Gerda and Olina became friends with Janice. Often when the men were working at the farm, Janice spent the day at Gerda and Olina's home, even helping them with handwork or cooking lunch for them while they finished a garment. In the evenings, Gerda, Olina, and August ate dinner at the farm. Everyone wanted to make the most of the time Lars and Janice were there.

One Friday night in September, all the family was gathered around the table enjoying another one of Mrs. Nilsson's wonderful meals. Gerda noticed that Gustaf seemed preoccupied. She wondered what was bothering him, but she didn't have long to worry.

"A few of the shingles on my house look as if they're damaged." Gustaf took another bite of the chicken and dumplings. Olina knew it was one of his favorite foods. He looked thoughtful while he chewed. "Since we don't have any other fields ready for harvest right now, I think I'll go over and fix the roof tomorrow." He looked around the table at his brothers. "Do you want to help me?"

Lars put down his fork and frowned. "I would like to, but Janice promised her aunt and uncle that we would spend the day with them."

Janice smiled at her husband. "It would be all right if you want to help your brother. I can go without you."

"No," Gustaf said. "You haven't spent much of your time here with the Braxtons. It's only right that you both go tomorrow."

"I can help you." August reached for another hot roll. "I haven't had a day off, except Sunday, for a long time. We aren't very busy right now."

Gustaf smiled. "Then it's settled. I'll feel better about the girls spending the winter in the house if I know the roof is safe."

The next morning, Gustaf and August arrived in time for breakfast. Gerda had told Olina that they would, so the young women had cooked extra bacon and biscuits. Gerda started the scrambled eggs while the men washed up for the meal.

Breakfast was fun, with light banter going around the room and keeping everyone laughing between bites. Olina looked at Gustaf. She liked having him sitting across the table from her. It was familiar and something she would like to continue for her whole life. Where had that thought come from? She sat stunned, wondering what it meant.

August pushed his chair back from the table. "We'd better get started if we want to finish today."

"Okay, Brother." Gustaf clapped him on the back before he went out the door toward the wagon.

Olina sat for a minute more, still stunned by the direction of her thoughts. Gerda quickly cleaned off the table. Olina jumped up and started washing the dishes while Gerda dried them and put them away.

"I'm going to the mercantile this morning." Gerda hung the tea towel on a hook near the sink. "Do you want to go with me?"

"Not today," Olina said. "Last week I bought a piece of wool to make myself a suit. I haven't even had time to cut it out. I want to get it made before the weather gets any colder."

"Do you want me to get anything for you while I'm there?"

Olina followed Gerda out of the kitchen. "Would you check and see if they have any cotton sateen? I want to make a new waist to go with the suit."

Gerda stopped and put on her bonnet and shawl. "What color?"

"The wool is navy. Maybe a light blue, pink, or even white would go with it."

Olina went into the sewing room and pulled the fabric from the shelf. She planned to make a skirt that wasn't as full as she wore in the summer. She liked a little flare, but if it wasn't too full, the skirt would be warmer. The wind was bad about blowing full skirts around, and the wind already had a bite to it. Olina wanted to make a fitted jacket with fitted sleeves. That style was also warmer than looser styles. If she had enough fabric, Olina was going to add a peplum to the bottom of the jacket. Maybe she would scallop it to give it more interest. She could even add scallops to the opening of the jacket, with a buttonhole in each scallop. The more she envisioned the new creation, the more excited she became. Spreading the fabric on the table, Olina went to work cutting out the suit.

❧

Gustaf and August quickly gathered the needed tools and wooden shingles from the wagon. While Gustaf carried them to the side of the house, August hefted the ladder on his broad shoulders.

It took several trips up and down the ladder before the men had moved all they needed to work with onto the roof. Soon they were pulling away rotted shingles and nailing new ones into place. While they worked, the brothers talked and laughed. They had always gotten along, and they worked well together.

It took them most of the morning to finish the back of the roof. Then they moved across to the front. Gustaf placed his tools and nails within easy reach, but they had used most of the shingles they brought up earlier.

"I need more shingles." Gustaf stood and stretched his muscles. He wasn't used to all this hammering and crawling on his knees. He rotated his right shoulder while holding it with his left hand. "How about you?"

"Sure." August laid his hammer down and pulled a bandanna from his back pocket to wipe the sweat from his forehead. "I've used most of mine."

"I'll go down and get some more." Gustaf started over the top of the roof, but one of the shingles he stepped on broke, and he lost his balance. Standing on a slope wasn't easy, and he couldn't regain his balance. He tried to clutch at anything that would stop him as he tumbled down the few feet to the edge of the roof, then he plunged through the air. A primitive cry forced its way from his throat before he hit the ground two stories below. Then everything went black.

❧

At first, the sound of the pounding had bothered Olina, but soon the rhythm was soothing. One of the men hit a nail, followed immediately by the other man's pound. It didn't take Olina long before she knew which pound was which. Although Gustaf hit the nails with power, because of his work at the blacksmith's, August's pounds were harder. _Ba Boom. Ba Boom._ The rhythm continued. It was a comforting sound, much like her mother's heartbeat when she had held Olina close as a child. The sounds would stop as the men moved to another spot, only to resume again.

Olina tried to keep her thoughts from wandering to Gustaf. She didn't want to make any mistakes as she cut out the suit. If she was careful, she could make the outfit the way she wanted and still have enough fabric left to make a matching reticule. She could line the purse with the fabric from the blouse she would make to go with the suit.

There was never a minute when Olina wasn't aware that Gustaf was on the roof above her. She knew when the men moved to the area above the sewing room, even though a bedroom was between the roof and the room where she worked. Once again the pounding stopped. She imagined the men taking a break.

"_Aaiiee!_"

The primitive scream was followed by a dull thump right outside the sewing room. For a moment Olina was paralyzed. Then she rushed to the window and raised it. What she saw caused her to catch her breath. Gustaf lay motionless on the ground.

Olina quickly leaned out and looked toward the eaves. August leaned over, gazing at his brother with anguish covering his face.

"What happened?" Olina's question sounded shrill even to her own ears.

August shook his head. "I don't know for sure. He was going for more shingles . . . and then he was—" August couldn't continue.

"Come down right now." Olina turned and hurried toward the front door.

She ran around to the side of the house and crumpled beside the still unmoving body. She doubled over and sobs tore from deep within her.

When August came around the house, he knelt on the other side of his brother. Tears were making their way down his cheeks. "He's not dead, Olina."

Olina looked up.

"See. He's breathing." August pointed to Gustaf's chest, which was moving with each breath.

"Should we move him into the house?" Olina looked toward the structure.

"That might not be a good idea." August stood. "What if something is broken? We could injure him more. . . . I'm going for the doctor."

Olina scrambled to her feet. "What can I do?"

"Stay with him." August strode across the yard toward his horse, but he swerved to head to the wagon, then stopped and turned to look back at Olina and Gustaf. "Maybe you should cover him with something warm."

Olina ran into the house and up the stairs to her bedroom. She jerked the quilt from her bed and grabbed her pillow. After hurrying down the stairs and around the house, she gently cradled Gustaf's head in her arms while she pushed the pillow under it. Then she covered him with the quilt and pushed it in close to his body all around. It became soiled, but she didn't care. Nothing was important except Gustaf.

As Olina gazed at his face, her heart felt as if it had burst open, and all the love that had been building for Gustaf poured forth. She loved him with her whole heart. Olina didn't know when this had happened, but she really loved him. More than she had ever loved Lars. More than she had realized was even possible. That love hurt because Gustaf was injured.

"Father God," Olina wailed. "Please help Gustaf." She pulled the bottom of her skirt up and wiped the tears from her face, but they continued to pour from her eyes. "I love him, Father God. Please don't take him away from me just when I've discovered that I love him."

Olina reached and pushed his hair from his forehead. Then her hand continued around his cheek and came to rest on his strong neck. Olina could feel the blood pulsing through the vein there. Surely he wouldn't die while his pulse was so strong.

"Please, God, I beg You. Let him not be badly hurt. I don't care if he'll never be mine. I love him enough to want the best for him. Let him be okay. I want to see him every day." The last sentence ended on a sob.

The first thing Gustaf became aware of was the cold hard ground beneath him. He fought to open his eyes but was unable to keep from drifting back into the blackness.

The next time he fought his way up out of the dark, he noticed that he felt warmer. Something soft was under his head, something warm had settled over him, and someone was tucking it in around his body. It felt good. He tried to open his eyes, but he still couldn't. Then he heard the voice.

Olina, sweet Olina, was praying. For him. She said that she loved him. He wanted to try to open his eyes again, but decided against it. He would wait to hear what else she had to say. When her hand touched his head, he almost flinched because it surprised him so much. As it continued down his face, he reveled in the feel of her soft flesh against his. He would remember the way it felt as long as he lived. When her hand rested on his neck, Gustaf knew she could feel his pulse. His heartbeat had quickened so much at her touch. He couldn't wait any longer. He had to look at her.

Olina was studying Gustaf's face when his eyes fluttered open. She tried to pull back, but one of his arms snaked out from under the quilt and his hand grabbed hers. When she relaxed, his touch became gentle. She was unable to tear her gaze from his eyes. They seemed to hold her captive, and she read an answering love in them. Could it be that he loved her as she loved him?

Before long, August, Gerda, and the doctor hurried around the side of the house.

"I see that he has recovered consciousness." The doctor's voice boomed.

Startled, Olina turned and tried to get up, but Gustaf didn't let her hand go, so she sank back onto the ground beside him.

The doctor set his black bag on the ground beside Gustaf and took out his stethoscope. He listened to Gustaf's breathing through his chest and took his pulse.

"Do you have any pain, Son?" the fatherly man asked.

Gustaf looked toward the man. "Yes. I kind of hurt all over."

"Is there any place that it is localized?" The doctor started probing his body, searching for broken bones.

"I don't think so, Sir." Gustaf moved first one arm and then the other. "Maybe I'm just sore. I know I had the breath knocked out of me."

"He was knocked unconscious for several minutes," Olina informed the doctor.

"Well, can you move everything?" The doctor watched as Gustaf moved his arms, his legs, and his head. "Does anything hurt worse when you move it?"

"Not that I can tell." Gustaf tried to sit up, and the doctor gave him a hand.

"Are you dizzy?" The doctor looked at Gustaf's pupils.

"No, Sir. Is it all right if I stand up?"

The doctor helped him to his feet. Then he looked at the ground where Gustaf had been lying. "If you were going to fall off a house, it's a good thing you picked this place to land."

Gustaf looked down, too.

"See? There's enough grass to cushion your fall, and there are no rocks to harm you." The doctor touched his shoulder. "Come inside, Son. I would like to do a thorough examination, to be on the safe side."

Olina followed the men into the house. She was glad that nothing seemed to be seriously injured.

19

*A*fter the doctor finished the examination, he and Gustaf came back downstairs. Olina looked up expectantly, waiting for the doctor's verdict.

"Well, young man, you are lucky." The doctor nodded his head as he spoke.

"I believe that God protected me," Gustaf told him. "Maybe my guardian angel caught me and lowered me to the ground."

The doctor glanced at the others before he answered. "If that's what you want to think." He put his bag down on a chair and dug through it. After pulling out a package, he placed it in Gustaf's hand. "This is Epsom salt. Go home. Take a hot bath and put some of this salt in your bath water. It should take out the soreness. Didn't I hear that your folks have one of those newfangled water heaters at your house?"

"Yes." Gustaf took the proffered remedy. "I'm glad we do. It'll come in handy today."

After the doctor drove off in his buggy, August looked at Gustaf. "You take my horse and ride home. I'll bring your wagon later."

"Why?" Gustaf looked as if he was going to refuse. "What are you going to do?"

August gestured toward the roof. "Go up there and finish what we started."

Gustaf shook his head. "I'll do it another day."

"No need for that. It won't take me long." August glanced from Gustaf to Gerda and Olina. "When I'm finished, I'll bring the girls home for dinner. By that time, you might be feeling better."

August accompanied Gustaf to the horse. It looked to Olina, who

461

was watching from the window, as though Gustaf was arguing about it, but August must have won, because Gustaf mounted the horse. August loaded more shingles onto his shoulder before he started back up the ladder. While he finished the roof that afternoon, Olina wished for Gustaf's part in the hammering rhythm.

When August, Gerda, and Olina arrived at the Nilsson farm for dinner, Olina was glad to see Gustaf sitting in the parlor. She stopped in the doorway and watched him. He was engrossed in reading his Bible. It allowed her a few undisturbed moments to study him. As if someone had told him that she was there, Gustaf glanced up. He smiled, then rose slowly.

"Come in, Olina," he said, his voice husky with emotion.

Olina caught her breath. "P—perhaps I should see if your mother needs any help with dinner." She turned to go.

"Come in, Olina. We are alone, and we need to talk."

Olina's right hand fluttered to her throat. "Right now?" Her question sounded breathless, even to her own ears.

Gustaf looked around. "Now would be a good time."

Olina took one step into the room. It seemed to be filled with the presence of Gustaf, leaving little space for her. She took a hesitant breath. There wasn't even enough air for both of them to breathe comfortably.

Gustaf walked toward her. "Are you suddenly afraid of me, Olina?"

She shook her head in denial. Gustaf stopped right in front of her, but he didn't reach out to her. Olina didn't know what to say to him. All afternoon she had wondered if he had heard any of the words of her prayer. He was standing so close that the heat of his body reached out and enveloped her.

"You weren't afraid of me this morning, dear Olina." The soft words were for her ears alone, and the endearment touched her heart.

Olina dropped her gaze to his muscled chest, but that didn't help her breathe any easier. "Why do you say that, Gustaf?"

A gentle chuckle rumbled from him, causing his chest to rise and fall. "Do you love me, Olina?"

Her wary gaze flew to his. Once again, she saw the loving expression from that morning. "Why do you ask?"

Gustaf reached out and pulled her into his arms. With her nestled against his chest, he rested his chin on top of her head. Olina was glad she had worn her hair in a simple chignon at the nape of her neck. Nothing was in the way of his chin. Its touch felt like a caress. She closed her eyes and sighed.

"I heard a voice calling me out of the darkness this morning."

Olina's eyes flew open. That startling statement answered the questions she had wrestled with all day. He had heard her. But how much had he heard?

As if she had spoken the question aloud, Gustaf answered. "I heard you praying for God to heal me. You told Him that you love me." He leaned back a little and placed one finger under her chin, raising it until her gaze met his. "You wouldn't lie to God, would you? Do you love me?"

A large lump in her throat kept Olina from voicing her answer, so she nodded.

"Enough to marry me, Olina?"

Olina's heart almost burst with happiness.

Before she could answer, Gerda came from the kitchen. "Olina, Gustaf—" She stopped short. "I'm not interrupting anything, am I?"

"Yes."

"No."

Gustaf and Olina answered at the same time. Then they burst out laughing, but Gustaf didn't release Olina from the shelter of his arms.

"Is there something you would like to tell me?" Gerda looked from one to the other.

"Yes."

"No."

Once again, they answered in unison.

Now Gerda was laughing with them. "Well, Gustaf keeps telling me 'yes,' and Olina keeps telling me 'no.' Which is it?"

Olina could feel a blush creep up over her neck and face while Gustaf answered. "Yes, we'll have something to tell you but not right now. You'll know what's going on soon enough."

Gerda rolled her eyes and went back into the kitchen. "Mother, is it time to ring the dinner bell?" Gustaf and Olina could hear her elevated tone. "Father and August are in the barn, but Gustaf and Olina are in the parlor."

The next thing Olina heard was the dinner bell. Although it was the most wonderful place she had ever been, Olina pulled herself from Gustaf's embrace and put her hands on her cheeks to try to cool them.

"That won't take away your becoming blush." Gustaf touched his forefinger to the tip of her nose, then turned toward the kitchen, but he whispered into her ear as he went by. "I will get an answer to my question before the evening is over."

The meal Mrs. Nilsson had prepared was a veritable feast. A succulent ham was accompanied by roasted potatoes, green beans, and the last tomatoes from the garden. Fresh churned butter melted into the hot rolls. Some of the butter dripped down Olina's chin when she took her first bite. She patted her chin with her napkin and glanced toward Gustaf once again. His face held a secret smile that touched her heart.

Although everything tasted wonderful, Olina couldn't eat more than a few bites. Her stomach did flip-flops every time she glanced up at Gustaf to find his intent gaze trained on her face. Soon she was moving the food around her plate instead of putting it in her mouth. Gustaf wanted to marry her.

Father God, is this Your plan for me? When Olina asked the question in her heart, she felt a peace there, but the turmoil in the rest of her body continued. What was the matter with her? Was this jumpy feeling in the pit of her stomach a prelude to some illness?

Olina was drawing circles in the gravy on her plate with her fork when she felt Gerda's foot nudge hers. She looked up to find every eye in the room trained on her. The blush that had died down once more stained her cheeks.

"I asked you, Dear, if you were feeling all right." Mrs. Nilsson looked concerned. "You've hardly eaten any of your dinner. I hope you're not getting sick."

"No." Olina smiled at her hostess. "I guess I have had too much excitement for one day." Olina didn't look directly at Gustaf, but out of the corner of her eye, she could see his smile widen.

"Yes, well." Mr. Nilsson harrumphed to clear his throat. "I wanted to tell you girls how proud I am of you."

Everyone's attention turned toward the head of the table.

"Why is that, Father?" Gerda asked.

"I can't help but worry about you." He looked toward Gustaf. "Of course your brother keeps me informed about how you're doing, but I wondered if you needed any monetary help." Olina started to comment, but before she could, Mr. Nilsson continued. "When I was at the bank this afternoon, I asked Mr. Finley if I needed to put some money into your account. He informed me that you each had a very healthy account indeed."

"It helps that Gustaf isn't charging us any rent." Gerda smiled at her brother.

He laughed in return. "No rent, except several hot meals each week."

"Which you don't need, since your mother feeds you quite well." Olina looked him full in the face for the first time during the meal.

His gaze was so intent that she couldn't look away. "It's a good time to make sure you are safe and don't need anything."

Everything around them seemed to fade away, leaving only Gustaf and Olina, with an invisible, mysterious connection—even across the table.

Finally, Mrs. Nilsson arose from her chair and began cleaning off the table. Gerda quickly assisted her. When Olina also started to help, Gustaf asked her if she would take a walk with him.

"I need to keep the stiffness worked out of my body." His eyes compelled her more than his words. "Please accompany me."

They strolled halfway down the long drive in companionable silence before Gustaf brought up the subject that was on both of their minds.

"Are you ready to give me your answer, Olina?"

At his words, Olina stopped and turned toward him. Before she could answer, he laughed. Gustaf took her hands in both of his. "Are you going to make me kneel and ask you again? It might be hard for me to get up afterward."

The picture of her trying to pull the tall, strong man up caused Olina to laugh, too. "Yes. I love you enough to marry you."

After a moment, Gustaf asked, "Do I hear a 'but' at the end of your sentence?"

"I want to marry you, but I need to make things right with Fader. When you shared that Scripture with me about forgiving as God would forgive, it made me realize that I need to forgive Fader as much as I must forgive Lars. I've finally come to the point where I have forgiven him in my heart. I was planning to write a letter to him asking his forgiveness for going against his wishes. Would you wait for the wedding until I can write him? I've come so far since I started listening to the Lord again, but I still feel I can't move on with my life without taking care of this matter."

Gustaf pulled her into his embrace again. Cradling her against his strong chest, he whispered, "You are so special. I'll wait as long as you need me to. I do believe that God intends for us to be together."

Olina nodded against his chest. "I do, too."

"It'll give me time to court you properly."

❧

Gustaf liked the feel of Olina in his arms. As they stood with her soft, warm body pressed against his leanness, he thought of her strawberry-colored mouth. He wondered how it would feel to press his lips to hers and savor the sweetness that was the essence of Olina. She must have sensed some of what he felt, because she raised her face from against his chest and looked up into his face.

Gustaf's gaze dropped to her trembling lips. He lowered his head slightly, then hesitated, to give her time to pull away. Olina's adoring gaze never wavered, so he continued his descent.

Gustaf had never kissed a woman. He had never felt this burning desire to taste a woman's lips before. The first touch was tentative and gentle. Gustaf savored Olina's sweetness, then settled his lips more firmly against hers.

For a moment, or an eon of time, he reveled in the feel of Olina. All too soon, Gustaf broke the earth-shattering kiss. He once again cradled her head against his chest. He felt sure she heard his heartbeat thunder against her ear. How easily he could have lost himself in their togetherness. But Gustaf knew that if they were going to wait awhile before marrying, he needed to protect Olina from his strong human urges. *Father, help me be the man she needs.*

When Gustaf and Olina gazed into each other's eyes, she felt it to her very foundation. She had never realized how strong the connection between two people in love could be. Then Gustaf's gaze dropped to her lips. She could feel the intensity of his attention. It caused her to lick her lips because they felt dry.

As Gustaf's head lowered toward hers, Olina held her breath. She knew that he was going to kiss her. For an instant, he hesitated. She recognized that he was giving her a chance to step back. But Olina didn't want to. She welcomed his kiss with all the love she felt for him.

Gustaf was so strong. His muscles were rock hard, but his lips were soft. His gentleness reached toward her. And then the kiss deepened. Everything faded from Olina's awareness except Gustaf. Wrapped in his love, she felt protected. Her arms crept around his waist.

Too soon, Gustaf broke the kiss, but he pulled her against his chest . . . and his beating heart. She could tell by the rhythm of the heartbeats that he was as affected by their kiss as she was.

Gustaf turned toward the house and started walking with one arm around Olina, holding her securely by his side. "Now we must tell my family, but I don't think they'll be surprised."

That night, Olina wrote a long letter to her mother, explaining all that had happened. She included another to her father, asking for his forgiveness. After writing a note to Tant Olga, she enclosed all the missives in one envelope addressed to her great-aunt. Olina sealed the envelope, then placed both hands on the thick bundle and prayed over it, asking God to direct every word to the hearts of those receiving them. When she finished this task, her heart felt lighter.

During the rest of the autumn, Olina and Gerda were busy with their dressmaking. News of their expertise spread, and some women even came from other towns to order dresses from them.

Olina no longer felt the need to protect her financial security as she had, so she and Gerda purchased things to make their cottage more homey. They chose fabric to make all new curtains and even bought a few small pieces of furniture. Tables and lamps added warmth to the living room. Scraps of fabric were fashioned into pillows that made the sofa more inviting.

Gustaf kept his promise to court Olina. He escorted her to every party and social that was held in Litchfield or at any of the surrounding farms. It wasn't long until everyone knew that the two planned to marry. They received many congratulations, even from Anna Jenson, who was being courted by one of the other young farmers in the area.

Olina hoped that she would hear from her father in a month or two after she sent the letter. By mid-November, she went every day to the post office, which was located in the mercantile, to check for a letter. Every day that didn't bring an answer caused a heaviness in her heart. She feared that her father was still angry with her. How would she ever have total peace if he continued to shut her out?

Thanksgiving was fast approaching. Olina had never experienced this holiday, since it was distinctly American. She was excited while the family began preparations. In addition to their grain crops, the Nilssons raised cattle. However, for Thanksgiving, August went hunting for venison. When he brought in a large buck three days before the holiday, the whole family worked on preparing the meat. The two hindquarters were smoked, much like the hams of a pig. The forelegs were roasted, and the rest of the meat was made into sausage, then smoked.

On Thanksgiving Day, their church hosted a community-wide celebration. A morning service allowed everyone to express thanks to God for their blessings that year. Olina thanked God for bringing her to America and giving her Gustaf to love, but a small part of her heart ached for the loss of her Swedish family. She prayed silently for God to intervene there, too.

The pews were moved into a storeroom, and tables and benches were brought in for the dinner. Everyone had prepared their best.

The Nilssons shared the roasted forelegs and one hindquarter of their deer. Others brought ham, pork chops, beef roasts, or chickens. Olina imagined that the tables groaned under the weight of all the food. Vegetable dishes, pies, cakes, pastries, hot breads, fresh churned butter. The aromas started her mouth watering long before the meal began.

Soon after Thanksgiving, everyone was preparing for Christmas. Olina and Gerda worked together to make all the members of Gerda's family some new garment. While they were visiting at the farm, Gerda sneaked around and measured her father's and Gustaf's shirts. The young women offered to do August's laundry with theirs, so they were able to measure his shirt, too.

Pooling the amount of money they could afford to spend, they bought the best fabric available in Litchfield. They made each man a new dress shirt. Mrs. Nilsson would receive a wool suit, complete with a silk waist to wear with it.

One week before Christmas, Olina went to town to pick out lace for the dress she was secretly creating for Gerda. When she finished making all her purchases, she went to the corner where the post office was located. Once again, she was disappointed to find no letter from Sweden waiting for her. With her head down against the cold wind, she started the walk toward the cottage. She didn't notice the vehicle driving by until she heard her name called.

Olina almost dropped her package. The voice calling her sounded so much like her mother's voice that tears pooled in her eyes. When she looked up, she saw August driving a buggy from the livery. The tears blurred her vision so that she didn't recognize the woman sitting on the other side of him.

"Olina." August stopped right beside her. "Look who has come to visit you."

He jumped from the buggy and turned back to help the woman to the sidewalk. Olina reached into her reticule and withdrew a handkerchief to wipe her eyes. When she looked up, she saw that her ears had not deceived her.

"Mor!" Olina dropped the package and threw her arms around the woman her heart had missed all these months. With tears streaming down her face, Olina hugged her mother as if she would never let go.

"Darling, don't cry." Brigitta Sandstrom said in Swedish, as she pulled back from the embrace to look at her daughter's face. "I only wanted to make you happy."

Olina was used to conversing in English, but she easily went back into her native tongue. "Oh, you have. These are happy tears." Then Olina looked around. "Where is Fader?"

Brigitta and August looked at each other. August picked the package up from the wooden sidewalk. "Olina, I'll take you and your mother to your house. We'll be there in a few minutes and then you can talk all you want."

"Could Fader not come?"

"Come, Dear." Brigitta took Olina by the arm. "This wind is so cold. Let's get in out of it, and I'll tell you all about it."

Olina was so pleased to be with Mor that she climbed into the buggy for the ride. Thankfully, it only took a few minutes.

Once they arrived at the cottage, Gerda hurried to the kitchen to make a pot of tea. Olina was glad that she and Gerda had baked Christmas cookies the day before.

Mrs. Sandstrom and Olina sat on the sofa holding hands and devouring each other with their eyes. "Mother, what are you doing here?"

Brigitta laughed at her daughter. "I've come to help plan a wedding." She pulled Olina into another hug. "Have you set a date yet?"

Olina leaned back from her mother's arms. "I wanted to wait until I heard from Fader. Where is he?"

After standing up, Mrs. Sandstrom paced once across the parlor. With her back still turned toward her daughter, she started explaining. "Your father couldn't come, Olina." She turned around and looked into Olina's face. "I brought some bad news."

Oh no. Please God. Her thoughts became jumbled. She wasn't even sure what she was asking Him for. She had realized when Moder didn't tell her anything in town that something bad had happened, but she hadn't wanted to believe it was possible. Now she could no longer deny it.

Mrs. Sandstrom crossed the room and sat beside her daughter. "There's no easy way to say this. Your father became sick. I believe it was his hard-heartedness toward you that brought the sickness on. I prayed for him so much, but he kept getting sicker and sicker."

She pulled a hanky from her sleeve and wiped the tears that were making trails down her cheeks. That caused Olina to realize how wrinkled they had become. As she looked closer at her mother, Olina realized that she had lost weight, and her hair, which had still retained the golden color when Olina last saw her a month before she left Sweden, was streaked with silver. When had her mother become old? It had only been nine months since Olina last saw her. Nine months shouldn't have done that much damage. Unless something terrible had happened.

"Finally, your father told me that we must contact you. He wanted to make peace with you. I told him that I would write you a letter the next morning, but before the sun came up, he left us."

Olina pulled her mother into her arms, and the two women cried together. They weren't aware of Gerda entering the room, but when they stopped crying, they found a tray—with a pot of tea, two cups and saucers, and some cookies—sitting on the table in front of the sofa. Olina poured each of them a cup of tea, but neither of them picked up a cookie.

After taking a few sips from the bracing brew, Mrs. Sandstrom set her cup and saucer back on the table. "That day, we received your letter telling about Gustaf and asking your father to forgive you. I'm so sorry he wasn't able to say this himself, but I know that he would accept your apology and welcome you back into the family."

Olina smiled at her mother through her tears. "I hope so. I wouldn't set a date for the wedding, because I was waiting to hear from Fader."

Mrs. Sandstrom patted Olina on the knee. "I know, Dear. That is why Tant Olga urged me to come to America and talk to you in person."

Olina smiled. "Tant Olga?"

"Ja, for sure." Mrs. Sandstrom returned her smile. "I already turned the farm over to the boys. When Sven got so sick, I couldn't help them at all. All my time was taken with caring for him. Then he died, and Olga asked me to live with her. That way the boys would know that the farm is theirs. Sven and I saved enough money for me to live on for the rest of my life. I won't have many expenses living with Olga, and she needs me."

Olina looked up as Gerda came into the parlor with a carpetbag in her hand. "Are you going somewhere?"

Gerda went over and hugged Mrs. Sandstrom, then Olina. "I wanted to give you and your mother some time alone. August put her luggage in my room. He and I have been having tea in the kitchen. Now he'll take me home. I'll stay with my parents for a few days."

Mrs. Sandstrom stood up. "You don't have to do that, Gerda. I can sleep here on the sofa."

"No need for that." Gerda turned and called August. "I'm ready to go."

August came in and took the carpetbag from her. Then he helped her into her heavy coat. "It's cold. You probably should take a blanket to wrap up in during the drive."

Gerda went upstairs and returned quickly with the cover. "Don't be surprised if Gustaf comes for dinner tonight. I'm sure he'll want to be with the two of you."

After Gerda and August left, Olina and her mother planned a special meal for when Gustaf came. It was good to work together in the kitchen again. Gustaf arrived as they were putting the finishing touches on the food.

Olina answered his knock. He gave her a quick hug before he greeted her mother. Soon they were seated at the table sharing the special meal.

"How long are you staying in Minnesota?" Gustaf asked.

"I planned to stay for awhile. It's such a long journey. One of my cousins is staying with Tant Olga until I return." Brigitta glanced at her daughter. "I want to be here for the wedding, and I know Olina needs some time to mourn her father's death."

Gustaf put his fork down and looked from mother to daughter. "For sure, that's right. I know Olina was anxious to hear from him." He reached over and placed his hand on Olina's shoulder. "How are you doing?"

Olina's eyes glistened with unshed tears. "I'll be okay. It will just take some time."

"I want to be here for the wedding." Brigitta took a bite of the gräddbakelse she had made because it was such a favorite of Olina's.

"Maybe we should set the date tonight." Gustaf studied Olina for a moment. "Do you think we could do that?"

"Moder, can you stay until April?" Olina asked.

"Ja, for sure."

Gustaf and Olina soon decided that they would exchange their vows on Saturday, April 9. That would give them plenty of time to plan the wedding, and Olina and her mother would have time to enjoy each other.

Since Christmas was only a few days away, Gerda and Olina were busy with a few last-minute orders for Christmas presents. Gustaf brought Gerda to the house every morning, so she and Olina could work together. After two days, he took Mrs. Sandstrom back to the farm with him to visit with her old friend, Ingrid.

That day Gerda and Olina went to town to purchase fabric so they could make Mrs. Sandstrom a suit similar to the one they were making Mrs. Nilsson. They finished in time for the family Christmas at the farm.

Olina woke on her wedding day to the sun streaming through her window. She was used to getting up at dawn and making breakfast, but Gerda must have beaten her to it. The fragrant aroma of coffee beckoned Olina to the warm kitchen.

"Well, Sleepyhead, I see you finally woke up." Gerda was pouring a cup of coffee as Olina entered the room.

"Yes. I didn't think I would ever go to sleep. I was so excited thinking about today." Olina stretched and yawned before she sat at the place Gerda set for her at the table. "When I did go to sleep, I slept like a baby." Gerda placed a plate filled with pancakes and sausage in front of Olina.

Olina gasped. It was so much food. "I can't eat all of this."

"You need to," Gerda urged. "You might not be able to eat lunch, and you must keep up your strength. I don't want you fainting before you walk down the aisle."

It was here. Her wedding day. Olina could hardly believe it. So much had gone into the preparations for the day. Her mother wanted to make her wedding dress. Olina and Gerda told Mrs. Sandstrom that she should learn to use the sewing machine, but she insisted on making the dress by hand. Her stitches were tiny and even, a labor of love.

The wedding was scheduled for one o'clock, because Gustaf and

Olina were catching the four o'clock train. They were taking a honeymoon trip to San Francisco.

❧

Gustaf stood beside the preacher at the front of the church. His father was standing at the back of the church with Olina's dainty hand resting on his arm. Since her father wasn't there to escort her down the aisle, she asked Gustaf's father. It made both Bennel and Gustaf very proud.

Gustaf caught his breath at the vision of loveliness. Olina wore a dress of white silk brocade. A single row of flowers, formed into a coronet, now adorned her golden tresses. She looked like an angel. His angel.

Tears formed in his eyes. *Thank You, Father, for bringing her to me.*

The pastor's wife began playing the organ, and Olina walked toward him.

I'll care for her, Father, as You have cared for me. I'll love her and cherish her.

Olina had never seen the suit Gustaf was wearing. He must have bought a new one for the wedding. She was amused. He wore a suit so seldom, but it meant a lot to her that he would purchase a new suit for their wedding. He was such a thoughtful man.

As Olina and Mr. Nilsson walked down the aisle, tears blurred Olina's vision. It didn't matter that she couldn't really see the people who surrounded them. *Father, thank You for what You planned for me. Thank You for helping me come to the place that I could recognize Your plans. I will love and cherish Gustaf for the rest of my life.*

Mail-Order Husband

by DiAnn Mills

To Lane and Katie Dyke and their precious
children, Hannah, Hayley, Jim Bob, and Jenni Beth.
Many thanks to Meredith Efken for her valuable
assistance in researching Nebraska.

Central Nebraska, 1880

ena Walker stiffened and glared into the face of the man before her. "I will not marry you, Dagget Shafer. Not now, not tomorrow, not ever."

His small, dark eyes narrowed, and despite the thick black beard covering most of his face, skin as bright red as a cardinal's feathers shone through. "You will change your mind, Miz High and Mighty. You can't run this farm by yourself and rear those two younguns. You'll either starve or get sick and die."

"I can work this land and raise my children just fine by myself," she said with a lift of her chin. Perspiration beaded her forehead and trickled down her back as she fought her rising temper.

"I dare say you'll live to regret your decision not to marry me. A woman needs a man to take care of her and tell her what to do," he shot back. "And if you had the sense to look around, you'd see there ain't many eligible men in these parts." He turned to face the entrance of the sod dugout, used as a barn, then whirled back around. "Of course, now I see you'd make a bad wife. I need a woman who knows the meanin' of doin' what her husband says and where her place is, not some sassy, purdy face. Miz Walker, you ain't got what I need. You ain't fit for any man."

Swallowing another sharp retort, Lena glanced at the bucket of water in her hands and, without thinking, tossed the contents into Dagget Shafer's face. Probably the closest thing he'd seen to a bath in a year. "Get off my land." Venom riddled her voice. "We don't need the likes of you."

For a minute she thought Dagget might strike her. She dropped the bucket, grabbed the pitchfork leaning against the dugout wall, and silently dared him to step closer.

Dagget must have sensed she meant business because he plodded toward his mule, muttering something she couldn't make out.

Lena started to challenge his view of her fitness to be a wife but held her tongue. She'd run him off, and that's what she'd intended. How could he think she'd be interested in a man who never bathed, had the manners of a pig, and refused to step inside a church? Her heart ached for his six children who no longer had a mother, but her sympathy didn't extend to marrying their unbearable father.

"Mama, you all right?" eleven-year-old Caleb asked, peering around the corner of a horse stall.

She took a deep breath to settle her pounding heart as Dagget rode away, his legs flapping against the sides of the mule. "Yes, Son. I'll be fine."

He picked up the empty bucket. "I'll go fetch some more water."

Lena nodded and laid her hand on her son's shoulder. "Thanks, Caleb."

He glanced up through serious, sky-blue eyes. "I'm glad you're not marryin' him, Mama. We do just fine by ourselves."

Suddenly the whole incident seemed funny. The thought of Dagget standing there with water dripping from his greasy beard to his dirty overalls, nary saying a word, was priceless. Caleb took to laughing too, and their mirth echoed from the sod barn's walls.

"We do need help," Lena finally admitted. "But it will be by God's hand, not by Dagget Shafer or any of the others who seem to think I'm begging for a husband."

"We work good together, Mama," Caleb insisted.

She smiled into the face of the boy who looked so much like his departed father, with the same dark brown hair and tall, lanky frame. "Right now, you, Simon, and I are doing all right, but tomorrow may bring something else. God will provide; I'm sure of it. But I need to talk to Him about the matter."

That night, after the embers from the cow chips no longer produced a flicker of orange-red, and the only sounds around her were her sons' even breathing, Lena prayed for guidance.

Oh, Lord, what do You want me to do? This place needs a man to run it, and the boys are too young. I know the men who have come asking me to marry them could run this farm proper, but Lord, none of them were fit. She shook her head in the darkness, dispelling the visions of the other two farmers who had indicated a desire to marry her. One of them was old enough to be her father, and the other reminded her of a billy goat—with a disposition to match.

Lord, Dagget made me awful angry today, and I'm sorry to have lost my temper. I'll apologize the next time I see him; I promise. It's my pride, I know. I'm sorry, and I'll do better.

Life simply didn't seem fair. Men could come looking for a wife, even place a notice in one of those big newspapers back East. They took advantage of women who had no one to help them when circumstances took a bad turn.

Suddenly an idea occurred to her. If a man could find himself a bride by placing an advertisement, why couldn't she find a husband?

1

Wanted: Christian husband for widow with two young boys. Must be of high moral character, refrain from drinking spirits, be even-tempered, and be able to run a farm in central Nebraska. Interested gentlemen apply by mail. Please allow two to three months for reply.

*G*abriel Hunters smoothed out the wrinkled *Philadelphia Public Ledger* advertisement. He'd read it several times during the past three days and had committed the words to memory. Tonight he'd crumpled it, certain the foolish notion would pass once the paper crackled in the fireplace.

But Gabriel couldn't rid himself of the hope bubbling between the lines of the print. He snatched the newspaper clipping from the sputtering flames, as though the words were more valuable than silver or gold.

Something foreign had occurred to him, something contrary to his hermetic way of life. He actually wanted to respond positively to this widow. A big part of him believed a home and family might fill the emptiness in his heart. Shaking his head, Gabriel suspected God had plans for his perfunctory existence, and the thought brought a surge of unusual emotions. He felt a strange and exhilarating strength in considering a home beyond Philadelphia. Many times he'd wondered what lay outside his world of private bookkeeping, a place where gossip and malicious speech didn't prevail.

Glancing about the sparsely furnished room, he concluded nothing really held him in Philadelphia. Mother had passed away two years prior, and his best friends—his books—could be taken with him. God could be providing a way to obliterate the past and start anew. Certainly a pleasurable thought.

Allowing himself to dream a trifle, Gabriel closed his eyes and imagined the tantalizing aroma of beef stew and baking bread, the sound of children's laughter, and the sweet smile of a woman who loved him.

He studied the newspaper clipping again. What did he know about being a husband and rearing children? He'd never courted a woman or known his own father. After much thought, he realized men had been husbands and fathers for thousands of years. Certainly it came natural.

Another thought occurred to him. Jesus was not much younger than Gabriel when He embarked upon His ministry. Perhaps this stood as a sign from God to answer affirmatively to the widow's notice. He could do this; the Bible would be his guide.

The dilemma lay in farming. He rubbed his hands together. Soft. No calluses. Mother had insisted upon a small garden behind her establishment, but all he'd done was pick a few tomatoes and green beans. The girls had managed the rest. All the work he'd ever accomplished amounted to dipping his quill into an inkwell. Gabriel grinned. *The Farmers Almanac* provided all the knowledge he might ever need to till the land. How difficult could it be to milk a cow or plant seeds and harvest crops? After all, men had tilled the earth since Adam and Eve. He'd spent most of his life submerged in books and had learned volumes of vital information, and he felt confident in his savvy. This new venture merely challenged his intellectual appetite.

Gabriel stood and stepped away from his oaken desk. He surmised Lena Walker must not be endowed with qualities of beauty or she wouldn't have had to resort to advertising for a husband. It didn't matter, for he certainly had not been given eye-pleasing traits either.

A husband and father. Something he'd secretly dreamed of becoming but had never thought he'd share in the blessing.

Monday, October 14, 1880

Lena pulled her frayed, woolen shawl around her shoulders as a north wind whipped around the train station. She shivered, not relishing an early winter, but at least she'd have a husband to keep the fires burning and a helpmate to share in the work. How pleasant to think of conversation with someone other than two young sons—not that she didn't appreciate their willingness to talk—but sometimes she felt hauntingly alone.

"Mama, I hear it," Caleb said, glancing up from where he'd bent his ear to the train track.

"I do too," six-year-old Simon chimed in.

Lena felt her heart pound harder than the rhythmic sound of the Union Pacific making its way toward Archerville, a small town north of Lincoln and not far from the Platte River. Fear gripped her. What had she done? Ever since she'd accepted Gabriel Hunters's aspirations to marry her and be a father to her sons, she'd begun to have serious doubts. Up until she'd posted her reply, the idea had sounded like a fantasy, a perfect solution to all of her woes. Of course she'd prayed for direction and felt God had led her to Mr. Hunters, but could she have misunderstood God?

Her stomach twisted and turned. This man could be a vagrant or, worse yet, an outlaw intending on doing harm to her and her precious sons. Advertising for a husband now sounded foolish. Accepting a man's proposal sight unseen sounded even worse. She'd be the laughingstock of the community, and that didn't help her prideful nature.

What had happened to her faith? Hadn't she heard clear direction from God about the matter? She'd received more than twenty replies from interested men, but none had piqued her interest like the man she expected on board the train. With a name like Gabriel Hunters, he must be the strong, burly type. In fact, his name lent itself to that of a lumberjack. Yes, a rugged wilderness man who lived by his cunning and wits.

Swallowing hard, she forced a smile in the direction of her lively sons. *Oh, Lord, make Mr. Hunters a likeable man who'll love my boys. They can be a handful, but oh, what joy.* Both looked identical to their father, but Caleb leaned more to a compassionate nature, and Simon always ran with the wind and whatever notion that entered his mind.

"It's getting closer," Simon said nearly squealing. "I wonder what Mr. Hunters looks like."

"I'm wondering if he'll be friendly," Caleb said in a chiding tone. "That's more important."

"He'll be whatever the good Lord desires for us," Lena said. "And the Lord only wants the best for His children."

She felt her mouth grow dry as the train chugged down the tracks, slowly coming to a halt and carrying the inevitable. Naturally if the man proved to be less than she expected, she'd refuse to wed him. They weren't to be married until three days hence, which gave both of them time to consider what the future held in store. She wanted to pray with him and talk about everything. No surprises for Lena. Mr. Hunters might be taking on a ready-made family, but he was also getting a farm.

Remembering his letter tucked inside her pocket, she fingered it lightly. His penned words echoed across her mind.

Dear Mrs. Walker,

This correspondence is in regards to your advertisement for a husband and father for your sons. I am thirty-six years old and have never been married, but I believe God will show me through His Word how to be a proper husband and father. I abstain from strong drink or tobacco, and I welcome the opportunity to share in your family's life and teach your sons what little I know.

I've studied agricultural methods and am prepared to be of assistance in this endeavor. I'm a modest man and not easily persuaded, but God has put our union in my heart.

Sincerely,
Gabriel Hunters

Lena assumed Mr. Hunters had an excellent education from his choice of words. How magnificent for her sons. She felt truly blessed and exhilarated—until the train's whistle sounded, the steam billowed with a *spwish*, and the train screeched to a halt.

Lena well knew her ability to act hastily. *Oh, Lord. I'm afraid I've made a terrible mistake. Please give me a sign.*

A man stepped down from the train, a tall, stout fellow who hadn't been able to fasten his jacket. A gust of wind caused him to suck in his breath. Wiry, yellow hair, resembling straw, stuck out haphazardly from beneath a tattered hat as though he might take flight. A patch of the same barbed-wire hair sprang up from his eyebrows, ample jaws, and chin.

Lena covered her mouth to keep from laughing, but then she saw no other man exiting the train. Oh, my, what *had* she done?

The man set his bag beside him and removed his hat, clutching it close to his heart. His hair lay matted like wet chicken feathers. "Mrs. Walker," he said, approaching her with a concerned frown. "Are you Mrs. Lena Walker?"

"Yes, I am," she replied and extended her hand. He grasped it lightly. It felt cold and clammy. Lena dare not look at Caleb and Simon for fear she'd burst into laughter—or tears.

"I'm Gabriel Hunters," he said with a gulp, his words jumping out like a squeak.

"It's a pleasure to meet you, Mr. Hunters." She released her hand and gestured toward her sons. "This is Caleb; he's eleven. And this is Simon; he's six."

Oh, Lord, help them to remember their manners. Help me to remember mine!

Mr. Hunters bent his portly frame and offered his hand first to Caleb, then to Simon. "It's an honor to meet you, Caleb and Simon Walker. I'm looking forward to an auspicious relationship."

His voice trembled slightly, and Lena felt compassion tug at her heart. She hadn't considered he might have reservations about their meeting.

Simon's gaze shot up at his mother. "Are we in trouble, Mama?"

Lena gathered her shawl closer to her; the wind had taken a colder twist. "I don't think so, Son." She took a deep breath, hoping her ignorance didn't show through. "Mr. Hunters, Simon isn't sure of the meaning of auspicious."

Still bending at the knee, he nodded and turned his attention to the small boy. "It means successful or promising."

Simon's blue eyes appeared to radiate with understanding. "Mama says a word like that when she thinks Caleb and I are doing something we shouldn't."

"Suspicious?" Mr. Hunters asked.

"Yes, Sir. That's it. Do you like chores, Mr. Hunters? Me and Caleb get real tired of 'em, and we're sure glad you're here to help." He reached out to shake Mr. Hunters's hand again. "I see you like to eat a lot, Sir, and your clothes appear a bit tight, but never you mind. Our mama cooks real good, and she can fix your clothes when they tear."

"Simon," Lena gasped, horrified. Hadn't they talked about proper introductions all the way to Archerville?

Mr. Hunters stood and tugged at his gaping jacket. "I apologize if my corpulent body is offensive."

"No, Sir. Not in the least," Lena replied before one of the boys could embarrass her further. She assumed the meaning of corpulent had something to do with his size. "Kindly excuse my son's bad manners. Caleb, would you like to carry Mr. Hunters's bag to the wagon? We can all get to know each other on the way home, and I'll cook supper while you boys show Mr. Hunters around the farm."

Mr. Hunters stared anxiously at the train. "I have another bag, but it's extremely cumbersome. Several of my books are packed inside."

As if hearing the man's words, the conductor scooted out a fairly large trunk. "Right heavy this is," he said, massaging the small of his back.

Mr. Hunters reached for his belongings and stumbled with the weight. Lena dashed forward with Caleb and Simon, but the man fell flat on his back with his bag quivering atop his chest and rounded stomach.

Instantly, the conductor stood by his side and removed the trunk, then helped the dazed man to his feet. Simon began to chuckle, followed by Caleb. Despite Lena's stern looks, the two boys laughed even harder. She found it difficult to contain herself, wanting to give in to the mirth tickling through her body. *Oh, Lord, surely I misunderstood!*

"Oh dear, are you all right?" she asked, trying desperately to gain control of her wavering emotions.

Mr. Hunters shrugged his shoulders and dusted off his clothes. "Ma'am, this is definitely not the proper image I wanted to present you. I sincerely apologize for my blunder."

"No need to fret about it," she said, and for the first time she caught a glimpse of his eyes—coppery brown, much like the color of autumn leaves, unusual for a person with blond hair. A second look reminded her of a frightened animal, cornered with no place to run.

Poor Mr. Hunters, and we're laughing at him. Immediately, she sobered. "I hope you don't mind, but I scheduled the wedding for three days hence. I thought we could use the time to get accustomed to each other."

His face turned ghastly white. "Ma'am—"

Lena gathered what had shocked him. "Sir, I intended to have you sleep in the barn until our wedding." Her face grew hotter than a Nebraska sun in mid-July.

He released a pent-up breath. "Those arrangements sound perfectly fine to me."

They moved awkwardly toward Lena's wagon. Caleb and Simon struggled with one bag, and Mr. Hunters heaved with the trunk. Moments before, Simon had embarrassed her with his endless prattle. Now no one uttered a word.

"You must be quite fond of books," she said, groping for something to say.

"Yes, Ma'am. I hope you don't mind, but I took the liberty of having the rest of them sent here in a few weeks."

"Of course not. The winter nights approaching us will provide you with plenty of reading time."

"Will you read these books to us, Sir?" Caleb asked, struggling with the heavy bag.

Mr. Hunters's shoulders relaxed. "I'd be pleased to, along with the Bible."

Lena swallowed. Mr. Hunters might not be what she envisioned, but this part of him was a relief.

They reached the wagon and, after much difficulty, loaded the trunk and bag. Caleb and Simon climbed into the back, curiously eyeing the outside of Mr. Hunters's baggage.

"Do not touch those," she reminded them.

Lena turned for the man to assist her onto the wagon seat, which he did with much effort. Huffing and puffing, he attempted a smile.

"Would you like to drive us west toward my home?" she asked, smoothing her dress.

His shoulders sank. "Ma'am, I've never driven a wagon before in my life."

2

*G*abriel wanted to step down from that wagon and make a running leap to board the Union Pacific back to Philadelphia as fast as his round and aching legs would allow.

His entrance into Archerville had been met with one disaster after another—and this last occurrence would surely conclude his demise. The boys, his future sons, had been beset with amusement when the trunk landed him on his backside, and his future wife had just learned he knew nothing about driving a wagon.

Defeated and exhausted from the laborious trip to middle-of-nowhere Nebraska, Gabriel realized he'd made a terrible mistake. And in three days' time, he might make an even worse one.

Oh, God, why did I think You willed this for my life? Am I once again to be made a laughingstock of a community?

"Don't concern yourself, Mr. Hunters. I've driven this wagon more times than I care to remember," Mrs. Walker said, but he couldn't tell if she sounded annoyed or simply tired—most likely the former.

He didn't blame her; he wasn't pleased with his lack of dexterity either. In less than ten minutes, he'd discovered that not all knowledge came from books. Apprehension rippled through him at the likelihood of the next twenty-four hours revealing a generous amount of his ignorance.

"Mr. Hunters," Caleb began. "What did you do while in Philadelphia?"

Obviously he didn't drive a team of horses.

"Bookkeeping," Gabriel replied. When he saw the rather confused look spreading across the boy's face, he added, "It's arithmetic. I help

492

business establishments add and subtract what they earn and what they spend."

Caleb nodded. "Like when Mama sells a cow, then pays our bill at the general store?"

"Correct, and what's left is profit."

"We don't have any of that," Caleb said with a much-too-serious look for a boy. "We simply pay what's owed and start all over again."

Gabriel saw a muscle twitch in Mrs. Walker's face. Farming a 160-acre homestead and raising two boys must be a real hardship. No wonder she needed a husband. At least she knew how to survive. His former confidence in farming had ended at the railroad station.

"But the Lord provides," Lena said quietly. "We have a house, clothes to wear, and food. Some folks aren't as fortunate."

"I pray I'll be able to make you more prosperous," Gabriel said firmly.

"Thank you, Mr. Hunters. I—"

"Are we going to be rich?" Simon asked, tugging on Gabriel's coat-tail. "I know zactly what I want."

"Simon," Mrs. Walker scolded. "Mind your manners. Now, you boys leave Mr. Hunters alone for awhile. He and I have things to discuss."

The boys scooted back to the end of the wagon and dangled their feet over the edge. They minded well. A good sign. He'd seen his share of misbehaved boys and the damage they could do.

Gabriel glanced at the sights of Archerville behind him as they pulled away from the small town. One dusty street was lined with a few necessary businesses: a general store and post office; a jail; a barber and undertaker; a saloon; and across from the liquid spirits and worldly entertainment, a freshly painted church—for a dose of the Holy Ghost.

The odor staggered him. Horses, pigs, and cows wandered through the town and contributed their droppings wherever they saw fit. Certainly nothing resembling the cleanliness or the hustle and bustle of Philadelphia. A burst of wind whipped around a barrel outside the general store, sending it teetering to the ground. A shiver wound its way around Gabriel's spine. As much as he'd looked forward to leaving the city, this new environment settled upon him like questionable figures in a ledger.

He'd been lonely before with people everywhere, but now he felt alone and afraid. Yes, fear did have a strangling hold on him, fear of the unknown and fear of the future. God did lead him here to Archerville, of that he had no doubt, but those thoughts did little to calm him.

Gabriel studied Mrs. Walker's horses. They appeared fine to him— shiny coats and not at all swaybacked. He'd expected mules. His gaze trailed up the reins to her hands, callused and deeply tanned. He'd never seen a woman's hands that weren't soft and smooth. Another oddity. Well, he didn't intend for his wife to work herself into an early grave. Wetting his lips, he stole a quick glance at her face. With all the commotion at the train station, he hadn't afforded a good look at his future wife.

Oh no. Shocked and disgruntled, he instantly changed his focus to the surrounding countryside, flat, bleak, and uninviting.

Lena Walker was comely, and he couldn't trust an attractive woman. She'd betray him just like his mother and the other girls. For weeks since he'd received Mrs. Walker's agreement to the marriage, he'd prayed for a plain woman, one who matched him in appearance. A man could build a life with a woman who'd never stray. He'd never have to worry about her participating in the activities his mother had.

Suddenly, Gabriel fought the urge to shake his fist at God. The One in whom he'd put his faith and trust had tricked him. He'd journeyed all this way only to find a woman who would hurt him more deeply than his mother. Although his mother had died and he'd forgiven her, he was smart enough not to fall into the same well again.

What should he do now? *Lord, cruel jokes are what the bullies did when I attended school. I can't believe this is from You. Even if she might be different, she'd never love the likes of me. Have You forgotten what I look like?*

"Mr. Hunters, forgive me. I had so many things to ask you, but now I can't seem to figure out where to begin." Mrs. Walker offered him a slight smile, then quickly stared ahead at the road.

Perhaps you're disappointed; can't blame you. "We're strangers, Mrs. Walker. We have much to learn about each other."

"Yes, that's true. Could we begin by calling each other by our given names and talking about ourselves?"

He nodded, although not so sure he wanted Lena Walker to know more about him. "Certainly, if it suits you."

She took a deep breath and sat straighter as though summoning courage for an arduous task. "My name is Lena Jane Walker. My family came to Nebraska from Ohio when I was a girl. I'll be thirty-one years old come February." She paused and urged the team of horses to pick up their pace. "I've been a widow for three years. I'm strong and healthy, and so are my sons. The Lord guides my life, but I do tend to make mistakes more often than not."

"We all do," he said solemnly, regretting the moment he'd considered her advertisement for a husband. Why hadn't she told him what she looked like?

"My biggest fault is my temper," she continued, as though bound by some unexplainable force to confess her worst. "I'll do my best to curb it, but I thought you should know."

When she looked his way again, the intensity of her green eyes captured his heart. Their gazes locked, and he could not pull away. Truth and sincerity with a mixture of merriment radiated back at him. The combination caused Gabriel to rethink his former conclusions about comely women. *Help, I'm so confused.*

Could it be Lena Walker held no malice? He knew God intended the best for him, and for a moment, Gabriel had forgotten His goodness. He'd proceed with caution, remembering more than one of his mother's girls had looked innocent as a child.

Mrs. Walker averted his scrutiny. "I want you to know the real reason why I contacted the Philadelphia newspaper."

"I'd be obliged if you would. Naturally, I assumed you needed help with your land and your sons."

"Yes, but I never thought a man would be interested in coming all this way, and when you did, I took it as a sign from God that this was His will. You see, three farmers asked me to marry, but I couldn't tolerate them. I felt advertising for a husband made more sense. I wanted God to send what I needed."

His stomach lunged. "Why didn't you wed one of the men who proposed?"

She shrugged. "They weren't God-fearing, or bathed, or good to my sons. When they came around asking, I threw them off my land. Guess they got a taste of my temper."

A mental picture of this woman tossing a grown man off her farm leaped from his mind. It sounded incredibly funny, and he stifled a laugh.

"You can laugh," she said, shaking her head. "Most folks around here do anyway. They think I've lost my mind by refusing to marry up with a man who'd take care of the farm." She stopped talking abruptly, as though she suddenly felt embarrassed.

Gabriel thought about Lena's confession, and a cloud darkened his mind. "Ma'am, are you desiring a husband who allows you to direct his ways?" *I may not be handsome or successful, but I believe a man is head of his household.*

Lena abruptly reined the horses to a halt. Her face paled. "By no means. I believe in the biblical instructions for husbands and wives—a husband guides and directs his home."

"As I do. A marriage must follow every God-given precept."

"Precisely. Now, tell me about yourself."

The tension seemed to grow worse. He didn't want or see a reason to reveal much about his person. He deemed a willingness to do right by her was all that held importance. "You already know quite a bit about me from our correspondence. My complete name is Gabriel Lawrence Hunters, and I've lived my whole life in Philadelphia."

"Are your parents living?"

"Mother passed on some two years ago."

"So your father is still in Philadelphia?"

Gracious, Woman, how much do you need to know about me? "I have no idea." He prayed for a diversion, anything to stop the questioning. "This is magnificent country."

She smiled. "Yes, it is. In late summer, prairie grass can grow taller than a man."

He studied the landscape in curiosity and in avoidance of Lena's inquiries. In the distance all he could see was flat land with miles of prairie grass, now limp and brown. According to his findings, this river valley hosted dark brown soil. Farmers near the Platte River grew mostly corn, but they also raised oats, barley, and wheat. Although Mrs. Walker's land lay farther south, he assumed the farming methods were the same. He tried to envision what fields of ripe corn looked like. From his research, he gathered tall green stalks with green shoots and a cap of brown silky-like tassels. He'd find out in the months to come.

Gabriel remembered Lena mentioning in one of her letters about a few head of cattle, but he'd neglected to find out how many or what kind. He should have asked, since he'd be working with the beasts.

A hint of excitement, a rather peculiar sensation, spread through him as he considered this adventure. For the first time in his life he'd watch things grow: corn, cattle, pigs, a garden, and two freckle-faced boys. He'd learn how to farm properly; after all, he'd read the books.

Three white-tailed deer leaped across the road from the tall grass, such wondrous creatures. My, how he admired their gracefulness. The call of a flock of geese perked his ears. Staring up into the sky, he watched their perfect V formation head south.

Winter. Philadelphia was frigid in the winter, but he'd heard Nebraska received bitter temperatures and several feet of snow, and that wasn't long in the making.

"It's all so serene," he whispered really to no one.

"Yes," Lena agreed, "but the same things making it peaceful can also turn on you if you're not careful."

"I don't believe I understand," he replied.

"Nature," she said simply. "Just when you think everything is perfect and a bit of heaven, it turns on you by throwing a twister over your land in the summer, or a prairie fire destroying everything in its path, or a blizzard to blind you in winter."

Like a beautiful woman. Gabriel studied her features beneath a faded bonnet. This time he took in the oval shape of her face and large, expressive eyes framed by nearly black hair. Her pursed lips reminded him of a rose bud. If only Lena Walker appeared a bit less lovely. Those looks could defeat a man—drive him to lose his principles. He'd seen it done too many times.

The regrets about Lena again plodded through his rambling thoughts. A plain woman whom no other man might covet had been his heart's desire. If blessed with any children, they might not look real pleasing, but he'd teach them how God examines the heart for true beauty.

Already Gabriel didn't trust Lena, and they hadn't even completed their nuptials.

3

*L*ena shoved a lump back down her throat. She'd made such a fool out of herself in trying to soothe Gabriel's humiliation. The laughter she'd felt for him back in Archerville had quickly turned to regret when she couldn't utter a single intelligent word.

They should be discussing the farm or arranging a time to talk about Caleb and Simon. She and Gabriel would be married in three days; they should be spending this time getting to know each other.

Fear gripped her like the time she'd sighted a cloud of grasshoppers descending on the fields ready for harvest. Gabriel Hunters was nothing like she'd pictured: He didn't look like he'd ever spent a day in his life on a farm. Well, she simply had to know the truth.

"Did you grow up on a farm?" she asked.

"Not exactly," he replied after a moment's pause.

The fright subsided to a rising anger. "Where then did you learn about it?"

"From books," he said simply, staring straight ahead.

His reply shook the very foundation on which she built her values. "From books? How can you feel the soil between your fingertips from a book? How can you tell the color of ripe wheat?"

"The written word is a valuable asset. I place complete trust in what I've read and studied." His ample chest rose and fell, while the buttons on his jacket threatened to break free. "Man has farmed since the beginning of time. If it were a difficult process, then human beings would not have survived."

I refuse to lose my temper. She clucked the horses to venture a tad faster. *I refuse to lose my temper.* "Many people have died due to crop failures or the natural hardships arising from living here. I hope you read *that* in your books."

"I have."

"And your conclusion, good sir?" She gritted her teeth to keep from adding a vicious retort.

"I have determined to be a farmer. There are many things for me to put into practice from the books I've read. If I had thought this undertaking an impossibility, I would not have answered your advertisement."

Mercy. What have I done? Lena glanced back to see Caleb and Simon still dangling their feet over the wagon. God had entrusted her with those precious boys, and she would guard them with her life. She'd see them grow to manhood and have children of their own. They needed a father—a man who had experienced life and knew its pitfalls. Somehow she doubted if Gabriel Hunters could fulfill those qualifications. She'd clearly heard God's affirmation in this strange union, but why? God must be punishing her for her pride and temper.

"Ma'am," Gabriel said just loud enough for her to hear, "I'd be grateful if you'd give me an opportunity to be the husband and father you need."

~❧~

Gabriel believed he had lowered himself as much as he could without some consolation in return from his future intended.

"I want to give you a chance, but you must understand how much I need a man who can work the land," Lena said, her eyes moistening.

He did not miss her tears, and immediately he wanted to whisk them away. "I will not disappoint you."

She hastily glanced away and pointed to a shadowing of buildings in the distance. "Up there is the farm. Besides the two horses, we have a mule for working the fields, a few pigs, chickens, ten cows, and a bull. Hopefully we'll have more cows in the spring."

Gabriel's first view of his new home and its outbuildings fell far below his initial ideas of a rural home. He'd seen the great farms in Pennsylvania, the clapboard homes and the well-kept barns and sheds.

The conditions here ranged close to the shanty life on the poor side of Philadelphia. Bleak. Desolate.

The cabin had been constructed of sod brick made from dried prairie grass and dirt. He remembered from Lena's letter that the cabin was called a soddy. These structures kept out the heat in the summer and shut out the cold in winter. Gabriel couldn't keep from wondering if it carried a smell. However, the structure did have two windows with real paned glass.

The roof looked like the same weathered sod laid over top some type of wood. From the bare spots with shoots of plant life sprouting up from them, he assumed the roof leaked. Obviously, carpentry would be his first priority, or whatever else he deemed necessary to make the home comfortable. Using a hammer and nails shouldn't be too arduous, if those tools were required. He hadn't seen any trees, and the quandary puzzled him. Where did one find wood?

What Lena referred to as a dugout more closely resembled a cave dug out of a hillside with a portion of the front built with the same sod bricks. With his keen insight into the world of mathematics, he should be able to calculate the length and width of sod necessary for repairs. Come spring, perhaps they could locate lumber to have hauled in for a good, solid barn.

Lena pulled the wagon to a halt. The boys jumped from the back and fell into the welcoming embrace of a mangy dog that had emerged from out of nowhere. Barking and wagging its flea-bitten tail, the animal eyed the newcomer suspiciously . . . and growled.

Gabriel hesitantly stepped to the ground. He didn't care for dogs. He'd never owned one or knew anyone who did, but he'd been bitten once when he'd bent to pat a dog while walking to the Philadelphia library.

"Just let him sniff you," Caleb said, when the dog growled at Gabriel the second time. "Turnip, you need to make friends with this man. He's going to be marryin' our ma."

The dog's name is Turnip? "We don't have to do this right now," Gabriel replied as he deliberated whether to help Lena down from the wagon or wait to see if the dog took a bite from the seat of his trousers.

"Put Turnip in the barn," Lena said to her son. "Gabriel can make friends later."

Once the dog followed the boys into the dilapidated dugout, Gabriel offered her his assistance. Immediately he noticed her firm grip—stronger than his.

"You have a fine-looking place here," he said.

She frowned. "Don't add lies to your deceit. Everything is falling apart, and you know it."

"I'm not by nature an egregious person," he replied.

Lena planted her hands on her hips. "Gabe, let me tell you right now. Those big words don't mean anything to me. Here in Nebraska, we don't have time to learn the meanings of such nonsense. Using them will only upset folks, make them think you are better than they."

Is she always this petulant? And the name of Gabe? No one has ever called me anything but Gabriel.

Lena whirled away from him. He saw her shoulders rise and fall before she faced him again. "I'm sorry, Gabriel. This is not how I wanted our first meeting. We're supposed to be getting to know each other, not quarreling. Will you forgive me?"

He wondered the extent of Lena's sensibilities, for he'd certainly seen a gamut of them in the brief time they'd been together. Could he endure a lifetime of irrational emotions? Of course, he must. His mother could flare at a moment's notice, then turn her sweetness toward an unsuspecting victim. His integrity lay foremost in his mind, and he'd made a commitment to the woman before him. After all, God had given him clear direction. Hadn't He?

"I can most assuredly forgive you and take into consideration your emotions. I'd be a fool not to comprehend that my credentials do not meet with what . . . with what you anticipated. But rest assured, I will curtail my vocabulary to something more acceptable. Making good friends is important, and a proper image is quite desirable."

"Thank you, and you can start right now. I never thought I was an ignorant person, but I'm having problems following your words."

Were all women so particular? His mother had been his only example, and she always had her mind set on business—and on her disappointment in him. Lena flashed her troubled gaze his way. He could make a few concessions, since she had more to lose in this endeavor than he. "I'll do my best," he said, carefully guarding each word. "I've never been called Gabe, but it does have a pleasant sound to it."

She brightened. "You like it? Wonderful. I know Gabriel in the Bible was a messenger, and I'd like to think of you in the same way, but shortened seems to fit you."

At last she appeared happy. He inwardly sighed. Now, on to other things. "Perhaps we can talk later after your sons are in bed?"

"I'd like that very much."

He could quickly grow accustomed to Lena's smile. He offered one of his own, then quickly turned to secure his trunks from the wagon. "Where shall I put my things?"

"Inside the cabin, in the boys' room for now." She folded her hands in front of her as though searching for the courage to say something else. "I hope the barn is all right for a few days," she finally said.

"Most certainly," he replied, lifting the massive trunk into his arms. He'd ache tomorrow from this work.

"I'll fix us some supper. I hope you like venison and carrots and potatoes." When he nodded, she continued. "The boys have chores and milking to do, so we'll eat as soon as they're finished."

Gabe felt the call of a challenge. "And I'll assist the boys as soon as these are inside."

His first view of the cabin, or rather what he could see of it, astounded him. It was dark even with two windows, but the sod bricks were nearly three feet thick, which made for a wide window ledge. Lena had a few dried wild flowers setting in a crockery jug alongside a framed picture of an elderly couple.

"Your parents?" he asked, adjusting the trunk in his arms.

"Yes." She tapped her foot on the earthen floor, then pointed to a quilt near the back. "That's Caleb and Simon's room."

He maneuvered through the meagerly furnished dwelling: a rocking chair in front of a fireplace, two small benches positioned around a rough-sawn table, and two other ladder-back chairs. A small cookstove rested in the corner where a few pegs held two cast-iron pots and a skillet. Glancing about, he saw a good many household items

hanging from the walls. Lena was a tidy woman. Another quilt separated the main living area from what Gabe assumed was her bedroom.
He tried not to stare at it, feeling his face redden at the thought of
sharing a bed with this woman. The plastered walls were a surprise
to him; he'd assumed they would be covered with newspapers.

The boys' room held a chest and two straw mattresses, and he
noted not much room for anything more. The earthen floor came as
a shock. He'd been accustomed to wood floors with a soft rug beneath
his feet. A bit of dried grass had fallen from the roof to the floor. *Surely
this leaks.*

A short while later, he plodded out to the dugout, the old twinge
of excitement fading to somewhat of an uncomfortable knot in the
bottom of his stomach. A distinct, disagreeable smell met his nostrils.
How sad, one of the boys must surely be ill.

As Gabriel entered the darkened dugout they referred to as a barn,
a horrific stench took his breath away, and he covered his nostrils.
This was worse than Archerville. "Caleb, Simon, is everything all
right?"

A voice replied from the shadows. "Yes, Sir. We're back here. Just
starting to milk."

He recognized Caleb and ventured his way. "I'd like to help. What
is that dreadful odor?"

Simon rushed down to meet him. "I don't know, 'less you're smel-
lin' the manure."

Ah. Why didn't I detect it? "I'm sure you're right."

"It's powerful bad," Caleb said. Gabe had yet to make out the boy
because his eyes were having trouble adjusting to the faint light. "Tomorrow we have to clean out this barn before Ma thrashes us."

"Perhaps I can be of assistance?" Immediately he regretted his
words. Hadn't he already decided to make repairs to the various buildings?

"Oh, yes," Caleb replied, a bit too enthusiastically.

By this time, he'd made out where the young boy knelt on his
knees, leaning into a brown-and-white cow. A *pinging* sound alerted
Gabriel to milk squirting into the bottom of the pail. *So Caleb squeezes
those conical attachments to discharge the milk.*

"When's the last time you milked a cow?" Caleb asked, grinning into his half-filled bucket.

Gabe refused to reply. "Do you have a stool?"

"He can have mine." Simon stood and peered up at him curiously. "I have one, but it's a little wobbly. Try balancing yourself with your leg."

The endeavor didn't look too difficult. He stepped over beside Simon's cow, but the stool, which was really a rickety nail keg, appeared a bit precarious. The youngest Walker bolted from his position, making room for Gabe. About that time, the cow made a woeful sound as though lamenting the milking process.

"Hush," Simon ordered. "And don't be kicking over the bucket either."

As soon as Gabe eased onto the keg, it gave way and splattered into a mass of wood pieces and a splintered seat.

"Goodness, Mr. Hunters," Simon said. "You've gone and done it now. Ma will have a word to say about this."

"You hush, Simon," Caleb said. "He couldn't help the keg breaking with his weight and all. Ma knows the difference between an accident and an on-purpose."

God help me, Gabe silently pleaded. "Boys, I can milk this cow in short order as soon as we can find a suitable stool for me."

"Ain't none," Simon said. "You'll have to bend down on your knees."

Gracious, is anything easy here? "I shall need to construct a new milking stool, but for right now I'll do as you suggest."

Gabe gingerly touched the cow. Its bristled hide felt strange, reminiscent of the short-haired dog that had bit him years ago. He wondered if cows bit.

No matter. He'd see this task to the end. All of a sudden, the appendages hanging from under the cow's belly looked rather formidable. Did he grab them one at a time or use both hands? Rubbing his fingers together, he realized the time had come to show his initiative. He reached out and grabbed an udder. It felt soft. Not at all like he'd imagined. Gabe squeezed it, and a stream of milk splattered his jacket.

"In the bucket, Mr. Hunters," Simon said impatiently. "Ma says waste not, want not."

"And she's so right," Gabe replied. "I'll not be shirking in my duties." His next attempt sent the milk into the pail. He sensed such satisfaction, but the twisted position of his body made it difficult to breathe.

"I bet you never did this before either," Lena said, towering over him.

4

$\mathcal{S}$omehow Lena restrained the doubts and ugly retorts threatening to spill out over supper. Ever since she'd entered the barn with the suspicion that Gabe Hunters knew nothing about milking and discovered she was right, her mind had shaken with anger.

How had he lived for over thirty-six years without learning the basics of life? Even city folks had to eat and survive. No matter if God had been involved with this husband mess she'd gotten herself into, come morning she'd be sending Mr. Gabe Hunters packing.

To make matters worse, she'd told Caleb and Simon to clean out the barn three days ago. The smell would make a person throw up their shoes. Lena tilted her head thoughtfully. After a night in the barn, Gabe would be more than willing to leave.

"Good food, Mama," Caleb said, breaking the silence.

The fire crackled, providing all the sound Lena needed while she ate. "Thank you. Most times we have cornbread, beans, and sorghum molasses," she added in explanation to their guest. "Tonight was . . . supposed to be special. In the morning—"

"We'll get right on cleaning the barn after we deliver the milk," Gabe announced.

Lena said nothing. She had learned a long time ago about letting her temper simmer rather than letting it boil over. That method didn't always work, but tonight, laced with prayer, her angry, racing thoughts were subsiding.

"I agree with Caleb," Gabe continued. "The food is delicious."

"Thank you, Mr. Hunters." She didn't dare lift her gaze to meet his for fear she'd give into temptation and tell him just exactly what she thought about his book learning. Maybe it was enough to know he had the company of animals tonight.

"When did you want to hold our discussion?" he asked, taking a big gulp of coffee.

She swallowed a piece of molasses-soaked cornbread. "As soon as the boys go to bed. Normally, we have Bible reading before their prayers."

"May I do the honors of reading tonight and conducting prayers?"

You're going to need it by the time I'm finished with you. She bit her tongue and tried to respond civilly. "Sounds like an excellent idea. I look forward to what you'll be selecting."

"What have you been reading?"

"Job," she said.

"Mama, I don't think Mr. Hunters wants to read about a man who had sores all over his body and his family died," Caleb said. Upon meeting her scrutiny, he quickly added, "Of course, what he reads from the Bible is his choice."

"Job is fine," Gabe said. "There's something for us to learn in every piece of Scripture."

Lena glanced at his barely touched food. From the looks of him, Gabe seldom refused a meal. She lifted her coffee cup to her lips. She hadn't much of an appetite either—too many emotions floating in and out of her mind. Feeling Gabe studying her, she lifted her gaze to meet his. Kindness poured from those coppery pools and along with it a sensation akin to hurt and desperation. Her father had given her a cat once that looked at her in the same way. The animal had been beaten and left to fend for itself until her father brought it home.

A smile tugged at Lena's lips. After all, she could be kind and show him Christian hospitality until she told him there wouldn't be a wedding.

To her surprise, Gabe suggested all of them help Lena clean up from supper. Soon the dishes were washed and the debris that had fallen through the roof whisked away from the floor. A moment later, he disappeared into the boys' room and returned with spectacles in his hand.

"Here's the Bible," Lena said, handing him James's weathered book with its turned-down pages. Someday she'd give it to Caleb. All of a sudden, she wanted to jerk it back. This man had no right to take James's chair for Bible reading. She choked back a sob. "We sit by the fire, and I read from the rocking chair."

"You have to be real careful," Simon said, finding his position on a braided rug. "If you don't say the words right, the devil will pounce on you while you're in bed."

"Simon," Lena scolded. "Where ever did you hear such a thing?"

He glanced at his older brother in one giant accusing glare.

Gabe chuckled, surprising her. "Well, Simon, I haven't been able to do much since I arrived here with any expertise, but I *can* read. And the devil doesn't come after you when you're sleeping just because you can't pronounce a word correctly."

Caleb found his spot near his brother and said nothing. Lena would deal with her older son later. The two boys faced Gabe, warming their backs against the fire. If Lena hadn't been so upset, she'd have treasured the sight of her precious sons looking to a man for Scripture reading. She pulled a chair from the table, hoping he hadn't lied about knowing the Bible.

"We're near the end of Job," Lena said. "I have it marked. Oh, it's the last chapter."

Gabe carefully put on his spectacles and cleared his throat. "Job, chapter forty-two. 'Then Job answered the Lord, and said, I know that Thou canst do every thing, and that no thought can be withholden from Thee.' "

Lena felt a knocking at her heart. *I know You can do every thing, and that no thought can be kept secret from You.* She shifted uncomfortably. *Lord, I do know You are all powerful.*

Gabe continued. " 'Who is he that hideth counsel without knowledge? Therefore have I uttered that I understood not; things too wonderful for me, which I knew not.' "

This is about Gabe, isn't it? Lena knew in an instant her belittling thoughts about him had not honored God, especially when she'd doubted the Father's hand in Gabe's coming to Nebraska. She didn't understand any of it.

But he doesn't know a thing about farming. Having him around and having to teach him will be like having another child underfoot.

Lena fidgeted; the sweltering realization of being under conviction brought color to her cheeks. She glanced Gabe's way, his reading perfect against the stillness around them. Even if she had to show him how to farm, how ever would she get used to looking at him? She peered into the fire. James had presented a striking pose, and his hearty laughter had brought music to her soul. But Gabe? Although he had nice eyes, she'd have to look at his portly body and pallid skin for the rest of her life.

" 'Wherefore I abhor myself, and repent in dust and ashes.' "

Lena wanted to scream. *All right, Lord.* She wouldn't tell Gabe he had to leave. She'd teach him how to farm and tend to animals. She swallowed and choked on her own spittle, causing Gabe to halt his reading until she was all right. Yes, she'd marry him. But for the life of her, she didn't understand why, except God had ordained it, and He had a plan.

"What do you boys think about Job's life?" Gabe asked once he'd finished reading.

Simon balanced his chin on his finger. "Hmm. Pick better friends?"

Gabe smiled and ruffled his dark hair. "That's one thing. Caleb?"

"I'm not sure, Mr. Hunters. I think we're not supposed to get mad at God when bad things happen."

"Yeah," Simon piped in. "The devil might be out looking for someone to hurt and give you a wife who wants you to die."

Lena hoped the warmth in her face didn't show. Her whimsical son always saw things in a different light, and he wasn't afraid to voice his feelings.

"You're both right," Gabe said. "We don't always understand why things happen, but we can always trust that our God is in control."

Lord, You've already made me feel awful. There's no need to do it again. "Gabe, would you lead us in prayer?" she asked, hoping he didn't hear the turmoil in her voice.

He nodded. "Father God, thank You for bringing me here to this fine home. Bless Lena, Caleb, and Simon. Guide them in Your infinite wisdom and keep them safe in the shelter of Your almighty arms. Amen."

"Amen," Caleb and Simon echoed. They glanced at Lena expectantly. When she nodded, they bid Gabe good night and followed her to their small bedroom behind a blanketed curtain.

All the while she tucked them in and planted kisses on their cheeks, Lena considered the man sitting by the fireplace. She'd made a commitment to God. Now, she had to echo that same promise to Gabe.

She'd rather plow her land without a horse.

Gabe twiddled his thumbs while he awaited Lena's return. He felt certain his heart would leap from his chest. What a fool he'd been to think he might belong here. Would she simply order him off her farm or tell him sweetly to take his fancy words and books back to Philadelphia? Not that he considered either request in poor taste. All his life he'd been labeled a failure, and circumstances were not about to change overnight. Learning new things and fitting into a family would take weeks, even months. Today, he'd ruined every opportune second he'd been given.

What now? *Lord, I wanted this to work. I could have learned how to farm and help Lena with those boys. I know she's not what I envisioned, but I don't think I'm what she expected either. I could have put my despicable past behind me and found confidence in being a husband and father. Oh, I know my confidence is in You, but is it a sin to desire a loving family?*

Turnip growled. Another member of the family against him. "You want to send me back on the next train too?" he whispered. He stared at the dog, trying to initiate some semblance of friendship with the mongrel.

The dog turned its mammoth head as though attempting to understand the man creature before him.

"We could have pleasant times together," Gabe continued, momentarily shoving aside his current disturbing situation with the members of this household. "Why don't you sniff at me a bit? I need a faithful companion."

Turnip focused his attention on the fire. Perhaps he contemplated Gabe's dismal mood. At least the dog wasn't growling.

"Gabe?" Lena asked quietly, interrupting his thoughts. "Would you like another cup of coffee while we talk?" She wrung her hands and offered a shaky smile.

"I'd like that very much."

"With milk?"

"I believe milk is just fine."

She felt her insides flutter while she poured the hot brew into a tin cup. "I guess we have much to talk about."

Gabe raised his hand. "Lena, I know I've failed miserably today, and I surely understand your aversion to me. I'm riddled with compunction. Let me simplify the matter. I'll leave in the morning, but I need to trouble you for a ride into Archerville."

"What is compunction?"

"It means I feel guilty and ashamed for building up your hopes, then disappointing you."

She inhaled sharply. "No . . . I'd rather you stay . . . and we follow through with our original plan."

"To marry? After I deceived you?"

She handed the coffee to him and slipped into the chair beside him. "I'm sure I have disappointed you."

Only that you are lovely. "You are exactly what God intended for me. God does not issue unfitting gifts."

His reply must have moved her, for her eyes moistened. "What sweet words. I must admit I had my doubts until you read from the Bible, but now I am sure we should marry as God put into both of our hearts—unless you have changed your mind."

He leaned forward in the rocking chair. "No, Ma'am. I came here to marry and help you, and that is what I still need to do."

She stared into the fire, and he turned his attention to the flames devouring a cow chip. Silence invaded the empty space between them.

"The preacher is expecting us day after tomorrow," Lena said quietly.

"I'll be ready."

Silence once again reigned around them.

"Caleb and Simon want to know what to call you," she finally said.

Gabe had pondered this ever since he boarded the train in Philadelphia. "I believe for now, I'd like them to call me Gabe. When and if they ever feel comfortable, they can call me something more endearing."

"Like Pa or Papa," she finished for him.

He smiled. "Yes. Our arrangement is not unusual, but I want Caleb and Simon to feel some sort of affection before choosing a fatherly title."

Again, Lena appeared moved as she brushed a tear from each cheek. "I'm pleased, Gabe."

He felt his heart lifting from his chest. "Now, I must seal our relationship properly." He slid to the front of the rocker and dropped to one knee in front of her. The effort caused him to take a deep breath. "Lena Walker, would you do me the honor of accepting my proposal of marriage? I promise to cherish you for as long as I live and to always consider Caleb and Simon as my sons." His heart softened as tears flowed more freely from her eyes. He prayed they were not shed in sadness, but in hope for a blessed future together. "I have much to learn, and I will always do my best."

Lena bit into her lower lip and smiled. "Yes, I will marry you."

5

$\mathcal{G}$abe slowly moved toward the barn, or rather the dugout, dreading the night before him. The thought gave a whole new perspective on cave dwellers. He carried a kerosene lantern in one hand and two quilts in the other, but the darkness didn't bother him, just the smell permeating the air.

"Why don't you let me make a pallet by the fire?" Lena had suggested just before he stepped out into the night. "I hate for you to sleep in the barn. The odor gags me, and I'm used to it."

"No. It simply wouldn't be appropriate. I refuse to cast any doubt upon your name. The barn will suit me until we're married."

Glancing up at a clear, star-studded night, he shoved away the unpleasantness of the sleeping arrangements by focusing on the various star formations. As a child, he'd studied them while he waited for his mother to come home. Usually he fell asleep before she stumbled in.

"Gabe," Lena called.

He turned to see her slight frame silhouetted in the doorway. The fire behind her filled his senses with a picturesque scene. An unexpected exhilaration raced up his spine. This woman would soon be his wife, and she'd been given the opportunity to negate the agreement. Maybe not all lovely women were the same. Maybe he'd been given another chance to make his life amount to something worthwhile.

"Gabe?" she called again. "No one will ever know you slept by the fire."

"I'll know," he replied, then waved. "Good night, Lena. Tomorrow I'll help the boys clean out the barn."

He whirled around, feeling a bit giddy. For one night, he could endure most anything. Then the smell violated his nostrils like a hot furnace. What manner of insects crawled in the hay? Would the animals bother him? It would be a long night.

❧

"All right, boys," Gabe said the following morning at breakfast. "We have a full day of work ahead of us, but I understand you have milk to deliver first."

"Yes, Sir," Caleb replied, reaching for a piece of cornbread.

"We share our milk with Mr. Shafer and his six children," Lena added. "He doesn't own a cow, and I promised his wife before she died that I would keep an eye on the children."

How commendable. "All right," Gabe said, turning back to the boys. "I'll go with you if your mother doesn't mind."

He glanced at Lena, whose pallor had turned ghastly white. "You might not want to go to the Shafers. Dagget is not the sociable type."

"Mama threw him off our land 'cause he got mad when she wouldn't marry him," Simon said. "He don't like us much, but the others are friendly."

"Simon," she uttered, her face reflecting the humiliation she must have felt. "Son, can't you ever leave well enough alone?" She stared into Gabe's face. "I feel sorry for his children since their mother died. The oldest girl, Amanda, has her hands full taking care of her brothers and sisters and dealing with her father. Caleb and Simon take the extra milk, but I don't ride along, and I don't think you would want to either."

Gabe had seen the surly type before; he'd go another day. "I'll take your advice and get started on the barn while they're gone."

Lena sighed. "I'll help until they get back. It's a nasty job." She gave the boys a stern look. "And it will never get this dirty again. Right, boys?"

"Yes, Ma'am," they chorused.

Gabe hadn't slept a wink last night, but he'd never admit it. Every time he moved, the broken ends of what little fresh hay he'd found jabbed his body like tiny needles. Before daybreak he'd nearly jumped through the roof when a rooster crowed his morning call right beside him. Then he'd discovered some sort of bites all over him. He didn't want to think what might have caused them. Although the manure smell curdled his stomach, the unaccustomed sounds of the animals—both inside and out—had also kept him awake. He'd have to ask the boys about the birds and animals in the area and how to recognize their calls. The possibility that the animals were predators flashed as a warning across his mind, not that he believed himself a fearful man, merely cautious.

In the morning light, he'd seen the structure housing the animals not only needed repairs but also existed in an overall sad state of disarray. How did they locate anything without designated areas set aside for tools, feed, harnesses, and such? This project would take more than one day, but he wouldn't be working on it tomorrow. That was his wedding day.

He glanced down at his newly purchased working clothes, thinking he should have obtained another set in Philadelphia. By tonight he'd be emitting the same stench as those animal droppings. With a shrug, Gabe headed outside, eager to begin his first day as a Nebraska farmer.

❧

Lena took extra pains to prepare a hearty meal the morning of her and Gabe's wedding day. She hadn't slept the night before due to the anxiety about the day swirling around in her head.

"I don't believe I've had such a delectable breakfast," Gabe said.

His clothes were wet. Surely he had not tried to wash them last night.

"Lena, your cooking certainly pleases the palate. Thank you. I apologize for not complimenting you sooner."

Simon eyed Gabe curiously. "How can a pallet please you? I'd rather sleep in my bed."

Lena turned her head to keep from laughing.

"Palate, p-a-l-a-t-e," Gabe said slowly, giving the boy his utmost attention. "It means your mother's food tastes good. A pallet on the floor is p-a-l-l-e-t. It's a common mistake, because the words sound the same but are spelled differently."

Simon shook his head. "Sure can stir up strange things in a person's head. Whoever came up with words should have thought about what he was doing."

Gabe smiled. "I believe you have a valid point." He turned to Lena. "Caleb said he and Simon haven't attended school since last spring." He scooped a forkful of eggs and bacon into his mouth, then bit into a hot piece of cornbread oozing with butter.

"The schoolteacher quit after the spring session, and Archerville hasn't been able to find another," Lena replied. "I try to teach them reading, writing, and some arithmetic, but they really need someone more educated than I. I know we were lucky to have a teacher when other farms farther out have nothing."

He reached for his mug of coffee. "I'd be honored to assist in Caleb and Simon's fundamental studies."

Lena recalled Gabe had been too tired to eat supper the night before after working all day in the barn. He'd barely made it through the Scripture reading before heading to bed. How would he find time to teach the boys?

"You're welcome to do whatever you can," she said.

"Perhaps in the evenings after our meal and before Scripture reading."

"Are you sure that won't be too much trouble?" Lena asked. "I'm thinking with you here, I should have more time to devote to their book learning."

Gabe rested his fork across his plate. "Their schooling is as important as food and shelter. I'll not neglect their education. The future of this country belongs to those who aspire to higher learning. How rewarding to someday see Caleb and Simon attending a fine university."

I'd never considered them going to college. Gabe is good for them. Thank You, Lord.

An hour later, alone in the house while the boys delivered milk and Gabe prepared for the ride into Archerville, Lena pondered the day ahead, her wedding day. She wiggled her fingers into a pair of ivory-colored gloves. At least they would hide her work-worn hands. She stared at her left hand and remembered not so long ago when her ring finger was encircled by a wedding band. Only when Gabe had informed her of his arrival date in Archerville had she removed it.

Mixed emotions still battled within her. Today she planned to marry a man she did not know or love. At least she knew James before they wed. A lacing of fear caused her to tremble. Although she believed God's hand was in this marriage, she still felt like a scared rabbit.

Smoothing her Sunday, cornflower blue dress, she examined her appearance in the small mirror above her dresser. She pulled on a few wispy curls around her face, then pinched her cheeks. Inside her pocket, she'd already placed a few mint leaves to chew before the ceremony so her breath would be sweet for her wedding kiss.

A slow blush crept up her neck and face, and a chill caused her to massage her arms. She felt sordid, as though remarrying meant she no longer valued her vows to James. But that wasn't true. He would have wanted her to remarry a good man. James had been so handsome—tall, darkly tanned, muscular, and he always made her laugh. An image of Gabe flashed across her mind: his fleshy stature, the wiry straw-colored hair, and his pale skin. How could she ever learn to love and respect him? He knew nothing about living on a farm, and she questioned if he knew anything about marriage.

Yesterday, with the boys, he'd cleaned out the entire barn and organized tools and equipment, which hadn't been done since before James's illness and not ever to the extent of Gabe's high standards. He'd planned on Friday, the day after their wedding, to build another milk stool and make roof repairs to the barn. The stool would have to wait, since lumber was too dear. Gabe had looked happy, satisfied with what he'd accomplished. She felt relieved about this part of him. Goodness knows what she'd have done if he'd been a lazy sort.

"We want to call Mr. Hunters, Gabe," Caleb had announced. "I'm not so sure he knows how to be a father. Why, Mama, I had to tell him what some of the tools were used for."

Oh, Lord, I know You are in this. Help me to be a good wife and not compare *Gabe to James. Hold onto my tongue and help me to be sweet-tempered.*

Lena heard the door to the soddy open. "Mama," Caleb called. "It's time to go."

6

*K*indly take the bride's right hand," the Reverend Jason Mercer instructed. He towered over Gabe as he cleared his throat and continued with the wedding ceremony. "Repeat after me."

Although he shook with thoughts of the future, Gabe repeated the vows word for word. "I, Gabriel Hunters, take thee, Lena Walker, to be my wedded wife, to have and to hold from this day forward, for better or for worse, for richer or for poorer, in sickness and in health, to love and to cherish, till death us do part, according to God's holy ordinance; and thereto I plight thee my troth." Nervousness tore at his whole heart and mind—to say nothing for what it was doing to his body. He stared into Lena's incredible green eyes and saw the same trepidation.

Poor lady, she'd said little on the ride here, and now her hand trembled like a fall leaf shaking loose from a mighty tree. How arduous this must be for her.

Standing alone in the church except for his soon-to-be family, the reverend, and a friend of Lena's, Nettie Franklin, Gabe appreciated that no one else gawked at them. He desperately needed solace.

"Repeat after me, Lena," the reverend said.

"I, Lena Walker, take thee, Gabriel Hunters, to be my wedded husband, to have and to hold from this day forward, for better or for worse, for richer or for poorer, in sickness and in health, to love and to cherish, till death do us part, according to God's holy ordinance; and thereto I plight thee my troth." Her voice quivered. Gabe held her hand firmly, understanding her fears for the day and tomorrow because he had just as many if not more. Only God could ease their uncertainty.

"Do you have a token of love?" Reverend Mercer asked.

"Yes, Sir," Gabe replied in a voice not his own. He reached into his jacket pocket and pulled out his mother's ring, a striking red ruby set in gold, not gaudy but dainty and elegant. It had been the only thing he'd kept of her possessions, because it once belonged to his great-grandmother.

As they joined their right hands, Gabe held his breath until he slipped the heirloom onto her left ring finger. *Thank You, Lord, for allowing Mother's ring to fit.* She'd left him something of value after all.

Behind Lena, Caleb and Simon stood solemn. No doubt Caleb, acting on behalf of the family, had misgivings about Gabe's qualifications as a provider. These first two days had been such a disappointment, and Gabe had to ask the boys about everything. He looked like a simpleton.

The two youngsters stared at him in a mixture of disbelief and confusion. From the looks of them—thick, mottled brown hair and wide, dark eyes—Lena's deceased husband must have been a dandy. Now, she had a man who held the same shape as a pot-bellied stove—painted white.

"By the power vested in me, I pronounce you Man and Wife. What God hath joined together, let no man put asunder." The kindly young reverend paused and smiled. "You may now kiss your bride."

I've never kissed a woman before. How am I supposed to do this? Should I have rehearsed or found a book?

Gabe stepped closer, his bulging midsection brushing against Lena's waist. He lightly grasped her thin shoulders and bent ever so slightly. She quivered with his touch, and he prayed it was not from aversion. Her lovely features settled on him in a most pleasing manner, reminding him of an angel depicted in a stain-glassed window at his church in Philadelphia. To him, Lena had given beauty its name. Maybe God had given him a woman he could trust after all.

"Thank you, Lena, for giving this lowly man your hand," he whispered.

Tears graced her eyes, and he seized the moment to offer a feathery kiss to her lips. "I am most honored."

The seal of their commitment, Gabe's first kiss, tasted warm and sweet with a hint of mint. Quite agreeable. In fact, he could easily grow accustomed to this endearment.

"Congratulations," Reverend Mercer said in a booming voice. Over the few years he'd served as clergy, the reverend must have repeated a thousand "amens," but none as meaningful as the one Gabe interpreted as a blessing upon this ceremony.

"Thank you," Lena said quietly to the reverend.

Nettie, a pleasant-looking young woman, reached out to hug Lena. "I'll be praying for you every day," she said.

The two women's eyes flooded with tears. "Don't make me cry. This is a happy occasion," Lena said, dabbing at her eyes.

"Yes, it is, and you deserve all the good things God can give," Nettie replied, offering a smile.

Gabe offered Nettie his hand in a gesture of friendship. "Thank you for witnessing the ceremony. I'm grateful."

"I'm sure you will be very happy," the reverend continued with a nod. For a young man, his hair had rapidly escaped its original seating. He grasped Gabe's hand. "I have a good feeling you will make a splendid husband and a fine father."

"I don't know about that, Reverend Mercer," Simon said with a deep sigh. "Mr. Gabe needs to learn some farmin' and how to ride a horse first."

Gabe glanced into the little boy's face, seriousness etched on his features. How should he respond when the boy spoke the truth?

Lena whirled around to face her youngest son. "Simon, you apologize this instant." She met Gabe's gaze. Her face had transformed from ashen to crimson in a matter of a few moments. "I am so sorry. I'll properly discipline him when we get home."

"No need," Gabe said as gently as possible. This was his family, and he needed to take control but not exhibit harsh or domineering ways. "I have a better idea, if you don't mind."

When Lena said nothing, he lowered to one knee and eyed Simon. "No one knows more than this man before you all the items I need to learn and experience, but you could have voiced your concerns in a more mannerly fashion. So, while you are feeding the animals this afternoon by yourself, Caleb will be teaching me the fine art of bridling, saddling, and riding a horse. When you're finished, you can offer any helpful advice."

Simon's eyes widened, and Caleb muffled a snicker. "Yes . . . Sir."

"Good." Gabe stood and caught a glint of admiration in Lena's eyes. "Is this suitable?" he asked her.

"Most definitely." Lena smiled, and his heart turned a flip.

Oh, Lord, help me to be worthy of this woman. If only she weren't so comely. Ignoring the misgivings pouring through his mind, Gabe offered her his arm. "Mrs. Hunters, may I escort you to our carriage? I will then take care of the monetary arrangements with the good reverend and drive you home, with your careful instructions of course." He shot a glance at Caleb and Simon, who thankfully chose to say nothing.

She linked her arm with his. Her touch exhilarated his spirit. *I'm a married man, and I have two sons!*

❧

Lena listened to the sounds of her son's laughter coming from the barn while she lowered the bucket into the well. She caught sight of the ruby ring, thinking once more how beautiful its brilliance and how out of place the ring looked on her weather-beaten hand. Gabe's mother must have been a highly educated and sophisticated woman.

"Mama," Caleb called from the barn.

She turned to see Gabe riding the mare toward her with no assistance. He sat erect in the saddle, and his hands held the reins firmly. Without his hat, the late afternoon sun over his shoulder picked up the pale blond of his hair, reminding her of ripe corn. *Gabe Hunters, I believe with a little physical work and the sun to darken your skin, you just might strike a fine pose.*

Immediately she detested her impetuous thoughts. The Bible clearly stated the measure of a man dwelled in his heart, not in his looks.

"How quickly you learn," she said, drawing up the water and setting the bucket aside.

"I believe my ability to progress is due to Caleb's excellent instructions," Gabe replied. He'd pulled the mare to a halt and talked to her while leaning from the saddle.

Crossing her arms, she laughed. "Mr. Hunters, you do catch on fast. Why you look like you were born in a saddle."

Gabe joined in her laughter. "We'll discuss my riding ability after I learn how to trot and gallop. Perhaps in time we could ride together."

"It's been a long while since I've enjoyed riding," she said wistfully. An image of her and James riding across the plains so many years ago flew across her mind.

He dismounted, a bit clumsily, but successfully. "You work too hard," he said, grasping the reins in one hand and picking up the bucket in the other.

"That's life on a farm," she said simply. His nearness served to remind her of the vows they'd shared earlier in the day. For a moment she'd forgotten, not really wanting to think about it all. Then she remembered the night and her wifely duties. . . . The unknown had always been frightening, and although farm life seemed insurmountable before, now she had a husband who knew less about toiling the land than her sons.

"I want to do all I can to make your land profitable."

His words sounded as though he'd read her thoughts.

"Thank you." She glanced again at her left hand. "My ring is far above anything I've ever owned," she murmured. "Is it a family heirloom?"

"My great-grandmother's passed to my mother." He smiled. "I'm glad you're pleased."

"I've never owned anything so fine."

"It reminds me of you and the thirty-first chapter of Proverbs. 'Who can find a virtuous woman? For her price is far above rubies.' "

Lena felt the tears spill swiftly over her cheeks. The precious gems flowing from Gabe's mouth came so natural. His words touched her heart with a special warmth and beauty of their own. *Must be from his books, and I can barely keep up with the boys' schoolwork.*

"Have I upset you?" he asked, his strawlike eyebrows knit together.

"No." She shook her head. How could she tell him, this stranger—her husband—all the fears, doubts, and questions racing through her mind about him and this ruse of a marriage?

She'd entered into this with only thoughts of herself. She'd wanted a farmhand and a model for her sons. Not once had she considered this person might have feelings and emotions. The very thought he might be sensitive with the potential of caring very deeply for a new family never had really occurred to her.

I am so selfish. Gabe doesn't deserve a woman like me. Rubies? Lena thought the verse about throwing pearls to swine best befit her.

"Lena," he whispered.

She knew her eyes held her turmoil when she should be happy this first afternoon of their marriage. Unbidden droplets of liquid pain coursed down her cheeks.

"I think it best if I continue to sleep in the barn."

"Why?" Had she hurt him so badly he could not bear being with her?

Gabe moistened his lips. She'd learned in the three short days they'd been together that he often did this before he spoke of important matters. "We do not know each other, and of utmost importance is for us to be friends." He cleared his throat. "Affection should be present before we live as man and wife, don't you think? And how else can we develop a fondness for each other unless we first appreciate our strengths and talents?"

Oh, Lord, is Gabe a saint or simply terribly wounded by my initial reaction to him?

⤜⤐

She detests me. My inadequacies have destroyed any hope of respect. Gabe wanted to place a hand on her shoulder, but he dared not see her recoil. Lena's tears moved him so deeply he feared if he didn't turn away, he too might weep.

All of his doubts about her beauty and possible unfaithfulness surfaced and drowned in his inward grief. He had spoiled what could have been great joy. In all of his grandiose ideas of learning to live on a farm and all it entailed, why had he fool-hardily thought he could experience the knowledge by reading books? Now, the theory burst in his face. As his mother always said, "Gabriel, you are an utter disappointment. I can't love anyone who is such a fool. Live your life in your books; see where it gets you. Nowhere, I tell you. Nowhere."

"I want what you want," Lena said, between sobs. "If this is how you believe our lives should begin, then so be it." She lifted her tear-glazed face. "Perhaps we should have corresponded more before your trip here."

Gabe felt his heart plummet. If they had written numerous letters, she would have detected his deception. "I'm sorry for allowing you to believe I knew about farming and living by the sweat of my brow. But I will learn—"

"I know you will," she interrupted, taking the bucket of water from his hand. She paused, staring at the water as though it offered the answers to the dilemma plaguing them.

"Do you want to leave?"

Gabe refused to answer, carefully forming his words. He took in a panoramic view of the farm—the work it needed, the work he didn't know how to do. He should give her and the boys an escape from the community's ridicule. They need not be the victims of his idiocy. Defeat wrapped a black hand around his heart and strangled the utterances he believed proper and fitting for the situation.

"No, Lena, I don't want to leave. I came here to start a new life, and I want to stay."

7

*L*ena marched down the front of Archerville's Gospel Church, where only four days earlier she and Gabe had spoken their vows. Nervousness had attacked her then, but not as much as the sense of every eye in the building studying her and Gabe now. What a sight they must present—Lena shivering like a new bride, her husband carrying his traveling hat with his wild hair and filled-up suit, and her barefoot sons pretending they weren't embarrassed by it all. To make matters worse, Riley O'Connor sat on the aisle seat midway down.

Oh, Lord, I'm so sorry, but I feel like the whole church is laughing at me. She glanced at her new husband and offered him a shaky smile. Gabe might not give the appearance of a Nebraska farmer, but he certainly had treated her and the boys well. Unless something changed, he was a giving man and anxious to learn about farming. But those resolves didn't help her face the forty people attending this Sunday morning service.

"Good morning," Amanda Shafer whispered. Unlike her father, Dagget, Amanda was a sweet, pretty sixteen-year-old who loved the Lord and took the best possible care—under the circumstances—of her brothers and sisters.

"Mornin'." Lena hooked her arm into Gabe's. "Amanda, this is my husband, Gabriel Hunters. Gabe, this is Amanda Shafer."

"A pleasure to make your acquaintance, Miss Shafer," Gabe said, his every word pronounced perfectly . . . and sounding foreign. "Or is it missus?"

"Miss," Amanda replied. "And these are my brothers and sisters."

After Amanda politely introduced her siblings, she added, "We're neighbors and see Caleb and Simon 'most every day."

"Amanda is a big help to her pa in raising these children," Lena hastily added, eyeing an empty pew two rows up from where they stood.

"Your father must be very proud of you. Is he here that I might introduce myself?"

Amanda's face flushed pink. "No, Pa is at home today."

He needs to be here with his family.

Reverend Mercer greeted Lena and Gabe as he made his way down to the front of the sod-bricked church. Thankful for the interruption, Lena urged her family to the empty bench near the front. At least there she wouldn't have to endure the stares from the rest of the congregation.

Lena attempted to concentrate on the sermon, but the topic caused her to cringe from the moment Reverend Mercer read from the Bible about God looking at a man's heart rather than his physical appearance. *All right, Lord. You shamed me, and I know You're right.* Sitting up straighter, she patted Gabe's arm and focused her gaze on Reverend Mercer, although her ears didn't take in another word.

At the close, Reverend Mercer stood before his small congregation and teetered back and forth on his heels. "I have an announcement to make. This past week I had the pleasure of marrying Lena Walker and Gabriel Hunters. Let's all take a moment to congratulate this fine couple. Mr. Hunters is from Philadelphia and welcomes the task of farming in our fine country." He motioned for Gabe and Lena to stand and face the people. Slapping on a smile, she nodded at the well-wishers and ignored the snickers. Caleb and Simon stared straight ahead at the door, and she wished she could do the same.

"Mr. and Mrs. Hunters, would you and the boys kindly join me in the back so each one of these fine people can greet you?"

Oh, no. Dagget may not be here, but Riley O'Connor is. Knowing that man's quick tongue, he's liable to say anything after I refused his improper advances. Sure glad I walloped him when I could. Instantly, Lena felt sorry for Gabe. He'd be caught like a snared rabbit, unsuspecting in the least of Riley's insults.

Gabe greeted each face with a smile. He appreciated the sincere welcomes from most of the people and their desire to be friends. But he also saw the wary expressions and mocking stares from a few. How well he knew the judgmental type, whether they lived in Archerville, Nebraska, or Philadelphia, Pennsylvania. If you didn't wear the clothes they wore, converse in their familiar words, or come from an acceptable family, then you were cast at the bottom of their list. He'd seen it too long and well recognized the characteristics.

Fortunately, he had an opportunity to prove himself capable and responsible to those who mattered—Lena and her sons. God valued him and had given him the distinction of being a part of this community. By His hand, he'd succeed.

"Good to have you here," a wrinkled elderly lady said after stating her name. She patted his hand and gave a toothless smile. Slivers of gray peeked beneath her bonnet. "Lena is a fine woman, strong and determined."

"Thank you, Ma'am. We'll be happy, I'm sure."

"Pure pleasure to meet you. Glad you're here," a balding man said. Dressed in a little better attire than most folks there, he introduced himself as Judge Hoover. "I'd like for you to meet my wife, Bertha." A round woman smiled prettily, but before Gabe could respond, the judge continued. "This is a growing town, and I praise God for each newcomer." He swung his arm around Reverend Mercer's shoulders and ushered him outside into the fall sunlight with his quiet wife behind him.

Then Gabe met the eyes of a tall, slender fellow who eyed him contemptuously. "Hunters, eh?" He kept both hands on a tattered hat in front of him. "Sure don't look like a farmer to me. Ya won't last here."

Remember, Sir, we are in God's house. Gabe had dealt with this type of person longer than he cared to remember. "Looks are often deceiving, as the reverend so eloquently established this morning," Gabe said. "The good Lord willing, I will succeed at my endeavors."

If the ill-mannered man could have spit in church, Gabe surmised he'd have done so. Furrowing his brow, the fellow turned his attention to Lena. Immediately, he became charming in every sense of the word.

"Lena." His words dripped with honey. "You look right pretty this morning." He smiled broadly, revealing a row of perfectly white teeth—not a common sight, and certainly an edge to any man wishing to impress a woman.

Gabe ran his tongue over his own teeth—fairly straight and not discolored from tobacco. *Have you forgotten she is my wife?*

Lena lifted her chin and glanced at the door. "Riley O'Connor, your horse is waiting for you."

"How soon before you get bored with this city feller?" he asked just loud enough for Gabe to hear. Leaning a little closer to the new Mrs. Hunters than Gabe deemed proper, Riley turned to Gabe and sneered. "She never minded my kisses. In fact she asked for more."

Lena lifted her hand as if she might strike him.

"It's all right, Lena," Gabe soothed, not once taking his gaze from Riley. He feared she was ready to unleash her temper, not that he wouldn't enjoy seeing this rude fellow with freshly slapped cheeks, but God didn't ordain this type of behavior and fighting as a means of settling disputes.

"Mr. O'Connor, I am currently overlooking your deficiency of manners, but when issues pertain to my wife, I thank you kindly to refrain from indecorous speech."

Riley issued him a snarl.

"In other words, Mr. O'Connor, Lena Hunters is a married woman and does not desire to hear your crude remarks." Gabe turned to Lena. "Is that a correct assumption, Dear?"

"Yes, it is," she replied and dismissed Riley in one seething glare. A young woman carrying a baby stood behind Riley. "Martha, your little girl is growing like a weed, and look at those sky-blue eyes. Can I hold her?"

Riley stumbled down the steps in a huff and headed straight to a horse tethered beyond the wagons.

Once the receiving line for Archerville's Gospel Church had diminished, Gabe expelled a long breath. He leaned down to Caleb and whispered, "How did I do?"

Caleb pressed his lips together in an obvious gesture to suppress his mirth. "You did right well. Judge Hoover shook your hand, which means he likes you, and he can be rather bad-tempered. And . . . you put Riley in his place."

"Thanks," Gabe replied. "I do believe I'm ready for the peace and quiet of our farm."

He glanced at Lena, whose face resembled a color somewhere between gray and flour white. *Did she and Mr. Riley O'Connor court before I came? Was his arrogance a result of being a jealous suitor?* Rolling the conversation with Riley around in his jumbled mind, Gabe could only dispel the despairing thoughts with a shiver.

"Shall we go home?" His question sounded weak.

"Please," she uttered, once again hooking her arm onto his.

Outside the sod church, Reverend Mercer lingered at the Shafer wagon while holding a little girl who hid her face in his jacket.

"Excellent sermon this morning," Gabe called to him.

The reverend turned and waved enthusiastically. "Thank you. Mighty glad to have you with us. See you next week?"

"We'll be here," Gabe assured him.

"Has someone invited you to dinner?" Lena asked the reverend. *Are you not wanting to be alone with me . . . because of Riley?*

"Yes, Ma'am."

Her shoulders relaxed. "We'd love to have you come next Sunday."

The reverend smiled and thanked her politely before handing the bashful child back to Amanda Shafer.

Seeming to ignore Gabe and Lena, Caleb and Simon chattered in the wagon, caught up in their own world of trapping animals and teasing each other.

"Are you displeased with me?" Gabe asked softly. He held both reins firmly as had been his instructions.

She gasped. "Oh, no." Shaking her head, she adjusted her sunbonnet. "I'm so sorry about what happened."

"You mean the saturated infant I was asked to hold?" He didn't want to upset her if she truly felt badly about Riley.

Her gaze flew to his, and she blinked back a tear.

Now, I've truly upset her.

"Riley O'Connor," she uttered, as though his name were a curse. "I'm so sorry for the things he said to you."

"To me? Ma'am, he insulted you."

She shrugged and stared up at the sky "He insulted both of us, Gabe. I want you to know that I never courted him. Not ever. I wouldn't allow him near me, which is probably why he was so mean today."

"You don't have to explain it to me—"

"But I want to! He asked me to marry him, and I refused. He's been like that ever since."

Another thought needled at Gabe. "Should I have challenged him outside? Did you expect me to engage him in a fistfight?"

"Goodness, no. You handled him much better than I could ever have."

When she sniffed, he yearned to extend consolation to her. "The situation is over and done. Perhaps he won't trouble you again now that we're married."

"I hope not." She forced a laugh. "I nearly blacked his eyes. Oh, I wanted to, Gabe."

Gabe laughed heartily. "I saw. I'll be sure to avoid making you angry."

And she joined him, laughing until the boys begged to know what was so funny.

8

*L*ena rocked gently in front of the fireplace, enjoying its familiar creaking like an old friend. She loved these moments: quiet, peaceful times while she tended to mending. The only sounds around her came from the mantle clock's steady rhythm and the comfortable rocker. Usually Gabe taught the boys their lessons during this time and then treated them all to a chapter in some magnificent book. Nightly he read from the Scriptures and led in prayer.

Tonight, the men in her family had hurried from supper to make sure the animals were all secure. The temperature outside had dropped considerably during the afternoon, and the wind whistled about their soddy like a demon seeking entrance. Snow clouds hovered over them all day, and she knew without a doubt that the sky planned to dump several inches of snow—possibly several feet—before morning.

Inserting her needle into Caleb's torn drawers, she worked quickly to patch the knees. He'd most likely need the clothing tonight. Fall had passed with no hint of Indian summer; suddenly the warm days of early September changed to a chilling cold in October and now November. The dropping temperatures alarmed her, and she prayed the winter would be easy. Usually the frigid weather waited to besiege them until at least December, with the coldest days landing in January and February.

Lena paused and stared into the crackling fire. A smile tugged at her lips. This past month as Mrs. Gabriel Hunters had been good and ofttimes humorous. Gabe was indeed a fine husband—maybe not exactly what she wanted or envisioned—but God knew best. Such a tenderhearted, compassionate man, but he had his unique moments. When he decided to complete a task, he refused to give in to the cold, time of day, mealtime, or lack of knowledge. Tenacious, he called it, but she knew better. Gabe had a stubborn streak as clear as she knew her name.

My, how she appreciated having her husband around. Praise God, Gabe hadn't mentioned the unfortunate incident with Riley again. Riley hadn't been back to church—for which Lena was grateful, especially given that hearing God's Word had done nothing to improve the man's disposition.

The sound of Gabe's hearty laughter and the giggles of her sons caressed her ears as if she'd been graced by the sweetest music ever sung this side of heaven.

"Mama, we're ready for a winter storm," Caleb said, once all three had made their way inside.

"I'm glad," she called from the rocking chair, smiling at her sons, then meeting a sparkle in Gabe's merry gaze. *He enjoys this work. Seems to thrive on it.*

"If you don't mind, Lena," he said, "we went over our arithmetic in the barn. So I'd like to work on our reading tonight."

"A story?" Simon asked. "When we're all done with our lessons?"

Gabe chuckled. "I imagine so, providing your reading expertise surpasses my expectations."

Caleb placed his coat on a peg by the door and turned to his younger brother. "That means we do well."

Simon crinkled his forehead. "I know what it means. I study my *vocaberry* words."

"Vocabulary," Caleb corrected. "The correct pronunciation of the English language is a declaration of our appreciation for education." He nodded at Gabe as though reciting before a schoolmaster.

Lena stifled a laugh. Caleb, who had not shown much interest in schooling before, had blossomed under Gabe's instructions. He actually looked forward to his schoolwork.

"I don't need to know how to say words as proper as you," Simon said between clenched teeth. "I'm just going to be president of the United States, and you're going to be a doctor."

"Both are worthy callings," Gabe said. "No point in brothers becoming adversaries. Neither profession is above the other or requires less expertise. Education is vital to any man's vocation."

"Even a farmer?" Caleb asked.

"Absolutely. A farmer needs to know how and when to till the soil, take care of the animals, how to make repairs, and a host of other necessities too numerous for me to mention."

Simon shrugged and sighed heavily. "Sounds like I will be tending to my lessons until I'm an old man."

"Precisely," Gabe replied and ruffled his hair. "We never stop learning; that's why God gave us eager minds. Now, gather your slate, so you can inscribe any words for which you do not comprehend the meaning while I read."

Thank You, Lord, for directing this man to my sons. I've never heard such wisdom.

"And what will you be reading this night, providing the boys master their work?" Lena asked, not wanting Gabe to see her enthusiasm at the prospect of another exciting tale.

Gabe thrust his hands behind his back and teetered on his heels. "I think a new book, *David Copperfield*, by Charles Dickens. I believe the boys will enjoy the tale of a young boy in England and his adventures. There is much to learn about life and England in this novel."

Lena caught his gaze and a faint shimmer of something she had not felt in years swept through her. *Lord, what a blessing if I learn to love this man.*

Gabe settled in beside her on a rag rug. He'd begun teaching the boys in this manner, stating they learned more when they shared eye contact. Obviously, he was right.

"Are you weary tonight?" he asked her quietly.

Her heart hammered. Why did Gabe ask her this? "No. Is there something that needs to be done?"

"Only my hair needs to be cut before church tomorrow. It reminds me of straw, and the longer it grows, the more unruly it becomes until I look like an overstuffed scarecrow."

She calmed her rapid pulse. *Oh my. I nearly had a fright.* They still remained as friends, with Gabe sleeping in the barn. For a moment, she wondered if he'd decided to claim his rights as her husband. "I'd be glad to. Perhaps I can help you since it wants to go its own way."

"I'd be much obliging," he replied. "I've never been able to comb my hair so it would lay smoothly."

Once Caleb and Simon finished their lessons and they all heard the first chapter of *David Copperfield*, the boys scurried off to bed amidst the rising howl of the wind outside.

"I'll bring in some more chips from the porch and a few corn cobs for the cookstove," Gabe said, reaching for his coat. "You know better than I do how much snow may fall, and I want to be prepared."

"Maybe a few inches, but most likely a few feet." Lena pressed her lips together. Snow always frightened her, more so than the other threats of nature. James had become ill in this kind of weather, then died of pneumonia. "I can cut your hair when you come back inside."

A short while later, she pulled a chair beside the fire, where Turnip rested with his face in his paws. Pulling her scissors from her apron pocket and securing a comb from the bedroom, she waited for Gabe to dump an armload of chips near the dog.

Once seated, he shook his head. "Only a miracle or losing all of my hair could help."

Lena laughed lightly. "I don't think you will go bald any time soon." She dragged a comb through his thick hair, all the while pondering its wildness and his wiry eyebrows. "Have you ever tried combing it in the direction it grows?"

"You mean straight up?"

She joined him in another laugh. "Not exactly, but do you mind if I try something?"

"Whatever you can do will be an improvement."

She touched his shoulders and felt him shudder. For certain, she hadn't been this close to him since he'd kissed her on their wedding day. "I'll do my best," she managed, remembering the shiver she'd felt with his gaze earlier. "Do you mind if I wet it a little?"

"Uh . . . well . . . certainly."

Odd, he's never been at a loss for words. Makes me wonder if something is happening between us. Lena shook her head. *Of course not, we've barely known each other a month.*

All the while she dampened Gabe's hair, she saw chill bumps rise on his neck. "I'm sorry this is cold. I used warm water."

"You're . . . you're fine," he said.

She glanced at his face—red, too red even for their position in front of the fire. *I can't stop now. What will he think?* Swallowing hard, she continued combing his hair, easing the coarse strands in the direction they wanted to go—straight back rather than to the side. The change amazed her. His face looked thinner, and his eyes seemed larger—like huge copper pennies.

"Have you not combed your hair back before? Why, it looks wonderful," she said. "I can trim it a little, but Gabe, you look positively dashing."

His face now resembled a summer's tomato. She hadn't meant to embarrass him, but he did look . . . well, striking. With a snip here and there, his hair rested evenly over his head. She couldn't help but run her fingers through the thick, blond mass. Instantly, she realized what she was doing and trembled. Whatever had she been thinking?

"Do . . . do you mind if I cut a bit of your eyebrows since they tend to stick up too?" she asked.

He shook his head and moistened his lips. *This is hard for both of us!*

Once completed, she excused herself long enough to fetch her handled mirror from her bedroom. "Just look, Gabe."

He took the mirror and their fingertips met—a gentle touch, but it seared her as though she'd stuck her hand in the midst of a hot flame.

Shakily placing the mirror in front of his face, he leaned closer. "You've worked wonders," he mumbled.

"No, I haven't. You have beautiful hair; it simply has a mind of its own."

He examined his image more closely, turning the mirror from side to side to catch every angle. "Even without a hat, it will not stick out like a porcupine."

She laughed and moved to face him. "Your hair looks good, and your face is pleasing too." *Now, why did I say that?*

"Uh, thank you, but I believe you've been isolated on this farm too long. It's affecting your judgment." He avoided her gaze, and she too felt terribly uncomfortable at her brash statements. "I think it's time I ventured to the barn."

Lena nodded, but another whistle of the wind alarmed her. "Gabe, the barn is simply too cold for you to sleep out there. Why, you'll freeze to death."

This time his ears reddened. "Nonsense. I will be snug and warm."

"I refuse for my husband to sleep in a barn when this soddy is where you belong."

He stood and strode across the room for his coat. "And I say, the barn suits me fine." He reached for the latch. "I have two warm quilts out there."

"Would you like a comforter?"

Gabe stared at her incredulously, and she grasped his interpretation in horror. "I mean a third blanket."

He hesitated. "If it will not inconvenience you."

On unsteady legs, Lena made her way to the blanket chest in her bedroom and brought him a thick new quilt. He thanked her and opened the door. An icy gust of wind hurled its fury at them.

"Please, Gabe, stay inside tonight."

"No, this is what I committed to do until we are ready to live as man and wife."

Your stubbornness will make you ill. She grabbed her coat and muffler. "Then I'm going with you."

9

ost certainly not!" Gabe replied, a little louder than he
intended.

"If you insist upon freezing to death, I will most certainly join you," Lena replied, shrugging into her coat.

Completely frustrated, Gabe toyed with the proper words to convince her of her absurdity. He'd tried so hard to refrain from using
the vocabulary that confused those around him, but his mind spun
with the terms familiar to him.

"See, you cannot even argue against me." She swung her muffler
around her neck and face.

"What must I do to convince you of this foolishness?" he asked
with an exasperated sigh.

"Be sensible and sleep inside by the fire."

I'll agree until you fall asleep. "All right. I concede to your pleas,
but I must get my quilts from the barn."

"If you aren't back in ten minutes, I'm coming out there."

Gabe nodded, speechless. He knew Lena meant every word. He
lifted the chain deep inside his overalls pocket holding his pocket
watch. From what he'd seen of his wife with Caleb and Simon, he
dared not proceed a moment past her ultimatum.

Odd, he used to have to tug on that chain to retrieve his pocket
watch. Glancing at the small clock on the fireplace mantle, he double-
checked the time.

"I'll be waiting," she said, folding her hands at her waist.

He'd seen that menacing look on her face before. The lightning
stare didn't occur often, but he understood the flash occurred before
the thunder. Truth of the matter was, he enjoyed Lena's feisty mo-

539

ments. She'd told him right from the start about her temper, but he'd yet to see it vex him. The few times she lashed out at the boys, they needed an upper hand.

The frigid air nearly took his breath away—a raw-bone cold that sought to solidify his blood. Gabe buttoned his coat tighter around him. Used to be the outer garment didn't fasten. Another oddity.

Loyal Turnip braved the cold with him. "Thanks," he said to the dog. "I believe we men need to form lasting bonds." Moments later he returned with his quilts, after giving himself enough time to check on the livestock.

Once he glanced at the roaring fire, he saw she'd made a soft pallet before the burning embers. All those less than comfortable nights in the barn plodded across his mind. The smells there were still offensive, but he'd grown accustomed to them, and the sounds of animals— both inside and out—no longer jolted him from his sleep. With the cold came the likelihood of fewer insect bites.

Then he saw Lena. She'd removed her outer garments, but she'd been busy.

"What are you doing?" he asked at the sight of her constructing a second pallet beside his.

"I'm staying here beside you until you go to sleep," she replied, not once looking his way. "Gabe, you're a determined man, and as soon as you hear my even breathing in the next room, you'll be out the door and to the barn. Won't happen if I'm here. I sleep like a cat."

Have I met my match? We'll see who falls asleep first.

"And why are you so insistent about my sleeping arrangements?" He chuckled.

She wrapped her shawl about her shoulders. "The boys' father stepped out into a blizzard and caught pneumonia. Before two months passed, he'd died."

Gabe frowned. "I'm sorry, Lena, but I'm overly healthy. Just take a look at my portly size."

"If you haven't noticed, you're losing weight." Her features softened. "I don't want to lose another husband."

With elegant grace, Lena slowly descended to the floor, sitting on the rag rug where he'd taught the boys their lessons. She pulled her knees to her chest and wrapped her arms around the faded blue dress she wore every day but Sunday. An intense desire to draw her to him and kiss her soundly inched across his mind—just as it had earlier when she'd touched him. He couldn't have this. Gabe Hunters had made a commitment. He'd feign sleep, then creep to the barn.

"Shall we talk?" he asked. "I'm not ready to retire."

"I'd like that," she replied quietly. "Is there anything you need? The pillow is nice and soft."

"No, I'm fairly comfortable, thank you."

Gabe studied her, this enigma before him. This puzzling, confusing, perplexing woman who bore his name. So unlike his mother, Lena's spirit heightened with compassion and tenderness, even when angered. He didn't want to learn to love her, not really. A part of him didn't trust or rather refused to trust a woman as lovely as Lena Hunters. But . . . in quiet moments like these, he allowed himself to dream of this genteel woman loving him.

"You are an excellent teacher for the boys," she said, resting her chin on her knees. "They are learning so much."

He smiled, recalling their impish grins and eager minds. "They are teaching me as much if not more."

"We've been married a month," she said, glancing his way.

"A good month. An abundance of work has been done."

"Some days, I think you work too hard."

"Nonsense. I must compensate for all the skills I lack in farming."

She sighed, and her shoulders lifted slightly. "I'm impressed with what you've accomplished. You're making yourself into a fine farmer." With lowered lashes, she stared back at the fire. As though mesmerized by its brilliance, she blinked and took another deep breath.

She's exhausted. My poor Lena, and she's concerned about my welfare.

"You need your rest," he urged.

"I will when you fall asleep. Shall I read to you?"

He pondered her question. "I believe so, then I'll read to you."

She nodded and reached for the Bible. "What would you like to hear?"

"I don't have a preference. Why not your favorite passage?"

So close he could see a shimmer from her fire-warmed cheeks,

Gabe listened to Lena read the book of Ruth. No wonder she chose this accounting of such a godly woman. Ruth, like Lena, was a widow who put her faith and trust in the Almighty God. He delivered Ruth from her poverty and blessed her in the lineage of Jesus Christ. How wonderful if Gabe could be Lena's blessing.

He listened to every word, concentrating on the musical lilt of her voice. She was tiring; too many times she shifted and straightened to stay awake.

"No matter how many times I hear Ruth's story, I'm impressed with her devotion to Naomi," he said when she completed. *I shall not say a word about the weariness plaguing her eyes.* "Now, I will read to you. Perhaps a novel?"

"Not *David Copperfield*," she whispered, covering her mouth to stifle a yawn. "The boys will be jealous. More of the Bible sounds fine, perhaps the Psalms. They are so soothing at the end of a long day."

"Excellent choice. I'll start with Psalm 119." Gabe thumbed through the pages, noting she grew more tired as time progressed. " 'Blessed are the undefiled in the way, who walk in the law of the Lord. Blessed are they that keep his testimonies, and that seek him with the whole heart. . . .' "

By the time, Gabe reached verse sixty, Lena had drifted asleep, her head resting on his left shoulder, her body completely relaxed. Being careful not to disturb her, he wrapped his arm around her frail shoulders. She snuggled closer, bringing a contented smile to his lips. He'd won in more than one way this night. Although he needed to quietly slip out to the barn, right now he wanted to close his eyes and bask in the joy of having her next to his heart.

He delighted in her face flushed with the firelight and her lips turned up slightly as if she enjoyed some wonderful dream. Tendrils of black had escaped from the hair carefully pinned at the back of her head to frame her oval face, and the thought of seeing those long silky tresses drape down over her shoulders filled him with pleasure. Such a sweet, altruistic soul. He felt dizzy with the moment, painfully aware of her nearness. Surely his sensibilities existed in an ethereal realm.

Daring to lean his head against hers, Gabe fought the urge to kiss her forehead. For the first time in his life he felt protective. *Oh, Father, is it so wrong of me to pray this angel of a woman might someday love me? I've vowed not to care that deeply, but she is breaking my will—or is it You acting on my behalf?*

How much longer he sat with Lena snuggled against him, Gabe did not know, only that this timeless moment must certainly be a glimpse of heaven.

Slowly he began to nod. As much as Gabe resisted allowing the closeness between him and Lena to fade, he must put her to bed. With more ease than he anticipated, he gathered her lithe body in his arms and slowly rose to his feet.

Lena neither stirred nor did her breathing alter. *I thought you slept like a feline.* As she lay against his chest, she sighed. Gabe wanted to believe she felt content because of him. Glancing down, he saw her face looked as smooth as a young girl's. She must have been a beautiful child.

He couldn't help but pull her closer, cradling her like he'd seen mothers carry their babies. He prayed she wouldn't waken, not because of his vow to sleep in the dugout, but because he wanted to relish in the softness of this sweet woman for as long as possible.

Gabe moved slowly into the bedroom. He clutched his wife with one arm and pulled back the quilts with the other. Gingerly he laid her on the straw mattress. The thought of removing her shoes crossed his mind, but he feared waking her. Instead, he covered her completely, tucking the blankets around her chin. No point in Lena Hunters falling prey to an illness.

Gabe studied her face. Even in the midst of darkness, he could see the peacefulness on her delicate features. It took all of his might to turn and leave, knowing the bitter cold of the barn awaited him.

"James," Lena murmured in her sleep.

Gabe shot a glance over his shoulder.

"James," she repeated barely above a whisper. "I miss you so much when you're gone."

10

abe felt as though the bitter temperatures outside had taken roost in his soul. His reaction to Lena's honest emotions vexed him. How mindless of him to consider she might one day grow to care. He, Gabriel Hunters, the illegitimate son a of a woman who once owned Philadelphia's largest brothel, would never compare to a decent man like Lena's deceased husband. How foolish for him to attempt such an inconceivable feat. He should have remained in Philadelphia, living in solitude and managing the monetary accounts of others. There his books were his friends, and they neither demanded of him nor ridiculed him.

Defeated before he even stepped foot on Nebraska soil, Gabe determined it best to return to the life he'd left behind. He could shelter himself from the cold, from people, and from the elements, and live out his days in peace.

Is that really what you want?

Shivering, Gabe ignored the inner voice.

Do you remember how My people grumbled after I delivered them out of Egypt from Pharaoh's cruelty? Were they not afraid and ready to return to slavery when they couldn't see My plan? Do you want freedom or a life enslaved in bitterness and loneliness?

Gabe's deliberations only took a moment: Caleb, Simon, and yes, Lena, promised more liberty than a ledger with worrisome numbers. Straightening, he turned his gaze into the fire. He could make an impact on these people's lives and learn how to farm. He could contribute useful information and encourage them in their spiritual walk with the Lord. Allowing the resentment from the past to take over his resolve meant the evil forces in this world had won. God hadn't promised him this family's love; He'd simply instructed Gabe to follow Him to Nebraska.

Turnip tilted his shaggy head as if the dog understood Gabe's silent turmoil. His tail thumped against the clay floor, offering no advice, only the gift of loyalty.

"Come along with me," Gabe whispered. "You and I have more in common than what others may cogitate." Slipping into his coat, he silently grimaced at the thought of one more night on a straw mattress. But with renewed confidence, he rolled up the three quilts for the trek to the barn.

Silently he made his way to the door with Turnip right behind him. The latch lifted with a faint click.

"And where do you think you're going?" Lena quietly demanded.

Gabe's gaze flew in her direction and he stiffened. *Caught.* "To the barn to sleep," he replied firmly.

In the shadows, his dear wife lifted a shotgun—the one that normally hung over the door. "I said that I did not intend to bury another husband. I know how to use this."

Gabe buried his face into the quilts to keep from laughing aloud and waking the boys or angering his wife. His earlier worries and fears, especially about James, contrasted with her resolve to keep him from the barn now seemed incredibly funny. He knew Lena's gun wasn't loaded. "Well, Mrs. Hunters, if I mean that much to you, then I shall surely sleep by the fire with Turnip at my feet."

❧

The following morning, three feet of fluffy white snow banked against the dugout and house and halted any plans to attend church. Lena gazed out at the dazzling display of winter's paintbrush. Smiling like a child with the first glimpse of a winter treat, she thought how much the boys would treasure playing outside this afternoon. She might even steal a moment with them.

Gone was the howling wind and threat of a death-chilling blizzard. In its wake, a quiet calm of white blanketed the land. The pure innocence in the aftermath of the storm reminded her of giving birth.

She watched Gabe trudge from the barn to the soddy. What had possessed her last night to pull the shotgun on him? This temper of hers had to be put to rest. My goodness, what if he had refused?

Once Gabe had resigned himself to sleeping by the fire, she'd crawled back into bed. Soon his laughter roared from the ceiling. In the next breath, she'd joined him, apologizing and holding her sides at the same time. If the boys woke, she never knew it, or maybe they simply enjoyed hearing the sound of merriment.

He is a delightful man, Lord. Why he puts up with my disposition is beyond me.

Leaning her forehead on the frosty glass window, she reflected a moment on the differences between James and Gabe. She hoped her contemplations were not wrong and quickly scanned her memory of the Bible to see if God would be disappointed in her comparisons. No particular verse came to mind, so she allowed her musings to continue.

James had enjoyed teasing her, sometimes unmercifully. After last night's episode, she realized Gabe possessed a delightful sense of humor too.

James didn't take much to book learning. He claimed nothing equaled the education of living life and taking each day as it came. Gabe placed a high regard on books and the importance of learning. Lena thought both men were right, but if she allowed herself to be truthful, she wanted her sons to have the opportunity of seeking professions other than farming if they so desired.

James sometimes grew so preoccupied with the workings of the farm that he neglected her and the boys—not because he didn't care for them, but because his love took the form of providing his very best. Gabe put his new family right under God. She'd seen him stop his work to give Caleb, Simon, or herself his undivided attention.

James's deeply tanned skin and dark hair had turned the heads of many women. Gabe's light hair and pale complexion reminded her of an albino mare her father once owned. With that horse, one had to look a little closer to find the beauty—but oh, what a gentle spirit lived inside. Lena had asked for the mare, and her father had consented, stating she recognized the value of a kind heart.

She held her breath. Remembering the albino and her father's words jolted her senses. Was there much difference between the mare and Gabe? A tear trickled down her cheeks as she realized the beginnings of love nestled in her heart.

How strange she could see so much of Gabe in such a short time. James and Gabe were notably different—each with their own strengths and weaknesses—equally good men. Before last night, she'd believed she'd never love another like James. But this morning's reflections caused her to think otherwise.

Gabe had carried her to bed, covered her, clothes and all. Not many men were that honorable. She sighed deeply and whisked away the tears. Now she understood the wisdom in Gabe desiring them to feel affection for each other before they consummated their marriage.

The latch lifted, and Lena waited expectantly for him to enter. Her heart fluttered, and she didn't attempt to stop it.

"Ah, Lena," he greeted, stomping his feet before stepping inside. "The boys and I have been conversing about all of this snow, and we'd like to take a stroll. Would you care to join us?" A sparkle of something akin to mischievousness met her gaze.

"Splendid," she replied.

He turned to leave, then added, "Leave the shotgun inside unless you think there's a wild beast that might threaten us."

Her eyes widened, and she giggled. "Oh, I don't know, Gabe. A nice wolf's pelt sounds like just the right thing." She pulled on her boots, then grabbed her coat, mittens, and wool muffler while he waited.

"Naturally, you'd need ammunition to protect us." They shared a laugh. "I do plan to take the rifle," he added. "Beauty can be deceiving."

"Yes, sadly so," she replied, feeling utterly content.

"In what direction is the school?" he asked a few moments later, as the boys chased each other in the snow.

Lena pointed northwest and squinted at the sun's reflection on the snow. "About two miles from here. Do you want to see for yourself?"

He nodded slowly. "Indeed."

"I imagine the soddy is in bad shape, being left empty and all. It needed repairs before we lost the teacher."

"Any prospects?"

She shook her head. "I don't think so. Haven't heard anyway."

They trudged along, stepping in and out of drifts. Gabe walked beside her, helping her through the deep piles of snow.

"It's unfortunate no one desires the teaching position," he said.

"Oh, the Shafer girl would love to fulfill it until a suitable person is found, but Dagget refuses. Says he needs her at home. Truth is, he's right."

"Is she capable?"

"I believe so. Amanda has a quick mind and certainly knows how to handle children."

"Hmm," Gabe replied, lifting the rifle to his shoulder.

"This matter will take some thought. Perhaps I should pay a visit to Mr. Shafer in the morning when the boys deliver the milk."

"He'll run you off," Lena warned, her pulse quickening at the thought of how loathsome Dagget could be. "He's mean and selfish— almost as bad as me." She laughed, then sobered. "Really, Gabe, he is not a good father—works all of those children much too hard. I know our staple diet is cornbread and sorghum molasses, but he could butcher some meat for those children instead of selling his livestock to buy whiskey. Wouldn't take five minutes for you to see he doesn't care about them or their schooling."

Gabe lifted a brow. "But I don't give up easily, and if his daughter would make a fit teacher—"

"Good luck," Lena said. "He's as contrary as a sow with pigs— and just as dirty."

The crispness of the afternoon nipped at their breath and stung their cheeks, but Lena felt warm inside. For the first time in a long time, she felt safe . . . and content.

"Mama," Simon called.

She glanced in his direction and saw three white-tailed deer at the edge of a snow embankment. Like statues in the landscape, the deer suddenly leaped and bounded away—so graceful and effortless.

"You should have shot one, Gabe" Simon said. "Since Mama showed you how to use the rifle."

"Another day," Gabe replied. "Today is for pleasure, and I don't want to be killing an animal just for the sake of drawing blood. We have smoked venison at home."

Simon studied him curiously, then shrugged and took out after his brother.

"I'll take the boys hunting soon," Gabe said. "One at a time, though, so I can establish individual rapport. And if I haven't said it before, I appreciate your meticulous instructions on how to care for and use this rifle."

"You're welcome. I was amazed at your marksmanship after only a few tries." She smiled in his direction. "Of course, the Winchester is only as good as the one who fires it."

"Well, we shall see how skillful I am after a hunting expedition." Gabe chuckled. "Do we have elephants and lions out here? I sort of fancy myself as a hunter of ferocious beasts."

"Not likely, but we had a band of outlaws pass through here a few times."

He cringed, no doubt for her to see. "I'll take to bringing down a few geese or rabbits, if you can show me how to remove their outer coatings." She shook her head. "We *skin* animals, and we *pluck* feathers from birds."

"I'll be sure to remember that."

Lena gasped and clutched Gabe's shoulder. "Oh, no. Dear God, no."

11

*G*abe's attention flew to Caleb and Simon. They stood motionless, paralyzed by a pack of wolves slowly encircling them. He heard the growls, saw the bared teeth.

Lord, no books ever prepared me for this. Help me. Help me, I beg of You. A quick assessment of Lena revealed a colorless face.

Wordlessly, he took careful aim at a wolf closest to Simon. "Pray, Lena," he said, shielding any emotion. "God must deliver this bullet." Although tense, he focused on Lena's careful instructions from the past and all he'd read about the capabilities of the rifle.

"Don't move, boys," he called evenly. From what he'd read, running could prove disastrous. Holding his breath, he squeezed the trigger. A sharp crack splintered the air and startled the predators. One wolf howled and fell onto the snow, its blood staining the white ground.

"Steady," Gabe called to the boys.

Breathing a prayer of thanks and noting none of the animals had inched closer, he sited another one, fired, and missed. He swallowed hard, neither looking to the right nor to the left. Again the wolves took a few steps back, and he squeezed a third in hopes they would disperse. "Get out of here," he shouted.

Help me, Father. Lena couldn't bear losing Caleb or Simon—and neither could I.

He dug his right-hand fingers into his palm, then released them before lining up a wolf straying too close to Caleb. This time, the bullet sunk into the wolf's neck. The cries of the injured animal pierced the air. In the next instant, Gabe fired at another one and missed. The rest of the pack moved beyond the circle, then one broke and raced in the opposite direction.

"Go on, get!" Lena cried. "Leave us alone!"

"Move back slowly," Gabe said to the boys. "Keep your eyes on those wolves, and do not panic." He fired another shot.

The animals watched Caleb and Simon's retreat, then turned and chased after the other lone wolf, disappearing into the scenery. Gabe studied the two he'd shot to make sure he'd killed them. One moved, and he sent a bullet into its skull.

"Thank You, Lord," Lena uttered.

Gabe heard her soft weeping and longed to comfort her, but she needed to embrace her sons and feel their young bodies safe and secure.

Simon and Caleb didn't show the emotion Gabe felt, but youth had a way of bouncing back after adversity. Once Lena had hugged them until they complained, Gabe dropped to one knee and wrapped his arms around them both. Tears filled his eyes, and he didn't strive to disguise them.

"I ain't, I mean I'm not calling you Gabe anymore," Simon said. "You're my pa, now."

Joy beyond Gabe's comprehension filled his very soul. *I never thought I'd be good enough. Thank You.*

"Some good shooting," Caleb said, staring at the dead wolves. "I don't think I'll ever forget today for as long as I live."

Tears coursed down Lena's cheeks. Gabe caught her gaze and her whispered words of gratitude. "Praise God for you, Gabe Hunters, and I bless the day you made me your wife."

He stared speechless, a rarity for him. Finally, he choked back a lump in his throat. "I think we can visit the school-house another time," he said with a sniff. "I'd like to skin those animals—if one of you can tell me how—for new hats and mittens for you boys. Let's tend to it and move toward home. I'm in the mood for a snowball fight." He hoisted the rifle onto his shoulder and tossed a smile in Lena's direction.

Simon grabbed his free hand. "You might not know a lot of things,

Gabe. I mean, Pa. But you stopped them wolves from eating me, and the other things don't matter."

Gabe couldn't reply for the overwhelming emotion assaulting him. He'd gone countless years without shedding tears, but today he'd made up for lost time.

"Listen to me, boys, while it's this cold and those wolves are venturing close, you won't be delivering any milk without me along, and I don't want you wandering far from home," he said.

"Yes, Sir," Caleb said with a smile. "Do you suppose you might teach me how to shoot, Pa?"

⚬

Gabe slept by the fireplace that night. Once Simon cried out with a bad dream, and Lena crawled into bed with him. Gabe surmised she needed her arms around the boy as badly as Simon needed the affections of his mother.

Unable to sleep, Gabe rose early to milk and feed the animals. He felt a new confidence about his role in the family—a position he'd desperately craved but certainly hadn't wanted at the expense of yesterday's ordeal.

Today, he'd approach Dagget Shafer. Hopefully the man wasn't as formidable as the wolves.

"I don't have a good feeling about this," Lena said, as Gabe lifted the pail of milk into the wagon. "Dagget has no respect for anyone, including himself."

"A friend might redirect him. Does he claim to be a Christian man?"

"Gabe, he refused to attend his wife's funeral because it took him away from his farm." A torch flared in her eyes. "He treats those children horribly."

And he wanted you to marry him? "I'm pleased you decided to accept my proposal instead of his, even if you had to run him off with a pitchfork." He chuckled, knowing the teasing would ease her trepidation.

She lifted a brow. "And how did you know about that?"

Gabe leaned over the side of the wagon and smiled into the face of this woman, this woman who had touched his heart like no one had before. "I'm having difficulty remembering. Perhaps it was the unsigned notice I received in Philadelphia warning me about your temper, or possibly the animals during those nights I slept in the barn—"

"Or Caleb and Simon," she interrupted. Covering her mouth, she shook her head, no doubt attempting to stifle her glee.

"But I have the distinction of you persuading me to your manner of thinking with a shotgun," he whispered.

She sighed and tilted her head. "Will you ever forget what I did?"

Gabe climbed up on the wagon seat and laughed heartily. "I rather doubt it. It's my ammunition." Calling for the boys to board, he picked up the reins and urged the horses on. "We'll return shortly, Lena, most likely a little better than an hour since I have business with Mr. Shafer."

"Do you have the rifle?" she asked as they pulled away.

"Yes, Ma'am. Danger won't find me unaware." At least he hoped not.

Gabe drove the team, a task he'd come to enjoy, while Simon chatted on about everything. Caleb, on the other hand, merely watched the landscape.

"You're quiet this morning," Gabe said. "Is a matter perplexing you?"

"I'm praying," the boy replied, picking at a worn spot on his trousers.

"Anything particular?"

He shrugged. "I don't want you to die like my pa. You didn't fit in so good in the beginning, but you do now."

Gabe realized the boy spoke from his heart. "A man doesn't choose what day God calls him home, but I have no intentions of doing anything foolish to quicken the process."

"I know that, but asking God to watch over you seems fitting to me."

"And I thank you. Life's been difficult since your father died."

"Yes, Sir." Caleb stared at the snow before them.

"Taking on the role as head of a household can be taxing."

"Yes, Sir."

Do I dare force his feelings out, Lord? Poor Caleb looks so miserable. "I'm sensing you didn't weep at the funeral."

A muscle twitched in Caleb's cheek, and his lips quivered.

Gabe continued. "My assumption is you knew your mother needed you, and so you pushed your grief aside."

Long moments passed with Simon's incessant talking to absolutely no one. A solitary tear slipped from Caleb's eye.

"Would you like to grieve the loss of your father now?" Gabe whispered.

Caleb nodded, his face so filled with sorrow that he threatened to burst. Gabe pulled the reins in on the horses and brought them to a stop.

"What's the matter?" Simon asked.

"Hush, Simon," Gabe chided gently. He turned to the older boy and enveloped him in his arms.

Caleb's tears began quietly, then proceeded to heavy sobs as his body heaved with the agony wrenching at his heart. *What do I say?* When God did not give him any words, Gabe remained silent.

For several minutes he held the boy, allowing him to spill out every stifled tear he'd ever swallowed. Gabe knew the healing power of physical grief; he'd been privy to it a precious few times when only God could comfort him. When Caleb withdrew from the shelter of Gabe's chest, he seemed humiliated.

"Don't ever regret showing emotion," Gabe said. "A real man attempts to experience all the happiness and sorrow the world contains. Only then can God use him in His perfect plan."

The boy offered a grim smile. "After today, He'll be using me for something big."

Meeting his smile, Gabe gathered up the reins and urged the horses on. *Is this what a father does? Lord, I'm exhausted from yesterday and today . . . but my spirit is exhilarated.*

The Shafer property bordered Lena's about forty minutes away, but instead of a sod-bricked soddy, the family's dwelling was a dug-out—at least that's what it appeared to be. Many folks used this type of home, and Gabe understood the majority of homesteaders didn't have time to construct a soddy when they first arrived. Preparing the fields for crops took priority, and dugouts were quickly constructed for shelter.

The Shafer home and the two dugouts used for barns fell short of being called in shambles. All looked as if the roofs would cave in at any moment. A pig had climbed the snow-packed hill forming the home's roof. Gabe envisioned it falling through in the middle of a meal. Didn't sound like a good dinner guest to him. More pigs rooted up next to the house, leaving their droppings outside the door—a sharp contrast to the white landscape. Gabe had no tolerance for the lack of repairs, filth, or the ill-clad youngsters who met them.

"Mornin', Simon. Mornin', Caleb," a thin, pale boy said. His feet were bound with rags, and he didn't wear a coat.

"Mornin', Matthew," the boys chorused. One scratched his head, and the other spit, reminding Gabe of old men ready to sputter about the weather and their rheumatism.

"This is our new pa." Simon lifted the bucket of milk from the wagon.

Gabe climbed down and offered Matthew his hand. "Pleased to make your acquaintance. My name's Gabe Hunters."

Matthew didn't appear to know how to respond. He lightly grasped Gabe's hand and muttered something inaudible.

"Is your father available to speak with me?" Gabe asked, once again taking in the boy's scant clothing. "I'd like to introduce myself."

"He's with the pigs." Matthew pointed to a dugout nearby.

"Thank you." *I can follow the smell—even in the cold.* Gabe rounded the dugout. He heard a list of curses much like he used to hear from his mother's customers. Already he didn't care for Dagget Shafer.

"I told you to take care of this sow before breakfast, and it still ain't done," Dagget shouted. "Guess you need a beatin' to learn how to mind."

Echoes of yesterday assaulted Gabe, causing him to tremble with rage. "Mr. Shafer," he called out, forcing himself to sound congenial.

Another string of curses was followed by an "I don't have time to see callers." Dagget shuffled toward him, smelling like the animals he tended. "And who are you?"

Once again Gabe stuck out his hand. "Gabe Hunters. I'm your neighbor. Lena Walker's husband."

The man narrowed his brows and ignored Gabe's gesture of friendship. "Lena, ya say? She must have been looking for money, 'cause you don't look like a farmer to me."

And you don't possess any qualities resembling a decent human being. "I'm learning. I just thought it was about time I introduced myself."

"Why?"

"To be friendly, neighborly."

By this time, a little girl about three years old emerged from the shadows. She appeared clean from what he could tell, but her thin sweater and even thinner dress caused the child to shiver. In the shadows, a dark discoloration on her cheek indicated a bruise. Gabe didn't want to think how she might have been injured. The vile image of this man inflicting the blow brought back a myriad of his own beatings.

Bending, Gabe stared into the little girl's face. "Good morning," he said softly. She looked fearful and stepped back. "I'm Gabe Hunters."

The child recoiled as though he intended to harm her. She raced from the dugout, her sobs echoing behind her. Dagget broke into raucous laughter, further irritating Gabe.

"I'm sorry if I frightened your daughter," he said, still confused with what he'd witnessed.

"Aw, she thinks yer taking her to the Indians," Dagget said, between offensive guffaws.

"Why would she believe such a thing?"

Dagget wiped his face with a dirty coat sleeve. "I told her she'd best be ready 'cause I'd sold her to a man who'd trade her for blankets from the Indians."

He doesn't deserve any of these children. "What right do you have to tell a child such a terrible story?"

"It ain't no story. I'd do it in a minute. She ain't worth nothing, and it's none of your business no how."

Gabe stared into the haggard face. He seldom grew angry, but causing terror in a child incited a fury so great that it alarmed him.

"You're right. Your daughter is not my concern, but I'm wondering why you don't pick on someone who can meet you as an equal."

Dagget narrowed his brows. "Like you? I'd make manure out of you in less than five minutes."

"Probably in less time than you might think, but I will say this. If you want to get rid of that child and any of your others, just bring them to our home. We'll take care of them in a proper manner."

Gabe whirled around and marched back to the wagon. What an insufferable beast and an even poorer excuse of a human being. No wonder Lena had refused his marriage proposal. He glanced at the dugout with an earnest desire to gather up every one of those children and take them home. Dagget would no doubt come after them once he needed work hands. Gabe looked to the heavens for answers. The thought of another child suffering through the same ordeal as he'd known infuriated him.

Lord, I know I utilize more of Your time than appropriate, but I'm pleading with You to look after these children. I've only met two of them and heard about four more, but You have them sealed in Your heart.

He'd met some wonderful hardworking people here in Nebraska—good citizens who loved the Lord and demonstrated their devotion to Him and each other in everything they said and did. Then there were a choice few who wouldn't know how to model the Lord if their lives depended on it. Gabe refused to dwell on Dagget another minute. He and Riley O'Connor were a matched pair.

Caleb and Simon stood near the wagon, still talking to Matthew. "Let's go, boys," Gabe said. "We have plenty of matters to tend to at home."

"Don't you be coming around here no more," Dagget shouted with a string of curses. "Them boys can bring the milk without the likes of you sticking your nose into my business."

Gabe took a deep breath and faced Dagget. "My sons will no longer be delivering milk. I will bring it each day but Sunday. If you want the milk for your family, then you'll deal with me."

He joined Caleb on the wagon seat, while Simon climbed onto the back. He released a labored breath and turned the horses toward home.

"I've never seen you mad," Simon commented a few moments later.

"I've never been so infuriated," Gabe replied. "Dagget Shafer places no value on his gift of children or the importance of the example he gives to them."

"I heard what you said to him back there," Caleb said. "I thought he was going to tear into you."

Gabe smiled grimly. "One punch would have flattened me, but I didn't care."

"I'd have helped you," the older boy said firmly. "We'd have done fine together."

Gabe wrapped his arm around Caleb's shoulders. The bond he and Caleb had formed felt good. *A father's love for his children.* "Your mother would have disciplined us severely for fighting, I'm sure."

"Naw," Simon piped up. "She doesn't like the way Mr. Shafer treats his children either. We don't tell her the things he says to us in the mornings."

A new surge of anger bolted through Gabe's veins. "Well, he won't have the opportunity anymore, now will he?"

12

You're right, Gabe. It's snowing too hard to attend church tonight," Lena said with a disappointed sigh. Already at midday, she could barely see through the window for the driving snow. "I'd looked forward to driving into Archerville for the Christmas Eve services."

"We can conduct our own," Gabe replied with a reassuring smile. "It won't be the same for you, because I know how you enjoy visiting with the other members, hearing the sermon, and singing, but we'll honor the Lord's birth just the same."

"Oh, I know you're right, and you've looked forward to tonight too," she said. "I've noticed how you enjoy the minister's company." She tilted her head. "Seems like Christmas Eve should be spent with others, but we'll make do just fine."

"Of course we will. I'd like to involve the boys in our own little service, and I do have something for each of you."

"You do?" *When did he purchase gifts?* The occasions they'd ridden into Archerville for supplies, she'd been with him the entire time.

He offered a wry grin. "I purchased gifts in Philadelphia before boarding the train there."

"Mine are very small," she said, "and not fancy."

Gabe reached for her hand—an infrequent action for him. "You, Caleb, and Simon are my Christmas treasures. With you, I am the wealthiest man alive."

His words moved her to tears, for she knew without a doubt he meant every word. Although no mention of love had crossed their lips, she felt it growing as each day passed.

"Gabe, I have never met a man with such a giving spirit. I feel as though you know our needs before we speak them."

His gaze met hers, sealing those words she wanted to say but couldn't—not until he spoke them first. "Next to God, my family is my life."

Oh, my dear Gabe. I never dreamed I could learn to love you, but you have made it easy.

That night after a hearty supper of ham, turnips, white-flour biscuits—which were a rare treat—and a pie made from dried pumpkins, they gathered around the fireplace to hear the Christmas story. Pushing back the rocker, all four sat on the rag rug. Caleb and Simon read from Luke, and Lena led in singing Christmas carols. Outside the wind whistled as it often did during snowstorms, but somehow it didn't sound threatening as the story of Jesus' birth unfolded before them.

"I have an idea," Gabe said, "one I think you'll enjoy. Caleb, I want you to pretend you are a shepherd boy. You've heard the angel's proclamation of Jesus' birth and are hurrying with the other shepherds to see the baby. Unfortunately, you must assist an aging shepherd who has difficulty walking. All the others leave you behind."

Caleb stared into the fire for a moment. He nibbled on his lip, then turned to Gabe. "Knowing me, I'd feel sad the other shepherds would see the baby Jesus before me."

"Only sad?" Gabe asked.

"Well, probably a little angry." Caleb glanced at his younger brother. "Sometimes when I have to wait for Simon to tag along with me, I get mad. He can't help being slow, like the old shepherd. Maybe I could talk to the old man so the walk would go faster."

"Very good." Gabe patted Caleb on the shoulder. "How do you think the old shepherd felt when the younger one had to help him walk to Bethlehem?"

Caleb brought his finger to his lip, seemingly concentrating on Gabe's question. "He might remember when he was young and didn't have to lag behind. I think he'd feel badly for the shepherd boy too."

"What would the two discuss along the way?"

"The angel's message?" Caleb asked without hesitation.

"Probably so," Gabe said.

Caleb took a deep breath. "And maybe how they all had been frightened when the angels appeared in the sky."

Lena listened in awe at the way Gabe taught the boys without them ever realizing it. *Caleb's always so serious. I wish he'd learn how to enjoy life before he's an old man.*

"And you, Simon?" Gabe continued. "What if you were the young shepherd boy?"

"Since the angels came at night, I might be a little afraid of wild animals."

"Much like the day with the wolves?" Gabe asked.

Simon's face grew serious. Nightmares had plagued his little mind since the incident. Many nights his cries awakened them all. "Yes, Sir."

"Don't you think if God cared enough for the world to send His Son as a baby that He might be watching out for all frightened boys?"

Simon gave Gabe his attention. "I think so. Do you think God cares about my bad dreams?"

Gabe ruffled Simon's hair. "I'm sure He does." He looked at each member of his family. Love clearly glowed from his gaze. "We all need to pray for Simon's nightmares until God stops them."

"I will," Caleb responded. "Those wolves were scary."

"Bless you, Son. We all need to pray for each other, in good times and bad." The room grew quiet, then Gabe spoke again, his tone lighter. "And now I have a gift for you."

The boys' eyes widened.

Gabe rose from the floor and walked to his trunk where he stored his books. The fire crackled, and Turnip rose on his haunches, his ears erect. "Easy, Boy. It's just the wind searching for a hole to get inside." Gabe retrieved a leather pouch and brought it back to the fire.

"You really did purchase these before you left Philadelphia?" Lena asked. "Why, you didn't even know us."

Gabe smiled, warming her heart. "I believed the future held something wonderful . . . and it did." He pulled out a small brown paper parcel. "This is for you, Simon."

The young boy grinned at his mother, then eagerly took the package. Inside, two carved wooden horses with soldiers mounted atop poised ready for a little boy to play with them.

"Thank you," he breathed, turning the toys over and over in his palm. A broad smile spread from ear to ear.

"And you, Caleb," Gabe said, handing him another parcel.

Lena watched her elder son slowly untie the string wrapped around his gift.

"A compass," Caleb whispered, moistening his lips. He peered up at Gabe with an appreciative gaze. "I will take good care of it always. I promise."

Gabe nodded. "I know you will. I know both of you take excellent care of your possessions." He turned to Lena. "And now for you." He strode over to the chest and pulled out a much larger package and handed it to her.

Oh, my. Has Gabe spent his money on something extravagant for me? It's large too. He gingerly placed the gift in her lap. "Open it, please," he said.

Lena swallowed a lump in her throat and slowly unwrapped the package, savoring the thought of Gabe's generous spirit more so than what was inside the package. She gasped, and her fingers shook as she lifted a cream-colored woolen shawl for all to see. "It's beautiful," she uttered, staring into his face. Never had he looked so handsome, so beloved as tonight. Every day his unselfish devotion amazed her, and every day her love for him grew. "Thank you so much. I've never had a shawl so grand."

"You're welcome." He smiled. "There's more for you." Gabe took the shawl and placed it around her shoulders.

Lena turned her attention to the remaining items in the package. Neatly folded yard goods in colors of light green and a deeper green plaid felt crisp to the touch. "How perfect," she whispered, examining the fabric and relishing its newness.

"I believe there's an ample amount of calico for a dress and jacket," he said.

"Oh, yes." She blinked back the tears. What was it about this man that drove her to weep for joy?

Gabe rubbed his hands together. "On our next visit to Archerville, I'd like to purchase the necessary items to make all of you new coats. And I believe new shoes and mufflers are also in order."

This time Lena did cry. She hadn't known where the money would come from to purchase the needed clothing for the boys. They grew so fast, and Caleb tended to wear out his clothes before Simon had an opportunity to wear them. "Oh, Gabe, you spent too much. Thank you, thank you ever so."

He lightly brushed his fingers over her hand. "I have a little put aside for our needs."

If I could only give to him what he's given to me and our sons. He loved her and the boys, of this she felt certain.

Lena hurried to the bedroom to fetch her own small packages. She'd saved for Christmas since last summer. For Caleb and Simon, she had bought peppermint sticks and had sewn them warm shirts. The ones they wore for everyday use were thin and had been patched many times. The boys thanked her and dutifully placed a kiss on her cheek.

She handed Gabe his package, believing he'd like it, but nervous nevertheless. Slowly he unwrapped the gift, and at first she feared he was displeased.

"Not a day passes I don't wish for a journal," he said, running his fingers over the leather cover. Still staring at it, he continued, "Humorous and serious bits of conversation, happenings I refuse to forget, something new I've learned, lessons our Lord has taught me . . ." He glanced up at her. "Memories are what keep us alive. Thank you, Lena. I'll treasure this always."

Her heart leaped to tell him those precious words, but she couldn't—not yet.

❧

"Stop it, Caleb!" Simon shouted as his face got thoroughly wiped with snow, courtesy of his older brother.

"What's the matter with a little snow?" Caleb asked, holding Simon down with one hand and reaching for another handful with the other.

"You know what I'm talking about." Simon sputtered and tried to punch him, but Caleb was faster and simply laughed. He coated Simon's face with the cold snow.

"Tell me," Caleb taunted.

"Pa," Simon hollered. "Caleb keeps hitting me in the face with snow that the cow did her business in."

Gabe groaned. *What would those two do next?* "Caleb, leave your little brother alone."

"Do you want to hear what he did to me this morning?" Caleb protested.

Not really, but I guess I will.

"He locked me in the outhouse for nearly an hour."

Gabe looked away to muffle his guffaw.

"You called me a runt," Simon retorted. "And took my quilt last night and wouldn't give it back."

"Boys, I have the perfect solution to this," Gabe said, wishing the boys could get along for one whole day without picking on each other. "Your mother is taking advantage of this cold weather by mending and such. The last I checked, she was preparing to darn socks—something each of you need to learn."

Simon stared at him incredulously. "That's woman's work!"

I feel a lesson coming on. "I believe your mother worked like a man before we married."

"That's right," Caleb said with an exasperated breath. "But since you've been here, Ma doesn't have to do that anymore."

Gabe lifted a brow. "Then show your gratitude. Inside, boys."

"Yes, Sir."

"Yes, Sir."

Caleb and Simon plodded to the soddy. Gabe grinned and turned his attention back to rearranging the tools inside the barn. He wondered what they'd think of next.

❧

Had four months really passed since Gabe arrived in Nebraska? The days flew by, each one blending into the next. He loved every moment of it, not once ever considering the natural demands of his family and farm as a hardship.

As had been his habit since the first morning, Gabe woke at the hint of dawn. He'd grown accustomed to sleeping on the tamped earthen floor by the fire, long since comprehending he had the warmest spot in the soddy, but this morning an eerie shriek of wind woke him. The howls carried a sense of foreboding, different than other bouts with high winds that ushered in heavy snowfall. Gabe's concerns mounted for the livestock. They had a goodly stock of supplies and provisions, but he feared losing any of the animals to the cold. When the temperatures had plummeted in the past, the dugout had provided sufficient protection to ensure the warmth of the horses, mule, and chickens. But the cattle in the fields could not huddle close to a warm fire.

After slipping his overalls overtop his trousers and pulling his suspenders up, Gabe quickly added chips to the fire. *Thankfully, we can keep the soddy warm.*

"You're up earlier than usual," Lena said quietly. "I'm afraid we're in for a bad storm." In the shadows her silhouette and soft voice comforted him. His love for her abounded in moments like these. The freshness of sleep on her lovely face tempted him to reveal his heart. Fear of her rejecting him always halted his confession. He believed she cared and often saw something akin to affection in those green eyes, but he could be mistaken.

"Winter winds are attacking us again," he said, making his way to the peg holding his outer garments. As he shrugged into his coat, he fretted over past snows. "Lena, how did you survive the winters alone? How did you deal with all of the work and responsibilities of this farm?"

"By God's grace," she answered. "When the wind tore around the soddy and snow banked against the door, or when in the heat of summer, tornadoes raged, I simply prayed." She walked across the room and took his muffler from his hands. Wrapping it around his neck, she smiled. "God's never failed me. Somehow I managed to make it through one perilous situation after another. Then He sent me you." Her last words were spoken barely above a whisper.

Gabe warmed to his toes. Was she conscious of what her sweetness did to him? The emotion bursting inside him sought to surface. He longed to take her into his arms and declare his love. *Oh, Lord, dare I?*

"Tonight, after Caleb and Simon are in bed, I'd like to discuss a matter with you." Gabe instantly regretted his choice of words. He sounded as though he wanted to propose a business transaction. "I mean, do you mind talking with me for awhile?"

"Is everything all right?" she asked, pulling her shawl around her shoulders.

"I believe so." He dipped his hands into each mitten. "It's not a topic you need to worry about, just a personal matter about which I wanted your opinion." He offered a smile and grasped the latch on the door. "Come along, Turnip. We have work to do. From the sound of the wind, I may be blown to Archerville."

She laughed lightly. "I'd come looking."

Would you, my love? "How far would you venture?"

"As far as Philadelphia, and if you weren't there, I'd look some more."

13

*O*utside, the biting cold and wind whipped around Gabe's body with a fury he'd never experienced. He fought to stand and instead fell twice to his knees. The very thought of Lena and the boys existing in this ominous weather filled him with dread. Surely God had watched over them.

Once the animals were fed and cared for, he gathered up the quarter pail of milk and trekked back to the house before dawn. Only one of the cows had not gone dry, and the others had been turned out to pasture when they'd stopped producing milk. He caught a glimpse of the winding smoke from the fireplace, and he knew his family welcomed him inside. As always, Lena would have coffee ready.

Although the faint light of morning tore across the sky, he couldn't study the clouds for the curtain of snow assaulting him from every direction. He'd studied clouds in his books and, together with Lena's teachings, had learned to read nature's map. This morning spelled blizzard, and already all he could see of the cabin was the fire twinkling through the window. Suddenly the wisp of smoke from the chimney vanished.

The Shafers would miss their ration of milk today, but he dared not risk losing his way in the snow. He'd missed bringing them milk before, and they had fared well. Obviously, this was a day to advance the boys in their lessons.

"Turnip," he called. Normally the dog came bounding. "Turnip." Gabe released a heavy sigh. He pondered looking for the animal. However, once he ventured out again into the blinding snow and ferocious wind, he abandoned his purpose, setting his sights on the beacon in the cabin window.

Turnip is probably in the house, lying by the fire all snuggly warm. Deserter.

Each step took his breath and cut at his face. He contemplated resting the pail on the snow and pulling the muffler tighter around his face but feared spilling the contents. If the blizzard raged on, they might need the milk.

"Gabe!" Lena called.

He glanced toward the cabin.

"Gabe!"

"Yes, I'm making progress," he replied, the wind stinging his throat. "I see the firelight in the window."

"I'm waiting for you."

The dearest words this side of heaven. He'd stumble through ten blizzards for that endearing sound. "Don't linger in the cold," he called to her. "You'll be ill."

"Not until you get here."

Stubborn woman, and he loved her for it.

Once he reached the front door, she opened it wide. A gust of wind sent it slamming so hard on the inner wall of the cabin that he feared the house would crumble. She stood covered from head to toe with the new coat, mittens, and muffler he'd purchased in Archerville. She reminded him of an Egyptian mummy he'd seen in a book.

"I should have given you a rope," she said, shaking the snow from her coat.

"To tie about my waist and to the house?"

She nodded. "Don't leave again without it. You could wander around for hours and freeze to death."

He chuckled. "I know you've expressed concern over that condition before." He hung his outer garments on the peg beside hers. The aroma of coffee mixed with frying cornmeal flapjacks filled his nostrils.

"Ready for coffee?" she asked, as if reading his thoughts.

"Absolutely." He walked to the fireplace and glanced around for the dog. "Isn't Turnip inside?"

She whirled around and stared at him. "No. He left with you."

Where is the dog? He shivered, both from the bitter cold and the prospect of Turnip caught in its grip. "I need to find him."

"Later, Gabe. You need to get out of those wet clothes." She hesitated. "You've lost so much weight I believe you could wear James's clothing. Let's take a look. We can deal with the dog after breakfast."

He followed her into the bedroom, feeling slightly uncomfortable with the unmade bed and the fresh scent of her lingering in every corner. If he were to wake up tomorrow and find himself blind, he'd live out his days with her face in his mind.

Lena pulled a trunk from beneath the rope bed and sorted through it. Gabe stood back, uncertain if he should invade her personal treasures.

"Here's a shirt and overalls," she said, handing him the carefully folded clothing. "I'm sure they will fit."

"Will this plague you or the boys? Seeing me in his attire?"

She shook her head. "He'd be pleased they'd come to good use, and so am I." She stepped from the small room and pulled a curtain separating the bedroom from the main room. "Do you mind if I let the boys sleep?"

"Let them," he replied, examining the shirt and overalls. He felt oddly disconcerted by the knowledge that they'd belonged to Lena's deceased husband. "Not much for them to do today with the blizzard." *And I need to find Turnip.*

Gabe donned the clothes and caught sight of himself in Lena's dresser mirror. *I look so different—not at all like the Gabriel Hunters who left Philadelphia. What happened to my portly body?*

In the midst of his second cup of coffee and a third flap-jack smothered in molasses, he looked up to see Caleb making his way through the blanket separating the boys' room from the fireplace and cookstove.

"Mornin'," he greeted through sleepy eyes. "Sounds like we have a blizzard. Strange, we haven't had one all winter."

"We do, Son," Gabe replied. "My first Nebraska blizzard, and it's everything this family has warned. We'll all stick close to the fire today; maybe do a little extra reading."

Caleb grinned. "Sounds good to me." Glancing about, he gave his mother a puzzled look. "Where's Simon and Turnip?"

Lena's face turned a ghastly shade of pale. She swallowed hard and called out. "Simon, are you using the chamber pot?"

No answer.

"I woke up, and he wasn't there," Caleb said softly. "He wouldn't have wandered outside, would he?"

Gabe rose and made his way to the boys' room. His coat. He prayed Simon's coat hung on the peg beside his pallet.

"Simon?" Lena called, her voice anxious . . . and scared.

"He's not here." Gabe hurried to the front door. He couldn't face Lena. First he'd lost Turnip, and now Simon had disappeared. "I'll find him," he said as he grabbed his winter garments. By the time he'd pulled on his mittens and wrapped the muffler around his face to bar the frigid cold, Lena had a rope.

"Tie one end around your waist and the other around one of the porch posts," she said shakily.

He couldn't avoid eye contact any longer. "I'll not disappoint you or Simon." Not waiting for her reply, he stepped out into the blizzard, praying harder than when he'd faced the wolves. At least then he could see his son and the face of danger. He felt his way to the right post anchoring the porch.

"Simon, where are you?" he called, but the wind sucked away his breath, and the words died in his throat. Securing the rope, he plodded toward the barn.

I've always had a keen sense of direction, but not even a compass could assist me now. Oh Lord, be my feet and lead me to Simon.

"Simon, Turnip," he tried calling again. The roar of the wind met his ears.

After what he believed was several minutes, he bumped into the well. He'd walked in the opposite direction! Making his way around it until he could grab the well handle, Gabe closed his eyes and turned in the direction of what he believed was the barn. Every second became a prayer. On he went, his feet feeling as though they were laden with weights. The way seemed endless, and ofttimes he fell.

"Pa." He strained to hear again. "Pa, I'm scared and cold."

Praise God. Simon must be in the barn. Guide me, Lord.

Gabe tried to speed his trek, but the elements slammed into him as though an invisible wall had been erected. "I'm coming, Simon. Have faith."

With his chest aching and each step an effort, Gabe at last touched the side of the dugout where he believed Simon awaited inside. "Simon, I'm by the barn wall."

Nothing. Not even the hint of sound indicating the boy rested safely inside.

Gabe repeated his words. *Keep him in Your arms. I beg of You.* Rounding the barn, he found the opening. A few moments later, he stepped inside and scanned the small area. A pair of arms seized him about the waist. Gabe wrapped his arms around Simon, wanting to shelter him forever from the cold and wind.

"You came," Simon said between sobs. "I thought I'd die here with Turnip and the animals."

Turnip's tale thumped against Gabe's leg. Never had the dog looked so good. "I heard you calling for me," Gabe said, carefully inspecting him from head to toe. Luckily, the boy had dressed warmly before leaving the cabin.

Simon shook his head. "I didn't call for you. I just waited and talked to God about being scared."

Thank You, Lord, for sending Your angels to minister to me and keep Simon safe. Joy raced through Gabe's veins, while he hugged the boy closer.

"You're the best pa ever," the boy said, clinging to Gabe's snow-covered body.

"We must give the credit to our Lord," Gabe replied, tucking Simon's muffler securely around his neck and face. "Oh, Simon, what made you decide to come looking for Turnip?"

"I didn't. I heard you get up early and wanted to help with the chores, but with the blizzard, I couldn't find the barn. Turnip guided me here, but you were already gone."

The dog nuzzled Gabe's leg, and he patted him. No doubt, God had used stranger-looking angels than a mangy dog.

"We need to head back. Your mother and brother are very worried. First, let's check on the animals and pray."

And they did, thanking God for taking care of Simon and sending His angels to help Gabe.

"Ready?" Gabe asked, dreading the walk ahead.

Simon nodded. "Don't let go of my hand, please."

"I'll do better than that. I'll carry you." Although Gabe wondered how he'd make it back with the extra load, he knew God hadn't brought him this far to desert him now. He'd follow the rope. Gathering up Simon, he whispered, "Keep your head down against the wind, and pray."

"Yes, Pa. I love you."

❧

Lena could wait no longer. Gabe had been gone an hour, with every minute taking a toll on her heart. She must do something.

"Caleb, I'm going out there. I'll follow the rope, so don't worry." Pulling on her heavy clothes, she ignored her son's protests.

"Then, I'm going with you," he said stubbornly, reaching for his coat.

"I won't lose two sons in this blizzard."

"And I won't lose my ma, pa, and brother either."

Bravery doesn't need to be so dangerous. "I want you to stay here, please."

Caleb stood before her dressed for the weather. "I'm going with you." He lifted the latch. "We'll both follow the rope."

Lena made her way to the post, but the rope was gone. She searched the other side of the porch. Nothing. She kneeled on her hands and knees, frantically searching for the loose end. She felt certain Gabe had secured his end to the right side. Caleb joined her. The wind stole her breath, but she refused to give up. The snow could have covered the rope in a matter of moments, but without it, Gabe would never find his way to the cabin. She prayed and wept—for Simon, Gabe, and the love she possessed for both of them.

Caleb tugged at her coat. She ignored him. He tugged harder and began to drag her back. "I found it," he shouted.

Lena wrapped her fingers around the frayed ends and clung to it as though she held the hand of God. She and Caleb managed to crawl back onto the porch and to the door. Securing the rope around the porch post had proved useless. She'd not let it go until she saw her family. *Help them, Father. Bring them back to me.*

"I'll stay out here and hold it," Caleb shouted above the wind.

"No, I'm stronger. Go back inside."

"I'm nearly twelve, Ma, and I'm staying."

He sounded so much like James, so much like Gabe—so much like a man. She didn't argue.

Lena's whole body grew numb with the cold. Every so often she stomped her feet and forced her body to move. Caleb followed her example. *Where are they?*

Then the rope moved. Perhaps the wind had grasped it and toyed with her mind. She felt another pull and grabbed Caleb's arm.

"They're coming! I can feel it." She laughed and cried at the same time, simply believing Gabe had Simon. After all, he'd said he'd bring back her son—their son.

The minutes dragged on before she caught sight of Gabe trudging through the snow, carrying Simon with Turnip beside them. For a moment, she feared her eyes might deceive her, but then Caleb called out to Gabe, and he answered. Tears froze on her cheeks.

Once the wind and snow lay outside and she saw Simon and Gabe were safe, Lena threw her arms around Gabe's snow-laden body and sobbed on his chest.

"Simon's fine," Gabe soothed. "He was in the barn with Turnip staying warm with the animals."

"I was afraid I'd lost you both. Oh, you dear, sweet man, I love you so."

14

he . . . she loves me? Surely I'm mistaken. She must mean Simon. Gabe pushed Lena's show of exuberance to the far corner of his heart. Later he'd contemplate those words when solitude embraced his mind and body.

A shiver rippled through Gabe's body, and he suddenly noticed that his teeth were chattering uncontrollably. Practical matters must be addressed first.

Gabe thought he'd be freezing till the day he crossed over the threshold from earth to heaven . . . and poor Simon. Even sitting by the fire and cocooned in a blanket, the boy still shivered.

A teasing thought passed through Gabe's mind. "When I was in Philadelphia, I read about this doctor who believes we all would be healthier if we took a bath every day rather than once a week."

Caleb and Simon's eyes widened in obvious disbelief.

"Might be a little cold to start that today, don't you think?" Gabe asked and caught an amused glance from Lena. "Although, if you want, I could bring in enough snow to melt for the tub."

"Not today," Simon replied. "I'd rather work on my lessons all day until it's dark."

Laughing, Lena kissed Simon's cheek. "Drink this," she said gently.

"What is it?" He stared at the cup of brown-colored liquid.

"Tea with honey. It will help you get warm on the inside."

Simon peered up at Gabe as though looking for his approval. "Yes, drink it. You'll be glad you did. I'm having plenty of coffee to warm me up. Our insides are cold, Son."

The boy nodded and reached through the blanket for the tea. Gabe smiled. Lena was right when she said Simon usually did the totally unexpected. He'd never offered to help with chores before. And to venture out on this horrendous day? No one in this household would ever doubt the presence of God. Gabe carefully recorded the story in his journal to read when the problems of life seemed overwhelming. After he'd told Lena about thinking he'd heard Simon's voice call out to him, she'd cried again.

Her endearing words when they entered the cabin still nestled deep in his heart. Had she really meant them, or was she simply filled with gratitude? Emotion often guided a woman's response to external stimuli, and he fully understood if she'd simply overreacted in her enthusiasm to find Simon safe. But he desperately wanted to believe otherwise.

She handed him another cup of coffee. "Are you doing all right?"

"Yes, thank you." Her very presence intoxicated him.

"Do you still want to talk to me about something tonight?"

Even more so. "If you're not exhausted."

She smiled and laid her hand on his shoulder. "I have a topic of my own, if you're not too tired."

Simply listening to your voice fills me with joy. "We will have a good evening together." Speaking more softly, he added, "You are an excellent wife, Lena. As I said on our wedding day, I'm honored."

She blushed, and her reaction surprised him. Clearly flustered, she rose and wrung her hands. "Ah, Caleb, would you like to get the Noah's Ark from the chest under my bed? I think Simon would enjoy playing with it."

"And when you're finished, I'll read to you," Gabe added. "I have a new book I believe you will enjoy."

"It's not about snow, is it?" Simon asked, holding his cup with both hands. "Or wolves?"

Gabe chuckled. "No, Son. The book is called *Moby Dick* by Herman Melville. The story is about a whale and a sea captain."

Simon grinned before taking a sip of tea. "I can hardly wait."

"Me too," Caleb echoed from the other room. "A real adventure. Might I read a bit of it aloud?"

"Most assuredly." In times like these, Gabe forgot the boys' pranks and mischievous ways and dwelled on his intense love for them and all they represented.

The day passed quickly with quiet activity. While Gabe read, Lena sewed by the fire. When evening shadows stole across the sky, she prepared corn in one of the thirty different ways she knew to use it. The challenge had become a joke to them, especially when they all grew tired of cornbread, mush, flapjacks, and molasses.

Lena possessed a radiance about her that he didn't quite under-stand; perhaps her glow came from the fact Simon had not frozen to death. These past four months had seen both lads in perilous circum-stances. Was this the way of raising children? He'd rather think not, but the logical side of him told him otherwise. No wonder parents' hair grew gray. He'd always attributed it to wisdom, but now he cred-ited the color difference to the hardships of parenting. In reflecting on his past, Gabe knew without a doubt that he wouldn't trade one moment with his family.

God, You have blessed me beyond my most secret thoughts. All I can say is thank You.

Once the boys were in bed, Lena tended to her sewing while Gabe wrote in his journal, recording every moment of the day.

I thank the Lord for His deliverance today, he concluded. *Now, I cannot let the words of my heart stay imprisoned any longer. I will tell Lena this evening of my love for her. To hold it back any longer would be to deny my very own existence.*

He closed the book and set it aside. Now that the words were in print, he must brave forward.

"Would you like another cup of coffee?" Lena asked.

He studied her cherished face as he mustered the courage to begin. "No, thank you."

She drew her rocker closer to his chair. "Are you plenty warm?"

"Yes, I'm content." His heart began to pound more furiously than drummers in a parade. "You mentioned your desire to speak with me about a matter."

She nodded and stared into the fire. Her cheeks flushed, kindling his curiosity.

"You're not becoming ill, are you?" He leaned up on his chair to view her more closely. The thought of touching her forehead crossed his mind.

"Oh, no. I'm perfectly fine," she hastily replied.

Easing back, he folded his hands across his once ample stomach. "Go ahead, I'm listening."

She rose and paced back and forth in front of the fire. "Do you remember what I told you this morning when you returned with Simon?"

She's full of regret. I surmised as much. "Yes, I do remember." With great effort, he stared up into her face.

Slowly, she removed her apron and laid it across the rocker. Inhaling deeply, she sat in front of him on the rug. "I meant every word," she whispered.

Gabe thought his heart had stopped.

She moistened her lips. "I've known for weeks, but I didn't want you to think of me as brash." Lowering her head, she picked at a loose tuft on the rug.

Have I heard correctly? Is this a dream? But when he glanced at the top of her head, he dared not lose his nerve. Gently he lifted her chin and smiled into those green pools he'd grown to cherish.

"And I have loved you for weeks, but I was uncertain of your response."

She looked innocent, fragile, her lovely features silhouetted by the fire, her pursed lips equally inviting. Gabe bent and kissed his wife. It was a soft kiss, a tender kiss, but a luxury that invited more . . . and more.

"I do love you, Lena," he whispered. "You are my life and my joy. I never dreamed I'd be so blessed."

She drew back from him. With a sweet smile, she pulled the pins from her raven-colored hair and allowed the long tresses to cascade down her back. Taking his hand, she said, "I believe it's time we became man and wife."

⁓

Lena woke and wiped the sleep from her eyes. Sometime during the night the winds had stopped. Gabe had risen in the wee hours of the morning and tried not to stir her, but she knew the instant he'd climbed out of bed. For two weeks now, they'd been true husband and wife, and she treasured their tender relationship.

"Go back to sleep," he'd whispered earlier. "The snowstorm is over, and I want to check on the cattle."

"I'll go with you," she said, unable to bear the thought of him leaving her side. She'd become unashamedly possessive.

He'd leaned over and kissed her. "No, my dear. I won't be long." For the first time in years, she felt loved and protected. Her eyes closed. How wonderful to love and be loved. Surely this would last for a hundred years.

Now, as morning graced the skies and the shades of rose and amber ushered in the dawn, Lena met the day with happiness and hope for the future. She had a husband who cherished and adored her—and considered her sons as his own. What more could she ever ask?

This morning he planned to ride over to the Shafers and make sure they had fared well during the storm. Most likely the snow held drifts in some places higher than the cabin. She and Gabe had already experienced the snow drifting to the top of their door, holding them captive within their home.

Lena sighed and listened to see if Caleb and Simon were up. She should go with Gabe. Dagget despised her husband, ridiculing him each morning when he brought milk. Gabe had asked him one day if he detested his presence so much, then why didn't he buy a cow. However today, the children wouldn't get any milk until the wagon could get through.

As she dressed, her thoughts drifted back to those first few weeks when Gabe had tried so hard to learn everything he could about the farm. He'd hammered his thumb, spilled a bucket of milk, spooked the horses while learning to drive the wagon, and nearly gotten sprayed by a skunk. The dear man did not give up, even when drenched by a downpour in the midst of patching the dugout roof.

She'd admired his courage and stamina. Every day a new adventure brought them closer—even the unpleasant and frightening challenges. There had been a time—and not so long ago—when she'd believed no man could ever take James's place. How wrong she'd been. God had indeed brought her the best.

❧

God had indeed brought Gabe the best. He treasured his family and their relationship. Two weeks ago, he and Lena had confessed their love for each other, and now he actually felt like a married man. Never had he dreamed his life might contain such fulfillment. Oh, there were disagreements here and there, and Simon would always be unpredictable, but to have his heart's desire fulfilled . . . well, he simply couldn't put a price on what it all meant to him. When Lena looked at him with her impish smile, he melted faster than the snow in spring.

This morning, he had a job to do. Neither the cold nor the snow could stop him from braving the elements to reach the Shafers. He worried about the Shafer children, especially when he noted the many times sour, old Dagget had been drinking by the time he arrived with milk. He'd seen the scurvy sores on the children's thin arms and faces, and Lena had sent dried fruit and vegetables to add more nutrition to their diet. Caleb and Simon had passed their old coats, mittens, mufflers, and hats on to them, but Gabe doubted if Dagget even noticed.

The Shafer children were mannerly, and Gabe had allowed Amanda to borrow a few books. She always thanked him, eager to report on what she'd read and often pointing out confusing words for his explanation. He appreciated her willingness to educate herself, especially in this part of the country where most women lived to bear children and work the farms. Amanda had done her best to school her brothers and sisters with a McGuffey Reader, but she didn't have any slates or chalk. Gabe found extra in his trunk so she could teach them to write and learn arithmetic.

Smoke curled above the dugout in the distance. He breathed a sigh of relief. He'd feared their home had caved in with the weight of the snow. An abundance of it had fallen in the last two weeks, so much he'd climbed onto the roof of his house and barn to clean them off.

The image of the little Shafer girl with her bruised face and obvious terror haunted him. Not once had he seen her since she ran from him, Dagget's repugnant laughter echoing through the barn.

Dismounting his horse, Gabe saw the door had more than three feet of snow banked against it. Not seeing a shovel, he used his gloved hands to scoop a path wide enough for the door to open. He knocked soundly. Amanda answered, her eyes red. A whimpering child could be heard in the background.

"Good morning, Mr. Hunters. I'm glad to see you are all right from the storm."

Something is wrong here. "I came by to see how you were fairing after the snowstorm. I apologize for not having milk, but the drifts are too high for the wagon. I believe the cow is about to go dry too."

Her round face, pale and rigid, looked distracted. "Thank you, but we are warm and have plenty of chips for the fire."

"And food?"

"We will manage. I appreciate you stopping by." She hesitated, then whispered, "I can't let you in, Mr. Hunters. Pa would thrash me for sure."

He smiled in hopes of easing her nervousness. "I understand, Amanda. Is—"

"Amanda, whata ya doing?" Dagget's slurred voice bellowed.

She glanced behind her. "It's Mr. Hunters."

"Shut the door!" A string of curses followed with how Dagget viewed his daughter and Gabe, certainly nothing complimentary.

"I'll not keep you," Gabe said to Amanda. "Let us know if we can be of assistance."

Amanda's eyes pooled as she slowly shut the door. Gabe offered another reassuring smile and ambled toward his horse.

"Wait," Amanda called from the doorway. "We do need help. Mary is awful sick—burning up with fever."

Gabe whirled around. "What have you given her?"

"I don't have anything but a little ginger tea, and I've applied a mustard plaster. Pa had me give her whiskey and a little molasses, said it would cut the cough and put her to sleep. Mr. Hunters, did I do the right thing? Ma always said spirits invited evil."

"Amanda, get in here now! I'll teach you to mind me."

Dagget had been drinking, that was obvious, but Gabe wasn't about to ride home and forget the little girl lying sick. He strode back to the door and entered the small dugout. It smelled rank from whiskey, vomit, and unkempt bodies.

The little girl stared up from a straw pallet with huge, cavernous eyes, the same child from the barn incident weeks before. She coughed, a deep ragged sound that rattled her chest. Her little body shook, and she barely had enough strength to cry. Nearby, Dagget sat sprawled in a chair with a bottle of liquor in one hand and the other clamped around Matthew's wrist. In the shadows, three boys ranging from about Simon's age to probably fifteen sat motionless.

Gabe clenched his fists and fought the rage tearing through him. He swallowed his anger, realizing a fight with Dagget would solve nothing. "A good father would put down that bottle and see what he could do about nursing this child."

Dagget lifted a brow. "She ain't none of yer business. So ya'd best be leaving before I find my shotgun."

"Not yet," Gabe said quietly, edging closer to view the child's pallor.

Dagget staggered to his feet and took a swallow from the bottle. Finding it empty, he threw it across the room. The pieces landed dangerously close to the boys huddled in a corner. "Git me my gun, Charles."

(15)

he older boy emerged from a corner, a strapping young man, tall and muscular. He glanced at his little sister suffering through another gut-wrenching cough, then at Amanda. "No, Pa. I'm not getting you the gun."

Dagget swung his arm wildly. He released Matthew and stood to stagger toward Charles. "Boy, you'll know this beatin' for a long time."

Lord, why are there such animals in this world? "You'll not harm him," Gabe said, surprising himself with his firmness.

"It's all right, Mr. Hunters," Charles said. "He's too drunk to do anything but talk, and we've all had enough. Truth be known, I could take him on, but I don't like the idea of fighting my own pa."

"Why you—"

Gabe grabbed Dagget's arm and shoved him back down onto the chair—the first time he'd ever touched a man in fury. "Stay put, because I intend to make sure this child is properly tended to."

"If only the doc didn't live so far away," Charles said, bending to feel Mary's forehead, while Amanda wiped her face with a damp cloth.

"It would take four days or more to get him," Gabe replied, thinking Dagget was angry enough without Charles adding more rebellion by leaving. "She needs attention now, and that's a rough journey for a grown man."

"No disrespect meant, but it's time I acted like a man and took better care of my brothers and sisters. Pa never acted like this when Ma was alive, and he treats Mary like a pitiful dog." Charles shook his head. "It's not her fault ma died giving birth to her, but Pa expects her to pay for it every day."

"Seems like she doesn't want to fight this sickness," Amanda added. "It's as though she's given up."

"I have to do something." Without another word, Charles reached for a thin coat on a peg beside the door. "I need to get help somewhere."

"Go to Lena. She has more tea and some herbs to nurse your little sister." Gabe began to pull off his own outer garments. "Here, take my coat. It's warmer. And my horse is already saddled."

Charles hesitated.

"Do take the coat and Mr. Hunters's horse," Amanda insisted. "You don't need to be ill too."

Reluctantly, Charles accepted the clothes. A handsome lad with light hair and strong features, he stole another glimpse at Mary. "Thank you, Mr. Hunters, and I apologize for not expressing my gratitude in the past for the milk."

"It's quite unnecessary," Gabe said. "Hurry along. The snow is deep, and it will take you a few hours to get there and back."

Nodding toward his father, Charles asked, "Do you want me to tie him up?"

Excellent idea. "No. I can handle Dagget just fine."

After he left, Gabe greeted the other children. They appeared a bit leery of their father, who only stared into the flames. He didn't bark any orders or curse. He simply sat.

Amanda made Mary as comfortable as possible, wrapping her in another blanket and moving her closer to the fire, while Gabe scooted Dagget's chair away from it.

Nearly three hours later, Lena and the boys arrived. Simon road on the horse, while the other three traveled on foot. Charles carried food, ginger for tea, and another potion of dried horseradish to brew for Mary. Lena and the boys carried dried elderberries, salt pork, a little milk, and a blanket.

"None of us wanted to wait at home when we might be of use here," Lena said. "The walk felt refreshing after being inside all day yesterday."

"I'm glad I didn't know you were trekking across the snow, but

I'm glad you're here." Gabe helped her remove her coat and kissed the tip of her nose—so natural a gesture, so easy now that she'd revealed her heart and accepted his love.

Lena's presence eased the heaviness threatening to overwhelm him. To him, anger had always been a characteristic of the weak, and a trait he'd refused to succumb to. The sins accompanying loss of control were vile. *I've never felt so angry. I don't know whether to apologize to Dagget or try to make him comprehend what he's doing to his family.*

Caleb and Simon urged the younger boys to head outside. Gabe surmised the Shafer children didn't share the luxury of free time very often, although their lack of proper clothing tugged at his conscience.

"Check on the hogs," Dagget bellowed. "And feed my mules."

Gabe said nothing for fear he'd strike the man. Every muscle in his body tensed, ready to shake him until what few teeth he had fell out.

He definitely did not feel like the model of a godly man.

"Why?" Dagget asked of Gabe a few moments later. "You bring milk 'most everyday. You're ready to fight me over—" He pointed to Mary.

"Can't you say her name?" Gabe asked, the ire swelling inside of him again. *Lord, I'm being self-righteous here. Dagget is wrong, but it's not right for me to condemn him.*

"She killed her ma." Bitterness edged Dagget's words.

Gabe glanced at the child. If she died, God would lift her into His arms in heaven. If Dagget died, what would be his fate? "God took your wife home and left you a gift. In fact, He left you with six treasures. Maybe it's time to cease your complaints about the children He's entrusted to you and start taking care of them before you lose them all."

"Easy for you to say," Dagget sneered.

Pain wrenched through Gabe's heart as he remembered his own childhood. "No, it's not easy for me to say. I understand little Mary's plight." Gabe stood and towered over Dagget. "Look at your daughter. She's not fighting the fever; she has nothing on the inside of her to want to live. Unless you give her a reason, she won't survive."

A bewildered expression spread over the man's face even in his drunken stupor. Gabe turned his attention back to Mary, disgusted at the drunken excuse of a man before him.

"Pray for me, Lena," he whispered. "I'm incensed with Dagget. I think I could tear him apart with my bare hands."

She lifted her gaze from Mary and touched his face. "You're a man who loves his family and doesn't understand why Dagget fails to see his blessings. I'll pray for you and Dagget." She studied Mary's face. "And this poor baby suffering here."

"If only Pa loved her," Amanda softly whispered. "Sometimes we hide her from him so he won't beat her."

"We won't let him hurt her ever again," Charles vowed. He took a deep breath. "I think I'll check on the animals."

Gabe stood. "I'll go with you. Staying inside is making me irritable."

~&~

Lena watched Gabe leave, her heart heavy with the sadness etching his features. She wanted to offer comfort, but the right words slipped her mind. Her childhood had been happy and full of wonderful memories, but she'd come to know something terrible had happened to Gabe as a child—something that weighed on him like a heavy yoke. Perhaps she should ask him about it when all of this was over.

She'd never heard Gabe raise his voice, and he really hadn't shouted at Dagget, but his anger had spilled over like a boiling pot. How well she understood the guilt of an uncontrollable temper. Each time she forgot her resolve to contain hers, a matter would irritate her, and her mouth acted before her Christianity set in.

Of course she understood giving it all to God would help, but Lena wanted to end it all on her own—to show God she could please Him. She hadn't been able to curb her unforeseen anger by herself yet. She glanced at Dagget. Drunk. Mean. Hurting those he loved, or should love.

I'm not like him. I'm a good mother and wife. I don't hurt anyone or use horrible language. I love my family, and they love me.

Lena unwillingly recalled the days following James's death when her heart had hardened against God and all those around her, even Caleb and Simon. She'd despised James for leaving her alone to raise two children and manage the farm. Her tears of grief had turned to hate for his abandonment. The turning point came when Caleb asked her why she didn't like him or Simon. Lena had cried and begged God and the boys' forgiveness. Since then, she'd managed her temper fairly well—but not to her satisfaction.

Obviously, Dagget felt the same way about Mary. Unfortunately, he hadn't recognized the poison brewing in his soul.

Lena pushed aside her disturbing thoughts. At present, Mary deserved all of her attention. She bent and kissed the little girl's feverish cheeks. *I'd take this child in a minute—all of them—and give them a proper home where they'd know the meaning of real love.*

"Do you think she will be all right?" Amanda's voice broke into quiet sobs. She sat on the other side of her sister and adjusted the quilt for what seemed like the hundredth time.

"Are you praying?" Lena asked quietly.

Amanda buried her face in her hands. "I don't know what to pray for. I've been Mary's mama since the day she was born, and I love her so very much. I even named her Mary Elizabeth after Ma, but Pa has made her life miserable. Perhaps she should be with Jesus and Mama. At least she'd be happy and loved."

Lena moved alongside the young woman and held her while she wept. "We all want what's best for Mary, and only God in His perfect wisdom knows the answers. He loves her more than we can imagine, and He knows our hearts."

"I want her to fight this and get well," Amanda said, lifting a tear-stained face. "I don't want to lose my little Mary." She turned to the child. "Please get well. I promise to take better care of you. None of us will let you be hurt again."

Lena cried with her. Children shouldn't ever have to suffer for adults' mistakes. "We must pray for God's healing. He can work miracles." Lena took a sideways glance at Dagget, who stared at them. In his slouched position with his chin resting on his chest, huge tears rolled down his face.

"Have I killed my little girl?" he groaned.

Lena recalled Gabe's earlier words. "She needs to hear you love her and want her to live."

Dagget curled his fingers into a ball and trembled. "Amanda," he said softly. "Do we have any coffee?"

"Yes, Pa."

"Would you mind getting me a mug full?"

Amanda tore herself from Lena and brought her father the coffee. Although steam lifted from the hot brew, he downed it quickly. All the while the tears washed over his dirty cheeks. He stared at Mary, wordless. Lena didn't know if his drunkenness had brought on the emotion or if he sincerely regretted the way he'd treated the child.

Mary's breath grew more ragged, and she cried out delirious in her half-conscious state. Lena tried to give her more tea, but the little girl couldn't swallow it.

"Oh, Jesus, please save this precious child," Lena whispered.

An instant later, Dagget scrambled to the floor beside his youngest daughter. He pulled her hand from beneath the quilt and held it firmly. "Mary, I want you to live. I know I've treated you bad, but if you'll give me a chance—if God will give me a chance—I'll make it up to you and your brothers and sisters."

The door squeaked open, and Gabe walked in with Charles. The youth had aged years in a matter of hours. Weariness and a hint of sorrow settled on his features. Gabe's gaze flew to Lena, questioning, wondering, and fearful.

"Charles wants to ride for the doctor, but I've explained the trek is too dangerous with all this snow. As long as there's sunlight, he can find his way, but on a cloudy day, he'll get lost."

Lena nodded in agreement and turned her attention back to Mary. She saw the sorrow on Dagget's face as he held Mary's hand and shed one tear after another. Each time the child coughed, her whole body shook.

"There's a bottle of paregoric under my bed," Dagget said. "Would that help?"

Paregoric. Lena knew it contained opium, and some folks got so they had to have it all the time.

Gabe cleared his throat. "I've heard of its being used for cough before, although its primary use is stomach ailments."

"Would it hurt her?" Amanda asked.

"I knew of a woman who became addicted to laudanum—a mixture of opium and alcohol—but we could try a little of the paregoric," Gabe replied. "It's up to you."

Silence resounded from the walls of the small dugout.

"I think we should try anything that might help," Charles finally said. He ran his fingers through his hair. "We have to do something."

Gabe moved to Dagget's bed and pulled out the small bottle from beneath it. "Let's give her a dose. In the meantime, why don't we call in the other children and pray together for Mary?"

A short while later, they all gathered together while Gabe prayed. "Lord Jesus, all of us have asked You today to spare this child and heal her. Now, we all are praying together. Hear our voices. We look to You for strength. Amen."

❧

Later that afternoon, with no change in Mary, Gabe realized the necessity of making arrangements for Caleb and Simon. Pulling Lena aside, he shared his thoughts. "The boys ought to get home. I'd like to escort you back. Then I'll return to spend the night here."

"Would you mind if I stayed the night instead?" She stared at the unconscious child, still and dangerously hot. Not once had she left Mary's side with Amanda and Dagget.

"Of course not," he replied. "Whatever happens, Amanda will need you."

She reached for his hand, and he assisted her to her feet. "I'll walk you outside."

While Lena pulled on her coat, Gabe stepped around to Dagget's side. "I'm going home with the boys, but Lena is staying the night."

He nodded. "Uh . . . uh thank you for . . . today. I'll not be forgetting it."

Gabe grasped the man on his shoulder. "I'll be by at daybreak."

Gabe and his family stepped out of the dugout. Once the door shut behind them, Gabe voiced his concerns to Lena. "Do you think Dagget is harmless?"

"Yes, I believe so. Right now regret is eating him alive."

"Do you think it will last?" Gabe remembered all his dealings with Dagget, and the thought of the man tossing his foul words at his precious wife alarmed him.

She shrugged and wrapped her arms around her. "I hope so. These children need him."

"But he's so mean, Mama," Caleb said. "I don't think he'll ever change."

"We have to give him a chance, just like the good Lord does for us," Lena said.

Gabe hugged her and planted a light kiss on her lips. "I love you, Lena Hunters. Now, hurry on inside, before you get too cold."

Caleb and Gabe trudged through the snow back to the farm, while Simon rode the horse. They all were quiet, including Simon, and it offered an opportunity for Gabe to reflect on the Shafers. Oh, how he wanted Mary to live, and how well he understood her desire to die. Children needed love to grow and flourish. Without it, they grew inward, as he'd done. Fortunately for him, he'd come to know a heavenly Father who'd changed his whole life.

"Pa?" Caleb asked.

Gabe gave him his full attention.

"Would you take all six of the Shafers and love them like us?" Caleb asked.

"What do you think?" Gabe responded.

"I believe you would."

"Do you feel my sentiments are wrong?"

Caleb did not hesitate to reply. "No, not at all. I think it's mighty fine."

"Of course, what is best for those children is for their father to love them."

"I'm sure glad we have you for a pa," Simon piped up.

"Me too," Caleb echoed. "We got the best pa in Nebrasky."

Lena had dozed by Mary's side, while Amanda slept off and on. Every time Lena awoke, she saw Dagget staring into his little daughter's face. He didn't eat the supper of salt pork and cornbread that Lena and Amanda prepared and refused anything to drink. The boys did their chores and silently went about their business until time for them to sleep, although Charles sat near the fire, watching Mary. The vigil continued with only the sounds of the younger children's soft snoring and Amanda's quiet weeping.

Just before four o'clock the next morning, Mary stirred. "She feels cooler," Dagget said. "Don't you think so, Lena?"

Immediately, Lena touched the child's forehead. "The fever's broken. Praise God."

Amanda and Charles awakened and scooted closer.

"Mary," Dagget whispered. "Can you talk to me?"

Through half-closed eyes, the child whispered, "I'm so tired."

"Sure you are, Honey. Now you just sleep, and I'll be here when you wake up."

"Are you my Jesus?" Mary asked a moment later.

Dagget sucked in a ragged breath. "It's your pa, Mary. I'm so sorry for being mean to you. I . . . I love you, Child."

Lena blinked back the tears. God had answered many prayers this night. What a dear Lord they served.

16

*L*ena ladled the freshly churned butter into a small bowl and proceeded to rinse it thoroughly before packing it lightly into a yellow mound. Gabe loved his bread and butter. Even when Caleb and Simon complained about the endless meals of cornbread, Gabe never said a word. Instead, he'd reach for a second hunk. At night, he loved to sit before the fire and feast on leftover cornbread with milk and molasses. Didn't take much to please her husband.

The snow this March came lightly and in inches rather than feet. A few more heavy storms might fall upon them, but the likelihood lessened as the days grew closer to spring. Lena loved the seasons, but she'd had enough of snow and ice.

What a winter, Lena mused, but a much easier one with Gabe to share each day. He'd changed so much since the first time she'd seen him at the train station in Archerville—and not simply in appearance. That alone proved startling enough. He'd shed all the excess weight, and the work outside had tightened his muscles and darkened his skin. One glance at his coppery-colored eyes could leave her breathless, and his thick blond hair, well . . .

In short, Gabe Hunters had transformed into quite a handsome man, but his heart had won hers from the moment he reached out to her and the boys.

I'm a pretty lucky woman to find a man who loves me as much as I do him.

So much had happened in the last month. Dagget had given his permission for Amanda to teach school, and the area farmers had pitched in to make the soddy presentable. Gabe had offered his assistance in helping Amanda form a schedule and arrange the classes.

He'd been guiding her through basic reading, writing, and arithmetic much like she'd done with her brothers.

Today, Gabe had gone hunting while the boys were in school, much to Caleb and Simon's regret. They'd have gladly gone along, skipping their lessons with Amanda in light of a few hours in the wilds. Gabe had taken to regularly bringing in game, and today he had his sights on taking Dagget with him. How strange that these two different men had grown to be such good friends.

"Hello," a voice called.

Lena strained her ears. She didn't recognize the voice. Her sights trailed to the loaded shotgun hanging over the door.

"Hello, Lena?"

She peeked through the window. Dread washed over her.

"Lena!"

She opened the door to see Riley O'Connor dismounting his horse. *Gabe will not be happy about this.* "My husband's not here," she said, crossing her arms.

Riley shot her a wide grin as he tied his mount to the porch post. "I hoped he'd be gone."

"Why?" she snapped. Remembering Riley's temperament when challenged equaled her own, Lena rephrased the question. "I don't understand why you need to see me."

"I think you have a good idea." He loped toward her, offering an easy smile. "I wanted to see you."

She didn't like him, not one bit. "Unless you have business with Gabe, then you don't have any reason to be here."

"You and I have unfinished business," he said low, standing dangerously close.

Lena stepped back and took a deep breath. *Hold your temper. He's bigger than you.* "We have nothing to talk about."

"I asked you to marry me, you refused, and now you're married to that city feller."

"Then everything is settled." Lena lifted her chin in hopes he understood her silent dismissal.

Riley's eyes narrowed, and he lifted one worn boot onto the porch. "You never gave me a chance."

"For what?"

"To win you back."

"You never had me. Riley, please, just leave. I am a happily married woman. I love my husband very much, and he's going to be upset when he finds out you've been here."

"Good, I'd like the chance to fight 'im."

She closed her eyes and fought for control. Anger bubbled hotter than a pot of lye and tallow. "My Gabe has better things to tend to than fighting you. In case you've forgotten, you and I never courted, never kissed—unlike what you told Gabe—never anything. As I remember, you rode up one day and stated you were planning to marry me. I said no then, and I would say no again, even if you were the last man in the world!"

Riley's foot slipped from the porch, leaving a clump of fresh manure on the edge.

"Aw, Lena, just let me come inside for a spell. I'm sure you'll change your mind."

"Get out of here."

"You're making a terrible mistake. Lots of women think I'm good to look at."

She gritted her teeth. "I don't. Take your charms to one of them."

A wry smile spread over his face. "Why don't we just see?"

Quickly, Lena stepped inside the open door and slammed it. "You best leave, Riley. I have a shotgun in here, and I'm not afraid to use it."

"I'm goin'! I feel sorry for your husband. You ain't worth the trouble."

Latching the door, Lena peeked through the side of her window's calico curtain to watch Riley gallop off. She closed her eyes and touched her pounding heart. *I've got to tell Gabe.*

That evening, while the boys tended to chores and Gabe skinned three rabbits—Dagget had brought down a deer—Lena stole over by the well where Gabe hunched over the animals.

"What's wrong?" he asked, lifting a brow. "You look upset."

She nodded and wrapped her shawl closer about her shoulders.

"It's too cold for you without a coat, Lena. Why don't you stay warm by the fire, and I'll be there momentarily."

"You don't mind?"

He smiled. "I'm finished, and I rather enjoy the opportunity to catch my wife alone."

A few moments later, Gabe joined her at the table. She poured both of them a cup of freshly brewed coffee and sat across from him, her mind spinning with Riley's unpleasant visit. For a few tempting seconds, she thought of not telling him at all. *Who would know the difference? No, that's wrong.*

Taking a deep breath, she blurted out, "Riley O'Connor paid a visit while you were hunting with Dagget." It didn't sound at all as she intended. Trembling, she wrapped her fingers around the mug of hot coffee.

Gabe stared at her—emotionless. "What did he want?"

"He was up to no good, saying things that weren't true."

"What did he want, Lena, and what did he say?"

Suddenly, she burst into tears. "Gabe, if that man ever shows up on our land again, I'm going to fill his backside with buckshot!"

"I'd like to know what happened." The cold tone of Gabe's voice nearly frightened her.

"He just talked about him and me . . . insinuating we used to court. I hurried back into the cabin and told him to leave or I'd get the shotgun after him."

Solemnly, Gabe rose from the table. "I believe I need to pay Mr. O'Connor a visit. I won't have this in my home."

She grabbed his suspenders. "No, Gabe, please. That's what he wants. I told him I was happily married and I loved you." She glanced up at him through blinding tears and repeated the conversation word for word.

Sighing heavily, Gabe lowered himself onto the chair. A distant look filled his eyes, and for a moment, she saw a stranger before her. "I'm glad you told me," he finally said.

"I couldn't keep anything from you. We're supposed to share everything." *This is not like Gabe. If I didn't know better, I'd swear he didn't believe me!*

A shadow of something she didn't recognize swept over his face. "I'm not sure what to do."

"Nothing, Gabe. I really don't think he'll be back. I made him plenty mad."

This time his gaze captured hers, and the grim look changed to the one she cherished. "Let's hope it deterred him, for if there is a next time, I'll be forced to take drastic measures. No one, I repeat, no one will accost my wife."

Lena said nothing as Gabe snatched up his coat from the peg and headed outside. A sick feeling swirled around her stomach. Why did she feel he doubted her?

❧

Gabe finished skinning the rabbits with a vengeance that frightened him. Dagget Shafer. Riley O'Connor. How many other men had vied for Lena's attention? Had she encouraged them? Was she still seeing Riley? Why did she have to be so beautiful? He knew the degradation of men when they became consumed by a comely woman. Jealousy enveloped their lives. One sin led to another. Drunkenness. Fights. Murder. Families destroyed and a host of other atrocities.

And I'm traveling down the same highway of destruction. My jealousy has to cease, or I'll shatter my marriage. He'd fall victim to the same wickedness he'd sworn never to enter. Gabe swiped at a single tear coursing down his cheek. His relationship with Lena ranked second to God. Only a fool would destroy something as good as the Father's gift.

Dropping the knife, he wiped his hands clean on the snow. If only he could eliminate the bitter memories as easily as he'd just washed his hands. Gabe stood and took long strides back to the cabin.

The moment he opened the door, he could see Lena had been weeping. He hated what he saw, knowing his insensitive response had ushered in her tears.

"Lena." He crossed the room and took her into his arms. "I apologize for not understanding how today affected you. All I could dwell on was Riley coming after you."

"You have nothing to be jealous of," she whispered, stroking his cheek and no doubt seeing his single tear. "You are what is most important to me—you and our sons."

He held her against him, his fingers running through her dark silky hair, her breath soft and warm against his neck. "I'm so fortunate to have you in my life. Please forgive me."

"Oh, Gabe. Don't be so hard on yourself. Riley O'Connor is a difficult man. You reacted like any man who'd been insulted."

"It's no excuse for me to be difficult too. We have so many fine friends, and I don't need to make a fuss over one ill-mannered scoundrel."

"I love you, Gabe Hunters. Nothing's going to change my heart."

He held her close, chasing away his fears and bitterness. Someday, he'd have to tell her about Mother and the others, but not now. For this moment, he wanted to simply cherish the woman in his arms.

17

$\mathcal{W}$inter slowly melted into the Platte River, and Gabe eagerly looked forward to spring. At last he could plow the fields and plant corn and other grains for a fall harvest. He wanted to help Lena plant a sizable vegetable garden, knowing she'd have to preserve the food while he worked in the fields. He'd learned so much about Nebraska since last October, and this new season promised to teach him even more. Without a doubt, the cold winter months had given him and his family time to get to know each other. They'd played in the snow, gone hunting, and Lena had taught him how to ice skate.

It has been a good season, he wrote in his journal. *My family is affectionate, and I am deeply grateful for their devotion. I believe we would not have grown this close if the winter had not closed in around us. Now I'm eager to do the work that will provide for my family.*

In the mornings, after milking and chores, Gabe listened for the birds. Through Caleb, he'd learned to distinguish the soft coo of a mourning dove, the unique call of the bobwhite, the obnoxious cry of the crow, and from time to time, the gobble of a turkey, which reminded him of chattering women. Near the river, ducks and geese abounded, and occasionally, he and the boys would bring one down for a fine meal.

Once he'd sowed the crops, Gabe wanted to take Caleb and Simon fishing. Of course, the first few times the boys would have to teach him how to properly operate a pole, line, and bait. No doubt, he'd provided yet another source of amusement—but he didn't mind.

Dagget and his family worked through their differences. Little Mary never left her father's side, nor did he object. Dagget had even bought a cow, which ended Gabe's morning visits. Still, a few times a week, Gabe ventured toward the Shafer farm just to keep his mind at ease. Shoots of spring plants weren't the only things thriving at the Shafers.

Lena and the boys had shown Gabe how to read the tracks of the white-tailed deer, coyotes, foxes, rabbits, and a host of other animals. He looked forward to seeing prairie dogs, for Simon found them quite interesting.

The wolves hadn't bothered them since the incident with Caleb and Simon, although Gabe still looked for them from time to time. He'd lost a few head of cattle over the winter: three to hungry wolves, two others to the cold.

Gabe wouldn't trade his new life for the biggest mansion in Philadelphia—or anywhere else for that matter. Being a husband, father, and farmer surely must be God's richest blessing.

Today, he'd begin the plowing. Like a child eagerly awaiting a spectacular event, Gabe hadn't been able to sleep all night.

"Gabe, it's hard work," Lena warned. "Your shoulders will ache. In fact, your whole body will hurt. You'll fall into bed dead tired only to get up before dawn and start again. I think I should help, Caleb too."

"Maybe Caleb—later," Gabe replied with a frown. "But not my wife. I'm the provider."

Before the sun offered a faint twinge of pink, Gabe hurried through his chores, then hitched up the mule to the iron plow. He slipped the reins over his shoulders and offered a quick prayer. Grinning like a love-struck schoolboy, he took out across the earth, all the while envisioning fields of waving corn and grain just like he'd seen in his books.

After one length of a field, Gabe realized the truth in Lena's words. Plowing was hard work! He looked behind him and saw his beloved wife watching. Waving wildly, he gestured to the completed row. Turning the mule, he began again. No point in letting her know she'd spoken correctly in her assessment of the plowing.

Tonight he'd be one sore man.

Midmorning, Lena brought a crockery jug of cold water wrapped in burlap and a cloth to wipe the sweat from his brow.

"Admit it, Gabe. This is hard work," she said while he drank deeply.

Not yet, maybe never.

When he refused to reply, she laughed. "I'm sure your books on farming didn't talk about the sweat pouring off your face or the way your back feels like it's breaking in two."

He tried to give her a stern look, but one glimpse of her sweet face melted his resolve. "The endeavor is satisfying," he said, clamping on his lip so she wouldn't hear his chuckle.

"Are you ready for me to help? Or can I send the boys as soon as they get home from school?"

"No, Ma'am. I'm a Nebraska farmer, and I'm excited about plowing my own fields."

"And you're sure about this? Caleb will be disappointed since he wanted to help."

He leaned over and kissed her. "I made it through the fall and winter—wolves, Dagget, blizzards, and Riley. Now I'm ready for the spring and summer and whatever comes with it."

She wrapped her arms around his neck. "Tornadoes. We get some nasty twisters in the summer. Prairie fires too." She tilted her head. "Back in '73, we had a horrible drought, and in '74 the worst plague of grasshoppers ever seen—ate everything to the ground. Even the trains couldn't run because the tracks were slick with 'hoppers."

"I'm ready." He grinned.

"I see you are." She stepped back from his embrace and laughed with him. "I'll bring you food and water in a few hours. Besides, you're beginning to smell like a farmer."

By noon, Gabe wondered how many days it would take to complete the plowing. It had taken him half a day to till one acre. No doubt by the time he finished, he'd be strong and muscular. He grimaced at the mere thought of Lena guiding the plow over the rough terrain and supporting the reins. No woman should work like a man.

After devouring dandelion greens and cornbread at noon, Gabe fought the urge to stretch out on the blanket where Lena had set their meal and sleep a few moments before submitting himself to the plow again.

I am a farmer. We don't shirk in our work.

"Close your eyes for a little while," she urged, coaxing him to lay his head on her lap. "The plowing doesn't have to be finished today, and you were out here before the sun barely peeked through the clouds."

"Now I understand how Samson felt," he said. "Next you will want to know where I confine my strength."

She stroked his cheek with her fingertips. Intoxicating.

"I'm a farmer, not a lazy city man," he mumbled. "I'm going to call you Delilah."

She combed her fingers through his hair; soon her touch faded into memory.

❧

Lena woke with a start. She'd fallen asleep! She'd planned for Gabe to rest before finishing the day's work. Shielding her eyes from the sun, she saw him in the distance struggling with the mule. Why, he'd gotten so much done. How long had she slept? From the sun's position in the sky, she must have napped for over an hour.

"Gabe Hunters, you tricked me!"

He heard her call and took a moment to wave. She wanted to shout at him, but the incident suddenly struck her as funny. Looking about, she saw he'd gathered up the remains of their meal and packed it nicely into the basket. Only the quilt beneath her needed to be folded and placed with the other items.

"Gabe Hunters, you never cease to surprise me," she whispered. Beneath her fair-haired husband's smile and gentle ways rested more courage and grit than any man around. *He's a warrior,* she thought. *The best there is.*

Humming a nondescript tune, she walked back to the house. The boys should be home from school by now and seeking out mischief if she guessed correctly. Perhaps her strong-willed husband would accept Caleb's help.

As darkness covered the farm and stars dotted the sky, Gabe came trudging in for supper with Caleb and Simon behind him. Although they'd washed at the well and their cheeks glistened from the scrubbing, the lines in their faces and their hunched backs betrayed their exhaustion.

"I have beef stew," she said brightly, "and a dried chokeberry pie with fresh cream."

"I'm starved," Simon moaned, dropping into a chair.

"I don't know why," Caleb said with a glare. "All afternoon you and Turnip chased rabbits, while Pa and I took turns at the plow."

"You didn't work that much," Simon replied. "I saw Pa do more rows than you."

Mercy, let's not argue. Gabe is tired enough without settling the boys.

Gabe ruffled Caleb's hair. "You both worked equally hard, and you spent a good part of the day in school. Caleb, you were a great help in the fields, and Simon, thank you for completing the evening chores without assistance."

"Why don't we eat so you men can get to bed," Lena said, filling their plates with the hot stew and a slab of buttered cornbread.

"It smells delicious," Gabe said. He chewed slowly as though every motion took all of his strength. "Do you boys mind if I postpone our reading of *The Last of the Mohicans* until tomorrow night?"

Caleb sighed. "I'm too tired to listen."

Simon agreed.

Shortly thereafter, the two boys went to bed with promises to say their prayers before drifting off to sleep. "School is just too hard for me," Simon said.

Lena captured Gabe's gaze and smiled. Their youngest son was not about to admit the afternoon's venture had worn him out. She watched the two boys disappear into their small room.

Gabe slumped into a chair, and she immediately stepped behind him, massaging the shoulder muscles she knew were tight and sore. He winced. "And so what has made you so tired?" she whispered.

He pulled her around and down onto his lap, offering a light kiss. "All the good food I ate today. Plowing is fairly simple."

She shook her head. "I suppose the pain I detect is a bee sting?" she asked with a tilt of her head and a smile she could not hide.

"Not exactly." Gabe tossed her a most pathetic look, reminding her of a little boy seeking sympathy.

"Is that the way you peered at your mother when you needed something?" Lena asked, pretending to be stern.

Immediately, Gabe stiffened. *What have I done?* She knew he never spoke of his mother, except to discourage a conversation.

"Maybe I should go to bed."

Lena despised her foolishness. "I'm sorry. I know you don't like to talk about your mother."

He gently lifted her from his lap. "It's all right. My mother behaved rather uniquely with her maternal instincts."

"She really hurt you," Lena stated, wanting to touch him but slightly fearful. The regret and anger in his face had only occurred once before—when he'd dealt with Dagget Shafer the night Mary nearly died.

Shrugging, he chewed at his lip. "I'm a grown man with a fine family. I determined a long time ago to rise above my circumstances. Revisiting the past is pointless." He stood and grasped her arms. She could feel him trembling. "Lena, I don't want to speak of my mother ever again. She's buried, and everything about her is best forgotten."

"I'd be glad to listen. It might help how you feel."

"No!"

18

*L*ena woke the following morning to discover Gabe had already left for the fields. She'd slept soundly, not her normal manner of doing things, but she'd had a difficult time falling asleep the night before. She'd cried before coming to bed, and not once had Gabe apologized or attempted to hold her when she crawled in beside him. This morning she was furious.

When she finally climbed out of bed, she discovered Caleb and Simon were outside doing their morning chores before school, and she hadn't prepared their breakfast or lunch buckets. Even with time pressing against her, the memory of Gabe's final words last night seared her heart.

Slapping together cornbread and molasses sandwiches, Lena roughly wrapped the lunches in a cloth and tossed it into the boys' buckets. She turned her attention to the boys' breakfast. Anger raced through her veins as she heated the skillet for fried cornmeal and eggs. *Look at all I've done for him, and this is how he treats me! Where would he be if I hadn't married him and taught him about farming?*

Without warning, Lena felt her stomach roll. *Now, look what Gabe's done—made me sick with his rudeness.*

Who has made you ill?

The gentle whisper penetrated her soul. She'd allowed her temper to upset her, the evil poison she'd sworn to overcome. Gabe had nothing to do with her churning stomach. Pulling the skillet from the fire, she dashed outside to rid her body of whatever had revolted in her stomach. Sick and feeling the pain of remorse, Lena realized she couldn't go on with the rage inside her.

After the boys left for school, Lena picked up the Bible. Oh, how she needed the Lord this day. Every part of her wanted to crumble in memory of her horrible temper. She remembered her thoughts the day when Mary hovered between life and death and how Dagget's ugly temperament had nearly killed the child. *Am I any different? Would I lose Gabe and the boys if they knew the horrible things I was thinking?*

Praise God, Gabe and her sons had been outside and not witnessed her tantrum. The One who really counted, the One she'd given her life to had heard every thought and seen every deed. Lena rubbed her arms; the guilt of her sin made her feel dirty. She thought she could resolve her temper without bothering God. One more time she'd failed. How long before she destroyed the affections of her family with her selfishness?

Opening the Bible, she leafed through page after page, reading the notes and underlined passages. Some Scripture she had marked, others came from Gabe or James. Remembrances of all the nights by the fire listening to her husband read and pray settled upon her as though she'd crawled up into God's lap.

Choking back her tears, Lena continued turning the pages of the Bible, allowing His Word to soothe her troubled spirit. The book of Romans graced her fingers; the first verse of chapter eight she had memorized as a girl: "There is therefore now no condemnation to them which are in Christ Jesus, who walk not after the flesh, but after the Spirit."

But I am walking after the flesh by not turning over my anger to the Lord. My rebellion is displeasing to the One who has given me life.

Catching her breath, Lena shivered. How could she expect to please God on her own? She must give Him her struggles at this very moment.

Heavenly Father, You have blessed me far more than I could ever imagine. I'm sorry for not giving You my problem with anger. In the whole six months Gabe and I have been married, not once has he ever raised his voice or initiated an argument. It's always been me. Take this burden from me, I pray, for without You, I will only sin more and more. Amen.

Closing the Bible and laying it on the table, she proceeded to tidy up from breakfast. Peace lifted her spirit. No longer did she feel sick or angry, but instead, she prayed about the problems plaguing Gabe with his mother. The woman must have hurt him deeply for him not to want her mentioned. Poor Gabe. Such a good, sweet man. He'd given her, Caleb, and Simon his devotion without asking for anything in return.

With a new resolve to live every moment of her life totally for her Father, Lena determined to never confront Gabe with any questions about his past. Let him come to her if he desired to talk. Until then, she'd pray for peace in his soul.

At noon she carried a basket of cornbread, newly churned butter, apple butter, boiled eggs, and a slab of ham along with a jug of buttermilk and another one of water to the fields. Gabe must be starved by now. They'd fared well during the winter with plenty of food—although they'd all gotten tired of cornmeal and molasses. With spring here, she could gather fresh greens, elderberries, and chokeberries. Later on in the summer, fresh vegetables would add variety to their diets. And as always, everything would be dried for the next winter.

❧

During the morning, Gabe had plowed with a vengeance, completing more rows than he thought possible. Dagget said the corn should be planted by the twentieth of May to insure its being knee-high by July fourth. At this rate, he'd be done with time to spare.

All the while he deliberated on the way he'd spoken to Lena the previous night. She meant nothing by her innocent remark, and he'd lashed out at her unfairly. If he admitted the truth, Lena should be told about his mother. The woman who had given him birth might have gone to her grave, but the wounds still drew blood. Not a day went by that he didn't ponder over something she'd said or done. This pattern of action made him think he hadn't truly forgiven her.

Lena had allowed God to work through her. She said and did the right things to instill self-confidence in everything he did. Every day he looked forward to what God had planned for him and his family. Lena loved him, and he loved her. The doubts he'd experienced in the beginning about her fidelity grew less and less as he viewed her true spirit. She trusted him, and he needed to trust her.

Gabe chuckled despite his grievous thoughts. His Lena had a temper. Feisty, that one. She'd warned him repeatedly about her outbursts, but he hadn't seen much of them. He enjoyed her free spirit. _I bet she's boiling over this morning._ The thought saddened him. Any repercussion from last night clearly was his fault.

He must apologize, but in doing so he had to reveal the truth of his past. _Can I tell a portion of my life without revealing the entire story?_ The answer came as softly as the breeze cooling his tired face. Truth didn't mean dissecting what he comfortably could and could not state.

Gabe stretched his neck and stared at the sun straight up in the sky. Glancing toward the house, he saw Lena edging toward him, carrying a basket. Bless her. He didn't deserve her bringing him food. An urgency knocked at his heart.

Lord, I'm afraid I haven't given You the past—not completely. I realize now if I had allowed You to share my pain, I would have been able to tell Lena about Mother. Take the bitterness from me and use my past to Your glory.

Shifting the reins around his shoulders and giving Turnip a pat, he proceeded to plow the row that brought him closer to his wife. Suddenly, the burden didn't seem so heavy.

Lena and Gabe met at the end of the row—she with her basket of food and he wearing an apology on his lips. Halting the mule, he dropped the leather pieces to his side and approached her. She wore a timid smile, a quivering smile. He felt lower than the dirt he plowed to submission beneath his feet.

"Lena," he said, "I apologize for the way I spoke to you last night, and in my self-pity, I neglected to tell you good night or kiss you properly."

She nibbled at her lip. "Would you like to kiss me now?"

"I smell of sweat and the mule."

"That's a farmer's smell." Lena offered a half smile. "I love my farmer." She set the basket onto the ground and reached out for him.

Gabe enveloped her in his arms, and she clung to him as though they'd been apart for days. He bent to claim her lips, tenderly at first, then more fervently than their first night together. At last, he drew himself back. "I never meant to hurt you. You are the sunshine to me each morning and the vivid colors of sunset each night."

"I wish I could state things as wonderfully as you," she whispered. "You make me feel special—pretty and pleasing."

"And you are; you always will be."

Her shoulders fell, and she shook her head. "I'm sorry for all the wicked things I thought about you," she whispered. "And the things I threw."

He could not disguise his smile. "What did you throw?"

She swallowed hard. "A ham bone, but I picked it up and brought it for Turnip."

Gabe roared with laughter.

"No, please," she said, her eyes misting. "You don't understand. That bone is what brought about my prayer giving God my horrible temper." She stared up at him. "I did it, Gabe. I surrendered my anger to the Lord."

Once more pulling her close, he realized he had not been the only one to confess sin this day. "His ears must be filled with the Hunters from Nebraska. The Lord and I had a talk of our own."

She waited patiently, a look of curiosity and love glowing from the luminous green pools of her eyes.

He lifted the basket. "Let's eat, and I will tell you all about it."

The food tasted wonderful, and the talk between them was light and flirtatious. Gabe knew he masked the serious conversation about to evolve, but the Lord promised to be his strength.

"Are you ready to hear a story?" he asked, wiping a spot of apple butter from Lena's lip.

"I always like a good story."

"This one has a remarkable ending."

"I'm ready, Gabe, for whatever you want to tell me."

He nodded and lifted his gaze to the heavens for a quick prayer before he began with the story only his heavenly Father knew. "My mother never knew my father. She worked at a brothel in Philadelphia . . . an exquisite woman whose parents were from Norway. I remember she had hair the color of the sun and eyes the fairest of blue, but her disposition didn't match." He paused, and Lena reached over to take his hand.

"Mother gave me the last name of Hunters, although I have no idea where she found it. I was an inconvenience and an irritation to her . . . well, her business transactions. At an early age, she left me alone while she worked. She drank to drown her own pain, which only made her even more disagreeable. She took her disappointments with life out on me, and so did many of the gentlemen she brought home. I quickly became their whipping boy. The tongue-lashings and beatings were unbearable until I learned to believe I deserved them for whatever reason they gave me." Gabe covered the hand touching his. "I know you've seen the scars on my back, and I thank you for not mentioning them before."

Huge tears rolled down her cheeks, and he hastily added, "Don't cry. This has a happy ending, remember?" With a deep breath he continued. "As I grew older, I became absorbed with learning. School was the perfect diversion for the abuse at home. However, when the other students discovered where I lived and what my mother did, I became the brunt of their ridicule. So I buried myself even deeper into my books. I grew infatuated with words. Their meanings gave me power, and that's when I started using them to fight back. No one else might have comprehended their meanings, but I did. It gave me an opportunity to consider myself better than the ones who shunned me.

"About the time I turned sixteen, Mother purchased the brothel and became the madam of the largest establishment of its type in Philadelphia. She enlisted me to work there, do her books, and keep her records straight. Also at the same age, I received a Bible from a well-meaning group of ladies from a nearby church who aspired to reform everyone living within the confines of the brothel. The women didn't want the book, so I began reading it." He paused, and she said nothing, as if knowing he would continue.

"Shortly thereafter, I started attending church. No one knew or cared, for they were all sleeping off the escapades from the night before.

"When I turned twenty, Mother developed a cough. The doctors couldn't find a cure. Her only temporary relief came from medication that she began to rely on as much as the alcohol. Remember when Dagget asked about giving little Mary paregoric, and I told him about the woman who became addicted to laudanum? That was Mother. By the time I reached thirty, she had to be nursed day and night."

"And you took care of her?" Lena asked.

"Yes. She depended solely on me. I resented it at first, but the Lord kept dealing with me until I forgave her—at least I thought I did. But the bitterness stayed with me." He squeezed her hand. "That's why becoming a husband and father meant so much to me. I had to make up for what had been done to me."

Lena nodded, the tears glistening on her face. He brushed them aside. "I understand, Gabe. I really do. You are a wonderful father."

"But a true miracle happened right here on this farm—the blessings of love. You have no idea of the joy that filled my soul the first time Caleb and Simon called me Pa. I would have died a happy man right then. But your love has been the finest treasure of all. God gave me all these gifts, but I could not release my resentment until this morning." He reached up to touch her cheek. "And my story has such a beautiful ending. I have the richest of blessings at my fingertips."

19

*L*ena wept with Gabe until they began to tease each other about their puffy and reddened eyes. *We are a pair, Gabe Hunters, you and I.*

"You look like you've been in a fight and lost," Lena accused, blowing her nose on his clean handkerchief—one of the items from Philadelphia that he still insisted upon carrying.

He lifted a brow. "And who rammed their fist into your face, Miss Blow-Your-Nose-Like-a-Honking-Goose?"

She wiggled her shoulders to feign annoyance. "My nose, Sir? I thought we were talking about your eyes. Maybe Turnip threw the punches."

He drew her into his arms and kissed the tip of her nose. "Promise me we will always have laughter," he whispered. "I want us to talk, to cry together, even to argue from time to time, and always to laugh."

Laughter. Yes, what a true blessing. He'd never laughed so much in his entire life.

"I'll do my best," she said with a smile. "You are much more handsome with a smile on your face." She took a deep breath. "Although today was necessary too."

"I agree," he replied. "I'm insistent about urging the boys and you to discuss your thoughts and feelings, but I'm not always so quick to adhere to the same advice."

"I really am sorry for your unhappy childhood," Lena said seriously. "We had our good times and bad, but my memories are sweet."

He stared at the fields, the cabin, and back to her. "When I reflect on it, I can't help but see the good resulting from those days."

"You mean your compassion for people? For children?"

"Yes. I could have easily drifted into Mother's manner of living and not come to know God."

"Did she ever accept Jesus as her Savior?"

He picked up a clod of dirt and sent it soaring across the plowed field. "I don't know if she ever asked Him to rule her life or not. I talked to her about the Lord and read to her from the Bible, but I never knew if she actually made a decision."

Silence held them captive. Lena felt eternally grateful for the day. They'd both shed ugly garments that not only threatened their relationship with the Lord but also their happiness as husband and wife.

"I have something else to tell you," Gabe said. "I hope when I've finished you won't feel I have deceived you in any way."

She stared at him curiously.

"Mother died a wealthy woman, which meant I inherited the brothel and an exorbitant amount of money. I dissolved the business, in case you wondered." He glanced teasingly at her. "And I donated the building to a church, which now uses it as an orphanage. After praying through what God wanted me to do with the rest of the funds, I gave to several churches and deposited the balance in a Philadelphia bank. When the time comes, we will be able to provide funds for Caleb and Simon's education. There is plenty there to expand the farm when we're ready and for other unforeseen expenses. Someday, I'd like to take you on a trip, anywhere you want to venture."

Lena felt the color drain from her face. "Why ever would you want a poor widow when you could have had so much more?"

"God had a plan, Dearest. A very pleasant one, I might add. However, I do believe I gained more than money from my adventure in Nebraska."

"I'm so very lucky," she whispered.

He gave her the smile meant only for her. "Nonsense. I am the fortunate man."

My dear, sweet husband. You try so hard. "Want to know my thoughts and feelings right now?" she asked.

"Most certainly."

She closed her eyes. "I want a kiss, a very nice long one."

"I can oblige."

"Not just right now, Gabe. I want one every day for the rest of our lives."

"I can still oblige."

"Even if we've quarreled or the things around us threaten our joy in the Lord and in each other?" she asked, tracing his lips with her fingertip. "No matter if snow blizzards keep us inside for days, or rain forgets to fall, or grasshoppers eat the very clothes we wear, or Caleb and Simon disappoint us?"

"I promise to oblige."

"Good, let's begin now."

❧

"How far is this town you're talking about?" Gabe asked, teasing Caleb and Simon about the three-mile walk to see a prairie dog town. They'd gone to church earlier, and the boys had been pestering him for days to visit this spot. "Is there a hotel? A sheriff? I'm really thirsty too."

Lena giggled. He glanced her way as they walked and captured a loving gaze. She still looked pale from being ill that morning, but the color had returned to her cheeks. She'd been perfectly fine the night before. The idea of his precious wife—or any of his family—falling prey to one of the many illnesses tearing through this land alarmed him. He squeezed her hand, sending love messages from his heart to hers.

A year ago he'd received her first letter. So much had happened since then. God had transformed him into a new man, taken away his selfishness, and worked continually to mold him into a godly husband and father. *Thank You, God, for the gift of family and their love.*

"It's not much farther, Pa," Caleb said. "We have to be quiet because once they sense we're around, they stop chattering and disappear."

"And what do they say?" Gabe asked. "Don't believe I've ever had a conversation with a prairie dog."

Simon frowned and shook his head. "You don't understand what they're saying; you just know they're talking to each other."

Lena nibbled at her lip, no doubt to keep from laughing. "Simon, why don't you tell him what they look like?"

"That's right. I haven't seen a good picture in one of my books." Gabe grinned. "Are they as big as Turnip?"

"No, Sir," Simon replied. "Be glad we left him at home 'cause he'd scare them down into their holes."

"They live in holes? I thought they lived in a town."

Simon shook his head in what appeared to be exasperation. "Prairie dogs are smaller than rabbits. They live under the ground, but we call them towns. When you see them, they sit on their back legs and wave their front legs like arms. Then they talk to each other. Remember how Miss Nettie Franklin used her arms when she talked that Sunday in church about drinking whiskey being a sin?"

How well I remember. I thought Judge Hoover would burst since he owns the town's saloon. "She was quite demonstrative that day and quite successful in gaining everyone's attention."

"Gabe," Lena whispered. "Let's not encourage Simon."

He winked at his wife. "Go ahead, Simon."

"Well, that's how those prairie dogs look when they are talking to each other, flapping their arms as if they are pointing out something that really matters."

"Hush, Simon," Caleb said. "We're almost there, and I don't want Pa to miss them."

The four moved ahead, being careful not to make a sound. In the distance, Gabe heard chattering—like a squirrel convention. As he inched closer with his family right beside him, he saw the humorous stance of the peculiar animals. They *did* resemble Nettie, and he stifled a laugh. What a town indeed!

Suddenly, the animated creatures detected humans and dived into their burrowed homes. Nothing remained but the doorways into their dwellings.

"Doesn't appear to be a good town to ride through," Gabe remarked a short time later, "especially if your horse stepped through one of those holes."

"True," Lena replied. "Of course there are a few people towns too dangerous for decent folk to walk through too."

"Is my philosophical nature rubbing off on you, Dear?" Gabe asked, slipping his hand from hers to wrap around her waist.

"Oh no," Simon moaned. "Does that mean Ma is going to start using all those big words too?"

"I might," she said with a tilt of her head. "Do you mind?"

The little boy's eyes widened, and he stared at his brother. "What do you think, Caleb?"

"Might be all right. Ma could take over teaching school for Amanda." His eyes sparkled mischievously, so much like his mother.

"That wouldn't do at all," Simon quickly replied. "Pa needs her at home. She wouldn't be happy teaching school, and then she'd be too tired to cook supper."

"And I'd miss her," Gabe added. "Amanda will have to keep the job until the town finds someone else."

20

*G*abe stared up at the sky. Black clouds swirled, and the rumble of distant thunder with a flash of lightning intensified nature's threat. Storms and high winds he could handle, and he'd learned that when it rained, the household items had to be shifted from one side of the cabin to the other—depending on the direction of the rainfall. But the green color spreading across the horizon bothered him.

Glancing at the barn anchored deep into the earth, he wondered if Lena and the boys would be safer there than in the soddy. Although the walls of their home were nearly three feet thick, a twister could still do a lot of damage.

With a heavy sigh, he wished Caleb and Simon were home from school. He focused his attention to the east, straining to see if they were heading this way. Nothing. A gust of wind nearly toppled him over. *This is not merely prairie winds, but a malevolent act of nature.*

Gabe wondered if he should set the mule and horses free to run with the cattle until after the storm, but if his family were safer in the barn, then those animals would be as well. The cattle were contained in barbed-wire fencing. Of course that could be easily blown down.

With a heavy sigh, he realized they'd had a good spring. The corn stood more than a foot high, and they'd been blessed with ample rain. He hadn't considered he might lose a crop. Suddenly, all those days of work twisted through him. Lena's words about the Lord providing for their needs echoed through his ears.

This spring, tornadoes had always managed to venture far from them—until now.

Drenched in sweat, he stepped outside and studied the southwest sky. In a matter of minutes, the temperatures had dropped, and the wind had increased its velocity. *Where were Caleb and Simon?* Then he saw his sons racing home against a background of a hideous green sky. The closer they came, the better he felt.

Thank You, Lord. I didn't mind You taking care of them, but I feel much better knowing where they are.

"Gabe," Lena called from the doorway. "This looks bad, and I'm worried about the boys."

"They're coming," he replied above the wind. "I see them. Are we safer in the barn?"

"I think so." She scanned the sky, then shouted, "Hurry!" to Caleb and Simon, although Gabe doubted the boys could hear their mother's call. By the time they'd all scurried into the barn, huge droplets of rain pelted the earth. Ear-splitting cracks of thunder resounded, and jagged streaks of lightning split the sky.

"I saw a twister touch down in the distance," Caleb managed to say, trying to catch his breath. "Looked to be heading this way."

Gabe skirted his family to the farthest corner of the barn cradled deep into the hill. He positioned the horses and mule in front of them in case of flying debris. The structure had been built facing the east, which gave him some comfort in their safety. He moved to the opening, seeking some sign of the twister. "It might miss us," he said, watching the wind tug at the roof of the cabin.

"We'll know soon enough," Lena shouted. "Gabe, please don't stand out there. You don't have any idea how the wind could snatch you up."

"I'm being careful." His gaze fixed southwest to where a dark funnel cloud moved their way. The fury of nature left him in awe. One minute it showered his crops with water and in the next it threatened to beat them to the ground.

As the twister soared across the fields, a roar, like the bellowing of a huge beast, sent a tingle from his neck to his spine. This was not a time to stand outside and challenge the wind. Foolishness invited a loss of life—his own.

"Gabe!" Lena called frantically.

"I'm coming," he replied, moving back.

Huddled against his family, Gabe listened to the creature spin closer. "I hope all of you are praying," he said. "Not only for us, but for others in the twister's path."

They didn't reply. His request didn't warrant one. In the shadows, he couldn't see the emotion on their faces, but from the way Lena, Caleb, and Simon trembled beneath his arms, he knew fright penetrated their bones.

"Aren't you afraid, Pa?" Simon whispered shakily.

"Of course I am. But God is in control, and at times like these we have to hold onto our faith."

"Wish I could see Him," Caleb said.

"You can, Son. God's in the quiet summer day, the blizzards last winter, and in the wind outside. Close your eyes, and you can feel Him wrapping His love around you."

Lena squeezed his hand, and he brushed a kiss across her cheek. "I love you," she said. "Seems like you always say the right things to make us feel better."

He forced a chuckle. "I'll remember that the next time I slip and use those long words you so despise."

A deafening crash of thunder caused Simon to jump and snuggle closer. "If I had known we all were going to be this close, I'd have taken my bath before Saturday night," Gabe said.

Caleb giggled. *Thank You, Lord, for Your comfort. Keep us in the shelter of Your wings. Peace, be still. Amen.*

As ferocious as the storm sounded, the wind finally ceased to howl and left only a steady fall of rain in its wake. Gabe released his family. He was grateful they were unharmed. Now he needed to see what had been done outside. Swallowing hard, he made his way to the front of the barn. Although the rain had continued to fall, the cabin stood with only minor roof damage. He glanced to the fields surrounding them. They looked untouched except for one in the direct path of the tornado. The corn planted there bent to the ground as if paying homage to a wicked wind god, but perhaps the stalks might right themselves in the next few days. Even if that didn't happen and the field of corn perished, they'd survive.

Sometimes he thought his optimism masked good sense, but he

always tried to buffer his decisions with logic. Leading his family was often . . .

Gabe searched for the proper word. Glancing back at the boys, he knew exactly what fit. Hard. Just plain hard. What a relief to know God held the world in the palm of His hand.

He felt Lena touch his shoulder. "Do you suppose we should check on the Shafers?"

He nodded. "I also need to make sure the cattle fared well, but I can do that on the way there. Any chance of the twister changing directions and heading back this way?"

She sighed. "Doubtful, though I've seen two touch down in the same day."

"We'll wait until the sky clears." He clasped the hand on his shoulder. "The Shafers' dugouts are in bad shape. I know Dagget plans to build a soddy once harvest is over."

"Amanda told me. She's very excited. Dugouts don't last much longer than seven years, and Dagget built that one ten years ago."

"Sure hope the twister didn't step up his plans," Gabe said, glancing at the distant sky in the Shafers' direction. It looked menacing in a mixture of navy and green.

⁓

The tornado had laid waste to the dugouts and fencing of Dagget's farm. From what Gabe could tell, the wind had hit them as if they were a child's toys.

"Hello!" he called, stepping down from the wagon. "Dagget, it's Gabe and Lena and the boys."

A pool of water streaming from the door indicated the inside trench used to keep out the abundance of water had overflowed. What a mess for them to endure.

The door swung open, and Amanda stepped out along with some of her brothers and Mary. "We're all right," she called, "but Pa and Charles rode out this morning to check on fences and haven't returned."

Gabe's insides twisted with fear. He didn't like the sound of those two out in that storm. Dagget had changed considerably since their first encounter. He'd become a caring man and wouldn't endanger his family. "Which way did they go, Amanda?"

She pointed to the southwest. "That way."

Lena nudged him. He hadn't noticed when she'd climbed down from the wagon. "I'll stay and see what I can do here. Why don't you go look for them?"

Their gazes met. She obviously felt the same concern he did. "The wagon might be necessary," he said.

She nodded, her thoughts evident in the lines of her face. "Do you want to take Caleb?"

Gabe studied the growing boy, now twelve years old. In some cultures he'd be considered a man. Still, he'd like to shelter him for as long as possible from the ugliness of the world.

"I'd like to go, Pa," Caleb said. "I'm nearly as tall as you, and I could help."

Placing a hand on the boy's shoulder, Gabe silently agreed. Life's lessons could be a difficult lot, but he'd rather they occur while Caleb was with him than for the boy to learn on his own.

The sheared path before them looked like someone had taken a razor to the field. To the right, barbed wire stood untouched. Cattle grazed peacefully on their left.

"Do you suppose Mr. Shafer and Charles are dead?" Caleb asked as the wagon ambled on.

Gabe's heart plummeted. "I don't know, Son, but we'll deal with whatever we find. Dagget and Charles know this country, and I'm sure they read the signs of the twister."

"I remember when my first pa died," Caleb went on. "He just went to sleep and didn't wake up."

I hope if God has taken them home, we don't find their bodies mangled. A vision of the wolves crossed his mind. He had the rifle. By now the sun shone through the clouds, and the sky gave no hint of rain or the earlier violence. Calm. Peaceful.

Within the hour, Gabe spotted Charles on the trodden grass, bending over his father. "I believe we've found them," he said, breaking the silence.

"Mr. Shafer must be hurt," Caleb said. "Sure hope he's all right."

Gabe merely nodded. Charles had not moved, and he surely had seen and heard the approaching wagon. Once Gabe pulled it to a halt, Charles lifted a tear-stained face.

"Pa's gone," he said with a heavy sigh. "We tried to outrun the twister. I didn't know he'd fallen."

Gabe surmised what else had happened. "Are you hurt?"

"No, Sir."

"Can I take a look at your pa?"

Charles swallowed hard. "When I looked back, the twister had picked him up. Then it slammed him into the ground. I thought it had knocked the breath out of him, but his head hit hard."

As Charles moved aside, Gabe saw the blood rushing from Dagget's crown. "Caleb, stay in the wagon for now."

From the looks of him, Dagget had died from the blows to his head. Charles dried his eyes, and together the two lifted Dagget into the back of the wagon while Caleb minded the horses.

Charles said nothing as they drove back to his home. Sorrow etched his young face. Upon sight of his family's farm, he finally spoke. "He's been a good pa since last winter. Before that, I don't know if I'd have grieved so much."

"Now you have good memories," Gabe replied softly.

"I want to bury him beside Ma. He missed her terribly."

"I understand. We'll get the minister and have a proper burial."

Charles wiped his nose with his shirtsleeve. "Thank you, Mr. Hunters. You're a good neighbor."

Gabe startled at the sight of the minister already there when they arrived. He'd ridden out once the twister blew through.

Odd. Why here at the Shafers? Gabe wondered until he saw the way the man looked at Amanda.

"I should have guessed the reverend would be riding out to check on things," Charles said. "He's taken a fancy to Amanda."

God had already made provision for the Shafers. It appeared to him that Jason Mercer needed that family as much as they needed him.

"Glad you had the foresight to come," Gabe said, shaking the reverend's hand.

"I couldn't let a moment pass without riding out," he replied. "I had a notion something was wrong."

The following morning, Gabe, Charles, and Caleb dug the grave for Dagget. The ceremony was short but meaningful to his family. Dagget had died a good man, filling his life with the things that mattered most—God and his family. Little Mary plucked some goldenrods and laid them atop the mound of dirt.

"For you, Pa," she whispered. "I'll always love you."

Lena edged closer to Gabe and took his hand. He felt her body shudder. For the first time he understood why she fretted over him and the boys. Love didn't stop death, it simply made it harder to say good-bye.

Gabe dipped his pen in the inkwell and wrote his reflections about the tornado, then ended his entry with Dagget's death.

Dagget was a good friend. Although we didn't start out this way, the Lord saw fit to bring us together. Lena believes Dagget learned a lot from me, but the truth is he taught me a few valuable lessons. Aside from hunting techniques, which I sorely needed, my friend confided in me about how it felt to love a woman, then lose her. I selfishly pray that when the Lord calls Lena and me home, we go hand in hand. The idea of ever having to part with her sears my soul. And yes, I know God would comfort me, but I'd hate to consider such a separation. This morning as we laid him to rest beside his wife, I wondered if I had thanked him enough for his companionship. Aside from my beloved Lena, Dagget Shafer was my first real friend. God bless him.

21

*L*ena finished covering the rhubarb cobbler with a cloth. Caleb had taken a ham and a beef roast to the wagon, and Gabe carried a huge pot of greens. She corked the crockery jug filled with fresh buttermilk and glanced about to see if she'd missed anything. Spotting the quilt she'd set aside to spread out for their lunch, she snatched it up and wrapped it around the jug.

Taking a deep breath, she massaged the small of her back and blinked back the weariness threatening to creep into the eventful day—to say nothing of the queasiness attacking her stomach. *I have to tell Gabe soon. As observant as he is, I can't believe he doesn't already know.*

"Is there anything else?" Gabe asked from the doorway.

Instantly she drew her hands away from her back to gather up the food. "Just what I have here."

"You certainly look pretty this morning. Do weddings and house raisings always brighten your cheeks?" He warmed her heart with his irresistible smile.

I'm pregnant, Gabe, and tonight I'll tell you. "My how you toy with a woman's affections, Mr. Hunters. I'm overcome with your flattery."

He winked and snatched up the jug and cobbler. "I'll remember those sentiments."

She blushed and giggled. For a grown woman, sometimes the way Gabe made her feel like a schoolgirl nearly embarrassed her.

Today promised to be such fun. Amanda Shafer and the Reverend Jason Mercer had been married yesterday morning, just one month after Dagget had died. The young minister declared his intentions shortly after the funeral, promising all he'd see to raising the Shafer children. Today, the community gathered together to build them a sod cabin.

Lena tingled with excitement. The mere thought of visiting with the women all day long pushed aside the sickness that had plagued her since earlier that morning. She'd stopped telling Gabe about the morning wave of illness until she knew for sure she carried their baby. The poor man didn't suspect a thing. She touched her stomach. The thought of new life, another child for Gabe, filled her with anticipation. But along with the joy came the reality of how lucky she'd been to give birth to two healthy boys who had aged beyond the critical years. She prayed her new baby would also thrive in this hard country.

Enough of these silly worries! Gabe will be so happy!

The wagon ride to the Shafers, now the Mercers and Shafers, seemed bumpier than usual, or perhaps the jolt rocked her queasy stomach. She continued to smile, praying her stomach to calm. Caleb and Simon hadn't done this to her. Perhaps she carried a girl. What a sweet, delicious thought.

With the musings rolling delightfully around in her head, she pushed away the sickness threatening to send her sprawling into the dirt. She could hear Gabe now—crowing like a lone rooster in a chicken house. And the boys, they'd be wonderful big brothers.

"Are you feeling all right?" Gabe asked, reaching over to take her hand into his.

Does he know? "I'm very happy," she replied.

"Happiness doesn't make one pale—or get sick."

Sometimes. "I'm perfectly fine," she assured him and reached over to plant a kiss on his cheek. "Today will be such fun. I can hardly wait."

"I agree. You can socialize with all the women while we men build Amanda and the reverend's new home."

She laughed. "Are you wanting to trade places?"

"Absolutely not. Besides, you spent three years laboring in man's work, and I plan to do everything in my power to make sure your life never involves that again. Women's chores are difficult enough."

"You're too good to me. I'm not so sure I deserve you." She grinned up at the early morning sun. Birthing babies was hard work, but it was a whole sight easier than farming or building cabins. "I hope it's not too late when we get home today."

"It's hard to tell, Lena. Being new to this, I don't know how long it will take to construct the cabin, but I imagine a good many folks will show up to help."

She nodded, busily forming the words she'd use to tell Gabe about the baby. *Have you ever thought about a child of your own? No, he considers Caleb and Simon his own. Maybe, wouldn't it be grand to have a little one? Or, do you think you could build a cradle?* The thought of holding an infant again and watching him or her grow filled her with joy. God certainly had blessed her over and beyond what she'd ever imagined.

Gabe and Lena were among the first workers at the building site. Amanda and the reverend had chosen an area beyond the dugout to construct their home. Like so many other farmers, they planned to use the dugout for a barn as long as it stood. Gabe didn't think it would last beyond another winter.

Eager to get started, Gabe helped Lena unload the wagon.

"Go on, get going," she laughed. "Simon can help me. Never saw a man in my life who loved work more than you."

He leaned closer. "Oh, there're a few things I enjoy more."

She blushed and glanced about them. "Gabe Hunters, someone will hear you!"

Gabe grinned at his wife and watched her and Simon unload food onto a makeshift table. He grabbed two spades for himself and Caleb and trekked toward the other men busy at work. The sod house would be approximately sixteen feet wide by twenty feet long, the size of most all the sod houses. Amanda claimed it would be a mansion in comparison to what she and her siblings were accustomed to.

"Mornin', Gabe, Caleb," a neighboring man greeted.

"Morning," he replied. Riley O'Connor walked with the man, but he didn't acknowledge Gabe or look his way.

I'm going to try to be civil. He can't help being lonely.

They hurried to a field of thick, strong sod where a few men turned over furrows for the sod bricks. Gabe watched in earnest, for he wanted to build a barn in the fall. He and Caleb helped trim the bricks to three feet long and two feet wide, understanding they must be equally cut to insure straight, solid walls.

"Sure glad you taught me how important it is to know arithmetic," Caleb said, measuring a sod brick with a piece of string Lena had cut for the occasion.

"Never underestimate the value of education," Gabe replied, tossing his elder son a grin. "Although experience is important too."

They shared a laugh, and as they worked side by side, Gabe reminded Caleb of the fall and winter and all the lessons the family had to teach him. So much there had been for Gabe to learn, and plenty more remained ahead.

The cabin raising went fairly quickly. The first row of bricks was laid along the foundation line, with younger children and some of the women filling the gaps with mud as mortar. Every third layer was laid crosswise to enforce the structure and bind it all together. They set in frames for a door and two windows and put aside sod to secure them later on. Shortly after noon, the walls stood nearly high enough for the roof, but tantalizing aromas from the food tables caused them all to stop and eat.

"Are you enjoying the day?" Gabe asked Lena, handing her his tin plate. He'd eaten in a rush so he could get back to work. As soon as all the men were finished, the women and children would share in the food.

Her eyes sparkled. "This is better than a church social. We've all brought Amanda gifts for her new home, and she's so very happy."

"What has she gotten?" Gabe asked curiously.

"Food, scented soap, embroidered pillowcases and handkerchiefs, a cornhusk basket, and some fabric scraps for a quilt. The poor girl has never known anyone to care for her like the reverend, and combined with the cabin and all, she's a little beside herself."

He stood and brushed the cornbread crumbs from his hands. "My compliments to all the women for their fine cooking." He winked and brushed her cheek with his thumb. How lovely she looked, his Lena. Her cheeks tinted pink and rosy, reminding him of wildflowers blossoming in the sun. The sky had seemed to dance with color, but not nearly as brilliant as the light in her eyes. "I love you," he whispered.

She wrinkled her nose. "I have something to tell you."

"And what is that?"

"Well, I—"

"Hey, Gabe, if you're done, how about giving me a hand with framing the roof?" a neighboring farmer called. "Since the preacher's gone to the trouble of having lumber hauled in, the least we can do is get it up right."

"I'll be right there." Gabe glanced at his wife, waiting for her to speak.

"I'll tell you later." Lena laughed. "The news can wait."

Gabe saw Caleb eating with a young man, laughing and talking, but at the sound of the neighbor's voice, Caleb glanced up.

"Finish your meal, Son. You've worked hard today." He remembered his own longing for a companion when he was Caleb's age and how much he valued the friendships in Nebraska. Yes, he was a fairly lucky man, as they said in Nebrasky.

❦

Leaning against the wagon, Lena crossed her arms and fought a wave of dizziness. She hadn't been able to eat all day for fear of being sick. Mercy, those boys hadn't made her ill like this, but soon she'd be four months along, and the sickness should leave.

"Are you all right?" Nettie Franklin asked. She'd helped Lena put her things back into the wagon.

"I'm fine," Lena assured her.

"You're pale, and I see you didn't eat a thing."

Lena nodded, nearly overflowing to tell someone about the baby. "Can you keep a secret for a day?"

The young woman quickly moved to her side. Her large, expressive eyes widened. "On a stack of Bibles, I'll keep a secret."

"I'm pregnant," Lena mouthed and looked around to make sure no one else had heard.

Nettie giggled. As the local midwife, she had a right to know about future babies. "So Gabe doesn't know?"

"Not yet. I started to tell him a few minutes ago, but Hank Culpepper hollered at him to come help with the roof." Lena wiggled her shoulders, the excitement of actually telling someone about the baby made her want to shout. "But I will tonight—if I don't bust first."

"Have you been sick much?"

Lena squeezed shut her eyes. "Every morning. What amazes me is Gabe usually doesn't miss a thing, and he has yet to question me. I can't believe he hasn't guessed it."

Nettie hugged her shoulders. "I'm so happy for you. What a blessing."

Suddenly, Lena felt her stomach roll. "What is that horrible smell?"

They looked to the cooking fire where a kettle of beans still simmered, but with the offensive odor Lena felt certain they'd burned.

The two scurried to pull the kettle from the fire. Another whiff of the beans sent Lena's stomach and head spinning. She swallowed the bile rising in her throat and blinked repeatedly to stop the dizziness. Blackness surrounded her. Nettie screamed for help just as Lena's world grew dark.

⁓

Gabe wiped the sweat from his brow with the back of his shirt. Water would quench his powerful thirst. Besides, he was curious over Lena's news. He looked about and saw there was a lull in the work right now too. Maybe he could take this opportunity to satisfy both desires.

"Be right back," Gabe called out, thinking how his vocabulary had shrunk since last October. But he fit in with these farmers because now he belonged.

Lifting his hat to cool his head, Gabe headed toward the spot he'd left Lena. Some kind of commotion had drawn the ladies' attention. Rounding a group of wagons, he moved closer.

Suddenly, Gabe felt the color drain from his face. All of his worst nightmares and misgivings about his wife were vividly realized in front of his eyes. Rage seethed from the pores of his flesh.

Lena lay in the arms of Riley O'Connor.

22

What is going on here?" Gabe bellowed. He clenched his fist, ready to send it through those pearly white teeth.

The crowd of women around Lena and Riley instantly hushed and made way for Gabe to reach his wife. He'd tear Riley apart with his bare hands. So this was Lena's news! All those words of love and endearing smiles meant nothing to her. *Lord, help me!*

"Riley, what are you doing with my wife?" he shouted.

Riley looked up. Surprise swept across his face. Gabe took a glimpse of Lena, who moved slightly in Riley's arms. She looked pale, ghastly pale, but no wonder. She'd been discovered.

"Answer me, Man." Gabe pushed his way through the mounting crowd. The women gasped. If they wanted to see a fight, then he'd give them one.

Listen, Gabe. It's not what you think.

He held his breath and attempted to control his rapid breathing.

Nettie rushed to his side. "No, Gabe. This is not what it seems. Lena fainted, and if it hadn't been for Riley, she'd have fallen into the fire."

His head pounded. Had he heard correctly?

"That's right, Hunters," Riley said. "I caught her before she fell. Nothing else."

"Gabe," Lena moaned. "Where's Gabe?"

Emotion clawed at his throat and threatened to choke him alive. Riley lifted Lena into Gabe's arms without a word. She felt light, fragile. "Lena, are you all right?" He didn't care that most of Archerville gawked at him. He'd already made a fool of himself—not once thinking about Lena, but only of himself. "I'm so sorry I shouted."

628

"I didn't hear a thing," she said and wet her lips. "I don't remember what happened to me, just got dizzy."

"Well, I'm getting you home and to bed. Tomorrow I'm riding to North Bend for the doctor. No more of this."

"No. It's not necessary. I'm fine, really." She stirred slightly, but he could see through her ploy. "This is natural, Gabe. The sickness will pass."

"What do you mean the sickness will . . ." He heard Nettie laugh, then slowly the other women began to laugh. "Are we? I mean, are you?"

Lena smiled and reached up to touch his face. "Yes, Gabe. We're going to have a baby."

"Ah, wh . . . when?"

"Mid-December."

He let out a shout that resembled a war whoop he'd heard at a Wild West show back East.

"Gabe Hunters," she laughed. "You sound just like a Nebrasky farmer."

❧

On December 10, Gabe paced the cabin floor while Caleb and Simon stared into the fire. Lena had labored with the baby for nearly four hours, and he'd had enough. She didn't cry out, but he'd heard her whimperings. Outside, the night was exceptionally cold, although only a sprinkling of snow lay on the ground.

"How much longer?" Caleb asked, breaking the silence from the ticking clock above the fireplace.

"Soon," Gabe muttered. "Can't be much longer."

He went back to pacing, keeping time with the clock. In the next moment, he heard a cry. He stopped cold and stared at the quilt leading into their bedroom.

"You have a girl, Gabe Hunters!" Nettie Franklin called. "A healthy baby girl!"

"Can I come in now?" he asked, frozen in his spot. "I want to see my wife and baby."

"Not just yet. Give me a moment," Nettie replied. "Oh, she's right pretty, but no hair."

Gabe waited for what he believed was an hour. Suddenly he couldn't contain his excitement a moment longer. He pushed through the quilt, his gaze drinking in the sight of his lovely Lena and the red-faced baby in her arms.

"She's beautiful," he whispered, tears springing to his eyes. "And you're beautiful." He kissed Lena's damp forehead, then her lips, before kneeling beside the bed.

Lena glanced up from staring into the baby's face. "Thank You, Lord," she whispered.

"Amen," he said, gingerly picking up a perfect, tiny hand. The awe of this miracle left him speechless. He memorized every bit of the tiny face, then kissed the baby's cheek. "I love you, Lena. You never cease to fill my days with joy."

"And I love you. She looks like you."

"Oh, I want her to look like you."

"Nonsense. She has your eyes and chin. They're just like her father's. I certainly hope she doesn't have my temper."

Gabe chuckled. "I want my daughter to have spunk."

"I'll settle for spunk. What shall we name her?" Lena asked.

He pressed his lips together. "Hmm. How do you feel about naming her after our mothers?"

Her eyes widened. "I think that's a wonderful idea."

"I've been thinking the best way for me to honor my mother is to name my daughter after her. What was your mother's name?"

"Cynthia."

"Cynthia Marie. What do you think?"

"Perfect," Lena said with a smile.

"Caleb, Simon. Come on in and meet Miss Cynthia Marie Hunters, your new sister."

Gabe's eyes pooled with joy. The Lord had showered him with so many blessings. Surely something he'd never have known from books. The intensity of his feelings for Lena and his family spread through him like sweet molasses. Never had he expected the love of such a fine woman, or two strapping sons, or the sweetness of an infant daughter. He was happy. He was content. He'd given and received the greatest gift of all.